Immortality
Kevin Bohacz

What if God is only a ghost in a cosmic machine?

Speculative fiction / techno-thriller

Immortality
Copyright © 2003, 2007 by Kevin Bohacz. All rights reserved under international and Pan-American Copyright Conventions. No part of this book may be reproduced, scanned, or distributed in any print or electronic form without written permission.

Published in the United States by CPrompt.
Printed and manufactured in the United States using the highest quality materials and workmanship available.
Printed on acid free paper.
7757002345923079391

www.kbohacz.com   www.c-prompt.com

Trade Paperback Sixth Edition: September 2008

A first edition was published in March 2007 with slightly different content.

Library of Congress Control Number: 2006910696

Publisher's Cataloging-In-Publication Data

Bohacz, Kevin.
   Immortality / Kevin Bohacz. -- trade paperback ed.

   p. ; cm.

   ISBN: 978-0-9791815-1-1

1. Immortalism--Fiction. 2. Nanotechnology--Fiction. 3. Plague--United States--Fiction. 4. Human evolution--Fiction. 5. College professors--Fiction. 6. Forensic scientists--Fiction. 7. Science fiction. 8. Techno-thriller I. Title.

PS3602.O33 I46 2007
813/.6   2006910696

About the Author: Kevin Bohacz is a novelist and a writer for national computer magazines as well as founder and president of an e-business consulting and software engineering company he founded in 1989, a scientist and engineer for over 28 years, and the inventor of an advanced electric car system, the ESE Engine System (circa 1978).

Born in 1957 in New York City, Kevin has lived in New York, California, Florida, Texas, Pennsylvania, Delaware, New Jersey and New Mexico. He can be currently sighted with his wife, Mazelle in one of their favorite cities in New Mexico, California, or Texas.

Other published novels: Dream Dancers (Hays & Associates 1993) – Science fiction / fantasy

Other published works: Various articles for national computer magazines including Smart Computing.

More information: www.kbohacz.com

Author's note, Human v2.0? Human evolution has always been partially under our control. In the hundred generations of recorded history and millions of years before, we have been self-evolving by enhancing our bodies with technology. The first artificial gains occurred thirty thousand generations ago in prehistoric times when we improved upon our fists with stone tools and clubs. Ten thousand generations ago, sharpened flint and fire removed more physical limitations. In the Bronze Age, eighty generations ago, we enhanced our muscles with wheels and metal. Fifty generations ago we extended our arms with blades of iron and sheathed ourselves in armor. Now, we are embedding electronics into our bodies, networking our thoughts, breathing in outer space, and engineering our genes. This self-evolution is accelerating at a breathtaking rate. It seems inevitable we will continue to enhance ourselves with machines and genetic manipulations. What will healthcare be like a generation from now? The environment? War? Will we still consider ourselves human or will we be human v2.0?

To Mazelle who helped me polish my dream.

To Maxine who left before the dream was finished.

Prologue

End of Sleep

I – Amazon Forest: January, present day.

The rainforest had a humid, earthy smell that reminded him of home. Diego was twenty-two years old and, like most of his village, he'd spent half his life away from home. The bulldozer he was illegally operating was idling in neutral. In front of him were a half dozen control levers and gauges. With a worker's rough hands, he compressed the squeeze-grip on a lever and pushed forward. He heard the sound of grinding gears. The tree cutter failed to engage. The huge dozer was thirty-year-old army surplus. There was a cable problem in the lever he was working. The problem sometimes caused the squeeze-grip to snap shut when the transmission grabbed. If he was not careful, the squeeze-grip could badly pinch his hand. Diego pushed harder on the lever. He could feel teeth missing in the gears from how the lever bucked back against his push. Without warning, the gears dropped into place as the squeeze-grip bit his palm. It was like a vicious dog. An angry welt throbbed in his palm. He cursed the dozer. He cursed the steaming heat. He'd drunk two quarts of water since breakfast, and lunch break was still hours away.

The rainforest was alive with insects. Diego had never seen this many in all the years he'd illegally logged the deep forests. There was a steady drone which was louder than the diesel engine he controlled. Tiny no-see-em's, biting things, had left a rash across the back of his neck that felt like sunburn. Earlier, he'd scratched it raw but now had a bandanna tied around his neck to remind him to leave it be.

The bulldozer rocked into a depression as the cutter began chewing through the trunk of a mahogany tree. Diego fed more fuel into the beast's engine. The dozer's treads dug in; there was a hesitation. He could feel the strain building. Tons of steel lurched forward pitching him in his seat. Another tree tumbled, its branches snapping like rapid-fire gunshots as it crumpled into the ground. The front of the beast was equipped with a chain driven saw instead of a dozer blade. The fixture had a pair of serrated edges that shimmied back and forth like steel teeth. Pieces of shredded green leaves and bark caught on the teeth's edges. Diego had long ago decided the beast was a sloppy eater.

The insect sounds of the forest had stopped. As far as Diego knew, these insects never stopped. He dropped the beast into neutral then switched it off.

There was silence.

Out of this stillness, a faint crackling sound rose from the distance, then disappeared, and then came again. He listened carefully. It took him a moment to realize the faraway sound was trees falling. The logging company operated a small army of dozers, far apart now; but by evening they would all meet up, connecting each of the separate cutting tracks into a solid plot. Diego swung round in his seat and gazed back. A swath of fallen tropical forest lay behind him: mahogany and cedar and even some rosewood along with countless varieties of plants and bushes. The largest trees were left standing so their canopies would hide the results of his work from the few government scouting planes that were not on the company's payroll. Heavy tractors would come through later to drag out the good logs. He got paid by the yard for mahogany, rosewood, and cedar; the rest was trash. Today it looked like he would earn a small fortune; tomorrow might bring nothing.

He lit a cigarette and left it hanging in his lips. After starting the engine, he ground the shifter into a forward gear and moved out. He drew cigarette smoke into his lungs then exhaled through his nose. No time to rest. He needed every bit of money he could earn. He didn't blink as a cloud of insects flew into his face as their nest was churned into rubbish by his dozer's teeth.

The humidity was so high that water had begun to evaporate into a fine mist. A steam cloud floated through the tops of the trees blurring the upper canopy into a milky green. Diego swung the beast around in a stationary about-face. The base camp was miles behind him by the river. The camp was a dock and tents with ratty screens. Beside the camp was a tree covered clearing that at night was filled with sleeping dozers and other heavy equipment. By now, a pot of beans would be simmering for lunch. A hunk of flat bread and canned beer would complete the meal. No meat. He'd lived worse. Everything here had been secretly brought in by river barge, including him and the other labors. With luck, he could cut a second swath back toward camp and arrive by lunch. Today would fill his pocket with more than two hundred *Reals*... a new record.

The logging ride out of the forest turned out to be easier than the ride in. The trees in his new path were an ideal size for cutting. Diego began thinking about his wife Carla and their dream. She'd been anxious to come with him into this hell. He had kissed her and told her no... no wife of his would suffer in a place like this. In seven months, he would be a father. The foreign company running this operation was taking good care of her. She'd written last week that the company had paid for a test with a machine that was like an x-ray but used sound. The nurse had told her the baby would be a boy. Diego smiled with that memory... it was a good one. He would have a boy who would grow up to be his friend. That was a new part of the dream; the old part was still a small house outside Maceio, the coastal city where Diego was born.

Diego instinctively slowed the dozer to the speed of a man's stride. He squinted watching a cloud of rain moving toward him along the path he'd just cut from camp. The rain didn't appear heavy, but when mixed with ground steam it was solid enough to bring a false twilight. Nothing could be seen inside the cloud. The dozer had a roll cage. A piece of corrugated sheet metal had been welded to the top of the cage as a roof. Diego switched on spotlights. Drops started hitting the sheet metal with rhythmic pings. The humidity grew heavier. The air surrounded him like a damp towel. He pulled off his t-shirt and wiped his face with it. A storm of birds fled from some trees his dozer was about to consume. Their colored shapes moved past him at eye level like watercolor paints in fog.

Diego cocked his head to one side. He sensed something wrong. Grinding the shifter into neutral, he idled the machine. As the noise of his engine simmered down, he was able to hear the far off sounds of a dozer racing at top speed. He heard an engine revving at its highest rpm... no, it was two engines. More than one dozer was racing through the forest. This was very unusual. A hollow feeling began gnawing inside his chest. He remembered stories of odd things that happened to people alone in the forest. He heard a different sound like a wet towel hitting the ground in front of him. He leaned forward, squinting into the fog.

A bird tumbled from the air bouncing off the cab, the sound startling Diego badly. The bird fluttered, then righted itself on the ground and took off. He saw another bird fall a couple yards away, then another, and another. They would roll around a bit, then fix themselves and fly off. This was very strange… too strange. He now understood why dozers were racing through the forest. Something very bad was happening.

He shoved the dozer into gear and slammed his feet into the pedals. The beast jumped forward at top power. He heard muck spitting into the air off the backs of the tread-plates. *To devil* with cutting the second track. *To devil* with the money. He was going to get out of here as fast as this dozer could race. The treads were clanking at an accelerating pace as the beast slowly picked up speed. He disengaged the tree saw to gain a few more drops of power. He plowed through the top of a tree he'd cut earlier, then another. He was doing close to ten miles per hour. A man might run faster, but not through this brush and not for the miles that remained to the camp.

Without warning, he felt dizzy, an ill kind of dizzy. The fingers on his right hand went numb, then paralyzed. He tried to move the fingers, but they were limp. Coldness was spreading up from his hand. The more he tried to flex his fingers, the worse it got. In seconds, his entire right arm was hanging flaccid at his side. Whatever had gotten the birds was working on him. He knew it. The trees kept moving past him in a blur. He realized with an odd disconnect that he was having difficulty drawing breaths.

He thought about Carla and the baby. His jaw squeezed tight. His lips formed a grim line. He would make it for them.

The dozer glanced off a large tree and kept going. The impact rocked him. He wheezed, attempting to draw air into his chest. Maybe two miles remained until base camp. He began veering off the trail. The saw-blade snagged on a mahogany six feet in diameter. Diego was pitched from his seat. Dizzy and unable to hold on, he fell from the cab. His shoulder hit a moving tread-plate, which tossed him off the rig. He was like a paralyzed sack of meat.

"Umph!" He landed on the ground. He thought how odd it was that he'd bounced. He didn't know people could bounce when they hit the ground. The tractor rumbled beside him. Without his feet on the pedals, the dozer had stopped. The left side of his face was a mix of blood and dirt. He tried to draw air into his lungs but failed. His mind felt like it was beginning to evaporate. His entire body tingled. He felt no pain. The muscles that worked his lungs were no longer responding. He thought of calling for help, but without his lungs he could do nothing. He gave up struggling and stared skyward at the treetops and thought of Carla. Moments later, his heart stopped beating. He felt calm as what was left of his mind faded into a warm nothing.

II – New Jersey: January

Sarah Mayfair opened her eyes. The nightmare was still around her. Her vision was not in this world but in some other. The nightmare was of underground water, great arteries of rivers and streams and lakes. Where the liquid pooled, it was cool and deep. She sensed this water was alive with thoughts, evil thoughts. A teaspoonful of it teamed with plans of death. She was floating deep under the water, staring as drowned people glided past her face sinking into the depths of a bottomless pool. Looking down, she saw a trail of countless tiny bodies slowly pirouetting as they drifted into the yawning darkness below her feet...

Headlights from a car traveled across a wall of her room. The lights dwelled on a wooden credenza, then moved on. She followed the glow with her eyes seeing reality for the first time. The simple act of seeing began to clear the veils of her nightmare. Her breathing slowed. She realized she was covered in sweat.

Outside, a subzero wind was blowing unimpeded through a forest of leafless trees and ice crusted snow. The windowpanes rattled and hummed. Small drafts snuck through the rooms. She shivered as the drafts caressed her dampened skin. She was in the living room of her home. She recognized the shadowy details of furniture and walls. Her boyfriend Kenny was in the bedroom asleep. She remembered getting up and walking out here to be by herself to think. The nightmares had grown worse, more of them with each passing week. She was starting to see the faces of people she knew in these nightmares. She sensed it was some kind of horrible parade of those who would die. She remembered Kenny's image from the dream.

Her body stiffened. A disembodied voice was whispering into her left ear. The words were unintelligible... garbled, but unmistakably evil. This can't be happening. She screamed out in frustration and grief at the seeds of budding madness.

Chapter 1

COBIC-3.7

1 – Wyoming: October, ten months later.

Mark kept up his pace hiking across the foothill terrain. The exertion had long ago passed from a conscious effort into machine-like automation. A trickle of sweat ran down one side of his face. His build was average, but his legs were nicely muscled and responded well to the exertion. He was wearing hiking boots, jeans, and a Sierra Club sweatshirt. His black hair had thin streaks of gray. A backpack pressed down on his shoulders. A pair of sunglasses hung from his neck by a nylon cord. The sun was extremely bright passing through the thinner air. He squinted but left the glasses off. He wanted to see this place the way it truly looked. He wanted no filters of polarized glass to alter the appearance of what nature had put here.

A breeze swept up the slope, pushing him from behind. The climb had been more difficult than he'd remembered from the trip half a year ago. In Wyoming, what the locals called *a hill* was a solid incline that went on for miles. These were the foothills of the Rockies. The ground was covered with boulders between which sprouted knee high grass and sage and small plants that carried burrs. Mark looked off into the distance. The rocky terrain ended a mile downhill where it blended into oceans of wild grass. He watched as the wind pushed huge waves through the grassy stalks. The sky was clear except at the horizon where a weather front was moving toward them. The storm was a bruised wall of clouds floating over the plains a hundred miles in the distance.

Six of them were on this expedition. They were doing *paleobiological research*. This was a relatively new science and Mark Freedman was its celebrated genius. At late middle age, he'd accomplished many of his early dreams. The only problem was that with each dream attained, three more had arisen in their place. He was a Nobel Prize winning molecular biologist, yet still worked as a professor at UCLA. He had been happily married but now lived with a female student less than half his age.

His five companions on the expedition were all graduate students from his classes. These expeditions were not games. The work was real. The goals were serious. He could have taken anyone on these outings, but these students were handpicked and brighter than many scientists he knew – and far more eager and easily led.

The destination of this outing was a site Mark had named A4, designating the fourth potential location in the region to be explored. A4 was a half-mile slope along the northeastern rim of the foothills. The terrain that had once been an inland sea was now a sea of grass. He hoped to find fossilized mats of bacteria deposited in the limestone croppings. The mats were remnants of a rare, still existing strain of *Chromatium Omri* bacteria named *Chromatium Omri BIC-3.7*. Mats previously unearthed by Mark had proven this strain was a throwback which had first lived 3.7 billion years ago. As the bacterium's discoverer, Mark had been the one who had named the creature and given it the acronym of COBIC-3.7.

Mark's COBIC was the oldest known form of motile life on Earth, the first cousin to protoanimals, the very nexus of the great kingdoms of plant and animal; it was literally the origin of an evolutionary branch which would eventually lead to all animals, including humans; and it was still swimming and living among us. Ten years ago, Mark had been able to link living specimens with the fossil mats. That link had proven his theories and earned him a Nobel Prize due to his solid research and a generous dose of luck. Winning this level of acknowledgement had changed his life and given him new reasons to dig even deeper into the questions surrounding this unusual microscopic creature.

Mark had recently developed a novel way of analyzing ground-penetrating radar images from satellites. The new technique revealed geological clues to where COBIC bacterial deposits might exist. The government had been happy to assist an eminent scientist in his work, especially if it might have defense implications. He had been given limited amounts of raw data from an older generation of military surveillance birds. His work with the satellite data had led him to over fifty possible sites, eight of which had already turned out golden, and heavy with mats of COBIC-3.7. That he had found any mats at all was remarkable. His bacterium was a free-swimming creature that resembled a capsule with a tail on it. Why had they ended up tightly packed into clumps of floating dead? In some cases, the mats were dozens of feet long with populations reaching into the countless trillions.

His fieldwork had uncovered the additional surprise that COBIC-3.7 was not as rare as originally theorized. His evidence showed that at one time COBIC had been a dominant species which had almost died out during the same extinction event as the dinosaurs. Mark was certain this line of investigation would earn him his second Nobel Prize. He was convinced the bacteria held an important clue to the mass extinctions of the Cretaceous period. He had formulated a theory that the dying off of his bacteria could have been one of the triggers of the *extinction events*. The tiny bugs could have been a vital link in ancient food chains; and without them, the greatest beasts of all had perished. By comparing fossil samples from different periods, his investigation had shown the bacteria were going through long cycles of population growth and decay, cycles measured in hundreds of millions of years. Mark believed that during the final cycle, it was the combined environmental strain of huge animals and climatic shifts that pushed COBIC-3.7 and other bacteria over the edge and took the dinosaurs with them.

Up ahead of Mark, a student named Marie stopped walking to take a drink from her canteen. The weather was far too hot for October, but this had been an odd year of fires and floods and droughts. Global warming was catching up with them. Mark stared at her, imagining the flawless body he knew was hidden beneath her loose-fitting clothes. Marie was one of those blonde haired, blue eyed flowers that grew wild on the beaches of Southern California – in her case, Venice Beach. He had once seen her at the beach in a small bikini and roller-skates, and he'd never forgotten that heart stopping image.

A mild shove came from behind. Mark stumbled half a step forward. Another of the gals had pushed him. "Get going, you dirty old man," she said.

Mark turned and stared at her. She had her hands on her hips and appeared stern, but there was a hint of a smile on her lips and in the corners of her eyes. The smile was contagious. Mark fought to keep a neutral expression.

"You made me into what I am," he said.

"Don't rub it in," she said.

"Love to... Your place or mine?"

The girl puckered her lips into an air-kiss that said, *not a chance.* Her name was Gracy, and Mark was certain he was madly in love with her. They had shared his condo in Marina Del Rey for more than a year. Their relationship had been anything but simple. Gracy was strong-headed and wanted *her way* in everything. Mark was the same, except stronger and more stubborn.

In the beginning, their relationship had been overheated. He was wild about her looks, and she was in lust with his mind and his fame. A year later, she had moved into his place. Gracy had made it clear that she wanted their living arrangement kept a secret at UCLA as much as Mark did. The sneaking around had been fun and had lasted for several months. But inevitably the word had spread, and now everyone in the department knew their secret. Gracy had been embarrassed by her new-found whispered notoriety. She was the grad-student who had bagged the infamous Professor, the most desirable faculty member on campus. She had tried to blame Mark for the leak, but they both knew the gossip had been spread by her girlfriends whom she'd sworn to secrecy.

Some of the students were straggling behind. Mark slowed, giving them the opportunity to catch up. Gracy continued to walk at her own pace which was taking her out into the lead. Mark loved her most when she was displaying this kind of independence. She was twenty-three years old and had the looks everyone considered the *natural* California girl. She had a perfect body and long straw colored hair that was real and not from a bottle. She could have been one of those girls seen on a beer commercial, and might have been except for one thing: Gracy was determined to be recognized for her brains, not her looks. She had one of the highest grade point averages at UCLA and was on her way to earning a Ph.D. a year ahead of schedule.

Mark stared at her as she continued to put distance between them. Her clothing was a mix of Wyoming and *The Coast*. She had on jeans, an old silver studded belt, a t-shirt, an insulated vest, and a funky western hat. She was getting too far out in front of him. Mark called back to the stragglers. "Come on folks! When we get there, it's Miller Time!" All he got in response were groans, but the pace did pick up.

The forced march ended at a rocky knoll. Mark laid a map out on the ground and pegged the corners with stones. Gracy sat opposite him and was busy with her field notes. The other students were resting and talking among themselves. Mark suspected the topic was mutiny and smiled. He switched on his GPS. The device was a military model the size of a cell phone and cost ten times as much as a commercial GPS. Most civilians were not allowed to own this kind of military hardware, but a Nobel Prize and called in favors got him altitude and map coordinates accurate to less than an inch.

"This is a good place to set up camp," he said. "Site A4 is all around us."

"Groovy... Why don't I break out the beers?" said Gracy.

"You know I never drink on duty."

"Sure," said Gracy. "And you never swear and always hold the door for ladies."

"Duddly Do-Right at your service."

Gracy opened the lid of what Mark called his specimen container. The Coleman ice chest would be filled with fossil specimens on the return trip; but right now inside were several blocks of dry ice, four six packs of Miller, and fifteen pounds of frozen ground meat.

The iced beer flowed down Mark's throat, taking with it any remnant of fatigue. Marie and Tony had gone off in search of wood and, Mark suspected, each other. He gazed around at the vast surroundings. On the west side of his hill were the beginnings of the Rocky Mountains. On the east side was the ocean-sized basin of grass. Gracy had the beer raised to her mouth. Mark reached over and tickled her sides. She spit beer all over him and the map.

"You bastard!" she yelled.

She grabbed him and they wrestled on the ground until he had her pinned. Her cheeks were flushed.

"Give up," said Mark.

"No!"

Some leaves were tangled in her hair. She squirmed under his weight, but he had her solidly pinned. He felt her muscles relax as she stopped fighting him. He knew she was trying to catch him off guard and didn't give her a break when she suddenly tried to roll him off.

"All right," she said. "What'll it take for you to let me up?"

"A kiss."

"Never!"

Mark kissed her on the lips then got off her cautiously as if she were a cat about to strike. Gracy sat up. She removed a leaf that was dangling over her face. Her hair was a mess of blonde tangles. Mark could tell by the look in her eyes she was plotting revenge.

~

The sun was creeping down toward the western rim of mountains. The storm clouds were half again as close as they had been in the afternoon. The team had been working the site for hours.

Mark looked over another piece of limestone. There had been several fossils of large marine animals but no mats of *Chromatium Omri*. This piece of rock was no different. Gracy had taken charge of the two students responsible for chipping off vertical slabs of limestone. The other three were off scouting.

The bacteria should have been here. Mark turned around and pitched a small piece of limestone down into the valley toward a pair of hawks that were circling in the distance. The hawks were in no danger. The rock sailed far enough out that it landed silently hundreds of yards down the slope.

"Forget it," he mumbled.

Gracy turned around and stared. Mark said it again, only louder. "Forget it." The day was shot. They had enough provisions to stay for two nights. If tomorrow was a bust, they would have to hike back into town to re-supply and then out again to a different site. He hated being wrong.

The sun was gone. The base camp was a collection of dome tents scattered across a hillside clearing. The arrangement of tents had been completely random. Several campfires illuminated the surrounding boulders and tents with flickering orange glows.

Mark wore his reading glasses. He was sitting on a folding stool outside his tent. A Coleman lantern hanging from a pole cast a white hot light onto the ground. Arrayed in front of him were poster sized satellite photographs. The photographs had a slight curl from being stored in a tube. The sensors that had collected these images worked in the infrared region of the spectrum. Plants and trees were a bright red. Ground formations were paler colors of blue.

The sounds of discussions and the sizzle of grilling burgers were drifting from the other side of the camp. The smell of food was working on Mark but he ignored it. Minutes ago he had stopped examining the COBIC sites and was instead looking at a satellite image of the American Northwest forests or, more accurately he thought, *what was left of the northwest forests*. The lumber industry had succeeded in harvesting far too much of that ancient place. Trees hundreds of feet tall and older than western civilization were gone. There were single trees that had been growing for thousands of years. He grew crazed seeing this evidence of mankind's idiocy. Humans were one of the few animals that went merrily along consuming its environment until it no longer supported life, then moved on; locusts were another. Someday there would be no place to move on to. It might take generations, but sooner or later we would run out of something critical, and then what? Look at our oil supply. Fossil fuel would be gone soon, and were we creating a replacement energy source? Not likely. What did we have to show for our concern? Not much except some rich politicians, a bankrupt Middle East policy based on our addiction to oil, and terrorists indirectly funded by our addiction who wanted to annihilate us.

Gracy walked into the wash of lantern light carrying two burgers and two beers. She put the food down in front of him.

"Stop pouting and eat something," she said.

"Look at this scarred earth," said Mark. "We're not going to be happy until the entire country is paved with concrete. Except for the farms of course, and that land will be so heavily polluted with pesticides and nutrient depleted that we'll all be eating hydroponic Spam or worse."

"I knew I shouldn't let you read before dinner."

"Come on, this is serious." Mark felt his body tensing up. "If it wasn't for endangered species like the Spotted Owl, logging companies would have clear-cut the last of the Northwest years ago. We have inconsequential endangered species protecting the last of the great forests on legal technicalities. Talk about shaky ground. I just can't fathom those loggers. If we let 'em do what they want and cut the forest, most of them will be out of work in ten years anyway. They want to trade ten years of income for one of the last strongholds of nature in America. What happens when their ten years are up? They'll all be on welfare – with us footing the bill – after they pissed on their own backyard and our national treasure. And what about the loss to science and medicine? In the Brazilian rainforests, every twenty seconds they're rolling the dice on plowing under the cure for cancer. Shit!"

"Cut the rant and eat your hamburger," said Gracy. "You're giving me a headache."

Mark stared at her through sore eyes. What was wrong with her? Didn't she get it? He sighed, then slowly shook his head. She did understand and she was *getting it* better than him. What could he do right now in the middle of nowhere except give himself indigestion? He needed to save it for the real fights that were coming in the years ahead. He had the ear of important people. He could make a difference and already had by working with the Sierra Club and powerful friends like Senator Ann Spector.

"Sorry," he said. "You know I'm a little crazy at times."

"I know," said Gracy. "Part of why I love you is your passion, but sometimes you make me nuts."

Gracy casually pulled a wrinkled joint out of a pocket. She lit it and passed it to him. She had brought along a quarter ounce of reality-altering Hawaiian pot. Mark took a series of hits off the joint, pulling the smoke deep into his chest. The smoke expanded as if pressurizing his lungs. He stared at his nighttime surroundings. This was a place where civilization had never reached. His head lightened. The glowing tents, the boulders, the plants, even the soil looked a little richer in detail. This piece of Earth was unspoiled. He relaxed and picked up the burger. His stomach grumbled with the first bite.

The fires were out. The lanterns were long ago turned off. Mark and Gracy were sharing a sleeping bag. The bag was unzipped. They had dragged it outside the tent and were enveloped in a world of stars. The air was so clear and thin that the stars no longer twinkled. Mark felt like he was being pulled into the depths of space. Gracy's head was nestled inside the crook of his arm. She was gazing up into the sky with him. He had just finished off the last bits of a second joint. Mark felt uncomfortable for reasons he couldn't understand. Moonlight was casting shadows into the house-sized boulders around them. He thought about his ex-wife and child. No, that was a road he was not going down tonight. To distract himself, he began telling Gracy a story.

"Did I ever tell you about my first political rebellion?"

"No, sweetie," she said dreamily.

"When I turned eighteen it was the middle of the Vietnam war. All I had was a choice between two ways of ruining my life. Either get drafted and play the Me Cong delta lottery or desert to Canada and become a draft resister. There was a great crisis of spirit back then. I had a lot of hate boiling up inside me. Hate for the government. Hate for big business profiting off the war. In my teens, I woke up every morning to news about body-counts, how many guys a little older than me had been killed in Vietnam the previous day. I knew in a couple years that was going to be me. I couldn't see any future. I marched in my first protest when I was fifteen – long hair, bellbottom jeans, and Hell no we won't go. We had to stop the killing."

"I had a history professor who said the peace protesters extended the war," said Gracy. "He believed that during the peace negotiations in Paris, the marchers gave hope to the North Vietnamese that America might pull out. A divided country was a sign of weakness."

"That's ignorance!" said Mark. "Without the protests, there would have been no pressure for Nixon to negotiate in Paris. If it was left up to those political sociopaths, we'd have kept on going until we ran out of kids to kill – or nuked Southeast Asia."

"Maybe you're right?" said Gracy.

"I am right. I was seriously involved back then. I was a radical before I turned eighteen. Later, I became a draft resister and burned my card. I was attending UCLA when things got violent. Students were shot at Kent State and the underground was bombing federal buildings. You can't imagine what it was like unless you were there."

"Sounds like homeland war," said Gracy. "People were killed by the police, right?"

"It was civil war," said Mark. "I got a letter from Uncle Sam telling me to report for selective service or else my butt would end up in Alcatraz. I dropped underground. Later, I met some people who belonged to the SLA and ended up tagging along with them."

"What's the SLA?"

"Symbionese Liberation Army... They're the ones who kidnapped Patty Hearst. Soon, I was breaking worse laws than draft resisting."

Gracy got up on her elbows and stared into Mark's eyes. Her expression changed. She punched him in the stomach.

"You're lying," she squealed. "You creep. I thought you were opening up and it's all a lie!"

"I really did burn my draft card," said Mark. He shrugged weakly. "I just never went underground or hooked up with the SLA."

"Yeah, sure. You're pathological. How can I believe anything you tell me."

"Forgive me?"

"Never!"

"Please."

"You are a bastard."

15

Gracy started tickling him. Mark laughed while trying to protect himself. The sleeping bag soon had him hopelessly tangled.

"Stop fighting me," said Gracy, "and take your punishment like a man."

~

Mark awoke with the morning sun in his eyes. The grass was dewy. The air felt crisp. Each breath was like a small drink of life. Gracy had already risen and was off somewhere.

Mark stood up and stretched. Every muscle had been worked during yesterday's hike. He ached with the pleasant sense of a freshly toned body. He ducked inside the tent. Inside his pack was a small plastic box that contained a digital instrument for measuring blood sugar level. In a separate thermal bag, next to a small block of blue-ice, were a bottle of insulin and a bottle of liquid vitamins. He pricked his thumb to draw blood. The meter read a little high. He prepared a small dose of insulin and injected it into his thigh. He'd been diabetic since early adulthood and had been fighting the inner battle ever since.

Mark heard the sounds of someone walking toward the tent. He quickly gathered up his supplies and shoved them into the backpack. Gracy crawled into the tent. She knew about his diabetes, but Mark couldn't stand for her to see the evidence. He couldn't stand for anyone to think of him as less than perfect.

"Ready for breakfast?" she asked.

"Maybe later..."

"You have to eat something. If you don't, you won't get any dessert tonight."

"Well, when you put it like that ..."

Marie, Tony, and Claire – the scouts – had reported they'd found an interesting site a half mile North of where the team had been digging the other day. Mark had decided to go alone to check it out. If it looked promising, he'd relocate the dig. The site was as promised: there were several indicators of a good fossil bed.

After the move, the team fell back into its normal rhythms. Gracy was supervising four students who were peeling off sheets of limestone. A rope grid was laid over the excavation to help identify the locations from which each fossil was removed. Mark was a short distance away with specimens scattered around him on sheets of brown wrapping paper. He sat on the ground with his specimens. He was examining a confused piece of fossil that contained several different types of marine animals. There were small crablike crustaceans and tiny fish and mussels. The sample looked like it was from the early Cretaceous Period. In one corner was something that might have been a speck of his matted bacteria but there wasn't enough to be certain.

Mark was hungry, and lunch was a missed opportunity from hours ago. The students had stripped down several feet into the limestone and were peeling off segments from an earlier period.

Gracy carried a sheet of limestone over to Mark. A crooked smile was on her lips. Mark caught the expression immediately and got up. The limestone had several trilobite fossils scattered across the two foot piece. He took the fossil from Gracy and began closely examining it. Trilobites were marine arthropods that were plentiful during much of the Paleozoic Era. Mark judged the sample to be from the middle of that Era. This dated the fossil at approximately two hundred million years before the dinosaur extinctions. In the upper left side was a band of fossilized bacterial mat. He saw the signature characteristic of COBIC: a waffled honeycomb of stone that would crumble if pressed too hard. The honeycomb was made of cavities the size of pinpricks and looked more like petrified foam than anything else. The frothy appearance was the result of billions of tiny bacteria having been packed into microscopic globs. Over time, some of the bacteria decayed. What remained was fossilized, leaving behind a fine latticework of imprints. The bacteria embedded in the honeycomb could be seen only under a powerful microscope. *Nanofossil* was the technical term for the remains of these microscopic creatures. It was impossible for Mark to lug into the wilderness all the equipment needed to conclusively identify these nanofossils, but this honeycomb structure was good enough for a preliminary identification. No other bacteria produced mats like these except COBIC.

"I need to get an exact date on this strata," said Mark. "It's not the right age to be extinction matting, but it looks like it'll fit into an earlier COBIC cycle. Tell the gang to move over a few yards and start sampling at the last Cretaceous layer and work down again."

He gently set the fossil on a sheet of wrapping paper, then knelt down and began scribbling notes into his PC Tablet. This was it. He could feel it. Discovering this piece meant they were in the right place. He had never been able to explain why but COBIC mats tended to form in the same location eon after eon like growth rings in some great geological tree. It would only be a matter of time before they found additional fossils. He noticed Gracy's shadow and realized she was still standing next to him.

"I want you to recheck the grid," said Mark. "We can't afford any mistakes. And keep them working at it."

"Yes, sir," she said. "I'll take that as a Job well done, Gracy!"

Mark had filled up the memory card in his digital camera with shots of the fossils. He could see Gracy recording the excavation work at the dig with a second Nikon. He pulled out a length of bubble-pack and started to box up the last sample. It was an excellent specimen. As soon as he got back to UCLA, this one was going under the electron microscope. He wished he could field-inspect the nanofossils. He was convinced this was his COBIC, but nagging doubt always plagued him until all the proof was in.

Two hours later, Mark had a prize specimen. This one was from the late Cretaceous Period, which put it within target range of the dinosaur extinctions. A more accurate date was needed for his work, but the estimate was close enough for now. He had what he was searching for – a huge slab of stone covered with the intricate froth-like patterns of bacterial mats.

The mother lode, thought Mark as he unpacked a field stereoscope. The device had a pair of binoculars eyepieces that were attached to what looked like a stubby microscope stage. The rig was mounted on a boom stand that floated it out over large samples. The scope could focus on a specimen from six inches away and magnify it a hundred times into a perfect 3D image.

Mark scrutinized every centimeter of the upper half of the slab, the area that contained the best preserved details. The telltale honeycomb structure screamed COBIC. He saw tiny pieces of seaweed twined into the mat and, a few inches away, a small fish that had lived during the Cretaceous Period. He cracked open a victory beer. It was the last one in the cooler.

The winds had picked up. Using the stereoscope, Mark had examined the entire the limestone sheet. A fat raindrop landed on his back. He ignored it. He rubbed blurriness from his eyes, then looked again. The mystery was still there. A piece of fossilized mat had come loose revealing a large insect hidden inside the fossil. He increased the magnification of the scope to fill his view with the prehistoric creature. The insect was embedded head first into the mat. A fossilized air sack and leg segments with fine hairs were visible – definitely a land creature. What was an insect doing in the middle of a marine fossil? Part of the creature's body was splayed out as if it had been crushed under a shoe. From what was visible, he had the impression it was some kind of large almond shaped beetle.

Mark heard crunching footsteps heading toward him. He sensed it was Gracy. He continued peering into the stereoscope. Gracy touched his shoulder. He looked up at her. She gave him a slip of paper, like a judge at the Emmys handing out the name of a winner. He was annoyed at the interruption but started to read. It was a more accurate field dating of the second fossil. The date was solidly in the middle of the dinosaur extinctions. Mark crumbled the paper as he made a fist. Some of that nagging feeling had just vanished.

"Yes!" he yelled. "I've got you!"

Gracy started to laugh. He pulled her down to him and kissed her. Losing her balance, she tumbled into his lap.

2 – Los Angeles: November

Mark set down the can of Pepsi. He was eating lunch by himself. The café was one of his favorites, close enough to UCLA to walk, with the best falafel in the city. The eatery was nothing more than a glass storefront on Kinross Avenue in Westwood, but every lunch hour it was packed and had a waiting line that extended down the sidewalk.

Mark had gotten there early and nabbed one of the prime spots, a small round table next to the only window. On the checkered tablecloth was a copy of the Los Angeles Times folded open to an article he'd been reading.

Children raised in Los Angeles County had twenty percent less lung capacity than the rest of the country.

The article explained that a UCLA study had established solid links between lung capacity and air pollution. Mark glanced at the folded paper. He thought about all the health food stores and restaurants in Los Angeles…in some areas they actually outnumbered the liquor stores. There was an odd counter-logic to it. The residents of Los Angeles breathed toxic air and swim in polluted bays but eat healthy and exercise as a way of making up for all the things they won't control.

Mark had returned from Wyoming this morning and gone straight to UCLA. The Physical Sciences Department had a scanning electron microscope. There was a waiting list months long for access to the machine. Mark had used his influence to get his specimens moved to the top of the list, even bumping a set of routine work-orders from UCLA Medical Center's Pathology department.

The technician operating the equipment had a set of photographs on Mark's desk an hour later. The black and white prints showed the Nanofossil outline of a single animal with the distinctive capsule shape and flagella tail unique to *Chromatium Omri 3.7*. In some ways, single-celled creatures were as complex as their multi-celled descendants. Even with all the bacteria catalogued by modern science, more were discovered each year with totally new structures and behaviors. Their diversity was as great as the stars in the sky. There were dozens of strains of living Chromatium Omri beside his COBIC-3.7. The oceans and fresh waters were teeming with Chromatium. He would have liked to work with living COBIC-3.7 again as he had during his days of Noble Prize research. Those had been heady times. The specimens he discovered and collected from hot springs had reproduced and grown into a breeding colony. The colony lived for almost a year in the lab before perishing from an infection of bacteriophages. He had a freezer full of uninfected, cryogenically frozen samples from that colony. All the common strains of Chromatium Omri were highly susceptible to pressure damage from freezing and were typically killed by the process, but COBIC-3.7 was an exception. The bacterium had a thirty percent reanimation rate. All he had to do was thaw some of his colony out to have a live strain again; but there was no scientific reason to do it, no new information to be obtained.

Mark checked his watch. The time was a few minutes past one. He took a last bite of falafel. It was time to drop in on Professor Ann Wilson. She was the dean of the entomology department. He had called and asked her to consult but had offered her no explanation over the phone. They both liked little games of intrigue.

Mark knocked on the open doorframe then walked in. The lab was cluttered with something new. An entire wall was stacked with one-gallon aquariums. Mark peered into a tank with his face almost touching the glass. A six-inch scorpion stared back at him. He'd never seen one that large. Its body was armored in what looked like dull black plastic. The monster skittered backward an inch. Its stinger curled up into the air. The spike was quivering. It looked ready to strike at Mark's face through the glass.

"Starting a pet store?" he called out.

Mark heard Ann Wilson walking over. He turned away from the aquariums and saw her. She was smiling behind a set of Ben Franklin glasses. Her gray hair was frizzed out enough to suggest the appearance of a female Einstein. She wore a white lab coat over a black sweatshirt, black sweatpants, and Nike running shoes.

"They're giant South-Asian scorpions," she said. "One of the most aggressive strains. They've been known to kill and eat small rodents. If your life insurance is paid up, you can pet one."

"Only after it's been stepped on, thank you very much."

"I hope your mystery's going to be entertaining," said Ann. "I had to put off a staff meeting."

"Sorry to drag you away from such an exciting afternoon."

"So what's so important?" she asked.

"A bug."

"I'd have never guessed."

Mark opened a metal lockbox the size of a dictionary. A segment of the fossilized bacterial mat was inside. Ann carefully placed the specimen under a customized stereoscope that was fitted with a video camera. A computer displayed a magnified image of the fossilized insect. She stared at the screen for several minutes, then looked over at Mark.

"My technical analysis is that we have windshield splat," said Ann.

"I think windshield splat's a little too broad in the old taxonomy department to help much," said Mark. "That's a marine fossil and that bug's not an aquatic animal, right?"

"Not unless its air sack was used as a floatation device."

Ann got up and selected a volume from a set of books that occupied an entire wall of her lab. The collection was a reference set that contained photographs and drawings of every known species of insect.

21

With one hand on the stereoscope and the other flipping pages, she went to work identifying the little creature.

"You're lucky the hind legs and air sack are intact," said Ann. "I should be able to figure this one out in no time."

"So how's your husband doing?"

"Don't ask. He dragged me out to a cocktail party the other night. Everyone there was a politician of some type. Harry was in his element. There was this one idiot city councilman who crossed over into my bailiwick, spouting off about how disorganized a species man was. He said we ought to look at how well run ant-societies were. Can you believe it? He thought we should organize into hives."

"Ann, the world's full of loony tunes."

She blinked a few times as if digesting what he'd said, then continued her story while simultaneously flipping through pages in the reference volume.

"This guy wouldn't stop ranting about how perfect a machine these ant colonies were. Finally, I just couldn't take it anymore and interrupted him. I told him that in ant-societies there are workers who sometimes blow a fuse and start dismembering their fellow comrades. Sounds a lot like some postal workers we've heard of, right? Anyway I told him how the ant-society deals with these sociopaths: a bunch of soldier ants show up and eat him. I said, I think we're already too much like ants right now."

"Sounds like you were the life of the party."

"Wait a minute," she motioned him to be quiet. "I think we've identified your little friend here... Yeah, I've got him."

Mark leaned closer to the monitor. She adjusted the scope to show a detailed view of the hairs on one of its legs.

"This baby is one of the all time winners in the evolutionary contest," said Ann. "Maybe that explains what it's doing mixed in with your marine critters."

"What is it?"

"Periplaneta Americana."

"Hey, that really clears things up for me," said Mark.

"Study your Latin, my boy. This is the king of all bugs. A giant North American Cockroach. This one was big enough to make a nice pet. I'd say about three inches long."

Mark felt a twinge in his stomach. That mess was a cockroach. His college job during his sophomore year was at a burger joint that had been infested. He'd hated those scampering vermin ever since, disease-infected rats of the insect world.

"Any guesses on how he got into the depths of an ocean?" asked Mark.

"Who knows," said Ann. "They get into everything."

"So what do I owe you?"

"Dinner."

"You're on. My place tomorrow night. I'll pick up your favorite dessert."

"I'm afraid to ask. What's my favorite dessert?" said Ann.

"Mint grasshopper mud pie."

"Ouch."

~

After Mark left UCLA, instead of driving home, he rode into Santa Monica. His car was a vintage '69 Mustang convertible. He had the top down. It was late afternoon; rush hour was just beginning. The streets were still moving freely. Mark decided the light traffic must have been a gift from the gods. The Santa Ana winds were picking up. The sky was clear except for a haze of pollution at the horizon. A full strength Southern California sun was flooding down. He was listening to NPR on the radio as he bathed in the sun. An interview was being aired with Professor Alan Minasu, a notorious environmentalist and an award winning marine biologist. Minasu had been arrested and served ten years for bombing commercial fishing ships in several states up and down the east and west coasts. For a one-year period of time, Minasu's presence was felt and feared any place where endangered fisheries were being harvested. The over-fishing practice had slowed and some environments were probably saved. No one knew who was behind the bombings until the end when the FBI apprehended him. To Mark, the man was an eco-terrorist of the worst kind, not a scientist. It was a shame that he was one of the most articulate and brilliant speaker on the environmental scene today. His past behavior had been forgiven. He was the G. Gordon Liddy of the environmentalists, convicted felon reborn as a media personality.

"The problem has been growing for decades with almost no public awareness," said Minasu. "Today, the Colorado River has been dammed in so many places and water is siphoned off to such a degree that what

flows out into the Gulf of California is often a trickle. For millions of years, the Colorado River provided twenty percent of the fresh water to the Gulf of California wetlands. These were vast breeding grounds for birds and sea life that flourished. Now, the wetlands are a desert of dry clamshells. For hundreds of square miles all you see are plains of these bleached white shells. All of that used to be the fertile bottom of wetlands."

"The Gulf of California is a key location where migratory birds lay over and whales come to give birth to their young. A thriving fishing industry is there, which harvests shrimp and fish. They are an important source of these foods."

"This is both a potential environmental disaster for the world and an economic disaster for Mexico. All it would take to defuse this ticking bomb is to give back a small percentage of the water currently being diverted in the United States. There are hundreds of locations along the Colorado River where water is taken for irrigation and drinking. If each state just took one percent less, this disaster could be averted. Several environmental organizations have been trying for years to get the states along the river to give back one percent. No one is willing to budge. With water rights and water laws in the way, getting one percent back will take an act of Congress. When talking with the individual water authorities for these states, you would think we were asking them for one percent of their tax base instead of what, in many cases, amounts to less than a fraction of a percent of their state's total water usage..."

Mark shook his head. Minasu was absolutely right and on-target as usual. He didn't know which was more frustrating: the blind eye we turn toward environmental crisis or having a jerk like Minasu as the representative to the world on such important matters. We were ignoring global warming, loss of topsoil, and water pollution to the point where we might not be able to feed the world's population by mid-century. What was hardwired so wrongly in us that we were this self-centered, this greedy, knowingly destroying the world our children would inherit?

Mark couldn't stand to listen anymore and turned off the radio. He was almost at his destination anyway. Wilshire Boulevard was sloping down toward the ocean. A man wearing a monk's robe stood by a corner holding a six foot wooden cross. A sign hung around his neck: '*They are threatened by our pillaging! The End is near!*' A small crowd had gathered. Two police officers were getting out of their car.

Mark felt sorry for the man. There were damaged people like that in every city of the world. One block from a cliff that dropped off into the Pacific Ocean, he cut over onto Lincoln Boulevard which ran parallel to the coast, then turned west on San Vicente. Mark parked his car on a small side street. Tall trees canopied the midsize houses along the block. The neighborhood was just a fifteen-minute walk from the Pacific, but it could have been a street anywhere in the country.

Mark walked to the end of the block and stopped. The house never seemed to change. It was a small two bedroom with Ivy covered trellises and olive trees. He remembered a moment from years ago…he and Julie in the front yard picking olives. He smiled with the memory. Julie had read a book on how to cure olives. One step was to soak them in lye. He had told her it sounded insane and that the book had to have been written by mad anarchists. Julie had persisted and the olives turned out to be the best he'd ever eaten.

The front door opened. His daughter Mary came running out. She was only nine but already looked so much like Julie. She had her mother's eyes and mouth and hair. She was wearing a private school uniform, a plaid skirt, white socks and shoes.

"Hi daddy!" she screamed.

He knelt down to her height. As she hugged him, he felt all the wonderful times: the picnics on the beach, the trips to the zoo, the endless rides at Disneyland. She whispered, "I love you, Daddy."

He looked past his daughter's hair and saw his ex-wife in the doorway. She was smiling warmly. He looked into her face. Memories surfaced and his happiness waned. There were the nights he never came home, the expeditions into the field – and always a coed to share the evenings, a different gal for each semester. What had he been looking for? What had he been running from? Julie smiled. She had forgiven him long ago, but he could never forgive himself. She had divorced him saying she loved him – and herself – too much to live like this.

Mary kissed him on the cheek and dragged him off to see her latest work of art. She had it pinned on the refrigerator with pink ladybug magnets. The painting was a watercolor of the ocean and gulls and an island in bright sunlight.

"Daddy, I want to show you my picture of you... I'll get it. Stay here."

Julie came into the kitchen. She was wearing a pair of jeans and a red blouse. Her eyes could say more than any woman he knew. Deep brown and moist like pools of warm emotion. They seemed to move over his face, taking in the new lines, the subtle hints.

"You look unhappy," she said. "Are you all right?"

"I'm fine... I was thinking of taking Mary to the beach this weekend."

Julie sat down in a chair beside him. She picked up his hand and rested it between hers. A vague sensation of electricity moved along his arm. The feeling was pleasant. She was leaning forward. Her eyes were only inches from his. He leaned back a little. He felt a sensation of dizziness. Had he taken his insulin this morning?

"Something is bothering you," she said. "I can see it. You're not drinking again, are you?"

"No, of course not. I know it's bad for diabetics to drink. Wreaks havoc with the old blood sugar levels."

"I'm worried about you…"

~

The sun would be setting in a few hours. The air was still unseasonably warm from the Santa Ana winds. Mark sat in a deckchair on his roof. His townhouse was on the canals in Venice Beach, a block from the Pacific. Over the roof of the building in front of him, he could see the ocean meeting the horizon. The water seemed to reach up to fill half the sky. The brine scented wind conjured memories of him and Julie sailing on the bay. A pitcher of margaritas sat on a glass coffee table. He was fixing himself his third. He wet the rim of the glass, then pressed it into a dish filled with salt. The iced margarita mix was still a cold slush.

His stomach grumbled. Gracy would be home from her classes soon. Maybe they'd go out for something to eat. He'd been on the roof for over an hour watching the ducks swim in the canal. For the first drink or so he'd been thinking about Julie and what he had done to her, but those thoughts had stopped and now he was just happy to sail on pleasant dreams. Occasionally, a few seagulls would show up at the canal's edge, poke around a bit, and then leave. He realized he was enjoyably drunk and slurped some more of his margarita.

The steel door leading to the roof opened with a familiar creaking. Mark looked up. It was Gracy. A gold colored beer can was dangling from one of her fingers by its plastic six-pack loops. She was wearing jeans and one of the tropical shirts that he'd bought her for their trip to the Bahamas. Her fingernails were pink. Her eyes were a coral blue. She was a stunning creature. His world never failed to change in her presence.

"What are you doing?" she asked.

"Having a party – want to join me?"

"I don't know. My mother warned me about guys like you."

"I promise to be good."

"Hope not," she said.

Chapter 2

Survivors

1 – Atlanta, Georgia: November

Dr. Kathy Morrison stared at her reflection in the mirror. An hour from now, a blind date would be knocking on her door. Her hair was okay but her makeup was not. She started to make her face over again. She knew she was acting crazy but couldn't help it. She was a very attractive woman but had never been confident in her beauty. During her years at Harvard Medical, she had dated an endless procession of soon-to-be doctors. None of the relationships had lasted, and with each ending she had lavished greater and greater blame onto herself. At the odd moments when she dared to look back, she saw an entire life filled with blame.

During her final year of medical school, she had met and married Barry Lakeman, a successful surgeon who had been brought in to lecture on liver transplants. Barry the great, Barry the ego. She had dumped his last name along with the marriage two years, twelve days, and – she glanced at a bathroom clock – six hours ago. She could still feel *that feeling* from the day when she had come home early, walked into their bedroom, and found Barry thrusting furiously between the legs of the neighbor's nineteen-year-old daughter. That evening, Barry's stellar defense had been that the girl was no virgin, just a neighborhood slut who had chased him relentlessly and caught him at a moment of weakness.

Kathy set her lipstick down. She was getting angry and knew from experience that applying makeup in this frame of mind led to undesirable results. She went into the kitchen, drank some Diet Coke, and tried to relax. This was only a blind date; she didn't have to marry him. A cat mewed from beyond the kitchen.

"Tolstoy, here baby," she called.

A gray Siamese with blue eyes sauntered into the kitchen. He stopped at her feet, batted her slipper once, then ducked out of sight behind the far end of the table. Kathy laughed and thought *typical Tolstoy*. He looked so cute at his games. He never cuddled and preferred catnip mice to food. Kathy wondered where the other little monster was hiding. The third member of the Morrison household was a seal point Persian named Socrates, 'Socks' for short, in honor of a past feline member of The White House.

Kathy considered the cats two of her best friends. She lavished them with everything she imagined they'd crave. She fed them almost exclusively on people-food and in the living room they had a kitty condo: a scratching post that ran from ceiling to floor, with lookout platforms and a cylindrical den at the top. The kitty condo had been very expensive before she'd had it recovered with the same Berber carpeting that was on the floor. One of Kathy's closer friends, of the human variety, had once said that she treated her cats better than she treated herself. Her friend was right.

Kathy opened a box of chocolate truffles to go with her Diet Coke. It was time to get a grip and climb out of this funky mood. She'd done well... hadn't she? At forty-two, she was a respected medical researcher. She had friends who really cared. She had a very desirable condo in the exciting Buckhead neighborhood of Atlanta, the Greenwich Village of the South, and she loved it. Countless distractions greeted her the minute she walked out the door: restaurants, movies, bars. Sure, there was crime; but what urban area was free of that particularly human blight? *Buck up kid*, she thought with a smile, *you're doing fine*. She slurped the last of her Diet Coke and returned to the bathroom to face her makeup and mirror.

~

Kathy was nursing her first drink of the evening. Jack, her blind date, was turning out to be far better than she'd expected. They were seated outside under a canopy while waiting for their table. It had rained earlier and the streets were wet and the air clean. There were reflections of colored lights dappling the roadway. Jack was talking about his job as vice president of marketing for CNN. Kathy was impressed. He was gorgeous and successful. Minutes ago she had started thinking about the condom in her purse. The condom had been there for over a year, buried under makeup and breath mints and keys. It was the kind wrapped in foil. She remembered rediscovering it a month ago and thinking that the edges of the wrapper had looked rusty just like her love life. She stared into Jack's face. Not hearing a word he was saying, she considered the unavoidable fact that she hadn't slept with a man for over a year. There it was – an uncomfortable truth. She found herself hoping that Jack would seduce her. She would never have the nerve to take the initiative.

The maitre'd appeared to usher them to their table. Jack slipped the man some folded money and whispered something to him. They were led to a quiet table separated from the others by a row of potted palms.

Two more drinks had arrived, and Kathy was starting to relax. Her half of the conversation was growing more personal.

"I feel like my life's been stuck in one of those cheap romance novels," said Kathy. "I was the orphan kid who grew up to be a doctor."

"Did you know your parents?"

"They died when I was eight. Killed in an auto accident. I ended up at an orphanage run by the Catholic Church. Up until then, I'd seen the inside of a church exactly twice, once for a distant relative's marriage and once for a Christmas mass. Almost immediately, the sisters at Holy Cross singled me out as a gifted student. It was like I was going to be their example of success, their reason for being nuns. Most of the time I resented it, but their little ploy worked. I got a scholarship to Harvard."

"Harvard's a good university," said Jack. "Me... I went straight from prep school to Yale law, and from there to upper management. It's sort of a family tradition. Yale, I mean."

Jack took a sip of his drink. He appeared so refined.

"Did I mention my cousin's running for congress in Virginia?" said Jack.

"No, that's got to be exciting," said Kathy.

Jack glanced at a woman at another table. He'd done that several times since they'd sat down. Kathy was trying to ignore it.

"I've been through elections before," said Jack. "My family's been in politics for almost a hundred years. We've had three US representatives and two state senators. I'm the black sheep for not going into politics."

"Why didn't you?" asked Kathy.

"Nothing there except wiping the behinds of a bunch of sniveling constituents and a government pension in the end. Now television, there's a career with a serious up-side."

He grinned with his mouth, but the eyes lacked warmth. They had an impenetrable sheen that seemed to deflect all feeling directed toward him and revealed nothing of what was inside.

"I'm a senior VP at CNN. In five years, with my connections, I'll be president of one of the majors. Forget politics. It's the media that controls this country."

As dinner blended into ordering dessert, Kathy began to notice one constant. Jack never stopped talking and the topic seldom veered from money. She knew how much his house cost, his Corvette, even his Armani dinner jacket. She was starting to wonder when he would get around to telling her how much his perfectly straight white teeth cost. Or were they just one more sign of the genetic perfection of his lineage? She just wanted to go home. How could such an enticing beginning have reached so disgusting a finish? At least now the entire evening made sense. Earlier, Kathy had been wondering how such an eligible man had escaped marriage for so long; now she knew.

"Don't look now," said Jack.

"Look at what?"

"The couple that just sat down behind you. That's Laurence De Pontane. He owns Jazz 24, that new club. The guy's in his sixties and that girl can't be more than eighteen. Gotta be a hooker... low cut black dress, black pumps... Wonder how much she's charging him?"

"Excuse me," said Kathy. "I need to visit the ladies room. If you're really curious you can ask her."

Kathy stood, picked up her purse, and headed toward the rest room and the lobby. She hoped she could find a cab fast. She couldn't believe she was doing this. She'd never run out on a date before, but Jack had succeeded in making her insane.

2 – Atlanta, Georgia: November

The morning sun barely penetrated the heavy rain clouds. The world was gray. The CDC facility was a nondescript multistory building of black glass. It was located in an Atlanta Suburb twenty miles from the city line. A small sign read *United States Government, 19002 River Road.* Circling the building and its parking lot was a fifteen-foot fence topped with barbed wire. The entrance gate was electronically controlled, requiring a magnetic badge to enter. The facility received few visitors, and those who did arrive had to be accompanied by a CDC employee. From every corner of the building, remote controlled cameras monitored all movement to the property's fence line and beyond.

Inside, past the reception lobby and security checkpoint was a research facility more tightly controlled than a nuclear lab, and far more dangerous. Samples of all known pathogens were stored in cryogenic vaults housed below ground level. Included in this little collection were quantities of the twelve known incurable viruses and bacteria. The scientists referred to them as the Twelve Apostles. This was the nation's most advanced civilian laboratory for research on lethal communicable diseases. Its official designation was BVMC lab, which stood for Bacterial and Viral Maximum Containment. The laboratory exceeded all level-4 containment regulations; it was the most secure facility in the country and probably in the world. The facility's funding was lavish compared to other CDC installations, due in large measure to its designation as part of the National Defense Network. Somewhat surprisingly, years ago, the talking heads in Congress had actually realized that diseases killed more people than bombs; and that these microbes were a much greater threat to this country than nuclear weapons. The tragedy of 9/11, anthrax mail attacks, the War on Terror, and killer flues had increased the funding to a point that they were running large surpluses every year.

Kathy unlocked the door to her office. The door had a cipher lock as well as a key. Several stories below ground, directly below her feet was the BVMC lab. Her left knee was sore. She'd twisted it last night while jumping into the taxi. That made three times this year she'd aggravated the old injury. She cursed her ex-husband Barry. A month after they'd been married, it had been his idea to go skiing and his encouragement that had led her into trying the advanced slopes. After three minutes of high speed downhill, her leg had been broken in two places and the knee seriously twisted. Her skiing career was over and her life with an occasional cane had begun.

Kathy set her cane against the side of the desk and eased herself into a chair. The cane had almost become her trademark around the office. She seemed to need the walking stick's support more often with each passing year. She placed an ice pack on the throbbing knee. She now kept a supply of them in a mini-fridge that was part of the office furnishings.

She looked around her second home. Half her desk was a layered mess of files and paperwork and open books. A large computer flat-panel display and keyboard occupied the only clear spot. Her bookcases were precariously stuffed with thick computer printouts and medical reference sets. She was the CDC's prized expert on immunological response to bacterial and viral pathogens. She was even mildly famous within a small circle of scientists. She had developed very novel ways of studying in vitro immunological reactions to every one of the Twelve Apostles. Her special status as *the CDC expert* gave her the privilege of working twelve-hour days, six days a week, but the pay made up for it. After six years she now pulled in almost as much as a general practitioner who was just starting their career. Barry had gone nuts when she began working for the government whose pay scale averaged one half that of the private sector.

Money had never been a motivation for Kathy. She became a doctor to help people. She'd decided to work for the CDC because no one was doing a more successful job wiping out the killer diseases. In her first year at the CDC, she'd worked as a rookie field agent for the EIS, Epidemiological Intelligence Service. She was sent to New York City where drug resistant tuberculosis was staging a comeback. EIS agents were the detectives of the medical community: they went into places where unknown killers were loose, tracked them down, and stopped them. No organization in the world was better at it. Working this job was the first time in her life that Kathy had felt whole. When she was on the trail of a disease, nothing else mattered, nothing else entered her mind. Her past was, for the moment, erased. What she did saved lives.

Kathy logged onto her computer. She clicked open a window and began to read her e-mail. The telephone rang. Dr. Jeffrey Renoir's voice greeted her on the line. He was a friend and colleague who worked at the main CDC campus in Atlanta. She put on a headset and continued to go through her e-mail.

"I have a problem with a disease. I'd like to go it over with you," said Jeffrey. "It's a hot agent, maybe a new species jumper; and I can't identify it. It fits no patterns in our database."

"Tell me about it."

"What we know of the early symptoms is limited because we haven't found a living subject or witness. So far, it's one hundred percent fatal. I have an EIS team in a Brazilian village ninety miles out of nowhere. They've sent me a couple of digitized pictures over a satellite link. It's ugly stuff – people lying everywhere, babies, women, men. It looks like it hit so fast that people were dropping in mid-stride. There are sixty bodies, the whole damn village. There's nothing left except dogs, livestock, and insects."

Kathy was no longer looking at her e-mail. Her eyes were staring at a team photo on the wall; but in her mind, she was seeing images of what Jeffrey was describing, images reinforced by things she'd witnessed during a stint with an EIS team in Africa during an Ebola breakout. Her voice was tense.

"I've never," she repeated, "never heard of a hot agent killing as fast or as completely as what you're describing. Jeffrey, you don't have a disease. You have a toxin. What's the military like down there? Do they have any history with chemical weapons?"

"That's what I'd thought, too. Believe me, I wouldn't be bothering you if I hadn't eliminated that possibility. We ran all the tests for chemical agents and came up with zero. Preliminary autopsy results indicate asphyxial deaths with secondary heart seizures – no signs of lung collapse, physical injury or fluid build up. These people just stopped breathing and their hearts quit. The only clue I've got is antibody counts that are through the roof, but nothing disease specific. The counts are uniformly raised across all antibody types."

Kathy went down a mental decision tree. Respiratory arrest. Pulmonary infarction or edema could be fatal, but they were caused by long term circulatory problems or injury. She shook her head. Not relevant. Lack of fluid in the lungs was the important clue. It was impossible to have a fatal bacterial or viral assault on the respiratory system without massive fluid build up. An extreme reaction to a toxin was the only thing that made sense.

"Broad immune response can be a symptom of an allergic reaction," she said. "People die from anaphylactic reactions to bee stings. I agree it's rare for an allergic reaction to cause asphyxiation, but then we don't know what kind of chemical you're dealing with."

"I'm telling you it's not a chemical! Assays of blood chemistry and tissue samples show zero trace of foreign agents," said Jeffrey.

"There's no way this is a naturally occurring disease," said Kathy. "How could an entire village succumb to the same pathogen at the same time? It's not possible!"

"Kathy, if you'd just look at the reports. I went through the same thoughts you're having and had the same doubts. A chemical potent enough to kill people would've killed the dogs and pigs too. It's not a chemical weapon. Who on earth could have come up with one that kills this quickly and this selectively? I give the military mad scientists a lot of credit for their inventiveness, but not this time. This one scares the hell out of me because I'm convinced it's of natural origin, and that means it could have come from anywhere and could be heading to anywhere."

"Is the report on Secure-Net?" asked Kathy.

She heard some keyboard clattering over the phone.

"I just gave you access and e-mailed you the link."

3 – South Atlantic near the Shetland Islands: November

Lieutenant Paul 'PJ' Orton was a confident man. His entire life was based on an inner foundation of stone. He could walk into a village of hostiles and survive simply because he knew he would. His theory had been proven in dozens of secret conflicts around the globe.

PJ was the team leader of a Navy SEAL special ops group. Currently he was missioned to a hunter-killer sub named Sea Wolf. They were somewhere off the coast of Argentina under the Antarctic ice cap. The water temperature was lethal. Direct exposure could kill a healthy man before he could swim a hundred feet. High salt content was the only thing that kept the sea from turning into solid ice.

PJ and his team were here to conduct top secret tests for Project Gail using an experimental diving system designed for super-chilled waters. Project Gail was a classified plan to use ice floes as a weapon of blockade. The SEAL team's task was to conduct placement and detonation runs, using plastic explosives to simulate the tactical nukes called for in the actual implementation plan. Project Gail was a strategy based on using tactical nukes to create massive flows of icebergs to choke off sea traffic through the straits at the tip of South America and South Africa.

The Captain of the boat walked into the ready room while PJ was briefing his men. A visit by the captain was unusual. Their eyes met. Captain Bradford's expression was rigid. When the mission requirements had been transmitted on board the other day, PJ had gotten an earful from Bradford. The man didn't like taking his boat under the treacherous Antarctic ice of this region. The bottom was nothing but rocky peaks that jutted up thousands of feet from deep water while, at the same time, broken ice floes reached down from the surface like drifting mountains.

Bradford had complained that navigating these canyons was like sailing into the maw of a huge animal while it slowly ground its teeth.

A sailor entered the ready room and handed Bradford a slip of paper.

"We've reached station," said Bradford. "Lieutenant, get your men wet."

The first thing PJ noticed as he exited the airlock was the water. There were no currents and it was clearer than anywhere he'd dived before. Rays of sunlight were slashing through it from cracks in the overhead ice. He adjusted a knob on his chest plate. A tiny stream of bubbles scrambled toward the surface. His buoyancy decreased. The automatic depth control was venting air. The device clicked off at 30 fathoms. PJ hovered weightless a dozen feet above and to the side of a narrow shelf of rock. He could see a few shrimp and crabs clinging to the rocks. The shelf itself stuck out from the top of a stone peak as if it were the remaining span of a long ago crumbled bridge.

Above him and to the right was the bluish-gray hull of the leviathan that was their submarine. Underneath PJ and the sub was an endless void. He could feel the depth pulling on his body. Below his feet, a trench reached down for miles into the blackness of the earth. He was literally floating alongside the top of a chain of submerged mountains. He could easily imagine something unknown sweeping up from the depths and devouring him and his men. No one would ever know what had happened. The captain had been right. This area was like the mouth of a giant monster. PJ's men joined up with him. They were able to communicate amongst themselves and the boat with voice-scrambled hydrophones.

"Hey, PJ," radioed one of his men. "I feel as warm as if I'd peed in my suit."

There was laughter...

"Shut up, Whale!" snapped PJ.

It wasn't until Whale had mentioned warmth that PJ noticed how comfortable he was and how uncomfortable he should have felt. This coldwater gear worked better than anything he'd tried before. The suit was as thick as standard coldwater latex, but inside its layers was a secret. There were thousands of tiny capillary tubes webbed into the material. Within the tubes circulated an anti-freeze mix that had been heated in a chemical reaction chamber. The solid fuel was a classified mix of acids and metal salts good for five hours of operation. The entire suit was airtight, including a full helmet similar to that worn by astronauts.

A vast school of fish swam into view just a few yards below his feet. There had to be millions of them. They were two inches long and the color of silver. They changed direction in perfect synchronization, zigzagging to the commands of an invisible director. The beginning and end of the school were lost in the natural blurring effects of the water; at a distance of twenty feet, small objects like these fish became invisible.

"Okay, girls," said PJ. "It's time for a little exercise. We're going to conduct a live explosives drill. Let's make believe that chunk of free ice is part of the Antarctic ice shelf."

PJ dialed up a new depth adjustment. A measured amount of air was shunted from his tank into a buoyancy vest. Like a mini-submarine, he rose to meet the ice. PJ's part of the mission was to observe the dexterity of his men using the new suits. He watched them from a few feet away. The water changed in tint as sunlight took different angles through the slowly shifting ice.

PJ was distracted when he noticed the school of tiny fish had swum up higher in the water. The entire school had returned to within a few yards from his feet. Maybe they were attracted to something about the new diving suits – the sound or the color? At different spots, single fish broke synchronization and collided into other fish, causing tiny areas of confusion inside the larger school. PJ maneuvered closer to the school to get a better look. This was odd behavior. He'd never seen anything like this in two decades underwater. After each collision, the culprit fish fluttered around a bit then caught back up with the synchronization of the school, effectively vanishing from view. The entire mass of fish seemed to be changing course, moving off toward the sub.

PJ turned toward his men. The water near his men was filled with tiny bubbles. For a moment, nothing odd registered. Then PJ realized none of his men were moving. They just hung there in neutral buoyancy. Thousands of two-inch fish darted past him on all sides. The school had reversed course and was moving by him like a blizzard of sequins. His mind snapped into action. His men! Instinctively, he was swimming toward them. He could tell by the limp drifting of their arms and legs that they were unconscious or dead. Something had to be going seriously wrong with the experimental suits. He radioed for help.

"Mayday, Mayday, Sea Wolf, this is PJ. I am declaring a mission scrub. I need help. My men are HIA – Over…"

There was no reply. He reached the first of his men. It was Whale. PJ grabbed him by the vest and lifted his faceplate into view. Whale's lips were a vivid blue. The capillaries in his eyes had ruptured. PJ knew the symptoms. He was dead from lack of oxygen. PJ checked Whale's gauges and tanks. Everything appeared to be working fine.

"Sea Wolf, this is PJ... Mayday, mayday! Answer me, over."

Still, no reply. The com must have failed. What was going on with this equipment? Every major system bugging out at the same time was impossible.

There was a metallic popping sound. PJ looked up toward the boat. It was moving. The hull was slowly drifting lower as tiny streams of bubbles vented from its sides. The air volume wasn't enough to be a response to a flood command; it was more like ballast adjustments used to trim a boat.

PJ swam to the next closest man. He was also dead. There was a tint of blood drifting from shredded fingertips. It looked like the man had died while trying to tear his helmet off.

A shadow moved across PJ. He turned around. The Sea Wolf was drifting lower; starting to nose down. His eye grew wide as the leviathan moved past him and into the void. The boat's downward momentum was increasing. This was not a controlled maneuver. The boat was dead. In less than a minute it had vanished into the endless black. The suits, the boat – what kind of colossal equipment fuckup was this?

PJ heard the horrible groaning of a hull scraping against rocky peaks. He imagined what it would be like to die in that disabled boat; then a thought grabbed him and shook him back into the present. He was stranded. PJ closed his eyes then opened them. Nothing changed. He was still in the water and the submarine was lost. He was going to die. His unfailing confidence was gone. No amount of SEAL training could help him survive this. Once he ran out of air, all that was waiting for him topside was the subzero weather of an ice flow.

4 – Atlanta, Georgia: November – a few days later

The shower was warm heaven. Kathy sluiced the soap from her body. She felt human again. Her ritual of waking was never complete until her shower. She'd been known to wander like a ghost for hours until revived by warm water.

The phone started ringing. At first she decided to let it go, but there was something about how it continued ringing that worried her. She grabbed a towel and padded across the bedroom. The phone stopped just as she reached it. She walked back into the bathroom and started to towel her hair. The phone started ringing again.

"Hello," she said.

"It's Jeffrey."

His voice sounded disturbed. Tolstoy was licking water off her toes. She barely noticed the small rough tongue.

"It's happened again," said Jeffrey. "Eighty-two dead, the whole scenario. Déjà vu."

"How close to the first site?" asked Kathy.

"That's what's spooked me. Try almost a thousand miles. We're not even talking Brazil. It's a fishing village in Cabo San Diego, an island off the southern tip of Argentina."

"Is an EIS team there yet?"

"Same team, same pictures, same test results. What the hell is going on?"

"I'm telling you Jeffrey, it's got all the symptoms of a chemical, not a disease. Mobility like this also rules out any kind of contagion vector unless we've got a walking-wounded that came from the Brazilian village, boarded a jet, and flew to Cabo-whatever to spread the disease there."

"I ran all the tests again," said Jeffrey. "There's no trace of chemical agents. It's biological and the director agrees with me."

"I don't."

"Well, you'll get a chance to prove it."

"What's that supposed to mean?"

"I just finished talking with the director. He's instructed me to give you all the assistance I can. You're the new head of this investigation. He's probably got his secretary trying to get you on the phone right now."

"Why me?"

"It's the antibody levels of the victims. It's the only lead we've got and you're one of the best when it comes to reverse engineering a pathogen from immune system responses. Kathy, I'm certain it's a bug. There's more proof than you know. I'm not authorized to share this, but you're going to know it all in a few hours anyway. There was a third incident. The Navy is sending us the body of a diver who died in this third incident. There's a lot of secrecy surrounding what happened. All I know is that this diver left port in a submarine two weeks ago and was swimming in a couple hundred feet of water when he died. The spooky thing is he died at nearly the same time as villagers of Cabo San Diego; but he was in the Antarctic, six hundred miles south of Cabo San Diego."

"That's impossible," said Kathy. "What are we dealing with here – simultaneous exposures of a Navy diver and villagers in Cabo San Diego plus an exact two-week onset period? What kind of bug acts like that?"

"I haven't slept in days. Now it's your turn to lose some sleep."

"Where's the body being sent?"

"The safest place in the world for it... the BVMC lab. Cadavers are also coming from Cabo San Diego."

Kathy took a deep breath, then let it out slowly. She was upset and confused. There was something very wrong going on here. Government agencies didn't go all out like this over events in poor countries unless there was a mountain of political pressure, so this was all about the Navy diver.

"Jeffrey, have you asked yourself why the United States government is suddenly moving so hard on this? I don't want to sound insensitive but, to politicians, what we have are a lot of dead South Americans and one Navy sailor. South Americans don't get to vote in U.S. elections. You practically have to kidnap a politician before they'll listen to you about any public health issue unless it's bio-weapons related. Remember the assistance we got with drug resistant TB? Zero. That monster had hospitalized or killed a hundred times more than this disaster. No, there's got to be something horrible that we don't know and the Pols do."

"I don't want to add to your paranoia," said Jeffrey. "But there's a media blackout in effect; national security has been invoked. This could turn into a stealth operation before you even get your hands on it. Someone very high up in the political food chain is worried about this bug, someone much higher than Director Shaw."

The moment Kathy hung up from Jeffrey, the phone rang again. Director Shaw's secretary was on the line; Shaw himself came on a few minutes later. Kathy knew the drill. The director was a very predictable political animal. He delivered a bit of the carrot, a bit of stick, and a not-so-subtle request to work twenty-four hours a day. Oh, and one more thing. The kicker and probable reason for the personal call: she was to funnel everything through his office, and that meant everything.

Kathy got dressed and packed a suitcase. She coaxed the kids, Tolstoy and Socks, into their kitty cage and took them out to her Jeep. She knew she wouldn't be home for days. The kids were used to the drill. They had a lot of human friends on the fourth floor of the BVMC lab.

~

The room was growing dark. Kathy looked around the ruin of her office. The floor was covered with papers. Her desk was a minefield of half empty coffee cups and partially eaten food; and worse, Jeffrey was snoring on her couch. At daybreak, he would be on his way to South America to supervise the field operation. His wife had called just before lunchtime. It had sounded like they were arguing about him leaving. When he'd hung up, Kathy had asked him if he was okay and had gotten only a shrug in response.

Kathy decided to let him continue napping. There was a backlog of work waiting for her. The analysis of blood and tissue samples would be available on her computer within the hour. Everything done at the lab revolved around the CDC WAN and Secure-Net. All data, both visual and written, was stored in massive servers. All laboratory equipment was computer remote-controlled. All lab work was monitored by digital video cameras and archived.

Kathy had ordered a full workup of the respiratory and cardiac control regions of the Navy diver's brainstem, including cross-sectional scanning of the regions, using the lab's newest 3D Microscopic-MRI imaging equipment. Since the sailor died because his lungs stopped operating and there were no other clues, Kathy decided to start reverse engineering by investigating the area of the brainstem that controlled respiration and heart. Maybe the chemical agent targeted this nerve tissue; and if it did, there would be traces. She was still convinced the cause of death was chemical and not biological.

Kathy clicked a bookmark on her desktop. A live video feed from the BVMC lab appeared inside a browser window. Her screen was twenty-five inches across and capable of displaying images with many times the resolution of the best high definition television. The BVMC lab had been designed so the scientists never had to enter the containment room. They typed work orders into their computers. From there, lab technicians wearing special biohazard containment suits, who staffed the facility twenty-four hours a day, carried out the procedures. The technicians were called lab rats by the staff and they wore this title with pride. The name strips on each of their personal containment suits read "Lab Rat" in small lettering below their name as if it were a title. By CDC policy, access to the lab was restricted to essential personnel only. Doctors and scientists were almost always considered nonessential. Kathy often broke this rule. It required thirty minutes to complete the entry procedure to the containment lab – and even longer to exit, but she didn't mind. Sometimes she needed to do things herself. She felt subtle details were missed if her hands couldn't touch the work.

She clicked opened the report on tissue and blood toxicology for the sailor's brainstem. After reading and re-reading the report, she couldn't find anything that appeared abnormal. This just didn't make sense. There had to be something. She knew she was staring at the answer and just not seeing it.

She opened the recorded images from the Microscopic-MRI and leaned back in her chair. The detail was amazing. The results of 3D Microscopic-MRI never failed to leave her in awe. In front of her eyes was an alien world she could navigate with a computer screen and mouse. The imaging equipment delivered about one micron of resolution. She could see great detail in structures only a few cells in thickness, and even see the shapes of the cells themselves. She started by examining nerve bundles that exited the respiratory and cardiac regions of the brainstem.

A half hour into her exploration, something caught her eye. A few nerve fibers in a bundle were severed. The fibers were so thin that it would take thirty of them to equal the thickness of a human hair. She looked but could not find evidence of trauma or penetration of the bundle's outer protective sheath. This eliminated the possibility of mechanical damage from a weapon or accident.

Minutes after discovering the first cut, she was identifying one cut after another. While the nerve bundle had not been severed entirely in any one location, all the microscopic cuts added up to the same thing. The bundle had been effectively severed. This was clearly enough nerve damage to cause death. She knew she was on the trail of the killer. The satisfaction of catching and stopping this thing was like a drug that had just flowed into her veins. Even if she had wanted to stop, she could never stop now.

Kathy ordered twenty different samples of damaged nerve fibers prepared for the electron microscopes and for toxicology testing. In the past, the task of locating and sampling microscopic regions would have taken days. Now this job was completely automated. All Kathy had to do was mark the coordinates on the screen; and within minutes, micro-surgery robots were at work taking samples with needle-like bores. Her adrenaline flowed. She was going to nail this killer in hours, not days.

On the computer screen, Kathy watched as a lab technician wearing a containment suit inserted specimen carriers into a pair of electron microscopes. One of the instruments was a Scanning Electron Microscope, a SEM. The SEM was used to view intricate surface structure using a magnification power of up to nine hundred thousand times. The other instrument was a Transmission Electron Microscope, a TEM. The TEM didn't show surface structure but instead was used to see through a prepared cross-sectional slice of a specimen revealing internal details. The TEM worked in the same way a flashlight shining through a piece of paper would show its grain; except instead of light, it used a beam of electrons. This specific TEM had a magnification power of up to two million times, which was enough to show the vague shape of a single atom. A message appeared on her screen acknowledging that her work order was completed and the first specimen was loaded.

Kathy double clicked on the control panel for the SEM. She wasn't sure exactly what she was looking for in the damaged nerve fiber. With the SEM she would be able to see tremendous detail. The instrument could show shapes in even the smallest viruses that were three nanometers in size (0.000 000 000 118 inches). The cellular tissues of the sample looked normal in every aspect. Kathy moved the magnification up and down as she examined an edge that had been left from the robotic bore. Several minutes passed before she realized she was mistaken in what she was looking at. The cellular structure was normal, but this edge was not. The precision-cut edge she was looking at was not the result of slicing and mounting the sample – she'd just found that cut; it was in a different plane and far more ragged. Whatever severed these nerve fibers had cut them with laser-like precision. No, better than laser precision. This was a microscopic cut that was clean to way below the level of cellular structure. A chemical cut could do something similar over a small distance but not over the length of this hundred micron cut she was examining. This definitely meant something, but what?

Kathy ordered examinations and samples taken from the same region of the brainstem on all the victims. The request took only minutes to fill out on a webpage; the task itself would take days to complete for every cadaver. Her only consolation was that she would start receiving results from the five cadavers at the lab within hours; and those five would be more than enough to uncover a pattern if one existed. Now that the lab had her orders, she returned her attention to the microscopic samples she already had in her possession.

Hours later, Kathy was still at her desk. She had been staring blankly for over an hour at the same microscopic view of damaged nerve fiber. Nothing was going through her mind; she just stared. Every detail had been scrutinized long ago.

~

Midnight had come and gone. Kathy had tried to sleep after reading reports on three of the cadavers. She'd been unable to shake off a psychosomatic tingling in the back of her neck where her brainstem ended and the damage had been done to all those people. Sleep was impossible. She was at her desk. A pot of coffee was in her stomach and a fresh cup was in her hands. Her thoughts were locked in arguments over a small set of facts that were not providing any useful answers. A lined pad of paper covered with her rambling thoughts was staring back at her. There had to be something obvious she was missing.

A soft rapping came from the other side of her door. Kathy looked up. There was a shadow under the doorway from a pair of shoes. She knew it had to be Jeffrey. He'd left his bags for safekeeping while going out to pre-mission briefings and dinner. An Air Force transport that would race him to a small piece of hell in the southern hemisphere was due to leave soon at a painfully early hour of the morning. Kathy straightened herself up a bit.

"Its open," she called.

"I though you'd be asleep," said Jeffrey as he peered in through the partially opening doorway. "Sorry, about not collecting my bags earlier."

"I may have found a link between our victims," said Kathy.

Jeffrey appeared to have completely forgotten why he was in her office. There was a stunned expression on his face.

"What link?" he finally asked.

Kathy picked up a stack of lab reports she'd printed for him and handed them over.

"A little light reading for your flight," she said. "All the victims I've examined so far have the same nerve damage in their brainstems. The region controlling respiration and heart were disconnected by microscopic cuts to key nerves. Toxicology is completely negative. This nerve damage is the cause of death, but I have no idea how it happened. The microscopic incisions were not caused by anything mechanical, and I can't figure out how a chemical agent could have dissolved fibers without affecting adjacent tissue."

"So you've decided it's not a chemical toxin," said Jeffrey. "The only thing left is biological. Does this mean you've come over to my side?"

"I can't see how a bacterium or virus could have done this either. It's just too clean."

"What, no little teeth marks?" said Jeffrey.

5 – The Nevada Desert: November

The Army helicopter bucked through an air thermal, dropping a good ten feet. General James H. McKafferty didn't blink, didn't flinch, he barely even noticed. The same was not true for the other four passengers who sat opposite him in the forward facing seats. Their faces were pale and clammy, as if all the blood had drained to lower parts of their bodies. McKafferty smiled at their weakness. Civilians, he thought. He was a bear of a man at six three and two hundred forty pounds.

The United States Senator glanced at him, then turned away with a trace of fear in his eyes. McKafferty was a truly ugly man. He knew this and liked the power it gave him. He had gotten that look of fear from others all day long and all the days of his life. His face was large and quarter moon shaped on profile. A pair of jug ears stuck out rudely from below a peach fuzz of gray hair. His skin had a ruddy leather complexion from too much booze and fistfights.

There was a black and gold braided insignia on his jacket just below his shoulder. The emblem contained a cobra coiled around a sword with the letters BARDCOM below it. This was McKafferty's command: Biological Armaments Research and Development Command.

"We should be reaching *The Zone* in a few more minutes," said McKafferty.

Senator Kitridge nodded, then continued looking out his window. Their destination was out in the middle of the desert on property annexed by Nellis Air Force base more than two decades ago. This was BARDCOM's primary facility. The site was so highly classified that it did not exist.

McKafferty had picked up the Senator at McCarrin Airport thirty minutes ago. The Senator had arrived in a Lear Jet owned by Caesar's World. This was his third trip to Vegas this year. He was the ranking member of the Defense Appropriations Committee and had oversight authority on McKafferty's command.

Across the left windows, the peaks that ringed Las Vegas like a giant crater drifted past. McKafferty forced a smile at the Senator's aide, a woman in her early twenties. She looked away also with that hint of fear he recognized as matter-of-factly as others noticed the weather or the temperature of their food. She'd have to be parked somewhere before he and the Senator finished their tour.

As *The Zone* came into view, McKafferty described it for the benefit of the passengers who were making their first tour. The structure looked like an octagonal concrete slab that had been dropped from the sky into the middle of endless sand. The structure measured eight hundred feet across with one story above ground and six below. The only markings were the white outlines of a helicopter pad on the roof. There were no roads. All supplies and personnel came by air. Ten thousand men and women were stationed there on permanent assignment; half were scientists, the other half soldiers. The facility was the size of a small town.

A coded message had come in a few minutes ago. The contents had left McKafferty distracted. He recited his welcome speech but his mind was on the Sea Wolf incident. The salvage operation had gone smoothly. A pair of deep submersibles had dropped down onto the sub. Luckily, it had settled onto a ledge that was only a thousand feet down. If the currents had been any stronger, the boat might have ended up in the bottom of a trench with its belly crushed like a cheap beer can, and the Navy would have never found out what had happened.

The crew had been evacuated. Ninety-eight percent of them were dead; three survived. The medical staff at BARDCOM had been unable to explain what had happened. The dead had been asphyxiated. Two crewmembers and a SEAL had survived without any signs of injury. What kind of hot agent could attack soldiers in a sealed environment like a sub? McKafferty was a man of conviction and honor, and with that came the ability to intuitively recognize things for what they were. He had no doubt that this event was an attack.

A satellite had picked up a garbled signal from Sea Wolf. One of the crew had apparently managed to launch a com-buoy but had no idea how to operate it. After the boat had failed to respond to a ULF alert signal, aircraft were dispatched for a look-see. The sub jockeys owed their lives to a half frozen SEAL lieutenant. After his air tanks were exhausted, the man had crawled up on an ice flow. When the search aircraft had shown up, he'd used plastic explosives to signal.

The SEAL had shown resourcefulness. McKafferty believed strongly in team initiative. For that very reason, he had used his political pull to bring the CDC on board. McKafferty was never fully confident in any one science team, so he had set the CDC up on a parallel competitive track with BARDCOM. He didn't care which team won the race. He just needed to know what this hot agent was and how it worked and, most importantly, if it could be controlled. The problem was that he couldn't let the folks at CDC in on the whole picture. Because of *need-to-know* security, this contest was being run with a handicap against the civilian side.

Though none of his science teams at BARDCOM had isolated any traces of chemical or biological agents, the team was leaning toward a chemical agent as the cause. They argued that the CDC's finding of cut nerve fiber was extremely similar to the effects of a highly classified U.S. chemical weapon code named ZRX661. The computer models all indicated to the contrary, with high probability that this was a biological attack, not chemical. After all, it was damn impossible to smuggle and then release a chemical agent inside a U.S. Navy sub or an airtight dive suit. McKafferty agreed with the computers as he often did. People made too many mistakes due to vested interests fogging their logic. Machines didn't have this problem. The helicopter touched down as a cloud of sand blew up around them like an abrasive curtain.

Chapter 3

Kill Zones

1 – Atlanta, Georgia: November

Dr. Kathy Morrison was frayed to the point of confusing simple things. She could use a solid eight hours of sleep. A week had passed and she was still trying to gain her first insight into what was now rightly or wrongly being called an epidemic. A week ago it had been a village in Brazil, a village in Argentina, and a Navy diver. Now there were three additional sites: one in Chile and two more in Brazil. The death count had risen to almost six hundred. An EIS agent in Chile had coined a phrase to describe these sites as *kill zones* and the name had stuck. Kathy thought the phrase was appropriate. *Kill zone* brought up images of a war, and that's exactly what this was... a violent, ugly war.

She had seen the worst types of epidemics that Mother Nature and man had so far devised. What was driving her to work almost twenty hours a day was the nagging doubt that this killer might not be a man-made chemical or natural biological, but something new and unimaginable; and if that was the case, all their calculations based on historical observations of epidemics spreading might as well be thrown out the window. For every kill zone they'd documented, there could be dozens of others they hadn't yet found. The BVMC lab was now working with more than three hundred samples of bodily fluids and tissues. While the database was growing, the knowledgebase had increased by exactly zero.

Kathy walked into her boss's office. Carl Green was usually an easy-going man, but in the center of this epidemic he was out of his element. He was a deputy director, not a military commander. At ten in the morning, his tie was already hanging loose around his neck. He looked haggard. His dark forehead was creased with worry lines. He was on the phone and waved Kathy to a vacant chair. She smelled tobacco on his clothes. A pack of Camels was on his desk. She knew he hadn't smoked in years.

"Senator, please, I promised you a full report by the end of this week. Right now we have nothing to add. Yes, Sir, I will. Have you considered Dr. Morrison's request to quarantine all goods and travel from South America? Yes, okay, I understand. No one wants the public scared with terrorist theories. Uhuh... The press blackout does make it difficult. Yes... yes... Good day, Sir."

Kathy knew there was no political will to quarantine South America because of the questions such an action would raise. Maybe the bureaucrats were right; maybe a quarantine was an overreaction, but it was the safe thing to do. If this was a chemical agent being used, then a quarantine would make it harder to smuggle the agent into the country; and if this was a biological, then a quarantine would help to block its spread. Either way, humanity didn't need another global scourge. We were doing quite well with AIDS and drug resistant TB and global warming and terrorism, thank you very much.

"So what have you got for me?" asked Green.

"I've registered a name for this set of symptoms, SAAC for South American Asphyxial Complex, and got it quietly listed in the CDC public records as a reportable disease."

"Well that was important," said Green. "Glad it's been settled. Now can we get to a few minor details like what the hell is it and how do we stop it!"

Kathy's fingers involuntarily tightened around the status report she'd brought. Carl was under pressure. It would only make things worse if she let this degrade into a shouting match. She wanted to tell him what he could do with this report. She stood up ready to leave. Carl's eyes locked on hers. The tension in his face held then began to fade.

"Sit down," he said. "Please go on with your report."

Kathy hesitated. Carl picked up a pencil and began to fidget. The strain abated. She sat down, glanced at the summary page of her report and then began.

"There's no disagreement from the entire research team on these three facts. One: all the deaths are caused by internal nerve fiber damage. Two: we haven't found a single instance of trauma or cuts to the nerve bundles' protective outer sheaths. Three: we've gotten no positive hits from all tests for toxins and pathogens.

"I've got part of the team trying an unconventional tactic to identify the cause by working forward instead of backward. They're trying to reverse-engineer it by going through all the possible way to replicate this kind of damage. We've identified enzymes that can break down nerve tissue and leave chemical micro-cuts behind, but there's no way an enzyme could have reached the nerve fibers without also damaging the surrounding protective sheaths. There's also no way these cuts could have been done mechanically or by radiation.

"I have someone working on what we're calling Jeffrey's bite theory. His idea is that bacteria are nibbling away at the nerve fibers, using enzymes. There are bacteria that eat steel, so a little nerve tissue is nothing. The only problem is the clean, straight cuts. If bacteria were responsible, we would see molecular enzyme cuts everywhere, almost like snail-trails weaving around and between the nerve fibers.

"I've got the lab processing every bit of tissue and cellular material from two of the bodies. It's a huge job. We're doing visual inspection, DNA, and spectral analysis. We're looking for anything that does not belong; but so far, nothing. The theory for a biological cause is supported by elevated immune system responses in all victims, but nothing disease specific. The theory for a chemical agent is supported by the fact that all deaths were nearly simultaneous. In the end, we still have almost nothing to go on. We're no closer today than we were days ago when I found the micro-cuts."

Kathy sighed and looked down at the desk. The room was silent for a while.

"How long?" asked Carl.

"How long for what?"

"Processing the two bodies bit by bit," said Carl.

"About four months if we're lucky, ten if we're not."

"Not good... What else have you got?"

"There's something no one's been willing to take a stab at explaining. There's a well-defined boundary around some of the kill zones. It's somewhat circular with a radius averaging a few hundred feet. Outside the perimeter, there are no deaths. On the inside, it's hell's picnic."

Carl took an ashtray and lighter from his desk drawer. He shook a cigarette from a pack of Camels and lit it. The entire facility was non-smoking, even outside. Kathy thought about saying something about his health and then realized how petty it would sound.

"You were talking about the kill zone boundary," said Carl.

"That's right… The best example of this boundary was in Chile," said Kathy. "Near a kill zone, a dozen villagers were fishing alongside a stream about four hundred feet from the village. They'd been fishing for a few hours when they heard a commotion – dogs barking, that sort of thing – and came running back to the village to find everyone there was dying. People were dropping around them, literally falling into their arms.

"Every one of the villagers by the stream were fine. They were tested and showed no signs of any toxins or biologicals. This means that we have an entire event measured in minutes or seconds, from exposure – to death – to an inert state that no longer kills. This makes everything including Ebola Zaire seem like a case of chicken pox."

"None of the EIS agents have found a reservoir for a disease or toxin or any indication of how it's transmitted or ingested. Hell, we don't even know if this thing is a chemical or a disease. I had CDC Atlanta run our symptoms through that new AI diagnostic computer program of theirs."

"What's the name of that program again?" asked Carl.

Kathy's thoughts went blank. Her brain felt strained. It took her a moment to remember the name.

"DTAVAS, Disease and Toxin Attack Vector Analysis System… Carl, you're not going to believe what it came up with. The computer program indicated a sixty percent probability that we're dealing with an insect-transmitted disease, with high probability of ticks or mosquitoes as the carrier."

"Wouldn't it be something if this did turn out to be insects?" said Carl.

Kathy leaned back in the chair. She closed her eyes for a moment. Her knee was bothering her for the first time in two days. She took a few aspirin from her pocket and swallowed them with coffee. Could it be insects? She picked up a photograph of the latest kill zone and stared at it. Hell's picnic. None of these people died with a peaceful expression on their face.

"What about Chromatium bacteria found in the Navy diver?" asked Carl.

Kathy felt immediately frustrated. She suspected Carl would get around to that question again sooner or later, just not so soon. Jeffrey had come across that scrap of information in the reports she'd given him to read during his flight to South America. He'd called Carl and told him he was convinced there was a connection. He argued that there was no explanation for the Chromatium found in the scalp tissue of the diver, as if lacking an explanation was so damn unique right now. Everything in this case was lacking in the explanation department. Kathy felt that Chromatium was an interesting curiosity, but she was equally convinced that it was a total waste of time.

"It's a dead end," said Kathy. "I told Jeffrey it was a dead end the first time he called me, before he started bothering you with it. Chromatium Omri lives in seawater and divers swim in seawater. We found no trace of Chromatium in any other victim. I know it's odd that some dead Chromatium were found inside epidermal capillaries on the diver's skull, but that strain is completely benign. It was not inside the blood brain barrier and not in nerve tissue. Even if it had made it inside the victim's nerve tissue, there's nothing Chromatium could do to cause the micro-cuts we're seeing. I promise you this is not the problem. Case closed."

"Did you set up a team to work on the Chromatium question?" asked Carl.

The man was unrelenting. He'd asked the same thing yesterday. The throbbing in her knee was growing worse and had spread to her temples. She took a deep breath to calm herself. The problem was they did not have enough top-level people to waste them on wild tangents.

"I know you've asked me to get this done, but I don't have the staff," she said.

"People are dying!" snapped Carl. "What if this thing has a breakout and makes it to The States? What if Jeffrey is right and there's a connection? The CDC has a multibillion dollar budget. Use it… Hire more people!"

"Carl, please."

"Please what?"

His dark complexion looked damp. Little veins were coming to the surface across his neck and face.

"You're a doctor, a scientist," said Kathy. "Listen to what you're saying. You know the answer is never throwing more bodies at a problem. When has that ever worked? If we just keep adding people we'll end up with a bureaucratic nightmare. People will be going off in all directions and important findings will be lost in the chaos. You know the biggest problem with this kind of work is centralizing and digesting information and then disseminating it to the entire team. Besides, if you're so worried about a breakout getting into this country, you should take your billions dollar budget and use it to quarantine the Southern US Borders."

"So we're back to that again!"

"Damn it, Carl! Why don't I just call a press conference and get it done myself, okay?"

2 – Los Angeles: November

Mark was wearing a pullover shirt, jeans, and sneakers. He was in an alcove of his microbiology lab that served as an office. The chair he was sitting in was an oversized executive model upholstered in aged brown leather. It was the same chair he'd used when he'd first discovered COBIC-3.7, the same chair he'd used almost twenty years ago when he'd begun his career in genetics. The chair squeaked in familiar ways. The leather's smell was familiar. It felt like home.

His office space was furnished with a bookcase, a desk, and a few chairs. Mark leaned back. He was staring at the screen of his workstation. His eyes were devouring what they saw. The screen contained columns filled with horizontal lines of different colors and thickness. Each column looked like a vertical barcode and that's almost what it was – a barcode that described life. The software was his own design, built exclusively for him by an engineering firm. The program was used to analyze DNA sequences including their interrelationships. This particular DNA sequence was from the engineered bacterium he was developing. There was a problem with the bug's longevity. He'd found a way of lessening the problem, but didn't fully understand why it worked and that troubled him.

Genetic engineering was his second obsession, a field of research completely opposite from paleobiology. Where COBIC-3.7 occupied the world of prehistory, his genetic work was part of the future. Bacteria were the machines of the coming centuries. They could be engineered to be construction workers that made plastics or new kinds of fabric. There were mutations which had been used to consume oil slicks and other environmental hazards. Through recombinant DNA techniques, simple bacteria could be turned into chemical factories that churned out custom protein strings for new super drugs. Their use in medicine was not something new. Long ago, the pharmaceutical company Eli Lilly developed a bacterium that mass-produced human insulin. Millions of diabetics around the world, including Mark, owed their lives to tiny *E. Coli* bacteria that had been converted into insulin factories.

Mark glanced at a framed micrograph of COBIC. The picture had been taken when his breeding colony was flourishing. He'd never been able to uncover why the colony had died off so suddenly. Next to the photograph was a chunk of COBIC fossil collected on his first expedition.

His eyes went back to the screen. The colored barcodes were becoming a hopeless puzzle. He needed to stop. He knew from experience that letting go of a problem brought perspective, and often with that distance came fresh ideas. He leaned back in his chair and surveyed the contents of his lab. On his desk was a mug of coffee long ago cold, and a drying sandwich with a bite missing. A lithograph of Albert Einstein hung on the wall above his workstation. The great man looked like he was staring out across a universe of time with those doleful eyes.

The clock on Mark's desk read seven. It was impossible to know if it was morning or evening. His lab was in a subbasement and had no windows. The room was large – fifty by thirty-five feet – a vast improvement over the days before his Nobel Prize when he'd worked alone in an off campus annex. Now he had a staff and was located in a newly refurbished section of a building located in the heart of the UCLA campus.

The lab was equipped with state of the art research tools, things to service the imagination of the University's pet Nobel Laureate. The equipment alone had cost millions of dollars. Half the funding had come from federal grants, the other half from UCLA coffers. His operating expenses were never a problem. The work he did was filled with splashy buzzwords that made it easy to obtain additional grants. He was a recognized leader in the genetic engineering of bacteria – designer bugs for designer times.

The only difficulty with his work was the large amount of security that surrounded it. The lab had solid steel doors and negative pressure ventilation. Nothing that he worked on was supposed to escape. To Mark, the security was a big joke. He was working on bacteria that, at worst, might overly increase soil nutrition. There were no pathogenic microbes here. Several months ago, a grad student had left the lab area with a gas-sampling probe which had not been sterilized the required six hours. The incident had been caught and investigated, and Mark had ended up with enough paper work dropped on his desk to make a dozen lawyers smile.

The telephone began ringing. Mark was cleaning his glasses. He put them back over his eyes. He tried to ignore the noisy intruder. A minute later, the phone stopped its complaining. He closed the computer window containing DNA barcodes and clicked another icon. A graph appeared showing the rate of reproduction for the latest variant of his designer bug, *Cri Thiobacillus*, CT for short. The graph was incomplete. As he stared, new line segments were added. In the background, a low priority computer job was running that simulated an entire bacterial ecosystem; and from that simulation, it predicted how his CT bacteria would multiply. The graph showed that under typical conditions, the little creatures could produce a new generation every fifty minutes resulting in fast exponential population growth.

Mark smiled to himself. CT was engineered to be an effective consumer of what had been considered non-biodegradable human garbage up to now. At its geometric rate of reproduction, small amounts of the bug could fan out to process huge quantities of waste. Once the garbage was consumed, their food supply would be gone and the bacteria themselves would die off. CT was an elegant solution to the problems of waste disposal.

Mark imagined someone with an eyedropper adding a small amount of CT to a pile of garbage. In a few days, the bacteria's enzymes would reduce the trash to a harmless sludge usable as fertilizer. The little critters were voracious. They could easily take over the world if it was made of what they were designed to eat, and that was the key to their success as a product. Living plants and animals had defense systems that could easily destroy the garbage eaters. CT bacteria were the ultimate scavengers, able to eat only things that could not defend themselves.

Mark knew that his bug wouldn't solve the entire waste problem. No technology could break the cycle of trees – into candy wrappers – into trash. CT couldn't stop man from converting the planet's ecosystem into recycled waste. In darker moments, he wondered if his bug might even make the problem worse. If society could easily dispose of its trash, would it produce even more?

He closed his eyes and thought about how CT spread out to consume all available food and then died their mass death. Such an efficient machine... His eyes opened. Was that part of the COBIC mystery? Had COBIC spread out over the world and consumed too much of its food supply, bringing self-extinction?

A buzzer sounded. Someone was at the lab door. Mark saw Gracy in the video monitor and pressed a button that unlocked the door. His eyes were drawn back to the computer screen as another line segment was added to the exponential growth curve. Was he looking at a mathematical model of extinction?

"Hi honey," called out Gracy.

Mark turned around in his chair. Gracy walked over and sat in his lap. She kissed him, then leaned back and looked into his eyes.

"You were supposed to be home almost two hours ago," she said. "We were going to have dinner with Mary and George just about now... Don't worry. I canceled."

"Sorry, you know I've got a broken sense of time."

Mark stood up, removing her from his lap. He pulled a book from his shelf and then glanced at the computer screen again. The graph had changed some more. The pattern reminded him of something.

"I tried calling you three times," she said. "I knew you wouldn't answer. You're too obsessive!"

"My obsessing just got us out of a boring dinner with Mary and George."

"Yeah, but that's no excuse."

Mark sat down in his chair again. He stared at the computer screen. He knew he'd seen a growth curve somewhere that reminded him of this one, but where? He opened the book.

"What about food?" said Gracy.

"I'm not hungry right now. You go on. I'll catch up with you later."

3 – Anchorage, Alaska: November

The day was gusty and clear with a robin's egg blue sky streaked with white. The seawater was a dark green. The freezing air was crisp with a chill that opened his mind. Harold Nakachia took a deep breath of the air into his lungs. He was high above the ground in the operator's cab of a shipyard crane. He had the side window partially open. He craved fresh air almost as much as iced beer. Looking through the glass, he could see out across the waters of Cook Inlet. He could feel the vastness of the sea beyond. Winds were buffeted his cab. Fall was long past, and winter was blowing hard through Alaska.

The nosepiece of his cab was a glass box. Harold sat in a bucket seat that had a control-stick built into each of the armrests. His footrests extended out over a glass floor. He looked down past his boots at a miniature army of longshoremen working cargo on and off the docks. The experience was like sitting suspended in midair over the edge of a cliff.

An order from the dock foreman, Pete Fulmar buzzed inside Harold's headphones. Harold eased back on a control-stick that operated the winch. He could sense the crane tightening under the load he was lifting out of the ship. The work was dangerous for the men below. Harold was a five-year veteran on the crane. He performed his job almost as an extension of the machine. Orders were whispered into his ears and his body obeyed without the mind interfering. Operating the crane was like walking: if he thought about all the motions that were needed, he might trip over his own feet. Today his thoughts were far away.

In a month, he and his cousins, Frankie and Toad, would be spending a week trout fishing along South Bear River to celebrate Harold's twenty-ninth birthday. He could hear the water running over the rocks. He could almost smell the trout bubbling away in a fry pan with a splash of beer and pepper and salt. His mouth started to water.

Harold smiled to himself. Life was good, sometimes hard, but always fair. He had grown up in a small town just outside of Anchorage. He was an Eskimo of the Yup'ik people. When he was little, some of the town kids had teased him, but once he reached twelve the ribbing had stopped. By the time adolescence had passed, Harold was six foot six inches tall and two hundred seventy pounds. So far he'd enjoyed, as his father liked to say, *a life stuffed with whole good memories like a plump roasted chicken.*

Harold gazed down at the docks and watched as Toad drove his flatbed cart, called a yard-vehicle, along a ramp. Harold drifted off again remembering how Tony had earned his nickname of Toad. It wasn't because Toad was a squat broad man with a smile that extended like a crack from ear to ear: he was, but that wasn't the reason. It wasn't because his voice was always a bit hoarse: it was, but that wasn't the reason either. The reason was because Toad used to be able to slip into the water and swim submerged like some great bullfrog up to where the girls were skinny-dipping. Harold and the other boys would be hiding in the bushes. Toad's mission had almost always succeeded with squealing females running naked from the swimming hole. Harold often wondered why the girls came back to the same place for their swim. He grinned with the memory. Maybe they liked being chased from the water so the boys could get a good look at them? If that was the case, their game had worked. Six years later, Harold had ended up marrying one of those girls – Sue.

Pete Fulmar relayed more instructions into Harold's ears. Harold moved a control-stick and the crane swung the load to the left as smooth as sliding on ice. The skill of his job was pure eye-hand coordination. Harold brought the container to a stop perfectly centered over a tractor-trailer chassis. No repositioning was needed before lowering the container.

"Fifteen minute break," the voice of the dock foreman crackled over the headphones. Harold engaged the winch lock. A few seconds later, his stomach was lanced with pain. He pressed his fist into his belly. The pain was less than it had been, but still felt like he'd swallowed a burning coal. It was only a few months ago that he'd returned to the job from a hospital stay. He'd made the trip down to the lower forty-eight on orders from the company doctor. Serious tests were run. Harold's Dad had died of stomach cancer. The results from the hospital had been both a relief and a curse. Harold only had the beginnings of an ulcer, but his love of eating had come to an end. At twenty-eight years old, no more chili, no more pastrami, no more tacos with hot sauce. He thought about the bag lunch Sue had prepared: tuna dry on white bread, carrot sticks, and an apple for dessert. At least he'd sneak a couple beers with Toad after work.

The shadow of a low cloud moved over him, momentarily dimming the sun. Harold looked out into the direction of the oncoming cloud and saw in the distance gray snow clouds moving toward him from the sea. The wind had been gusty all day, but now the harbor waters were turning into a heavy chop. Spray was beginning to whip up over the docks. He could feel the crane vibrating from the gusts. He looked at the wind speed gauge. The needle was wavering up and down, peaking at close to thirty miles per hour. Union policy mandated that work stopped if the sustained wind speed reached thirty-four miles per hour.

Close to the shoreline and low over the water, a flock of seabirds were searching for fish. The patrol worked its way past his crane and then edged back out over deeper water. One of the birds bumped into another. The collision sent both birds somersaulting into the water. Less than a few seconds later there was another collision. Stupid birds. It was as if they were drunk. A coughing sound came over the radio. Harold pressed the talk button.

"Hey, Pete; that you hacking in my ear?" he asked. "You smoking those roll-your-owns again or what?"

There was no answer. Harold looked down at the dock and saw men collapsing. Their small forms made them look like toys. Some were motionless while others were trying to help. Harold stood up in the cramped cab and leaned forward. All rational thoughts had stopped. He braced his hands against the glass. His cousin's yard-vehicle disappeared underneath a stack of crates that toppled over him.

"Toad!" he yelled.

There was a peal of thunder that increased to the sound of an explosion. His cab windows rattled. Harold wrenched his eyes from Toad and saw a small patch of flames rising off the water; above the flames, reaching towards the clouds was a growing mushroom of gray smoke. At its origin were two ships that had collided. Harold recognized one of them, the cargo ship *Chica Misteria* out of Venezuela. He'd unloaded her the other day. The second ship must have been carrying a cargo of chemicals. He could see liquid flames spilling from her belly out across the water. Smoke from the fire was already approaching the docks.

Harold was climbing down the crane, his face streaked with tears. Above his head, the opened cab door slapped back and forth in the wind. He gripped the ladder rungs sloppily as he raced down the scaffolding. A safety cage surrounded the ladder like a tunnel of steel bars. He slipped, then caught himself with one knee hooked through a rung. His entire body hurt. It was the end of the world. He was sure of it. The air was foul with the taste of burning tar. He was out of breath and coughing. Brown smoke was blowing across the dock, at times obscuring it from view.

Harold didn't remember actually reaching the dock. He vaguely remembered using a six-foot pry bar to shift the crates that had fallen on Toad's yard-vehicle. He remembered a guy that came to help shift some of the crates. A minute later the guy was dead. There was no way to see it coming. The light in the guy's eyes just went out as he crumpled to the ground.

That was the past. Now there was only a world of raw pain that was threatening to stop his heart. He looked down into Toad's eyes. They were lifeless orbs of glass. Scattered across the dockyard were hundreds of bodies that had once been friends. There was no one alive. The world had grown oddly still except for the wind.

4 – Airborne over the Northern Rocky Mountains: November

By his will alone, General McKafferty urged the jet transport faster. He and his men were on board an Air Force high speed transport that was approaching mach two. In forty minutes they'd arrive at Elmendorf Air Force Base in Anchorage. Two hours had passed since the port had been hit. The goddamn disease – or weapon – or whatever the hell it was – had now been used on *United States soil*. McKafferty banged his fist into the armrest. He'd revised the armed force's bio-containment plans years ago after 9/11 and the anthrax mail attacks. Back when it had been completed, he'd prayed they would never need it. He now knew that God had not been listening to a sinner like him.

The Port of Anchorage was under martial law. Army teams had been mobilized from Fort Richardson which was eight miles outside of Anchorage. The Arctic Warriors were in control. All points of access had been sealed. A wing of Blackhawk helicopters lifted off from Elmendorf Air Force Base carrying McKafferty and his team. They were flying directly toward a plume of smoke that looked like a colossal mushroom cloud. Part of its head had merged into the ceiling of clouds. Its base was five miles out over the water. McKafferty felt dwarfed by the sight. The towering darkness was like the rage of an angry God.

The local authorities were out of control. Calls had been placed to the White House demanding help. The governor was throwing a screaming fit and McKafferty was racing into the middle of the storm. His helo was vibrating badly as it cut through turbulent air. The engines were at their maximum power settings. McKafferty, his team, and everyone else at Elmendorf were wearing NBC suits – Nuclear, Biological and Chemical protective gear. The clothing was a major upgrade from equipment worn by soldiers who'd worked the scenes of the anthrax mail attacks. McKafferty's communications officer tapped him on the shoulder. She was Lieutenant Alice Rivers, twenty-four years old, and on her first tour with the General.

"Sir, we've gotten word that CNN is sending in a crew to do a video shoot from the air."

"Damn it! I knew they'd try to weasel around the quarantine orders. Send this message to Elmendorf: I want fighters in the air circling that port. Give 'em orders to drive off any approaching aircraft – hell, tell 'em to shoot the bastards down if they have to."

"General!"

"Yeah right... leave off the part about shooting 'em down."

"Yes, Sir."

The helos swung in low from the east. McKafferty's helo orbited the docks while three other birds landed. He watched his men disgorge from the crafts and fan out. He felt anger reddening his skin. Whatever the hell caused this devastation; he would put a stop to it.

A small private plane came out of the setting sun and swooped low over the docks. McKafferty saw the glint of a camera aimed out the window. Where the hell were his Air Force sentries? That looked like CNN going live right now. Things were unraveling. He needed to contain this horror until his people understood what was happening. If news of this spread, his job would get a lot tougher. He didn't need political toadies crawling up his ass.

"Lieutenant Rivers," he yelled. "Raise the operations officer at Elmendorf. I want to talk with him now!"

"Yes, Sir."

"Goddamn reporters are coming in for the kill."

"Sir, I have him on the line, channel eight."

"Who am I speaking to?" said McKafferty.

"Captain Bennett, acting CO."

"Captain, do you know who I am?"

"Yes, Sir, you are OPCON, General James H. McKafferty United States Army. Your communications officer made that very clear."

"Well son, then you know how big a club I carry. If you don't want to catch it swung full force against the side of your head, I suggest you get your fucking F16s in the goddamn air and over here right now!"

"Yes, Sir, your orders were received minutes ago and we're processing them priority one. The Eagles will be in the air within fifteen minutes."

"Processing, hell! Make it five minutes and don't disappoint me, son."

"Yes, Sir!"

McKafferty knew that Air Force fly-boy was probably raising the middle-finger salute right about now, but there wasn't anything that an

Air Force Captain could do about a General with full operational control of the mission. McKafferty switched his com-channel over to the helo pilot's.

"Let's swing this bird around and head on out to the civilian staging area."

A police barracks had been selected as Safe-Point-One, a civilian staging area for police and rescue teams. The barracks was almost twenty miles from the Port of Anchorage and well outside the two-mile quarantine line. As the helo touched down in the parking lot, a garbage can tipped over, sending a stream of litter across the road. McKafferty climbed out. He pulled off the hood of his NBC suit. His communications officer did the same. McKafferty noticed a tense expression on her face.

"Lieutenant, you don't have to do this," he said. "You can stay in the chopper with your suit on."

"It's my job, Sir... and I know the NBC team has checked and cleared this area. So it's safe... Right, Sir?"

"Rivers, you're a good soldier."

A man wearing a parka with 'Police Captain' stenciled on it came out of the building to meet them in the lot. McKafferty had already been briefed on Captain Eastwood. He recognized the man from a photograph in his file. Eastwood looked young for the job, clean shaven with a mop of blond hair. By now, the Army had every road leading in and out of Port of Anchorage under military control. He knew Eastwood would have his questions about the deployment, and the man's suspicion would only make it harder for McKafferty to sell him on the cover story.

"Hello, Captain Eastwood," said McKafferty as he extended his paw.

"General McKafferty?" asked Eastwood.

"That's right, son."

"General, will you please tell me what the 'H' is going on?"

"I'll make you a deal. I understand you have someone named Harold Nakachia in your custody and that this man is an eyeball witness. You give me access to Harold and I'll tell you what I can, within limits of national security, of course."

Eastwood seemed to think it over for a moment.

"Harold stays in my custody?" asked Eastwood.

"Of course."

"You got a deal."

"Okay, Captain, here's what I know. An NBC team from Fort Richardson has run preliminary sweeps of the docks and found traces of an unidentified chemical toxin. Right now, our best guess is that it came from a leaky container on some ship. The Army's position is that the container is not United States government property but may contain agents used in the manufacture of chemical weapons."

"I don't care who gets blamed," grumbled Eastwood. "I just want to know if my people are safe here. We don't have chemical gear for everyone."

"Your people are safe," said McKafferty. "We'll find the source in no time. Our sniffers have picked up nothing a quarter mile from the port. There is no chance the chemical will get this far, no matter what it is."

Eastwood's face showed relief. McKafferty smiled as warmly as his ugly visage would allow. The man had bought the story and hadn't asked about the Army shutting down roads. Harold was not a real bargaining chip; McKafferty already owned him. Once the cover story was leaked to the press, the speculation would be that the disaster was caused by military chemicals, and that was fine with McKafferty. The Pentagon could take it on the chin as long as the real truth didn't get out. Control of the population was paramount at times like this. Rumors of terrorists or killer plagues would make control far more difficult, and in the end that could cost more lives than the incident itself.

McKafferty took off the rest of his NBC suit. Underneath was an insulated khaki officer's field uniform. On it was the cobra and sword insignia of BARDCOM. McKafferty walked into a jail which was attached to the barracks. The air smelled of disinfectant. As ordered, an NBC team had set up a medical isolation tent four feet out from all sides of the cell which held the survivor. *Just as a precaution* was the story the Army had given Captain Eastwood. McKafferty was relieved that nobody had asked why the Army was treating a chemical spill like a biological attack. Steel bars and heavy, double–walled, floor-to-ceiling plastic separated the survivor from the outside world. The survivor had been brought in wearing an NBC suit to isolate him from his jailers. On the floor in the hallway was a ventilator that was fitted to the tent. The ventilator disinfected both the air being blown into the tent as well as recycled air being drawn out. All the sites in South America had indicated zero risk following a kill zone. The scientists were not as worried about this survivor spreading any disease as they were worried about contaminating their prize subject with the normal dirty environment of human habitation. They wanted him unadulterated until they could run their medical tests.

Harold Nakachia was sitting on a chair inside the plastic tent, his lunch untouched in front of him. The NBC suit he'd worn when he arrived was lying in a pile on the floor. McKafferty's first thought was that the man was a big son of a bitch; then he recognized the vacant look in Harold's eyes. McKafferty had first seen that look in Vietnam on the faces of recruits who'd lived through their first day of bloody combat.

"Hello, Harold. I'm James."

"Hey, James. What's the Army doing here?"

McKafferty realized this man was sharp. The vacant look was gone from his eyes. Harold stood up. Anger was radiating from his body. He was not going to be easy to control.

"The Army was called in because we have experience with things like this," said McKafferty.

"And exactly what are things like this?"

"A chemical leak," said McKafferty.

"That's some hell of a leak. What happened? Some war toy blow a fuse and you're the clean up crew?"

"No, son, I am not the clean up crew. Why don't you tell me what happened."

Harold went through his story beginning with birds acting oddly and ending with an NBC squad evacuating him. He went on in detail about how horrifying it was to see all his friends crumpling to the ground. McKafferty wondered what Harold would think if he could see the docks now. The shoreline was littered with dead fish, birds, and marine mammals. After his team had dumped toxin in the water to simulate a chemical weapons leak, everything living there was now dead except Harold. As far as the scientists could ascertain, Harold was the first person to be exposed at the epicenter of a kill zone and survive. He could end up becoming a walking antidote factory.

"Okay, you saw a vehicle run into a stack of crates," said McKafferty. "Are you sure that happened after everyone started dying? Maybe it happened before? Maybe whatever killed everyone was in the crates?"

"You're not listening, man!" yelled Harold. "First the fuckin' birds were butting heads, then Toad and a lot of the other guys dropped like rag dolls. This wasn't any dock accident. This was a goddamn rerun of the Twilight Zone. Rod fuckin' Serling was standing down on the docks saying *Consider this if you will...* Get it?"

"Harold, just take it easy."

"Fuck you!"

"You're in shock and you've got the sequence confused."

"My story isn't changing, James. I saw what I saw, and it's just too bad if that doesn't fit your official version of lies. What the hell happened here? One of your chemical weapons go off? Huh? You mother fuckers kill all my friends?"

McKafferty's radio beeped. He turned his back on Harold and listened. The signal was from Lieutenant Rivers with more bad news. CNN had received footage broadcast from that private plane, and they were outside in the police parking lot right now with lights and a minicam broadcasting live.

"Shit!"

McKafferty walked out of the infirmary and cornered a deputy.

"You got a TV with cable in this place?'

"In the Captain's office."

McKafferty stood in front of the set. This was a disaster. A reporter dressed in an NBC suit was laying out carefully worded rumor and speculation as fact. Their need for "a scoop" was going to cause hysteria.

"To Repeat: A major incident has occurred in Anchorage Alaska at two p.m. Alaska Standard Time – six p.m. Eastern Standard Time. The incident, which occurred in the Port of Anchorage, may have been the work of terrorists. Nothing has been confirmed or denied yet. Authorities are providing very little information. We have eyewitness accounts that hundreds of people are dead, and that the cause is an airborne chemical of undetermined nature. We have film from a spotter plane that flew over the scene one hour ago at five p.m. local time."

The television showed an aerial view of bodies lying across the dock, with men in space suits walking around them. McKafferty was beyond anger. He was in that silent place where rage brewed into lethal concentrations. He knew the political opportunists would be sharpening their knives. Those animals were better at sensing wounded prey than a pack of wild hyenas.

5 – Atlanta: November

The alarm clock buzzed. The time was eight-thirty in the evening. Kathy reached out and deftly hit the snooze button. She yearned to go back to sleep. Her body's cycle was totally confused. She sat up, draping her legs over the side of the couch. Her mouth was dry. She picked up a can of warm Diet Pepsi and drank some. Slowly, her brain started to grind through the facts. She got up and walked past balled up clothing and books and papers sprawled everywhere. Her office looked like a locker room. She'd been living out of it for eleven days. One dead end after another had kept her grasping to find new leads. Nothing she had learned over the years seemed to apply anymore. This monster evaded every framework for detection that medical science had ever devised.

The BVMC lab had originally been designed to support twenty-four hour operations in case of emergencies. Senior staff offices on the fourth floor were set up for extended stays like small hotel rooms with stall showers, toilets, and sleeper couches. Kathy walked into her tiny private bathroom and flipped on the light. Tolstoy was in the sink, peering over the rim at her. He looked so proud of himself. She smiled then saw her reflection in the mirror. The smile faded. Was that really her? There were deep bags under her eyes. Her T-shirt was wrinkled and the shorts she was wearing hung limp from her thinning body. She removed Tolstoy from his hideout and filled the basin with water. During the next fifteen minutes, she washed her face and put on simple makeup. The results left her feeling human again.

Kathy was riding the elevator down to the cafeteria to eat whatever was left over from dinner. Her thoughts were elsewhere. Carl had gotten his way days ago on Chromatium. Kathy had been forced to retest all the victims – with zero results. The Navy diver was the only one with the bug in him. She also had several primate test trials running with Chromatium. Before heading down to the cafeteria, she'd received an e-mail on one of those waste-of-time trials. Lab techs had been running twenty-four hour relay shifts to complete the trials. The CDC had obtained a breeding colony of Chromatium Omri from a research center up in Rochester, New York. Living Chromatium had been injected into the blood stream – and even the brainstems – of lab monkeys. The animals' immune systems ignored the bacterium, not recognizing it as a threat. So far, in every case, the Chromatium had died within forty-eight hours, essentially from starvation. For Chromatium, there was nothing good to eat inside a monkey. None of the lab monkeys were showing symptoms of SAAC. A warm-blooded circulatory system did not appear to be a great environment for this particular bug.

Kathy wandered into the empty cafeteria. The clock on the wall showed it was almost a quarter after nine in the evening. She was exhausted. She put some leftover pizza into a microwave and wondered, not for the first time, if amphetamines might not be such as bad idea. A week ago, she'd been certain they'd have found important pieces to the puzzle by now. Instead, all they had was a growing list of questions. If she could just figure out how to recreate those microscopic cuts in nerve fibers. Maybe the killer was some kind of unknown microbe that moved in straight lines, leaving a trail of nerve tissue-dissolving enzyme that vanished without a trace? Kathy sighed and closed her eyes. Yeah right... and maybe the tooth fairy had turned into a sociopath and was bumping off bad South Americans that didn't believe in fairies. The microwave beeped.

Not surprisingly, the pizza had been unsatisfying. Kathy turned a corner in the hallway. She heard her phone ringing and ran for it. Her pager started going off. Her skin felt like an electrical current was crawling all over it. Instinctively, she knew something bad had happened. She tripped over a pair of sneakers in the middle of her office floor, but still managed to grab the phone before the caller gave up.

"Hello!" she gasped.

"Switch on CNN." It was Carl.

"What is it?"

"Just turn it on. You need to see this."

The television was a twenty inch model sitting on a stand, with a digital recorder below. Using a remote, Kathy switched on the set. It was already tuned to CNN. There was an aerial view of a dockyard with bodies lying all over the ground. Nearby were three military helicopters that had landed on the dock. Their rotors were turning slowly. Men in biohazard gear were examining the scene. Kathy sat down behind her desk. The phone receiver was still pressed to her face. A reporter was in the middle of his story. The title read *Anchorage, Alaska*.

"...It's hard to describe what I've experienced tonight. I have to keep reminding myself that this is happening. One hundred-six confirmed fatalities, no survivors. Earlier I spoke with a medical worker who said that all the victims' lips and fingernails had turned blue. I was told this is a symptom of suffocation. The government has issued a statement that this is not a terrorist attack. There are strong rumors that some type of chemical weapons leak has occurred; but whatever has happened, the results are terrifying. Along with the human toll, the shores are littered with thousands upon thousands of marine animals. The Harbor is under martial law. No one is allowed in or out. CNN has attempted several times to again fly over the zone but has been driven off by F16 jets that are now patrolling the area. Orwellian and ominous are the feelings one gets when seeing this horror, as I did from the passenger seat of a small plane. I remember thinking, this can't be real..."

Kathy was stunned. This incident had to be SAAC, and it had now jumped to North America; but there should have been no dead animals, just people. If this thing was now killing animals, then it was a species jumper. And if that was true, then this was a clear sign of mutation. And chemical agents did not mutate; that little trick was reserved for living things like microbes.

"Carl, who do we have on site?"

"I've been trying to get an EIS team in there, but the Army has a lid on it. They didn't even alert us. The folks in charge want our help but we're not allowed any direct contact. They don't want news leaking out that we're dealing with an unknown epidemic."

"That's crazy. We have to be there. Get Director Shaw involved."

"It's already come from the top. The Army's in control of this. And forget about the dead animals. Apparently some genius decided to kill off a good part of the marine life in Cook Inlet just to support their cover story about a chemical weapons leak."

Kathy massaged her temple with her free hand. The burgeoning headache lessened a small amount. She wasn't sure which was worse: the Army killing things to support their lies, or the disappointment that the hot agent was not a species jumper and she had just lost what could have been an important clue. On the other end of the phone, she heard Carl lighting up a cigarette.

"Okay," said Kathy. "The government wants us to stop an epidemic, then ties our hands by restricting us from going on site. Is there any theory how SAAC ended up in Alaska?"

"A ship registered to Venezuela was in port."

"Damn it, I told you we needed quarantines!"

"And I told Director Shaw, and he told the President, and look what it got us: nothing. Forget quarantines."

"Well, tell them all again! Because of no quarantines it's now on American soil. Where's this Venezuelan ship? If we can get some blood samples from the crew and test the cargo, I can..."

Carl interrupted her.

"The ship's a ball of fire. It collided with a vessel carrying highly flammable chemicals."

"How convenient," sneered Kathy.

"I'm going to tell you something and I want you to stay calm. An Army liaison officer told me they have a survivor. The man was in the middle of the kill zone and is in perfect health so far. Zero side effects."

"What! How soon can we get him?"

"We can't. The Army has him locked up in Anchorage and that's where he's staying."

"I have to examine him. I'll put on a uniform and pretend to be an Army nurse. I'll do anything they ask; just get me in there."

"They won't let you see him. Believe me, I've already jumped through the hoops. They've agreed you can interview him over the phone. And they'll collect blood samples and perform any tests you request."

"That's crazy. The entire country's in danger, and we can't get quarantines but the Army can. We can't examine patients, but they can. What's next? Are they going to take away my magic decoder ring because the Army could use it?"

"I'm sorry, Kathy."

"What's happening to you? Whatever happened to fighting for what's right?"

~

The light from her office window was growing pinker. It looked like in another hour sunrise would be flooding the sky with pastel shades.

Kathy had been on the phone several times going through a chain of Army officers, including a doctor who had custody of the survivor. She had not been given the patient's medical history, travel history, or even his full name. Blood and tissue samples were on their way to her lab by military courier, along with a small square of cloth cut from his shirt, but that was it. Field tests done on Port Anchorage casualties had shown elevated immune responses matching those found in South America. She wished they could have somehow checked for micro-cuts in victims while still at the scene; but with the optical microscopes and the other portable equipment at their disposal, that was impossible.

Major Garvey, an expert on chemical and biological countermeasures was on the phone with her now. Kathy had quickly realized obtaining information from these people was almost as difficult as getting a straight answer from a politician. At least Major Garvey wasn't trying to insult her with the same propaganda that was being fed to CNN. She apparently had the necessary security clearance to avoid that lie. They discussed the connection to South America and the fact that all the military experts believed the killer was a biological agent. In an attempt to get more out of Major Garvey, Kathy had resorted to baiting him by arguing that the killer-agent had to be a chemical, though she no longer saw how it could be unless someone had figured out how to make it randomly toxic. Completely unaffected survivors were just not found in the middle of a lethal chemical exposure.

"How could anything biological kill all those people at the same instant?" said Kathy. "Even if they were all exposed at the same time, some of them were healthier than others. There were differences in body mass, metabolism, age. Onset times would have to vary. The symptoms I'm seeing are much closer to a chemical agent than a bug. Maybe your cover story inadvertently turns out to be true? That would confuse everyone. Government news leak found to be accurate; story at eleven."

"You're a medical doctor," said Major Garvey. "You cure people. There's another side to medical science; one I am more familiar with than you are. I've seen what renegade countries have engineered to kill on a mass scale. There are weaponized strains of Hemorrhagic Fever that can wipe out a city in 24 hours. I can easily imagine an engineered bug that could cause what's happened in Anchorage."

The Major paused to speak with someone on his end. Kathy heard muffled voices. He came back on the line and continued where he'd left off. "Four hours after the Anchorage incident, the Army had a dozen monitoring teams set up around the perimeter of the harbor. These teams have the best equipment. They can pick up a change in air chemistry from someone opening a bottle of chlorine bleach miles away. The equipment is designed to sniff out traces of chemical weapons up to a hundred miles from the battlefield. If this incident was caused by a chemical agent, our equipment would have picked up traces of it by now and it hasn't."

"So you're convinced we're dealing with a biological weapon?" said Kathy. "What if the chemical agent is something totally new, something your equipment's not calibrated to detect?"

"I never said it was a biological weapon. I said a bug could have caused what happened at Anchorage, a naturally occurring microbe of a type yet unidentified."

The Major was ignoring the interesting part of her question and getting defensive about the term 'biological weapon.' Kathy wondered what that meant. Carl's secretary poked her head into Kathy's office. She apologetically walked in, dropped a green slip of paper on her desk, and then disappeared. The slip was a phone message. The call Kathy had been waiting for was on another line: the survivor, Harold N.

Kathy was pacing back and forth in a fifteen-foot trail that led from her bookcase to her couch. Her knee was starting to feel raw. She ignored it. Her phone conversation with Harold N. had been the strangest of her career. Before the survivor had been put on the line, she had been informed that the conversation would be monitored and recorded. She was limited to pre-approved topics. Any deviation and the phone call would be terminated, no second chances. The lone witness's description of what had happened had left her dizzy. The killer-agent was far more potent than she'd originally understood. Most the dockworkers had died in less than a minute. If broader exposure occurred, this thing could take out thousands of people in the blink of an eye. And who would survive? Who would be the next Harold, and why? For the first time in a very long while, Kathy felt completely inadequate for the job.

She stopped pacing and slumped down into her chair. She opened a computer window that displayed an enhanced view of the microscopic cuts. She had to find a new direction to approach this problem. What she was doing right now wasn't working. So far, all she had was unexplainable microscopic nerve damage and heavy immune system reactions to nothing that could be identified. The bodies of the victims had apparently responded to the attack with every possible biological defense and been soundly trounced in less than a minute.

The samples from Harold N. would be arriving in less than an hour. She had no idea what to do, except run the same tests that were performed on the victims and look for discrepancies. Where were the great insights she'd had years ago when working as an EIS agent? Where was the innovation she'd shown in her work on immune system reactions? Maybe the Army was right in keeping Harold N. to themselves? They were probably more qualified....

~

Kathy was stunned by the Army's postmortem report. She'd read it twice from beginning to end and still couldn't believe it. Chromatium Omri had been found in the bodies of eighty-nine of the Anchorage victims. Frozen samples of Chromatium taken from each of the bodies were on their way to the CDC, courtesy of the U.S. Army. Thanks to Carl's stubbornness on the issue, all the South American victims had been double checked days ago. No Chromatium had been found. There was no reason to run the tests a third time. The inconsistency between the South American and Alaskan finding didn't make sense, but she could not ignore the numbers. Eighty-nine out of a hundred-six victims of the Anchorage kill zone had small unexplainable infestations of Chromatium Omri. Apparently the Chromatium had been found in isolated pockets, either in water that had been frozen on the face of the victims or in epidermal capillaries of skull and facial tissues. The numbers of bacteria were small and they were not distributed through the body, which suggested this was not a pathogenic contagion.

Kathy now had two unexplainable things that had to be connected in some way; Microscopic nerve cuts and Chromatium. She was miserable. If she hadn't been so obstinate, so set against looking into Chromatium, they might have found something useful by now. She might have even found the answer, and hundreds of people that were dead might still be alive. Carl had been right and she had been fatally wrong. What else had she been wrong about?

~

Every surface of the ready-room was hospital white. Kathy was don-
ning the protective clothing worn inside the BVMC lab. The containment
suits were made by the same manufacturer that supplied NASA with
space suits. The gear was in fact similar to equipment used by astronauts.
Kathy pulled up a large plastic zipper that sealed the torso-section of
her suit. The zipper had an oversized grip on the slider and a tongue-in-
groove seal that could withstand a thousand pounds of pressure before
separating. The material of the suit itself was completely impervious
to liquids and gases. This airtight quality made the rig uncomfortable
because of rapid buildup of perspiration. Unlike the astronauts' model,
the cooling system for the lab's model was limited to simple air circulation; the weight and cost of a refrigeration unit made that luxury
impractical. To partially compensate, the room temperature of the lab
was kept at sixty degrees. Lab techs worked on three-hour rotating shifts
in the BVMC lab. The reason for the short work period was discomfort
and realization that accidents occurred when workers were distracted.

Kathy tucked her hair up in a net, then pulled on a helmet. The glass
visor was off-center as she jockeyed the helmet back and forth, until it
rested in the metal groove of the suit's collar. She then fastened a pair
of clamping levers and switched on the system to perform a pre-check
for leaks. There was a hissing sound as the suit pressurized. The suit
was completely self-contained with an air supply good for a maximum
of four hours. The extended breathing time was accomplished by mixing bottled air with exhaled breath that had been scrubbed of carbon
dioxide by a re-breather system. To achieve the high containment levels of the BVMC lab, the suits could not use external air supplies and
hoses. At level four facilities, workers were connected by air hoses to
spigots inside the lab. This allowed extended time in the lab, but it also
meant that extremely small amounts of airborne contaminants which
had come to rest on hose connections and spigots could be vented into
a suit during hookup to an air supply. Even the most restrictive air filters on suit inlets were not considered safe enough for the BVMC lab.

While Kathy had been suiting up, the first and second stage airlocks
were cycling to a condition where the automatic safeties would allow
the entry door to open. Both airlock stages were currently flooded to
the ceiling with Zydex, a chemical sterilization solution developed for

the military. The blue colored solution was a witch's brew of highly activated sterilization agents which could kill any living substance on contact. The only problem with Zydex was that if not neutralized in about an hour, it would start to eat away at an entire host of materials. Before cycling to allow entry, both airlocks were flooded with Zydex solution for twenty minutes and then drained and refilled with a bath of neutralizer.

Two airlocks were used in series to reduce the possibility of contamination caused by seal failure or other door malfunctions. In addition to multiple airlock stages, the containment lab operated one quarter below normal atmospheric pressure to prevent contaminants from escaping in the unlikely possibility that all other safety measures failed. The first stage airlock would be pumped down an eighth in air pressure from the outside before the middle door would open. The second stage airlock would be brought down another eighth before the door to the lab would open. The entire process of entering took thirty minutes; exiting took forty. During entry, in each of the two stages, occupants were drenched in high pressure sprays of Zydex and then neutralizer. A shower of sterilized water followed each chemical treatment to wash off any remaining neutralized Zydex. The sprays of sterilization liquid, neutralizer, and rinse came at the occupants from every direction, out of thousands of jets that were mounted in the floor, ceiling, doors, and walls of the airlocks. Once each cycle completed, the hatch safeties leading to the next stage would release. Exiting the lab took longer than entry; instead of spray-downs, lab workers were sealed in each airlock stage as its high pressure sprays completely filled the chambers, effectively immersing workers in Zydex sterilization baths. Whether exiting or entering, workers emerged from the airlocks a little disoriented and drenched in sterilized water. Just outside each entry hatch in the lab and in the ready-room were drying stalls where a set of warm air blowers and vacuums whisked off all dampness.

Kathy sat down on a bench and waited as the suit's automated pre-check continued. The ready-room always reminded her of a whitewashed locker room, except for one thing: the entranceway. From the outside, the ready room was a vault identical to that used in a bank. Both a magnetic badge and a numeric pass code were required to open it. Security was the sole concern of one tenth of the entire BVMC staff. Some days, it seemed there were guards at every doorway and television cameras in every closet. The hallways leading to the BVMC lab were monitored by cameras every twenty feet. There was no possibility of even a cockroach sneaking by.

Kathy tried to stretch her legs. She was already getting stiff inside the suit. The pre-check finished with a series of beeps which indicated all systems passed their self-tests. She glanced at the air supply gauge on her wrist. The gauge was like a digital stopwatch running backwards. Her reason for being here was the package from Alaska, and it was due to arrive any minute. The airlocks had completed their cycle. A green light above a numeric entry pad indicated she could enter. She felt perspiration dotting her forehead. She tried to think of other things while she waited.

Kathy looked up to the sound of metal bolts sliding into their receivers and then a faint hiss, as the vault door slid open. Two men in military uniforms entered. One of the men was carrying a metal container that looked like a cross between a small ice chest and a safe. Inside it were the Chromatium samples from the victims of the Alaska kill zone.

After what felt like an endless spray of toxic liquid, the final stage airlock door opened with the whir of electric motors. Kathy stepped over the foot high threshold into the lab. The flooring by the door was a steel drainage grate which continued as a walkway to a set of drying stalls. High power UV sterilization lights glowed partially out of sight beneath the grate. There were times when entering the lab felt like she was stepping onto the surface of the moon. This was one of those times. In the lab, she was more completely separated from the world than anywhere else on the planet. The unspoken fact was if accidents occurred, those trapped in the lab handled it themselves or died. As far as help was concerned, they may as well have been on the moon.

Kathy was aware of the hiss of bottled air being released with each of her inward breaths. This was something she normally did not notice. She set the metal container down on a lab bench and unlocked it. Inside, immersed in a super-chilled bath of concentrated hypochlorite solution was a rack of sealed specimen pipettes. Each glass pipette was the size of a thin bar straw sealed on both ends. The hypochlorite was there to kill anything dangerous if the container or the pipettes broke in transit. Using a pair of tongs, she removed the rack from its hypochlorite bath. She kept one of the pipettes and placed the rest in a cryogenic freezer.

Two of the lab techs, Alan and Claire, were setting up equipment to run high speed comparisons of key DNA sequences from this new sample versus live Chromatium from the Rochester colony. Kathy placed her pipette inside a glove box. The glove box was like a large glass aquarium, roughly four feet square with a door in the front and oversized sealed rubber gloves that passed through to the inside. She lowered the door, set the controls to recirculate, then switched the glove box on. A ventilator began to purify the air inside the box, one of many precautions used to lower the chance of airborne microbes contaminating a specimen.

Kathy took longer than normal to prepare a sample for the TEM. She was working carefully to avoid all sources of contamination. During the entire procedure, she kept feeling that this held the answer, that her fingers were touching something that would save lives. The feeling was irrational. There was no logical reason why she would find any answers now. Her mind was working on theories. Maybe Chromatium was the carrier and not the killer. A mosquito borne illness suggested last week by the DTAVAS computer program might not have been so crazy after all. Maybe the killer was a virus or something else living inside the Chromatium? She barely noticed when Alan came over to collect the remainder of sample she had been using. She was so anxious that her hand was shaking as she inserted the first carrier into the electron microscope.

The computer screen was the same high resolution model as the one in her office. She set the TEM at one thousand diameters and began searching for Chromatium by programming the system to slowly move the sample in widening circles ranging out from the center. She hit the pause button when several bacteria came into view. She centered the best specimen and upped the magnification. The cross-section of Chromatium grew to fill the screen. The bacterium was approximately the same size as a human blood cell. The specimen had been dead for twenty-four hours and was slightly misshapen from pressure damage. It no longer appeared as a perfect capsule shape; it was mildly shriveled as if it was a tube balloon that had lost too much air.

Kathy increased the magnification, zooming in on the Chromatium. Details of the cellular membrane and the internal cytoplasm with its ultrastructures were now visible. She was looking for any signs of viruses or indications of abnormality. She slowly ran the imager along the bacterium, examining its nucleoid, storage granules, ribosomes; there was nothing that looked out of the ordinary. She needed to find an expert on this microbe; until then, chemical testing would yield more information than visual inspection. Claire came up beside her and waited.

"Yes Claire."

"You need to see this... It looks like our little zoo's far from dead."

"What do you mean?" asked Kathy.

"I was transferring some of the Chromatium into a centrifuge tube when one of them put up a fight. It scared the heck out of me. Didn't you hear me screaming on the radio?"

They had live Chromatium samples that had survived freezing. This was amazing luck. Kathy had every tech in the lab running in circles to prep the scanning x-ray microscope. The scope was a relatively new instrument called an SXM that had been specifically developed to study microscopic aquatic life. The SXM used soft x-ray technologies to display both the external and internal structure of specimens. By varying the intensity of the x-ray beam, different levels of translucency could be dialed in. The resulting image looked similar to that seen through a standard optical microscope, only with far greater detail. The revolutionary aspect of this instrument was that it used a scanned soft x-ray source to reduce dosage to a level not immediately harmful to living tissue. This meant that living biological specimens could be studied in their natural aquatic environment and with terrific detail. Electron microscopes only worked with carefully prepared dead specimens, which often had to be dehydrated as well. The preparation was always lethal; and even if it were not, the electron beam and evacuated target chamber of most electron microscopes would kill any living sample. The magnification level of the SXM was its limiting factor. Under ideal conditions, the SXM could deliver a magnification factor of just under three thousand, which was trivial when compared to the capability of electron microscopes which could reach magnifications of two million or more.

A liquid specimen of a few drops of water and Chromatium was loaded into the SXM. The microscope was switched on, but the screen remained an empty white image. Kathy wondered if the scope was broken. The sample should have been teeming with Chromatium. The magnification was set at two hundred fifty. She tried varying the intensity of the x-ray beam but nothing seemed to change. Using a joystick to control a 3-axis mechanical stage, she moved the sample around. Her heart jumped as something flitted across the screen. The scope had been working; there had just been nothing to see. Using the joystick, Kathy moved the specimen carrier trying to catch up with the animal while at the same time adjusting focus. A Chromatium snapped into view, then darted off screen.

Kathy caught up with a different Chromatium and increased the magnification to fill the screen. The image was otherworldly. The surface detail was amazing. She could almost see the microbe respiring or moving or something. Bacteria didn't breath, but there was such a powerful sense or illusion of biological life. With all its computer processing of the image, the SXM microscope gave this incredibly altered and real perspective. She felt as if she were viewing a living thing the size of submarine, not an insignificant creature smaller than a speck of dust. The Chromatium twitched and was gone from view before Kathy could get a detailed look. Another ghost shape shot across the screen from a different angle. She tried to follow it and failed. She was puzzled how they could have survived being frozen. Some bacteria could turn into a spore and survive almost anything short of a nuclear blast, but that was not Chromatium Omri. This little guy was an aquatic animal that was easy to kill. Yet these had survived freezing and thawing, which was typically a death sentence for this strain.

"We need better images," said Kathy. "Alan, you're in charge. I want you to get something set up so that we can constantly monitor these Chromatium. It's too hard to keep them in view. Maybe we can use some bait to corral them into a smaller area. What do these guys eat?"

"From what I've read, sulfides and B12 vitamins," answered Alan.

"Okay, gang, let's get on it," said Kathy. "Sulfides and B12, probably a better lunch than I'll get! I am out of here. I'll check back with you in an hour."

Kathy headed toward the airlocks. Above the hatchway was an illuminated emergency sign. Next to the hatchway was an instruction plaque with a skull and cross bones on it. Exiting the lab through the decontamination locks was frightening, even after having done it so many times before. She checked her oxygen supply. The gauge read fifty-eight minutes remaining. She stepped into the chamber and hooked her boots into floor shackles which automatically locked. The hatch closed with the finality of a tomb door. Inside a chamber which would soon be filled with Zydex liquid, if her feet were not firmly strapped down, the buoyancy of her containment suit would have her bobbing around the ceiling; which was not a pleasant thought. The high pressure sterilization spray started coming from every direction and filling the room like a shower with a stopped-up drain. The clear blue liquid was up to her knees and rising. She could feel a coolness penetrating the suit. The experience was claustrophobic. It felt worse than being in a lab where a vial of some deadly toxin had spilled. At least in the lab, she was surrounded by air, deadly air maybe, but it was still something she could breathe, something her mammalian mind could work with. The Zydex was up to her chest. This liquid could kill her instantly. All that separated her from a nasty death was the face shield of her helmet. She knew the smell in the room would be overwhelming at this point. One breath of that toxic mist and she'd pass out; a few more breaths and she'd die. The liquid rose up past her face and over her head. That was it. She was now submerged in a metal tank flooded with toxic blue liquid; and when she was done with this bath, she had to walk into the next airlock and do it all over again. She looked at the seams where the face-plate connected to the helmet and said the same prayer she always did.

"Please... Please don't leak..."

~

A school fire bell was sounding. Kathy woke up with a start. The room was silent. There was no bell, but she could still hear its echo. She glanced around to be certain she was in her office and not the BVMC lab. Minutes passed before her nerves settled.

She looked at the SXM display on the computer screen. The last surviving Chromatium was moving back and forth in its little prison. The creature's movements had been restricted to the microscope's field of view by reducing the amount of water it had to swim in. Alan had been unable to coax the microbes into remaining at a fixed observation point by baiting them with food. The Chromatium had ignored the food. This was odd because bacteria never ignore food. It was almost as if they had known they were being held against their will and wanted to escape. Microbes barely possess what were considered primitive instincts. They sought nutrients, fled adverse environments, and reproduced; that was it. They ran on pure hardwired instructions. They did not have memory and they did not display new behaviors.

Most of the Chromatium had died within the first hour. They shriveled a little like the original dead specimen; and then, within a minute, all movement ceased. Kathy assumed the cause of death was what she had started calling freezer-burn. The animal's cellular structure must have been damaged from pressure changes associated with freezing and thawing. The real curiosity was that they came out of a frozen state and were able to reanimate at all.

The lone Chromatium was still moving, repeating the same activity for the last few minutes. The bacterium nudged up against the edge of the water drop as if trying to push through; then, it moved to a new spot and tried again. This behavior was very unusual. As Kathy watched, the Chromatium shriveled, then stopped moving. The last one was gone.

Carl Green knocked on her doorframe. The sound startled her. He wandered in and sat. She could see he was in a gloomy mood.

"Tell me something good," said Carl.

"The DNA comparisons are showing a close enough match between Anchorage Chromatium and the Rochester colony to identify our bug as a strain of Chromatium Omri. I would have preferred that the key DNA sequences didn't match and that this Chromatium was some new and deadly species. That would have answered a lot of questions, but at least this match narrows down what we have to consider… and that's a good thing."

"So, no reason to experiment with more monkeys to see if this Chromatium is lethal," said Carl. "It was just a dead end after all."

"I'm not so sure," said Kathy. "I'm going to run more primate exposure trials. I want to inject Anchorage Chromatium into some of the monkeys on the chance that these Chromatium are carriers and not the disease. If they're carrying something, then we could get a reaction."

"Long odds?"

"Carl, I know what I said before about Chromatium being a dead end. I think I was wrong. I can't ignore the fact that we now have a diver from Antarctica and a whole group of Alaskan victims with Chromatium Omri in their bodies. This has to be a piece of the puzzle. I just have no idea what that piece means. I want to get an expert on Chromatium Omri to consult with us. Can you find me someone?"

"Consider it done. I think I'll get something to eat," said Carl. "Want to join me?"

"Sure."

~

Kathy stared at the computer screen and felt disoriented. It was late at night. There was no other light in her office except the glowing monitor. The largest window on the screen contained a video feed from the BVMC lab. Alan Trune was drawing blood from a series of primates that had been injected with a concentrated extract from the Anchorage Chromatium. So far, all the tests using Anchorage Chromatium had failed to cause any of the SAAC symptoms: no raised antibody counts, no respiratory problems, no microscopic nerve damage.

Kathy was starting to believe she was dealing with a contagion that shared the same environment, the same pond with Chromatium. The killer might even be a symbiont, possibly a bacterial parasite, but it did not require this specific strain of bacterium to exist; that much was clear. In the end, Chromatium might prove to be a key that unlocked the door to discovering this killer ghost; but it was almost assuredly not the killer itself. The killer was probably some kind of stealth microbe, a contagion that attacked ferociously, then went dormant and hid in the victim's body masquerading as a normally present organic. There were precedents for stealth behavior like this, though nothing quite as advanced as she suspected of this killer. Viruses could mutate and, over time, alter their protein shells to mimic organic molecules normally present in the body of their hosts. This adaptive behavior caused the host's immune system to ignore the virus until it was too late. Bacteria also used this kind of survival strategy. The antibiotic-resistant strains of staph and tuberculosis were just two examples of a growing category of diseases scaring doctors to their very core. Granted, these examples were the result of natural selection; but didn't nature have a way of learning from her successes? Was this killer ghost simply using the next evolutionary step in the survival tactic of camouflage? Could a microbe sheathe itself in a chemical disguise, dialed-in to match its environment like a chameleon changing colors?

So many disturbing aspects surrounded this crisis. The idea of a chameleon-like microbe was troubling. The idea that each outbreak was limited to a small geographic zone was inexplicable. The idea that this thing killed so rapidly was terrifying. Kathy was making progress; but for every step forward, new unanswered questions were revealed. She was grateful the Army had sent her the Anchorage Chromatium samples, but their action was a stark contradiction when compared to their secretive behavior surrounding the only Anchorage survivor – Harold N. They had provided limited lab samples and reported finding no Chromatium in him, and that was the extent of their cooperation. Was she just being paranoid? No, there were troubling questions. Why had the Army been looking for Chromatium in the first place? The fact that they had found the bacterium so quickly had to mean that they were actively looking for it. Before the Anchorage kill zone, she had given up on Chromatium and was only humoring Carl. All objective evidence supported no reason to actively pursue Chromatium; yet within 24 hours of Anchorage, the Army had zeroed in on, found and catalogued Chromatium in eighty percent of the victims. Their findings were just too good to be accidental. They had to know more than they were sharing.

Kathy's head was throbbing. She was so tired, so very tired. She switched off her monitor and with it went all the ideas tormenting her mind. The room was dark. She sat in silence. The absence of everything was soothing.

Chapter 4

Discoveries

1 – Black Creek, New York: November

Black Creek Village was an ideal middle class suburbia, a small community only miles from Niagara Falls. A slow river meandered through the landscape amid wild grass and trees. The development was young; it was only a few years ago that the last house had been completed. The majority of the homes had been built upon freshly trucked-in soil, on which a landscape had been carefully shaped and planted to create an ancient rustic facade. Every aspect had been engineered to conceal the horror of its past.

In 1978, this small part of the world had received its ten minutes of notoriety. Black Creek Village had a different name back then. In 1978, it was known as Love Canal. Beginning in the late 1950's, developers built homes and an elementary school over a site where 20,000 tons of toxic waste had been dumped. The poisons were gifts from a company named Hooker Chemical and the complicity of a local government. Many residents were left with permanent reminders of their years at Love Canal: birth defects, low grade cancers, and odd little tumors that came and went.

Through the years, the betrayals had been forgotten by outsiders and the site had been cleaned up. A new developer arrived and purchased some nearby land at what he considered an excellent price. He held documents that assured him the land was safe, certified by the EPA. On his fire-sale lots, he built a dream, a model bedroom community of luxurious homes in Black Creek Village. Unfortunately, many upstate New Yorkers remembered the area and the original name. Soon, the developer had to lower his asking price and advertise in cities hundreds of miles away.

Tina loved her new home. She had just turned seven, and it was the best present she could have hoped for. She had a big room of her own, a new bike, and her dog Santana had a yard to play in. She should have been happier than any time in her life but she was sad. This morning she'd stared out the window, barely touching her breakfast. She missed all her friends who still lived in New York City.

Her Mommy had been saving for as long as Tina could remember, to get them out of the City. Mommy called it escaping. Tina thought it was like running away. It had taken every penny of mommy's savings, but they had the down-payment; and Tina and her aunt Margaret and her Mommy moved into a brand new home.

There were still plenty of empty houses on the block, and her Mommy had said that's why they had gotten such a great deal. Tina wondered if there were other reasons. When she played in the neighborhood, sometimes it felt like the empty houses were filled with ghosts.

A month ago, Mommy flew off to visit Grandpa Arturo for a whole week. After feeling ill, Grandpa had gone back to live in Venezuela. Mommy's airline ticket was so expensive, but Grandpa was successful and had paid for her ticket himself.

She loved Grandpa Arturo. His smiling face and bushy white mustache were constantly in her thoughts. He had been the father she'd never known. When they lived in the City, every Sunday he would come to their home with food to cook. Their life in the city had been hard then, before Grandpa had sold his store to the big company and retired wealthy.

Tina ate a spoonful of cereal, slowly chewing, not wanting to swallow. She remembered how Grandpa Arturo had proudly walked her to school everyday. His stick cane would click on the sidewalks signaling the young gangsters to lower their eyes in respect. The sound of that cane had been like the security of a warm blanket. She remembered how good that sound had made her feel when she'd heard it while waiting in the afternoon for him to arrive and escort her home. She could hear him coming, long before he turned the corner. There was always a special gleam in his eyes when he saw her. Tina knew she was his favorite.

Once a local tough guy had pulled a knife on her and Grandpa. Grandpa had not hesitated an instant. He'd struck the gangster with his cane as if he were punishing a child for being naughty. That gangster was never tough again.

Grandpa Arturo had called last week, and Mommy said he would be coming to visit this Christmas. Tina's spirits had lifted for a day or two, but even the thoughts of Grandpa Arturo's smiling face and his gifts were not enough.

Tina pushed the bowl of cereal away. The milk sloshed a tiny flotilla of Cheerios. They'd lived in their new home for over a month and she still hadn't made a single friend. Yesterday, some of the kids at the arcade had whispered things and started to laugh. She knew they were talking about her. One of them had pointed. She had cried the entire way home. While half-running down the sidewalks, she'd heard the faint echo of Grandpa Arturo's cane and knew it was only a wish.

Tina got Santana's leash from the kitchen drawer. The metal chain jingled. A huge black Labrador came bounding into the room. Tina decided that a long walk in the woods behind their house was exactly what both of them needed. The other day, she'd found a field dotted with wild flowers. She had laid on her back and looked up at the clouds. Maybe she would do the same today. It was a place for dreaming.

The trail was narrow. Twigs and leaves crackled under her sneakers. The woods were alive with wonderful sounds. Bird noises were something new to Tina. Growing up in the City, the only birds she knew were pigeons. The shrill musical notes of the forest enchanted her. She wanted to dance and twirl amid their sounds. A small wind cut through the trees and tickled her face and hair. There was a faint smell of something like syrup.

A bright red bird landed on a branch less than ten feet away. The bird had a feather crown on its head and seemed very proud. He stared, tipping his head to either side until Santana barked. The bird was beautiful. Tina decided to ask Mommy for a book on birds so she could learn all their names and what they liked to eat. She would feed them and make friends.

The trail turned to the left and began to follow a slow moving stream. Tina wondered what kind of animals lived in the brown water. There must be frogs and turtles and fish... maybe even something special that lives nowhere else but here? She stopped under a huge weeping willow tree. Its branches hung like vines dipping into the water. Winds moved the tree as if it were sweeping the top of the river. Santana walked into a foot of water and tasted some.

A bird landed in tall grass five feet away from Tina. Santana hadn't seen it. Tina crept closer, amazed with her good luck. She was only a yard away. Maybe if she was very slow and gentle, the bird might let her touch him? She leaned over a clump of grass for her first peek. The bird looked like it was getting back on its feet. It seemed wobbly. The bird cocked its head to look back at her for a moment and then took off with a flutter.

Santana started yapping in pain. Tina got up and ran to him. Was he having trouble in the water? She yelled his name. He came bounding out of the stream toward her. He looked fine. Tina began to feel weak for no reason. Her legs became like rubber. She stumbled under the weeping willow tree. Her head struck a rock. Everything was spinning. She tried to call Santana but couldn't breathe. She managed to roll onto her back and watched as birds fluttered in the trees above her. She tried again to fill her lungs. She wanted to scream for help. All that came from her lips was a squeak. Her breath was gone. Oddly, she no longer cared. Her eyes stopped working as her brain drifted into dreams of Grandpa Arturo and fields of wildflowers.

~

The weeping willow vines in water were tangled in debris of leaves and litter. Like broken toys, a small flotilla of junk cans and bottles drifted by on a slow current. Soon they were washed around a muddy bend. Crickets, birds, and the occasional rustle of leaves were the only sounds in the forest. The zone of death had been small, a few hundred yards in diameter.

Santana had come home without Tina and had acted very upset, but not nearly as upset as Tina's mother. Tina was found the next morning.

A week later the police ruled the incident as suspicious because of Tina's head wounds; but with no leads to follow, the case was filed with a dozen other unsolved deaths. No paperwork was sent to the State Health Office. The incident didn't fall under the guidelines of events that had to be filed. The police were overworked and understaffed. There were cases that could be quickly solved and that's where the limited manpower went.

2 – Los Angeles: November

It was raining in Los Angeles, an unusual event even during the rainy season. The sky was dark with clouds that were swirling low and threatening to touch the ground. Mark stood beneath the overhang of a side entrance to the building which housed his lab. It was lunchtime. He took a bite of his turkey sandwich and watched the rain. A chill worked its way up his body. Most of the drops missed him, but a few made it to his face and glasses. The tiny spots of water brought childhood memories.

He'd always loved the rain, the *tears of the earth,* was what his mother had called even the worst of storms. Most of his friends hated the rain, calling it bad weather; but to him the storms were powerful and exciting, especially lightning storms. The very dark ones seemed to charge the world with energy. He could remember when he was ten years old, standing in a field with lightning flashing around him while he tipped his head back and drank the rain. That taste would be with him his entire life. As he grew a little older, he became able to distinguish the source of a storm by its taste. Ones that came off the ocean had a fresher flavor. Those that came off the mountains had a slightly earthy taste.

A student with books over her head ran down the sidewalk, seeking shelter. Mark looked out into the rain and felt its mist; for a moment, he was part of it. He wanted to go out into the downpour and taste it, but he knew that the rains were different now. The air was poisoned and so was the rain. If he did drink some, he knew there would be an acid taste – the telltale markers of an industrial state – particles and sulfides and carcinogens from the exhaust pipes of highway traffic. He had grown to hate Los Angeles because of what it had done to the rain.

"Mark..."

The woman's voice surprised him. He turned to see Donna Brooks, a professor of biochemistry, and a man he did not recognize. The man was probably in his late forties, with silver sideburns and a camel hair overcoat. Donna was fortyish, with long hazel colored hair and eyes that were very blue from contact lenses. Mark and Donna were friends and sometimes had lunch together. A long time ago, they had dated. The relationship had never gotten sexual and Mark was glad it had worked out that way. Instead of a few weeks of easy gratification, he now had a lifelong friend. The corners of Donna's eyes had the beginnings of tiny character wrinkles when she smiled. She was a very appealing woman.

"Mark, this is my friend Jack Harris. Jack's an MD specializing in infectious diseases at Bethesda Medical."

"I thought you had to be Navy to work there?" said Mark.

"It helps," said Jack. "You can call me Commander Harris if you like."

"Jack's been moonlighting for the NIH," said Donna. "He's involved in some kind of hush-hush research and has something he wants to talk with you about."

"So talk," said Mark.

"Do you have a place a little more private?" asked Jack.

"Sure," said Mark. "My lab sound good?"

"Fine," said Jack. "Donna, I'm sorry but you can't tag along."

"I've got a class in ten minutes anyway. I guess you boys are just going to have to get along without me."

"I'll call you later," said Jack. "Around six."

Donna gave Jack a peck on the cheek, then went off into the rain. Halfway down the steps, she opened a red and white umbrella. Mark felt a small twinge of jealousy. They obviously had plans for a date.

The metal door to the lab clanked shut. Mark walked over to the coffee machine and poured himself a cup. The warmth felt good on his throat. He glanced up at the lithograph of Einstein.

"Commander Harris, want some coffee?" he asked.

"No thanks. What I want to talk about can never leave this room."

"Damn, I've always wanted to say that."

"I'm serious. I need you to sign a secrecy act before we go on."

"Can I see some identification?" asked Mark.

Jack Harris removed a laminated card from his wallet. Mark decided it looked official, not that he had any idea what a Navy identification card should look like. Information on the card listed Jack Harris as a medical doctor with a rank of Lieutenant Commander in the United States Navy.

"Okay, Commander, tell me why I should sign this piece of paper?"

"Why not?" said Harris. "What have you got to lose? And I might have a very interesting story to tell you."

Mark's nature was to be suspicious of the military and the government; but this man was right: what did he have to lose? He read the document quickly and signed all the copies.

An hour later, Mark was pouring himself his third cup of coffee. He was having difficulty believing everything he was hearing. The CDC was operating in secret under a national health emergency. Some unknown pathogen was taking out villages in South America and now had apparently made the jump to Alaska. Almost a thousand people were dead from what amounted to an epidemic, and just as disturbing was the idea that a complete news blackout was in effect. Mark was listening carefully to what the military officer was saying. Mark had brought up the conflicting news coverage of Anchorage. What the Commander was saying implied not too subtly that the news broadcasts were intentional misinformation, including the part about a chemical weapon's leak possibly being involved.

"Why would the military take that kind of blame?" asked Mark.

"There are more important issues and soldiers follow orders."

"Why should I believe you?"

"Why would I lie?"

"Do you answer every question with a goddamn question?"

"Look Mark, we need your expertise. This disease may have an onset period measured in minutes. We don't know if the cause is bacterial or viral. We don't know where it's coming from. We don't even know if it's contagious."

"What can I do?" said Mark. "I'm not an MD. This isn't my area of research."

"Chromatium Omri has been found in the bodies of eighty percent of the victims in Anchorage. The bacterium is benign; but human blood is not exactly a native environment for this bug, so we're assuming there's a connection. We've established that the bacterium found in the victims closely matches the known strains of Chromatium Omri. One of our scientists believes it could even be a strain that's genetically close to your COBIC-3.7. We need *the expert* on this bacterium. Your name came up."

Mark felt like he'd been steamrolled. He actually felt dizzy. Harris was still talking but Mark was no longer listening. He was trying to focus on the chunk of fossilized COBIC on his desk. His thoughts were running in wild circles. Could it be a close cousin to *his* Chromatium in the blood of these victims? The government seemed to think that was a possibility. If true, this was certainly a dark form of luck. He felt energized, then conflicted, then horribly guilty. This could be a clue to the solution of one of the greatest mysteries of ancient times – mass extinction, and he would be right there to collect the data. He felt guilty that such a self-centered thought had even occurred to him; but if it was true that a closely related strain to his COBIC was connected to these cluster deaths, these mini-extinction events, then another Nobel Prize was in his future.

"Who exactly is working on this?" asked Mark.

"The CDC is where you'd be going, specifically a top research group that operates out of a secure facility in the Atlanta suburbs."

Mark stared into the man's eyes.

"When do I start?"

Commander Harris handed him a satchel-briefcase with the top open. Inside were manila folders with the words Top Secret stamped on them. Shiny orange and white striped tape was folded over the edges of the folders. The tape made the edges look like smaller versions of the orange and white traffic barricades used at construction sites. Commander Harris handed him a key for the briefcase.

"You can begin now," said Harris. "This is all the relevant data the CDC has collected. Keep it secure and keep it with you at all times until we pick it up. Don't make copies. It's a federal crime. Oh yeah, take a look at the folder labeled five. It seems this bacterium can be frozen and, when thawed, a large percentage reanimates."

Mark was stunned. This bacterium could be more than a close cousin; this could be *his* Chromatium. In all the papers he'd written, there had been no mention of viability after freezing. The detail was a small piece of information he'd kept for himself like a chef leaving a single ingredient from the recipe. At the time, it had seemed curious that COBIC-3.7 had been able to survive freezing and thawing. While it was not at all unusual for other species of bacteria to possess this trait, his discovery made COBIC-3.7 the only strain of Chromatium Omri with this resiliency. COBIC-3.7 flourished in superheated hot springs, so at the time it had not been that surprising they were heartier than the common strains in more than one way.

3 – New York City: November

The City was experiencing an unusually warm day which was breaking temperature records for November. The air was a pungent mix of food and car exhaust and sweat. Artie Hartman pushed open the taxi door with his foot. The door's rusted hinges groaned. He was a young man dressed in an expensive business suit. He was half Japanese and half English. His features were a smooth blending of the two races. He was tall and muscular with a Caucasian build but Asian complexion and features. His eyes were more round than almond, with the color of blue sky.

Artie lifted his gaze slowly upward and drank in the expanding view. What he saw was good. No, better than good. Twelve stories above him was a set of windows, his and Suzy's new windows, his and Suzy's new apartment. The rent was three thousand dollars a month and the apartment was small, but it was in a great part of town and had a uniformed doorman and a marble entrance hall. So what if the marble was cracked and the doorman smoked cigars?

Artie gave the cabby a generous tip. The doorman smiled and said, "Good day, Mr. Hartman." It was a good day, decided Artie. Life was working out better than he could have hoped. Fresh out of law school, he had landed his dream job, a prime cut assignment as an assistant DA. For a poor Asian kid from the Bronx, this was the American dream come true. The job had started a month ago, and today they were moving into their new place. Suzy would be home from work in a few more hours. She was a location camerawoman for *Hello! New York*. The local morning show had average ratings and aired pointless stories, but it had easily paid their bills during Artie's last two years of law school. In her off time, Suzy had worked on a pair of documentaries for a nonprofit organization. Her documentary about homeless people had been aired on PBS. Documentary filmmaking was where her real passions lay. Artie felt good knowing that soon it would be his turn to support Suzy in her career move.

Artie wiped the perspiration from his face. He'd unpacked ten boxes filled with books. He leaned against the kitchen doorway and poured gulps of beer down his throat. In spite of all his work, the room still looked just as filled, stacked from floor to ceiling with more boxes. Had they secretly materialized from another dimension? Where had all this stuff come from? He felt walled in. It was time for a break. Fifteen minutes later, he was in the elevator with a mountain bike slung over his shoulder.

Traffic was heavy. Artie clicked up through the gears of his bike. He flashed past long lines of cars bottled up at intersections. There was a rhythmic noise, something like the sound of riding swiftly beside a picket fence. He was doing almost thirty mph at mid block and on a ruler-straight line toward Central Park. Speed was freedom. He had worked his way through undergraduate school as a bicycle courier. In those days, he'd spilled over the hoods of more than a few cars but had never been tagged by the wild bumper. He had earned his right of way over the cars. He was the one going for speed, cutting the corners, jumping the lights.

Anger was warming the skin of his face. The rage had been there, simmering all day long and now it was coming to the surface. The anger had begun after court at eleven o'clock this morning. The gangbanger he was prosecuting had an arrest record eighteen pages long, but only one prior conviction. This time he'd been picked up for breaking and entering a grocery store after hours. The creep had vandalized the shelves and made off with two cases of Pepsi. The punk was stupid as well as violent. Busted six blocks from the store for Pepsi theft, this time the gangster had also been wanted for raping a sixteen-year old girl.

The crime scene photos splashed up vivid memories in Artie's mind: a small Latino girl with a swollen eye and a split lip and bruises that ran all along her torso. She had been raped several times over a period of hours.

Artie's attention jumped back to the street. His teeth clenched tightly as he squeezed the brakes skidding to a stop at an intersection. The cross-flow of cars rushed past him like the maw of some huge deadly machine.

The gangbanger had gotten off, case dismissed, because the girl had been too scared to pick him from a lineup. The cops only had him on circumstantial evidence, no fingerprints or DNA. As far as the judge was concerned, it wasn't enough for a trial.

This afternoon, that piece of human dirt had shaken Artie's hand in the hall outside a courtroom and thanked him for coming today. The animal had leaned close and whispered through a mouth decorated with two gold-capped teeth.

"Hey five-0, the little bitch 'id wanted it, liked it. She turned pissy when I wouldn't give her no mo'. I know you know what I mean... homey."

Artie had knotted up with rage. Every inch of him had yearned to follow the animal outside and put him down.

The light changed to green. Artie pushed off. By the time he was across the street and through the park gates, he was moving flat out. He swung wide around Cherry Hill fountain and headed back toward the gate. It was time to push the limits.

Suzy hated the way he rode. She was constantly trying to get him to stop. Kamikaze riding was the name Artie's old gang had given it.

He knew that rapist punk better than he wanted to. Ten years ago, given a few more problems, it could have been him.

Artie started working the pedals with everything he had. Sweat was soaking into his shirt. His legs were fleshy pistons driving the machine. The speedometer was reading high thirties. He jumped the curb and shot through a line of traffic. The horns faded as he whisked down a corridor of buildings, still gaining speed. He glanced down at his left wrist. The mark was still there, the gang tattoo.

Artie closed his eyes for a moment and listened to the wind. Danger was a rush. He opened his eyes and yelled into the wind. The memories were still there along with the tattoo. No amount of penance would erase the things he'd done and seen. He'd been fourteen when he was initiated into the Red Dragons. The ceremony was called being beat-in. First he was hugged by the guys that were going to beat him. They were in a vacant lot. Gutted buildings towered around him like the ramparts of some destroyed castle. He was bigger than all the others, but in minutes he was driven to his knees by the circle of ten hitters. He'd fought back hard. He was no punk that would just take it and lie there. He was determined to prove himself. One of the hitters had ended up with a smashed nose.

Once Artie had recovered enough to stand on his own, he was led off to a crash house. He was given a quart of beer and a joint; and told one of the local girls was waiting for him in a small bedroom. She was a nice girl, too scared and too proud to be wilded by any gangster that came along. She wanted the protection of her gang. This was her initiation too. Girls had the choice of being sexed-in or beat-in. After he was done with her, others had lined up. This serial abuse was the first train he'd seen, and not the last. After several years he'd earned the nickname caboose. He was always the last in line. He didn't like this thing they did; but if he didn't participate he was out, and that was almost always fatal. There was a gauntlet of knives to walk before a gangster became an ex.

Artie had told Suzy nearly everything about his past. The trains were something he could never discuss or explain to a Japanese girl who had grown up in the affluent suburbs of New Jersey.

The day after his initiation, Artie was given his mark. A local tattoo shop had etched onto his left wrist a red dragon coiled around a dagger. The mark was three inches long and directly over the major arteries. If a blood ever failed his brothers, he vowed to cut the serpent in two. There were rumors about some who had done it; one voluntarily, the others under threats of things far worse.

Artie was covered in sweat as he carried his bike into the apartment. Suzy peeked around the corner between the kitchen and hallway. She was home early. She stared at him with those eyes that never missed a thing. The smile vanished from her face. She knew he had ridden wild. He took his bike out everyday and almost never Kamikazied. How did she know? Sometimes Artie wondered if she was a witch.

"Sorry baby," he said.

Silence was her weapon. Artie went into the bathroom to take a shower. He felt like a dog. The soap and hot water cleaned his body but not his thoughts.

Dinner was quiet. Suzy had made dumplings and noodles. When she was through picking at her food, she watched him eat. At first her eyes were hard, but slowly they softened. By the time Artie was through with his first helping, she smiled.

"Do you forgive me?" he said.

"Remember rule number twenty-six?" she said. "Forgiveness is for suckers."

Artie laughed. He figured he knew about half her rules by heart. He loved her more than anything he could have imagined being able to feel, and sometimes even more. She had this smooth healthy complexion and when she smiled the entire room grew brighter. She was an exotic woman, high cheekbones and a smallish nose. Her hair was short and black and reminded him of pictures he'd seen on the cover of Vogue.

~

A faint smell of dinner lingered amid the cardboard boxes. Artie was on the couch with a glass of red wine. The boxes were piled around him like a fort. Suzy had been off doing something for the last hour, probably tracking down some of her stuff. The stereo was playing softly. She came into the room and cuddled up next to him. She took a sip of his wine, then gave him a small piece of plastic with a blue dot in the center. Artie was confused. There was something mischievous in Suzy's eyes.

"What is this?" he asked.

"Guess."

Something in the back of Artie's mind clicked. His nerves jumped. He'd seen these on television. The blue dot was a home pregnancy test. He hugged her and kissed her until she was laughing so hard that he had to stop. He realized he was babbling, gushing, but didn't care. He was in love with the girl of his dreams and they were going to have a baby.

~

Artie awoke in the middle of the night. His stomach felt sore as if all the muscles had cramped up minutes ago. He was sweating. The air felt thicker and was hard to breathe. There was a stench of burned meat. Something was very wrong. He was on fire. He screamed until his lungs were empty. He gasped awake for the second time. The air was fine. The room was fine. His death had been a dream, but so real....

4 – Atlanta, Georgia: November

Mark was dead tired. He hated flying and was glad that part of the trip was behind him. He was yawning. He couldn't stop thinking of sleep. He'd flown into Atlanta on the red eye, tossed his bags through the open door of a hotel room, then piled into a rented Ford to drive out to the lab. The radio in the car was broken and the CD player had just finished eating its breakfast, his favorite CD. *Morrison Hotel* by the Doors was hopelessly jammed in the player. The great god of rental cars was frowning on him today. He knew he should have rented the Lexus.

At the CDC facility, Mark was expected. A security guard parked in a green Dodge was waiting at the gate. Mark followed the green Dodge with its government plates to a set of reserved parking spaces.

With his uniformed escort, Mark walked into the lobby of the CDC facility. Mark was wearing a tweed sport coat, Greenpeace t-shirt, jeans, and a pair of beat-up sneakers. The security officer working the front desk disliked him on sight and hated him even more when he found out Mark was the VIP they were expecting. The security officer gave him a six-page questionnaire to fill out for a temporary badge.

A half hour later, a young woman in a blue dress and white lab coat arrived to escort Mark through the building. They passed through a security checkpoint which included a metal detector and an x-ray machine for bags. Mark noticed people were being screened both entering and leaving.

Following his escort, he walked through a revolving door that required his new magnetic badge and was deposited into a long hallway of faux marble. One side of the hallway was the building's back wall, which was solid glass. The other side of the hallway was a long row of doors leading to offices, elevators, and other rooms. The woman started chatting small talk. She was very much his type, young, full of energy, and a little reckless around the edges – a lot like Gracy. He noticed she had no ring on her left hand.

"So, I understand you are going to be staying in Atlanta for some time," said his escort.

"Maybe a week."

Suddenly, Mark began feeling dizzy and stopped walking. He tried to conceal his dizziness by leaning on and starring out the glass wall. The view overlooked a wooded area of some kind. He'd taken his insulin on the flight. Maybe those two vodka martinis six hours ago had not been such a great idea. The young woman had stopped a few paces away and was staring. He noticed she had blue eyes; then he realized he didn't remember her name.

"Are you okay?" she asked.

"Yeah, I just feel a little run down."

After a few minutes, they started walking again. The woman asked him where he was staying. The dizziness was waning. His insulin was back at the hotel, but he suspected he'd be fine without it. She opened a door and ushered him into a large office.

"Dr. Carl Green and Dr. Kathy Morrison are on a conference call. Can I get you anything... coffee?"

"A gallon would be nice... black, extra caffeine. In fact, hold the coffee. Just give me some raw beans to chew on. I had a long flight."

"Coming right up."

"No... You know what... wait a minute. Do you have some orange juice instead? I need a little sugar in my system."

The woman smiled, "Sure."

5 – Atlanta, Georgia: November

Kathy was walking down the hallway with Carl. She was not happy. With every step, she was closer to meeting Professor Mark Freedman and that made her nervous. She was surprised that Carl had been able to bring in a Nobel Laureate as a consultant. She was worried that what her team had pieced together so far was meager and that she'd look foolish and premature for calling in a scientist of his stature. She'd done her homework on Professor Freedman, even phoning a college instructor of hers who'd worked with him in the past. The consensus was that Professor Freedman was brilliant and eccentric in equal measure, with a lot of drive to be the best.

As she walked into Carl's office, a good looking man rose to shake her hand. So this was a Nobel Prize winning scientist. He looked younger than she'd imagined, something closer to forty than fifty. His handshake was firm, not wimpy. He had dark hair with a little gray in it and very intelligent eyes.

"So, I understand you found Chromatium swimming around in the blood of some of the victims of your top secret epidemic." said Freedman.

"Not my secret," said Kathy, "and not just blood. Chromatium were also found trapped in ice on the face and scalp of some of the victims."

"I've got to be up front with both of you," said Freedman. "I've been thinking about why Chromatium might invade an animal's body and you're not going to like my conclusion. There is no explanation, none. If any organization including the CDC had made this claim under different circumstances, I'd think drugs were involved and not the legal kind. There's nothing in blood for these bugs to eat. It's a completely wrong environment for them to expand into. There are only two things that motivate these critters, food and reproduction."

Kathy nodded and agreed. She was starting to feel intellectually comfortable, but warning signals were flashing and she had just realized the reason. She was not sure in what way, but Mark Freedman reminded her of Barry, her ex-husband.

"How do you think Chromatium are related to this epidemic?" asked Freedman.

"If we knew that," said Kathy, "we'd be out of a job and the country would be safe."

Kathy had no idea why she had just acted so rudely. Freedman was staring at her with an odd expression. She glanced at Carl. He looked aghast.

"So..." said Freedman, "I haven't had a chance to eat anything except a snack at the airport. No food worth eating on flights anymore. How would you folks feel about an early lunch? My treat. We can continue talking in a more relaxed setting."

"There's a great Italian restaurant fifteen minutes from here," said Carl. "We can take my car."

"Great," said Freedman. "My rental's been a real pig on the ride out here."

"Gas?" asked Carl.

"No, CDs. The little road-toad ate my favorite Doors album."

"We had another incident today in South America, Guatemala this time," said Kathy. "Forty-one people died."

My god, she did it again! What was going on with her? Was she going for the bitch-of- the-month award or something? Freedman was going to think she's off her rocker.

"Listen, why don't we eat here," said Freedman. "On my way in, I passed the cafeteria. It looked okay to me. So Dr. Morrison, I understand the outbreak in Anchorage was limited to the dock area."

"So far; and the Army's maintaining a quarantine for public appearances, which is a good thing, even if it's for the wrong reasons; but I can't be sure we've contained anything since we don't know the cause or method of transmission. Too bad it's not Chromatium. If that was the case, then we'd know we were dealing with a waterborne vector and we'd know how to contain it."

"I've been thinking," said Freedman, "I believe we can safely go with the idea that the killer is waterborne. There's good circumstantial evidence that it's connected with Chromatium, which means they are sharing the same environment, and for Chromatium Omri, that's water."

In the background, a lunch tray clanked against a table. Kathy took another sip of Diet Pepsi. So far, she had managed to swallow half a dry tuna on wheat. She had no appetite. Carl and Freedman had done most of the talking. The conversation had turned to something that was insanely boring, professional sports. Kathy was content to drift off into her own thoughts. Carl wiped his mouth and then stood up. He shook Freedman's hand.

"I have to get back to my office," said Carl. "I have a conference call to make. Kathy can finish the tour and fill you in on whatever you need to know."

Great, thought Kathy, as she swallowed the last of her Diet Pepsi. She realized when she had drifted off, she had been thinking about George. She hadn't thought about that adventure in over a year. She was a little embarrassed to have thought about it now. The affair had happened on a trip to the Cayman Islands one month after her divorce had been finalized. Before that trip, she had never gone anywhere alone, not even the movies. Something had happened to her there. The complete separation from her old life had transformed her into someone far bolder. Every aspect of her personality had been amplified. She had become almost a caricature of herself in a bathing suit and sarong; and then without warning there was George.

6 – Atlanta, Georgia: November

Mark decided the remote control systems in the BVMC lab were brilliant. He was looking over Kathy's shoulder as she manipulated software controls on the screen. They were in an office that had been assigned to him. A large computer window was open. The screen magnification within it increased, revealing live Chromatium swimming in liquid. At Mark's request, a small army of them had been thawed. From that thawing, nearly twenty percent had revived. There were hundreds of them moving in what resembled a swarm of capsule-shaped tadpoles or sperm. For the most part, they were swimming in random directions; but occasionally a smaller group would standout from the swarm by suddenly schooling like fish. They would swim together and change direction at nearly the same instant. The coordination only lasted seconds; then the small group would disorganize and vanish back into the swarm. The image was of choreographed chaos. Their synchronization in those brief moments was remarkable. It couldn't be the result of random turns and dives. These animals were swimming with each other in some controlled way. He'd never seen this behavior exhibited by any bacterium including COBIC-3.7.

"Is this being recorded?" he asked.

"Everything is automatically recorded and saved for at least thirty days unless you tag it to be saved permanently or deleted. What you're seeing is real time from a scanned x-ray microscope, but I can switch to a digitally recorded playback at any time."

Mark had a great deal of experience with scanned x-ray instruments but was not sure what the lab's computer system could do with recorded data.

"Can you digitally zoom out and play it back in slow motion? I want to get a broader look at their interaction with each other."

"No problem. This system is like a super-Tivo with unlimited hard disk space."

Kathy clicked a few times and entered some numbers on what looked like a tape recorder control panel. The image jumped backward at high speed, then zoomed out and began running forward at quarter speed. There was no mistaking the synchronization of some of their movements. The organization did look like the behavior of schooling fish, but that would have required intelligence, something bacteria did not possess. Maybe they were just reacting to some invisible stimulus? Maybe they were sensitive to the microscope's soft x-ray beam? Mark needed to study this more before he discussed it openly. There was something else not right about these Chromatium. The capsule shape was a little rounded in the area where the nucleoid was located. The bulge was something like the bacterial equivalent of a mild potbelly.

"Kathy, can you freeze and zoom in on one of these bacteria? I'd like to see a full frame view with a superimposed ruler or grid... something to measure the animal's dimensions."

Kathy entered a set of numbers and commands. The instrument's magnification went up. The system continued recording as Chromatium swam by in the enlarged view. In a few minutes, Kathy had the real-time image replaced by a perfect freeze frame of a single animal with a calibrated grid superimposed. Mark studied the shape. The size was about twenty percent larger than baseline Chromatium Omri, just like COBIC-3.7. However, COBIC-3.7 did not have that rounded bulge; and the nucleoid itself appeared to be the cause. The nucleoid was enlarged and less opaque than it should have been. His initial impression was that it almost looked like a bubble was trapped inside it. Mark had Kathy switch the view back to live Chromatium.

"How far have you gotten on a complete DNA sequence?" he asked. "I need to know which strain of bacterium we've got."

"The sequencing is done. We sent it out to GenTech who agreed to run a priority job."

"It's done!" said Mark.

"When GenTech's CEO was told in confidence what was happening, heaven and earth got moved. They turned the job around in twenty-four. From what I heard, we tied up their entire production capacity for most of the day. The sequence contains matches to published DNA fragments for twenty strains of Chromatium Omri, including COBIC-3.7. Apparently there are a lot of junk sequences which are causing false positives. Matching to a specific strain is beyond what my team can do quickly, so I guess that job's on your plate."

There were eighty-six identified strains of Chromatium Omri. In a gene pool of that limited diversity, there were a lot of chances for common sequences and junk sequence matches. Only an expert on Chromatium would know which lengths of DNA should be checked and which should be ignored. Indiscriminate matching of all the COBIC sequences that Mark had published was evidence a microbe could be COBIC-3.7 but conclusively proved nothing.

Mark was feeling distracted and anxious. Kathy had been silent for several minutes. She seemed transfixed by the screen. He noticed that the number of live Chromatium appeared to be decreasing quicker than he had been warned by Kathy to expect. There was no reason for them to be dying unless they were running out of nutrients or were damaged. He could see there were more dead bodies floating around than live animals. He watched one shiver and shrivel a small amount as if the cellular membrane had ruptured, but there was no evidence of cytoplasm being jettisoned. All the dead Chromatium had the same shriveled look. The damage was one more oddity to consider, but right now what he wanted to focus on was the nucleoid bulge. That was an obvious difference between COBIC-3.7 and these Chromatium.

"Can we get a few shriveled and unshriveled specimens mounted up for the TEM? I want to get a detailed look inside both," asked Mark.

"I think we can fix you up," said Kathy.

Kathy turned from the computer. Mark had been leaning over her shoulder and was now very close to her as she turned to face him. He could feel her discomfort and backed away. She stood up.

"Come on; I'll introduce you to the lab staff. They can take care of the rest."

Mark was fascinated. Kathy's idea of introducing him to the lab staff had turned out to be meeting the team that was going on-duty in the ready room during shift change. The last stage of the airlock was rinsing away leftover sterilization solution. The process was like a human carwash. Through heavy plate windows, he could see into both stages of the airlock and the BVMC lab. Radio chatter from the lab team in the airlock could be heard over speakers in the ready room. The five members of the team going on-duty were getting into their containment spacesuits. The process was cumbersome and involved stepping into the suit backwards through an opening in the torso. Mark felt like he was meeting astronauts, and there were similarities. Kathy had explained that the team inside that containment lab was cutoff from the outside world. If a problem occurred, the team had to solve it themselves. They were at least forty minutes from help; the time required to get through the airlock system. If someone in there had a heart attack, the odds were fifty-fifty they would not make it out alive. To minimize risk, all personnel entering the BVMC lab had to undergo monthly medical examinations and all were trained in emergency first aid.

Mark knew that due to his medical problem the BVMC lab was permanently off limits for him. Which was alright, but at some level he was oddly envious. As a young boy, he dreamed of being an astronaut, and this lab was a way of experiencing some part of that dream. The team was putting on their helmets and checking each other's suits. Mark could remember being very young and hiding under the covers, looking at picture-books of spacecraft with his flashlight. He'd built tree-forts with levers and handles that controlled imaginary rockets. He remembered watching in awe as the first steps were made on the moon. With their helmets on, the team going on duty was now using radios to communicate. Kathy and Mark were standing in the same room with them, but to talk required a set of headphones and a radio. This was the first step in the isolation process: all direct human contact was gone.

~

Mark was alone for the first time in his temporary office. He pushed down on a lever to lower the height of his chair. Perfect. He opened the center desk drawer. There were signs that someone had recently vacated. A few dry pens were in a tray along with some unused tea bags, a lottery ticket from last month, and a small bottle of aspirin.

It would be at least another hour before his Chromatium samples were ready. The lab was having problems getting unshriveled samples of Chromatium into the TEM. The animals shriveled while being prepared for mounting. It was unusual that they were so easily damaged. If the bulge was a sign of injury from freezing and thawing, then all their Chromatium samples might have the same problem. The techs were trying different chemicals to prepare the specimens. They needed to find a technique that would completely solidify the Chromatium's structure from the inside out before they shriveled.

Mark woke the computer monitor from its screen saver sleep. After several minutes of exploring, he opened a window with a view of the lab. A series of software buttons and knobs were just below the window. One of them was labeled volume. He grabbed it with the mouse and rotated it higher. Voices started coming from the computer's speakers. The back and forth conversations were the same intercom traffic he'd heard in the ready room. He recognized Kathy issuing a rapid-fire barrage of orders. He was surprised that she was in the lab. As he listened, he realized that she must have gone in to personally supervise the preparation of his specimens after the problems had started piling up.

He wondered if he should share with Kathy his theories of COBIC-3.7 and its possible connection with mass extinctions. For now, it didn't seem wise. In all likelihood, whatever was going on right now had no connection to past extinctions or COBIC's connection to them. There was no value in scaring people needlessly over an unproven theory that might not be relevant even if true.

Mark located some pre-recorded images of shriveled Chromatium that Kathy had told him about. The images had been recorded four days ago in the TEM. He might as well get a head start looking at the shriveled model. The way things were going, it might be a long time before he had a side by side comparison with the fully inflated version.

Mark focused in on the nucleoid. The volume of DNA material inside it seemed to be a little less than what he'd normally expect to see. Also, there was no lower density area in the nucleoid to explain the hollowness he had seen in the living samples. He tried to increase the magnification but found the view was already as digitally enlarged as possible for this recorded image. He examined what he could of the animals' other structures. Except for the differences in the nucleoid, it looked like his COBIC in every way.

Mark looked at the stack of optical disks he'd brought with him from California. The full DNA sequence of COBIC-3.7 was on them. Why was he digging around the edges of this question? Either this was COBIC or it wasn't. The time had come to take a thorough look at the DNA. He'd been distracted by structural and behavioral oddities long enough. He wondered if those detours were just ways of postponing the inevitable. Half of him wanted the DNA to conclusively match, while the other half feared that it would. He did not want COBIC-3.7 to be connected with so many deaths. Extinction had been only an academic mystery when he was studying COBIC's connection with the end of the age of dinosaurs. This was very different.

After digging through some online manuals and calling the help desk twice, Mark finally had DNA sequences from the suspect Chromatium and COBIC-3.7 loaded into a Department of Defense supercomputer that the lab timeshared. He wished he had his custom software here. Almost everything at the BVMC lab was years ahead of what he had at UCLA, except for his genetics software. He watched as the system did best-fit comparisons of the long key sequences of DNA that he had tagged. The supercomputer was shockingly fast. The results were done in minutes. The outcome was as close as matches got in genetics. All the key sequences that he'd published – and those that he'd kept secret – had been found in the right locations. Nucleoid bulge or not, this animal was COBIC-3.7. He felt dizzy and switched off the screen. He couldn't bear to look at it any longer. *And so it begins*, he thought.

7 – Atlanta, Georgia: November

Kathy was in her office reading a lab report on the Guatemalan kill zone. She'd had a fruitless afternoon trying to mount unshriveled Chromatium samples for Mark. He'd gone back to his hotel looking disturbed. The lab was still trying. She was fighting against eyes that wanted to close. Just a little longer and she'd be finished. Her eyes refused to pull the words from the screen. She tried rereading the sentence; but by the time she reached the end, she had forgotten the beginning. Grudgingly, she decided to rest for a few minutes. The moment her head touched her folded arms, she was asleep on her desk.

Her dreams were confused. She was in grade school, but was thirty years old. All the kids from her past were there, and oddly that felt normal. The uncomfortable part was that the school was the BVMC lab and the children were all lab techs. They were teasing her, calling her Moron Morris. *She'd show them, she'd show them all. She'd become a famous doctor. They would read about her in the papers and see her on television.* The school bell rang. It was a strange sound, more like an electronic chirping than a metal school bell. All the kids started to pile into the airlock. The sterilization liquid splashed around them, raising a mist. The bell continued to ring... the bell.

Kathy woke. She was disoriented for a moment. *She'd show them...* The bell was still ringing. The phone! She snatched up the receiver.

"Hello?"

"Dr. Morrison?"

"Uh huh"

"This is Dr. Nancy Potter. I'm the senior agent on the EIS team working Brazil. We have sort of a developing situation here. I sent out teams of agents to check into rumors we've been hearing from locals about undiscovered kill zones. The locals hadn't seen anything – they were just reporting what other villagers had told them. Well nothing turned up for a while; but a few hours ago, I got confirmation of a previously unknown kill zone; then things started piling up. So far we've found fourteen KZ's and counting... All of them are tiny, a hundred feet in diameter or less. Apparently this thing has been at work for some time. One of the villages might have been hit as long ago as six months. So far, the total number of deaths has jumped to four thousand."

"Do you have documentation on this?" asked Kathy.

"Sure do, including full field reports. I already sent it to your e-mail address."

"Okay, good... I don't know what to tell you at this point. I need to go over the reports."

"I understand. How are you folks doing on the research end? We got an update the other day that a Nobel Prize winner has been called in to help."

"Yeah, that's true. He just got here today and is settling in. Seems like a brilliant guy. Don't worry, Dr. Potter. We're on top of this and we'll find an answer soon. You just keep up the great work you're doing."

"We will. Thank you Dr. Morrison."

"Goodnight."

Kathy hung up the phone. Her eyes were wide open. Her fight against sleep was just won. Her hands were clammy and the psychosomatic tingle in back of her neck had returned. Four thousand dead. Yesterday the number for South America was in the hundreds. She wondered how many more hidden kill zones they'd find. Were there small outbreaks in the United States that no one had noticed? Anchorage was a media circus, but who would have covered the deaths of a few campers in the middle of nowhere?

8 – Morristown, New Jersey: November

The clock read four a.m. Sarah Mayfair sat bolt upright in her bed. Her pulse was racing. Her fingers were hooked into the sheets, nails grated across the fabric as she squeezed. She was repeating the words to herself like a mantra.

"All dead... everyone dead..."

This was the second time she'd had the nightmare in as many days. Prior to last night's dream, it had been over six months since the recurring nightmares had troubled her. Seeing the psychiatrist had worked. She'd thought the horror was over, gone forever; but now it was back and far worse than before.

Her boyfriend Kenny stirred next to her and then settled back into his sleep. She had been dreaming of a subterranean ocean as still as a pool, but this water lived and hated and schemed. It had swallowed Kenny alive. She could still see his lifeless body drifting down into the blackness of that yawning cistern to meet hundreds of thousands of other bodies collecting into a landscape of horror at the bottom. Everyone she knew, and in turn everyone they knew, and so on, and more, all the people from this part of the world, all were dead at the bottom of that still ocean. She could feel Kenny's last thought, a single question whispered in darkness, "*Why?*" Earlier, she remembered knowing the answer, but now she could no longer grasp it. The idea was too large to fit into her head. "*Why?*" His last thought was like acid, burning that single question deeper into the flesh of her memory with every passing second. She rubbed tears from her eyes. She had gotten control of the nightmares before and been rid of them. She would master them again.

A shiver passed through her. Her skin was clammy with sweat. The shivers came again, this time harder and longer. She sensed a malevolence prowling below her bed, below the floorboards, deep underground. Through a forgotten way, she perceived subterranean water flowing in the darkness of rock and gravel thousands of feet below her.

As a child, she remembered having grandpa's gift of finding water with a sapling branch. They were a family of water-witches, going back for generations. People used to pay grandpa to dowse for drinking wells. Grandpa had been gone now for many years.

Her night chills came again, this time thankfully weaker. The shivers faded to a dim electric tingle. She knew it wasn't the underground waters themselves that were evil. It was something that existed in the water that scared her. Like a poison, death was flowing in the currents. She pushed the idea from her mind and refused to think about it. She scorned superstition and knew her thoughts were childish – but she couldn't shake the belief that just thinking about this evil might summon it to do terrible things.

Kenny murmured in his sleep. Sarah touched his cheek lightly with her fingers. She could feel the soul that animated his flesh. She wanted him to wake. She wanted him to hold her and comfort her and say that everything would be okay, but that wouldn't be fair. He worked hard and needed his sleep. Construction work was a difficult living; and besides, what she was feeling was crazy. There were no such things as water monsters or telepathy or clairvoyant dreams. She knew that her memories of Grandpa were just a child's way of seeing things. The dowsing couldn't have been real. The memories were just of a game Grandpa had taught her. If they found water, it was luck. There had to be millions of underground streams in New Jersey, with all its rivers and marshes. Maybe she never even walked around with a twig in her hands looking for water with Grandpa? It could have all been a child's make-believe.

Sarah quietly got up and went into the bathroom. She clicked the door shut and found the dangling light chain. The harshness of the light blinded her for a moment. As she washed her face, her toes sought out the familiar cracks in the tile floor. The water was bracing. Patting her skin dry, she stared at her image in the mirror. She was twenty-three years old. Her honey colored hair was a tangle of wavelets. Her skin had a light olive complexion. She angled her head a little to one side. Her eyes were her best feature. They were a startling emerald green. She would have considered herself pretty if it hadn't been for that nose.

The nose was a gift from something swimming in her father's gene pool. The shape was the same as his. She smiled. She often thought of herself as the perfect mutt. Tracing her ancestry was a complicated thing. She was part Jewish, part Catholic, part English, part Indian, part Moroccan, and the list went on. Her ethnicity was often mistaken by the eyes of the beholder: Italians thought she was Italian, Middle-Easterners thought she was Middle-Eastern, Indians thought she was Indian, and Brits thought she was British. Staring at the lines of her face, she wondered about the future tribes of man. If terrorists didn't poison or blow the whole mess up, she was probably the way people would look in a dozen generations. No more races, just one family of women and men, one tribe. Sometimes, she was troubled thinking about how America had continued changing from a melting pot of immigrants into a collection of tribes all wanting to be set apart for special treatment. The racial and class frictions were growing, the fuses burning. During work each day, she witnessed the escalating violence. She prayed that the American experiment would turn around and that its current failures were not a sign of things to come.

~

The morning sun was casting dusty shafts of light across the bedroom. Classic rock was playing from the clock radio on her dresser. Sarah had been unable to get back to sleep. The breakfast of oatmeal with bananas and yogurt was a pleasant lump in her belly. Ralph, a huge Rottweiler, was curled in front of her shoes. In a full-length dressing mirror, she adjusted the visor of her cap to form a perfectly straight line with the bridge of her eyes. The emblem of the Morristown Police department was polished to a flawless shine. Her image made her proud. She was a three-month rookie in what she considered the best police department in New Jersey.

A gust of wind sent tree branches of dried leaves chattering and whistling. Sarah looked through the parted curtains. Outside, fall was progressing toward winter. Piles of leaves were everywhere. She intimately sensed the cycles of nature and felt them working deep inside her body. Small animals were out collecting food to last through winter. Newborns from months ago would be facing their first cold. This cycle was the alchemy of life, fall flowing into the ritual death of winter; and then with eyes closed, all would wait for the rebirth of spring. Sarah was fascinated with how the works of nature formed patterns within patterns, small cycles of dependency that, when broken, could destroy so much more than the small part that had suffered the original damage.

Velcro straps chafed against her ribs. She unbuttoned her shirt to readjust the bulletproof vest. The body armor that she wore underneath her blues was just another tool of her job. The vest was one of the better models made from a mix of Spectra-Shield and Kevlar 129. The material was much lighter weight than pure Kevlar but still padded her torso, giving her a muscular look that wasn't real. Department policy did not require vests for beat cops, so it was something she had to purchase herself if she wanted one. Kenny had bought it for her. The vest had cost him over a thousand dollars. He'd made her promise to wear it every minute she had that uniform on. She had no intention of breaking her word. The vest made her feel safer. Her partner had warned her about the superman complex that a vest could give her. She was certain that it hadn't affected her judgment.

Sarah crinkled her nose. There it was – the aroma de jour. The bedroom was starting to smell of burnt toast, eggs, and bacon grease… and something else… maybe oven cleaner? Below them on the first floor was *The Acropolis,* a Greek – American diner. She turned down the radio and heard the two brothers who ran the grease pit yelling or arguing in their native tongue. *Another month,* she told herself; then, she and Kenny and Ralph would be out of here. With her paycheck added to Kenny's, there would be enough to rent a small house including a yard for Ralph to play in.

Sarah went through the living room searching for her keys. She had already looked everywhere. This was her second sweep of this room. The apartment was decorated with clean but threadbare furniture. Sarah was proud of what she'd accomplished with so little. She had meticulously collected each piece by scouring flea markets and used-furniture stores. She started turning over cushions hoping the keys had slipped between.

Kenny snuck up on her and grabbed her from behind. She squealed. They tumbled onto the couch. He was wearing jeans and no shirt and was fresh from the shower. He carried a scent of baby powder.

"That's assaulting an officer, Mister," she said. "You want me to take you in?"

"Will you handcuff me?"

"Maybe for your birthday," she said. "I've gotta go."

Sarah untangled herself from him and got up. He pretended to pout. She kissed him on the forehead and barely escaped his arms as he made a fresh grab for her. After another ten minutes, she found her keys in the refrigerator on top of a six-pack of cola. On the way out, she gave Kenny a long kiss, then bent down to let Ralph lick her face.

"Glad you said goodbye in that order," said Kenny. "Dog germs, yuck!"

"Ah, Ralph, you know he doesn't mean that. Daddy loves you."

"When are you getting off tonight?"

"Five o'clock shift, but I've got classes later."

The huge Rottweiler rolled onto his back to get his belly scratched by Sarah. His tongue hung out to one side, forming a pink slab that curled at the end. Kenny looked disappointed that she'd be home late. There was an uncomfortable silence. They'd been through it all before. Sarah wished she could spend more time with him, but she needed to work hard if she was going to get her degree in two more years. The Bachelors in psychology was not only something that fascinated her, it was also a ticket into federal law enforcement; and her grades, which were all A's, didn't hurt.

~

The police firing range was inside the basement of an old National Guard fort, long since converted for police use. Sarah pushed a nine-millimeter bullet into the clip, then inserted the clip into the stock of her Beretta. She thumbed the release lever down. The gun-slide jumped forward with a reassuring sound of metal colliding with metal as a bullet was chambered. She put the gun into her holster, then drew into a one-armed stance. A shiver brought memories of the night chills. In rapid fire, she emptied the clip into the silhouette of a man. All fifteen rounds were gone in under eight seconds. A ragged hole the size of a coffee coaster was missing from the man's chest. The smell of cordite and gun oil swirled around her. The shiver was forgotten. She knew the feel of her gun intimately. She had fired the Beretta thousands of times. She could feel the subtle changes in trigger pressure as she squeezed toward the point where the hammer-catch would release, capping off a round.

Sarah gazed at the target with its perfect hole. She smiled to herself. That ought to throw off the scoring curve. She knew she was the best marksperson on the force. She'd been handling guns since the age of ten and had gone out hunting with her dad and brother every chance she got.

Sarah removed her hearing protectors and safety glasses. She'd been on the range for almost an hour. It was time to get back to patrol duty. Trent was probably already waiting in their Black and White. As she headed toward the exit, she spied Sergeant McCormick making an intercept line toward her. She felt anxiety in the hollow of her chest, much like a deer must have felt sensing the wolf. She knew what was happening. Trent had warned her. Some of the cops had a tradition of trying to initiate the younger females in the backseat of a patrol car. McCormick was the defending champ, not that any of them had ever scored except in their own sick little minds. His claim to fame was that he'd supposedly nailed two rookies, both now conveniently long gone from the force. The history was all big talk and lies, but the harassment was not. A patrolwoman named Kacy Jefferson, who was already gone from the force, had complained to her brother-in-law who was a District Attorney. The game had retreated underground for a time, with memos flaming and one officer on administrative leave.

McCormick reached the steel door the same time Sarah did. Somehow he'd managed to corner her. The maneuver must have been something genetically programmed into cavemen.

"Mayfair, you're really good with that pistol," he said. "I've been keeping a special eye on you."

"You're pretty good yourself, McCormick."

"Do you think you can show me some of your tricks?"

"Sure anytime... You know I shoot all-pro at the situation contests. Took third place last year in the state finals."

Somehow his hand ended up on one of her hips. His finger hooked into her belt loop. He tugged at her a little and smiled. With his crew-cut hair, he looked like a Nazi rapist.

"No kidding," he said. "State finals huh? Hey, have you ever fooled around with a machine gun? I'm asking 'cause a few of the guys and me have a range set up on my uncle's farm near Newton. I've got a nine-millimeter UZI, full auto. We've killed a bunch of old cars and refrigerators. It's righteous stuff. You and me could take a drive up there after work and mess around."

"Take your hand off my hip," said Sarah.

McCormick's eyes narrowed in what must have been Neanderthal cunning. He looked amazingly stupid and dangerous. He tugged on the belt loop again. Sarah was breathing rapidly. She tried to pull back from him. His hand stayed in place.

"Shooting that UZI 'll be real hot," he said.

"Do you have a problem with English?" said Sarah. "TAKE YOUR HAND OFF MY HIP!"

"Ah, baby, don't be like that."

A deep voice broke in, "Leave her alone, McCormick."

Sarah looked up and saw her partner Trent. The man was at least fifty pounds heavier than McCormick and it was all thick muscle. By any standard Trent was a large man. His skin was a rich chocolate brown and his eyes were hazel. He smiled warmly at her. Over by the firing line, a few of the guys started to snicker. McCormick's hand vanished from her hip.

"Hey, just getting to know the rookie," said McCormick.

"Uh huh..." said Trent.

"McCormick you're such a loser," called one of the guys from the firing line.

9 – New York City: November

Artie wandered through the museum drinking in the paintings and sculptures. The afternoon crowds had been thin, even for a rainy workday. He stood alone in the exhibits gazing at the dreams of Monet and Renoir. He remembered a time years ago when he and Suzy had first wandered these halls. They had stopped in a vaulted passage between two exhibits. Her hands had been hooked around his elbow, her perfume lingering in the air. She had leaned close and whispered 'I love you Artie'. It had been the first time she'd said those words. The feelings of that moment were forever etched in his mind. He had come back to this place many times since then, mostly when he needed to think.

The rain outside was worsening. Artie could feel the weather. There was a cold dampness growing in the air. He stood before his favorite Monet and was unmoved. Though his eyes stared, his mind was far away. The chemical accident in Alaska was troubling him. Things were not making sense and it was personal. He had an uncle who worked in Anchorage for the Department of Fish and Game. Uncle Peter was there to monitor the long-term effects of the Exxon spill and clean up.

Artie had been watching the eight o'clock news the night of the accident. He'd picked up the phone while the first reporter was still talking. On the screen was an aerial view of soldiers in chemical suits sorting through a wreckage of bodies and fractured packing crates. His uncle had answered on the tenth ring. Everything had been okay then. The accident had been some ten miles away and downwind. His uncle had told him that a quarantine encircled the area and martial law had been declared.

CNN had reported nothing about quarantines and martial law, which was odd; and still days later, all that was on the news were commentators rehashing what everyone already knew. The story of the year – and no one was covering it with any depth.

Artie had tried to call his uncle the next day and been unable to get through. Since then, he had tried dozens of times. The recorded messages had varied: all circuits were busy, lines temporarily out of service. He had contacted the telephone company, misleading them into thinking he was the district attorney and needed to get through as part of a criminal investigation. No matter who he talked to, their story had been the same. The lines were overloaded with traffic. There was nothing anyone could do. He had called the airlines; all flights were booked for the next two months. A strange collection of evidence was building. He had no idea what it all meant, but he had a feeling something was deeply wrong.

He had no way to go there, no way to call there. Someone had put a glass bubble over Anchorage. There had to be other people experiencing the same problems. Why wasn't that on the news? Suzy had told him not to worry. He'd kept silent for days. He knew people would think he was a paranoid, someone who saw conspiracies under every rock; but more and more, he believed that was exactly what was going on. He'd thought about flying to British Columbia, and from there driving to Anchorage, just so that he could know the truth. He wondered if there were roadblocks at the city limits; or worse, maybe he could enter but never leave.

Chapter 5

Escape

1 – Atlanta: November

The sun cast long shadows through Mark's office. Soon it would be night and the sky would be glowing with a full autumn moon. Something very big, sounding like a subway moving slowly through a station, had just rolled past his closed door. He looked up from his computer. So much activity was going on inside the facility. The pace of work was becoming frenetic. Since the discovery of smaller, previously undetected kill zones all over South America, the facility had been the scene of one lab reorganization after another: people were being reshuffled, equipment moved. Everyone involved now believed this killer had been active for months, maybe even years. The pattern of kill zones was one of escalation, and no one believed they had seen the worst. The unspoken fear was that countless small kill zones had been occurring undetected for some time in North America which meant the infection could be here all around them. The wall of arrogance between the industrialized northern hemisphere and the less developed southern had been shattered. Gone was the safety of considering this an exotic non-domestic disease.

Mark had been at the BVMC lab for three days. During the last twenty-four hours, he'd been obsessed by a peculiar discovery of COBIC's ability to cloak itself from the immune system of higher animals. There was no Darwinian advantage for the microbe to be able to cloak itself from a danger that didn't exist in its normal environment. Why did COBIC have this characteristic? A theory suddenly dawned on him and the idea was as startling as it was obvious. The invisibility wasn't from active camouflage or some other special ability. There were no chemical factories cranking out cloaking molecules that matched the bacterium's temporary host. COBIC was not a chameleon. The bacterium was simply invisible. It was a ghost. The genetic structure of the bacterium was so primitive that much of its DNA sequences could be found embedded in all living things. This creature was like the seed from which all higher life had grown. For an animal's immune system to attack the microbe, it would also have to be in some ways targeting its own body.

Mark set his glasses down on the keyboard. It was ironic. Evidence that the bacteria's DNA sequences were embedded in higher organisms was part of what had won him his Nobel Prize. COBIC was one of the earliest life forms on earth. How could he have not considered the implication for all these years? COBIC was a natural born invader, a natural born carrier. The bacterium's DNA was coded for stealth. Something terrible was coming to the world. He could feel it. Was COBIC-3.7 bringing extinction to its children a billion generations removed?

By accident, they now had a sustainable colony of the COBIC-3.7 bacteria taken from victims. One of the techs had placed an entire sample pipette in a bacterial incubator to thaw for processing later that day and had forgotten about it. The incubator was a lightless box that was temperature and humidity controlled. A day later, when the pipette was found and examined, they'd discovered almost ninety-five percent of the COBIC had reanimated. The animals placed under a microscope died within an hour, but those left in darkness remained alive. After a little more experimenting, they confirmed that the bacteria died when exposed to light but lived indefinitely in darkness. Light aversion was not a normal quality of COBIC; in fact, the bacteria normally required light to thrive. Mark was unable to explain it; and worse, he was not finding the usual correlations in his growing list of unexplainable things. Every time he thought about the list he could feel something nasty coiling up in his stomach.

2 – Atlanta: November

Mark leaned back in his chair and rubbed his eyes. The remnants of his dinner, some cartons of Chinese food and a bottle of Diet Pepsi took up a third of his desk. The images on the computer screen were blurry. His mind was blurry. It had only been a day ago that Kathy had come up with the answer for getting Anchorage COBIC into the transmission electron microscope. The bacteria shriveled too quickly during preparation. None of the usual mounting chemicals has been able to solidify the specimen fast enough. Kathy's solution was elegantly simple. Her idea was to keep the Chromatium frozen during the entire process of preparing, slicing, mounting, and viewing the specimens. By keeping the specimen frozen, the bacterium would not have a chance to thaw and shrivel. The task required preparing specimens in a walk-in freezer. The process would have been easier if the entire microscope could have been relocated into the freezer, but the temperature would have wreaked havoc with the calibration of its focusing elements. Instead, Kathy had come up with an ingenious way of keeping the specimens frozen. She had tiny discs of dry ice the size of nickels fabricated and placed one on top of each frozen specimen slice. The dry ice would evaporate directly into carbon dioxide gas as the TEM's specimen chamber was evacuated of air. The evaporation would uncover the frozen bacterium just in time for the TEM's electron beam to begin imaging it. The bacterium itself could remain frozen for minutes after the dry ice was gone. This would give them enough time to record images before the specimen thawed and shriveled. The first time they'd tried the procedure, the dry ice evaporated as planned; and perfect images of Anchorage COBIC were recorded.

Mark had been watching as the first image came on the screen, clear and detailed. While studying the image, he kept expecting the specimen to shrivel once it finally thawed; but it never did. Somehow, cross-sectional slicing of the bacterium had disrupted whatever process was causing the animal to shrivel. He could not figure out how sectioning a frozen bacterium could prevent what he'd believed was a spontaneous chemical reaction. Was the shriveling some metabolic function of the animal while it was dying?

In a perfect cross-sectional view of the bacterium's nucleoid, Mark had found what he was looking for: something to explain the bulge and the shriveling. There was a circular shape approximately four microns in diameter inside the nucleoid. The mysterious structure looked like the cross section of a hollow tennis ball. The outer membrane or shell appeared to be exceptionally thin. The shape resembled a virus but was a hundred times larger than any known strain. Mark was certain it was not a virus. Besides being too big, the object also appeared to be hollow. All viruses were filled with genetic material. The structure could have been the result of some kind of damage or bubble; but if that were the case, its shape would have melted once the bacterium thawed. All the other specimens he'd examined had this same structure. Whatever this object was, this thing did not belong inside COBIC. No specimen he had worked with over all his years of research had anything remotely like this inside it.

Mark had gotten the lab to prepare samples of exposed nucleoids for the SEM, so he could study the three-dimensional shape of this object. The lab had used an ion mill to carefully spray off atom-thin layers of frozen cell membrane and nucleoid until the desired results were achieved. The sample was then coated with a microscopically thin, artifact-free, layer of vaporized metal. The metallic coating was applied to reflect the SEM's electron beam so surface structure could be seen. Without metallic coating, the electron beam would penetrate the sample, showing only a vague blob without detail.

The SEM images revealed an object that was spherical. The surface of the object was not smooth. The outer shell was marked with dimples, which made it resemble a golf ball. The chilling thing about the object was that it looked man-made. The pattern on its surface was not random but looked almost machined. At points across the surface of the golf ball, there were bundles of very fine roots sprouting from it. The roots snaked out like veins into the cytoplasm of the bacterium.

In the midst of examining the roots, the entire structure dissolved. Ten minutes had elapsed since the specimen had been loaded into the SEM. Mark had watched in astonishment as the roots, then the entire ball, dissolved in seconds. What remained of the object looked like sludge melting into the cytoplasm of the cell. He realized he had just witnessed the mechanism that caused COBIC to shrivel. As the structure of the ball broke down inside an intact microbe, the bacteria's cellular wall in the surrounding area would wrinkle inward.

In the following hours, Mark watched sample after sample dissolve a few minutes after they warmed. Thinking about possible reasons why the TEM samples did not dissolve, Mark requested a frozen sample prepared for the SEM, with the top of the ball milled off. All the samples for the TEM were cross-sections of the ball. Maybe slicing the object in half was the answer? It had taken dozens of tries, but he finally had a sample that was milled down to remove two thirds of the top of the ball. This sample did not dissolve. Viewing the milled area using very high magnifications, he saw traces of internal structures. There was a set of three tubes joined at right angles to each other and a pattern of lines crisscrossing like the weave of a fine cloth. The ball was not hollow, even though it had appeared hollow in the TEM images. The only explanation was that the ball was composed of material that was far more transparent to an electron beam than common cellular matter. The fact that the ball did not dissolve when cut open hinted at the idea that the ball itself – and not the bacterium – controlled the disintegration. Did that mean the ball was alive and capable of reactions?

Mark had fallen asleep while leaning back in his chair. The office was dark. He was restless and had been vaguely aware of talking in his sleep for sometime. His eyes snapped open but the nightmare continued. He was walking along high cliffs that ran parallel to the Hudson River. On the opposite shore was the skyline of New York. There were millions of bodies choking the river like a carpet of autumn leaves. The evil that had done this was still present but unseen. He had a visceral feeling that it was in every drop of liquid and in every spot of dampness. The killer moved in the water. It invaded through water. He climbed down to the garbage strewn shoreline and inched his way over discarded tires and rubbish to get to the river's edge. He was reaching down to touch the brackish water. Didn't he recognize the danger? He screamed and screamed.

He woke up. His heart was pounding in his head. He was shaking. Mark hadn't experienced nightmares like this since he was a child. From the age of six until adolescence, he'd suffered from recurring nightmares. Later in life, he sometimes tried to remember but could never recall what the childhood nightmares had contained. He felt a strong connection between this dream and those of his childhood. His face was covered in sweat. He rummaged through Chinese food cartons and papers around his desk looking for a napkin to wipe off his face. The clock on his computer read a quarter to midnight. His computer screen contained a perfect TEM image of COBIC that was not shriveled. Mark blotted his forehead with a napkin then looked again at the screen. Hundreds of other COBIC were in the same specimen. The bacteria were in various states of damage and cross-sections. The image on the screen was the best of the lot and it had changed how Mark felt about this animal.

"What are you?" he asked.

His thoughts began to fall back into place as the cobwebs of sleep faded and he returned to his obsession with work. He clicked on a printer icon. On a table next to his desk, a high-resolution color printer started to whirr. In a few seconds he would have another photo to add to the growing stack. Included in that pile were several images of an intact ball resting in a bed of cellular material and close-up views of the faint structures he'd found inside the ball.

Mark took a sip of warm Diet Pepsi. He laid out all the photographs one next to the other. They covered his desk like the frames from some impossible comic book. The function of that ball was a mystery. The telephone rang. Mark reached for it absentmindedly, staring at a picture of a ball caught in the midst of dissolving.

"Hello?" he said.

"Hi, Honey."

The voice was Gracy's. He hadn't talked with her in days. He felt guilty during the lover's small talk that ensued and was having difficulty following the conversation. His eyes kept returning to the photographs on his desk.

"...I miss you," said Gracy. "Since you're stuck there, can I fly out to visit?"

"Yes... no, I mean things are crazy. I'd love it if you came, but you wouldn't see much of me. I'm working day and – "

There was a crash from next door. Mark stared at the wall separating his office from Kathy's. There were fainter sounds of some kind of commotion.

"Sweetheart, can you hold on a second?"

"Sure."

He could hear the muffled sounds of a voice, then silence. His door was partially open. The hallway was darker than his office. He saw a wash of light from another office door being opened and then closed. A moment later, he saw Kathy peering in. He cupped his hand over the phone receiver.

"It's bad," she said.

Kathy stepped into the light of his office. She was dressed in a pair of gray sweatpants and a loosely fitting wrinkled t-shirt. She had obviously been sleeping.

"Three kill zones," she said. "Three in the last two hours."

"I have to call you back," said Mark. "Something's come up... I love you."

He hung up the phone. Kathy looked like she was fighting off an illness. Her eyes were haunted. Her shoulders were limp. Mark was troubled just from the message of her body language.

"Emergency response teams are on site and have reported asphyxial symptoms. Everything's the same as the others except this is big; thousands could be dead."

"Where?" asked Mark.

"New Jersey... all three sites are in New Jersey. It's a nightmare. The worst hit areas are located around the swamplands near the Hudson River."

~

CNN was on the television in Kathy's office. Mark felt as if he was having an out of body experience and was somehow looking down at everyone, including himself, while they all played out a scene from some movie. He felt like this moment – his entire life – everything was pre-planned and there was nothing he could do about it. He was sitting on Kathy's couch. Carl Green was next to him. Every few minutes, a new emergency broadcast fax dropped into the output tray of a laser printer in the corner. Kathy had set up her computer to monitor all e-mail coming in from the field. There were entire conversations taking place on her computer screen. Mark focused on the report he was trying to read. Snap out of it, he thought.

Kathy had changed into a pair of jeans and a sweatshirt. She was sitting behind her desk reading a summary emergency field report. Mark had the same report in his hands. The news was getting worse. Small kill zones had been reported in both Ohio and Toronto. He was confused and overwhelmed. He had talked to Julie and his daughter, and then to Gracy. The telephone calls had been strained. They were all looking to him for advice. What was he supposed to tell them – run and hide – hide where? This killer had hit in the remotest jungles and now in the cities. He had no answers except that he'd call them back in a few hours – and stay away from all water. He wondered if he should fly to Los Angeles to be with them. Mark looked up from the paper to the television. A CNN senior anchor was standing outside in the cold next to a wall of New Jersey rescue vehicles. Their red lights were splashing the scene. The Anchor was running through a litany of recent developments. Snowflakes were falling from the sky.

"...Most of the New Jersey and New York areas are still blacked out. Downed power lines have shorted large portions of the grid, causing breakers to trip. Some news services have been reporting similarities between this tragedy and what happened at Anchorage ten days ago. Unofficial sources are confirming that the cause of death is the same, but this was clearly not a chemical accident; and we have information from a reliable source that Anchorage was not a chemical accident either, but a cover-up."

"Along with that damning revelation, CNN has learned that the Anchorage incident was not the first. It appears that similar deaths have been occurring in remote sites around the world for the last month or more. I want to stress again that there appears to be no connection to terrorism."

"Anchorage was allegedly the first time one of these incidents occurred in the United States. We have been assured by federal authorities that they are doing everything possible to contain whatever it is that's causing these deaths. Did these same authorities have prior knowledge of the alleged cover up? We do not know."

"For now, everyone is advised to stay at home. The cause is still unknown. Speculation of a cause is running wild, and this network has no intention of getting into the speculation game. All we can tell you is that the Center for Disease Control has been actively tracking these incidents. I want to stress that no one has stated that this is a disease. The official name for it is South American Asphyxial symptoms. The unofficial name is kill zones."

"CNN is well informed," said Carl. He looked directly at Kathy. She looked away. The image faded from the reporter to a helicopter view of a housing development. The caption read 'Mount Hope, New Jersey.' Mark swallowed reflexively. Under the glow of a searchlight from the helo were bodies lying in the driveway of a suburban house. The helo dropped lower until its rotor-wash began to gently buffet the scene.

Mark wanted to look away, but was held captive and unable to even blink. The searchlight moved on; wherever the circle of light wandered, it revealed more bodies. The light passed over houses and out into a pasture. There was a jeep on its side with a body pinned beneath. The Jeep's headlights were still bright and shining out across the field. The Anchor spoke over these images.

"Unofficial death counts have reached into the tens of thousands. This is the worst disaster in our nation's history. Two more kill zones have been reported: one in Ohio and one in Toronto. Initial government reports are referring to these as small events with under fifty victims. How can the death of even one person be called a small event?"

The Anchor's voice was straining to hold back emotion. Mark felt nausea and dizziness. He knew he was watching the end of everything. Humanity had built such greatness and suffered far too much for an end like this. He looked over at Carl. There were tears running down the man's cheeks. He turned to Kathy. A sheet of paper was partially crumpled in her fist.

"Mass extinction," said Mark. "I'm not a religious man, but that's changing."

Kathy's stare locked onto him. Hers eyes were bloodshot and livid. Mark thought about his extinction theory. He needed to tell them what they might be facing.

"I've been working on a theory," he said. "For years I've been compiling evidence that links COBIC with the great prehistoric extinctions. There are very rare mats of COBIC layered into the fossil records at the same time as the Cretaceous extinction which took the dinosaurs and before that during the Permian extinction. We could be witnessing the same cycles that killed back then."

"And you believe this?" asked Kathy, her voice was odd; there was an undercurrent of something seething.

"I don't know," said Mark. "What we're seeing right now could be another piece to some very old puzzle."

"Mass extinction?" she said. "The end of the world? No, it's not!"

Kathy pushed back from her desk. She got up and started wandering around the room. She moved like a caged tiger walking in front of bars that separated it from something to kill. Carl seemed oblivious to the entire exchange, his eyes never leaving the television screen.

"Fuck!" yelled Kathy. "Fuck... fuck... fuck! What are we doing wrong? We can't even figure out what's causing this. Do we have a virus, a bacterium, an act of God? What?"

"It's a seed carried in COBIC," said Mark. His voice was calm.

"What are you talking about?" snapped Kathy.

"That ball inside COBIC is a seed or spore or something. It doesn't belong there. Look, just because we can't tie it directly to the cause of death doesn't mean it's an oddity we can put on a backburner *just a speck of mystery junk inside a microbe* – that kind of dismissive thinking will lead to disaster. We need to separate out the seeds for study. My gut is telling me it's the killer."

"All right," said Kathy. "I'll buy into this for now. There's nothing else in the store that I can buy. What else does your gut think?"

"I think we better keep the bacteria frozen, and keep it in the dark, and not give it a chance to escape."

Kathy stared at him as if he was either crazy or the smartest man alive. Mark was not sure why he'd said what he did. Microbes trying to escape... The idea wasn't even a hunch. It was totally irresponsible to say such a thing. He had no evidence to support the claim, but his gut was telling him COBIC had some kind of basic awareness and was actively trying to escape capture the same way a cockroach flees when a room light is turned on. There were tantalizing clues that it was capable of this kind of behavior – things like synchronized swimming in schools, its conspicuous absence from over half of the victims, even the seed's disintegration could be considered the act of a creature programmed to die rather than be captured. Suicidal microbes, now that was crazy. Part of Mark knew there had to be rational explanations for everything. Bacteria did not act with even rudimentary awareness. But then again, maybe rational ideas had nothing to do with any of this...

3 – Morristown, New Jersey, before the kill zone: November

The night was quiet. Sarah felt like nothing was happening anywhere in the entire state. She looked up through the window of the patrol car. She was on the passenger side. She lowered the partially fogged glass for a better view. Cool air touched her skin. The sky was filled with millions of stars and a full moon. She heard her partner Trent muttering as he walked into the woods, small branches snapping under his shoes, as he found a place to answer nature's call. They had been parked for hours on the same strip of gravel. The spot was a railroad "right of way" that had been cut parallel to the road. They were part of a two-car team stalking speeders, the most highly sought criminal type in the state of New Jersey. They were working a road that was fed by Interstate 287. Broadly spaced houses and trees lined the road. They were on the edge of a bedroom community for upwardly mobile professionals and stockbrokers that commuted to New York.

Sarah's car had the role of catcher. The second car, the pitcher, had its radar buzzing and was tracking cars moving down a steep six-mile decline. During rush hour, it felt like they'd tagged half the county; but since then, things had quieted some. Still they'd made thousands of dollars in fines for the state. Cars hitting a fire-breathing thirty-five mph down that hill were fair game at a nickel over the speed limit. Sarah knew the importance of traffic safety, but what they were doing felt like something other than justice. This downhill stretch of road could easily have been driven at sixty by gray-haired grandmothers, two of which had received tickets this night. She was uncomfortable balancing the scales of law and revenue. It had been hard to look some of the offenders directly in the eye.

The driver's side door opened. Trent piled in and pulled the door shut. The vehicle seemed to weigh down. His bulk made the inside of the car feel smaller. Sarah was keenly aware of his physical presence and strength. She admired the man. He began rubbing his hands together to warm them.

"Damn it's cold out there," he said. "I am not watering that tree again no matter how much coffee…" He stopped before completing the sentence. "Patrolman, what do you have that window rolled down for?"

"Fresh air," said Sarah. "Need some more antifreeze?" She picked up a thermos of coffee.

"Just close the window."

"Trent."

"Yeah."

"Don't you feel wrong about what we're doing here, I mean the nickel-speeders?"

"Nope, if they're breaking the law they deserve to go down. Simple as that. The law is the only thing that keeps this country from self-destructing. If you're speeding, or killing, or robbing it doesn't make any difference. You gotta know there's a price to be paid. Think of what it'd be like otherwise."

"Would you feel that way about some kid who's shoplifted a pair of sneakers because he doesn't have any money and never will?"

"Poverty's no excuse."

"You really can't believe that," said Sarah. "I've read all these studies which say poverty is the number one cause of criminal behavior.

Think about some kid staring at a TV filled with stuff he can never have. He's being brainwashed into believing that self worth is measured in dollars, and that poverty is something to escape at any cost."

"Excuse me Dr. Sarah, but that is simple bullshit. I grew up poor and never stole a thing. I worked my way through high school and college, and I'm here to tell you that what causes crime is moral poverty. That stuff about monetary poverty causing crime is one of the great lies of our times. There have been poor and rich since we took a bite of the apple. The vast majority of the poor are not out there committing crimes. They are just as moral as rich people. In the equation of life, money does not equal morality. True, some people are driven to desperate acts by lack of food; but most evil is committed for a hot car, cool clothes, or to get laid."

"I wasn't saying all poor people are potential criminals," said Sarah. "I am saying that if you're poor, and you see no way out, it's more likely that when opportunity knocks, you'll go for it."

"Uh huh... and what about all those rich people committing white collar crimes – that whole Wall Street gang? Are they poor because they need a few million more to buy that estate they've always wanted? Bull; they're doing it just like poor criminals, because they do not understand right from wrong. They're criminals because either their role models set a bad example or they're sociopaths."

"I guess we're never going to agree," said Sarah.

"I'll agree to that. I'm gonna take a short nap. It'll be your turn next. Wake me if those guys up the road zap any more speed offenders. I feel a powerful need to stop some speed."

Trent closed his eyes. There was a smile on his face that hinted at the innocent child still alive inside him. Sarah thought about how she genuinely liked Trent. If he wasn't married and there was no Kenny, she would have dated him.

The wind had picked up a bit. Sarah watched bare tree branches swaying back and forth in the moonlight. She thought about her weekend plans. She had promised Kenny they'd go somewhere, just the two of them. He'd picked his family's cabin in the Kittaninny Mountains. She loved those forests as much as he did. The area was filled with ancient trees and streams and places people hadn't walked in hundreds of years. Dozens of trails wound through those hills. Years ago they'd found a side trail that wasn't on any map. After a mile of hiking, they had the woods to themselves. They had made love on a blanket in an open field. All they'd brought was food and the blanket and themselves. She closed her eyes and thought about Kenny. His love was the center of her life. Once she had followed him when he went out to work. The tailing had started as a lark and her way of completing a homework assignment she'd been given during her police training. She'd just hung back and watched him do all the things he did when they weren't together. The experience had made her sad that she couldn't be in every part of his life. She rested her head on the padded doorframe. Her breathing slowed as she fell into a gentle sleep.

Sarah awoke gasping air. She was terrified. Her fingers were locked on the grip of her gun. She'd been trying to pull it in her sleep. The holster's safety strap had kept it secure. One of her nails was broken off inside the trigger guard. She glanced over at Trent hoping he'd missed the embarrassing spectacle.

Trent looked like he was asleep, but there was something wrong. His face seemed too still. His mouth was open. His chest didn't look like it was moving. There was a numb feeling in her fingers like the sensations from holding a glass of ice too long. She sensed the world had just made a wrong turn down a road that led to... to what? What was it that felt so odd?

"Trent."

There was no response.

"TRENT!"

He just sat there with his hands folded in his lap. She leaned closer. Her vision seemed to focus down like a tunnel onto Trent's face. She could see his pores. She touched his shoulder. He slumped forward into the steering wheel. She knew he was dead, knew it, but still tried to deny it. She had to do something. Her thoughts froze as she noticed a sound. The warbling was almost musical, very faint. The sound could have been anything, a distant stereo from one of the homes. Why had she focused on this noise? Why did it make her feel so uncomfortable? There was a suffocating quality to it. She hated it. She was close to hysterical when she realized the sound was car horns. They were far off and mixing together into a single bleating warbling tone.

Sarah's confusion snapped. Her training took over. She jumped from the car, opened the trunk, and removed an oxygen mask and bottle. Trent was her friend. He had to make it. She opened his door. She pushed with all her strength to roll him onto the passenger side. She fixed the mask over his nose and mouth, then fastened his safety belt. His skin was still warm.

Gravel sprayed into the fender wells as Sarah pulled out onto the road. The tires screeched on the pavement, inscribing a half circle of rubber and smoke. She hit the lights and siren. In seconds, the speedometer was touching eighty. She reached for the microphone. "Dispatch, this is car seven-one-one, over." There was no answer only a faint hiss. She tried again, "Dispatch, this is car seven-one-one, over." Still no answer. Damn it. The radio was broken. This problem had happened before.

Approaching the top of the hill, she was doing over a hundred. The engine was growling and pulling faster with surprising power. She knew something larger than Trent had gone wrong in the world.

There was a peculiar orange glow at the top of the hill. She squinted while cresting the gently slopping ridge. Sarah jumped on the brakes too late. Her arms were locked straight. The car plowed forward, her windshield filling with the image of cars piled into each other and fire. She gripped the wheel. The sensation was as if she was falling into the fire. Still skidding at high speed, she plowed into the tangle of wrecked cars. Something white hit her face. The door buckled, plunging sections of its inner workings into her ribs.

Sarah opened her eyes partway. The inside of the car was dimly lit with an orange glow. There was a terrible smell of rubber fumes and gasoline. Nothing made sense. Why did her entire body hurt? She tried to move and felt a stabbing pain in her left side. She began to collect her thoughts. A deflated air bag hung from the steering wheel into her lap. The windshield had shattered into a spider web of glass. The dashboard was covered with cubes of safety glass. Reflections of nearby flames danced in the small pieces of glass. She looked over to her right and saw Trent. His neck was broken. His forehead had a bloodless gash. There was a crater in the passenger window the size of a basketball where his head had impacted.

Pain stabbed her again. She looked down at her left side, and saw a piece of door metal ending at a torn hole in her jacket. In a controlled panic, she slowly backed off the metal spike. She expected to see blood. There should have been lots of blood but there was nothing. She examined inside her jacket. She touched and felt pain. It took her several seconds to realize that her body armor had saved her life. Her ribs were sore, probably broken, but her skin was not punctured.

Sarah tried to open the door. The hinge and metal creaked. She couldn't budge the door more than a few inches. Her injury made it impossible to push with any strength. With each shove, her ribs reminded her she was not okay. She checked the other doors. They were all jammed from the collision. She could hear the fire crackling outside. She pulled an emergency rescue hammer from its mount and smashed out the side window.

Sarah's cheek was on the pavement. She didn't remember passing out or how she had gotten out of the car. She sat upright, and looked across the street. She could see Shepherd and Cussack sitting inside their cruiser not twenty yards away. From the looks of it, they had rolled into a shallow ditch and were stuck. What the hell was wrong with them? Where were the emergency vehicles?

Sarah walked toward the cruiser. She was staggering slightly and leaning to the left, babying her injured ribs. There was a growing feeling that she was invisible and not part of this world. The cruiser's headlights were a faint yellow. The engine had stopped running. The battery was almost drained. She stared in the passenger window. Shepherd looked like a wax museum mannequin. She opened the door. The dome light glowed a dying amber. She touched his face. The skin was cool, and soft, and pale. His eyes were open. Sarah held onto the door as she bent over and heaved out her last meal.

She wiped her mouth on the sleeve of her jacket. Without looking at Shepherd or Cussack, she reached in and tried the ignition. The headlights dimmed completely. The engine clicked a few times but didn't turnover. She was actually relieved there was no reason to pull Shepherd and Cussack from the cruiser so that she could drive it.

She looked down the street at a row of homes. All the lights were on. She refused to accept how odd it was that no one was out on the street after all the noise these accidents had to have made. She popped the trunk and got a flashlight and hand-held radio from it. She tried to call for help: still nothing but static. She set the radio on the car's roof. She pulled her hair back into a ponytail. She pulled harder and harder until it hurt. None of this was real. The radio had to work. Everyone couldn't be gone. She let go of her hair. She ordered herself to get a grip. She was a police officer. She was trained to deal with disaster. She would get though this. She picked up the radio and headed toward the nearest house.

Sarah knocked on the door with the butt of her flashlight. She didn't expect an answer, and there was none. She turned the knob. The door was open. She went inside. "Hello," she called. No answer. She spotted a telephone, and picked it up. There was a tone. She dialed the station. With each button she pressed, the dial tone came back. She tried pressing the buttons at random. The dial tone never switched off. She gave up and wandered deeper into the house making her way toward the back. She got as far as the kitchen. There was a man and woman slumped over a table. There was a stew bubbling on the stove. She turned off the burner and left.

The weather was growing colder outside. Sarah took a deep breath. She couldn't remember breathing the entire time she'd been inside that house. She felt dampness on her cheek. She rubbed it and came away with blood. She stared at her fingers for a moment then dismissed it. She no longer cared if the blood was hers or from someone else.

Sarah started down the center of the roadway. She played her flashlight back and forth across the street as she moved. A dog trotted in a confused manner into an intersection pulling an empty metal leash. The canine's eyes glowed demonically in the flashlight before it ran off.

Her foot hit something. She shined the flashlight down and saw a child crumpled on the frigid pavement. She moved on without allowing the thought to register too deeply. The flashlight illuminated other bodies in yards and in the street. She was growing numb to the insanity.

She thought about her nightmares where something evil lurked in underground rivers. She came to the dark opening of a sewer drain cut into a curb and stopped walking. Her legs refused to move any farther. Something evil was there below the ground. She could almost feel it waiting for its chance to get her. Half of her wished it would. She shook off the feeling and moved on.

The blocks drifted by. Periodically, she forgot where she was going; then, remembered. She was heading home. She wouldn't allow her thoughts to wander any farther than that. She refused to imagine Kenny like the bodies she'd already seen.

Sarah gazed at all the silent homes and cars. She'd thought about trying to steal one of the cars but couldn't bring herself to add to the trespass of all this violence. Abruptly, several of the house lights stuttered on and off in unison; then the electricity failed. The streets went black except for moonlight. The puddles of darkness grew impenetrable. The small noises of modern civilization that usually went unnoticed were now gone. The void felt as deep and still as the night.

Sarah didn't understand what had happened. Were they at war? Had terrorists done something with poison gas? The world felt silent but wasn't. There were sounds of wind and the rustle of dried leaves.

She stopped and listened. There was a dog howling somewhere far off and another one answering. The woods were alive – she sensed smaller animals moving in there. No weapon of man could have done this – killed all the people and not harmed the animals. She wondered if all this destruction was the wrath of God.

Sarah felt like she had been walking for her entire life. She was exhausted. The city of Morristown was still miles farther, and her home was eight miles beyond that. She had begun checking cars that had been in accidents along the way. While they all had keys, none of them had been drivable. She walked up to a Mercedes that was idling. A man was slumped against the driver's window. The side of a pickup truck had stopped the car in a low-speed impact. Around the car was a scattering of leaves that had recently fallen. Her feet crunched on them.

Sarah opened the door. The man remained behind the wheel as if frozen in time. His seat belt and shoulder harness were properly fastened. In his hand was a miniature voice-recorder. Sarah folded back the man's fingers. They felt like cold sausages. She extracted the voice-recorder. The digital memory had been completely filled. She pressed the play button and heard wind buffing through a car. A radio was playing a news show. The man was dictating a letter to his secretary. He coughed and then moaned softly. She could hear the car swerving, brakes being applied, and then the crunch of a bumper meeting the soft middle of the pickup truck. Sarah glanced at where the car had struck. The recorder was emitting the distorted blare of a horn being repeatedly hit. Maybe the man was trying to call for help? The recording grew silent except for the sound of the news show. There was some kind of commotion and then the news show went silent.

Sarah stopped the recorder. The world came back. Her breathing was shallow. She slipped the tiny recorder into her coat pocket then dragged the man from his car and deposited him on the sidewalk.

The Mercedes had a very expensive digital FM radio and CD player. The radio was picking up nothing. She had it scanning from one end of the dial to the other in an endless loop. Headlights from an overturned car shone at eyelevel through her side window as she drove slowly past it. The Morristown police station was located five blocks from the town square which was an historical landmark. Morristown was considered the military capital of the Revolutionary War and much of its history remained. Sarah parked the Mercedes at the opposite side of the square. An old church towered over her. The streets were an impassable pileup of cars. A fire hydrant was sending a geyser into the air. Some of the water had frozen into a thin glaze of ice. Nothing felt real. There was a sense she could almost reach out and change the channel to a better story. Some of the buildings still had emergency lights running. Sarah looked in through the windows as she walked passed them.

She stopped walking in the middle of a block. At the end of the block facing her was the silhouette of a woman. Sarah gasped. She slowly directed her flashlight onto the woman's face. Someone else was alive! The woman's cheeks were smeared with water and soot. A baby was in her arms.

"Don't be afraid," said Sarah.

The woman shook her head no. Sarah took a single step forward. The woman appeared ready to either flee or run toward her. She looked like she was fighting back inner demons.

"Let me help," said Sarah.

"My baby," cried the woman.

"What's your name?"

No reply...

Sarah slowly edged toward the woman, trying not to frighten her. Within arms length, she stopped. The woman was soaking wet. The baby was dead. The little face was as still as a doll's. The eyes were like glass. The woman was shivering. Sarah guessed she was in shock. She needed to be kept warm. Sarah looked around. There was a clothing store two doors back.

"Wait here... I'll get you something warm."

The woman nodded while fresh tears flooded her eyes. Sarah went inside the store. A sales clerk was slumped over a register. Several customers were splayed out on the floor. She was surrounded by the smell of human waste. Sarah grabbed the first coat she saw and went back outside. The woman was gone. On the sidewalk was the tiny bundle of infant.

Sarah ran to the end of the block and looked both ways. No one. The woman might not survive the night. Sarah heard a thumping sound almost like a pillow being fluffed. The sound was coming from down the block to her right. She ran along the sidewalk, stopping frequently to reorient to the sound. At the end of the block, she stopped and looked up. The sound was coming from the side of a building. She expected to see a face looking out, someone banging on the glass with their palms. There was no one.

A bird flew out of the darkness and into the side of the building... thump. The creature fluttered halfway to the ground and then took to the air. A few seconds later, the bird came at the building again... thump. The world had gone mad. Sarah turned away and headed back toward the station.

Sarah walked in the front door of the police headquarters and stopped. The lights were on. The emergency generator in the basement sent a subtle vibration through the floor. There were bodies everywhere. Their faces were contorted. Some had claw marks on their throats. Sarah steeled herself to walk back to the communications room. On her way, she passed the cellblock. Glancing into the guard booth, she saw movement on one of the television screens. All the cells were occupied by the dead except for one. The guy was banging at the lock with what looked like a piece of toilet. Sarah picked up the log entry for that cell. The guy was in for a third count of aggravated assault. She looked back at the screen. Stupid bastard was still banging away at the lock. Sarah left him.

The radio room appeared to be working. Most of the equipment had glowing lights. Sarah had no idea how to operate it beyond the basics. She repeatedly tried changing channels and keying the microphone. She called for help. There was no response to anything she tried. She began to wonder how far the destruction extended. Did it stop at a dozen miles, a hundred miles? Was civilization still there?

Sarah went out to the parking structure. She got into her antique Nissan and cranked it over. She had to try a few times before the old engine caught. The chassis vibrated from a rough idle and then smoothed.

Sarah headed out of town, taking the back roads to avoid any heavily trafficked areas that could be blocked with wreckage. The moon drifted behind a bank of clouds. The world grew darker. Sarah could feel the power of civilization waning along with the moonlight. The dark ages were coming back. How long would it be until the machines they depended on rusted into decay? How long before their cities were reduced to indistinguishable rubble?

Sarah was within two miles of her home when she gave up on the roads. Half the streets she'd tried had been blocked. She felt like a rat in a maze. She had driven across people's lawns to get as far as she'd gotten. Twenty minutes ago, the hand-held police radio had cut in with a distant signal. For a moment, there was a human voice saying something about an emergency. The signal had drifted off. Sarah had been broadcasting every few minutes since then, trying to get the voice back. She stared at the radio, her only link with the world. The radio was drawing power from the cigarette lighter. On its built in batteries, the radio wouldn't last long if she kept broadcasting every few minutes. Reluctantly she turned off the engine, unplugged the radio, and climbed out.

The street was lined with old trees, mostly oaks and a few maples. Sarah stuffed extra batteries into her coat pockets. She switched on her flashlight. Car wreckage completely blocked her way. She slid over the hood of one of the cars. A twinge of pain in her ribs reminded her to take it slowly. She began to walk down the middle of the street. The occasional sounds of animals seemed to be amplified by the silence of humankind. She found more signs of life here than in town. A bat flittered across the sky. A cat ran from under a car and out into the woods. Still there were no people except for bodies in cars and on the streets; and they weren't people anymore. Sarah no longer fully noticed them; her mind was defensively filtering out the horror as if it were part of the natural scenery as much as a fence or a lamp post.

Suddenly it was quieter. Sarah froze. There was complete silence, not even a breeze. Slowly, she turned in a circle playing the beam of her flashlight over fronts of houses and thickets of trees. She saw nothing but felt exposed and vulnerable. The urge to run was overpowering. She positioned her fingers over her holstered gun and started walking. The sound of her shoes on the roadbed echoed along the street as her pace quickened. The air seemed colder.

A twig snapped. There was movement off to the left. Sarah crouched, drew her pistol, and aimed it along with the flashlight. Someone had been stalking her from behind that tree. She was certain of it. Her breathing was tense. All she could see were branches and shadows and empty lawn. There was no place to hide. It was impossible for someone to have been there, but still her heart raced. A breeze swirled through dragging with it a scattering of dried leaves. She looked down and saw a body less than ten feet in front of her. Had it moved? Was one of them playing dead and just waiting for her to turn her back?

"Get a grip." she scolded herself.

She was disturbed realizing she hadn't registered seeing all the bodies until now. Subconsciously, she must have been absorbing everything. What kind of imagined dangers were being conjured inside her as a result? She put the gun away and forced herself to walk normally without looking back. By the end of the block, the sounds of the night had returned.

Three blocks to go until home, Sarah told herself. The street lights flickered on, then went dark. They had been doing that for the last half hour. The power came again, and this time with force. Houses lit up. There was a faint sound of music. The streets were flooded with light. Sarah looked about her. She decided it was better in the dark. The lights only added a carnival atmosphere to the dead.

Sarah walked up the outside flight of steps leading to her door. The wooden slats creaked as they always had. They were weather-worn and in need of paint. The entrance to her apartment was in back. The only entrances on the ground floor were for the Acropolis diner.

Halfway up, Sarah stopped climbing. The inside wooden door was open. The outer screen door was destroyed. A strip of screening was dangling over the edge of the landing. The house lights appeared to be out. Sarah's chest was filled with dread. A tiny rivulet of sweat trickled down between her shoulder blades. She tried to call Kenny's name, but only managed a croak. She tried again.

"Kenny!"

There was no answer. Kenny might have been out somewhere but Ralph should have been here. He should have heard her coming up the steps and been waiting at the door. Sarah drew her gun. She reached inside the door and flipped on the house lights, then walked in, keeping her back always to a wall. The living room was empty. She edged into the bedroom... empty. She checked the closets. She checked the bathroom. She checked the hall. The apartment was deserted.

Sarah thought about the Stephanopolis brothers downstairs. Maybe Kenny was in the diner. She ran and half-stumbled down the steps, around to the front of the building, and in the door to the diner.

She was panting as the plate-glass door closed behind her. The air reeked with burnt food and smoke. Patrons were spilled over the tables and the floor. One of the Stephanopolis brothers was sitting with his back against a wall. Sarah looked away. She didn't see Kenny anywhere in the room.

There was a sizzling noise coming from the back. Sarah went to investigate. She was praying that she wouldn't find what she suspected was there. She walked through the swinging doors into the kitchen. The second Stephanopolis brother lay face down on a gas grill. There was a stench of something burnt. Her stomach contracted. She knew she had to get him off the grill and shut it down before the place caught fire. She closed her eyes, opening them only long enough to grab him by the belt. She pulled hard, yanking him to the floor. Her injured ribs knifed her with pain. Without looking at the corpse, she found the gas knobs and shut the grill down.

Sarah walked out into the front of the diner, and threw up for the second time this night. There was nothing left in her stomach. She glanced around into the faces of corpses. She retreated to her apartment, locked the door, and pushed an oak bookcase up against it.

Sarah struggled out of her clothing, her gun belt, her uniform, her vest. She walked into the shower and turned on the tap. Water spewed into her face. Her body shivered violently in the cold deluge that slowly grew hot. Steaming water poured through clumps of her hair and trickled down along her chest. The despair felt like it was frozen so deeply inside her that nothing could ever thaw it. In time the water began to cool. She adjusted the taps to get the last moments of warmth. She looked down to examine her left side. There was a welt surrounded by a bruised area larger than her outstretched fingers could cover.

Sarah sat down at the kitchen table. She pulled her bathrobe tightly around her shoulders. Her uniform was piled on one of the chairs with the gun belt hung over the back. She stared at a salt and pepper shaker set, a porcelain boy and girl holding hands. Her eyes moved to a dent in the wooden tabletop; her fingers lightly touched the spot. Sarah had scoured secondhand furniture stores for months until she had found this solid oak table. It was the prize of her small furniture collection. Kenny had looked sheepish as if the dent had been completely his fault. She remembered the day it had happened. Kenny had been carrying in a bag of groceries. The bottom had ripped open. Cans of Progresso Soup had tumbled out, minestrone. He had tried to fix the top, but had only made it worse. He'd felt so guilty that it had taken her all week to convince him that she didn't care.

Tears ran down Sarah's cheeks. She knew Kenny was gone. She knew it by the hollow feeling in her chest. The place where she'd always felt his love was now empty. The ceiling light was blurred into shimmers from her tears. She pulled the gun belt off the chair. The Beretta's clip was loaded with hollow points. She clicked off the safety. The tiny sound made her heart jump. She turned the barrel toward her eye and stared down it. She could see the bullet's copper jacket inside the gunmetal bore. She hooked a thumb inside the trigger guard. On the wall next to the refrigerator was a framed picture of her and Kenny. He had his arm around her. They were both smiling, both knowing that their love would last. She stared at that picture while her thumb squeezed down on the trigger. She could feel it approaching the point where the hammer would drop free, the moment that oblivion would take her. The gun was an unfocused blur in her vision. With all her strength she kept her eyes on the image of her and Kenny, and squeezed farther on the trigger. Her arms were trembling. She was holding her breath. Applying that last ounce of pressure was as hard as lifting a car off the ground. She wanted the nightmare to end.

She exhaled abruptly. She couldn't do it. She set the gun down onto the table next to the dents that Kenny had made.

The kitchen window was open just a few inches. The air had a faint acrid taste. Sarah stared at nothing until the pangs of hunger finally moved her. She went to the refrigerator for a glass of milk. She drank it in greedy gulps and then looked at the clock. A rustling sound came from outside. *Just the wind*, she thought, and filled the glass again. A branch snapped.

Sarah got up. She tried to see out the window but couldn't get a good view. She went to the backdoor, pulled away the bookcase, and opened the door part way. She still couldn't see anything. There were no lights out back. The trees at the edge of the parking lot were like a wall of fuzzy blackness. She stepped out onto the porch and waited for her eyes to adjust. She checked the shadows by the cars and the garbage bins. She didn't recognize any of the cars; they must have belonged to the diner's customers. Sarah went down a few steps. There was a sound of bushes rustling. She froze. Her heart beat faster. Something was definitely in the woods.

A dark shape ambled out from the trees. Sarah stifled a scream. The shape was coming straight at her. She tripped over something that snagged her ankle. She scrambled up the steps on all fours. Just as her fingers reached an edge of the open door, she heard the creek of something mounting the steps behind her. She wheeled round to kick at it. She was weakened from all the trauma and knew there wasn't much fight left in her. Why had she left her gun inside?

The shape was coming low to the ground. It was an animal. The shape's eyes seemed to glow. Halfway up the steps it moved into a pool of light. Sarah blinked. It was Ralph. The world jumped back into motion. She was too drained to call his name. Briars were stuck to his fur and a length of rope trailed behind him. She could only guess what he'd been through and wondered who would have tried to tie him up. The only answer that made sense was Kenny. Ralph hesitantly climbed the stairs. He sniffed her and then splashed her face with his tongue. She violently hugged him. She could feel the strength in his muscled neck. He raised his head a few inches, lifting her entire weight up with his movement. Sarah was crying and couldn't stop. She wasn't alone anymore.

"Ralph, don't you ever scare me like that again."

Sarah thought about the broken screen door. The damage had to have been from Ralph getting out.

"I don't want you ever leaving home without me."

Ralph whined something and then licked her as if he understood he was being scolded. Sarah hugged him with every ounce of strength she had left. He was such a powerful animal that it was impossible for her to hurt him.

Sarah got Ralph a bowl of water and half a can of food. They had to conserve. No telling what the supermarkets were like. She went into the living room and tried the phone again. She pressed the first digit of her parent's number. Unlike before, this time the dial tone went away. She punched in the remaining numbers. She heard the clicking sounds of a connection being made. A rapid busy signal cut in. Sarah knew from her police training it was called an intercept-tone. Hearing it meant the system was working but the circuits were overloaded with calls. She glanced at the clock and decided to try again in a half hour. She looked at the television. The set was old and didn't receive all the channels. The screen was filled with a civil defense pattern. A message scrolled at the bottom of the screen advising her to stay tuned for specific instructions.

Sarah woke without remembering when she'd dozed off. She was in the living room with the Beretta in her lap. She heard the approaching wail of a motorcycle coming down her street. She got to the window in time to see the red glow of taillight wash fading on the trees at the end of the block. Had it been real or was it just a ghost rider of her mind?

Sarah went back to the couch. Ralph was curled into a ball at one end. Her throat was dry. She took a sip of bottled water. As she nestled back into the cushions, her eyes opened wide. The civil defense pattern was gone from the television. She recognized the face of someone from a New York news channel. A gas mask hung loose from the reporter's neck. He was inside some kind of military vehicle. The transmission kept cutting out and then returning. There was a window in the lower right-hand corner of the screen. The window contained a shaky view of what must have been a night vision gun sight on the vehicle. A set of cross hairs bisected the image. A Burger King sign passed across the view, followed by more buildings and cars. The main image zoomed in on the reporter who was saying something. Sarah turned up the volume.

"....The areas of central and northern New Jersey have been placed under martial law by order of Governor Fairchild. The National Guard has been mobilized along with the Red Cross. I have witnessed un-imaginable things, bodies lying in the streets, in cars, inside stores. Few of the reports coming in can be confirmed. What I can tell you at this point is that a catastrophe of major proportions has struck New

Jersey. No one in authority is stating that they can categorically rule out some kind of biological attack. The dead are numbered in the tens of thousands. The cause is still unknown at this time. The Governor's office has issued a statement indicating that some type of...."

The transmission went to static for almost a full minute, then,

"....All I can tell you is the Army Support group that I am with is very nervous. The vehicle I'm riding in is airtight and hardened for chemical warfare, but I still don't feel safe. I can only imagine what it's like outside. For the millions of people in the affected areas the only advice the authorities are offering is, 'Stay home with the windows closed....'"

Sarah heard herself laugh. She raised her warm bottle of water in a toast to the screen. The advice was idiotic, she thought. The minions of hell are marching on your homes. Shut the windows and bolt the doors; and while you're at it, boil some water. Do something, anything to take your mind off the fact that you're dead. You may be breathing now, but you're as good as dead!

~

Sarah opened her eyes. Outside her windows was darkness. She was shivering. The clothing she'd fallen asleep in was soaked against her skin. The night chills were back. She remembered her dreams and wished she'd forgotten them. They were vivid and real. She'd dreamt she was asleep on the couch with a dousing rod in her hands. The rod pulled as if it were seeking water. She opened her eyes and saw Kenny leering at her. She knew he was dead. His skin was like wax. His eyes were solid black marbles. There was no hint of expression on his face. Standing with him were her parents and her brother Tim. They were all dead like Kenny – waxy skin and black marble eyes. Brackish pond water was dripping from their hair and clothing, forming puddles on the carpeted floor.

Sarah tried to push the dream from her mind. She turned on all the lights and pulled Ralph into her lap. She stared at the floor where they'd stood – night chills were shaking her body. Something deep inside her believed the dream was real. She got up and touched the carpeting to see if it was damp.

4 – New York City: November

Artie was looking out the window of his apartment. Orange flames were reflected in the glass. Far below him, a car was burning in the center of the street. No one had come to put the fire out. A teenager had wandered by a few minutes earlier and stopped. The youth had dropped his pants and emptied his bladder into the flames.

Feeling exposed, Artie moved back from the windows. He imagined some crazy with a rifle sitting on top of a building just waiting for easy targets. As the reports of looting and fires had increased to citywide, Artie had found himself staring at the front door and the additional deadbolt he had installed after they signed the lease. At the time it had seemed like overkill; now he wished he had installed far more.

The television was glowing with aerial photos of the MetLife building covered in flames. The devastation looked like the terrorist attacks all over again. Artie took a deep breath and tried to calm himself. The air was laced with an acrid smoke. Each breath left a taste in his mouth. The fire department was taxed to its limits. The city was in a stranglehold. The news reports reminded him of a documentary Suzy had done on Rodney King and the Los Angeles riots. In Los Angeles, gangbangers and local kids – and even adults – had gone wild on the day of the Rodney King verdict. Suzy had footage of them dragging innocent people from cars and fatally beating them. Tonight, the mob's only excuse was the smell of death from across the Hudson River. With all this city had been through at the hands of terrorists, with all the hope for mending racial and class divisions, it seemed nothing really deep in the bones of this city had actually healed. There had been an old wound waiting to open and now its festering had been revealed.

From across the room, Artie studied Suzy's posture and face. She didn't notice him. Over the past few hours, she'd called everyone they knew. Dozens of tries were required before each call broke through the logjam of other people doing the same thing. Artie knew the world was coming undone. He saw the signs everywhere, even in Suzy's eyes. He wanted to protect her but there was nothing he could do. He could tell by the look on her face that she was in shock. Normally he could have expected at least one recital of a rule-for-life from the mental book she carried in her head. All she'd done for the last four hours was stare at that television and sip whisky from a coffee cup that was long empty of its original brew.

Artie sat down next to her and put his arm around her shoulder. She curled into him so completely that it was almost a total collapse of will. There was a pizza sitting on the coffee table that no one had touched. The pizza had long ago grown hard like a giant scab of cheese. Suzy had picked their dinner up on her way home from work when the world had still been sane.

A faint pop echoed down the street. The sound was quickly followed by several more in rapid succession. Artie knew those sounds all too well. They were sounds that had awakened him many nights when he was a child. The gangs were out conducting their business of fear. He kissed Suzy on her cheek and got up.

In the bedroom, Artie dragged a metal footlocker from a back closet. The locker was a heavy steel model, Army surplus, with a Master Lock dangling on the front. He turned the combination lock and opened a doorway into his past. He rummaged through the artifacts of a lost youth. In the bottom under some clothing was a handgun wrapped in oil rags. It was a stainless steel Smith and Wesson .357 magnum. He opened a box of ammo and loaded six rounds. The bullets were huge at an inch and a half long. Each round could hit a man with enough force to blow off entire pieces of human anatomy.

The gun fit Artie's hand like an old memory and relaxed his nerves better than any drug. He turned it over inspecting both sides, looking more at its shine than for signs of wear. His eyes wandered back to the footlocker. He set the revolver down on the carpet and bored deeper into his past. He removed a double-edged knife from the trunk and laid it on the floor beside the gun. He stared at the engraving on the blade, a dragon with a fiery tail.

An hour later, a circle of objects surrounded him on the floor. Along with the knife and gun were a set of throwing-stars, a Tae Kwan Do black belt, and a photo of him and his buddies Kelo and Tony. Kelo was gone now and Tony was in jail. Old memories were boiling up to the surface, heated dangerously by the flames of a burning city.

By the time Artie was sixteen, he'd spent half his life on the streets and the other half studying Tae Kwan Do with an uncle who was raising him and trying to show him there were alternatives to the gangs. Artie had earned a black belt and had been well on his way to a first stripe. He was very good at martial arts and had proved it to himself many times by sending members of rival gangs to intensive care; one of them, due to a bad fall, hadn't left the hospital alive.

A few months after his first and only murder, a gang war had exploded on the streets like a tank of gasoline going up in the night. The war had started on neutral party ground under an expanse of train track in Queens and ended as one of the deadliest gang wars of New York urban legend. There had been over forty soldiers on each side along with girlfriends and kids. Artie's side, the Dragons, had been lightly armed and expecting a good time. The Warlocks had come with ice chests full of guns. Many Dragons had been left to die drowning in their own blood that night. The next day Artie had bought his first gun. The open hand of his uncle's Tae Kwan Do didn't go far enough on the streets of a modern city.

Three weeks later to the day, the cops busted Artie. He spent a year in juvi-jail for mayhem and a concealed weapons charge. Jail had taught him the hard way. The path he was on was a dead end – and the end would be an early grave. He started thinking about his future for the first time. He remembered what his uncle had tried to jam into his thick skull for so many years. When the courts finally put him back on the streets, he had a high school diploma earned in jail, a clean record, and was enrolled in City College. He never looked back. He worked nights and weekends. Toward the end of law school, there had been no need to work so hard because of Suzy's help; but he had kept up the ninety-hour weeks just the same. Six years after getting out of juvenile hall, he passed the New York City bar exam. It had been a sad and happy day. His uncle had died a few months too soon to see him walk that final mile. The only solace was that the old man had known that Artie's future would be a solid one. Fourteen years earlier, Artie had lost his father and mother. Both had been killed during a robbery of a neighborhood store. Rumors were that someone from a local gang had done the shooting. Suzy was the only family he had now, and his protectiveness of her was a fire that burned with searing heat.

The television's shifting images were reflected on the glass coffee table. Artie was back with Suzy on the couch. The Smith and Wesson was within reach under a cushion by his side. The New Jersey kill zone was being covered on every channel. At first there had been only reports with no video; then came the direct feed. Television defined life; nothing was real anymore until it was shown on that screen.

Artie looked at Suzy. Shadows from the television moved across her face. She glanced at him, then back to the screen. Her eyes were ringed with tears. Her nails dug painfully into his thigh. He should have made her stop, but somehow the pain felt right. He should be hurting when he saw pictures like this. CNN had revised the body count to over thirty thousand.

Artie wondered how they got those numbers. His mind was moving down several different paths at once. If this had been a normal night, he would be conducting a round-table, talking with kids from the outreach program. He tried so hard to make sure they didn't repeat the mistakes he'd made. They were just a bunch of teenage boys and girls. One of his kids had called an hour ago. Lyle had been a fourteen-year-old on his way to full membership in the most American of institutions, the Crypts. Artie felt good knowing he'd pulled one kid from that pit of death. Lyle had actually called to see if he and Suzy were okay. It was difficult to imagine a tough kid like Lyle placing that call. Artie wondered how many of his kids were on the streets right now taking advantage of a one-time fire sale. He wondered how many wouldn't make it through the night.

A gust of heat and wind rattled the windows. Artie could see from his seat that a building across the street was going up in flames. He got up to look out the window. Suzy started to panic. She grabbed him and pulled him back to her. The window glass glowed with a yellow light as bright as the sun.

"Don't look out the windows," she cried. "The world's dying out there. I won't let you die with it. Promise me you won't do anything crazy. Promise me!"

5 – Morristown New Jersey: November

New Jersey had been suspended in four days of grief. The sky brought rain several times, but nothing could wash away what had happened. There was too much loss, too much grief, to ever recover what had been before.

Ralph was staring up at Sarah with expectant eyes. It was obvious he knew something exciting was about to happen. Sarah wondered if she was doing the smart thing. A week ago she'd never doubted her control over where she was heading. She was the strategist piloting a course from one accomplishment to the next. Now, life was a collection of things that were just happening to her, things she didn't understand. The loss of control left her feeling panicked for hours on end. She knelt down and tied a bandanna around Ralph's neck. He tried to lick her ear but ended up with nothing but air. He looked handsome in his new neckwear.

Sarah absentmindedly touched her side. The damaged ribs were fine. The pain was gone, the bruise was gone. She was glad the injury had healed, but it was odd that it had cleared up in just four days. She wondered if the plague had anything to with abnormal healing. Maybe the disease killed some people and helped others? She knew this kind of thinking was only survivor's guilt, but still it was odd how quickly she'd healed.

The television was playing in the next room. A tired-sounding reporter was relaying the latest statistics. Statewide, one out of every fifty was dead; but in the towns heaviest hit, less than one percent had survived. The litany eventually segued into a list of notable violent crimes that had occurred in the last twenty-four hours. The list was very long. Sarah tried not to listen, tried not to think of what people were doing to each other – wasn't this plague enough? The darker side was coming though. Last night, the sound of an automatic rifle going off had awakened her from a dreamless sleep. At first, she thought the sound was someone hammering nails, but then her mind had cleared. It was time to leave.

Sarah pulled the compression sack tightly around the sleeping bag and then inserted it into her backpack. The pack was a professional model. The frame had a torsion-link harness designed for carrying heavy loads without loss of balance. This was the same equipment used by elite military troops. Sarah had grown up on trips through the woods. She felt more comfortable in the middle of a forest than on her own couch. She filled the remainder of the compartments with food and water for her and Ralph. She knew the pack was heavy, probably ninety pounds, but it would be lighter in a few days if she couldn't find replacement food. She tested it on her back. Her legs felt the strain, but right now she only had to carry it the two miles to her car. She hoped to make it out of New Jersey without resorting to more foot power than that.

The National Guard had been given the assignment of clearing wreckage from neighborhood road. According to news reports, the task was daunting. Sarah had seen no sign of cleanup on her street or any of the streets she'd explored. She hoped the highways were in more passable condition. She'd tried to get information on road conditions, but had failed. Nothing up-to-date was available from government agencies. Even the news now seemed to be covering the story from a distance. The constant outages of television and radio only made it worse. With all the modern equipment at their disposal, it seemed insane that none of the networks were reliably on the air. The only things Sarah knew for certain came from civil defense messages repeated every fifteen minutes instead of commercials. There was a dusk to dawn curfew and the National Guard had orders to shoot looters on sight. All police were ordered to report in. She had started to call, but intuition had left her fingers hovering over the number pad.

The kitchen table was cluttered with what she was leaving behind. Sarah took a long last look at a photograph of her and Kenny and then shifted her eyes to a photo of her family. She had packed no pictures, no letters, nothing to remind her of what had been. She was leaving forever. She was certain that everyone she loved was dead. The phones had started working the day after the plague had struck. She had tried every number in her book. No one had answered, which was not a surprise. Somehow she'd known they were all gone. She'd touched each name with her fingers before calling. They'd all felt cold and empty.

The sounds of a car coming down the street leaked into the kitchen. Sarah's heart leapt. She turned to the window. For an insane and glorious second, the car was Kenny's. At any moment he would come through the backdoor. The sound of tires faded. Sarah fought against the icy void lodged in her chest. If Kenny was alive, he'd have been here by now and she wouldn't be feeling this emptiness, this absence of connection. She looked at the door and imagined herself taking that first step across the threshold. That would be it, final admission that Kenny was gone. She wiped tears from her eyes with a sleeve, and then with her hands, when the tears refused to stop.

Sarah felt alone and began sobbing. She slid from the chair to the floor. Legs of the kitchen table and chairs in front of her were like bars to a prison. She thought about her family. Her chest was rising and falling in huge gasps of air. Yesterday she'd walked the fifteen miles to their home in Mount Freedom. Their house had been quiet. The porch door had been moving in a breeze. She'd gone inside and found the place looted. Everything of value had been stripped from the home; even some of the furniture was gone. Every cushion and mattress and pillow had been split open. Stuffing had lain across the floor like the entrails of a violated life.

Out in the backyard, she'd found one of her mother's dresses trampled in the dirt. The garden was ransacked. Clumps of uprooted plants were scattered about like wounded people. Against a growing pressure of emotions, she'd walked back to her father's tool shed. The beat-up wooden door seemed as imposing as gates leading down into hell. She'd known what was inside. She could swear that there had been visual flashes, premonitions of what had been waiting for her beyond that door. Later trying to explain it away, she decided she must have been so traumatized that her memories had become scrambled.

Someone had dragged the bodies of her loved ones from the house. They had been dumped nude, one on top of the other like so many broken dolls. Sarah had spent the remainder of that day and a good part of the night digging respectable graves. Unable to go back inside the house, she'd slept on the porch for a few hours and walked home at first light. Through it all, Ralph had stayed close and made no sounds.

During the long hours walking home, Sarah had relived the burial again and again. She saw the dirt falling from the tip of her shovel onto her father's face and knew it was an image she'd keep until death took her mind. The words she had spoken over the grave kept repeating; they were words she'd heard somewhere else but couldn't remember where.

"It's not a man that is covered with soil, but a seed. As a man, he affected other people's lives and will live on through his touch on their souls and their children's souls in an ever expanding tree of life."

~

Sarah was in the bedroom getting dressed. The electricity winked out for a moment, then came back. In the living room the television was playing an earlier speech by the president. Sarah slid an optional trauma plate into the front of her body armor. The plate was a flat piece of ceramic material designed for added chest protection. Bullets striking a vest could cause severe bruises or even bone damage. The plate prevented that type of trauma and also slowed high velocity rifle rounds that would otherwise penetrate the vest. She readjusted some Velcro straps for the added thickness.

Over the armor, Sarah tugged on an extra large sweatshirt. The gray cotton hung from her shoulders like a tent. She also had on a pair of jeans and high-top sneakers. She racked a shell into her Beretta and then concealed it inside a jogger's belt-pack that had a special quick draw compartment designed for the gun. The pack was standard police detective issue. Another part of the pack had a flap used to hold her police shield. In the normal part of the pack went extra clips and as much ammunition as she could fit. All the ammo caused the pack to weigh down against her tummy like a sandbag. She put on a baseball cap that had the Morristown Police logo stenciled in white on the front. She pulled her ponytail through the adjustment strap in the back. Her look was complete. She hoped it would attract little or no attention. She started to put on some lipstick but then stopped and gazed at her reflection. The only adornments she wore were a set of pearl stud earrings. She dropped the lipstick onto the floor and walked away.

Sarah felt disconnected from the world. At eight in the morning on a clear fall day, she slung on her backpack and picked up her walking stick. She noticed how her fingers wrapped around the time-smoothed wood. The paint on the walls had a more pronounced texture than she remembered ever seeing. She noticed a faint buzzing from the kitchen clock. All her perceptions seemed to be slightly skewed, a bit like a dream that was vanishing just before waking. She called to Ralph. He came trotting into the kitchen. He was jittery and clearly psyched for a great adventure. From past experience, he connected the walking stick and backpack with trips to the country.

Sarah opened the door and stepped out. She started walking with little thought beyond the moment, just one foot in front of the other. Hiking back to her Nissan, she tried to keep everything she saw as snapshots in her memory. The trees had lost most of their leaves and what remained were muted autumn colors. The world looked almost normal. What was missing were the sounds – no squeals of children, or people chatting on porches, or cars, or the other million different sounds of an industrialized world. There were the occasional barking and bird noises, but that was all. Some of the more aggressive wild animals were already staking out new territories in yards and alleys and other places they had never been. A raccoon was on a roof trying to pry up a lose shingle. The first into the ecological void would reap the bounty.

As they walked, Sarah explained her plan to Ralph. They were heading south. He seemed okay with the idea, then ran off to chase a squirrel. A minute later he came back with a look of pride on his face. As they turned a corner, Sarah noticed a pack of dogs on the porch of a house. One of them, a large German Shepherd, came down the steps toward them. The animal was crouched and moving directly at them. The dog was not growling or barking. The animal was completely silent. The remainder of the dogs followed behind what was probably the alpha male. They were behaving like a wild pack of hunters. Ralph's hair bristled on his back. He began to move at the leader. "No," shouted Sarah. He stopped but kept his focus on the alpha dog. Ralph was much larger and stronger than the Shepherd. The pack continued in a cautious advance. They began to spread out in a semicircle across the yard. Sarah drew her gun and fired two shots in the air. The pack broke and fled in different directions.

The Nissan was just as she'd left it. Sarah had been worried that it might have been vandalized or towed from the front lawn where she'd parked it. The officials in charge of cleanup must have thought it belonged to whoever owned the house. The engine turned over on the first try. She made a right turn onto Washington Street; route Two Eighty-Seven was less than a mile away. The car radio was receiving news reports. Her police walkie-talkie was plugged into the cigarette lighter. The volume was set low. There were continuous radio calls sending State Troopers in one direction, then a minute later turning them around and vectoring them off toward higher priority incidents. The system was being taxed beyond all limits.

Sarah took a sip from a gallon jug of Arrowhead water. She had no clear idea of a final destination. Anything away from this hell was a good start. For now, she headed south toward the New Jersey border. She had a vague plan of not stopping until she reached the Gulf of Mexico and then heading west along the coast. Texas sounded appealing; all that deserted sand and camping sites along its thin coastal islands, a warmer place as far away from this nightmare as anywhere in the country.

Sarah exited Route Two Eighty-Seven onto the New Jersey Turnpike. The tollgates were up. There was no one to collect money. Wrecked cars were piled up on a shoulder just past the gates. Sarah stared at the hills of metal. There had to be hundreds of cars and trucks in there. The shoulder was like a giant scrap yard. She looked straight ahead. The road was an empty three-lane strip of tar that disappeared into the horizon. She'd imagined the toll road would have been clogged with people trying to get out. She'd lived in this area her entire life and had never seen the Turnpike without heavy traffic. There was something very unsettling in all of this desolation. She pressed down on the accelerator. The Nissan moved up to sixty-five miles per hour; if she pushed it any faster, a front wheel shimmy would set in.

The highway was lined with patches of trees and buildings. Car-to-car police radio calls had been going back and forth for the last ten minutes. Sarah knew from the codes that the Staties were trying to corner a gang of teenage looters pulling hit 'n runs on stores throughout the area. One of the calls included a code for shots fired; another quickly followed with a code for high-speed pursuit.

Sarah was listening to a world that had lost its self-control; violence was becoming the coin of the realm. She wanted to leave it all far behind. She was just fifty miles from the state line where the highway would cross over into Delaware.

Every few miles there were pockets of mangled cars pushed deep into the shoulder. Sarah noticed sections of the pavement looked like a huge dozer blade had scraped it. She assumed the marks were from whatever had plowed off the wreckage. Car parts were scattered along the roadside like the fossil bones of some bygone era.

Ralph was sitting in the front seat. His muzzle was sticking out a partially-open window. One of his ears was pushed back by the wind. Sarah patted his back. He seemed to be enjoying the ride. He was probably tasting and remembering every smell that went past. He was a very intelligent animal, always curious and driven to explore anything new in his world. Sarah imagined his journey would be marked by a collection of smells, just as hers would be remembered by the images in her mind.

A shiny black Caddie flew past Sarah on the left. The car clipped her while cutting over into her lane. Sparks flew as if a power line had landed on the hood. Mayhem took her world. The wheel felt like one of her tires was gone. She spun sideways, then recovered only to lose control again. She was off the road and skimming along a grassy incline. Her teeth were clamped tight. At any moment she would be tumbling. The Nissan came to a stop in the grass. The engine puttered. Her heart was beating so fast that her body tingled. That Caddie must have been doing over a hundred. She could have been killed.

"Bastard!" she yelled. "Fuck you!"

She kicked the underside of the dash then kicked it again. A pair of State Police interceptors screamed past like ground-locked jet fighters. They had to be going half again as fast as the Caddie. Get him, she thought.

Sarah looked over at Ralph who'd ended up on the floor. The dog gave her a remorseful look. The poor guy had not enjoyed the auto-acrobatics.

Sarah got out of the car to check the damage. The front fender was crumpled into the tire. Some of the tread had been sheared off like the skin of an apple. She tried pulling on the fender. No use. The wrecked metal wasn't moving.

Her hands were covered with road grime. She sat down on the ground and stared at the damage. Her car was going nowhere. That wheel didn't have enough clearance to make left turns. Ralph let out a soft woof. He was looking out the window at her.

"No use, baby. We're stuck here, screwed big time."

Sarah slowly shook her head. She couldn't believe how bad her luck was turning. Not an hour into her exodus and she'd already lost the Nissan. If they had to walk from here, it would be days before they reached the Delaware border. That was, of course, as long as some gang didn't rape or kill her along the way. Get a grip, she thought. She couldn't just sit here. She had to do something. She got into the car and turned the steering wheel to check how much of a left turn she could make. The tire pushed into the sheet metal. She heard a soft groan as the power steering applied too much pressure. Her eyes grew wide. *Mechanical power – that's it!*

"We're okay, baby!"

She hugged Ralph then jumped out of the car. She opened the trunk and pulled out the spare tire and jack. She left the tire lying in the grass. The jack was a small hydraulic model. In a few minutes she had wedged the jack between the wheel and crumpled fender. She carefully began cranking the jack up one pump at a time. Slowly, the piston began to dig into the sheet metal, pushing it up and away from the tire. The metal started to rip, but her idea was working. After pushing one piece of sheet metal away from the wheel, she moved the jack over and started working on another section.

An hour later, Sarah stepped back from the Nissan to admire her work. Her face and hands were covered in grime but she was smiling. After the sheet metal damage was cleared, she'd exchanged the tire with the spare. The car looked like hell, but who cared? She was in business again.

~

Sarah pulled onto the left shoulder of the turnpike. She was only a few miles from the Delaware Memorial Bridge and the state line. Traffic was completely stalled beginning at the last tollbooth before the bridge. Some people were milling around on a grassy area of the roadside. A couple of kids were tossing a Frisbee back and forth. A section of the barrier between North and Southbound lanes had been removed. There was a steady stream of cars making u-turns through the opening. Not far up the road, Sarah could make out an Army Humvee ambling along the shoulder. The vehicle was moving in her direction. She watched it stop for a minute and then move on. She wondered if they were giving out information. Ralph put his paw into her lap.

"Stay here, baby," she said. "I'm going to see what's up."

Ralph let out a short bark as if saying, *okay with me.* Sarah got out and walked over to the nearest group of people. The gathering looked like a father, a mother, and three children. The smallest was a girl of about four years old. She was occupied with a box of animal cookies. Sarah addressed the father.

"Hi there," Sarah called out. "What's going on?"

She extended her hand. The man shook it. His grip was firm.

"Well, no one's sure when they're going to open the bridge up. We've been here since four o'clock this morning. Right honey?"

The woman nodded and pushed some hair out of her face. The man continued, "Seems they've blocked the bridge and they're not letting any-one in or out of Jersey. Some Army guys came by and told everyone that the state's been temporarily quarantined by orders from Washington."

"Since when?" asked Sarah. All of a sudden two-plus-two was not equaling four.

"I'm not sure. There's a sign up ahead that says the Army has orders to shoot anyone trying to sneak across. Guess they're serious about keeping the plague from leaking out. The folks up there..."

The man pointed to a group of people that had set up a barbecue. "...they've been here for two days. They said they heard gunshots the other night; and someone else said a man and woman had been shot dead on the Jersey side of the bridge."

Sarah started walking back toward her car. She felt lightheaded. These were just rumors. The Army wouldn't kill anyone that way; but a quarantine – now that was something believable. Sealing off the bridges leaving Jersey had to be what was going on. All these folks were not camping here because this highway was a lovely spot for outdoor recreation. Sarah noticed Ralph was watching her from a distance through the windshield.

Why hadn't she heard anything about a quarantine in the news? An entire state being sealed off was something CNN wouldn't have missed. Sarah stopped walking. She looked down at the ground for a moment. She nudged a rock with her toe. Think it through. The television and radio had been cutting in and out for days. She'd blamed the poor signal on emergency equipment. The interruptions could have just as easily been censors doing their job of keeping the population tranquil and at home. Once word got out that soldiers were surrounding the state, people trapped inside might just panic and nasty confrontations would result. A news blackout like this couldn't be sustained much longer. This news had to be getting to the rest of the country. People outside had to be watching what was going on. That talk about a man and women being shot was crazy. There would be an outcry if the Army started slaughtering innocent citizens.

Sarah decided she was getting ahead of herself. Right now, she didn't know a single thing that was not in large part guesswork. She let Ralph out of the car. He sniffed around at the ground, then looked up at her. She got a bottle of water and a dish from the car. While Ralph lapped up his water, Sarah put on her belt-pack with the Beretta inside. She clipped a small water bottle to the belt and stuffed some food and a pair of binoculars into a nylon gym bag. She thought about it for a moment and then took her badge from the belt-pack and hung it around her neck.

It was a nice day for a walk. The sun was just nearing its noonday high. She patted her thigh calling to Ralph. He came to her and heeled. They started out toward the river.

Sarah rounded a bend in the highway and there it was in front of her: the impossible. She knelt down to hold Ralph close. Her first thought was this must be a mirage. Nothing like this happened in the United States of America. What she saw reminded her of something from the History Channel about Eastern European dictatorships. She no longer had any doubts that the news was being censored. The bridge was fortified with armored vehicles, including tanks. Hundreds of soldiers were moving around. Searchlight trucks flanked both the north and southbound spans of the bridge. This was no temporary measure.

To Sarah's right was a small strip of grass and trees that separated the highway from a canal. To her left appeared to be a large park that ran all the way to the river. A short distance behind her a service road exited into the park. Sarah and Ralph walked along the curving service road which eventually came to a field bordered by trees; behind the trees she could see the Delaware River.

Sarah pushed back her cap and wiped the moisture from around her eyes. She was crouched among a row of trees which lined the river. The water was a dozen yards beyond the trees. A few hundred yards to the south were some waterfront homes. She got out the pair of binoculars and focused them on the bridge. She watched as an armored personnel carrier backed out from a chokepoint it was blocking. A Humvee stopped beside it. An exchange occurred and then the Humvee was waved through to cross the bridge. The armored personnel carrier returned to its road blocking position. On the Wilmington side of the bridge, she saw what looked like civilian cars being turned back into Delaware and a small force of news broadcast trucks with satellite dishes.

Sarah realized she was trapped. New Jersey was a very easy state to blockade. The entire western state line was the Delaware River. The eastern edge was sealed first by the Atlantic Ocean and then the Hudson River. For all practical purposes, New Jersey was a peninsula. The only point of direct land contact was its northern border with New York State.

The Delaware River was known for its dangerous currents. Farther upriver were rapids and undertows that had claimed many lives. The water was broader and slower here, more like a choppy sea. She wondered if she could find a boat a few miles upstream and sneak across at night. She looked again at the news trucks and saw what might have been the glint of cameras pointing back in her direction.

A deafening staccato sound came from upriver. The noise sounded like some kind of aircraft. The noise grew as it reverberated off buildings and walls. Ralph began barking. Sarah covered her ears. An Apache helicopter zoomed by so low, it flew under the bridge instead of over it. Loaded missile pods hung from the helicopter's sides. The Army bird banked to a stop, hovered for a moment, then wheeled around and headed back upriver.

The helicopter was the most advanced attack bird the Army flew. The machine only seated two and was a devastating killer. Sarah was in awe. She knew a lot about military hardware from television and books but had never seen an operating war machine this close. It was like a giant armored insect in the air. The experience was intimidating. She now understood the psychological effect weapons like these had on an enemy.

The Apache was a show of overwhelming force intended to discourage exactly the kinds of things she'd been thinking about. The bird had electronics that probably gave it better vision at night than at day. No boat would make it across this river. Sarah was scowling. The depth of her anger surprised her. She knew she would die if she remained in New Jersey. She had stared down the barrel of her gun a few nights ago. If she stayed, she might look down that barrel again. She had to put as many miles as possible between herself and those memories she'd left behind. She was going to get out of this prison. She had no other choice.

~

Sarah had been driving along the Delaware for over two hours. She had passed bridge after bridge that were blocked off by soldiers just as heavily as the bridge at Wilmington. She'd decided that if she didn't find a way across before reaching the northern border, then the New York line would be where she'd make her escape.

The border between New Jersey and New York was dense forest. On a folding map, Sarah had looked at the few paved roads that snaked through the forest. There were dozens, if not more, forgotten dirt roads which appeared on no maps; and that's what she'd have to use, the forgotten paths. She knew a few of them from camping trips. This area was old mining and timber country from pre-revolutionary war days with horse and wagon roads, and before that there were Indian trails. She hoped it was impossible for the Army to have sealed off all the ways out in the few days they'd had to dig in.

The Delaware Water Gap had turned out to be the most fortified crossing point of them all. At its edge was where Interstate Route Eighty came to a stop. For decades, the highway had run from coast to coast, from New York City to San Francisco. Not any more.

Sarah decided the river was impassable. She'd seen more Apaches and also military patrol boats. The woods were probably filled with soldiers. This was the place they expected everyone to try crossing. It was time to explore the northern forests.

After hours of two-lane country freeway, Sarah turned down a dirt road she knew. If it was blocked at some point, she'd have to find some old engineering maps and check them for service routes. The local courthouses usually had a selection of those maps; libraries were another good source.

The road she was on was used by campers. She'd taken it many times. The road circled Greenwood Lake along the bordering hills. One side of the lake was in New Jersey while the other was in New York. She'd always thought it was odd that the Coast Guard rather than local authorities patrolled the lake. Years later as a cop, she learned the Coast Guard had jurisdiction because the water crossed state lines.

So far, the road was deserted. As best she could figure, she might already have crossed into New York State. A few minutes ago, Sarah had put in a CD. The reggae sounds of Soup Dragon's song *"I'm Free"* echoed in the car. She started to relax, getting into the music and the woods outside the car. She began singing the choruses *"I'm Free"* to Ralph. The windows were rolled down. There was a wonderful smell of pine and leaves. Sunlight winked through the branches like yellow kisses.

The road became rougher. There were spots where water had left small gullies across it. Sarah had to slow to a few miles per hour. She leaned forward squinting. What was that up ahead? She switched off the CD. Damn it! There was a tree in the road. She started to think how she could clear it. Maybe she could push it with her car? As she got closer all hope faded. On the far side of the tree was the roofline of an Army Humvee. The vehicle had been parked on the shoulder behind plant cover. Looking closer, she saw two soldiers staring at her from the shadow of a tall pine.

Sarah stopped the car a few yards from the barricade. There was no place to turn around. The road was only a few feet wider than her car. One of the soldiers stood up and walked towards her. He was carrying an M16 rifle. He couldn't have been more than nineteen. His uniform was National Guard, not Army. He was sloppily dressed with a shirttail hanging out below his jacket. His buddy stood up and walked into the light. He also had an M16. His face was covered with acne.

Sarah wondered if she could reason with them. She was a cop. She rolled up the windows to keep Ralph from jumping out. No point in getting him shot by some trigger-happy kid. She took out her badge and climbed from the car.

The kid stopped three feet in front of her with his M16 pointed to the side. He was too close and his stance was arrogant. His breath reeked of beer. Sarah looked the area over spotting the remains of a six-pack near where they'd been sitting. She smiled to herself. They'd be in serious trouble if their commanding officer found out about the beer. Drinking while on duty was a jailable offense. She held out her badge.

"What's your name?" asked Sarah.

"What's yours?" said Beer-breath. "This area's off limits to civilians."

"I'm a cop."

"So..."

He backed up a few steps and pointed the muzzle of the M16 toward her. Ralph started barking in the car.

"Hey, *Zit Face* get over here and check her for weapons."

"Wait a minute!" shouted Sarah.

"Shut up!"

The kid with acne edged a little closer. He looked worried. Sarah began to wonder what the hell was going on here.

"Shit, *Zit Face*...If you're not going to do it, cover her for me."

Acne-face leveled his M16 at her chest. Sarah didn't know how many rounds her vest could take before one got through. The kid appeared tense. He kept glancing over toward a section of trees. Sarah looked where he was glancing. For a moment she saw nothing, then her eyes started to pick out details. There were more empty six-pack cartons, and mixed up in the leaves were some clothes and two open suitcases.

Beer-breath had walked up to her and started to pat her down. His hands lingered on her. He was enjoying this. He twisted her around with a rough shove so that she was facing away from him.

"What you got in the car?" he asked.

She knew they intended to rob her or worse. She turned and pushed his hands off her. His eyes were glazed with alcohol and something darker. It was cruelty. He reached out to touch her. She backed away and took up a stance that looked casual but was a well-balanced position to fight from.

"Let her alone, Gordy," whined Acne-face.

"Who's gonna know?"

"What happened before wasn't right."

"Who cares?... Shit – what's with you?" said Beer-breath. "You're such a pussy."

"Fuck you!" yelled Acne-face.

Beer-breath's expression grew vicious. He turned and took a step toward his buddy. Sarah waited until he was at the perfect distance then snap-kicked him between the legs. She felt the toe of her sneaker reach bone. There was a moist sound from the impact. Beer-breath crumpled to the ground moaning. Acne-face lowered his rifle then let it fall into the dirt. Keeping her eyes on the kid, Sarah reached slowly down and picked up Beer-breath's M16. Acne-face seemed unwilling to do anything. It was almost as if he wanted her to shoot him. Sarah backed up toward her car. As she opened the door, Ralph tried to pile out. She shoved Ralph over to the passenger side, then, put the Nissan in reverse and floored it. The rear wheels spun kicking up dirt and rocks. The car was hard to control going backwards, the steering was jittery, but she had no intention of slowing down. She realized she was crying. She'd actually been happy for a few lousy minutes. She'd been singing to Ralph and then she'd run into those two bastards.

The road went through a turn and then straightened out. The weekend warrior children had to be at least a mile behind her and their Humvee was parked on the New York side of a downed tree. If they were after her, it would be on foot.

Sarah stopped the car. She couldn't keep driving backwards. The road was narrow. She needed to turn the car around. After several minutes of back and forth, she still wasn't facing the right way. She was starting to feel trapped and panicked. She inched back farther than the last try. There was a sound of crunching metal and a final jolt as rocks scraped under the rear of her car. She put the car in drive and gave it some gas. The rear wheels spun. She put it in reverse to see if she could get traction that way. More scraping. She was hung up.

"Damn it! God Damn it!"

She laid her forehead on the steering wheel. A moment later, she looked up half-expecting to see a Humvee racing into view. The road was empty, but for all she knew they might have some way of raising that tree barricade. She checked the M16. The automatic weapon had a full clip and one in the chamber.

Chapter 6

Ghosts

1 – Atlanta: November

His mind was wandering into empty space. Mark was tired but couldn't sleep. It was too early in the morning to be working but that's what he was trying to do. The sun would be coming up in a few hours. He hadn't slept much since the New Jersey kill zone. He was suffering from mild insomnia and then nightmares when he did manage to sleep. Horrible things were occurring around him and nightmares were a normal part of coping. But one nightmare was different. The dream had occurred only once and was far more real than the others. He was in a city that felt like Los Angeles, but all the streets and buildings were from somewhere he didn't recognize. In this city all human life had been erased as if by some act of God. Everyone had vanished – there were no bodies or other signs of recent habitation. It was a city of ghosts and he was condemned to wandering its streets and buildings in a state of amnesia, searching for someone he had lost but could not remember.

This new nightmare caused Mark to wonder about his earlier dream of people floating dead in the Hudson River. That dream had come only once and had seemed far too real; then later that day, New Jersey had been hit. The mind was a funny thing. Faces of actual victims were haunting him and had become indistinguishably blended with his memories of that earlier dream. Now this new dream left him insecure and scared, but reality was far more frightening and immediate than a childish fear of dreams. The government death count in New Jersey – the one that was kept secret – was still rising. Conservative estimates were a hundred and thirty thousand dead. Mark felt a terrible guilt. COBIC was his discovery, his Nobel Prize; he should have known more, suspected more. He should have done something. He was more convinced than ever that the focus of his life's work was now in some way the instrument of a terrible plague.

His office smelled stale to him. A fourteen-inch flat screen television was positioned on the corner of his desk. The sound was turned low. CNN had been on the air without commercials for the last five days. Right now, they were showing scenes of the Army turning back refugees at a bridge. Mark shook his head. He wasn't sure which was worse: the plague or the all-too-human response and overreaction.

The volume of information from his research was growing. He had a thriving population of millions of thawed COBIC-3.7 to work with; but it was impossible to ignore that this colony had come from the sacrifice of so many lives. The guilt made work very difficult and at times impossible. Mark had seen one of the lab techs cry as she prepped a sample. The woman had reached up to wipe away tears, only to have her hand blocked by the faceplate of her helmet. The image had haunted Mark for days.

Only a small number of the victims in New Jersey had traces of COBIC. After an exhaustive study, tests determined that nine percent of the victims had COBIC infestation. In Anchorage, the figure had been eighty percent. Mark was unable to explain the variations from zero COBIC in Latin America to eighty percent in Alaska.

He had again confirmed his earlier finding that any wavelength of light caused a dramatic effect in this animal. As long as COBIC was kept in lightless metal containers, the population levels remained constant. Exposing a small colony to light caused what could almost be described as mass suicide. In an hour or two after exposure, most of the creatures would be shriveled and dead, with no apparent physiological explanation. Odder still was the fact that the population level could remain constant. When kept in their lightless containers, none died; but even more strangely, none reproduced. He had tried to stimulate reproduction by providing foodstuffs and adjusting alkalinity along with other chemical characteristics of the water. Nothing had worked. As far as he could tell, not a single bacterium had reproduced in captivity. The COBIC breeding colony he'd worked with years ago during his Nobel research had reproduced nicely under identical conditions. Those original COBIC had also not been micro-vampires like these light-adverse specimens. The original COBIC had thrived in light and, in fact, needed light to remain active and healthy.

On his computer screen, Mark opened a particularly good SEM image of a seed. He now had a library of over two hundred images of this object taken at various levels of magnification and dissection. Tests for organic composition had just come back from the lab – all negative. No known organic structures were found in this object: no protein, no DNA, no organic carbons, nothing. The seed was semi-transparent to visible light, much like a bead of glass. As far as the lab could ascertain, this object was a non-organic lump of matter composed of silicon, carbon, and traces of various rare metals such as gallium and silver. It was like a pearl inside the bacterium. He could find no reason for its existence and no apparent effect that it could have, other than being an irritant to the microbe.

Mark was studying at high magnification the semi-transparent structures inside the seed. Because of how SEM microscopes work, optically transparent objects like the fine glass-like structures of this specimen appeared as solid and opaque as a metal surface. The image was a full frame shot of the opening of one of the tubes that Mark had previously discovered. The three microscopic tubes intersected at right angles to each other, forming a three-dimensional axis that was centered inside the seed. Surrounding the tubes, the seed itself was packed with a crystalline silica material that had a dense microscopic structure of rectangular bumps and pits that were interconnected with thread-like channels. The structures looked like the aerial view of a giant chemical factory: the channels were like intersecting pipes while the pits and bumps were like mixers and storage tanks. He wondered what purpose the tiny bumps and pits served. If the seed was some kind of quasi lifeform, were these structures organs of some kind, chemical reactors? Millions, possibly even billions of these nano-structures were inside the seed. Mark was also curious about the woven structure of the tube walls which appeared to be constructed from millions of ultra-thin ceramic donuts stacked together to form the tube. Tests had shown it was a complex weave of carbon, hydrogen, silicon, and trace metals. *What are you?* he wondered. He could not get past how man-made this thing looked. He knew that it was just an illusion. When highly magnified, many natural things could take on an appearance of being man-made.

Mark leaned back in his chair and put his foot up on the desk. He took a sip of coffee. Violating all security rules, he had e-mailed some of these images to colleagues. The e-mails contained no explanation or background, just a single sentence: *"Does this look like anything you've seen before?"* Mark hoped someone would recognize at least part of this microscopic pearl. He glanced at his in-mail box. There was nothing, not even a piece of spam. Kathy entered Mark's office and dropped down onto his couch. She looked surprisingly alert. The only clue to her eighteen-hour day was the wrinkles in her lab coat.

"I saw your light," she said.

"I was studying the seed's plumbing. I have no idea how this thing functions or even if it functions."

"Have you read the report on COBIC infestation?" asked Kathy.

"You mean that COBIC was found in only nine percent of the New Jersey victims?" he asked.

"Yeah, that's in the report; but there's something else I noticed that could explain why it's only nine percent. The answer's freezing temperatures. All the victims with traces of COBIC were found in frozen conditions. All the victims that didn't have COBIC were in warm conditions. In New Jersey, we found COBIC in all the victims that were outside in the cold. Victims that were in heated rooms had no COBIC. I am betting that COBIC was present in all the victims. We just couldn't find it because it was already gone."

"It can't be that simple," said Mark.

"I've checked every victim we have records on. The pattern holds up one hundred percent."

"Okay… let's say the pattern is real. How does this help us?" Mark shook his head. "Every lousy clue we get adds confusion."

"I've been thinking about it," said Kathy. "The only thing I've come up with is that COBIC is getting trapped in frozen layers of skin while exiting the victim's body. It's crazy. It's almost like the microbes are trying to flee the scene of a crime."

"Now you're starting to sound like a lunatic," said Mark. "Welcome to club paranoia. Remember when I said almost the same thing about them trying to escape?"

Outside, the dawn sky was drifting from black to gray. The parking lot lights were still on. Mark knew without looking the lot was over half full. Kathy rose and walked over to stare out the window. Mark saw her reflection in the glass. Discomfort showed on her face as if she were fighting some internal battle.

"I've got something that will make you think I'm crazier than you are," said Mark. "I've watched COBIC swimming and, I swear to you, once in awhile they seem to move in a synchronized way like a school of fish. It's got to have something to do with those seeds."

CNN Breaking News music came faintly from the television. Several times an hour there was some breaking news story that wasn't very breaking. Mark glanced at the screen out of habit. His vision was a little fuzzy. The news story was a live-feed from Los Angeles. In the background were palm trees illuminated by floodlights and an entrance to some kind of military base. A female reporter was standing with a microphone. It was still hours from sunrise on the west coast. Mark stared at the image dumbly for several seconds until his brain managed to command his fingers to turn up the volume.

"What is it?" asked Kathy.

Mark didn't answer. He couldn't speak. His hands were trembling. Kathy walked over behind his desk to stare at the screen with him. The reporter sounded like she was talking about New Jersey, but the caption read Los Angeles. The reporter was at a military airfield. A group of helicopters was lifting off, their strobe lights flashing as they disappeared into the darkness. Kathy's pager started beeping.

"....All power has been lost along with telephone and most radio communications. The military is preparing to deploy in a sixty-mile radius around the city. The deployment line will extend north to Santa Barbara, south to Newport Beach, and as far inland as Pasadena. This includes half of L.A. County. Initial reports are disturbing. By all accounts, this kill zone may exceed New Jersey by two or three times in landmass with a potential of ten times the number of fatalities. Over twenty million people live in the affected area. We have a team of reporters standing by to accompany the Army and Red Cross once they are ready to move in to aid survivors."

Carl Green wandered into the office wearing a bathrobe. One side of his hair was matted from sleeping on it. His eyes looked haunted.

"I've just gotten a call from our San Diego office," he said. "The unofficial word is that this one's going to make New Jersey seem like a practice run."

"Carl – Think!" hissed Kathy. "Mark's family's in L.A."

I've failed them, thought Mark. His eyes were flooded with tears. He thought about his nightmare of a ghost city. He thought about Mary and Julie. He started to dial the phone but stopped halfway. Gracy, what about Gracy? He imagined her body lying in the street. His face tightened into a mask that would prevent any more hurt from getting in. He wondered if this was the moment he would go insane. The CNN reporter was saying something. Mark's head tipped to one side.

"What?" he mumbled to the screen.

The news had to be a mistake. Maybe he could wake up now? At some odd level of detachment, he watched as his mind grasped, like a small cornered animal, at delusion… at denial… at anything to shut off this incoming reality he could not accept.

2 – Dobbins Air Force Base, Atlanta: November

Mark tightened the safety harness around him. The Air Force combat cargo jet was jammed with FEMA personnel, soldiers, and Red Cross supplies. Military transport was the only way into or out of the Los Angeles area. All commercial flights had been banned.

The cabin was claustrophobic; there were no windows. Seats were bolted to the floor facing inward with their backs against the fuselage. They had been waiting on the runway for over an hour. A moment ago, the plane had lurched forward. Finally, something was happening. Mark could feel the aircraft jouncing along. They were making some kind of turn. He hated flying. He realized that not being able to look out only made it worse. He glanced at Kathy. She was half asleep. Without warning, the jet throttled to full power and clawed its way into the air. They climbed at a steep angle, metal compartments rattling, engines roaring. There was no attempt at matching the smooth ride of a commercial airliner.

"I hate this," he muttered. His voice was lost in the drone of engines.

Kathy was asleep. Mark wondered how she could do that. He was just as tired, but there was no chance he would catch up on sleep here. He stared at her face. She looked calm, so out of place amid the military equipment and soldiers.

He looked away. He could feel the unheated cabin growing colder. He thought about where they were heading. He imagined smoldering ruins and mobs of people growing savage. In so short a time, the world had changed. Overnight reports had come in describing in lurid detail over a hundred thousand dead in Los Angeles. The entire world was in shock and mourning and fear of contagion. France had closed its borders; the remainder of Europe was expected to follow. As it stood right now, there had been no word from Japan, or Korea, or China, nothing... international calls were not even getting through.

Mark pulled out a pint bottle of vodka from his coat and took a long drink. The cheap vodka was the only liquor he'd been able to find on his way to the airfield. He twisted the cap back on and put the bottle away. How had things gotten this far out of control so fast?

The world he'd known was gone. The new one reminded him of an old man who'd given up the fight and was waiting to die. The *Los Angeles Event* was now being called the big one. A month ago, who would have guessed that it wasn't going to be an earthquake that swallowed the Southland alive? He studied the soldiers who were checking their weapons. One had his rifle in pieces and was coating the inner workings with oil. Every face he glanced at had an air of confidence mixed with unasked questions.

Mark tortured himself with how useless he'd been to his family and Gracy. Why hadn't he done something to get them out of Los Angeles? Working in Atlanta, he'd scarcely thought of them until this had happened and now it was too late. In the past day and a half, he'd tried calling more times than he could count. The lines were scrambled, nothing worked. He had no idea if they were dead or alive.

Mark pulled a secure PDA phone from his pocket. The device had been issued to him just before leaving the CDC. It looked like a normal PDA phone but allowed him to make secure calls and access the Defense Department net and Secure Net as easily as the Internet. He'd been told the dual mode wireless connection worked worldwide at high speed and could also automatically connect to the Defense Department's higher speed wireless network when the handset was in range of military access points. All that mattered to Mark was that wherever he was in the world, this thing allowed him to stay in touch using e-mail, voice, and web. He looked at a display listing e-mails and phone messages. The LCD was empty except for a "sex with slutty college girls" spam which had snuck through the filters. Disgusted, he deleted it.

Hours ago, he had begun calling friends who lived outside the quarantine line. He'd reached Donna Brooks who had a house in Ventura country. It felt like years ago that she'd introduced him on that rainy day to Commander Jack Harris. It was because of his decision to listen to Harris that Mark hadn't been there for those he loved. Donna was crying when she answered the phone. She'd lost her son. The call had ended with Mark not knowing how to comfort her.

What kind of god created a world like this? Mark noticed a soldier staring at him. The soldier looked so young. He could have been a teenager. Mark looked into his eyes. There was no emotion, only a willingness to do what he was told – and questions, so many questions. Mark sensed the young man regarded him as a figure of authority, someone who knew what was going on, someone who knew what they were flying toward. Mark had no answers. The young man finally looked away.

The warriors of our county, thought Mark, the protectors of our moral decline – so innocent and so lethal. They would go where they were told and do whatever was asked of them. Too bad the morality of the world's leaders was not worthy of the trust and sacrifice of these young men and women. Too many leaders were obsessed with gaining power and money. So much energy was squandered inventing better ways of slaughtering each other just to steal the other's shiny beads and women and oil. What had mankind given the world? Hydrogen bombs, exotic chemical agents, and anthrax letters... Humanity was a mess! We kill off a new species every day and replace their habitat with life sustaining concrete. Perhaps we had indeed earned our well-deserved extinction. The universe would be a better place without us. Mark felt like he was poison to himself. How ironic that the tool of god bringing this prophesied ruin had turned out to be a lowly microbe.

Mark's throat felt dry. He got out his bottle of vodka. He could almost taste the warmth. Kathy touched his arm as he started to raise the bottle to his lips. He stared at her. He looked directly into her eyes. He noticed for the first time they were brown. Her gaze was unblinking and strong. Her touch was light. He suppressed a powerful urge to kiss her and then felt disgusted with himself. Gracy could be dying somewhere alone.

"We're going to be there in a few hours," said Kathy. "You're not going to be any good to your family if you're drunk."

Mark took a swig of vodka anyway. He struggled a little to hold it down in his stomach. The liquid had been his only lunch.

"Thank you for all the concern," he said. "Now, butt out."

Kathy seemed unfazed. Mark felt a heat on his face.

"I've arranged for a helicopter at Camp Pendleton," said Kathy. "I was told the roads are solid traffic jams. The helo pilot has clearance to fly anywhere we want. I've had your home address and your ex-wife's address radioed to him."

Mark stuffed the bottle into his pocket. He felt sick. He closed his eyes for a moment and tried to compose himself. She was trying very hard to help him. Why was he fighting her?

"I'm sorry," he said. "I didn't mean to be so defensive. I'm grateful for all the strings you're pulling. Don't think for a moment that I didn't hear Green taking his pound of flesh. He didn't want you going to L.A. before the military had complete control and he sure didn't want you taking me."

"It'll work out," she said. "Carl can be a little too careful at times. I need to investigate and that can't be done by remote control. If I'm going to understand what's happening, I need to see this killer up close and personal."

"Investigations, huh..." he said. "And none of this had anything to do with helping me?"

Kathy smiled. She looked good with that smile instead of the clinical intensity that at times seemed to be a natural part of her being. Mark was convinced the emotional detachment she so often displayed was the very tool that allowed her to successfully wrestle death to the mat. He envied her resolve. At this moment, he had no idea where that kind of strength came from.

~

Mark walked outside alone. The rollup door of the aircraft hanger was large enough to drive a commercial jet through. The sun was directly overhead. He was wearing the red colored NBC suit that both he and Kathy had been issued. He'd been told the suits were lighter weight next generation military gear. The suit didn't seem very light. Following instructions, he'd left the hood and gasmask off. Even though the temperature was sixty degrees outside, the suit was already causing him to sweat. Kathy walked outside to join him and together they started off across the airfield. Their pilot greeted them at the helicopter, a huge red and white Coast Guard bird normally used for sea rescue missions. The pilot also wore a red NBC suit with his mask off. The helicopter's markings were unusual and included a large red triangle inside a red circle. The same markings were also on the hanger.

Inside the cabin were more passengers. The door slid shut on rails. The jet engine's whine grew to painful levels as the overhead blades started to whoosh. The noise was deafening even before takeoff. A Marine Sergeant helped Mark and Kathy get into the rest of their gear. First came a pair of noise canceling headphones. A microphone jack was plugged into Mark's gasmask; then, both the microphone and head-phones were plugged to a radio clipped to his belt. Despite the din, with the headphones on he was able to hear again. The masks had clear stick-on labels with a barcode, plus name and rank, affixed to the top of the faceplate. Mark's had his last name and the words 'Civilian-Scientist.'

Abruptly, the vehicle lifted into the air. The sensation was eerie, and felt as if some levitation field was working on them. Mark's ears popped. He glanced out the window and saw the ground shrinking be-neath him at a surprising rate. The view gave him a sense of vertigo more powerful than anything he could have imagined. The pilot's voice came over the wireless intercom.

"I've just been given clearance to throttle up to full cruising speed. For you ground-grunts that's about a hundred and ninety-five miles per hour. We should be at the Santa Monica LZ in about thirty minutes. Enjoy the ride."

The Marine Sergeant continued his instructions to Mark and Kathy. He showed them how to pull up the drawstring hood and seal it firmly around the gasmask with a kind of peel and stick adhesive. He explained how to monitor the operation of the air filtration gear and suit pressure.

"There's a blower inside the filter pack on the back of the suit. It's not just there to supply you with clean air. It's there to keep the suit over-pressurized in case of an accident. If your suit has a small rupture, you'll have plenty of time to repair the damage before the positive pressure is lost and outside air gets in. If the rupture is large, then you're screwed. This NBC rig is as advanced as it gets, but it can't work miracles."

"So, Sergeant," asked Mark, "What happens if this marvel of en-gineering fails and some polluted L.A. air gets to me?"

"Well, then you get to stay with the rest of the Angelinos for the duration. Tent-city-time. Standing orders are: no one who's exposed leaves the zone in a vertical state of being."

The ride was surprisingly smooth. Mark had expected some kind of up and down shimming from the lift of the rotor blades. He gazed out at the landscape. He guessed their altitude was about a mile up. The terrain looked like a huge patchwork quilt of urban construction. Army Blackhawk helos crisscrossed the air below them as if following a master plan. In the distance, he could see columns of smoke rising from Los Angeles. The apocalypse had come home. He sensed pockets of death as they passed over them. He closed his eyes and felt in the cavity of his body horrible voids growing and then receding. The voids were scattered across the landscape like blotches of winter cold amid the warm sun. He'd read reports that the plague had hopped across the basin like a killer tornado. There seemed to be clear dividing lines where people had survived or died. The pattern was difficult to explain, but there was actually more uninfected area inside the zone than infected.

The helo took up a northerly course following the San Diego Freeway. Mark began to recognize the terrain. Cars were bottled up on the roadway. Exits were blocked. Most of the vehicles looked abandoned. Mark wondered how many of them held decaying corpses. The world's largest road system had turned into a mausoleum.

After reaching the halfway point, Mark began to relax and almost tolerate the ride. The downtown buildings of Los Angeles grew in detail. What had been at first fuzzy needles in the horizon, were now discernable buildings. He noticed the highways were clear up ahead, then, saw the reason: a formation of Army tanks fitted with oversized bulldozer blades. He watched tiny colored squares – Mercedes and Chevies – being crumbled together into drifts of metal. The helo was losing altitude. Soon they were skimming buildings and trees at no more than a few hundred feet. Their speed, previously masked by altitude, was now unnerving. They whisked over a ring of camouflaged Army trunks. A dozen bonfires raged in the center. This was the source of one of the columns of smoke he'd seen. Men in red NBC suits were carrying stretchers toward the flames.

Mark tried to blot the image from his mind. An afterglow from the fire remained in his retinas. He tried to think about all the things he and his daughter had done together – the zoo, the beach – there would be more in the future. There had to be. He saw the Pacific coastline growing and, with it, his anxiety. The buildings and concrete of Santa Monica ended abruptly at a blue ocean. He could pick out the street his family lived on. The helo pitched backward in the air as it decelerated to a hover. Below them was a Von's Supermarket. The parking lot had been converted into a helipad. They descended and touched down with a jolt.

It felt good to be standing on the solid ground. Mark turned to help Kathy from the open hatch. Her knee had been bothering her. She stumbled a little and ended up against his chest. He almost lost his balance with her. Their faces were pressed together with plastic visors separating them. He could only see her eyes and the upper half of her cheeks. The rest of her face was hidden behind parts of the gasmask, but her eyes managed to communicate a deep feeling of unease. She took a step back.

A man's voice came over the intercom headphones. Mark had difficulty figuring out which direction to look.

"Freedman and Morrison," said the disembodied voice, "behind you."

Mark turned and saw a man in a red NBC suit. The faceplate's label had the abbreviation for a Navy Lieutenant and the last name of Peters.

"Please follow me. I've arranged for a driver and vehicle."

The Humvee had gotten them to within a few blocks of his old house. The road was blocked with an overturned Federal Express truck. The back was opened like a huge wound. Torn open packages were scattered across the road. Their driver stopped the Humvee. Mark opened the door with his gloved hand. He started walking and then was soon running down the street. He heard Kathy calling for him to wait over the radio intercom. He couldn't stop himself, he began running faster.

At the corner he glanced back to see if she was behind him. She wasn't trying to keep up but was following. There was a noticeable limp on her right side. He heard the driver saying something over the radio but ignored it. He was running again. His rubberized boots landed on the pavement with a slapping sound. The suit was difficult to move in. It was almost like the material was tugging back at his limbs.

Mark stopped running in front of his old house. He was drenched with sweat. Julie's car wasn't in the driveway. He hesitated at the front door. A trellis of ivy fluttered in a silent unfelt breeze. The suit cut off all sound and sensation from outside. Memories washed over him. His breath was returning to normal. A drizzle of perspiration ran down his face. He couldn't reach inside the visor to wipe it away. A vague aching began in his temples as he turned the doorknob. The door was unlocked but shouldn't have been. The door swung in, revealing a growing view. The room looked normal. He'd expected mayhem. He walked inside. His eyes were searching for signs of life. Nothing had been disturbed, but there was a building sense of desolation. This was a house of ghosts. He knew deep in a hidden part of his heart they were dead. In the kitchen there was a half empty cup of coffee in the sink. On the rim was an imprint of red lipstick. He touched the stain with a gloved finger accidentally smearing it. Tears welled up in his eyes. He smeared the remainder of the imprint away with his thumb. She was gone.

"They're not here," he said over the intercom.

Minutes later, Mark was running along the block yelling hello and banging on every door he passed. No one answered. He was at the end of the street. Someone had to know what had happened to his family. He needed to find out. Not knowing was sending him into a panic. Across the street at a house where he'd knocked, he saw a young couple staring at him through a front window. He crossed and knocked on their door again. When they didn't answer, he went to the window. They continued staring at him through the glass.

"I'm not going to hurt you," he yelled. "I need to ask you a few questions."

They stared right through him as if he wasn't there. Mark then noticed the young man was holding a handgun at his side. The weapon was pointed at the ground. Mark went back to the door and started pounding with his fists. His vision burned with their image. What was wrong with these people? He took a step back to kick the door in. Someone touched his shoulder. He spun around. Kathy had caught up with him. She picked up his gloved hands and examined them, turning them over. Mark looked at his hands at the same time. Across the heels were smears of green paint from the door, but nothing was ripped open.

"Maybe Julie and Mary were evacuated?" she said. "We should look for them at the shelters."

Mark stared at the people in the window.

"They can't hear you," said Kathy. "No intercom."

Mark untangled himself from her hands and walked away. He was surprised at the violence that had been inside him. What would he have done once he'd gotten in that house? Would he have tried to beat an answer from them? For the first time, he noticed the burnt hulk of a car that was sprawled across the sidewalk. He must have walked around it on his rampage down the block. How could he have missed it? Kathy was keeping pace next to him as he headed back toward his old home. A lone seagull drifted in the air.

"I don't think they were evacuated," he said.

"What makes you say that?"

"My gut. I know they ended up in one of those bonfires."

"Stop it! They could be at a refugee shelter or with friends. They could be anywhere."

"Mary's room still had all her toys. Nothing was packed. Her favorite dolls were scattered on the bed. It was like they'd be coming home at any moment, but I know they're not."

"You don't know that," said Kathy.

"The front door was unlocked. Julie would never leave the house like that."

"There's no telling how quickly they might have had to get out."

Mark stopped in front of his old house. He gazed at the olive trees that had been a part of his and Julie's life. He knew it was the last time he'd see this place. His stomach felt empty. The front door was half open. He went in then came out a moment later with a piece of paper and some tape. He wrote a short note and taped it to the door. Some part of him deep inside hoped it wasn't pointless.

The helo lifted off and headed south along the coast toward Venice Beach. Kathy had the helo's radio patched through into the phone system. She was busy exercising her clout as the CDC's chief on site. Mark listened as she talked. She had someone named George Gallo on the line. He was the deputy director of the local Red Cross operation. They apparently had a growing list of survivors which had not been made public yet. Kathy gave the names of Mark's family and Gracy. Mark heard the sound of a computer keyboard being worked. There was silence for a minute or two.

"Sorry, they're not on the list," said Gallo. "But that doesn't mean much. Right now we only have about three percent of the survivors entered into the database."

"Do you have a list of identified bodies?" asked Kathy.

"I've already checked. They're not listed there either, and that list is far more current than the other one. We have photographs of everybody that's been found and cremated; about a third have no names. You're welcome to go through the stacks of photographs."

"Thank you for all the assistance," said Kathy. "I'll get back to you about the photos."

Mark stared out the window at the Pacific Ocean. He'd heard every word, but gave no indication. Photographs of ghosts, the idea of going through those images looking for faces he knew made him feel dead inside. The helo slowed over a stretch of beach and began to descend. His house was a block away. The helo rotated during its landing, giving him a three hundred and sixty degree view.

Mark slid the door open and jumped into the sand. He'd never seen Venice Beach this empty. The place appeared frozen like the still shot of a postcard. He had to look closely at the palms to see their leaves moving and know this was real. He turned toward the ocean and watched the waves in complete silence. Not far off the coastline was a huge Navy aircraft carrier. The gray vessel had helicopters flying in a circle around it. One lifted off from its tail. Venice was the most California of beaches. It was a place where girls in bikinis roller-skated on the strand while sidewalk musicians played for dollars dropped into an open instrument case. The world had come to an abrupt halt. He glanced up toward the alley that ran behind his house and began walking. Wind blew a paper cup along the sidewalk.

Mark was not aware how long he had been standing in front of the outside door. This no longer felt like his house. He was staring at a clear plastic envelope stapled to the door. Inside the envelope was a death certificate. He was empty. His skin was cold. The certificate included a photocopy of the decedent's driver's license. The photo was Gracy before she'd cut her hair. Mark was having difficulty breathing. He recognized the symptoms of mild insulin shock, but didn't care. He finally managed to turn the key he'd brought with him. The deadbolt released. The door swung opened on its own. There were tracks of mud leading in across the carpet. He hadn't noticed until this moment that Kathy was with him. Her hand was on his back. He wondered how long she'd been there.

In the living room, Mark knelt down to pick up a newspaper crossword puzzle. Gracy had been working on it. She always did them in pencil first. Her box letters were as perfect as typeface. For a moment, she was real to him. They were on the roof sipping margaritas. The newsprint slid from his fingers and fluttered to the ground like a dying bird. He wanted to be with her. He wanted to say how sorry he was that he'd failed her. What was the point? He thought about Mary when she was three and just learning to swim. How she laughed in that water. He couldn't bear to leave the memories behind. He wanted to stay. He couldn't breath. He started to undo his hood. Kathy struggled with him. She was screaming for him to stop. He tried to push her off. She was strong. He couldn't get free of her grip. He twisted sideways yanking loose.

"Stop it!" she yelled.

He raised his hand to strike her. She brought up her arms to shield her face. He didn't move. He was breathing hard. Each breath carried with it fresh pain. He squeezed his eyes shut. The tears burned like an acid that cut him to his core.

~

The helo lifted off creating a storm of sand. Mark had a shoebox in his lap. Inside were photographs. Memories were all that he had now. He stared at Kathy and saw tears running down her cheeks inside the mask. Seeing her cry made him feel worse but also oddly better. Her tears were comfort because he was not completely alone. The helo took up an Easterly course. They were heading inland toward a refugee camp to drop off passengers then back to the clean zone.

The Marine Sergeant was giving instructions to Kathy on how to drink water through a straw built into the gasmask. Mark tried using his. The straw led to a sealed canteen on his hip. The water tasted good. He drew on it for minutes on end. He hadn't realized how dehydrated he'd been. Kathy returned to the seat next to him. Light from a late afternoon sun spilled through the side windows in pail yellow rays. Bits of dust swam in the light.

"You know, we used to ride our mountain bikes on the strand almost every day," he said. "Gracy was always a little faster. She always had to be in the lead. She had to do everything first."

"It's not your fault," said Kathy.

"I know. Sometimes we'd put the bikes in an old pickup I own and head for the mountains, the Sierras mostly. We'd bring a tent and go so deep into the forest that it felt like we were the only people alive. It was good between us..."

"I'm so sorry."

Mark watched as the refugee shelter came into view. The shelter was a vast landscape of tents next to a highway that was backed up for miles with buses waiting to unload. He had listened to a conversation between Kathy and some Army doctors who were heading to the shelter. These doctors were clearly dedicated and a better breed than most people. The shelter was a few miles inside the Eastern edge of the quarantine line. Almost thirty thousand people were already warehoused in this tent city. The old, the young, the hopeful, and the distraught were mixed together; and like all colors of paint blending into a single color, the result was a dismal gray that Mark could see even before they began their descent to the helipad. The land in every direction for countless miles was open desert. The shelter was divided into a clean and dirty zone. A double fence of razor wire and armed guards separated the two worlds. In the small clean zone, pressurized rubber tunnels formed passageways from one inflatable structure to the next. It was considered safe to remove NBC suits inside the sealed and filtered environment of the unsoiled part of this little hell; but once a suit was removed, the person was banned from leaving the quarantined area for the duration. Everyone working at the shelter had to remove their suits if for no other reason than basic human necessities.

The helo lifted off immediately after the doctors had disembarked. The doctors would be there for the duration. Mark looked down and saw faces of survivors staring up at him. They were like newly arrived prisoners in a concentration camp. His heart broke as he scanned the rapidly shrinking faces for Julie and Mary. He was deserting them. They could be there right now. What was he supposed to do? Santa Monica, their home was being evacuated. If they were anywhere, they'd be in one of these places. Red Cross workers were collecting names and notifying relatives. If Mary and Julie were alive, he'd know where they were soon, and then he'd use every scrap of coercion to get them out of refugee hell or join them.

The sun was gone. The helo vibrated as it flew through the darkness. They had crossed over the southern quarantine line a few minutes ago and were over what the solders were calling *safe-land*. Running lights strobed red through the windows. Mark had decided he needed to go through the stacks of photographed bodies that the Red Cross was compiling. He needed to know if there was reason to hope. Without hesitation, Kathy had made arrangements to get him there this evening.

The pilot announced they would be landing at a quarantine control point momentarily. Mark could feel the distance between himself and the ground vanishing as if in freefall. There were clicks as landing gear locked into place. He saw hangers, various small buildings, and a control tower as they touched down. The suit intercom switched on with a recorded message that was apparently coming from the airfield.

"This is quarantine control site Baker-Zulu-Three. All personnel are ordered to disembark for decontamination processing. Proceed to the building with the red triangle inside a circle designation over the hangar door."

The message repeated as Mark walked toward the hangar. Chain-link fencing with razor wire on top funneled everyone toward the hangar entrance. The entire area was flooded with powerful lights. It was brighter than daylight but the artificial lights made everything seem flat. At the hangar, sentries in white NBC suits stood on the other side of the fence, the clean zone. They were armed with machine guns. At the entrance, a sign directed women to one side and men to the other. Mark walked into the men's area which was tented off with thick semi-transparent plastic sheeting. Inside, he saw more armed guards but these were in red NBC suits. There were bins overflowing with discarded suits, clothing, and shoes. A large hanging sign gave instructions to disrobe. Naked men were walking into a sealed room up ahead. On the other side of the plastic sheeting, Mark saw the vaguely distinguishable shapes of women doing the same as the men.

Marked pulled off his mask and headphones. The noise of the world returned. The hangar was filled with the clattering and spraying sounds of a carwash. A loudspeaker played a recorded message.

"Remove all clothing and personal items. Place the NBC, all cloth-ing, and footwear into one of the laundry bins. Place your personal property, no clothing allowed, into an empty plastic bin, firmly seal the lid, and fill out the tag on the lid with your name and serial number or social security number. Your personal property will be forwarded to you as soon as it has been processed."

"No deposit, no return," said a guy in front of him in line.

Mark looked at his box of photos. He was suddenly terrified of losing it. He tried to back out of the line, then stopped. The hangar door had been sealed behind them. There was no way out; and even if there was a way out, what choice did he have?

With his heart beating in his throat, Mark snapped shut the plastic bin containing all that remained of Gracy. There was a rubber conveyor belt that looked like a luggage handler used at airports. He placed the bin on the conveyor and watched as Gracy slid away. Up ahead was a room filled with portable stall showers and sinks. He could see people gargling and spitting. There was a folding table stacked with abrasive sponges, small bottles of mouthwash, nose drops, and instructions. The air smelled strongly of disinfectant. Mark recognized the odor. It was like Lysol; ingredients: phenol mixed with alcohol. Great, he thought. A large red sign warned not to swallow any of the decontamination spray. A recorded message started to play.

"When ready, close your eyes, press the green start button, and step into the decontamination spray. Do not open your eyes at any time during this process. Injury may result. You will remain under the decontamination spray for five minutes. The spray will then change to water and you will hear an announcement confirming the change. You will remain under the water for two minutes. During the decontamination spray only, you will vigorously rub your skin with the TACM sponge. You must drop the sponge immediately when the water rinse commences. If you do not follow the procedure exactly, an attendant will order you to repeat the process."

His new gasmask smelled of fresh rubber. Following directions from an Army clerk who was providing flight information, Mark walked out a door on the opposite side of the hangar. The airfield in front of him was busy. Above his exit was a large white triangle inside a white circle. He had on newly issued Army fatigues, underwear, socks, a barcoded plastic identification card on a chain around his neck, and over all of it, a white NBC suit. A sign in the locker room had explained the color-coding scheme: red for going into the contaminated zone and white for leaving. From where Mark stood, floodlights beamed out onto the airfields. Several helos and planes were pinned in the crossfire of lights. He identified the Blackhawk helo he was flying out on by its tail number. The aircrafts and tarmac were shiny with some liquid and a residue of white foam. All the aircraft on this side of the field had a single large white triangle inside a circle painted on their sides. Mark walked toward his Blackhawk. Vapor was rising around him like curtains of fog. Whatever they were using to scrub the aircraft was very strong. He felt odd breathing normally in the middle of what had to be toxic air. The oxygen filters and scrubbers in these suits were amazing. He heard Kathy's voice over the radio intercom.

"Mark?"

Someone tapped his shoulder and startled him. She was right there. The noise suppressing headphones worked too well. It was uncomfortable to miss the sounds of someone walking up behind him.

"That was refreshing," said Kathy.

"How long do you think it'll take before our personal items catch up with us?" he asked.

"You mean our Tupperware... No idea. I think they have bigger things to worry about. Did you know they have a communications problem right now? I tried to ask one of the guards for directions, but their radios didn't operate on the same frequency as ours. I felt like I was trying to talk to a Star Wars storm trooper."

After a short fifty mile ride in the Blackhawk, they were on the ground in a parking lot. Ahead of them was an old elementary school that had been taken over by the Red Cross. After being given permission by the pilot, Mark peeled off his NBC suit. They were like portable saunas. Kathy was right behind him. They left the suits inside duffel bags on the Blackhawk. The NBC gear would be recycled when the helicopter made its return trip to the quarantine control point. Kathy looked at home in the Army fatigues. Mark felt a little odd that now even the clothes on his back were Government Issue; another layer of personal control had been peeled away.

They had checked in at a front desk and were being guided by a middle-aged, male Red Cross volunteer down a hallway lined with lockers toward the back of the school. There was some kind of meeting going on in a gymnasium as they passed. Most of the classrooms had been converted into field offices and were occupied. In a classroom next to the library was where the Red Cross was collecting digital photographs of the dead; there were over a hundred thousand images and the number was continuously growing. The raw images were on optical disks which were not available to the public yet; copies of the photos were printed for public use on four-inch wide strips of paper that were stored inside shoebox-sized cartons. The boxes were stacked on newly erected metal shelves that reached to the ceiling. Several printers were feeding out fresh images of ghosts. There was a small stepladder next to the shelves. A folding lunch table had been pushed up against one wall. On the table was a coffee maker, ashtrays filled with cigarettes, and plenty of space to view pictures of dead loved ones. The room smelled of smoke and something Mark could only describe as despair.

He walked over to the shelves. The side of every box was labeled with a postal zip code and groups of streets from where the bodies had been removed. The Red Cross volunteer had said there were over two thousand boxes and a new one was added every half hour.

As if the printed strip was soiled, Mark gingerly lifted the first image from the first box. He stared at it and, to his surprise, felt nothing. The anticipation was gone and reality was not as terrible as he'd imagined. The photo was of a middle-aged woman. She was lying on a drab green tarp. There were four images: one full length and then headshots of front, left side, and right side. She was dressed in a skirt and a silk blouse. Her name was printed on the bottom – Ann Martin; below that was her driver's license number. She looked like a nice woman, someone who hadn't deserved to die. He picked up the next image, a young woman. She had short blonde hair and was dressed in a t-shirt and jeans: Jane Doe, no driver's license number.

The room had grown hot. Mark stepped down off the stepladder with another box. After failing to find Mary and Julie on neighborhood streets, he began checking every location they might have been. He'd lost count of how many boxes he'd gone through, and how many faces he'd stared at. The parade was having a dehumanizing effect. Some people looked like they were sleeping while others were disfigured from death. The worst ones had been in auto-accidents. Some of them were charred and barely recognizable as human, but oddly they had become easier to look at than the unmarred. Death was supposed to be unsavory. The photos that disturbed him the most were the ones that looked at peace. How could they have been murdered and only look like they were sleeping? He was becoming haunted with a feeling that something supernatural was working inside this plague.

After almost two hours of searching, Mark felt lost. Mary's and Julie's images were not among the ghosts, but he was having difficulty accepting the possibility that they might be alive. With an odd feeling in his chest, Mark climbed up the ladder one last time and pulled out a box for Venice Beach. He had glanced at its label dozens of times while searching the other boxes. This box was the only one with his zip code and street name. He knew what could be inside.

Mark sat down at the table and opened the lid. He wasn't sure why he was doing this. Maybe he just needed to feel greater pain? Near the top of the stack was Gracy. Her eyes were closed. She was wearing a beat up sweatshirt that she used when hanging out around the house. Her expression was serene. She was one of the peaceful dead. It almost would have been better if she'd appeared upset or pained. He looked closer trying to understand what it was like to die. He started to sob.

Mark didn't stop sobbing until his body was empty of the pain. His face was slick with tears. His breathing was still ragged. He looked at Gracy once last time. He noticed her arms were oddly positioned and realized the obvious fact that someone had posed her. Someone had touched her. He set the picture back into the box and closed it as if shutting a tomb.

He looked down the aisle of shelves. The shoeboxes were tiny coffins. The musty air was difficult to breathe. He forced it into his lungs. This stack of miniature coffins was a symbol of a mass grave for all humanity. Someday, would a historian find his picture inside a box like these? Would there be historians? Would anything human survive?

The time was just after 9:00 p.m. when the Blackhawk set down at Camp Pendleton. A full CDC command post was under construction on the base. They had taken over a large warehouse. Two-by-fours and plasterboard were being erected by soldiers into a maze of walls inside the building. The construction was going on around the clock. A lieutenant met them at the entrance and escorted them to a huge central office space which was the command center.

Faces looked up as Mark and Kathy walked into the bullpen full of desks. Kathy seemed to know everyone there. She made an attempt at introductions, but there were too many people. Mark started to forget the names as quickly as they were given. After the greetings, the lieutenant led them toward a wall of doors. The officer stopped at one that had a cardboard name plaque which read 'Mark Freedman' and opened it. Inside was a fully equipped prefab office and sleeping quarters.

Mark felt both guilty and important that he had a private room. He and Kathy and four others were the only personnel with that privilege. The rooms were small and completely filled by a large metal desk, chairs, an army cot, and a footlocker but this was pure luxury when compared to the alternative accommodations which included sleeping in a nearby barracks and no private space at all.

Mark was weary as he stood at his office door and looked out at the city of desks that filled the command center. There were no windows. The ceiling extended up to the metal rafters of the roof from which hung lights and air ducts. On the far wall was a large mosaic video screen which showed a computerized world map and several smaller screens which contained what looked like real-time satellite feeds. Kathy was in an open area in the middle of the room conducting an impromptu meeting. A ragtag crowd had formed around her. She was issuing orders and people were taking notes.

"I want at least a four-to-one statistical sampling from both healthy and deceased. That means drawing blood from at least 25 percent of the people in refugee shelters and every, I mean every, cadaver from now on. There's to be no cremation before we have our blood and tissue samples.

"Also we just heard from Atlanta CDC that COBIC has been isolated in the spinal fluid of one of the New Jersey victims. This is the first time we've found COBIC inside the nervous system. I can't stress enough how significant this is. I want spinal fluid samples from all the cadavers. Harry, I want you to arrange for spinal fluid samples from volunteers at the refugee shelters. I want people who have been exposed and lost at least one close family member. We have to find out if we need to be concerned about COBIC being in the cerebral fluid of any of the refugees."

"Dr. Morrison," interrupted a young woman. "What if we can't get enough volunteers at the shelters to do a reliable statistical sampling?"

"The entire L.A. basin is under martial law," said Kathy. "We'll get what we need. We have no choice – they have no choice."

Mark went back into his office. He was disturbed by what he was hearing. The people in those shelters had suffered enough. They were already third-class citizens that had lost their freedoms and now they were going to become lab animals. Blood and spinal fluid was the order of the day. How many times would they be forced to submit to medical experimentation? How long would it be until every one of them was ordered to give spinal fluid or something even worse? The discovery of COBIC in spinal fluid was an important link between the microbe and the nerve damage that was the cause of death. He knew for scientific rigor this testing had to be done and assumed the same testing was going on in New Jersey. The entire county was in danger but this was not the way a free and open society was supposed to operate. The most basic rights of the defenseless should never be sacrificed for the good of the healthy.

He slumped into his chair. He tried to rid his mind of everything except the job at hand. He might be the best hope the CDC had at understanding what role COBIC played in this crisis. There was nothing he could do about the abuse of refuges and nothing he could do about locating Mary and Julie before some abuse happened to them.

An IBM workstation with a high-resolution flat screen was set up at his desk. The walls weren't even dry yet, but they had working computers. He logged onto the network and found the BVMC lab online. There seemed to be no delay in accessing data. The government must have leased dozens of dedicate fiber trunks between here and Atlanta.

Mark watched as a SEM image of the golf ball object was loaded on the screen. People were starting to follow his terminology by calling it a seed. The name was appropriate. He was more suspicious than ever that this seed was the carrier of the holocaust. He leaned closer and stared at the internal structures made of silica. The object was unearthly. What was this thing? Days ago, in a more paranoid mood, he'd speculated that it could be some doomsday weapon created by the military or even a rogue state. Maybe terrorists had gotten their hands on it and put it to their own unique kind of use? He knew these thoughts were crazy; but when lacking good ideas, even the bad ones started to seem plausible. He checked his e-mail hoping to find a response from at least one of his colleagues to whom he'd sent the classified images. The only e-mail in his box was from Alan Trune, something about the breeding experiments. Another failure, thought Mark as he clicked on the e-mail.

As he read, Mark subconsciously leaned forward in his chair. This was no failure. Alan had completed Mark's experiments of placing

COBIC in various combinations of field water samples. The idea was a shotgun approach to research, sloppy science, but Mark had been running out of ideas. Pond water containing normal Chromatium Omri had done the trick, sort of. COBIC infected with seeds had still failed to reproduce; that was not the success. The success was that Alan had managed to infect normal Chromatium Omri with seeds. This meant the seeds had reproduced even if the bacteria had not! Alan's e-mail included a link to a video stored on Secure Net.

Mark clicked on the link. The download took almost a minute before the video began to run. He saw a magnified SXM image of COBIC swimming in dirty liquid. The soft x-ray beam's intensity was dialed just high enough so seeds were clearly visible as voids inside the microbe's nuclei. Alan narrated the video. He had taken a census count of the normal Chromatium Omri present in the drop of pond water. Mark watched as Alan released a known number of seed-bearing COBIC into the liquid. The video paused, then started again three hours later. Alan had taken a new census count and found only seed-bearing COBIC. In fact the numbers were almost perfect. With only a two percent error, there was one new seed bearing COBIC for every missing normal Chromatium that had originally been in the drop of pond water.

The video was now showing Alan's method for taking a census of the infected microbes. In superimposed visible and x-ray images, Mark saw Alan herding the light-averse COBIC with a low intensity beam of light. The beam was from a visible laser with no more power than a penlight. The laser was part of the microscope's auxiliary illuminator setup.

Mark was astounded. The bacteria coaxed by the laser were swimming together in a loosely defined herd; non-infected COBIC were left unmoved by the light. How had Alan come up with an idea to do that? Obviously, not knowing something was impossible was a good way to accomplish the impossible. Mark wasn't sure which was more amazing: the reproduction of seeds or that COBIC could be herded with a beam of light. Alan was clearly unaware of the ramifications of this herding phenomenon. For COBIC to collectively respond like that, they had to be much more neurologically evolved than what was considered possible for a bacterium. They were displaying behavior equal to that of a primitive multi-celled animal.

Mark rubbed the sides of his head. There was a throbbing ache in his temples. No matter that more questions were raised than answered, this was a break-though. Reproduction was often the first step in understanding how a disease killed. Side effects from reproduction frequently turned out to be critical factors in the progression of a disease. Knowing that seeds were somehow being Xeroxed was a beginning. The unanswered question was how the seeds were multiplied. The most likely theory was that they grew in the same way as kidney stones. To find answers, Mark needed to capture images of seed reproduction and microbe infection while it occurred. It was too early in the morning to get Alan on the phone in Atlanta. Mark began hammering out a priority e-mail with detailed instructions.

3 – Yosemite National Park: November

The sun was creeping over the mountaintops. The grass was dewy and fresh. In the distance, clouds hinted at an afternoon sprinkle. Then it happened. The kill zone was small and silent. The animals fled in terrified packs as if running from a wildfire. Behind them, the ground was littered with bodies. Some were still moving in the final twitches before death. The epicenter of chaos was a section of forest that had been over-harvested last fall as part of the previous administration's federal partnership with private industry for woodland preservation. In the midst of a clearing, a squirrel ran in circles, chasing itself until exhausted. The little animal slumped onto its side panting. Some kind of palsy racked its body. In minutes, it was dead. The squirrel joined a legion of dead harmless things – mice and woodchucks and raccoons. There was a pond less than a hundred yards to the South. Extending out from the shoreline, an almost perfect semicircle of water was skimmed with a layer of bloated and dying fish.

The sun was strong. The area soon wafted with the smell of decay. Insects arrived to claim their bounty. The air was abuzz with clouds of tiny flying things while, higher up, birds circled unwilling to land and take advantage of the easy meal.

~

Jennifer and Chris worked for the Parks Service as rangers. They'd met on the job and had decided to celebrate their one-year wedding anniversary reliving how they'd met. At first light, they hiked out past the last ranger station to a cabin used by wildlife researchers. There was a fireplace, a potbelly stove on a screened in porch, and a view of untouched fields and mountains. The first snow of the season was late and not expected anytime soon.

The fireplace was crackling. The air was fragrant with dried leaves and wood. The sun was on its downward slope. Jennifer unpacked her clothing. She smiled thinking it would probably go unworn. Chris hugged her from behind. She turned into his arms. They held each other tightly. She loved him with all her soul and thought that if they created new life within all this warmth, it would be so perfect.

Chris got out of bed and went over to his pack. Jennifer watched him, her eyes glancing over the lines of his nude body. She felt her cheeks flush. He returned holding a bottle of champagne.

"I forgot about it," he said. "It's probably warm, but we have to toast us."

"I love you," said Jennifer.

Chris peeled off the wire clamp and started to inch out the cork. The bottle exploded. A warm gush of champagne spilled all over them and the bed. Chris was laughing. Jennifer started laughing. The entire bottle had emptied itself. Still giggling, they embraced with tiny bubbles tickling her skin.

The cabin's porch had a bench and pair of chairs. They had dragged their warm sleeping bags outside at sunrise to use as blankets and lit the potbelly stove. On the knotted planks rested a large plate containing remnants of their breakfast of cheese, bread, and fruit. Jennifer was content reading a book she had brought. The morning sun was spilling down onto open pages. Chris was beside her on the bench daydreaming. His arms curled warmly around her. They were breathing together as if they had blended into a single life. She closed her eyes for a moment and was asleep.

Jennifer awoke with Chris nibbling on her neck. She smiled, pretending to remain asleep. The sun had grown warmer. In the distance was the sound of wind rustling the trees and farther off than that, the sound of a stream. She took a deep breath. There was a powerful odor of bad breath. Chris licked her sloppily across the side of her face. Her eyes grew wide. She didn't feel his body pressed next her. The tongue was too big, the breathing too deep, almost a grumble. Her entire body froze. Her senses became acute. Something very big was next to her on the porch. Her mind ran through the mental list of what type of animal would act this bold. She knew the answer but refused to accept it. Afraid to move and draw aggression, her eyes stared helplessly out across the field. She saw Chris emerge from a crop of trees. He was carrying his fly fishing gear. From half a field away, she saw his expression turn to fear, then panic. He dropped his gear and began running toward her shouting and waving his arms. He was trying to drive off whatever it was.

A large paw shoved her over. Jennifer remained limp, trying to play dead, not even sure if it worked. She saw the animal's muzzle and heavy fur. It was a grizzly bear. A cataract haze covered one of its eyes. The animal was old and huge, maybe six hundred pounds, and it looked insane. Its behavior was unnatural. The bear kept jerking its head as if inflicted with palsy. Jennifer involuntarily sobbed. The animal's eyes narrowed in on her face. The monster had heard her. It knew she was alive.

4 – New Jersey – New York border, November

Sarah opened her eyes. Through the smeared windshield of her car, the sunrise glowed orange and red. Greenwood Lake was over fifty miles away from this forest clearing where she'd parked for the night. The clearing was off a deserted mining road which was little more than a furrow of dirt and small rocks. No guardsmen or anyone else had driven by in the time she'd been here. She opened the car door and crawled out. Ralph watched her for a moment and then put his head down and returned to sleep.

The other day, it had taken her almost an hour to get the car unstuck while anxious that Beer-breath and Acne-face might show up at any moment. Wedging branches and stones under the tires had finally done the trick. She had driven aimlessly for hours, putting miles between herself and those punks before feeling comfortable enough to stop running. She had found detailed hiking maps in a small fish and tackle shop that catered to locals. Her search for supplies had been less successful. All the stores she had stopped at along her path had been emptied of food and water.

Sarah trampled down an overgrown path that ended at a nearby stream. She wore a sweatshirt and jeans. The Beretta was in her belt-pack that was looped over her shoulder. She had a pair of empty Arrowhead water containers – one in each hand. She could hear the sounds of the stream growing louder. The promise of freshness pulled her on.

Sarah ladled up a handful of water and splashed it over her face. The water was clear and cold. She was at the bottom of a trellis of flat stones. The spring cascading over the stones was like a natural fountain. She drew some water into one of the gallon plastic bottles by angling it sideways into the stream. She'd selected a location on the downstream side of the rock trellis where the water would be at its freshest. She dropped in a purification tablet, shook up the bottle until the tablet dissolved, and then tasted a small amount. The natural filtration of stones had left the water pure; the tablet gave it a bitter aftertaste. She drank some more and then began filling the bottles one at a time. She gazed at the broken reflections in the rippling water.

Behind her, the sun vanished within charcoal clouds. Without warning, a chill crawled up her arm and into her spine. It was almost as if a mild electrical current was flowing from the stream. Her fingers released the plastic bottle. River currents immediately snatched it beyond her reach. The world was spinning. She tried to catch her breath. The experience was like the night chills from days ago. Suddenly she understood. This water came from an underground stream. Inside her stomach, she could feel what she'd drunk. The liquid was settling there like a lump of dirty ice chilling her from the inside out. This water was a gift from something evil that lurked in subterranean rivers. She shivered uncontrollably. The spring's purity was an illusion. It had bubbled up from a world without light. She thought of all the death left behind her. A question that was haunting her came again – why had she been spared when so many others had died?

A gust of wind stirred a huge elm tree mixing autumn leaves into the air. Sarah sat on the ground with her back against its trunk. In front of her was a field of tall grass turning winter brown. The clearing would have been a nice place to build a home. She'd been here for hours thinking and planning. The sun had warmed all the dampness from the fallen leaves and grass.

Sarah had reached a calculated decision. In her lap was a pad of paper. She was doodling on it. There was a childishly drawn house with smoke curling from a chimney and a forest leading off into the horizon. Below the drawing was her list of pros and cons. Both lists were long, but the pros had more entries than the cons.

Ralph was busy chasing imaginary rabbits through the field of stalks. He obviously had no idea that big decisions were being reached. Sarah had decided to leave the Nissan behind and hike out through the wilderness between New Jersey and New York State. After her run-in with those National Guard adolescents, she'd given up on the idea of finding a safe road. Just thinking of those creeps weakened her stomach. The only way out of New Jersey was through terrain too dense to patrol. On one of her maps, she'd marked out a ten mile trek through forests into a small town in New York State named Boarburg. She figured that if she and Ralph started out by eleven in the morning, they'd easily reach the town before nightfall.

"Hey Ralph," she yelled.

A huge black face peered up out of the dried stalks.

"Do you think we should go it on foot?"

Ralph barked once then disappeared back into the sea of brown. Either he thought the plan was a great idea or he'd cornered another one of his imaginary rabbits.

~

Using a compass, Sarah had managed to keep off the marked trails and hold a steady northerly course. She was proud of her abilities. The ground was hilly and covered with a thick mat of pine needles. She'd been walking under the mantle of old growth evergreens for the past two hours. The air was heavy with the scent of pine. Some of the trunks were almost two feet thick and straight as telephone poles. The forest was a catacomb of wooden pillars. Without a compass, she might have wandered for days only to end up where she'd started. The evergreen canopy was low, beginning twelve feet above her head. Few scraps of blue sky were visible through it. Dim light had kept brush growth to a minimum, which made walking deceptively easy. Once already, she'd stepped into a hole concealed under a blanket of needles and pine tar. She was lucky her ankle had been spared.

Walking under the canopy gave her a feeling of passage. It was as if she was moving through a cavern that would end in an opening to a new life. There was a warm light at the end of this struggle. She could feel it as strongly as she felt an evil soaking into the ground of her old home.

The first two-thirds of her route would be uphill, no way to avoid it. Sarah's legs were growing sore. The incline seemed mild and was deceptive in its ability to sap her strength. How much farther was it to the ridge? Sarah knew how to measure her progress. She started counting out her strides during ten minutes of walking. Each stride was about two and half feet. When the time was up, the count had reached three hundred and forty – and that meant her progress was far too slow.

"Damn it..." she muttered.

Ralph walking ahead of her disappeared into a clutter of small brush. She'd been hiking for three hours. Multiplying it out was depressing. She'd guessed the distance she'd covered was on the low side, but not this low. She'd gone only about three miles. She was averaging a puny one mile per hour. Her little hike was going to last far longer than she'd planned. At this rate, she and Ralph would be camping in the woods tonight.

Perspiration dripped from her forehead. Sarah had picked up her pace and turned the hike into a forced march. She had to stop, just for a few minutes. She wedged her pack against a tree and leaned back on it. She guzzled water then poured some into a cup for Ralph. He lapped it up then sat down by her feet. She pulled out a granola bar and slowly munched on it. The treetops were filled with birds. Their songs were almost hypnotic. She drifted into a nap of exhaustion.

Sarah awoke startled and disoriented. The light had changed to a stone gray. Her cheeks were damp with tears. Words were still whispering from her lips.

"All dead... everyone dead..."

For several long seconds, she had no idea where she was sitting. She only knew she was scared and that an entire city had been wiped out. Slowly, she gathered up the torn fabric of her dream. In it she'd been a little girl in her daddy's hardware store; but instead of Mount Freedom, the store was in the heart of a huge city. There were rows after rows of buildings that seemed like tombstones. The air was acrid looking with a brownish tint of pollution. Streets were wide and filled with millions of abandoned cars; while the sidewalks had stars embedded in them. Sarah looked down at pine needles stuck to her palms. The needles fell one by one onto her jeans. She recognized the place as Los Angeles. Could the plague have reached there already?

"Stop it..." she whispered.

Another city couldn't have been hit by the plague. She had to stop thinking like this. A chill wandered through her body leaving her weak. Could it be worse than just Los Angeles? Maybe the entire world was gone? The end could happen and she would never know about it in this forest.

Ralph barked. He was a dozen feet away and staring up into a thicket of branches. His posture was tense with aggression. His eyes were locked onto something. A growl came from deep in his chest. His gums pulled back to expose teeth. This was not an imaginary rabbit.

Sarah grew alarmed. She thought about the M16 lashed to her backpack and unreachable. Her hand slipped inside her jacket. Her fingers curled reassuringly around the stock of her Beretta. The weapon should have calmed her, but she was confronting the unknown. She pulled the gun and stood up. Her senses were sharpened to the point of aching. Her chest pounded. Fear was feeding upon itself and growing. Looking up, she scanned the lattice of branches and deep shadows. What was up there? She called Ralph to her side. He glanced at her scornfully and then turned back and continued his aggressive stance.

"Ralph, get over here now!" she snapped.

He hesitated and then came to her side while glancing back every few steps. He circled her legs and turned to face where he'd been look-ing. She patted him. He jumped from her touch.

She heard a loud rustling as if something had leapt from the tree-top. Dried pine needles fell to the floor of the woods. The sounds of the forest returned. Sarah hadn't realized they'd been missing until now; or had they? She looked at Ralph. The tension was melting from him. Whatever had been there was gone. What kind of animal was big enough to scare a hundred and twenty pounds of Rottweiler? Sarah remembered television images of people that had been driven violently insane by the plague. The medical explanation was that the cause was psychological, but what if that was wrong? What if the madness was directly caused by the plague? Could the same thing happen to ani-mals? Her stomach tightened as she thought of that bird in Morristown repeatedly flying into the side of a building as if it had gone mad.

She looked around her. The woods were filled with creatures nature had armed far better than her. She wondered which animal would be the worst to face. The eastern wolf was again being spotted in these hills. An animal like that could hunt anything… and what about black bears? Her nine-millimeter didn't have that kind of stopping power. Even solid hits might only enrage a bear. Blood loss would eventually kill it, but she'd be dead by then. She holstered her Beretta and unlashed the M16. The thought of sleeping in these woods filled her with anxiety. Ralph laid his muzzle against her open hand. Sarah kneeled down to stare into his face. She scratched him behind both his ears.

"I don't know about you, but this place gives me the creeps."

Ralph licked her face. Sarah hugged him and then stood up. The forest was getting darker by the minute. How long had she been asleep? She glanced at her watch. It was almost three. She was relieved that she'd only been out for an hour. It had seemed like much longer. Things felt changed as if months had passed. The woods, Ralph, herself – everything felt different. At first Sarah thought it was endorphins mixed with fear affecting her; but the more she thought about how she felt, the more she realized these were not random feelings. She sensed something instinctual was now guiding her; then she thought about her nightmare of Los Angeles.

Sarah's pace had grown quicker by the hour. She was sweating heavily but wouldn't let up. A few minutes ago, she'd crested the ridge and was now on the long downward leg of her trip. She'd already made it into New York State.

An hour later, the pine trees opened to reveal a valley nestled between two tree covered mountains. In the distance, a stream and a road paired together and then wandered through the valley like two serpents intertwined in courting ritual. Below her, the forest thickened again. The pine trees were gone; instead there was a mixture of maple, and oak, and walnut.

A quarter of a mile downhill, Sarah almost broke into a dance when she pushed aside some branches and stepped onto a footpath. "Hey, Ralph, I love you!" she yelled. Ralph looked at her and then started barking and bounding down the path to check it out.

The trail appeared to have been abandoned for years. Plants were well on their way to reclaiming it as part of the forest. Leaves and branches scratched against her sides as she walked, but it was a pleasure to be on clear ground again. She counted her strides and found she was going at about three miles per hour. Maybe she wouldn't have to spend the night in these woods after all?

The world was dark when Sarah emerged from the forest. She stepped onto a dirt road filled with tire tracks. It was ten o'clock. She should have stopped hours ago and camped, but an ember of fear kept her moving. She clicked off her flashlight and walked by the light of the moon. The map showed Boarburg was approximately two miles away. The road she was on led into the back of a gravel pit. She disassembled the M16 and hid it inside her backpack. She had a story ready in case anyone asked, especially local police. She rehearsed it once more in her mind.

Boarburg was a medium size town. A siren wailed as a police car flew past the front of the Boarburg Inn. A second car followed less than a minute later.

"They've been going wild around here since the quarantine lines went up. Probably another bunch of trouble makers trying to sneak across..."

The lady at the front desk focused her eyes on Sarah. On a corkboard behind the lady was an official looking set of pages released by the CDC. A second copy was on the counter. The document explained procedures and protocols for maintaining the quarantine. In bold characters was a phone number to call if a citizen saw anything suspicious.

Sarah had learned the lady's name was Marge, and Marge wasn't excited about allowing a dog to stay in one of her deluxe rooms. The rate had gone from fifty a night to seventy-five. The lobby was clean but faded. The carpet was worn in a trail from the front door to the stairs.

"I'll take it," said Sarah.

Marge looked as if Sarah had just told her that the earth was flat. Her eyes narrowed. She was a heavyset woman but looked strong, not flabby. Please, thought Sarah, don't let her say no. Sarah was ready to beg. Her entire body was sore. Her left heel was blistered. This was the only place to sleep in town. The idea of being turned out made her eyes water. Ralph curled around her feet. As if on cue, he was playing the role of good dog.

"So honey, you haven't mentioned what you're doing traipsing around at night."

"I was staying out at my uncle's cabin near Bear Falls."

Sarah held her breath and then realized that the lady wanted more. Sarah hated lying.

"Me and my boyfriend were planning on staying for a month. The day the plague hit, my boyfriend had taken the car into town. He hasn't been back since. I don't know what happened to him. I ran out of food. I was scared. I had no choice except to walk out. I left at nine this morning."

"Bear Falls is almost twenty miles from here. You walked all that?" Sarah nodded. Marge appeared to be impressed. The skeptical gleam was gone from her eyes.

"Men can be such unreliable heathens," said Marge.

While shaking her head, Marge turned the guest book around on the counter and handed Sarah a pen.

"It's past supper time, but I've got some hamburger macaroni if it interests you?"

Sarah started to tear up again. The food interested her a lot, but having someone show even the smallest kindness touched her deeply. She wished she could have told Marge the truth.

5 – Camp Pendleton, California: December

Almost half a week had passed since his arrival in Los Angeles. Mark slept late into the day. It was the first long sleep he'd had and was mostly from drugs prescribed by Kathy. This sleep wasn't good sleep, but it was better than insomnia. There had been nothing restorative in it other than the absence of nightmares.

The Army provided fatigues and bedding; everything else had to be purchased at the PX. Mark stood in the men's bathroom, opened a vial of pills, and dry swallowed his first of the morning. Kathy had prescribed the valium two days ago just after he'd gotten the telephone call.

A mirror hung over the basin. Mark leaned closer. His face looked like someone else's with the dark stubble and bags under his eyes. This life didn't feel like it belonged to him anymore. It was as if he'd awoken in a stranger's body and was fighting to hold onto a fading dream of who he used to be. He could pinpoint the exact moment when everything had changed. The moment had been when he'd walked out of the Red Cross building leaving behind those boxes of ghosts. There was a new and horrible world being defined in that classroom commandeered by the Red Cross. Mark stared into his own eyes in the mirror and saw an image of someone dying staring back.

Word had come almost two days ago that Julie's car had been found at the bottom of a cliff on Mulholland Drive. Mulholland was a treacherous road that snaked through the Hollywood hills. Two bodies were in the car, a woman and a young girl, both badly damaged. The woman's driver's license bore the name Julie Freedman. Deputy Red Cross director George Gallo had personally called with the news.

Mark looked at his wristwatch lying next to the basin. It was almost time for lunch. He wondered if it would be canned franks and beans again. It took a conscious effort to continue breathing and eating. He considered going back to sleep. His room was dark. There were no windows. Crawling back into the cot and closing his eyes would have been so easy.

He turned on the water and drenched his face and hair. He retrieved his Army issue shirt from a wall hook and buttoned it while walking toward the bathroom door. The fluorescent lights in the hall hurt his eyes. He put on a pair of sunglasses that had been in his pocket and wandered down the plasterboard tunnels toward food. Every doorway had a very clean military sign identifying the name and function of the room beyond. People had already started using alternate names. The blood chemistry lab had been given the nickname Mosquito Alley. The morgue was called Hotel California. Mark thought about the lyrics from its namesake song by the Eagles. *You can check out any time you want, but you can never leave.* He suspected the dark humor was a way of coping with the horrors of a world that was upended and sinking.

The officer's mess was filled with sounds of silverware tapping on plates, the low murmur of conversations, the creaking of metal chairs. Mark set his tray down at an empty table next to a television. The set was permanently tuned to CNN. Their coverage was providing better global intelligence than the CIA. Eighteen kill zones were now documented across the world; after Los Angels, no more had punished the United States. Overnight, parts of Athens had been heavily hit near the Gulf of Saronikos. Tens of thousands were reported dead. Similar bulletins were coming in from cities along the Loire River in France and from an area just outside of Zagreb near the Sava River. The Los Angeles event still held the record for most killed. Estimates had long ago topped the three hundred thousand mark.

Even through the fuzz of valiums and pain, Mark was still trying to analyze things. It was impossible to completely stop being who he was. He was still a scientist with an insatiable need to understand. He thought about how outbreaks were always near bodies of water: Athens had the Gulf of Saronikos, Los Angeles had the Pacific, there was the Loire River in France, and the Meadowland Swamps in New Jersey. This made sense because COBIC was a waterborne microbe. The CDC should recommend that all water should be boiled throughout the country… or had they already done that? He made a mental note to check on it, a note that he knew would probably be forgotten with many others.

The television continued to babble in the background. Mark tried to eat but couldn't. The bologna sandwich was dry. The coffee tasted like sewer water. He dumped the contents of his tray into a garbage can and left. He wandered the halls in the general direction of his office. Kathy was on her way to the Los Angeles kill zone for the third time this week. He thought about how she'd tried to get him to eat something for breakfast the other day. Her concern reminded him of how Gracy would come down to the lab and drag him out to some restaurant to make him eat. Gracy was gone. He would never see her face or hear her voice again. His eyes burned as if he was about to cry, but nothing came out. He opened the door to his office and went inside.

Mark hadn't heard anything from Alan Trune today. So far, all of Alan's attempts at capturing seed reproduction or infestation on video had failed. Mark was staring at the video of COBIC being herded. The recording had been running all night in an endless loop. With nothing else that he was capable of doing in his limited mental state, Mark started working through the test logs for water samples. The endless lines of numbers made the work tedious and repetitious, but it kept his mind off other things. Every source of water in Southern California was now being tested using COBIC traps that Mark had designed. The idea had come to him while he was writing Alan that first e-mail with instructions for capturing seed reproduction. The trap was elegant and simple. Infected COBIC appeared indifferent to all food items that normally interested it. So the standard technique of setting traps with food didn't work; but since infected COBIC were drawn to non-infected

Chromatium Omri, the non-infected bacteria could be used as bait. Tens of thousands of bacterium traps filled with non-infected COBIC, along with sulfide food, to keep them viable, were placed throughout all the local bodies of water including the beaches. The traps were small test tubes plugged with a microscopically porous membrane, through which bacteria can easily swim *in* but have a difficult time swimming *out*. So far, even though thousands of traps had been collected and replaced, only the results of a few had been tested and they had all checked negative. Testing was a slow process; and the data group was currently so small, the results meant nothing. The experiment itself was too new to even have a baseline for what to expect. The traps might need to be in place for weeks or even months before useful results were obtained.

The building began to sway. Reflexively, Mark looked up at the ceiling to be sure nothing would fall on him. The earthquake was mild. He'd been through dozens over the years. The intensity increased. His computer display started to jiggle. He thought about getting under the metal desk. The sounds of rattling increased from every direction. A coffee mug used as a pencil holder walked off his desk and shattered. The overhead lights flickered.

"Stop it," he yelled.

The motion settled down almost on cue. His breathing slowed but the tension lingered in his body. His legs felt wobbly as he stood. His equilibrium was off. He knew he had a mild case of earthquake sickness. He began checking for damage caused by the quake. His office looked fine except for the pencil holder. He left his office and headed toward a shipping dock to check his samples which were packed for delivery to CDC Atlanta for testing. The thousands of samples were the fruits of a second round of large scale collection from his baited traps.

The dock was empty except for six stainless steel drums large enough to hold twenty-five gallons of liquid each. The drums were stenciled with biohazard emblems. The lids were padlocked. Mark had been present when they'd been packed. The drums were filled with a potent solution of hypochlorite. Immersed in the liquid and suspended within each drum in a nylon cradle was a cylindrical twenty gallon thermos container. The hypochlorite served as a self-destruct mechanism in case anything ruptured or leaked from the thermos. Within the thermos were stacked slabs of dry ice. Each slab was drilled to hold hundreds of small pointed glass tubes called micropipettes. Each micropipette was two inches long, an eighth of an inch wide, and sealed on both ends. The slabs were like beds of deadly hypodermic glass needles. Each pipette was filled with a frozen slurry of sample water, non-infected bait COBIC, and possibly infected COBIC. The hypochlorite was mixed with a florescent dye which made leaks easy to spot. Mark inspected the outer drums for leaks using a handheld ultraviolet light. All the drums checked out. He had no way of knowing if any of the micropipettes were broken without unpacking all the containers, which was impossible unless he delayed shipment. He didn't feel checking inside was worth the effort or the delay.

Without any real purpose, Mark wandered toward the lab where the original test tube traps were kept. The lab had a Level-4 containment classification, which was as high as any place in the country handling deadly pathogens except the BVMC facility. The lab was built from prefab units brought in by the military. A pair of soldiers had just finished inspecting for earthquake damage when he walked into the prep room.

Mark got into a bubble suit and entered the lab without signing the entry log. He hooked up to an air supply line which was dangling just inside. He was alone in the lab. His sample collection was stored inside a vault resembling a meat freezer with a top-opening hatch. He punched in a numeric code and opened the hatch. The temperature was held at just above freezing. Inside were cardboard boxes filled with traps containing raw water samples and bait COBIC. Each test tube trap was the size of his little finger. Each one was hermetically sealed with a Teflon plug and a wire cage much like a champagne cork. He picked up a trap. The label indicated it had been collected from a wetland in Marina Del Rey. He held it up to the light. The liquid looked brackish like bad pond water. The brown-green color was Chromatium Omri.

He felt an insane urge to open the trap and drink it. He could do it. No one could stop him. He could take off his suit in seconds and down the liquid. What would it taste like? In this small glass vial teemed the creatures that had made him famous – and maybe a few of the infected ones that were now well on their way to destroying the world. The sample was probably not infected and wouldn't kill him, but drinking it was certainly a one-way ticket to a refugee shelter for the duration... and what if it did kill him? Why not finish the job a little quicker? There was poetry in that. Civilization was probably doomed and justifiably so. Our species was really little more than a self-centered mob ravaging the body of Mother Nature. Mark swirled the glass test tube and looked closely at the stirred up sediment in the water. He knew he hadn't lost all self-control. He knew he wouldn't really drink it... would he? How many times had he thought about the irony that this lowly bacterium, something little more than a swimming vegetable, was bringing down the most advanced species in the history of the world... then he thought about Mary and Julie and Gracy.

Mark realized he was breathing hard enough to make himself dizzy. It felt like insulin imbalance. His fingers holding the vial were trembling. He set the vial carefully back into the freezer-vault, next to its cousins. He stared at all the traps for a moment longer before sealing the lid. They had been gathered from storm drains, aqueducts, beaches, and thousands of other sites across L.A. County. The fact that virtually the entire county was riddled with sources of unprocessed water was significant. The obvious theory which he'd told Kathy was that the city's water was one huge reservoir for this microbe and the disease which accompanied it.

Mark leaned against the freezer-vault with both hands. The valiums had lowered his blood pressure, anger only made him feel worse, and now his diabetes did feel like it was stirring. He fought to hold his train of thought. He sensed there was something important in it. The problem with proving the water theory was that the sampling times were random, and no traps had been in place before the kill zone. Tests could prove the presence of infected COBIC if they found it, but they could never prove its absence.

Pushing the uncertainty aside, it was still a logical assumption that people were drinking this water after it was contaminated and then became infected themselves or was it a logical assumption? The water could have been infected at the same time and from the same source as the people. There were hundreds of documented cases where a spouse or roommate had left town just before the event and had survived. In some cases, moments of air travel time separated survival and death. They had one case of a jet with thirty percent mortality on the runway, while the jet in front of it with zero mortality had lifted off moments before. They had found not a single case where a spouse or roommate had died while out of town. All this was statistically impossible if simple exposure to contaminated water was the source of contagion. A critical clue lurked here but Mark could not even get a glimmer of it. He just repeated the facts again and again until his brain was too tangled to think.

The bubble suit Mark had used was being sterilized as he headed back to his office. Thoughts of drinking some of the gin that was hidden in his desk drawer were comforting. He could almost taste it. Images of Gracy and Mary and Julie seemed to float with him down the hall.

They were ghosts illuminated by his guilt. He knew their deaths weren't his fault, but knowing made no difference. He hoped the gin would dull the pain.

6 – Camp Pendleton, California: December

The helo was one of the new specially outfitted Blackhawks that were environmentally sealed. Masks and hoods were optional until they landed, but noise cancelling headphones were needed in order to arrive with hearing intact. Kathy was sharing the bumpy ride on this outbound shuttle to Los Angeles. An Army Major sat across from her. He was wearing an unusual NBC suit – it was camouflaged instead of the red and white color coding. The suit was also a different model than what everyone else was using. There was an insignia stenciled on his arm just below the shoulder: a cobra curled around a sword. The emblem was reminiscent of the medical profession's symbol, the Caduceus. On the bottom of the insignia was the word BARDCOM. His name and rank was stenciled on the suit above his breast.

The Major looked up and caught her staring at him. Kathy looked away just as he smiled. He was a handsome man with a large frame and sharp blue eyes. The ride was getting rougher. The pilot had explained they'd be hitting shears caused by Santa Ana winds. Kathy had learned on her second day here that Santa Anas were heat-driven winds that came off the Mojave Desert and turned the Southland into a temporary paradise or prickly hell, depending on their mood.

The helicopter shook. Kathy clamped her jaw tight. Some of the bumps were hard enough to jar her tailbone. Her kidneys were beginning to ache. This was like riding in a truck with a bad suspension. She thought about how Mark would have hated this flight. She hoped he would be alright. She'd been torn between leaving him alone and trying to get him to come along and help. He was so depressed and filled with self-anger. Getting out and doing some work might have been good for him, but it was still very early in the grief cycle. In three days he'd lost his daughter, lover, and ex-wife. He was entitled to his emotions; and besides, it was impossible to help someone who didn't want to be helped. He'd made it clear he wasn't ready to give up his guilt. He was such an asshole the other day when she was trying to coax him into getting some food into his stomach.

"Hello Miss Morrison, I'm Major Kenny Smith," the voice came over her headphones.

Kathy was startled but hoped it hadn't shown. How did he know her name? She keyed the mic on her headphones.

"Have we met?" she asked.

The major smiled and pointed from across the aisle at her gasmask which was in her lap. She looked down. Her last name in block letters was on the faceplate label along with the words 'Civilian-CDC.' She looked at his eyes. He was flirting with her. She became terrified.

"I don't bite," he said. "Unless of course you like that."

"I do... I mean I don't... I'm Kathy."

Damn it, she could feel herself blushing. She was reacting like a schoolgirl. She thought about her last disastrous date, the one she'd ditched at the restaurant. She tried to calmed herself. Did she find this guy interesting?

"What do you do?" she asked.

"I'm a problem solver."

"So am I," she said. "I was wondering earlier what that insignia is for? Boy Scout merit badge? I can't make the letters work."

"So that's what you were looking at. And here I thought you were checking me out."

"No, I'm just fascinated with merit badges."

The major unbuckled his seatbelt and moved next to her, but not too close. A pleasant chill tingled over her skin. She was caught off guard by how gentle his eyes looked.

"The insignia is for my unit. We're specially trained to handle these kinds of situations."

"These kinds?" said Kathy.

"Chemical attacks."

"But this isn't a chemical," said Kathy. "It's bacteriological. We know it's linked to a bacterium called Chromatium Omri."

"Probably true; but the profile matches the chemical warfare scenarios we've been working with, so they activated my unit. But I don't want to talk shop. Tell me, Kathy Morrison problem solver, where are you from?"

"Atlanta. I'm a doctor with the CDC."

"The Peach State. I've never made it out to Atlanta, but I've always heard there are some very nice things in Atlanta."

"Thank you," said Kathy. She was starting to enjoy the attention being lavished on her. "Where are you stationed, soldier?"

"Nellis Air Force base in Nevada."

"Las Vegas, ahuh..."

"And what's that 'ahuh' supposed to mean?" he asked.

"Are you a gambler?"

"Only in love... Would you like to have a drink with me when we get back?"

" I'll give you favorable odds."

"Maybe we can..."

The pilot cut into their conversation over the intercom. Kathy wondered for the first time had people been listening? The pilot announced that they would be landing in ten minutes; time to put on their masks and hoods. Kenny helped her. His fingers touched her cheek and she involuntarily responded with a movement of her chin as if he were going to kiss her. She felt a little embarrassed, but he seemed so natural about it all. It had been a long time since she'd felt the touch of a man like that.

The helo landed and Kenny got out, but not before getting her phone number. Kathy stayed on for the next hop. She was going to a Red Cross facility to interview three specific patients. Something odd and significant had been discovered while sifting data through a computer model. The anomaly was something that might explain why all the deaths had occurred in the space of less than an hour and why not a single additional person had died in days. This contagion hit with a vengeance and then disappeared. At first, Kathy had thought it was possible that survivors of the first hour had built up an immunity of some kind, which would explain why they hadn't fallen victim to the disease a day or two later. This new computer model had put an end to that line of speculation.

The model showed that kill zones were areas of fatal exposure never more than a few hundred yards in diameter, and that large events were actually clusters of these smaller zones stitched together like the cells of a deadly body. There was even more controversial data from the model that suggested some zones might be almost perfect circles. So what at first had appeared to be a single large kill zone in Los Angeles was in fact a cluster of thousands of small zones. The model also showed that the random killing – or sparing – by this disease was actually purely the result of the geographic pattern of smaller zones. Location was the ultimate arbiter of who lived or died. If someone was unlucky enough to be within one of the small zones, the person had a ninety-nine point nine percent chance of dying. If someone was outside the boundary of a zone even by a few feet, they survived one hundred percent of the time. Kathy had compiled a short list of people who had lost everyone they were living or working with and who had survived while surrounded by their dying companions deep inside a zone. They were the exceptions to the geographic grim reaper. She believed she would find another Harold N. in this short list of haunted souls. She was searching for that one person out of a thousand who survived even though the computer model indicated they should be dead. She had other CDC investigators searching out the same kind of anomalous people in New Jersey.

The prior day, Kathy interviewed two survivors who fit the profile; but after careful questioning, it became clear that both of them had to be disqualified. One had lied on the questionnaire, in hopes of getting out of the refugee camp; another had apparently been a hundred feet outside of the epicenter of death at the critical moment.

The helo lifted off as Kathy walked away from it. The rotor wash blew bits of debris past her feet. This was her second trip here. This refugee camp was far nicer than all others she'd visited and included the only fully rated surgical field hospital and mental ward. Like the other camps, this one was also divided into clean and dirty zones. The difference here was that the clean side was almost unused. This camp was mostly staffed by personnel who had been exposed to COBIC. The tents were set up across a closed municipal airfield. Running water, sewage, and electricity were provided in each barrack sized tent. The people here were better cared for, but they displayed the same detachment as in the other shelters. There was the ever-present vacant look in their eyes and lethargy in their expressions. Kathy found herself thinking a shelter is still a prison, only with a kinder name. A barbed wire fence patrolled by guards with dogs still encircled these people.

As she was escorted to the field hospital, Kathy glanced into the open entrances of some of the tents. Most people were sleeping on cots. Those that were awake were playing cards or eating. The very energetic were treading along the miles of footpaths, brief sprints of energy between long hours of nothing to do. It must have been miserable for them to watch red-suited visitors that could come and go at will, the new upper class born of tragedy. Isolated incidents of violent attacks had occurred at other camps. A doctor had been killed in one attack and several people injured in other incidents, which was the reason a pair of armed marines now escorted her through all of the shelters she visited. She tried not to make eye contact with the people. She told herself it was out of respect, but inside she knew it was guilt.

The field hospital was clean and well staffed. Many of the workers were not clothed in NBC suits. Most were either local volunteers or exposed medical personnel; but a few were outside doctors that had chosen to go without protection, as an act of solidarity and a statement that these people were not dangerous.

A Dr. Estevez greeted her at the entrance to a waiting room and took over for the marine guards who remained outside. Dr. Estevez wore no NBC suit. Kathy wondered if he was one of the doctors that had chosen solidarity. She wanted to ask but, out of respect, kept quiet. He wore a headset with an attached microphone. Clipped to his belt was a transmitter tuned to her intercom frequency. He was two feet away and still needed a radio to talk with her. Without the radio, her noise canceling headphones would have reduced even his loudest yells to an indistinguishable mumble. Society truly had two new classes of people: the clean and the unclean. How was she going to interview these people when she couldn't even establish the simple rapport of talking directly with them? Their eyes would touch, but they would never know what she looked like or whether she was smiling. Their conversation would be as intimate as a call from a telemarketer.

Kathy walked into a large room where almost a hundred people were seated in metal chairs. A movie was playing on a big screen television. There were free snack machines with the money slots taped over. Coffee and trays of food were laid out on tables. A few eyes glanced up as she walked in, but most remained glued to the movie. There was a group of children in the front who were sharing a bowl of caramel corn. Dr. Estevez offered her a sheepish smile.

"We've set up a table and chairs in this side room. I'll bring the patients to you one at a time."

Kathy was impressed that he considered all these people his patients. They were all physically healthy, no signs of illness or damage from the plague. The man seemed to hold himself responsible for everyone in the camp.

"I was told you have a large number of severely emotionally disturbed cases here," said Kathy.

"I've done a lot of work with that subgroup of patients. Some of them are so severely disturbed they're comatose and can no longer manage simple bodily functions. We are doing what we can for them."

Kathy looked down at the table. She had no idea how to respond.

"This entire interview process makes me feel terrible," she said. "I feel like an elitist, slumming to ease my conscience. I should be here working closely with these people to comfort them and not here to play some clinical game of Q and A."

"That's ridiculous, Dr. Morrison. It's you and people like you that have the best chance of saving us all. Anyone with half a brain will realize that; and if they don't, if you'll excuse my Latin, cluck 'em."

Dr. Estevez left to bring in the first of the three patients. Kathy found herself thinking the man was a gifted healer. In a few minutes of conversation, he had repaired a gaping wound in her heart.

7 – Washington D.C. December

General McKafferty had flown into Andrews AFB in Maryland on one of the Presidential Jets. There had been no intended honor, just luck that it had been at Nellis Air Force Base getting refitted with new avionics. He'd hitched a ride to Washington on it, saving taxpayer money. The overstocked bar, video entertainment system, and full bedrooms had nothing to do with his decision.

McKafferty was waiting in an antechamber just outside the Situation Room in the White House. He hated waiting and lit up a cigarette. The *No Smoking* sign on the table was a cut crystal stand that had been engraved with gold colored lettering. He stared at it for a moment, then drew in a chest full of smoke and exhaled it toward the sign. A smoke-free White House born from the smoke filled backrooms of politics. What a concept, thought McKafferty. Too bad we couldn't have a politician-free White House and Congress. Now there was something that would improve the health of everyone in the country.

A female aide came in to usher McKafferty into the meeting. He noticed she was young, maybe thirty, and had a nice little figure. She stared at his cigarette. He looked around for an ashtray. There was none. He snubbed it out in a potted plant. The aide looked like she was about to say something but withered as McKafferty rose from the couch. He could tell this was the first time she'd set eyes on a man who was a flesh-and-blood war machine. He turned his man-in-the-moon face at an angle that accentuated its size and then smiled. The woman gave him a wide berth as she held the door for him.

"McKafferty, you old warrior, how have you been?" said Admiral Burk.

The Joint Chief of Naval Operations was acting warmly. McKafferty immediately suspected something was rotten. The JC was not one of McKafferty's biggest supporters.

"The president will be arriving in about fifteen minutes," said the Admiral. "We all wanted to get a preview of your briefing."

McKafferty glanced around the table. He knew everyone there. Heads nodded. All the military representatives were present. The civilians had yet to arrive, late as usual. McKafferty took a deep breath and began.

Forty minutes later, the double doors opened and in walked the President. The National Security Advisor Eric Volloski and the Chief of Staff Martin Ross accompanied him. The officers rose to attention.

"Sit down, gentlemen," said the President. "I'm running late so let's cut to the meat of it. General McKafferty, I'd like to start with your report."

McKafferty got up and took the podium. He had brought a few visuals with him. He knew the President responded to that kind of information. The first image came up on the giant flat screen behind him. The image was a map showing all the kill zones, color keyed by death counts.

"The agent is definitely biological, not chemical. I'll get to those details later. Right now I want to emphasize that there's no intel that this is anything other than a naturally occurring microbe. This was not an engineered weapon, but its effects are better than anything we have in our arsenal. Close proximity kill ratios are near a hundred percent. Some of the BARDCOM scientists believe we are looking at an agent that kills in seconds; but scientists being what they are, they're squirming out of providing hard intel.

"I set up a parallel investigation using the CDC and had one of my aides recruit a top molecular biologist who is the expert on Chromatium Omri. The expert is convinced the killer is a virus-like object found inside a strain of Chromatium Omri that has remained unchanged for three billion years. The man's won a Nobel Prize for his work on this very creature. So I'm buying into his story for now and for as long as my gut tells me he's on track."

"Excuse me, General," said Chief of Staff Ross. "I want to back up a bit. How can you be so convinced this isn't a covert attack of some kind?"

"I never said this wasn't an attack. I said this was not an engineered bio-weapon. The two are not always mutually exclusive. At this point, every major country has been hit by at least one kill zone. The intelligence geeks are having a hard time coming up with a list of suspect states."

"Fine, what about a Middle Eastern terrorist group?" said Ross.

"I wouldn't rule anything out at this point," said McKafferty.

"I'll rule something out," croaked National Security Advisor Volloski. His voice was the harsh whisper of a chain smoker. "My best analysts are saying this is not an attack. Case closed."

"Please continue your report, General McKafferty." said the President. The topic was being shelved for now, but McKafferty was not quite ready to drop it. He had an opening to make a point and he was going to use it.

"It is my opinion that it's foolish for us to only focus on the eradication of this microbe," said McKafferty. "We need to learn how to detect it and weaponize it as much as we need to learn how to destroy it. It could take decades to eradicate in the wild. Smallpox took that long to wipe out and it can still be brought back, and so could this little bastard. If this bug can be used as a weapon, someone will put it to that use sooner or later. Gentlemen, do not fool yourselves. Right now, every religious fanatic in the world is thinking about this microbe. Can you imagine *mullah whoever* with a beaker of God's Wrath in his fist? We need to keep countermeasures a high priority; we need to know how to recognize a weapon because once these nut-jobs know what to look for, it will only take a dollar-fifty mason jar to start harvesting this bug. Think about it. Step right up. Yard sale, weapons of mass destruction. Get your jar of concentrated death, only thirty-six virgins plus shipping and handling. They could sell this horror on the Internet. This is a self-replicating weapon. Once you have the bacterium, it doesn't get any cheaper to manufacture than this.

"You have made your point, General." said the President. "I will take it under serious consideration."

"Very well, Sir; I'll move on. I have a team monitoring the progress of the CDC group. I am allowing no information exchange between the CDC and BARDCOM teams until confirmable breakthroughs occur. The CDC team does not even know of the existence of the BARDCOM team. This will ensure we keep each think-tank free of the Estelburg effect."

"The Estelburg effect?" asked Chief of Staff Ross.

"The negative effect of two research teams locked in a heated competition and, as a result, pursuing each other's leads, which may be dead ends, instead of pursing fresh ideas," said the President.

McKafferty was impressed with the President's knowledge. A few heads were nodding. He moved on to the list of scientific findings. He discussed clustered kill zones, described how the seeds were discovered inside COBIC, and the observed quasi-intelligent behaviors of COBIC. His knowledge about the teams' results was encyclopedic. He discussed possible countermeasures and the difficulties of searching for a vaccine.

"The CDC is running experiments to observe seed reproduction and infection of neighboring bacteria," said McKafferty. "While that intel will be very useful, we in the military are a little more practical. BARDCOM has come up with a way of recording the bacteria in the act of killing. We have set up experiments in every major city located near water. An outbreak in any of these cities will give us hard information on how this thing ticks and, from that, how to control it. I like to think that while the civilians are trying to spy on it fucking, we are watching it to see how it kills."

McKafferty noticed the National Security Advisor checking his watch. He was taken aback and stopped talking. The room was silent for some time; then, National Security Advisor Volloski started speaking. His damaged voice was soft. McKafferty had to listen closely to hear what he was saying.

"Does anyone realize what the implications are if we can inoculate for this plague or in some way protect our people from it?" said Volloski. "If we're slow to share our new found countermeasure and we let the global situation continue for awhile, some of our less hospitable neighbors in the Middle East and Asia could be removed from the game in a very convenient way."

The National Security Advisor's remarks registered on everyone. The President, the officers, all eyes were focused on Volloski. McKafferty felt a lump in his throat that was more like a jagged rock. Volloski was a dangerous man.

"Enough," said the President. "That topic is closed."

The President turned toward McKafferty. "How is BARDCOM going to capture this bacterium in the act of killing?"

"With all due respect, Sir" said McKafferty. "I believe you need plausible deniability on that topic. It's better if I say nothing more on methods."

McKafferty was grimly nodding his head. He knew his face, which was normally ugly would now look almost sinister. The men and woman around the table involuntarily looked down or away. The President stared for several long seconds into McKafferty's eyes, as if taking a measure of him. Finally the President nodded. McKafferty's respect for this President was growing.

"Very well, General. I'll accept your reason for secrecy for now. Next question. Why is the CDC not involved in the search for counter-measures while BARDCOM is expending half their resources on that track?"

McKafferty cleared his throat. "At BARDCOM," said McKafferty, "we have world class experts on toxicology and weaponization, and we have Harold N. who is the only verified survivor of a kill zone. The CDC team has no expertise in this area and no guinea pig. CDC scientists are the ones who will figure out how to track this bacterium and control its spread. I want them to focus on that. It's what they are good at. Military training teaches us to deploy our warriors in positions where they can have the greatest effect."

"Do you have anything promising in countermeasure research?" asked Admiral Burk.

"Right now, Admiral, all we have are theories."

"There is a potential problem in all this," said Volloski. "Once we do come up with a countermeasure and start protecting our people with it, other countries might think that we came up with a solution a little too fast. Maybe they'll think we're the ones that released this killer in the first place. Maybe they'll retaliate. The Russians still have a sizable nuclear arsenal and there is no shortage of Russian paranoia. When we get a solution, we need to time its distribution very care-fully. Better to lose a few thousand of our civilians than start a war."

"Sir, I have to interrupt," said McKafferty. "The Russians aren't going to nuke their salvation. If we're the ones with the magic pill, they'll want to take good care of us and not blow us up in some crazy mutual-suicide play. I realize we're just blue-skying this issue, but can't we keep it a little closer to the boots on the ground?"

The President looked as if he might be smiling to himself. The National Security Advisor was glaring at McKafferty. The room was again silent. McKafferty wondered if he'd just scuttled or advanced his promotion from brigadier to two stars.

Chapter 7

Circles

1 – Camp Pendleton: December

They had been cleared for takeoff. The whine of the four jet engines cut through Mark's head like a band saw. The rpm kept increasing. He felt a dull but commanding pain whose roots were in too many days of emotional hurt and alcohol and valium. Kathy smiled at him. Mark thought it pleased her to see him in pain instead of mildly sedated. She'd lectured him the other day on guilt and that medication was no way to cope. What the hell did she know about the emptiness he was feeling, about the guilt that was eating away at his soul? How had she shown her empathy – by first medicating him with Valium and then taking it away; typical doctor obsessed with the ailment instead of the patient.

The Air Force cargo jet lifted off the ground in a mild climb and then without warning veered upward with a surge of power. Mark felt blood draining from his head. His duffel bag slid along the cabin floor into the empty cavern behind him. He clenched his teeth as his stomach balled into a knot. He hated flying. This pilot was a sadist.

The jet was a brand new supersonic cargo hauler sprinting back empty to Dobbins Air Force Base in Atlanta. The only thing in the cargo hold besides him and Kathy was a single pallet with eight well secured stainless steel drums. Inside the drums was the latest round of water samples collected using Mark's traps. The flight would take three and a half hours. There was no heat in the cargo hold. They wore heavy parkas courtesy of the Air Force. Regulations prevented them from occupying the flight deck, which was the only heated space on the craft. Wool blankets were tucked under the seats if the coats proved inadequate.

Something from the rear began to rattle. Mark looked back at his samples to make sure nothing had broken free. The first round of traps had captured infected COBIC at three percent of the sites. He expected the same would be true for this lot. He planned on examining each bacterium sample for subtle differences, a mutation that might explain why some people died and others lived. At least that was the general idea. It was a competing theory against Kathy's computer model, reasonably good science, and would probably take him months to complete. As far he was concerned, that was all right. With any luck, there would be no need to finish the research. Let someone else find the cure. He had a vague second plan to see how much alcohol and sedatives it would take to erase the memory of your average Nobel Prize winning scientist.

What would be the loss? He had nothing more to contribute. Kathy had been doing fine before he'd shown up, and she would do fine with him out of the picture. She'd found a second Harold N., a 43-year-old woman named Gloria Martinez. In the center of a kill zone, the woman had held her children in her arms while they and several friends and relatives had died around her. There was clearly something medically unique about this woman. She was already at the CDC in Atlanta undergoing a battery of tests. It was possible she was a walking, breathing cure for the plague.

Mark felt thirsty. He got up to retrieve his flight bag. Thankfully it hadn't wandered far. The bag had been snagged by a row of bolt heads twenty feet aft. He sat down and strapped back in. Deep inside the bag was a fresh pint of gin, an airline sized mini-bottle of vermouth, and a water glass stolen from the officer's mess. He was, if nothing else, developing into a discerning drinker and had planned on self-medicating himself for the ride. The alcohol was his in-flight relaxation and entertainment system.

Mark discovered it required a certain skill to make a martini in his lap on a moving jet. He took a sip and decided it was worth the trouble. He heard Kathy say something but couldn't catch the words. The jet engines were loud enough to make talking difficult. He was surprised that Kathy had said anything. He'd expected the silent treatment once she saw him drinking. He now had the option of leaning closer and hearing her rebuke or pretending not to hear. Talking would lead to a fight. He leaned closer to speak into her ear.

"What did you say?"

Kathy's parka stuffed shape pressed against his shoulder. In that outfit, she was like a nicely stuffed down pillow.

"I said, 'You got your doctorate from UCLA didn't you?'"

Mark was confused. Where was this going?

"Ahuh," he said.

"Mine was Harvard Medical."

"I know. I read your bio," he said.

"Were you on scholarship?" she asked.

"No, UCLA was almost free back then. Plus I worked part-time. Took me a few extra years to earn my undergraduate."

"I had a full scholarship that included room and board."

"Lucky you." What was her point?

"When I heard you were coming to advise us, I went out and read the entire set of research papers that led to your Nobel Prize."

"You're kidding. There must have been thousands of pages. I don't think I've even read them all, and I wrote them."

"I have to admit I was searching for flaws," said Kathy. "I wanted to find something to make us more equal."

"And..." said Mark.

"It was brilliant."

"Wow, I mean thanks. Would you like a drink?"

"Sure."

Mark was baffled by the change in her. From his flight bag he pulled the bottle of gin and wondered where he would find a second glass. She took the bottle from his fingers and swallowed a couple gulps. He saw her eyes water up. She took another sip, this time smaller, then handed the bottle back.

"Can I be honest with you?" she said.

"Anyone that can drink gin straight from the bottle can say whatever she wants."

"I know that your feelings are overwhelming you, but there are other things even more important. You know COBIC better than anyone."

"Look, Kathy, you don't need my help. Never did. I'm not a medical doctor. I engineer microbes and poke around in fossil beds. I know in detail how bacteria work inside the human body, but so does every first year med-student."

"That's so much bullshit. You're the one that precisely identified this strain of bacterium. You're the one that discovered an object inside its nucleus that will probably end up being the disease vector itself. You're the one that came up with a way of collecting this strain of COBIC and more, much more. I ought to beat you silly for saying you've contributed nothing."

"Sorry honey, I won't do it again."

"Can you be serious for one minute? We need you. What we're doing will lead to stopping this killer. Probably hundreds of groups around the globe are working on this bug; but we're the ones who found it, and we're the ones who have the best shot at figuring it out."

Kathy opened the bottle of gin and took another sip. What could he say about this lecture she just gave him? Surprisingly, it left him feeling good; and judging from her expression she'd meant every word of it. She looked like she was ready to hit him if he disagreed with her one more time.

Most of gin was gone. The conversation had long ago drifted to more personal topics. Mark felt a solid glow from the alcohol, but it was nothing compared to how good Kathy was making him feel. She'd told him about one of her fantasies, getting a small horse ranch with an apple orchard and a stream. He'd told her about the high of winning a Nobel Prize, and his guilt about the way he'd ruined his marriage to Julie, and how it was now too late to even apologize.

"I can understand some of what you're feeling," said Kathy. "I was eight when I lost both my parents. I felt that somehow it had been my fault. If I'd only been a better kid, if I'd only kept my room cleaner or not had bad thoughts, then maybe God wouldn't have taken them from me."

Mark found himself looking at Kathy and seeing the person inside for the first time. He liked what he saw and that scared him. His heart was beating faster than it should have been. He was past scared; he was ready to run. He changed the subject amid a flurry of conflicting emotions. He tried to talk about safer things; but after a short period of time, he had drifted back to what was troubling him… or was it Kathy who had steered the conversation along?

"You know they're in my mind every minute of the day," said Mark. "Not a moment goes by that I don't play the 'what if game.' What if I'd let Gracy fly out to Atlanta? What if I'd told them to leave L.A. right after New Jersey was hit? What if…"

His voice cracked. Mark stopped talking. He realized he was on dangerous ground and close to losing it. He wasn't going to cry.

"I'm sorry," he said. "I shouldn't dwell on this guilt."

"Don't apologize."

The ride had gotten rough several minutes ago. Turbulence was buffeting the airframe. Kathy had been rocking back and forth with the sway of the jet. The motion had been bringing her face closer and father away. For a moment he thought he was going to kiss her. He was certain that a kiss was the farthest thing from her mind. She picked up his hand and squeezed it.

Mark's PDA phone vibrated. He fished the gadget out his pocket. There was no call coming in, it was an e-mail alert. Someone on his personal alert list had sent him e-mail. The message was from Professor Karla Hunt. It had been over a week ago that he'd e-mailed her the classified pictures of seeds. She was a leading expert in biomedical engineering. Her research was the direct interfacing of computers with the human brain. Her dream was to create prosthetic vision and hearing. She had achieved limited success with prosthetic vision. The e-mail was almost a week old and marked as spam. There must have been some kind of foul up in an e-mail server somewhere. The message itself was short and took Mark's breath away.

Hi Love,

Looks like some kind of next generation, carbon-based nano-tech circuitry. Something like the molecular computers IBM has been messing with. So what is it? Is this something IBM cooked up? Computer controlled micro golf balls? What? Did I win the prize?

Cheers,
K

2 – Boarburg, New York: December

Sarah had been staying at the Boarburg Inn for over a week. Marge, the owner, front desk clerk, cook, and maid, had proved to be a mountain of emotional support. Sarah was grateful. She hated lying to Marge about how she'd gotten here by crossing a quarantine line, but that had been the only lie and Sarah had taken solace in that. When Sarah told her she was a cop, Marge had acted as proud as if Sarah was her own child. The price for the room dropped to thirty-five dollars a night and food was on the house.

Sarah sat on the front porch sipping her third cup of coffee and thinking. She had been conducting this same ritual for the past few days – greeting the morning light. An orange sun was rising through tree branches casting everything in rich fall colors. She was thinking about her dream of a ghost town Los Angeles. How could she have known while hiking in the middle of a forest what was happening on the other side of the country? If it had only been that one time, she could have rationalized it away as coincidence; but what about her premonitions of New Jersey before it was hit?

The word *premonition* scared her, but what worried her even more was this impulse she felt, this deep urge to go south. It was a powerful need, almost like hunger. She wondered if this was anything like the instincts animals felt when it came time for them to migrate south. At times, she could see the entire route she would take; and at other times it was nothing more than an impulse to flee. Was she running from the plague like an animal fleeing a burning forest or was it more mysterious and less specific like responding to the sense of a warm place to nest that was far away? Sarah rose to go inside. She needed Marge's help and advice.

The street was empty. The air nipped at her face. Sarah zipped her goose-down coat to the collar. Dried leaves blew past. There were small patches of ice on the ground. She was on her way to talk with someone named Hank Swenson. He owned the local Exxon and used car lot. Marge told her to warn Hank he'd better give her a good deal on a car, or his days of half price meals were over. Ralph had stayed behind with Marge who now loved the dog. When Sarah had left, Ralph was in the process of making a bowl of leftover stew disappear. Sarah had called to him. He'd looked up at her and then went back to the stew. Oh well, doggy love only went so far when stew was concerned. Marge appeared to be getting ready to give him seconds. Sarah smiled to herself. Ralph would miss Marge as much as she would.

Hank Swenson turned out to be nothing like what Sarah expected. Instead of a gangly auto mechanic, he was a stocky blond in his early fifties and spoke with an accent. At first she'd thought his moving into her space while talking was part of his European upbringing, but then he'd started with the hands. He kept touching her arms or shoulders. Sarah put up with it in the hopes of getting a car she could afford. She was prepared to spend most of the six hundred and twenty dollars she had. She could find work once she got farther south. His only car in her price range was a twenty-year-old half rusted Ford. The price scribbled in soap on the windshield was seven hundred dollars. Gusts of cold wind buffed her face and hair. Hank's nose was red from the cold.

"Sarah, you know I like you," said Hank. "I just can't let the car go for five hundred. It's ugly but it runs like a watch."

"Five-fifty," offered Sarah. "It's as far as I can go and I really can't afford that."

"Maybe we can work something out?"

Hank Swenson put his arm around her waist and started to walk her away from the car. Her body stiffened.

"Let's go inside. It's getting nippy out here. I'm sure you'd be more comfortable in my office."

His fingers were now curling around her hip. Sarah looked back over her shoulder at the junk heap of a car. What was she going to do? She needed to leave and she needed a car. Her legs froze when she saw the office door. Hank continued trying to inch her forward.

"I'll give you six hundred and twenty dollars," said Sarah, hoping she could do cleaning work for Marge to earn back some of the money before leaving.

"There's only one way to drive off in that car for six hundred and twenty dollars," said Hank.

He skillfully backed her against a wall. The alcove for the doorway was concealed from the street. He tried to kiss her.

"Get off me!" yelled Sarah.

She pushed at him, but he was heavy and strong.

"Be nice," said Hank. "You can have the car for five hundred if you're nice."

He kissed her neck. Tears were streaming from her eyes. She was angry and breathing through her teeth. The emotional burn, instead of clouding her thoughts, added a peculiar detachment. In her mind was the remembered voice of one of her police instructors and diagrams of karate moves that were almost like dance steps. Sarah worked one of her legs into a crossed position behind her attacker's calves and planted her foot firmly on the ground. Hank seemed to react as if her change in body position was sexy.

"Up yours," she hissed.

She slapped both his ears at the same time. The dual blows hopefully ruptured his eardrums. Hank yelped and grabbed his ears. Taking advantage, Sarah brought up an elbow ramming it into his nose. The blow knocked Hank off balance and covered his lips in blood. He teetered backward tripping over her leg which she'd planted behind him; his feet were swept from the ground. The man went down hard. His head crashed into the doorframe. He was hurt. Seeing him in pain felt great.

"Cunt!" he groaned. "You get t..."

That was all Sarah heard as she was running from the lot. Her tears dried almost at once. Her heart was still racing as she slowed to a walk.

"That bastard!" hissed Marge.

It was the closest thing to a four-letter word that Sarah had ever heard the woman say. Marge was behind the front desk. She had the phone in her hand and was dialing.

"*That man* is not getting another scrap of food or business from me. In fact, I'm gonna call Sheriff Johnson and tell him what *that man* tried to do."

"Please don't," begged Sarah. "I don't want anyone else to know what happened."

Marge scowled at the front door for a moment.

"All right, honey. I don't want to make you feel any worse. It's a good thing you had all that police training. No telling what else *that man* might have tried."

Marge smirked.

"So you think he hurt his head good on that doorframe?"

"He didn't come running after me."

~

The clock on the nightstand read midnight. The room lights were out. Sarah was wide awake and sitting on the edge of her bed. Moonlight poured through the frozen window pane. Ralph was leaning against her side.

"I wish you'd been with me, sweetie."

Sarah smiled just a little, picturing Ralph biting Hank Swenson in the groin. That man deserved it... deserved worse. He was a rapist. No telling how many women hadn't been as fortunate as she'd been. Had he tried to force himself on high school girls for a tank of gas?

"That fucker!"

Sarah leaned over Ralph to switch on the bedside lamp. She had an idea. It would be justice. In fifteen minutes, she'd stuffed everything she owned into her backpack except the Beretta. She left the backpack in the closet for a quick getaway when she returned. She checked the Beretta to make sure a shell was not in the chamber, then tucked it into the waistband of her jeans and pulled the sweatshirt over it. She knelt down close to Ralph's face.

"Mommy will be back in a few minutes," she whispered. "You be a good boy and don't make any noise."

Ralph licked her on the nose. Sarah scratched his head as if ruffling the hair of a little boy. The hallway was lit from the end by a single lamp. She crept down to the kitchen, pausing at the occasional groans of floorboards under her feet.

Sarah put a goodbye note on the table just in case something happened and she didn't make it back, then borrowed a large screwdriver, wire cutters, and a pair of vice grips from the tool drawer. The spring loaded backdoor creaked as she went out. The noise was far softer than the sound of the wind but still seemed horribly loud to Sarah. The air was freezing outside. Her breath left in puffs of steam.

The alley was unlit. Even so, she was taking no chances and kept to the shadows as much as possible. The Exxon was only six blocks away. The lot was brightly lit. Sarah stood at the edge of the alley concealed behind a dumpster and decided which car she liked best. The vintage 1968 Pontiac Firebird was a shiny olive green with a black racing stripe and custom wheels. She knew the car came standard with an eight-cylinder engine that belonged in a racecar. The car was in perfect condition, not even a spot of rust. The price was marked at fifteen thousand! She decided it was for her.

Sarah hoped her police training was about to pay off again. As a normal part of school, every rookie was taught the methods criminals used in their acts against society. Theft of older model cars was amazingly simple. She clamped the vice grips to the shaft of the screwdriver. This turned the screwdriver into what the police manual called a *forced entry tool*. She ran across the exposed stretch of road and ducked down by the passenger-door. This side of the car offered a greater amount of concealment. Next to her was the Ford that Hank had wanted to trade for who knows what kinds of perverted favors.

"Fucking pig," mumbled Sarah.

She pushed the flat end of the screwdriver into the Firebird's door lock. She tried turning it with the added leverage of the vice grips but only succeeded in tearing a round hole in the lock. She silently cursed. She needed to get the flat end in deeper. She looked around for something to use as a hammer. She saw a piece of split firewood chocking the rear wheel of the Ford. The car probably didn't even have brakes.

She took the wood and used it to pound the flat end of the driver deep into the lock. The noise was loud, but she figured the night was cold enough that everyone would have their windows tightly closed. Forcing the lock this way was a calculated risk. She twisted the screwdriver and was rewarded with the sound of metal scraping and the latch popping open.

Sarah jumped into the car and lay prone on the seat. She began to hot wire the ignition. The principle was very simple, and made simpler because this was an older car with none of the theft deterrents of newer models. The key was mounted low in the dashboard with the wire bundle completely exposed under the dash. She used the cutters to clip the ignition and starter wires and strip off their insulation.

Sarah froze at the sound of a vehicle driving slowly down the road. She didn't know whether to run or stay. She was too close to getting her car to quit now. Tires on gravel… a police spotlight snapped on and played across the cars in the lot. She wondered if someone had heard her and called in a complaint. She knew she should have run. Now she was trapped. The spotlight winked off accompanied by the sounds of tires on gravel moving off the lot and back onto the street.

Sarah twisted the ignition wires together. The dash warning lights came on. She touched the starter wire to a bare piece of metal on the underside of the dash. There was a small spark. The engine turned over and idled in a low rumble. Sarah popped up in the driver's seat, put the car in gear and headed for the alleyway. She was grinning like a fool. Crime was easy.

~

Sarah had picked up Ralph and her belongings without incident. She drove until the early morning before she was forced to stop. She pulled off into a rest area somewhere in Pennsylvania after falling asleep behind the wheel twice. The last time had scared her. She'd been off the shoulder and onto the grass before a jounce had awoken her. Ralph had slept through it all. What would a dog do without his human slaves?

The rest stop was empty, but Sarah was no longer taking chances. She got out her Beretta and jacked a cartridge into the chamber. She put the loaded weapon onto the floor within immediate reach, then pulled her coat around her and started to doze. Half asleep, she visited old childhood memories of helping her mom sift flour with a huge metal sifter. There was something innately soothing to her about helping to bake things in a kitchen. Sarah's lips curled into a dreamy smile as her mind took the final plunge into deeper sleep.

3 – Dobbins Air Force Base, Atlanta: December

Mark looked up as the jet's landing gear dropped into position. He was startled and disoriented for a moment, and then surprised with himself, when he realized he'd fallen asleep. He'd never done that before. With no windows for reference, he felt like the jet was swooping down out of the sky. He thought about the e-mail from Karla Hunt. If she was even partially correct, the implications were unthinkable. Where could something like this have come from? He felt a drag on the wings and the pilot correcting to hold the nose up. The plane began jostling and fighting with the air. Whoever was flying this jet was operating it like a stunt-plane. There was a solid bounce followed by a screech of rubber. They touched down without warning and were still moving fast. A powerful shudder worked the fuselage as the thrust was reversed. Something small in the cargo area rattled loose and fell.

"Air Force pilots," grumbled Mark.

Kathy stood up and stretched. Mark stared at her for a moment remembering all they'd talked about and, more importantly, what they hadn't talked about. He had mentioned nothing about the e-mail. He picked up his bag and headed toward the forward hatch. Kathy was right behind him.

The entrance to the pilot's cabin opened. A thirty-something woman dressed in an Air Force flight suit stepped out. She had a small canvas briefcase in one hand and captain's insignias on her uniform. Her name patch read 'Capt. N. Carter'. The captain smiled. She was a very attractive woman. Mark stopped walking. He couldn't think of anything to say. If she'd been a man, he would have said something snide about barnstorming with a jet bigger than half a football field.

"Did you enjoy the flight, Sir?" asked N. Carter.

"Flawless," said Mark. "In fact I'm thinking about cashing in my frequent flyer miles just so that I can take the return trip."

"I'll look forward to it. My name is Nancy Carter. Maybe next time we can find room for you on the flight deck."

"Thanks for the nice flight," said Kathy.

Her voice was flat. Mark got the impression his flirting with the pilot annoyed her. He smiled to himself as he walked off the plane.

Mark was surprised that a Lincoln Town Car with government license plates was waiting for them. Apparently Kathy had been expecting it. The driver wore army fatigues and a sidearm. He took their bags and stowed them in the trunk. Mark opened the passenger door. It was unexpectedly heavy and well balanced like a vault door. The inside panel was twice normal thickness and the tinted glass looked like it was three inches thick by itself. Mark looked over at the driver and tapped the side window with his knuckle. It felt like plastic instead of glass.

"Bullet proof," said the driver. "Same for the entire car."

Kathy got in and stretched out her legs. Mark sat down next to her. A glass divider separated the front and back seats. Two telephones and a television were built into the front seatback. The leather was buttery soft. Through the tinted glass, he could look out but no one could see in.

"What's going on?" asked Mark. "Why the VIP treatment?"

"Frequent flyer miles." said Kathy.

"Very funny… When I told Captain Carter I'd cash in my miles, I was just being friendly."

"Fine with me."

"So what are we doing with this car and driver?"

Kathy opened her purse and took out some makeup. There was a fold-down mirror above the passenger door. She began fussing with her eyes. The town car pulled out. Mark noticed the driver had not asked for directions.

"Where are we going?" asked Mark.

"Like my new car?"

"Fabulous, but I prefer the Bentley to the Armored Lincoln."

"Got any Grey Poupon?" Kathy giggled.

"Ha ha," said Mark.

"Alright, alright! Our little ride is courtesy of the Department of Defense. The military is now providing all transportation and security for the CDC. The driver is also a bodyguard."

"Nice perk if you can get it," said Mark. "Little bit of overkill?"

"There have been death threats. They're trying to protect us."

"Or keep track of us," said Mark. "So what does Department of Defense get out of this?"

"Nothing big… We save the world."

~

Mark's eyes popped open from a nightmare. He'd fallen asleep on the couch in his office. The lights were still on. A book on nanotechnology was propped open on his chest; several more were lying open on the floor. His hand felt sore; then he realized it was cut. A broken water glass was on the floor near where his hand had been resting. He sat up groggily remembering the dream. He'd had this dream once before. He could still see the nightmarish scene of bodies floating in the Hudson River. The last and only time he had that nightmare was the day of the New Jersey kill zone; and unlike his normal dreams, many of the details had remained crisp for days afterwards.

A feeling of dread was growing in Mark's chest as he cleaned his cut palm. A thin stream of blood ran down the sink basin and into the drain. What if the dream was some kind of premonition? No, that's crazy. The dream was just a dream. His mind was playing tricks on him, but still, what if it was a warning?

4 – Central Pennsylvania: December

Sarah kicked a littered soda can with her sneaker. Smack. The can skittered across two lanes of highway. Both directions were deserted. This stretch of Interstate 81 had been cut into the side of a mountain. The view was spectacular. Off to the right and below as far as she could see was an unending pelt of trees, leftover autumn colors, empty branches, and pines mixed into a blur that reached to the horizon. There was not a town or man-made structure in sight other than the highway.

The day was half over. The backpack felt heavier with every step. It had been hours ago that the Firebird had died. Exactly one car had driven by in all that time. There had to be towns somewhere nearby. Sarah imagined people were barricaded in their homes and pretending that the plague was happening to someone they didn't know. She had to imagine that's where all the people were hiding. If she stopped imagining for a second, the quiet of her mind combined with the empty landscape to conjure fears that all life had vanished from the Earth. What made everything worse was a powerful sense of deja vu. She had walked this highway before in a dream.

Miles behind her were the smoking remains of the olive green Firebird. She wondered if it was instant karma that had caused the engine to die in the middle of nowhere. Before it had died, trails of smoke had poured from its tail pipes like the contrails of a jet.

Ralph came bounding after her from the edge of the woods after checking out an enticing smell or some other canine adventure. He was spending a lot of time investigating the trees. Sarah patted her leg. He stuck his muzzle into her hand and then licked her palm. He was excited. Sarah was glad at least one of them was having fun. She was damp with sweat and decidedly in the 'life sucks' camp right now.

There was a low humming sound. First Sarah felt it in the ground; then she heard it more clearly. A car was coming on her side of the highway. She stuck out her thumb. She knew it was dangerous to hitchhike, but she couldn't walk south the entire distance to the Gulf of Mexico. Besides, she had two guns and Ralph and months of police training.

The car came around a bend in the highway. The vehicle was low slung and moving fast, some kind of sports car. She couldn't tell what make it was from this distance. In less than a minute, a brand new black Porsche was close by and slowing. A pair of adolescents stared at her. Ralph came trotting back from the woods. The driver spotted Ralph and sped away. Great, thought Sarah. What was it with her? How did she keep attracting trouble? It might have been her imagination, but she could have sworn the driver had mouthed something lurid to his buddy before spotting Ralph. She let out a sigh. Maybe walking wasn't such a bad idea after all? It was great exercise.

Sarah would have sworn that hours had passed but she knew it was far less. Her sweat had turned into a low grade salt burn that lingered just below perception. The straps of the backpack were starting to work dull aches deep into her shoulders. Sarah had paid little attention when the clouds had started to roll in; but now it looked like rain, or if it got a little colder, maybe snow. The sky was growing increasingly grayer by the minute. She hadn't brought a tent with her. She hadn't given any thought to sleeping outside in bad weather. She'd assumed there would always be a motel or a car to sleep in.

She reached the crest of a hill. In the distance was a green rectangle that she hoped was an exit sign. The valley was still mostly trees, but there was a distant clearing that contained what looked like buildings. Four other cars had passed her since the Porsche. The first two she had ignored; but with her strength waning, she had tried to thumb a ride with the last two. Both had sped past her. Few people seemed interested in stopping for someone who might be infected with plague and accompanied by a hundred and twenty pound Rottweiler. She'd thought about changing into a pair of shorts and a tank-top – someone lecherous was sure to stop before she froze to death. The idea was stupid and made her smile.

Walking downhill felt good. The green rectangle was growing and was definitely an exit sign. She couldn't read it from here but hoped the sign was for a town and not some highway interchange.

"Alright, Ralphy baby, it's all downhill from here."

From nowhere, a fat drop of rain landed on her face. The drop had hit with surprising force. The water was very cold. She could sense a distant wind picking up strength. More drops started spattering around her. She glanced about in the pointless hope of finding shelter. There were only trees, not a great place to wait out a storm. The exit sign was about a half mile away. Just after the exit sign was an overpass, but more importantly the underpass was shelter.

Sarah's stomach grumbled. She was sitting on her pack. A tiny river flowed past her sneakers along a drainage path; small leaves and bits of road debris floated by in the water. The underpass was like being inside a cave. She wondered if life was like this for early humans, huddled and cold with no one to help them except themselves. A curtain of rain was falling at each side of the underpass. Occasionally the curtain parted with the noise of a vehicle blasting through. The black Porsche had passed in the other direction about twenty minutes ago and had slowed to a crawl. Those kids could not have been the real owners of that car. It was either their parent's or stolen. Sarah was betting on the latter. She noticed the driver was wearing a baseball cap turned backwards. His stare gave her a cold chill. The creep had his leering act down pat. He must have had a lot of practice.

After that drive-by, Sarah had taken out her Beretta and made sure a cartridge was in the chamber. She tucked the gun back inside her belt-pack and left the pocket open so she could draw it in a hurry. Ralph sensed her distress and stayed close to her side. Sarah didn't want to use the gun. She hoped those kids were only window-shopping.

Without warning, the water curtain parted and the Porsche cruised through again. This time the passenger had his window down. They were moving at no more than a few miles per hour. Ralph didn't like this at all. He pulled back his gums and showed a set of teeth that were as menacing as a wolf's. The two hoodlums didn't seem to notice and that worried Sarah. Did they have something with them that could take out a huge angry dog?

Hey baby, you want a ride?"

Sarah said nothing. The only place for her to ride in that car was in the passenger's lap and there was definitely no room for Ralph. Her hand was inside the belt-pack. Her fingers wrapped around the handgrip of her Beretta. She'd already picked her targets. First shot would be a "close miss" just to scare them off – unless she saw a weapon. If that happened, she'd unload the entire clip into the passenger door and windshield. The sixteen rounds in her gun would be enough for these two.

The passenger smiled. The driver shrugged and sped off into the curtain of rain. Sarah got up and walked to the edge of the downpour. Ralph was next to her. The Berretta was in her hand. She wanted to see if they had really driven off or if they had stopped just out of sight and were circling back on foot. A sneak attack seemed like something that fit their style.

"Police... Don't move!"

The voice came from a short distance behind her. The voice was male and amplified electronically. Sarah froze. Was it really the police? For all she knew, it was highwaymen with guns pointed at her back. Ralph was growling in his low rumble. He was in attack mode.

"Easy boy," she said. He could get them both killed.

"Slowly put the gun on the ground, turn around, and walk toward me."

Sarah started to do as she was told. The male voice did not sound like an adolescent. As she turned she saw a State Police cruiser. Relief spread through her body. The officer was alone in the car. As he got out, Sarah saw the shotgun for the first time. Ralph growled.

"Lay down, Ralph," she yelled. "Bad boy!"

Ralph turned to look at her with a hurt expression on his face. Sarah felt a pang of guilt for being harsh with him, but it was better than a face full of buckshot. He laid down but kept his eyes on the man.

"Ralph won't attack you," she said.

"Uh huh."

"I'm a cop," she said.

She noticed the man's eyes focus on the police emblem on her cap. His body language seemed to show a little curiosity, but he obviously wasn't buying it.

"Do you have ID?"

"I have a shield and police ID in my belt-pack."

"Okay, you come toward me and lean up against the car. If that dog moves I will shoot him."

"Ralph, stay!"

He cuffed her hands, frisked her professionally, and then told her to sit down while he verified her credentials using his radio. She was tense and hoped there would be nothing on file about her illegally crossing quarantine lines. Five minutes later, they were fellow cops. His name was Henry. He was in his mid-twenties, had a weight lifter's body, and the gentle demeanor of someone who had nothing to prove. Sarah told him about the joy riders.

"That sounds like some local trouble who live about a dozen miles from here. Their parents are loaded. Not bad kids, nothing criminal anyway, just out of control. I doubt they were doing anything more than looking, and I can't arrest them for that. Not that a few days in jail wouldn't do both of them a world of good."

"A lot better than the bullet or dog mauling they might have caught if they'd pushed it too far," said Sarah.

The storm had picked up and was beginning to freeze. Sarah could feel drops of water blown in from the curtain of rain and sleet. Henry was leaning back against the car's fender.

"It's against regulations, but I will give you a lift," he said.

"I don't know since it's such a nice day and all."

Henry smiled. Sarah had known by instinct this was a good man. After a half hour on the road, Ralph was fast asleep in the back, a clear sign that he approved of Henry; and Ralph was a better judge of people than anyone Sarah knew. She leaned back in her seat. After all those miles of walking, the police cruiser felt like deep luxury. The miles were melting away even though the speedometer never went a hair past the posted speed limit.

Henry was good company. Sarah had already learned he was stationed out of the Allentown barracks, had been with the Pennsylvania State Police for two years, and was married with a baby girl. Sarah told him her lie about being in New York State at the time the kill zone happened. She added a few details about finding out from the Red Cross that her family had been killed.

"I've got no family left. So now I'm just going south," she said. "Seems as good a direction as any."

"You can get a bus or train out of Allentown," said Henry.

"No, I don't think they're going to let Ralph sit next to me. I can't bear the idea of crating him up and loading him like some piece of baggage."

"Yeah, I can understand that. So you're gonna just keep on walking?"

"No, maybe I'll get some kind of job in Allentown and work until I have enough for a car."

"You know, you should head down to Virginia. There's an interstate quarantine line being set up. They're major league short-handed and looking for all the help with police training they can find. Right now, they don't care which side of the line you're coming from; but that can change tomorrow if something bad happens."

"Well, maybe?"

"No, really you should do it. When you get there, look up Major Frank Warton of the State Police. He was one of my instructors at the academy. We've stayed in touch. Tell him I told you to call."

"Thanks."

Sarah realized her smile was beaming. This was a really nice guy.

They had been driving for over an hour and had turned off Interstate 81 onto a smaller highway that ran parallel to the Delaware River. The storm had let up. The view was damp and beautiful in spots. Sarah found it hard to believe that it was only a short time ago that she'd been on the other side and desperate to get across. The past week had seemed like a year, but she had made it and was now being escorted by the state police.

They came to a high point on the road. Sarah looked out and saw a bridge blocked with military armor. Her stomach felt queasy. For a crazy moment, she expected Henry to exit off onto the bridge and turn her over to the military for deportation back to New Jersey.

"Son of a bitch!" yelled Henry.

He pulled onto the shoulder and flipped on the lightbar. At the opposite end of a small decline, Sarah caught sight of a man in ratty clothes standing next to a tree. The man looked like he was in a trance. To the left of the man was the beginning of a deep forest. To the right was a clear view of the Delaware River and the fortified bridge.

"I've got orders to assist in capturing anyone that looks like a dirt-eater or a line jumper, and that sure looks like a dirt-eater to me."

Henry got on the radio and called for assistance. He was told to keep the subject under surveillance from a distance until the Hazmat Team arrived. He was not to approach the subject or risk contamination in anyway. If the subject refused to cooperate and tried to flee, 'shoot to injure' was authorized.

"Stay in the car," said Henry.

He got out and cautiously walked a few yards down the grassy embankment. The subject was about thirty yards away. Ignoring what Henry had just said, Sarah immediately got out of the patrol car and joined him. Henry looked at her and shrugged. The subject had not moved. He was not even looking at them. His eyes were staring off in the direction of the bridge and its military cordon.

"What did you mean by dirt-eater?" asked Sarah.

"You don't watch much television do you? Some of the people in the plague areas are going crazy. And some of the crazies end up as mindless wanderers who act like peeping toms and cause mischief. Quite a few have been spotted eating garbage, so the name dirt-eaters stuck. Anyway, the CDC is looking for anyone that survived inside a kill zone. Someone in the department figures these crazies fit that description. This one looks like he's been on the move for some time. Look at those rags he's got for clothes. He must have somehow swam the Delaware River."

Sarah went back to the car and got a pair of binoculars from her pack. She used the binoculars to study the dirt-eater close up. He seemed odd but harmless. His hair was matted with twigs and dirt. A small bug was crawling across his forehead. There was no body motion whatsoever. The man was acting more like a vegetable than a human. His face was expressionless and perfectly average in appearance; but still, something about that face gave off an impression that was unmistakably haunted. It took Sarah a few minutes to realize what was so unnerving. The man's eyes never blinked and the pupils never moved. His gaze was locked on that bridge.

"Do they always act like this?" asked Sarah.

"Beats me. This is the first one I've seen. I've got no idea how I am supposed to restrain him if he starts to run. Got any suggestions?"

"You're not going to shoot him?"

"Not likely. I have no idea what kind of moron came up with those orders."

The dirt-eater screamed something at them, gibberish, then turned and fled into the woods. At the same time a pair of police vans pulled to a stop. In seconds, the dirt-eater was out of sight. He moved with the speed of a wild animal.

"Jesus! Did you see that?" yelled Henry.

"Unreal," said Sarah. "Welcome to Mutual of Omaha's Wild Kingdom."

"There is no way anyone is going to catch that thing," said Henry. "I wonder if there's more like him?"

"I wouldn't be surprised if there was an entire tribe by now."

Once they got to Allentown, it was late and Henry was coming off his shift. He insisted that Sarah spend the night at his house. Henry's wife Karen turned out to be just as nice as promised. She offered Sarah some clothes and the living room couch to sleep on.

In the morning after breakfast, Sarah gave in to Henry who was pressuring her to call about the job in Virginia. She called Major Warton. He was not in his office, but his assistant gave her the number for the barracks running the quarantine line. The assistant was very helpful. Along with other details about the job, Sarah learned the quarantine line was called I64 – which referred to Interstate Highway 64. Apparently, a length of the highway which ran west through several states had been converted into a single quarantine line.

Feeling a little more confident about her prospects, Sarah made the second call. All the folks she spoke with at the I64 Operations Center knew Major 'Tommy' Warton. After a short telephone interview and a quicker computer records check, she was offered a job patrolling the line. They were even willing to pay for her airfare. She ended up on the phone with Mary in Human Resources.

"Would it be all right if I drove?" asked Sarah.

"Well, we need ya'll as soon as possible," said Mary.

"It's because of my dog that I want to drive, but I can do it nonstop."

"No, honey, that's fine. Take a day or two. Drive safe. The job will be waiting."

"Thank you, Mary. Umm... there's one more thing. Since I don't need airfare, can the department loan me the money for a rental car?"

"Sorry honey, we can't loan money, but Virginia State PD has a reimbursement arrangement with Hertz," said Mary. "I'll make a call and set up a car voucher. All you have to do is go to any Hertz, show your ID, and secure the car with a credit card."

"What if I don't have a card?"

Henry gave Sarah and Ralph a lift into Allentown. He used his credit card for the security deposit. Things were moving almost too fast. In one day, she'd gone from leaving behind a stolen car and hiking down a lonely highway to having a job in Virginia and a new friend willing to trust her with a rental car on his own credit card. Something had to go wrong.

Sarah kissed Henry on the cheek. He looked like he might blush. Sarah got into a brand new Ford Taurus and shut the door. She just sat there for a moment watching Henry as he walked away. Ralph was sitting in the front seat. He had on a new red bandanna that was a gift from Karen. Sarah wiped the tears from her cheeks. She started the engine and pulled out onto the road.

5 – I64 Quarantine Line, Richmond, Virginia: December

The midmorning sun shone through the windshield of the patrol car. Sarah picked up a pair of sunglasses from the seat. She wore the uniform of a Virginia State Police officer. The world was again a place where she fit in. It felt good to be working, but there were things about the job that disturbed her. A week ago, the New Jersey quarantine had been her prison and now the same kind of barrier was her lifeline.

So far, the day had been uneventful. A radio dispatch came in to increase her speed to ninety-five. She adjusted the cruise control and leaned back. Similar orders came in about every fifteen minutes. Central dispatch acted like an air traffic controller maintaining all the cruisers at different but constant distances apart. At any given time, over a hundred cars patrolled the I64 Line. To a stationary observer, the cars appeared to be randomly spaced at intervals of up to ten minutes. Predicting the gap was almost impossible and that made it difficult for jumpers to time when to break through the barricades and cross the highway.

The Line was the largest quarantine barrier in the country. The barrier was over a thousand miles of patrolled highway stretching west from Virginia Beach to Louisville, Kentucky where it turned south on I65 until it reached the Gulf of Mexico in Mobile, Alabama. The Line separated a supposedly uncontaminated southeast from a north pockmarked with death. A new world order was beginning here where societal classes were defined by acceptable exposure risk instead of education or money.

Patrol cars running back and forth shared the southern lanes of the highway. A barrier was being erected in the median or the northern lanes, when the median was not wide enough. Construction was still going on everywhere. The barrier was being deployed in four stages. The Army, National Guard, and hundreds of private construction companies were all involved in this massive expenditure of taxpayer dollars. Stage one was a razor wire fence eighteen feet high. Stage one had been completed for the entire length of the line. Stage two was floodlights and wireless video surveillance. This stage had been completed for most of the line, though it was a guarded secret that fully fifty percent of the video cameras were nonfunctional decoys. Stage three was an additional eighteen foot razor wire fence spaced twenty feet behind the first fence. Stage three had been completed through Virginia and some of Kentucky and Alabama; the other states were lagging behind. Stage four was the construction of vehicle obstacles in the 'no man's zone' between the two fences. The types of obstacles varied. At its simplest, the obstacles were piles of construction debris which was mostly broken concrete and stone. At its most advanced, the obstacles were prefab military barriers made from a reinforced concrete pad with a tangle of steel spikes as teeth. The spikes were made from sharpened, six inch diameter pipe set into the concrete pads. The spikes varied in height up to two feet, protruding from the ground like a bed of spears. The obstacle could disable anything short of a battle tank or heavy bulldozer. The spikes could impale tires, engine blocks, tread, and even whole vehicles. At a spot near Charlottesville, a punctured delivery truck had been left in place to illustrate 'by example' what the obstacle did. Stage four was complete through most of Virginia while other states lagged seriously behind. Virginia was clearly the poster child on how to put up a good barrier. So far, no one had made it to the other side. People tried, but no one made it.

Sarah spotted car number one-twenty-five heading in the opposite direction. All that separated them was a dotted white line. They closed on each other at a combined speed of over two hundred miles per hour. When they passed, air pressure first pushed them apart then a vacuum pulled them in. Sarah adjusted the wheel correcting for the pull. This was the most excitement of the day, and it came about every five minutes. She wondered what the accident rate was at night when officers were sleepy at the end of a long shift. The barracks was run on a non-rotating schedule. Sarah suspected it was to make sure that everyone was fresh for their shift, and that no one was out there on two hours of sleep.

Sarah was nearing the halfway point of her patrol. Her route was from Richmond to Virginia Beach and back. She ran the loop three or four times a day. She passed a Coppertone lotion billboard. The ad was from an old-fashioned campaign that had recently been reissued. There was a small blonde girl whose tan line showed as a dog tugged her suit bottoms down. There was something oddly exploitative about the image that bothered Sarah.

She thought about the billboard for a while and tried to figure out what specifically bothered her. Her leather uniform jacket was folded on the seat next to her. She unconsciously withdrew a miniature voice-recorder from a pocket. The device still contained a recording made on the last night of old New Jersey. She played it. From the tiny device came the sounds of a car moving, and wind, and a radio news show. A man's voice was dictating to his secretary then coughing. She heard the crunch of an accident and car horns, followed by a stillness filled only with a doomed radio news show which soon went off the air, leaving nothing but a hiss. The haunted recording immersed her into the night when the world she knew was destroyed. She had played it countless times before. Tears streamed down from her eyes. She was tugged by an instinctive urge to leave this place and travel farther south. She felt like a creature that was not finished with her migration, trying desperately to put down roots.

~

The sun was bright and warm as Sarah pulled into the Command Center at Richmond. Her shift was over and she needed to unwind. Another car pulled in next to her. She recognized the officer; she'd chatted with him a few times before. His name was Alex Breaux, a very attractive older guy, maybe in his forties. His shift ran the same as hers, four in the morning to twelve noon.

"Hey, Alex."

"Sarah."

"Another day, another fifty cents..."

"What, you got a raise? Damn, that fries me."

Sarah smiled. She liked Alex and thought of him as a possible friend. She'd been here a week and had socialized with no one except a few people she worked with.

"Want to grab something to eat?" said Alex.

He'd never asked that before.

"Sure," said Sarah. "As long as I pay my own ticket."

"I never argue with a lady."

Sarah was pleased by the opportunity for some conversation and food. Lunch turned out to be a Cajun hole-in-the-wall that served the spiciest food she'd ever eaten. The blackened catfish was out of this world, if she could only get her eyes to stop tearing and her nose to stop running. Alex seemed to think her suffering was funny. He had this Creole accent that was one part French and one part country. Sarah liked the way he spoke even when he teased her.

"You remind me of my kitty when she went after a piece of cayenne pepper shrimp," said Alex. "Her eyes watered fiercely, but she wouldn't stop eating that shrimp. There's a lesson in that, I think."

"What? Good things make you cry?"

"Maybe, but how about it's that we all have to feel pain so that we can appreciate life."

"Well, thanks for that nice thought."

"Hey, all us coon-asses are philosophers at heart, philosophers of life."

"Well, Mr. Philosopher, mind if I try some of your crab?"

"Help yourself."

Sarah picked up a claw with her fingers and snapped it open. She drew out the meat with her lips and, only afterwards, realized how provocative that might have looked. Alex didn't seem to notice.

"How long have you been working the line?" asked Sarah.

"From the first day, before they added all that wire and other Berlin Wall paraphernalia."

"Do I detect a bit of sarcasm?"

"There's something not right here, and I don't mean the moral stuff about keeping people from crossing state lines or other dribble like that. I mean cold hard irreversible wrong. People have been shot crossing that line."

"I'd heard gossip and seen reports," said Sarah. "But no one's willing to talk about it."

"I'll bet. Especially if you're the someone who pulled the trigger."

"Have you?" asked Sarah.

"No, but what if I see a family who's made it over the fence, women and children? What if they're almost into the woods, and there's no chance of stopping them any other way? Am I gonna shoot them?"

Alex shook his head. There were deep wrinkles in his expression.

"I just don't know," he said. "I just don't know."

Sarah hadn't wanted to think about it. A state of emergency and Martial law were in effect. The orders were that jumping the line was a capital offense, and standing policies were to use deadly force to prevent it. The justification was that a jumper might be bringing in a disease that could kill thousands. They were potential mass murders, but line-jumpers were not violent criminals. How could she kill a man or a woman for doing something she herself had done a week ago in New Jersey and then again, with state permission when joining the I64 Line? She couldn't and that was that. She'd have to let them run for the woods and hope she wasn't killing thousands. No, she couldn't do that either. She couldn't risk thousands of lives to ease her conscience. She would shoot. Had to...

"You know the worst of it?" said Alex. "There're rumors that the CDC suspects this bug isn't contagious and that it's something you catch from water. All this police state oppression and murder could be for nothing."

Alex tossed another empty can of beer into the lake. He was leaning against the front of the patrol car. Sarah was sitting next to him on the hood. Her legs were crossed Indian style. The sun was almost gone. She watched a bird flying to its nest across a darkening sky and then took another nip from a pint bottle of Southern Comfort. She was pleasantly warm from the liquor. The full moon was already a quarter of its path across the sky. In the twilight, the lake was turning an oily black. At the shore, the water was speckled with reeds. Small fish jumping at insects made occasional splashing sounds that were like bubbles popping. Neither she nor Alex had said anything for quite sometime. They were just sitting there in the simple unspoiled beauty of this place. Sarah glanced over at Alex. His expression gave the impression of deep thought. She felt herself drawn to him. She touched his shoulder. He turned toward her. Impulsively she kissed him. There was chemistry between them. She felt it. Alex backed away from the kiss.

"Don't," he said. "You're a bit drunk and that's no way to start something."

"Don't you like me?" said Sarah. She was confused. She knew what she'd felt and knew he'd felt it, too.

"I'm old enough to be your daddy."

"Maybe I like older men."

"I'm damaged, Sarah. You don't want to get involved with me."

Sarah picked up his hand and squeezed it. She forced him to look her into the eyes.

"What are you talking about? Tell me," she said.

Alex let out a sigh which seemed to drain something dark from his body.

"I was in a shooting a few years back. I got who I was aiming at, but the kid also got me. A pair of bullets kicked around inside my belly and chest and chewed me up pretty good. The doctors were amazed that I'd survived, but they were wrong. The old me died that night, and what's here now is damaged inside and out."

"You look all right to me; and I'm not sure if I've ever met a kinder, more thoughtful man than you."

"Sarah, that's nice; but it's not true. I killed a teenager that night and I was killed that night. And maybe on the outside I look okay, but the heart and the plumbing just don't work right anymore."

"Oh God, I'm so sorry." Her cheeks were flushing. "I wouldn't have kissed you if I'd known."

"No, no, you don't understand," said Alex. He was almost laughing. Her expression must have been awful. "Not that kind of plumbing. The sex part works fine. Maybe it would have been more humane if it didn't."

Sarah was now even more intrigued but at the same time wasn't sure if she could handle any more. Alex seemed to want to talk. Now that she'd opened the box, the least she could do was listen.

"I haven't slept with a woman in over two years," said Alex. "It's left me kind of mixed up."

"I don't understand," said Sarah. "If you're umm, functional, why not?"

Alex lifted the bottle of Southern Comfort from her fingers and took a long drink.

"The injury left me with multiple bypasses on two big arteries. I've also got a shortened intestine, a pacemaker, and an amazing collection of scars. I can pop-off and die without warning, and that's just not a fair burden to lay on someone you care about. And besides, what's left of my body is not the prettiest thing for a woman to see, especially if she's anticipating romance. You should have seen the look in my wife's eyes when she saw me without a shirt. It was an ocean of pity, edged with revulsion. In that split second, I saw my future and knew it was over between us. Oh she said nice things and tried to be there for me, but she never once touched me again. To her, I was ugly and fragile. She left me a year ago and remarried."

Alex drank some more of the Southern Comfort and then handed it back to Sarah.

"You can't imagine what it was like," said Alex. "One moment you're the same as everyone one else; then, the next instant, there's this emotional and physical canyon you can never bridge. You're now and forever different. Sometimes I catch myself watching a couple while knowing I can never have that again. I'm damaged goods. I can't run up a flight of stairs; I can't hike in the mountains – nothing that will heavily tax my body. I want to do some of those little things that everyone else does. It's corny, but it's true: you never appreciate little things until it's too late and they're gone.

"The doctors said there's nothing more that can be done to repair the damage. Their opinion is that I'll probably be dead before I turn fifty, but you know what? I don't care. I've lost so much of my old life that losing what's left doesn't matter as much as it might have before. But for some reason I'm careful and I keep going on.

If I do all the right things and don't pop too soon, hey, who knows? Maybe there's a chance some new treatment will come along. It's funny, sometimes I catch myself thinking that I can just go out and get a few new parts for my body like you would for a used car. It's hard to believe that with all this technology there's nothing for me."

Sarah wanted to hug him but held back.

"Alex, you shouldn't be working as a cop," she said. "It's too stressful. You're crazy to be doing this job."

"You can't tell anyone!" His eyes were wide with a look of someone who was far too alone. "I've lied about my health records. The shooting happened in Louisiana and there's privacy laws covering medical records. If the Captain found out, he'd stick me with a desk job or worse. I love being a cop – even this lousy detail. It's the one job where I can make a difference. Every day I wake up is a day that I might save lives. I have to leave some good behind when I'm gone. After I was shot, I never thought I'd get the chance to work as a cop again. It's horrible and I feel guilty that a new chance for me came out of this plague. The police are desperate for hands and aren't looking too closely at the applicants. If you have some kind of proof you worked as a cop, you're hired on the spot."

"I won't tell anyone," said Sarah.

She kissed him lightly on the lips, and wanted him all the more, wanted him for his vulnerability, for his honesty, for his haunted soul. A relationship was hopeless. He looked so desperate.

The moonlight reflected across the lake as streaks of silver. There was a soft lapping of water at the shoreline. Some time ago, they had moved inside to the front seat of the patrol car and rolled down the windows. Both Sarah and Alex were quietly intoxicated from a second bottle of Southern Comfort. She was warmly aroused and sensed Alex was in a similar mood. Maybe if she was gentle, so very gentle? With a sense of shyness, she began to unbutton her shirt. The shyness turned into a smile as she saw a mixture of fear and boyish desire flushing Alex's face.

The moon was gone. With their tangled clothing straightened and back on, they had lain in each other's arms for hours drifting in quiet talk and half dreams. Sarah knew that if they had enough time together this man could grow to love her. He was such a caring soul. How could any woman have rejected him the way his wife had? She gently hugged him to her chest in a desire to nurture the man and his soul. He had opened himself to her so completely and vulnerably. She wanted to do the same. She sat up. In the protective cocoon of their world, she told him her deepest secrets – how she'd survived in plague-ruined New Jersey and fled across quarantine lines. She described everything. Her past came out of her in huge gushes of emotion that she couldn't have stopped even if she'd wanted to. Through it all, Alex had sat facing her, staring wordlessly.

"Look at my eyes," said Sarah. "They look normal, don't they? God, it's hard to imagine these normal-looking eyes could have seen all those horrible things. I don't understand how they can still be eyes. Why haven't they been rotted away by what they've absorbed? Alex, it's like I was a different person. I buried my own parents in holes I dug myself with these hands. I've seen so much death, felt so much heart-ache. I'll be scarred and fleeing from what I've been through for the rest of my life; and when I sleep, the dreams… the dreams are worse than what really happened."

It was done. She had emptied herself and stopped talking. It had felt good to unbottle her soul like that without any holding back. She knew they were now in some way married by their shared secrets. They each knew things that could ruin the other. Sarah waited in silence for Alex to say something…

6 – New York City: December

Artie had no memory of coming to the window. He had no idea why he had been looking down from their apartment at the exact moment when it had happened. The rush of people returning from lunch was crowding the streets. On the sidewalk people began falling in their tracks. Out-of-control cars went into a chain reaction of collisions that were chewing up everything in their path. The noise was horrible. Artie was speechless. At some point, Suzy had come to the window. He became aware of her crying. The horror quieted down for a moment; then, he saw a bus coming along the avenue amid sparks from glancing impacts with stationary cars and trucks. The bus was gaining speed. Cars were whacked out of its path, some torn in half as if they were made of foil. A channel of crashed vehicles held the bus on course down the middle of the avenue until a gap in the wreckage allowed it to escape. The bus veered toward the curb and over a wedge of flattened car that sent it airborne in a graceful leap. The thirty-ton missile came to ground at the base of a newsstand, obliterating the structure in a spray of wood fragments, fiberglass, and cement. The bus careened a hundred feet more, straight into the side of a building, and stopped; but its engine continued to run, its rear wheels trying to jam it deeper into the building. He could see the tires slipping and then gaining traction. Something in the bus exploded with a bang that rattled the glass in his face.

An hour later, Artie and Suzy were sitting in the living room of their apartment. Fear was in Suzy's eyes. Artie was certain his eyes looked the same to her. The television screen was filled with static. The drapes were pulled tight. The radio came back to life with an updated news bulletin on the disaster which had begun an hour ago: New York had been hit with the plague at one in the afternoon. The entire city and its suburbs were affected. Chaos and mob violence were ruling the city. Artie had no idea what to do. He had to save Suzy and the tiny life they'd created in her womb. With all he had done in his secret violent past, with all he knew about survival in the streets, there had to be something he could do. He knew with conviction that he was ready to die to save her.

The sun was fading. They had been sitting in silence on the couch for a long time. The telephones had not worked for hours. Like clockwork, every hour Suzy would mechanically pick up the phone and dial her parents in Washington. Artie was grateful that his parents had not lived long enough to witness this kind of end. He had his arm around Suzy and felt her sobs come again. She squeezed a pillow against her chest as if she were trying to wring the pain out of this world. A tone came from the television. Suzy jumped.

"This is the emergency broadcast system. The civil defense has declared a state of emergency in your area. Please tune your radio to seven sixty on the AM dial."

Artie felt worse than useless and it angered him. The same message played from the television every ten minutes. The radio was tuned to seven-sixty, but nothing had come through since he changed the channel. Earlier, the news had been horrible; but now any news was better than this emergency message which seemed to come from a system that no longer had people manning it. The last piece of information he'd heard was that the National Guard was being mobilized. The flames of anger grew hotter in Artie's chest. The only National Guard he'd seen was a Humvee that had gone out of control and crashed into the first floor of their building. A fire truck siren began wailing far off in the city. The sound faded; then, was gone. A terrible thought occurred to Artie. What if the Humvee started a fire? He stood up. Suzy looked at him.

"Where are you going?"

"Downstairs to check on that Humvee."

"No! You can't. You have to stay here."

Artie sat back down and hugged her.

"I have to take a look," he whispered. "What if it starts a fire?"

Suzy went limp in her embrace. She was letting him go.

"I'll be right back."

There was this look of fear in her eyes that hurt him. He felt she was preparing to watch him die. He would be alright. He had to do this. He had to protect her. He picked up the loaded .357 magnum from the coffee table and left the smaller nine-millimeter behind for Suzy. Not that she would touch the gun, but he hoped if she was scared enough, survival instincts might take over. He locked the door behind him without glancing back. In the hallway, he put a scarf over his mouth and nose. He was worried about contagion. He walked up to the elevator, then thought better of it and took the stairs. He had a flashlight in his back pocket in case he needed it.

The lobby was in shambles. Water from a broken pipe was draining like a small river out into the street. The Humvee was embedded in a wall. The driver and his passenger were both dead from bullet wounds to the head. Artie didn't want to get too close. He heard the crunch of a footstep in broken glass and swung around with his gun pointed.

"Whoa, partner," said the man.

Artie recognized him from an occasional nod in the hallways. He was a big man with a western accent and wavy gray hair. He held a pump shot gun with a flashlight attached to the barrel. The muzzle was pointed at the ground. He wore a gasmask, the kind used by rescue workers. The man's face was completely visible behind the mask's visor. He had deep wrinkles around his eyes.

"I'm Jesse, Twelve C" said the man. His voice had an odd vibration caused by the gasmask.

"The name's Artie…" He held out his hand, but didn't give his apartment number. Suzy was there by herself.

"You been down here long?" asked Artie.

"'Bout an hour. I figured someone had to look out for the building and check into things. Glad to see at least one other man's thinking the same way."

A series of faint pops echoed from outside in the street. The sound was dozens of blocks away. Someone was killing his fellow New Yorker – nothing new, just more obvious. Jesse walked over to what remained of the front doors. Glass crunched under his boots. He shook his head.

"Looks like the party's finally over," said Jesse. "You know, for a long time I thought if it came, it'd be a terrorist with an a-bomb trying to finish what they started at the twin towers. Who'd have figured it'd be some goddamn natural born germ that'd take down all we built?"

"I'm not giving up," said Artie.

"Neither am I, son. All I'm saying is our way of life is over. The world's crashing out there; and I suspect for years to come, it isn't going to be pretty. All those angry people living in poverty just got their lottery ticket cashed, and you can bet they're gonna be joined by lots of other folks who feel entitled."

"I've got to go check on my wife," said Artie.

"You do that, son; and remember what I said. I know what I'm talking 'bout. You see something that doesn't look right – you either run or shoot. Don't give the bad one's a second chance, 'cause sure as shit they won't be handing out any breaks to you."

"See you, Jesse."

Wyatt Erp, thought Artie as he walked toward the stairs. Then it hit him. He remembered hearing from a neighbor about this guy. He was as rich as they came and made every penny on his own. He started as a roughneck on oil rigs down in South America. There had been a story about him in the Wall Street Journal or some other paper.

Artie turned around to say something more, but Jesse was gone without a sound. Artie walked back out into the lobby and looked around. The man had vanished. There was only the sound of water draining out into the street.

The hike up the stairs was taking a long time. What Jesse had said about everything being over was starting to really enrage Artie. He wouldn't let it end like this. Halfway up and badly winded, Artie was thinking about using the elevator; but getting stuck was worse then getting tired.

As Artie entered the front door, Suzy leapt into his arms. She kissed him and hugged him fiercely as if he'd been missing for years.

"I was so scared. I'm sorry about what I said."

Artie had no idea what she was talking about. What had she said?

"You were gone so long. I thought you might have been hurt or worse." Suzy began to cry. "I hadn't told you I love you."

"I'm here, Suzy. It's alright. I'm sorry I was gone so long. This guy was in the lobby and..."

The emergency broadcast symbol dropped from the television. A reporter was speaking from a helicopter. The channel was re-broadcasting CNN. Entire blocks of the city were on fire. The aerial views reminded Artie of 9/11, only worse. The image shifted to a telephoto view of groups of people breaking into storefronts. The scene was lit by fire as much as by building lights. A piece of amateur video came on showing a gang member walking out into the middle of traffic and shooting someone in their car.

"The streets are impassable. There are no fire companies to respond. Government estimates are placing the dead and injured at over one million. The spirit of community and pulling together that stood out during 9/11 is nowhere to be found. We have received numerous reports of gangs roaming the streets, killing and robbing at will. There has been a complete breakdown of law enforcement. The governor has made an urgent request to the federal government for the Army to be sent in. We understand that several companies of soldiers are on their way to assist the National Guard and will be on the ground within a few hours. These are troops who have been trained for urban warfare. Those who are trapped inside the city appear to be on their own until then."

The video image shifted to another piece showing a mob of soot-faced people raging down the streets, breaking into stores, setting fires. Fights were erupting spontaneously within the mob. Someone grabbed the camera. The video went black.

"Those aren't gangs," said Artie. "Those are just people. They've all gone fucking insane!"

Artie knew the gangs were there too, growing stronger, feeding off the mobs – maybe even inciting it all. They would emerge as the new rulers of this world. Long live the Bloods, and the Crypts, and the Dragons.

The television screen switched to a female reporter standing on the George Washington Bridge. Spotlights from the New Jersey Quarantine line had been turned around and were being used to help people find their way across. Soldiers were mixed in among the people and trying to help. The plague lands of New Jersey were now sanctuary. A gust of wind stole the reporter's scarf and carried it over the side of the bridge. She glanced at it and then turned back to face the camera.

"Reports are coming in from the other bridges and tunnels. They are all jammed with auto accidents. People are climbing over the wreckage in a panic to get out. If you are listening to me from your homes, please stay there. Stay inside wherever you are. It is not safe to try to leave."

The image shifted to the anchor desk. A man with splotched makeup stared back.

"We are receiving information from Reuters that kill zones have occurred again along the New Jersey coast. One minute please. Atlantic City, Seaside, Wildwood. What?...   Please stand by... Yes..."

He pressed in on his earphone with his fingers.

"Something is happening in Philadelphia. We have received an unconfirmed report that the Philadelphia area has been struck by what has been described as a large kill zone. Reports are now starting to come in over the wire. There are names of cities, areas that have been hit. These events are taking place almost simultaneously. We have no idea of the magnitude. These could be small or large events. The names are scrolling too fast to read. London has been hit, Zurich, Moscow, Chicago... Excuse me..."

The man's voice cracked. His eyes flooded with tears. His face was red. He took off his microphone. The camera shifted to a female anchor.

"This is Laura Martin. John Ackerman's family lives in Chicago. I will try to continue keeping you informed. The reports of outbreaks are in the hundreds. We are receiving information of widespread deaths in Asia, Okinawa, Hong Kong. No place seems untouched by these events. God help us... God help us all."

Artie laid his head down on Suzy's lap and cried. He'd never cried before, but what he was feeling was too much... it was all too much. Suzy curled up with him on the couch. She nuzzled against him. When the pain finally dimmed, he opened his eyes. His vision was blurred with water. The screen was showing coverage from Washington, D.C. People were lying on the sidewalks by the reflecting pond. The camera was canted to one side and there was no one to level it. In the background the Washington monument was brightly lit against a darkened sky. Wind blew leaves across the ground. Suzy's parents lived on the outskirts of D.C. He reached for the remote and turned the set off. Suzy never saw it and thankfully the reporter had said nothing specific about D.C.

"What are we going to do?" said Suzy.

Artie got up and then lifted her to him. She looked awful. There was age showing on her twenty-three year old face.

"We are going to stop watching this tragedy on TV and we're going to get out of here. We are getting out before it's too late."

"We can't go!"

"Yes, we can, honey. Listen to me. We can't stay. What happens if we lose power? What happens when the food runs out?"

"The Army will be here by then."

"Look at what they're showing. The Army isn't coming to save us from this. There aren't enough soldiers in the entire world. The longer we stay in this island death trap, the worse our chances will be."

"There's no way out. The bridges are jammed." She wiped the tears from her cheeks with a shirtsleeve. "There are mobs killing people in the streets. We'll be murdered if we go out there. I'm not going, Artie. I'm not!"

"We're going to wait until the sun comes up. Most of these crazies will be tired after a long night of fun. We are going to drive as far as we can and walk the rest of the way if we have to."

7 – I64 Line, Virginia: Before the NY kill zone, December

The plague had been mostly quiet since the Los Angeles kill zone almost two weeks ago. The day was clear and very warm for December. It was almost twelve noon. Sarah would be off the clock in a few more minutes. Her speedometer read eighty-five. She glanced into the back seat of her patrol car. Ralph looked happily in the midst of some grand canine dream. Next to him were a beach blanket and a small ice chest with lunch inside. The timing was perfect. She'd be off the clock at a location on her patrol nearest Virginia Beach.

At precisely twelve noon, she cleared the radio for the day and got permission to open up the throttle and head east for a little R-and-R. The beach was the nearest thing to heaven she could imagine. She'd find a deserted spot and nap amid the sound of waves and gulls. Ralph could spend the day chasing birds and getting petted by kids.

At first, she had thought about inviting Alex; but she needed time alone to think. They'd been together every minute they weren't working for the past two days and they were thrilled with each other. Sarah was starting to get cold feet. She was afraid something bad had to happen. Things were just coming together too perfectly. She and Alex had made love again last night just before their shifts started. His health seemed fine. In fact, he seemed to be growing younger.

Sarah bit her lip as she drove. The only black mark today had been when a CDC request had come in via fax and e-mail. The request ordered authorities to increase their efforts to locate and detain what were being called 'sole family survivors.' The orders included a questionnaire for potential subjects to answer. The CDC was searching for people who were immune to the plague. Sarah knew they were looking for people like her and so did Alex.

Alex had become upset. He wanted to know what pencil pusher idiot had come up with this idea of a questionnaire. What were they expected to do? They had orders to shoot to kill anyone trying to cross the line.

"Excuse me, sir. I know we just told you to back off and go fuck yourself, but would you mind terribly taking the time to fill out our little questionnaire?"

The police radio broke her thoughts. The report was a line-jump attempt in progress near Williamsburg. Someone on a motorcycle had used a hand-grenade on the razor wire and gotten through onto the southern lane. Williamsburg was less than fifteen miles behind her.

The patrol cars were equipped with transponders which radioed exact position automatically every second. She picked up the microphone.

"Dispatch this is ten-ten. Do you want response?"

"Ten-ten negative. Perp is west bound at a hundred and fifty plus. We have closer units. Nothing you can do, Sarah; besides, you've earned your day off. Hit the beach and bring back a little sand for the rest of us."

"Ten-four, Alice."

Someone trying to jump the line in daylight was unusual. This perp was either stupid or desperate or maybe a little of both. Sarah's heart was beating fast even though she was far from the action. People she knew were responding to the call. They were playing a dangerous game. She'd had a tense moment the other morning. At five a.m., she'd been first responder to a tripwire alert. She'd had to draw her weapon to hold back the jumpers. She'd been alone for minutes that had seemed like hours. Never before in her career had she been so close to using deadly force. Several guys with wire cutters were trying to snip their way through the second fence. Apparently unarmed and intoxicated, they'd ignored her warnings because she wasn't a man. They'd called her sexy. She knew if they'd opened the fence, her gun would have been the only way to stop them. Finally, backup had arrived. Sam got out of his cruiser and jacked a shell into a riot gun as he walked over. As soon as they saw a policeman instead of a policewoman, the jumpers gave up. The entire event was insane. She could have been forced to shoot them because they were too stupid to believe she'd use her gun. Sarah shook her head. All in all, she'd been lucky and knew it. So far, she'd only had that one incident. Nighttime line work was a high encounter patrol. The radio squawked again.

"All cars on pursuit zulu-five, backed it down to one double zero miles per hour. Put some distance between you and the perp. We have air coming in."

Sarah was stunned. 'Air coming in' meant an Army Apache had been dispatched. They wanted this one stopped fast. He must have been nearing some exit point where they could lose him.

"This is dispatch. Air confirms: splash one jerk on a bike."

"Shit, Bobby did you see that! That fucking Bushmaster chain-cannon turned 'em into a self-igniting red spot. Goddamn… Score one for the Apaches!"

"Copy that."

Sarah was torn between relief and cynicism. The thermostat was definitely being turned up on her job. The official number of kills for this week was now ten. A secret war had been declared on civilians trying to jump the line. She wondered what Alex would say about this one. She'd been on the job only a week but already understood how things worked. It wasn't just fear of contagion that was powering the line; it was greed powered, too. Rumors had been circulating through every city, town, and squatter's camp that the plague didn't like warmer southern regions. If millions of people started migrating, the infrastructure of the southern states would be strained to the breaking point. If expensive social programs weren't enacted, there would be mass starvation and crime. Those in power were in no mood to take on the care and feeding of hordes of godless northerners. To some, an old fashioned plague was just not as serious a problem as financial drain. Sarah sped past the Norfolk Naval Base at almost a hundred and twenty miles per hour. In another fifteen minutes, she'd hit Virginia Beach.

Sarah pulled her cruiser into a secluded spot. She didn't want a passerby to see an officer of the law stripping in her car. She wrapped her uniform inside her Kevlar vest and stowed it in the trunk along with her weapons. She wore a two-piece bathing suit under her cut-offs, t-shirt, and sandals. The weather was cool enough that she figured the bathing suit would never see sunlight today.

Sarah pulled a small cooler from the backseat. Ralph was already prancing through clumps of reeds and sand. He let out a short bark as a pelican took to the air. The sudden movement startled Sarah. She looked up just as the pelican flew directly over her head, less than ten feet above her. The bird was huge and prehistoric in appearance like a flying dinosaur. Ralph must have been startled too, because he came back to her and hung around until they both ventured onto the sand together.

Sarah had little trouble finding a deserted stretch of sand – almost the entire beach fell into that category. She laid out her beach towel a hundred yards from a small group of people and sat down. There was a distant smell of barbecue. She could see small children playing in the surf. The scene was almost like a slice of some earlier age that had been lost to this newly troubled world. She was saddened that those people and their joy now seemed so out of place.

Sarah remained on her towel a few more minutes and then stood up. Maybe a walk would get her more into the spirit of things. It was her day off. Why was she this depressed? She left her sandals near the towel and walked barefoot along the surf.

The water was up to her ankles. The damp sand felt good as it formed into the contours of her feet. She stopped for a moment and let the water move past her. As it receded, it pulled back some of the sand from beneath her. She could feel it slipping between her toes. There was a bitter sweetness to it. The sand was like her life that had slipped away.

"Damn it," she muttered. "Stop moping, and get with the program."

She picked up a thin piece of driftwood and tossed it into the waves. Ralph charged past her and into the water. A wave came over him, throwing spray into air. A titanic struggle ensued. He emerged with the wood firmly between his teeth. Sarah could swear she saw him grinning. He was the conquering hero with his prize. He dropped the trophy at her feet. She picked up the wood and threw into some scrub grass. He yelped and was off to fetch it.

A cool breeze was coming off the ocean. The sky had grown a little overcast. The deepening mix of charcoal and blue gave the sky a bruised look. Sarah strolled the beach without aim or direction. At some point she picked up a scallop seashell. The shell was perfectly formed. She studied it for a moment before deciding to keep it. She was closer to the group of people. She could hear the squeals of children blending in with the calls of gulls. A huge flock was patrolling the sands between her and the people. There were hundreds of birds. She'd never seen so many in one place. Their calls were eerily like the sounds of a crowd of people at a cocktail party. Sarah wondered why so many birds were drawn together like that? As she strolled, she looked down at her feet and noticed for the first time that the water was teaming with hatching fish. Countless thousands moved like tiny silver darts in the tidal water. The gulls were here for the feast of baby fish.

Sarah felt disturbed. She looked down the shoreline. A father was walking knee deep into the waves to retrieve his child. He scooped up the little girl and set her on his shoulders. She had memories like that – memories of a wonderful father and an entire life she had been trying to forget. She looked at the seashell that was still in her hand. The shell was an artwork of nature. She stared at its intricate pattern of radiated lines and concentric circular ridges. A chill worked through her. There was a powerful feeling of déjà vu. She looked around and recognized her surroundings, but it was almost as if she was also somewhere else.

Ralph charged into the flock of birds, sending them into the air. There were so many, and they seemed to have become accustomed to dogs because they only flew off when he was within a couple of feet of each one. It was as if he were a tornado sending up a debris field of flying creatures. There was a queasy feeling beginning in Sarah's stomach. The bird sounds were loud, but something beneath their sounds – or within them – terrified her. A fog was coming in off the ocean. She thought of the miniature voice-recorder and its message of doom. Remnants of that message were here now. The signs were faint, but she was certain bits of it were hidden within the cries of the gulls and the sounds of the waves. She looked around. Everything seemed normal, but the message was now stronger and seemed to be growing with the approaching fog.

Sarah felt cold and hugged herself. Her t-shirt flapped in the sea breeze. She realized she was holding her breath. She suspected what was coming and wondered if she'd driven here to meet it. A gull stumbled on take-off and then landed awkwardly. Ralph stopped motionless amid the flock of birds. They were no longer fleeing. He looked confused. His head was cocked to one side as if listening to something. Sarah's heart was breaking. She could feel an invisible wave of death coming toward her from the ocean. The wave was building, tumbling, and would soon be crashing down on her. The wave reached shore. A startling cold rushed past and through her as the wave of death hit. The sensation was of ice crystals forming across her skin. She felt a terrible cold, but knew the air was tepid and not the source of her freezing.

Her brows wrinkled. She sensed there was another dimension to what was happening. She became aware of a subtle intelligence within the cold. Something was thinking inside it. An avalanche of strange thoughts tumbled into her. The language was unknown, unintelligible. She gasped and went to her knees as if driven down while staring into the face of God. She saw Kenny, her family, all gone in an instant like candles extinguished in a wind. Images came from nowhere. Bright and vivid with colors, scene after scene was seared into her memory. She was seeing through other people's eyes, hearing with other people's ears, perceiving other people's thoughts. The vantage points changed rapidly from doorways to rooftops to windows. All the views contained different scenes of the same event. In the streets and buildings of New York City, men and women and children were dropping to the ground like discarded toys. Cars out-of-control were coming to rest in one colossal accident after another. A bus plowed through a corner newsstand, obliterating it and then hit the side of a building. The view jumped to inside a subway careening out of control through a tunnel. The view jumped to looking up at a helicopter spiraling down from the sky. The view jumped to a street corner where the dead and dying lay at her feet. Somehow, she understood that all these witnesses of the horrors were left unharmed by the scourge. They were all 'passed over' as if from the ancient Hebrew story of God's wrath.

"Take me," she moaned. "Please take me."

She felt her body control was failing, paralyzed. Her lungs were empty. She knew another breath would never fill them. There was a pressure from the cold intelligence squeezing in on her from all sides. The thing was crushing her with the weight of its concentrated thoughts. She clamped her eyes shut to embrace her death and waited.

Another breath came and shouldn't have, then another. Her eyes fluttered open. Light poured in as an ache in the sides of her head. She was still breathing. She had never stopped breathing. She began to realize those feelings of paralysis had not been hers, but someone else's final moments. Hesitantly, she began to accept this entity had not come for her. On her knees, surrounded by the dying embers of so many souls, she wondered if this thing was God and began sobbing. The entity was something other than life, something ancient and aware, and dangerous. Within that vast mind were plans and deep memories. She could almost grasp the designs. Her eyes opened wider as if to see the ideas better, but she was unable to open her mind wide enough to drink them in. Amidst her failure to embrace the panorama, she managed to sense one thing: there was no emotion within this awesome power. The entity was a mind of all-encompassing, pure logic; and it did not care nor understand the pain it inflected.

Ralph yelped. The thread snapped. Sarah was back on the beach. She realized he'd been yelping for sometime. She looked toward him as the danger registered into a single thought. No, not him!

First on all fours, then half standing, she scrambled in the direction of his cries. The oppressive weight of the strange intelligence was gone. Gulls were flying in the air like a swarm of gnats. Their cries were otherworldly. She couldn't find Ralph amid the clutter of flapping wings. His yelps changed to drawn out howls. She stumbled and fell onto the sand but continued crawling. Her eyes were flooded with tears. The cloud of birds thinned enough so that she could see Ralph sitting on his haunches with his head raised. The howl coming from him sent a spike of ice deep into her chest. She tried to yell his name but remnants of the phantom paralysis restrained her.

"Ralph!" she croaked.

His head turned in her direction. He looked confused. She called him again. He leapt off toward her at full speed. He looked okay! Oh God, was he alright? As he got closer, what she saw in his eyes took her breath away. His stare contained a very human expression of fear. He came to her and started barking. He wanted her to do something. Make it stop? Run?

"It's okay, sweetie."

Streamers of grounded sea-fog drifted across the beach like wind-blown veils. Sarah looked at the flock of birds; many had already fled; another group took to the air. She watched as one trailed off from the fliers, lost speed, and then fell. The bird recovered before reaching the sand and flapped off in pursuit of its companions. Sarah looked down the beach to where the people had been barbecuing. They were still there. A few were looking toward her, probably at the commotion she and Ralph had caused. The children were still playing. To Sarah it was as if they were all ghosts in the fog.

A little girl with a pail was chasing a man. The girl fell. The man turned back to pick her up and then he collapsed. Sarah felt numb as more people started to drop. Some just went down as if they were marionettes with their strings cut, while others farther away from the center of the group seemed to die in stages as they ran to help their companions. They dropped to seated positions, then to their sides, and then finally they too were motionless.

The world grew silent as if all life had stopped. Sarah knew what was happening reached far beyond this beach and far beyond her visions of New York. Something all-powerful was swinging its scythe through the fields of humanity.

People were lying dead less than a hundred feet away. Sarah blinked as if, by that simple act, the illusion would revert to what she wanted it to be; yet it remained. Her face was damp with tears. She noticed blood on her fingers. She carefully opened her hand which still clasped the seashell. The shell had caused a serrated wound. She was surprised that she'd held on to it through the entire ordeal. She looked at the pattern of concentric circles in the shell. She looked at the sand, littered with victims. There was something connecting the two. She stood and walked toward the bodies. In this sprawl of death she saw evidence that the intelligence she'd sensed behind this plague was real. All the bodies lay within a large circle. The pattern was unnatural. She remembered people running in toward the center of the group and then dropping in mid-stride. She looked at those bodies and realized they had died immediately after crossing some invisible circular threshold which was now marked by the position of their bodies. She wondered if some would still be alive if they hadn't immediately run to their companions.

From a nearby street came a crashing sound, followed by the noise of raining glass. A beachfront community was just beyond the dunes. Sarah didn't turn in the direction of the noise. Instead, she looked at the dead and then out to sea. The fog was thinning where she stood, but the clouds were still thick out over the water. Sarah now understood that the malevolent force she had long sensed lurking in underground streams was in all the waters of the world. She was now aware of it everywhere and in everything living.

Sarah heard people crying from the direction of the streets. Ralph whined at her feet. She looked once more at the bodies lying in front of her and then glanced toward the dunes. She was an officer of the law and had taken an oath to serve and protect. She had shunned that obligation in New Jersey. Maybe this was her second chance? She trudged toward the dunes to see what needed to be done on the other side. Behind her, she left a trail of footprints in the sand.

8 – Southern New Jersey: December

The Dodge minivan started right up. Ed Devlin put it in drive. He was an average man, or at least that's how he'd always been proud to think of himself. Average height, average weight, an average family of two kids and a dog. He worked at Northridge Avionics as a technician assembler of components that went into the advanced fighter jet program. He'd never quite understood exactly what he was building, but that had been okay. He worked inside a clean room. Everyone wore white jumpsuits and masks like a surgical team. The air in the room was as free of pollutants and dust as modern science could make it. The electronic things he built were so sensitive that a speck of dust in the wrong place would make them fail and take a multimillion-dollar jet along with it. Now, the job was gone. He had the plague to thank for that. His foot pushed down on the accelerator a little. The speedometer crept up to sixty-five. The road he was on was a two-lane county freeway that ran along a scenic part of the coast that his wife Katy always loved.

He turned the radio off so that he could better listen to his own thoughts. He hated being average now. Average meant that his family had died. Average meant that his future was gone. Average meant that he had no hope of doing anything about it. His entire family had died together in their house while he tried to save them with first-aid he'd learned from television. Mouth to mouth resuscitation, chest massage, nothing had helped. If he'd only known more, he might have been able to save at least one of them. He felt drunk but had no alcohol in him. He knew from the doctors that were treating him, he was suffering from posttraumatic stress.

"These symptoms are nothing to worry about," the doc had said. "The feeling will wear off in a few weeks at the most. A lot of survivors have it to some degree."

Ed made the turn a little sloppily and then realized his speed was nearing eighty miles per hour. He slowed back to sixty-five. His eyes watered as he thought about Katy dying in his arms. Why hadn't he died with her? He rubbed his eyes with a coat sleeve. On the seat next to him was a copy of the local newspaper. On page three was a questionnaire from the Center for Disease Control and a follow up article. The CDC was looking for survivors like him. Sole family survivors were needed to help find out how to stop this plague. He wasn't sure if he was going to volunteer. That's why he'd gone for a drive. Often, driving helped him make up his mind.

He'd read the article several times and still couldn't remember half of it, not that this was much of a surprise. His memory had become awful since the plague. Sometimes he forgot where he was going and would have to drive all the way home, only to remember and head back out again. The doc told him this sort of thing was to be expected until the emotional problems wore off.

Ed wondered what it would be like to face the images in his head without the numbing effects of posttraumatic stress. He thought about his children lying on the floor of their bedrooms and sobbed out loud. He wanted to hurt this thing that had taken his children. The blare of a horn jolted him to his senses in time to swerve back into his own lane. A car shot past in the opposite direction. His nose was running, giving him the sniffles. He experimented at closing his eyes while on a straight piece of the road. His heart pumped faster. The experience was scary and seductive. He opened his eyes. There was a powerful side to being stress-intoxicated and having no reason to live. He could do things he'd never dreamt of trying before. He pushed down on the accelerator. The speed went up to eighty, then ninety. He watched the entrance to an overpass growing in the windshield. He closed his eyes and put his life in the hands of God. If he survived it would be the CDC for him. If not, well then....

9 – New York City: December

Sunrise was still an hour away. Estimates were that throughout the world millions had perished during those dark hours of the previous day. Artie leaned against the window frame, staring at the street while listening to the local news on the television. Fires were still burning in several parts of the city. The air had a bitter smell and taste. There were periods when it was difficult to breathe. He was waiting for Suzy to finish getting ready. As soon as the sun was up, they were leaving. Suzy was in the shower. She had decided to make the most of it since there was no guessing how long it would be until she got another chance. Artie was growing anxious but had no intention of rushing her. She'd shown more life this morning than in the last several days combined. He was willing to do whatever it took to keep her in this frame of mind. They were heading south and had plans of going through Arlington where Suzy's parents lived. There had been no word from them, but Suzy's hope was enough to sustain her. Artie turned up the volume on the television with the remote control.

A few minutes ago, the station had reported the Army was taking control of the streets, using armored vehicles. There was video of armored personnel carriers heading out of the Lincoln tunnel and down 42nd street. Artie had yet to see anything roll by his windows. All that was down there were bodies amid a twisted ruin of cars and riot debris. Occasionally, a body would move and then rise up to reveal itself as one of the party-goers sleeping off a hard night of fun. A pair of scientific experts were on the tube. Artie walked over to the couch and sat down.

"Have all the latest outbreaks occurred in the hot zones you've described in your report?" asked the reporter.

"Yes," said Professor Minasu. "If we look at the latitudinal lines that circle the globe, we see that kill zones are clustered into a pair of neatly arranged hemispheric bands; one in the Northern hemisphere and one in the Southern hemisphere. The equatorial and polar regions have been left relatively unscathed. The majority of the kill zones, 92 percent in fact, have fallen into this pair of bands that are about eight hundred miles wide. Now I'm not implying that the plague is following geographic lines of latitude just for the heck of it. I believe the bands are areas which are attractive to this pathogen. All the kill zones have hit areas that are environmentally damaged. So that is the first attraction. All the kill zones have hit areas that have a lot of water, beaches, rivers, lakes, marshes. So that's the second attraction, water."

"So, what does this mean in a practical sense?" asked the reporter. "Are you suggesting the population be relocated south of these danger bands and away from water and pollution?"

"Not simple pollution, environmental damage. There is a difference. For example, clear-cutting forests is not pollution but it is environmental damage. Another example would be water pollution that is severe enough to result in environmental damage. The Hudson River is a good example of that. Now, getting back to your question, I'd put it this way: if you live between the thirty-eighth to the forty-eighth parallels, northern or southern hemispheres, you are eight times more likely to die from the plague than if you lived in Miami which is on the twenty-sixth parallel. There is generally more environmental damage in these two hemispheric bands than in the equatorial and polar regions. This bug may be something which thrives in environmentally damaged places where its natural predators have been eliminated or beaten down."

"Los Angeles is latitude thirty-four," said the reporter. "Up until the New York kill zone, Los Angeles was the worst hit location in the world. Doesn't that disprove your hemispheric bands theory?"

"All the scientists I have talked with agree that L.A. was a statistical anomaly. My personal bet is that Southern California's extreme environmental problems made it a very attractive place for this bug to flourish."

The scientist sitting next to his colleague nodded in agreement. Artie stood up, walked over to the television and ripped the cable from the back of it. He didn't want to hear trash like that. He didn't want Suzy to hear trash like that. These people were insane. How could anyone call hundreds of thousands of people dying a statistical anomaly?

Artie and Suzy walked out the doors of their building. Sunrise had not brought much light with it. Clouds of smoke were blocking the sun. The smoke carried a peculiar scent that was pungent and earthy. Artie suspected the cause of the scent but refused to think about it. Ash was falling around them like snow. Everything was lightly coated with a dusty gray powder. They both had bandannas over their mouths and noses to filter the air into something breathable.

Artie's eyes were roaming in every direction, checking for possible threats. The tools of survival were all coming back to him like old habits. The streets were his home. He wore a black winter jacket; underneath it the Smith and Wesson .357 magnum was strapped to his side in a shoulder holster. On his hands were an old pair of fingerless black gloves made from a stitched, double layer of leather. He thought of them as his fighting gloves. Many times, they'd protected his knuckles from being ripped open on someone's jaw.

With Artie in the lead, they walked down a ramp into the garage. The electric gate opener still worked. Suzy's car, a brand new Toyota, was parked near the front. Artie had already made several trips alone to the garage. The trunk was filled with food and water. The rear seat was piled with warm clothes and personal items. He didn't think they would be lucky enough to make it out of the city with the car, and there was too much in it to carry very far on foot; but it was worth a try. He planned on trading at least half of the goods for some type of transportation when they reached New Jersey. Artie got in behind the wheel.

"Ready, honey?" he said.

"Yeah, I got my safety belt buckled."

He thought he saw the lines of a smile underneath her bandanna. Suzy's eyes were dry. She reached over, took his hand, and lightly squeezed it. This was the end of everything that had been their dream.

As Artie edged up onto the street, he could feel glass crunching under the tires. He kept the headlights on. The streets were empty except for the smoky fog. In the pre-dawn world, he could make out bodies of people lying in odd places amid a ruin of debris. He imagined what it would be like as the air warmed and sunlight filled in all the shadows.

He glanced over at Suzy. She'd brought some of her professional video gear with her and was videotaping through the window. Her face was pale and stiff. He could tell she was fighting to keep her grip – and succeeding. He wondered if this was the documentary producer in her; in any event, it was a personality he had never witnessed until now. He tried to imagine what it must be like to look through the focused lens of a camera and see bodies drifting in and out of view amid shadows and dust.

As they went though an intersection, Artie saw the burnt-out tail of a helicopter protruding from the ground floor of an expensive apartment building. A fire had gutted parts of the building. Neither of them talked. Artie looked at his left wrist. The tattoo of a red dragon coiled around a dagger was partly visible between the glove and jacket sleeve. He turned onto Riverside Drive and headed north toward the George Washington Bridge. Artie was under no illusions that New Jersey would be an ideal haven, but at least it wasn't a cramped little island with no resources other than abundant hate.

The sun had risen higher and was now a red circle enlarged by projection through a screen of smoke. The orb hung over the city like a bleeding eye. They had traveled fifty blocks north with another twenty to go. Artie had made countless detours and had been forced to drive on sidewalks more than once. The Toyota bore fresh scars from wreckage that he'd pushed out of the way with it.

He was growing nervous. They seemed to be the only car moving down these streets. Kids in gang colors were loitering everywhere. Some held weapons in plain view. Heads followed their car as they inched past at no more than ten miles per hour. He knew terrible things had happened here amid the darkness of night. People had done unimaginable things to their neighbors. He'd seen a young man's body tied across the bumper of a car. His chest looked like it had been crushed open from repeated impacts. On an iron gatepost, someone had jammed the decapitated head of an elderly man; and on the opposite post, a young woman. It was the artwork of sociopaths. Artie wondered when the first attack would come.

He slowed the car to a crawl. The road ahead was flooded. A hydrant had been sheered off at street level and was spouting into the air. Just past it, a van was smashed into the side of a building. Debris floated in the water: a red high-heeled shoe, a chair cushion, a plastic garbage bag bloated with trash. His window had been slightly open so that he could hear approaching danger. He raised it. They passed under the geyser. Water landed on the roof with a sound and force as though people were jumping on the metal above his head. Suzy had picked up her camera and was shooting video of the water as it cascaded down the windshield. Artie was certain the attack would come now while they were temporarily blinded. He reached inside his jacket. The waterfall started to clear. He could see shapes moving in front of him. He expected an army of gangbangers brandishing Uzis.

The water abated. The windshield drained. There was nothing except an empty street. Artie was stunned. A trickle of sweat ran down his forehead. He'd been certain this was the moment his past would catch up with him. Instead, it was almost as if the deluge had washed all the evil from the streets. Suzy looked at him. Her eyes were the only part of her face visible above the bandanna. He saw them wrinkling at the edges and knew she was smiling because she'd felt what he was going through. A bullet zipped through the windshield. Artie yelled something meaningless and guttural. He floored the gas pedal. Time seemed to expand. One second was an eternity. His head was clear. He was doing what he had to do. Another bullet punched though the rear window on Suzy's side and exited in a small spray of glass less than a foot behind his head. Suzy was still sitting up. He popped her seatbelt, grabbed the back of her coat, and pushed her down toward the foot well. Gunfire was exploding around them, but little was hitting the car.

They were moving fast and accelerating. Two blocks from the attack, Artie swerved left onto a cross-street that connected with the Henry Hudson Parkway. A fast escape was what he had in mind. The middle of the block was barricaded with the remains of an accident. He tried to stop, but the road was slick with something like oil. They smashed into the wreckage, adding their own car to the growing collection.

Suzy moaned. The force of the impact had jammed her into the foot well. Artie carefully helped her up. She seemed groggy. He was panicked waiting for the sight of blood.

"Are you okay?" he said.

No response, but also no blood.

"Suzy, are you okay?"

"Think so…"

The gunfire was still going. It sounded like a war zone. Artie realized what was occurring. He looked back at the opening to Riverside Drive. No one was coming down the street after them. The gunfire let up for a few seconds and then started again, punctuated with a small explosion. Suzy was clinging to him.

"We're safe," he said. "I'm positive we're safe. They're shooting at each other. We just got caught in the middle of their war."

Artie looked at the wreckage in front of them. He had to make a decision. Should they leave the Toyota behind and climb over the wreckage to the other side? He looked back at the corner. The block across the intersection was clear of wreckage. The Toyota hadn't collided that hard. The car was still drivable. He could turn around and race across the intersection. They'd be exposed to gunfire for maybe two seconds, but then they would still have the car. If they'd been walking and had stumbled into that firefight, they'd both be dead. Having a car had saved them. There was really no choice. He was going to do some Kamikaze driving with Suzy's Toyota instead of his bike.

Artie gunned the engine. He had positioned the car up the street past where the slickness began. Suzy was back in the foot well, this time by choice. He floored it; then, dropped the transmission into drive. The front tires spun. The car accelerated hard. He fought against it swerving. They entered the intersection. Artie cringed; then they were through it. Suzy peered up over the dash.

"Stay down," he yelled.

"The hell with that," screamed Suzy. "The next time bullets are flying I'm going to be shooting footage."

"You do that and I'll take away your camera and ground you for the rest of this life and the next."

"Nobody takes my camera, Mr. Bully man!"

Artie smiled. That's it, baby, he thought. They'd just been through gunfire and she was shrugging it off. He was proud of her. They were going to make it.

The Toyota had held up better than he could have asked. Artie shut the trunk. The last box of food was lashed onto a cart that he'd fashioned from a dolly they'd rented for the move into their new apartment. With leather belts that were buckled together, he had made a harness to pull the cart behind him. He lifted the front of the cart by pulling the belts over his back and shoulders. He dragged the rig a few feet. The cart was crude but workable. Suzy slung a duffel bag over her shoulder. The video camera hung from a chest sling. A camera-belt loosely circled her waist. Tucked into the belt's pockets were spare tapes and extra battery packs. They walked the last hundred yards to the tangle of huge steel cables that marked the edge of the George Washington Bridge.

Artie looked down the Manhattan Expressway from the entrance ramp where they stood. The Expressway ran across the George Washington Bridge and turned into Interstate Route Eighty on the other side. At the far end of Route Eighty was the Pacific Ocean.

There were no cars moving across the bridge, only people. Artie and Suzy stood motionless and watched the sea of humanity shuffling by: dirt smudged faces, people with knapsacks, people carrying small children, people with shopping carts. There were tens of thousands filing across the bridge like a tide of lost souls. The exodus reminded Artie of images he'd seen on television of mass migrations from the famines and wars in less fortunate countries. He used to think about how hard life must have been in those places. Now, in one night the entire world had been equalized.

Artie listened to fragments of conversations from the people slowly filing past. The lines would stop for a brief time and then start up again. There must have been rumors of every sort circulating like bad colds. One man was talking about a telephone call he'd made to his brother.

"My brother said Idaho is fine. Stores are open, people are going to work. Looks like God spared the heart of this country."

"Idaho's just next," said a guy behind him. "When you finally get there, it'll be just like here."

Suzy was videotaping the two men. She lowered her camera and pulled off her bandanna. Artie watched her take a deep breath. He pulled off his bandanna and joined her.

"Do you remember rule number four?" asked Suzy.

"No sweetheart," he said. "What's rule number four?"

"Everything humanity ever accomplished started with a single wish."

He kissed her and wished for a new home and a healthy baby. They picked up what they had and stepped into the stream of humanity.

10 – Atlanta: December

The CDC Facility in Atlanta had become an armed camp. There was now an entire detachment of Special Forces assigned to guard the facility. They had dogs, machine guns, armored vehicles, and two helicopters. The armored vehicles blocked the roadways. No one was getting inside uninvited. The presence of a protective force would have been comforting except for one problem: no one was leaving without permission from the military. The facility was now sealed off from the outside world. Mark had wanted to go to his hotel room for the night. He had been denied permission to leave. The soldiers were very polite and respectful and they did dispatch someone immediately to collect his belongings. But no matter how many times they addressed him as 'sir' and saluted, the inescapable fact was that he was now a prisoner of the United States Government.

The Army set up provisions for bunking, food, and sanitation. Mark, Kathy, Carl Green, and others fortunate enough to have senor staff offices on the fourth floor had what amounted to small hotel rooms. Everyone else had to accept using locker room showers and sleeping in shared offices or barracks set up in conference rooms. Supplies were stockpiled in every inch of available space. Cases of freeze-dried food were stacked to the ceiling in Mark's office. Army tents the size of houses were erected in the parking lot. There were satellite dishes and portable generators next to a huge camouflage-painted mobile home which was a military computer and communications command center. All these preparations sent a clear message that someone higher up was planning for the staff to remain under government control at this armed encampment for a very long time – or if necessary, forever.

Since his return from Los Angeles, Mark had immersed himself in his work. He hadn't had a drink or other medication and had no intention of crawling back into that refuge. The unfiltered reality heightened his feelings of loss; but along with the pain came a new sense of life and purpose, a purpose which the horrors of New Jersey and Los Angeles and New York only strengthened.

The holocaust had grown quiet as rapidly as it had burst onto the hapless planet. On December twelfth, more than a hundred large kill zones had hit around the world. None had occurred in the two days since then. There was endless news footage of people who were numb yet struggling to hold together what remained. The news shows had theme songs and special logos for their coverage. Different rumors and pet theories were being hawked by an army of talking heads. The hemispheric band theory being pushed by eco-terrorist Minasu had made a big splash on CNN and was now being treated as if it were scientific fact. Truth was an early casualty, but paranoia was in no short supply among reporters either. A talk-show host had stated that the I64 line's placement parallel to the bottom of the northern band was proof that the government had known about the *Minasu Bands* all along and was doing nothing to protect the public-at-large. This rumor was immediately picked up by lazier reporters and regurgitated in every way imaginable. Due to this rumor and others like it, hundreds of thousands of refugees were now camped at the I64 quarantine line, with more arriving every hour. The quarantine had become a symbolic line between hope and despair – and was covered by the media in that light. Mark suspected that all the quarantine lines were pointless. He was beginning to believe infected COBIC was wherever water could be found and that it was mostly dormant for now. Deep inside, he feared this small reprieve would not last. In the week since he'd received Karla Hunt's e-mail, he'd proved that infected COBIC was in fact some kind of artificial device, a hybrid of Chromatium bacterium and computerized nanotech machine. And like all computers, this thing had to be running a program, which meant there could be a schedule of kill zones it was following. He felt lost every time his mind drifted to visions of trillions of microbe-sized ticking bombs scattered across the globe like dust.

The technology was many decades beyond anything he could find in research papers. He was in daily consultation with Karla Hunt and several other experts in related fields, who formed his newly assembled nanotech advisory panel. All those bright minds were stumped as to where this technology could have come from; and if it was not a weapon, why it had been created? One expert suggested the device could be the result of a self-replicating and evolving nanotech experiment which had gone wildly out of control, but no one was able to adequately address the hurdles this theory raised. According to the panel, the technology did not exist to build a machine like these seeds. The most advanced nanotech work was being done at IBM, and theirs was an autonomous machine ten times larger and thousands of times simpler. The head of IBM's project was Dr. Param Marjari, one of Mark's experts. Some panel members were suggesting the nanotech was a 'black' defense department weapons project that escaped, while others were openly discussing alien technology and accidental infection from space. Speculation was running out of control. The simple answer was that there was no answer. Mark was confident that little green men were not the source of this device. His advisory panel evidently had far too much imagination. They were looking for complicated answers while Mark knew that core truths were often very simple. We humans had proved to be endlessly imaginative in coming up with ways to kill each other. This device was probably nothing more than the latest gift from that dark region of our psyche.

At least progress was being made on other fronts. The knowledge that they were dealing with a machine made it easier to study and even coerce reactions from the hybrid devices. Mark was certain that infected COBIC had some level of computer intelligence and was actively trying to avoid detection. By using low energy observation techniques and bait of untainted COBIC, he had been able to capture video of seeds reproducing and infecting their host bacterium. Reproduction only occurred in material-laden water, with seawater proving to be the best medium. The process was barely visible due to limitations in the type of low energy x-ray microscope that had to be used. The assembly of a new seed occurred over a one hour period. The process was thought to be similar to the growth of a crystal and looked like nothing more than ghostly scaffolding slowly materializing into view. The best theory so far was that raw material was harvested from seawater and assembled at a molecular level into a new seed. The assembly of each new seed always occurred within microns of a bacterium already infected with a seed. The unproven assumption was that the existing seed was either building or causing the self-assembly of the new seed. The proximity between new and old seed was so close that, in some cases, the forming seed appeared to be touching the cellular wall of the infected bacterium.

Once complete, the free-floating seed would slowly travel in a straight line directly toward the closest uninfected COBIC using a means of mobility that was both invisible and undetectable. The free-floating ball appeared to be nearly identical to an embedded seed. The only difference in appearance was a complete absence of the threadlike roots which connected an embedded seed to its host. Once in contact with an uninfected bacterium, the free-floating seed would pass through the bacterium's cellular membrane and into the nucleoid where it would take root. Dissection had confirmed that within minutes after invasion, the host's nucleoid and cytoplasm were completely entwined with nearly invisible threadlike roots. Both the seed's passage through cellular membranes and root growth were new mysteries. The bacteria's cell wall appeared to open and then reseal without any sign of trauma. Mark suspected some kind of molecular manipulation was being employed, much like the assembly process which was used to create each new seed. If this was true, it meant seeds might be able to pass through almost any physical barrier by simply rearranging the barrier's molecular bonds. Mark had learned that this kind of molecular assembly was one of the holy grails of nanotech research.

After the latest mass deaths, corporate America and the government had sent ever more money and resources flowing into the CDC. Mark had requested and received specialized equipment developed by IBM for molecular-level microelectronics research. The piece of equipment called a Mole had a ten-year waiting list. The system was delivered and installed in less than a day. It looked like the equipment had been pulled from an existing installation. A custom fixture had arrived by courier the next morning. The Mole was able to image objects in real-time at a level of magnification equal to an electron microscope; and it had nanomanipulators that could move and grip structures only hundreds of molecules in size. Mark hoped this equipment would allow him to see the hidden details of seed assembly. If he could capture that information, it might yield clues to the inner structure and workings of the nanotech device.

The nanotech advisory panel's daily teleconference had just taken an unexpected direction. Mark almost knocked over his coffee as he hastily retrieved a research paper from a stack on his desk. The paper was about something called emergent behaviors. Mark's understanding of emergent behaviors was that super-intelligent group actions could spontaneously arise from the random interactions of very primitive creatures. The interesting thing was that these super-intelligent actions were in essence unguided and accidental. Through natural selection, successful emergent behaviors were encoded into a species and passed on to future groups. The paper used honeybees, termites, and ants as examples. As a collective, ants carried out plans far beyond the brainpower of their species. With zero I.Q., they developed means of constructing cities, waging wars, building tools, and even hunting in groups. The theory being discussed in the conference call was that these nanotech seeds could be operating in a similar manner. The idea was incredibly frightening. What Mark had originally thought of as a very simple computer was now starting to sound like some kind of artificial intelligence.

Mark had seven experts on the conference call, seven minds and egos wrestling with one another to be right. After an hour of conflicting speculations, Professor Karla Hunt delivered what Mark considered the genesis of a second revelation about COBIC. Her question was so obvious and simple and inexcusably overlooked.

"Does anyone think the actions of groups of seeds are coordinated?" she asked.

It became immediately clear that everyone had assumed consensus where none existed. Some experts believed the actions were coordinated by a kind of collaborative supervisory program; others assumed the mechanics of random stimulus and emergent behavior with no master plan.

"I can't believe you actually think trillions of these hybrid devices are coordinating their actions," said Dr. Snow in a shrill voice. "There's no collective supercomputer working here. Do you honestly think these specks of nanotech dust function as a single networked supercomputer?"

"Naturally so." said Dr. Marjari. "If their actions are limited to only emergent behavior as you suggest, then how can you explain countywide kill zones being composed of smaller kill zones sometimes separated by miles? All the small zones occur at the same time and in an orchestrated geometric pattern. Random emergent behavior does not spring up in a synchronized way. Two beehives separated by miles do not simultaneously swarm with a coordinated plan."

"There are ways to explain how emergent behavior could result in synchronized events," said Snow. "The devices could be reacting to the same area wide stimulus or signal. For example, sunrise could light a fuse for an event that occurs hours later and appears coordinated, when it was only synchronized to the rising sun. Your theory has a huge problem. If the actions are intelligently coordinated, how are the seeds hosting this mythical supercomputer of yours? An impossible amount of network bandwidth would be needed."

Mark stopped listening to the arguments. His head was spinning. They were all overshooting the point. They were all too interested in winning their arcane arguments. The important question was not which kind of *program design* could best reproduce these behaviors. The important question was much simpler and less technical. Were the seeds communicating? This was the real question and maybe the crux of it all. If the seeds were communicating, then breaking their lines of communication might stop them in their tracks.

11 – Atlanta: December – a few days later

Kathy wandered into Mark's office. She hadn't intended to go there. She was troubled and needed to talk with someone. His door was open. He looked completely absorbed by something on his computer screen. He hadn't noticed she was standing five feet away. She liked the changes she saw in him. A week ago he was drugged and depressed. Now he was back in control of his life. He glanced up. Instead of showing surprise, he smiled and took off his glasses.

"Got a minute?" asked Kathy.

"Sure. What's up?"

Mark rubbed his eyes. Kathy walked over to the couch and sat down. The coffee table was littered with computer printouts of articles, handwritten notes, and some of Mark's personal things. She picked up an old Rubik's Cube and toyed absentmindedly with it while talking. In less than a minute, one side was already a solid color. She had tried Mark's idea for automated testing of blood samples for infection. Lab techs had worked straight through the night setting up the needed equipment and software. After a two hour incubation period, the test was able to screen samples in rapid succession. Once scaled up, they would be able to test entire populations of people.

"We got results on Gloria Martinez's blood," she said. "Your new test worked great. The computer did all the work and turned up a positive count on all her samples. Her spinal fluid was loaded with infected COBIC."

"That's good, isn't it?" asked Mark.

"It's something to investigate, but it's not what I was hoping to find. Everything we know says she should be dead with that much COBIC in her. I was hoping to find no COBIC – I was hoping her immune system had wiped them out and that's why she'd survived. Now I'm not sure where to go with this. How do I discover a negative? This isn't a disease; it's a weapon. Out of millions of possibilities, how do I uncover why the weapon didn't kill her? Did her body interfere with how it kills or was some electronic signal just blocked by accident?"

Mark sighed. "I'm trying to nail down how seeds communicate over a distance of miles while you're trying to figure out why someone survived inches away from her dying children."

Kathy put aside the Rubik's Cube; all four sides were now solid colors. Mark sat down next to her on the couch and began rummaging through some of the material on the coffee table. She felt a kind of energy from him that sent tingles through her body.

"Does your think-tank have any idea how far seeds can transmit?" asked Kathy.

"Assuming it's radio waves, the estimates range from fractions of an inch to about a yard. No one can see how a single seed could transmit over a range of miles. The most likely solution is they relay the signal from one seed to the next, something like the way our nerve cells work but without connecting fibers. The only problem is explaining large kill zones. An area the size of Los Angeles would need to be covered with pockets of COBIC every few feet or less. If the signal can only travel a fraction of an inch, then the amount of COBIC needed to blanket an area like Los Angeles is too large to even consider. We would be finding COBIC in every spoonful of dirt – and COBIC lives in water, not dirt."

"What if they worked together? I mean, what if a group of seeds could cluster together to form a high power transmitter?"

"Fascinating idea," said Mark. "They could work from centralized transmission and relay locations. Each seed in a large area receives the same broadcast signal. That could really explain it."

He was staring directly into her eyes. She felt herself leaning toward him, drawn to him. Was she about to embarrass herself? What if he didn't feel the same attraction? Kathy was suddenly terrified. Her heart was beating faster as she leaned closer still, unable to stop herself. Her mind flashed on an image of that rusty condom all scrunched in the bottom of her purse. She felt confusion.

There was a knock on the doorframe. The door was partially open. Kathy froze in panic. She saw Carl Green with a woman dressed in a Navy uniform. The woman was young, blonde and petite. Kathy felt embarrassed and invaded.

"Uhhh… Dr. Morrison and Dr. Freedman," said Carl. "This is Lieutenant Kateland from Naval Intelligence."

"Call me Jessica," said the woman as she walked straight in and shook hands. Her handshake was firm.

"Have a seat," said Mark.

Lieutenant Kateland rolled an office chair over to the coffee table. She opened a briefcase and took out a PC tablet that was inside a transparent plastic sleeve which resembled a larger version of the anti-shoplifting devices used in stores. The sleeve had the words 'USN Top Secret – LIM2 Eyes Only' written across it. Lieutenant Kateland broke the security seal by snapping an end of the sleeve off and removing the tablet. Kathy had seen these security seals before.

Lieutenant Kateland set the PC tablet on the coffee table. Using a pen stylus, she signed in on the tablet and opened a set of files that looked like aerial reconnaissance photos. Kathy noticed how Mark was leaning forward. He looked interested in the photos and maybe the Lieutenant.

"This morning we received these images from one of our birds," said Lieutenant Kateland.

"Birds?" asked Kathy.

"Spy satellites," said Mark. He picked up the tablet. "What kind of bird took these? They're higher resolution than any military surveillance stuff I've worked with."

"I can't comment on that," said Lieutenant Kateland. "See anything curious in those photos? The Navy analysts sure did." She pointed to something that looked like streams of smoke billowing just under the surface of the water. "These are plumes of…"

"Bacteria," said Mark.

"Exactly," said Lieutenant Kateland. "Navy intel decided anything dealing with waterborne bacteria could be connected with the nano-virus. So here I am."

Kathy noticed the woman's uniform had the same gold braided BARDCOM insignia as the Army Major she'd met on a helicopter flying out to a Los Angeles refugee camp. Kathy remembered the Major had said the insignia was for his unit which specialized in chemical warfare. What was a Navy Lieutenant doing wearing an insignia from an Army chemical warfare unit? Kathy did not trust this female Lieutenant. She was not who she appeared to be.

"Now look at this location," said Lieutenant Kateland.

She addressed Mark and pointed with the stylus to a section of a burnt orange plume. All the colors in the image were unnatural – probably the results of computer enhancement to bring out details.

"This feature measures sixty by eighteen nautical miles," continued Lieutenant Kateland. "Notice how far the plume has moved. If the drift continues, it will hit the New England coast in a few days."

Lieutenant Kateland selected a different image of the same piece of ocean. Unlike the previous image, this photo had normal coloration.

"This image is raw visible light, magnified of course, but no other computer magic. You can see the true color of this plume is a blue-green that almost matches the color of the water. Now let's compare this image with one from ground penetrating radar…"

Kathy was annoyed that the Lieutenant had not addressed a single sentence to anyone in the room except Mark. Soon, the simple fact that she was annoyed began to bother her. Between suspicion and annoyance, she was having trouble paying attention.

"It looks like something's missing," said Mark. Why was he smiling?

"Sorry about the blacked-out areas," said Lieutenant Kateland. "Navy censors have to do something to justify their paychecks. This ground penetrating radar image is color-coded for depth. Blue is sea level; the colors shift toward red to indicate greater and greater depth. This image shows the plume is running almost two hundred feet deep at spots. I've been told this kind of depth is very unusual for Chromatium, if that's what we've got."

Lieutenant Kateland zoomed in on the image, using the stylus to draw and select a rectangular area. She rolled her chair around the coffee table so she was beside Mark and viewing the image from the same perspective.

"Look at the pattern of graininess," said Lieutenant Kateland. "That's not our equipment. The analysts concluded this plume varies in density, forming a pattern with bands of higher and lower concentrations. One of our analysts said it resembles what low frequency sound waves would look like."

"Can I get a sample of this bacterium?" asked Mark.

"It's being done as we speak. A Navy helo stationed on the carrier Roosevelt is outward bound to the plume. When the helo returns to Roosevelt, a Navy fighter will fly the samples to Atlanta. You should have them tonight."

12 – Atlanta: December – later the same day

Mark absentmindedly turned the DVD mailer over in his hands. How could a small cardboard box contain something that would have the power to change everything? The package had arrived a few hours ago by military courier. There were no markings or information indicating who had sent it. The DVD which was now playing had a serial number written on it and nothing more. Light from the screen flickered on Kathy's face. Her expression was long and unreadable. Without any idea of what was on the DVD, Mark had viewed it before showing it to Kathy and Carl Green. The DVD had left Mark deeply disturbed. He'd lost track of how many times he'd seen it since then.

A secure video conference including his panel of nanotech experts was in progress. A notebook computer's screen displayed a set of video headshots for each conference call member. A video camera clipped to the top of the screen was capturing Mark, Kathy, and Carl.

The room was silent. The DVD contained no soundtrack. Dozens of questions arose when the beginning was shown to the group; but once the terminal sequence began to play, all questioning had ended. The DVD started with a time and date counter displayed in the lower corner of the screen. The date and time was that of the New York kill zone. The image was windowed. There was a wide angle Microscopic-MRI view of a living human brainstem along with several magnified views of specific regions. There was no civilized way to explain the images. Clearly, people were being used as test subjects. The screen had medical telemetry traces running superimposed over the top edge of the display.

Mark felt his pulse increasing even though he knew what was coming next. Activity started when a flood of blurry capsule-shaped microbes swam onto the screen in time-lapse video. The microbes were just above the resolution threshold of the Microscopic-MRI. They were unquestionably infected COBIC. The microbes could be seen swimming through veins and then capillaries as they converged on the brainstem from several directions. The movements appeared systematic and coordinated.

As the microbes reached the brainstem, they stopped moving; but something just below the resolution of the Microscopic-MRI kept going. What showed were pinpricks of disruption passing through solid tissue. The consensus was that the disruptions were seeds leaving their hosts and burrowing directly through the material surrounding the brainstem. The tissues came back together and resealed behind the disruptions. No evidence of passage was left behind. The mechanism was nothing less than disassembly and reassembly of living cells. The burrowing process changed once critical nerve tissues were reached: the speed picked up and reassembly stopped as each disruption began to trail a tunnel in its wake. The disruptions moved across vital fibers in an organized pattern leaving severed nerves behind them. In the cross-sectional view of the MRI, the tissue appeared to open up as if it were cut with an invisible scalpel. Mark knew it was clear to anyone medically trained that they were witnessing fatal injuries to a nervous system. The EEG traces grew erratic, blood oxygen levels were dropping; then, the EKG began to fail. Within a minute after brainstem penetration, the subject's EKG was a flat-line and the pinprick disruptions were moving back in the directions they had come. As the disruptions burrowed through solid tissues, the flesh was again being reassembled in their wake. The disruptions entered back into the circulatory system and seemed to disappear near the bacteria. The microbes slowly twitched back to life and then swam away. Mark thought it was a safe bet they were on direct paths to exit points from the victim's body. The EEG ran for a short time longer before also flat-lining.

Kathy had the remote control. She ran the video back and began replaying a zoomed-in image of a single nerve fiber as it was sliced into sections. Mark looked away from the screen. He had seen more than enough.

The DVD left too many questions unanswered for him. While it was proof that the seeds infecting COBIC were the killer, it did nothing to explain the mechanisms at work. The images demonstrated coordination of attack but offered no clues about how the coordination was orchestrated or how these things navigated a human body. Was there constant wireless communication or was each seed running autonomously once an attack was initiated? Mark tried to wrap his mind around the now inescapable fact that during the small time span of a kill zone, synchronized inside an entire population of people, these seeds moved through their intended victims' bodies, attacked their brainstems, and then fled. The entire idea was astonishing, impossibly grotesque, and all too consistent with what had already been discovered.

"Has anyone thought of the medical implications of this?" asked Kathy.

"I'm not sure I follow," said Mark.

"These seeds can slice tissue and then restore it without a trace," said Kathy. "If we can figure out how it's done, this would be a huge advance for surgery."

"Almost any physical ailment could be caused or cured," said Carl Green. Both Kathy and Mark turned to stare at Carl. He had not said a word since the first viewing of the DVD.

"That's right," said Kathy.

"Wait a minute," said Mark. "That could be a missing piece. Since we found out the seed was a nanotech device, we've all been asking the same question again and again: where did these things come from? We can't name anyone who was close to developing this kind of technology. So it has to be a radical breakthrough, right? So why would some company or government in possession of this technology create something this odd? I mean despite the death toll, far more effective weapons could have been built with this technology if a weapon was the goal. So maybe they weren't working on a weapon. Maybe this thing is a nanotech medical tool that went horribly wrong."

"Weapon, medical tool... you're all blind!" interrupted Dr. Snow. Even in the small video image on the notebook screen, she looked harried. Mark could see deep bags under her eyes. Her hair was held on top of her head with a clip from which large clumps fell out at odd angles. She was wearing a silver cross and chain that he hadn't noticed before. "Everyone's refusing to consider the possibility that we're dealing with something not created by us. Why does everyone continue to think of this amazing and intelligent creation as man-made? This work is godlike in its breath. Now we realize that it can heal as well as destroy. How much more proof will it take for you scientists? Maybe this isn't technology at all? Can't any of you see we're dealing with something that was written about in the Bible? The end of days..."

Mark had wondered how long it would take before people began to bend or break under pressure. A few days ago, Dr. Snow had argued there was no artificial intelligence running this technology; these were just dumb specks of dust following a simple but deadly program. She'd made her case that possibly even simple emergent behavior was beyond its capabilities. Now she was saying the seeds were an extension of God. Maybe some kind of holy invaders bringing divine wrath to our wicked world? Slowly, carefully, Mark studied each of the faces on the teleconference screen. Right now, they all needed each other's help to win this battle. He felt a small panic growing in his gut. Which one would be the next to snap?

13 – Northern New Jersey: December

The New Jersey side of the George Washington Bridge was no different than the New York side. Suzy leaned against a concrete abutment amid waves of people. Artie had been gone for over an hour, hunting for transportation. She was worried even though he'd said it could take all afternoon. Trying to distract herself, she played one of her tapes through the camcorder and jotted editing notes.

Soon, she was staring at all the passing faces again. She was both scared and exhilarated. There were people, hundreds of thousands of people, filling six lanes of highway to the horizon. Life had become surreal. The sound was the most amazing thing. The ground vibrated with the collective voice of humanity. The din had the timber of a monastic chant combined with the sense of a great force held back by the weakest of dams. The relative quiet could erupt into deadly chaos with no provocation. Suzy watched as an occasional scuffle turned into small whirlpools of people inflicting pain. It was almost as if human bodies were plugging holes in the social fabric by surging inward toward vacuums caused by the conflicts.

She set up her camcorder and started wandering around, careful not to stray far from where Artie would expect her. The equipment she had was the smallest pro model available. The camera wasn't much larger than a big consumer camcorder but was easily recognizable as professional gear. She knew the camcorder had the magical power of shielding its owner against violence. The logo of her employer NBC was decaled on the side of the camcorder. Few people would attack someone who looked like a press photographer. Everyone wanted to be on TV. She talked with people, taping them, asking them their story. A little girl and an elderly man caught her attention. It was the contrast between young and old. The man's face was a wrinkled map. The girl's skin was pink and her eyes so large she seemed owlish. The two were sitting on a bundle of clothing. The girl's tiny hand was enfolded in the huge palm of her elder. Suzy started the taping with a close-up view of the hands, and then slowly zoomed out to fill the frame with the man and child.

"Is she your granddaughter?" asked Suzy.

"My daughter's child," said the man. His voice started to break up. "I'm too old to have lived to see this. My daughter's gone. Her husband's gone. Me and Amy are all the family that's left. Now I've got to keep going for her."

"Amy, sweet heart, how old are you?" asked Suzy.

The little girl didn't answer. She leaned in close to her grandfather.

"It's okay," said the man. "This is a nice lady. You can talk with her."

"Three," said Amy.

Suzy felt her eyes tearing. She took a deep breath and told herself to hold on.

"Do you know where you're going?" asked Suzy. She had directed her question to the grandfather.

"Uhuh," said Amy. "We're going to find mommy."

"She doesn't understand," said the man. "I don't have the heart to tell her."

Suzy sat on the curb. She thought about that little girl and grew teary again. So many had died. When she and Artie got to Washington, would her parents be gone too? Was she going to become like that girl? She touched her womb and sensed the baby that was alive within her. What kind of world would their child inherit? She looked up and saw Artie parting the crowd. Just seeing him yanked the anguish from her chest. He was her future. His face seemed older. She ran into his arms. Her cheeks were damp with tears.

"You alright?" he asked.

"I'm fine. Just hold me."

"I've got us a car," he said.

"Where is it?"

"About a mile from here on a surface street. I want to get back there fast before anyone gets any ideas. I left our food in the back."

Suzy carried her camera gear. Artie took the duffel bag. They headed straight for the opposite side of the highway and over a guardrail. There was a hill of grass and trees. The far side of the hill led down into a backyard. Artie helped her down over an eight foot cement wall. As Suzy stood, she was captivated by the silence. It was as if all the people were gone. The thousand of voices had been stilled. Here there were trees, and grass, and birds. An old crow was staring at her from a second floor ledge. She had stumbled into another world that existed only hundreds of yards from where she'd sat on a highway curb. She stood there in awe until Artie tugged at her hand. She followed after him, feeling as if she were walking through a dream.

The car was an old Volkswagen camper with a single bench for a front seat. As Suzy climbed in, she saw boxes of food piled in the back. There was more than what Artie had left with and none of it looked familiar. What was going on? Suzy had noticed over the last few days that he'd gradually been taking on more and more of the appearance of a gang member. She didn't know everything about his past, but it was as if the streets were reclaiming him.

"Was the supermarket having a sale?" she asked, not wanting to know.

Artie pulled out a key ring that wasn't his and started the engine.

"I had to trade all our food for the Volkswagen; so before I headed back, I did a little shopping."

She noticed a scratch on his cheek.

"No one got hurt, did they?" she asked.

"The supermarket was being cleaned out fast. I was amazed no one had hit it before now. There was a little shoving. No big deal."

He avoided her eyes. Something was different about him; he was remote and a little sad. She decided to leave it alone for now.

"Does the radio work?" she asked.

"Yeah, but it's the funniest thing. It only plays music. Somehow I just can't seem to find a news channel."

He smiled for the first time since he'd come to collect her.

"Well, let's hear it," she said.

Artie turned the stereo on and selected the CD player. She immediately knew the music. It was an old Joni Mitchell song, Court and Spark. The song was what had been playing when he'd asked her to marry him. Tears welled up in her eyes.

"How'd you find it?"

"The people that I got the camper from threw in a box of CDs. Said they didn't have another player, so what would they need 'em for? When I saw Court and Spark, I knew everything was going to turn out okay."

He reached behind the seat into a box and came back with an orange and handed it to her

"You should eat this for the baby," he said.

Suzy leaned over and kissed him on the cheek.

They'd been moving at a steady crawl for hours. The surface road they were on had passed through the nicer suburbs, large houses, well groomed lawns, and the occasional main street of a town. They were at the crest of a large hill. Ahead of them was an open blue sky. Suzy momentarily aimed the camera back through the rear window. The ruined spires of New York were still visible amid the smoke. The scene through her viewfinder was 9/11 all over again. Traffic was snarled in front of them. There were cars which looked like they'd been pushed to the side after running out of gas or breaking down. Most of the people on the sidewalks were carrying weapons in plain sight.

Suzy focused her camera onto a mother and teenage daughter waiting by the curb for someone or something. The girl had a canvas shopping bag. The mother was holding a shotgun. Suzy zoomed in on the woman's face. As they drove past, the woman looked straight into the camera. There was no change in the woman's expression. Her eyes were cold and shiny black. The pupils were as wide as dimes. Suzy set her camera down. She'd had enough for now.

14 – Northern New Jersey: December

After hours of bumper to bumper traffic, Artie was frustrated and had started using the back roads. He was relieved when it turned out to be a better strategy. Suzy played navigator with a folded paper map, jumping them from street to street. Every dozen miles or so, he headed back toward the interstate to check out the congestion. At a point halfway across New Jersey near a town called Dover, they got back onto Route 80. The highway was almost empty. There must have been some kind of wreck behind them blocking all traffic.

In forty minutes, they were crossing a bridge through the Delaware Water Gap into Pennsylvania. The Delaware River was a ribbon of blue a couple hundred feet below them. There were several small craft heading downstream toward the ocean. Little remained of the military barricades that Artie had seen on the tube. He saw a trailer with a broken searchlight and the burnt out shell of a Humvee. A piece of the bridge was missing. Concrete and twisted reinforcing bars rimmed the crater. He hadn't heard anything about this destruction in the news, but it was clear a battle had been fought. People had died here.

The distant smoke had worried Artie the moment he'd seen it. He'd been watching it for the past several miles as they drove closer, and this was close enough. He pulled the camper to the shoulder and got out, leaving the door open. The spiral of smoke was less than a half mile downrange. He got out a riflescope that he'd liberated along with the Volkswagen and a deer rifle. The lens quality was poor. He made a mental note to find something better. He could see a tractor-trailer rig blocking the eastbound lanes of highway. Near it were several wrecked cars, one ablaze. Maybe a hundred people were milling around; most appeared to be heavily armed. Gang signs were being flashed. Lines were queued up in front of what looked like kegs of beer and food. Just immediately west of the tractor-trailer, the highway had been turned into a parking lot filled with motorcycles. Artie looked back at the tractor-trailer. He couldn't see any damage. He wondered if it was intentionally parked to block the highway. His eyes moved to a bonfire. He couldn't tell what was burning, but it didn't look like wood. Maybe car seats or cans of oil?

He stopped moving the scope, tried to focus it better. The image remained fuzzy. What he saw was a naked body staked out with ropes on the ground. He moved the scope a little to the right and saw another body next to the first. Someone walked by and flung the contents of a beer mug at it. A head lolled to one side. The hair was long. The captive could have been a woman. Artie's mind started working. He knew what this was – a party, but not any kind he wanted to attend. Memories of a past he'd tried hard to forget flooded back into his brain.

Artie set the scope onto the driver's seat. He thought about the guns he was carrying. The magnum would be useless, the rate of fire too slow and the deer rifle was even slower. That was a gang at war, and a huge one from the looks of it. They must have been using the tractor-trailer as a portable roadblock. If he hadn't seen the smoke or been more curious than cautious, he and Suzy could have been the next guests of honor.

"Something wrong?" asked Suzy.

"No big deal," he said. "The road's blocked by a huge accident. We'll have to turn around and find another route."

The sun had been fading for the last half hour. The sky was a deepening purple-blue. Even thought he'd driven a hundred miles from the gang roadblock, Artie felt like it wasn't far enough. They were parked on a shoulder. He'd been watching a rest area from the cover of some trees. There were a lot of people there and more than a few guns, but there were also kids and dogs. He watched cars pull in and then later leave unmolested; more than a few had been offered food. The rest stop looked like a huge roadside barbecue. A fifty-five gallon drum had been split lengthwise to make a pair of cooking pits. Suzy stood behind him with her hands on his shoulder.

"Let's check it out," she said. "I can almost smell the food from here."

"Looks okay," said Artie. "But if I start talking about going to find my parents in Maine, that's the signal something's wrong and we're getting out fast."

"You worry too much. We haven't seen anything bad since New York."

The evening was almost over. Suzy was curled into his arms. She was half-asleep. The food had been great. The price was barter or labor – or free if someone could offer neither. He'd eaten two burgers and more hotdogs than he could remember. Artie was on his third beer and enjoying the conversation. A half dozen men and women were sitting in a circle around a small campfire. This must have been the way news traveled hundreds of years ago. He caught himself wondering if maybe there was some hope after all. The plague was forcing people to leave their homes and band together in ways that hadn't happened in centuries. The arbitrary walls that society had erected were being torn down. Henry, a heavy set man with a beard, was talking. Artie had learned that Henry and his family had been on the road since the first New Jersey kill zone.

"I've heard they call themselves The Pagans," said Henry.

"Yeah, I was told the same thing by an ex-cop from Philly," said a woman named Claire.

"They travel in a pack as large as a thousand. I've seen it," said Henry. "They've got military hardware. There's a rumor going around that a lot of them are deserters. I was passing through Atlantic City when they were laying siege to a police station. Me and the wife and kids almost got spotted by 'em. We hung back behind some cover and watched. Nothing else to do. They were using heavy machine guns mounted on Humvees. Those guns were punching holes clear through concrete walls. The cops inside were being slaughtered. I'll tell you, it put a chill down my spine."

"Might have been fifty-caliber," said Artie. "That stuff was designed to cut through armored vehicles."

"Man! Where the hell's the Army when you need them?" said another guy. He tossed an empty beer bottle into the fire where it popped like a small grenade.

"Wish I knew," said Henry. "There was a report on the radio that parts of Atlantic City were under control of what they called rival gangs... Rival gangs, my ass. They're not reporting the truth. It's one gang and they're not rivaling among themselves. They're after us."

"I heard from the same ex-cop that Philly was in total chaos," said Claire. "He said it was the Pagans. I'll tell you what: me and the boys are heading south to the safe zone. We'll find a way through that damn line."

"Satan's Crossing," mumbled Henry in a softer voice.

"Huh?" said Claire.

"That's what people down there call the I64 line – Satan's Crossing."

Artie was barely listening at the moment. He was thinking about what he'd seen earlier today. That tractor-trailer party on I-80 could have been the same gang. If half of what he'd just heard was true, these animals were not only well armed, they were winning.

15 – Atlanta: December

Something felt out of place. Mark opened his eyes. Light beamed onto his face through a crack in the shades. He was lying on the couch in Kathy's office. A blanket was covering both of them. She was cuddled into his side and, as far as he could tell, she was not wearing anything. Her skin felt hot. He realized he was naked.

Memories of the previous night came back to him. He carefully got up and retrieved his shorts and jeans. While dressing, his gaze returned to her. She was so attractive. She stirred a little as if she knew he was looking at her and then returned to her dreams. They had both ended up so drunk last night. He remembered feeling they were each trying to find enough nerve in the alcohol to do what they had finally done. He was in the cobwebs of a mild hangover and was worried he'd made a mistake. He looked at her sleeping face and was drawn to her; no, last night had not been a mistake.

He set up the pot to make some coffee and went to wash up. When he came out of the bathroom, she was still asleep. He poured her a mug of coffee and held the mug so she could smell it. She opened her eyes.

"Want some coffee?" he said.

She nodded sleepily and then sat up on the couch while keeping the blanket fully wrapped around her like a robe. After a few sips, the sleep was gone from her eyes, replaced with a sheepish expression.

"Can you please turn around?" she asked.

"Oh. Sorry."

He heard her getting up, the blanket sliding across the floor, the bathroom door closing. He found his shirt and put it on. A few minutes later, she came out of the bathroom dressed in last night's clothes and fresh makeup.

"It went too far last night," she said. "We went too far."

Her eyes were staring out the window, at a bookshelf, at the floor, anywhere but at him. He couldn't take his eyes from her.

"We both needed an escape," she went on. "We'd just be kidding ourselves to think it was anything more."

Mark was confused. This was not how he imagined their morning-after conversation going. He didn't agree with anything she was saying. His entire body was tense.

"Maybe you're right..." he said.

"Last night never happened," said Kathy.

"Never happened."

Mark was starting to feel angry. He looked around for his sneakers. He found them under her desk and wanted to fling them across the room but instead began pulling them on. There was a rap at the door.

"Oh God!" whispered Kathy.

Mark quickly finished dressing and then unlocked the door. Carl was standing there. He was wearing clothes that were so wrinkled he must have slept in them. He walked in, removed some papers from a chair and sat down.

"The plume sample promised by the Navy finally arrived," said Carl. "Alan ran some preliminaries on it. The stuff is loaded with COBIC; about half is infected and half is clean; and there's more. A plume about the same size was just spotted in Lake Superior."

"Where's all this bacterium coming from?" asked Kathy. "It's spreading too fast."

"Maybe not spreading," said Carl. "I think this might be part of the answer."

He handed copies of a CDC report to both Mark and Kathy. The title page had the name of a water testing program that was still underway.

"The Ogallala aquifer is contaminated," said Carl. "Low levels: one part per million; but what if there are plumes down there? We'd get low readings like this unless we accidentally drew directly from a plume. It's like that parable of the blind men and the elephant."

"What kind of aquifer is this?" asked Mark.

Kathy looked pale.

"A big one," she said. "The Ogallala is like an underground ocean that runs from Nebraska to the Texas Panhandle. It's all sand and gravel, a lot of water capacity; and it may be connected to other aquifers, maybe even the ones feeding out of the Great Lakes."

"Tests of other aquifers are in the works," said Carl. "Odds are the entire underground supply is contaminated. For all we know, it could have been that way for some time. Hell, the aquifers could be its adopted home. This infected bacterium may not be spreading. It may be everywhere already. Water purification is blocking it from the tap; but what about irrigation and livestock? The infection vector could be our food supply."

Carl and Kathy appeared to be growing more distressed by the second. Mark's thoughts were oddly consumed by a sense of deja vu. In his mind he could see mats of fossilized COBIC forming and imagined how this giant plume in Lake Superior might wash up on shore and collect into thick layers, which a million years later would look exactly like his fossilized mats. Everything felt like events were changing for the worse. The nanotech seed was a modern problem, but this massing behavior of COBIC was as old as time, and it only happened during extinction events. The dinosaurs met their end the last time large mats of COBIC occurred. He couldn't explain a connection between a hundred million year old extinction and this modern nanotech monster, but he felt a link was there.

"I need to go to Lake Superior," he said. "This massing is starting to look more and more like the beginning of something entirely new and disturbing."

~

Mark stared out his office window at the activity below him. He needed to clear his mind. A helicopter was on its way to pick him up for the initial leg of his trip to Lake Superior. This would be the first time the roof's helipad would be put to its intended use. When he closed his eyes, he saw Kathy's smile and bedroom eyes and was stung by the denials of this morning. He could not work the emotions out of his system. His conflicted feelings were coloring everything. He had to try to focus on his job.

He thought about the daily briefing he'd read a few minutes ago. The briefing was very unsettling. A series of isolated and unusually small kill zones were being reported spread out across the northern part of the U. S. and Canada. Details were sketchy, but it looked like dozens had been discovered so far. Most of them had resulted in few deaths. All had occurred within the last week, with the majority hitting in the last forty-eight hours. The charts suggested events were accelerating.

This kind of small-scale horror could have been occurring at a slower pace for months and simply gone unidentified and unreported until now. The other possibility, the one which frightened him more, was that these small zones could be part of some change in pattern connected to the plumes. Someone had run a computer simulation that plotted this pattern of attacks into the future. The results indicated an escalation in fatalities. If the pattern held, these small kill zones would inflict far more death than the huge catastrophes of Los Angeles and New York combined. The simulation showed that in a matter of months, every acre of the northern hemisphere would be ravaged, one small bite at a time.

Mark picked up his overnight bag and headed up to the roof. He walked out the covered doorway and continued to the edge of the building. He leaned his hands on a railing. The wind in the trees reminded him of ocean waves. There was a distant sound of rotor blades. He squinted into the sun looking for the chopper but couldn't see it yet. He turned around. Kathy was there with a shoulder bag.

"Thought you were staying here?" he said.

"Forget that," she said. "You think I'm going to let you hog all the credit for this field trip?"

Mark smiled. Her eyes were clear and gazed directly back into his.

"I welcome the… umm… competition," he said.

"Thought you would."

A Marine helicopter landed on the roof. In minutes, they were on their way to Dobbins Air Force Base. The ride brought back memories of arriving in Los Angeles for Mark.

An Air Force tactical command and control jet was waiting on a runway. The aircraft was small, about the size of a Lear Jet but far sleeker. There was one other passenger, Lieutenant Jessica Kateland. The cabin was narrow; its walls packed with electronic monitoring equipment, radar screens, and computers. The seats were mounted on locking swivels facing the equipment consoles instead of facing forward. Mark strapped himself into a seat using a shoulder harness. In front of him was a set of computer displays containing what looked like satellite and radar images of the Great Lakes. Kathy took the seat on his left. He could not stop sneaking glances as she settled in. He was fascinated with everything she did, like the way she adjusted her clothing or toyed with her bracelet. He'd caught her smiling to herself several times today as if she were thinking something clever. Had she just started doing that or had she done it all along? He'd never looked close enough before to notice.

The jet started taxiing. Lieutenant Kateland came back from the cockpit to show them how to lock their seats facing forward. She then returned to the front of the aircraft. They lifted off fast and climbed harder than anything Mark had experienced. In the rush of engines, he felt himself browning out as the blood was drained from his upper body.

"Wow!" he said.

"Wow is right!" said Kathy. "How do I get off this ride?"

After takeoff, Kateland came back from the cockpit. She had them swivel their seats to face the equipment displays and then sat down next to Mark. He could smell her perfume. He noted there was no wedding ring. On the surface, her attitude appeared to be all business, but he couldn't help wondering if everyone got this much personal attention. He was surprised that it made him feel uncomfortable.

"This display is showing a real-time visual of Lake Superior from a Keyhole Bird," said Kateland. "It's like an orbiting microscope. By changing this value, you can adjust the level of magnification."

She typed a number. The screen zoomed in to show a small portion of the shoreline. Mark felt like he was staring over the side of a tall building. He could see boats tied up at a dock, cars and people moving around. The screen looked more like a window than a computer display.

"Why do I get the idea this thing is a version of NASA's latest space telescope, only aimed at the Earth instead of Mars?" he said.

"I really can't comment on that," said Kateland. "By the time the bird moves off target, all this data will have been processed by our land systems. You can then call up different computer-enhanced displays and selectively magnify areas for closer inspection.

"By pressing this button, you can switch the display to penetrating radar. This darker area is the plume. These fuzzy lines that look like a spider's web are surface wave clutter. The images I showed you the other day had been computer processed to remove random noise like wave clutter."

Kateland switched the display back to the telescopic view.

"If you look closely, you can see a slow change in the angle of view on the image. As the bird's orbit passes over the plume, its sensors have been tasked to track the plume. As it gets closer to the point of departure, where it goes out of range, you'll see the angle changing faster and faster. See, look. Here we go."

The image was changing, moving to a sideways view instead of straight down. There was a clearer sense of the height of objects and shadows. The screen blurred out for a moment, then was filled with an image of a forest.

"That's it for real-time," said Kateland. "In a minute or two, we'll be able to uplink all the computer processed data."

~

After a half-hour of learning how to work the equipment, Mark had the satellite display replaying an image loop of the plume. The clip was a sped up time-lapse sequence showing plume movement. The loop looked a lot like the animated clouds on a news weather map. Kateland had also shown him how to operate a ground facing video camera mounted on the belly of the jet. The camera was aimed with a joystick. Its lens was image stabilized and zoomable with a high level of magnification. The entire setup was apparently the same equipment used to aim laser guided smart-bombs at targets. For some time, he'd been watching the screen as a forward-looking view of the ground moved past at supersonic speed.

The jet was soaring across a part of the heartland that had been ravaged. Mark could almost feel the hell that must exist forty-thousand feet below. He stared down at a view of a sinuous waterway bisecting the land. Mixed in with the river and streams were all the works of man. He watched as the roads and buildings of a city went past. What would they look like after years without people to maintain them? Plants would grow between cracks in the pavement. In time, the pavement itself would be overturned, the steel would rust, the wood decay, the great cities would slowly flatten to gigantic mounds. In time, it would all be reclaimed as habitat.

He thought about the fossilized mats of COBIC. How many cycles of wide-scale extinction had happened before? They had clear evidence from millions of years ago, but could it also have happened more recently? Could ancient civilizations have reached heights equal to current times or even higher and then been wiped out by a cyclical killer? Our entire civilization had been built in the geological blink of an eye. In a few hundred years, mankind had gone from iron tools to outer space. All our great technology was fragile. If our world ended today, all signs of our technological achievements will have been wiped away by the elements in a thousand years. Near-extinction of mankind could have occurred before. Maybe that was the riddle of the Sphinx and the pyramids? Were they relics from an advanced world that was mostly lost? All we really knew of civilization was limited to a span of a few thousand years; beyond that, prehistory stretched out as the great unknown.

He looked back at the screen showing the plume's movement sped up in time. He watched the swirls of COBIC moving through the water. He watched its center thin out and then thicken, disorganize and then reorganize. The loop was replaying endlessly. He noticed that the bacterial cloud was disrupted as it flowed over the same area of water that was a dozen miles long and a few hundred feet wide. The disruption was probably caused by an unusual current of some type. The more he stared, the more he saw a rhythm and pattern to the spiraled motion. The circular flow was leading the plume into a collision with a southern shoreline.

He slowed the replay to normal speed and zoomed in the view. Focusing on the southern shore, he could easily make out stones and even pieces of litter which had probably blown in from nearby landfills. It was eerie watching the plume of bacteria being beached and concentrated into foamy mats. He felt like he was looking through a window into the distant past; a living example of something he'd only seen fossil evidence of until now. Knowing there was something akin to a microscopic computer in some of the bacteria made what was happening even more surreal. Someone had hijacked an ancient player in mass extinctions and combined it with advanced technology. Was the creator of this monster trying to send a message or was the choice of carriers nothing but a sick coincidence? Why use a bacterium that was connected with prehistoric extinctions? What message or benefit was in that? The choice didn't make sense. He leaned closer to the display. Maybe COBIC's selection only made sense if this destroyer was something entirely beyond human creation. Could the seeds actually be a doomsday machine that was thousands or even millions of years old? He'd ridiculed this kind of thinking after the seed was first identified as artificial. He'd refused to even acknowledge the possibility. Why was he considering it now? COBIC had been massing like this for millions of years. The thought that this advanced nanotechnology could also be millions of years old was madness. If it were true, he would have found seeds in his fossilized beds of COBIC. The seed was a glass-hard pellet of silicon and carbon. The material would have survived... or would it? Why couldn't the seeds have dissolved, leaving no trace behind, just like the captive lab specimens? Mark felt a cold chill and turned off the display. The thought was too wild to even consider.

16 – Northern Wisconsin: December

McKafferty was en route to Lake Superior. The huge cargo helicopter streaked across the ground at tree level. In his lap was a PC tablet which displayed the original NSA analysis that had led to planning this kind of emergency action. Behind his lead bird was a small armada of helos filled with soldiers and equipment. The NSA precursor alert had come in hours ago. The alert was the same as the others he'd received during the past two weeks; but from the moment he'd seen this one, he'd felt a twinge of fear in his gut; and fear was something McKafferty never felt. Fear was an enemy he worked hard to crush in his men, fighting it in himself was new. He lit a cigarette and drew deeply on it. The experiments they were carrying with them would confirm or disprove a critical NSA theory. What unnerved him was that the theory could prove to be true; and if it was, then they might have their first real weapon in this fight. He wanted it to be true. He needed this weapon – the world needed this weapon. What he could not handle was the spark of fear that this new hope would turn out to be nothing more than a statistical error. He looked down at the report and read through it again.

Two weeks ago, NSA analysts, while reviewing their take from orbital birds, had uncovered something unexpected. This prompted them to re-examine old data where they found the same signal had been hidden all along. They were picking up an increase in what the geeks called 'low frequency background signal noise' or white noise. This noise preceded and accompanied all kill zones. The background noise originally appeared to be of natural origin, until specialized computer programs had picked out an organized pattern in it. The spy birds were designed to intercept all radio signals, from low frequency submarine chatter to high frequency microwave. To accomplish this feat from near earth orbit, the satellites were equipped with antenna arrays that were miles in diameter. The arrays were really nothing more than thread-like wires that had been stretched out in space by sets of tiny maneuvering engines the size of cigars. The result was literally an invisible spider web that caught radio signals. The system was so sensitive it could pick up the electromagnetic impulse when someone flipped on an electric shaver. An immense amount of computer wizardry was necessary to filter out all the earth's background noise – and that was the rub. The seeds' signal was part of the noise that was usually tossed out. The NSA was working double time right now to completely re-engineer their programs, so they could focus on this seed noise and ignore all the communications signals that were previously so important to them.

Five days ago, McKafferty had successfully used the first ever precursor alert the NSA had issued to pre-position his team's brainstem experiments in New York. They'd received less than thirty minutes of warning and had barely succeeded in getting everything into position. No warning had been issued to the population. At that time, no one was certain the prediction would pan out. The prediction had; and as a result of his quick action, McKafferty had gotten two things he desperately needed: images of COBIC killing and a way of predicting future kill zones. He consoled himself that giving New Yorkers thirty minutes of warning might have actually caused more deaths through panic than it would have saved; and at that time they hadn't even been sure kill zone predications were possible.

They now understood these signals were how the microscopic robots coordinated their actions. If the NSA could break the encoding, they'd be closer to finding out who was behind this assault. But for now, there was something even more important. According to the NSA, this massing of bacteria had turned up a possible weakness. It looked like the nanotech bugs were being affected by a top secret radio installation in Lake Superior. Near the end of the cold war, the United States Navy had buried a ten mile long, low frequency transmission antenna under the lakebed. The antenna was used to communicate with submarines. The cloud of microbes appeared to be drawn toward the antenna and then repelled when they got too close. It was like moths flying at a bare electric bulb and then being driven off by the heat. The reaction certainly looked like proof that these microbes were sensitive to powerful radio waves. The implications of this NSA theory were big. The idea was that these bugs could be controlled or deterred with radio signals.

Whoever had built and unleashed this computerized weapon possessed technology beyond anything the U.S. government owned. In McKafferty's mind, he saw a terrorist version of Einstein. There had to be a genius madman mixed up in this attack. The insanity of what this enemy had done was almost justification for Project Big Boy.

McKafferty shook his head. No, Big Boy was even greater insanity. He could not let them do it. He wondered exactly which group of Pentagon fools had come up with the idea of using tactical nukes to sterilize large swatches of the country with electromagnetic pulses which should fry the nano-circuitry in this bug. The idea was being promoted as a kind of nanotech firebreak. What a brilliant idea, thought McKafferty. Let's poison the globe with radiation to save the chosen few. The world was filled with crazy people. There had to be a scientific principle at work that caused most of them to gravitate toward seats of political power – maybe a law of the massively stupid attracting like-minds?

17 – Near Duluth, Minnesota: December

Mark and Kathy found a four-wheel drive Chevy Suburban waiting at the airfield. Two soldiers were milling around the truck; one was a driver, the other was a heavily armed bodyguard. Wearing an NBC suit again felt ominous to Mark. These were a different model than he'd worn in Los Angeles. They had winter camouflage coloration, a full faceplate instead of a gasmask, and combat audio which made it possible to hear his surroundings with intensified detail. The dirt road they were on was narrow. A trail of dust and gravel was being kicked up behind them as they raced along. The terrain was mostly trees, scrub grass, and rocks.

The truck slowed and then stopped at the edge of an embankment. Just below them, Lake Superior stretched out like an endless sea. Water loaded with COBIC was lapping up on the rocks, leaving greenish-blue deposits behind. Mark opened the door. He had an odd feeling as his feet touched the ground. It was as if he was stepping onto a dead planet. There was work to do. He heard Kathy's door slam shut.

Mark edged his way sideways down the embankment. The body-guard accompanied him; the driver, who was now also heavily armed, had stayed with Kathy. Mark had a canvas shoulder pack filled with empty specimen jars and an aluminum pole with a fixture designed to grip the jars. He was nearing the water. The vista fascinated and repelled him. The entire area was saturated with lethal bacteria. He thought about how easily seeds passed through human flesh. Could it pass through NBC suits as easily? The idea made him feel like thousands of insects were crawling over his skin. A primal fear urged him to run. He could almost sense death seething like a poison within the lake. The bacteria were piling up at the shoreline into mats that were several inches thick. The plume itself spread out across the water like a slick of oil for as far he could see. He recognized that, without a doubt, he was looking at the creation of the same fossil mats he'd collected. As impossible as it was for him to believe, he was now certain he was witnessing the same kind of event that had wiped dinosaurs off the face of the earth. He couldn't shake the reoccurring insane question from his mind. Could COBIC have contained the same nanotech seeds millions of years ago?

He started to attach a sample jar to the end of the pole. The work was difficult with gloved hands. The jar was the size of a pill bottle and had a locking cap that, once closed, required a special tool to open. The jar slipped from his fingers and cracked on the stony ground. Kathy had come up beside him along with the driver. She said nothing. He knew without looking she was experiencing the same instinctive fears. Dotted along the coast, scientific groups were setting up equipment: meteorological monitors, cameras, air samplers. The human figures were too far off for Mark to be certain, but it seemed like their movements were stiffened with fear.

The afternoon sun was a bright glare on his faceplate. He was having some difficulty drawing air into his lungs. He felt like he was breathing dust but knew it was only in his mind. He forced himself to ignore the suffocating feeling and attached a jar to his sampling pole. He dipped the jar into the water and drew out a chunk of mat. The sample was thicker than he'd imagined, almost gelatinous. He capped the jar. Kathy helped him by logging the jar's serial number in a lab book. Their eyes met for an instant. Her pupils were wide. He could see the tension and fear in her. He slid the jar into a padded section of the canvas bag.

Mark slowly worked his way down the shore. Along the way, he took samples from thicker parts of the mat. Kathy had gone back to the truck. He knew he couldn't endure being here much longer. All his instincts were screaming *run*, again and again, in growing crescendos of panic. With extreme effort, he was just remaining calm enough to work. Without warning, he began to feel dizzy, almost to the point of fainting. The symptoms came on fast. What was wrong with him? He felt like his diabetes was acting up. He heard the bodyguard fall with a thud. He turned and stared at the man in disbelief. Commotion from a dozen voices filled the radio link.

"Mark!"

Kathy was shouting in his ears over the radio. He turned to where she'd been standing by the truck. She wasn't there. Panic gripped him; then, a new wave of dizziness hit that left him spinning. He stumbled to one knee. He looked up toward the edge of the embankment. Kathy was by a group of trees. The driver was restraining her.

"Mark!"

He weakly got up and looked down the shoreline. People in NBC suits were dropping to the ground. One fell into the bacterial soup and disappeared amid a thick splash. From nowhere, a bird fell into the dirt in front of him. The animal fluttered a bit; then, took off. Nothing seemed real. Time was running in slow motion – seconds were being stretched into minutes. He looked out across the water. The thick matting of COBIC appeared completely inert, yet he knew it was the source of this murdering. The illusions of safety were peeled away, the supposed protection of all their technology – like NBC suits – were false. What remained was a visceral understanding: he was about to die. He was in the middle of a kill zone. He heard through the suit's combat audio the sounds of death. He saw a truck rolling slowly uncontrolled out into the lake. He looked up at Kathy. He heard her crying over the radio. She was so scared. He had to get to her. He started up the embankment. Everything was spinning badly. He stumbled drunkenly. Lacking the muscle control to stand, frustrated, he tried clawing his way forward on hands and knees. The world dimmed.

18 – Near Duluth, Minnesota: December

McKafferty was ten minutes away from the landing zone when word reached him. There was confusion. First, there was an NSA warning that an imminent precursor signal was being detected from Lake Superior. Now, five minutes later, he was getting sketchy reports of a localized kill zone occurring at the lake. The decision was his: continue or turn back. The experiment was too important. Soldiers were paid to take risks. If he didn't go, the delay might prove costly in civilian lives. The NSA could warn him if another kill zone was coming and they could bug out fast. All they needed was a quarter mile of altitude from the zone to be safe. He put his hand on the shoulder of his communications officer, Lieutenant Alice Rivers.

"Instruct COMS we're continuing with the mission."

"Yes, Sir."

"Lieutenant."

"Sir?"

"Do you have a husband or kids?"

"Yes and no, Sir. I've been married for a year now, but no kids."

McKafferty nodded to himself. The responsibility of this job was wearing on him.

"I've been married for over twenty years," he said. "Haven't been that great of a husband, Lieutenant Rivers."

"Yes, Sir?"

"Transmit the message."

19 – Near Duluth, Minnesota: December

An embankment a few hundred yards away was littered with bodies, while other dead floated near the shore in the soupy layer of bacterium. Survivors were moving among the dead, kneeling down, checking. Mark hadn't fully lost consciousness. He'd experienced none of the respiratory or heart failure symptoms of SAAC. Sitting on the ground in his NBC suit, he felt his strength returning. Kathy was kneeling in front of him. He heard her talking over the radio link to someone at the CDC. She was describing his symptoms. She and the driver had felt nothing. They must have been just outside the radius of the kill zone. He had been within the radius and should have died. He heard the radio call to the CDC disconnect.

"Mark," said Kathy.

"Yeah, Doc," he said.

"You know we could have all been killed," said Kathy. Her words hung in the air for a minute.

"I know," he said. "I also know last night was not a mistake."

Mark was surprised he'd said what he'd been thinking all day, and surprised he'd just said it over an open radio channel. Apparently almost dying had a way of cutting through all the unnecessary emotional blockage. Kathy stared at him. Her eyes were level and direct. They moved back and forth over his face as if she were able to look deep inside him and see every corner of his being.

"I don't know what to think," she finally said.

"Maybe you should stop thinking?" said Mark.

The ground began to tremble. There was a powerful thumping. A blast of wind and dust hit them from nowhere. The NBC suit fluttered against Mark's skin. He looked up and saw the belly of a huge helicopter coming in low overhead.

"What the hell?" he yelled as the shadow passed over him.

The helo angled off over the water, sending circular waves out below it. Other helicopters followed the first in close formation. They landed several hundred yards away. Some of the helicopters were larger than anything Mark knew existed. The rotors had to be a hundred feet across. Rear platform hatches dropped open on the big ones. A Humvee drove out the back of one, while soldiers in camouflage NBC suits piled out of others.

"Looks like the cavalry's landed," said Kathy.

Many people had died while others had survived. The newly arrived soldiers ignored the bodies on the ground and the survivors who had to be overwhelmed by what surrounded them. The military's priority appeared to be something other than rescue. Scientific equipment was being set up. Some of the soldiers were using laser-surveying equipment to map the area, while others deployed remote controlled robots similar to those used by bomb squads. One of the soldiers pointed a rifle out over the water. A large torpedo shaped projectile was fixed to the end of the barrel. The rifle bucked hard, noticeably shoving back on the man's torso. A moment later, Mark heard an echoing report. Trailing a wire, the projectile arched high in the air and hundreds of yards out across the bacterial plume before splashing down. The wire filament drifted to rest behind the projectile, sinking into the infected water.

Mark turned to see if Kathy was watching. She was working on her field notes using a PC tablet. He looked back toward the shore and saw a Humvee ambling toward them.

"I think we're about to have visitors," said Mark.

Kathy came over and stood next to him. The PC tablet was still in her hand. As the Humvee neared, Mark was able to make out three soldiers inside, wearing camouflaged NBC suits. The Humvee stopped ten feet away. A very large man got out the passenger side, followed by someone much smaller, possibly a female. After a few hand signals and mistakes, they were all on the same communications channel.

"I'm General McKafferty," said the man. "And I believe you're Dr. Kathy Morrison and Dr. Mark Freedman, correct?"

"Have we met before?" said Mark.

"No, we haven't had the pleasure; but I've been following your recent work."

Mark noticed Kathy staring at an insignia that was stenciled on the General's NBC suit, a cobra coiled around a sword. He felt her nudging his elbow. She was trying to tell him something. He glanced at the insignia again and then remembered Lieutenant Kateland had the same thing on her uniform.

"I'd like to have a little chat," said McKafferty.

"You're part of BARDCOM," said Kathy. "Funny, how I keep running into you folks."

"We're a large team," said McKafferty. "And you've just run into the commanding officer."

"Honored," said Kathy.

"Dr. Freedman, I'd like to ask you a question or two," said McKafferty.

"Depends on the questions," said Mark.

"Fair enough," said McKafferty. "We're all working toward the same goal."

"Are we?" said Kathy. "Why aren't you helping survivors down there?"

"Doctors, I'm a soldier who's sworn an oath to protect his country." said McKafferty. There was an understandable edge to his voice. Mark was surprised at how Kathy had baited him. "I take my oath very seriously and would give my life for my country and its people. There aren't many who can say that and mean it. Help is on the way for those folks. I'm here to learn more about what we're up against."

Mark believed what the man was saying.

"Ask your questions," said Mark.

"Do you have any ideas that explain the movement of that bug infested plume?" asked McKafferty.

"Haven't given it much thought. Water currents probably?"

"Come on, Doctor. I know you're far too intelligent to have missed that the plume is moving on its own," said McKafferty. "Real-time marine and air charts show the water is moving to the southeast, away from this corridor. That pile of bacteria is moving against prevailing winds and currents."

"Impossible. If you're thinking they're swimming, you can forget it," said Mark. "Bacteria are too small to move that fast. In still water, a very determined Chromatium might be able to cover a mile in about a year."

"Well, these must be some very determined critters. We've been tracking the movement of that plume and it's going against the current at a rate of approximately a mile every few hours."

"There's something wrong with your data. Maybe sub-surface currents are pushing them?"

"I don't think so. We keep a very close eye on this particular body of water. There are no northerly crosscurrents. Take my word for it."

"What you're saying defies the laws of physics," said Mark. "A flagella microns long can't create enough propulsion to swim even a foot an hour."

"I've always noticed that when scientists start using absolutes or Latin words, they're either trying to convince themselves or hiding behind obfuscation," said McKafferty. "Which one is true for you Dr. Freedman? I think you're trying to convince yourself. Let's look at it from another angle. How many bacteria would you say are out there, trillions? How much propulsion could a trillion smart bugs produce?"

"Not enough, " said Mark. "Impossible."

"Sometimes, you have to open your mind and accept the impossible," said McKafferty. "Let me introduce you to another impossibility."

McKafferty took what looked like a pocket computer from one of his men. He turned the device on and passed it to Mark. The front of the device had a cell phone sized keypad and a color LCD display with a horizontal graph calibrated in units of radio frequency. A red line with small ripples moved across the bottom of the graph.

"It's an RF Spectrum analyzer that's been retooled a bit," said McKafferty. "Are you familiar with these kinds of instruments?"

"A bit," said Mark.

When either of them talked over the radio link, a blip appeared on the red line in the 900 megahertz range, which Mark knew was the radio frequency of the links.

"It measures RF radio waves and shows you their frequency and strength. Keep an eye on that graph and follow me," said McKafferty.

He started down the embankment toward the shoreline. Mark did not want to go down there again. He looked at Kathy. She wasn't budging, which was fine with him.

All right, he thought. *I'll play your game.* He followed the General down the embankment. An armed soldier accompanied them. The General stopped at the edge of the lake. Mark's mouth was dry. He was sweating heavily. His face was actually wet.

"Go on and move the box close to that goo," said McKafferty. "And keep an eye on that graph."

"What am I looking for?" asked Mark.

"You'll see."

As Mark got closer to the mat, the graph started to change. A broad shallow bump grew in the graph in the single digit hertz range and smaller bumps in the 100 to 1000 megahertz range.

"What is this?" said Mark.

"That's the million dollar question," said McKafferty. "The NSA first picked up on it a little while ago. We have no idea what data the signal is carrying – if anything, but we do know this concentrated bacteria is transmitting what's called white noise."

"How could everyone have missed this?"

"The geeks tell me this radio signal, if you can call it that, is what's normally considered natural background noise. Every piece of radio equipment we use is designed specifically to filter out this noise."

"They're very smart," said Mark.

"Who's smart?" asked McKafferty. "The nano-critters?"

"No. Whoever built this nightmare."

"Yeah, they're smart. But they've made mistakes... Everyone does. We haven't found 'em yet, but we will; and when we do, we'll use those mistakes against them with extreme fucking prejudice."

Mark and the General climbed up the embankment. As Mark got to the top, he had the distinct sense that Kathy wanted to embrace him. There was an emotion showing in her eyes that was hard for him to read. The feeling, whether real or not, lifted his spirits. He handed the Spectrum analyzer to the General.

"I'm going to tell both of you something that's classified," said McKafferty. "I'm doing this because I know it'll help the CDC. Most of it's a poorly kept secret anyway. Buried in the bed of this lake is a very large antenna used to transmit ULF radio signals. The transmission power is very high: we are talking global reach. It's in constant use. This bacterial plume has been congregating around the antenna. When part of the plume passes over the antenna, it breaks up like smoke in the wind, then reforms after it drifts away, and then turns right back toward the antenna."

Mark remembered the video display on the jet, the hypnotic motion of the cloud dispersing at the same location in the water and then reorganizing. The General was offering an explanation for what he'd seen, but all the pieces didn't fit.

"You're telling me that infected COBIC are attracted and repelled by low frequency radio waves," said Mark. "Okay, after what you've shown me, I'll buy that's possible; but it still doesn't change basic physiology. Microscopic animals simply cannot move that fast."

"Back to that again, are we? Listen, I'm just giving you a set of facts: that plume is acting very funny at a specific spot in that lake. It's one hell of a coincidence that a ULF transmitter is pumping this same spot full of radio signal. That's why I'm here. We're setting up equipment to measure any reaction of the plume during ULF test transmissions we've got scheduled."

"When the kill zone hit, what was the Navy transmitting?" asked Mark.

"That information is classified; but if I thought those specifics were relevant, I'd tell you."

The general checked his watch.

"Gotta go. Stop by our camp if you're interested in a tour."

The general turned and walked away. Mark thought about how odd the entire exchange felt. Suddenly, it seemed like everything had been rehearsed and that a pile of disinformation had just been dumped on him. He was starting to wonder if all the information they'd gotten from the military from day one had been intentional misdirection.

He thought about the video of a living brainstem being murdered as seeds burrowed through vital nerves. Was that a fabrication, too?

"General," yelled Mark. "I forgot to ask if you like high-tech slasher movies."

McKafferty turned in his tracks. He marched back and stopped within inches of Mark's faceplate. His eyes stared into Mark's eyes; the General's were soulless and featureless black orbs. Mark recognized that deep within them was the heart of a killer. The General didn't say a word for almost a full minute as an ugly smile slowly grew on his lips.

"Do you mean videos that show seeds slashing nerves inside a human brain?" asked McKafferty.

"Yes," said Mark.

"Never seen it."

The Humvee pulled out. Mark felt like a professional mugger had just worked him over. He wished he could have had that spectrum analyzer checked to make sure it wasn't a hoax. The General had shown up after a kill zone, dumped a very compelling piece of information or two on the table, and then faded into the background. The act was all too slick. Mark knew when he was being manipulated; but this was so obvious, so blatant. Didn't the government have more finesse than that? Was everything the general said all lies within lies or was there some truth to it? He hated dealing with secrets, but that seemed to be the only currency in this dying world that still had any value.

"Enigmatic man," said Mark.

"I don't trust him," said Kathy.

"Neither do I, but what if he's telling the truth? I have to check out what he said. On the flight back, I'm going to see if Kateland will give us a copy of the satellite data. That will show the movement of the plume. I can get wind and water conditions from the coast guard. Before McKafferty's ULF radio wave story, I thought the plume's movements were due to water currents. But if the plume was scattered by radio waves, and it's scattering against wind and water currents then that reaction proves the plume is moving under its own control and at a speed that's just not possible."

"It's hard to accept anything when it comes from someone who looks like that," said Kathy.

"What do you mean?"

"McKafferty, he looks like a criminal… ugly…sly…"

"I think I need to go over and take him up on that offer of a tour of their experiments," said Mark. "Let's see if they're really doing what the ugly, sly general said."

"Count me in," said Kathy.

McKafferty's crew had set up camp a mile down the shoreline. Mark's and Kathy's four-wheel drive Suburban didn't have as much ground clearance as a Humvee. Their driver had to park about two hundred yards away. Some of McKafferty's men were guarding the perimeter. Neither their bodyguard nor their driver were permitted to enter. Mark told them thirty minutes at the most and they'd be back. He and Kathy went on by themselves down a footpath that led toward the helicopters. Not far from the footpath, a pair of bodies in protective suits lay motionless on the ground. The sight made Mark's stomach squirm. He wondered how long the bodies would remain before someone claimed them.

"Dead!"

The voice came from somewhere nearby. Mark spun around to see a man standing behind them. He was dressed in the bottom half of a civilian NBC suit, no mask and hood. He was chewing on something. Brown juice was running down his chin. Mark edged closer, putting himself between the man and Kathy.

"Dead," said the man.

He tipped his head almost like a bird while his eyes remained glued on Mark's face.

"Dead… Dead… DDDDeeeeeaaaaad!" he screeched.

Mark inched Kathy and himself backward. He had to glance down to keep from tripping. The man sprang and knocked him into the dirt. Mark didn't know what had happened. The lunatic was on top of him. His hands were instinctively battling for control. Mark wasn't wrestling with a man, it was an animal. The thing's jaw began snapping in vain attempts at a piece of flesh. Mark had it by the hair and was pulling the head back. He was looking for a weapon. Spying a fist-sized rock, he let go of the hair with one hand and stretched for the rock. The lunatic twisted out of his grip and sank a mouth full of teeth into his shoulder. Pain lit up through Mark's body.

Kathy was screaming for help over the radio. Mark tried to get the attacker off him. The maniac was thrashing its head from side to side, trying to penetrate the NBC suit, trying to rip off a chunk of flesh with its teeth. The NBC material was heavy enough to prevent punctures, but the clamping pressure went deep into his shoulder. Mark pushed backward with his legs, shoving both himself and his attacker across the dirt. The rock was now within reach. He grabbed the stone and swung it into the side of the maniac's head. No effect! He swung again. The attacker released its teeth, but the crazy bastard was praying mantis quick and bit into the back of Mark's hand before he could react. The rock fell from his grip. From nowhere blood and pieces of meat spattered across Mark's visor. An instant later, came the crack of a rifle. The attacker was no longer on him. Mark sat up. He saw a lifeless body sprawled on the ground. Half its face was gone. Mark looked at his hand. There was blood dripping off his fingers and palm. The pain was excruciating as each injury competed to hurt more than the others. Salty sweat was burning his forehead. He couldn't see any rips in his glove. The blood wasn't his. He wiped the mess from his visor, leaving a thin smear. Kathy made him lie back, then took his hand and examined it.

"Keep still," she said.

Her eyes were concerned. She turned his hand over several times.

"No openings," she said.

She went to his shoulder. The whole upper area of his arm and shoulder was throbbing and felt wet. A moment later, Mark saw General McKafferty's face loom behind her and then saw another man with an M16. The General actually looked like he had some kind of pity in his eyes. Mark looked back at Kathy.

"The suit has a tear in it," she said. "The skin is broken. There's also a deep contusion."

"I feel like hell," said Mark. "A kiss would make it better."

He knew from the way Kathy's eyes wrinkled at the corners that he'd gotten a real smile. The attacker's saliva had mixed with his blood.

"Contaminated," said McKafferty. "Any direct exposure calls for immediate quarantine. Lieutenant Rivers, I want a medivac here in five minutes."

"Yes, Sir," came a female voice in reply.

Mark eyed the General. He had no idea what this man was capable of doing. Cold detachment was in McKafferty's stare. The pity was gone. Contaminated. He sensed McKafferty no longer considered him human. Had he just been added to the experimental subjects list? Were they going to film seeds burrowing through his brain next? Mark had heard the rules of martial law on the drive from the airfield. They were the same as in Los Angeles. Anyone exposed was not allowed to leave. Kathy took the General's arm and led him a short distance away from the other soldiers. Mark heard their radios switch off channel.

The pain was fading. He saw Kathy gesturing at the General. More than once, he saw her poke at his chest. Her jabs looked as effective as poking at a wall of rock. She glanced at Mark and a moment later came walking back. She kneeled down next to him and turned off her radio then turned off his. She leaned forward so their faceplates were touching, and he realized, so that the sound of her voice would conduct through the glass.

"You're coming home to the CDC with me," said Kathy.

"How am I doing that? This whole place is under military law and I am exposed. You heard the man."

"The General's going to help. We're going to get you a new NBC suit and they'll destroy this one. You're going to have to wear the suit all the way back to Atlanta. The General is going to take us out of here on his helicopter. I had to assure him we'd keep you isolated once we get back."

"What else did you do to convince him to go along with this?"

"Common sense – that you can do more good to end this nanotech virus working at the CDC than sitting on your hands in a refugee shelter."

"And?"

Kathy shrugged.

"I got the sense he was just waiting for me to ask with enough emotion. He's got to know he can use this as blackmail. He owns us. One word and you're shipped off to a camp and I get a visit from the military police."

Mark didn't like any of this. General McKafferty came over. He stood there smiling with that ugly face until their radios were turned back on. He helped Kathy up.

"Fucking dirt-eaters," muttered the General.

"What?" said Mark.

"Dirt-eaters. The bastard thing that attacked you! Some eggheads are saying it's the result of posttraumatic stress. My guess is the seeds sliced up a different part of their brain and not enough to kill them, so they end up as walking wounded. Dirt-eaters have caused a lot of problems in Los Angeles and New York. Lucky for you, one of my sentries saw what was happening and put the man down."

A pair of soldiers arrived with a gurney. At first, Mark protested but Kathy insisted. Her logic was annoyingly convincing. She was concerned about the contamination spreading. He needed to keep exertion to a minimum. His heart rate and blood flow would determine how quickly the bacterium could spread through his body and reach his brain. Mark didn't like that he was starting to feel like a patient. The image of infected COBIC swimming through his blood was something he immediately tried to push from his mind and failed.

20 – Alexandria, Virginia: December

They'd been on the road for three hours. The coffee and fried Spam breakfast had left Artie's stomach feeling raw. Tension was growing as they neared Alexandria. He was afraid they would find a pair of decomposed bodies that were once Suzy's parents. He tried again to engage Suzy in conversation. She was if anything more withdrawn. The rain had stopped an hour ago. The roads were slick with water and autumn leaves. Sunlight beamed through the branches of naked trees. Many of the streets looked like something from the third world: gutted houses, missing windows, doors hanging by a single hinge, every vertical surface tattooed with spray paint.

Artie turned left on Bishop Street; Suzy's parents lived on this block. He slowed to a crawl, trying to recognize the house. Thankfully, the last few miles of houses had appeared untouched. He wondered how much longer that would last. He stopped short as Suzy abruptly swung opened the car door. She was out and running toward a house he now recognized. She reached the front door and knocked, then tried the knob, then started banging. He killed the ignition, leaving the camper angled half out in the road. By the time he got to the house, Suzy was going around to the windows trying to peer in. She had her hands cupped over her eyes.

"They're not answering!" she cried. "Why won't they answer?"

"Shhhh, baby. Come here."

Artie put his arms around her. She was tense and struggled against him.

"They're probably not home. That's all. They could be anywhere," he said.

Artie sat her down on the steps and then went around the house checking every window himself. They were all locked. The back door was locked. He looked through a side window of the garage. There was a bare concrete floor. They own a single car and it was gone. This was the first good sign all day. He went around to the front. Suzy was back at a living room window trying to see inside.

"Their car's gone," he said. "They might have gone out to get something or they could have been evacuated. Everything's locked tight."

Artie walked to the curb to check the mailbox. Suzy followed him. The box was empty. He looked up and down the street. The neighborhood was abandoned.

"The only way in is to break a window," he said. "Do you want me to do that?"

"Can't you just jimmy something?"

"No, it's either break a window or kick in a door. The window will be a lot easier to fix."

Suzy hugged him and started crying.

"What if they're inside?" she said.

Artie led her back to the front steps. He looked around the foundation for a rock. He found a cluster of river stones used for landscaping a hedge.

"We're gonna feel really dumb when they show up five minutes from now," he said.

Suzy smiled meekly. Her cheeks were damp with tears. Artie carefully broke a side window and tapped out the remaining shards instead of opening it. He didn't want to set of a burglar alarm. He laid his jacket over the windowsill and climbed through.

The inside of the house looked lived in. Magazines were scattered on a coffee table. The air smelled of carpet powder. He spotted a burglar alarm panel. It was unarmed. He thought about checking the upper floors but knew Suzy would be kicking at the door in a couple more seconds. He'd seen enough and was convinced the place was empty. He twisted the dead bolt and opened the door. Suzy's eyes skimmed over his face checking for signs of bad news.

"Looks like they just stepped out," he said.

She glanced around quickly and then went straight for the stairs. Artie caught up with her half way to the top. All the doors on the second floor were open. Nothing appeared to be disturbed. Some hangers were on a bed. Suzy went to her mother's closet. She started going through dresses, then shelves, then shoeboxes.

"The suitcases are gone and so is my Mom's favorite dress. I think one of her coats is missing, too."

Artie sat down on the bed. He felt tired. His sinuses were beginning to ache. He worked his knuckle in small circles against one of his temples. The pressure relieved some of the aching. Suzy had started going through drawers and closets. She found a jewelry pouch hidden inside a secret place in her mother's vanity table. Inside the pouch was an antique locket and chain.

"She left it behind for me. I know it."

He watched her open the tiny locket.

"The picture's still there," she said. "It's the three of us when we lived in Jersey. I think I was five then."

Hours later, Artie was hungry. The house now looked like a burglar had carefully worked it over. Suzy dropped onto the couch beside him. She looked smaller somehow. She had gone over every inch of the place.

"Why didn't they leave a note?" she murmured.

~

Traffic was light. They were ninety miles south of Alexandria. Night had fallen hours ago. Artie pulled the Volkswagen off the two-lane highway onto a service access. This was the fourth one they'd tried. His eyes were sore. He was exhausted. The path was made of dirt and barely wide enough for the camper. A hundred feet in, the dirt road widened into a circle and then angled out to the main road again. He cut the lights and the ignition. This was exactly what he'd been looking for. They were out of sight from the roadway but could get back to it in a hurry by two different routes if they had to flee.

They shared a can of Vienna Sausages and a can of spaghetti, both warmed over a tin of sterno. There was apple juice to wash down the candlelight dinner. They slept in the back on the floor. The rear seats had been jettisoned the other day to make room for additional supplies. They kept warm by wearing their coats and cuddling under a quilt and two blankets. The temperature had dipped rapidly with the sun. Artie considered occasionally running the engine to warm the inside, but he had no way of knowing how far it was to the next working gas station.

In the middle of the night Artie stirred. He felt something was wrong; then he heard a distant sound, like the rumble of hundreds of engines at idle. He opened the door. The outside sheet metal was like ice. His skin adhered to it. He carefully pushed the door closed until it clicked. Suzy didn't stir. The sound was louder outside. He took a few crunchy steps. His breath formed clouds in the moonlight. He shivered and, for the first time in years, wished he had a cigarette. Whatever was out there scared him. He put his hand over the bulge in his coat to make sure the gun was still in its shoulder holster.

Artie moved carefully through the trees and brush. He could see road lights moving up ahead. The ground cover was crisp from the freezing cold. He kept behind cover while angling toward the highway. The noise of his shoe snapping a single twig immobilized him for minutes until he was sure no one was close by and had heard him. After an endlessly slow and tense progress, he'd picked his way to within a dozen feet of the pavement. He knelt low to keep from being spotted and peered out between a lattice of branches. A column of cars, trucks and military vehicles were moving at about five miles per hour. There were heavy armored vehicles with gun turrets. Their weight shook the ground as they crawled past. Searchlights probed the tree line. Slivers of light licked through the branches, illuminating things well behind him. Disembodied voices came and went. He was certain it was the Pagans. A collection of motorcycles rumbled past, followed by armored Humvees. He was watching a Halloween parade of the damned. A thin shard of spotlight cut through the trees and glowed white hot on his chest like a laser. He froze, not even breathing.

21 – Atlanta: December

Kathy had been pushing herself for over 24 hours without sleep. After their return from Lake Superior, she'd ordered blood and spinal fluid drawn from Mark. The first spinal fluid test had come back positive for COBIC; so had the second and the third. Oddly, the blood tests were all negative. His brain and spinal cavities were saturated with infected bacteria while other areas of his body appeared to be clean. Even though seeds could easily penetrate the blood-brain barrier, whole COBIC bacteria could not. The presence of COBIC in his spinal fluid while absent in his blood could not be explained by normal blood circulation from an infected bite that was only 24 hours old. The only clinical explanation was that Mark had been infected long ago. She had run every available medical test on him. Other than COBIC, he was healthier than he should be, given his age and pre-existing medical problems. A soldier standing next to Mark had died during the kill zone while Mark had not. She was convinced infected COBIC had been inside Mark prior to the Duluth kill zone, and that made him just like Gloria Martinez. And just like Gloria Martinez, Kathy had no clue why he was alive. She felt she was missing something obvious, some tiny but critical detail.

Thoughts about Mark's condition and their intimacy had left her frightened that he might have infected her. She'd submitted to the same tests as Mark and had received a clean bill of health, but was still worried. What if she was infected in some way that didn't show up? She could easily imagine this smart bug evading hypodermic needles which were probing and sampling its environment.

Mark's acceptance of his condition surprised her. He was sealed in an airtight bubble of a room that was more like a prison. In every way, he had become a lab specimen just like Gloria Martinez. She'd expected anger or depression. Instead, without missing a beat, he'd asked for a computer and for one of the lab techs to be assigned to work exclusively for him.

She looked at a window on her computer screen. Inside the window was video surveillance from Mark's isolation cell. His medical telemetry was in a second window. Mark was working with his computer. His back was to her. He had on a shirt, a sweater vest, and jeans. She remembered how his eyes looked. He had such strong eyes. Since they'd slept together, she'd tried very hard to bury her feelings. There had been moments when they were talking that she'd wanted nothing more than to hold him and promise that he would get through this. Walls of glass separated them and she knew it was a lie to say that everything would be all right. She suspected it was something that she needed to believe more than he did. He'd already started discussing ways the seeds inside him might be triggered with the unspoken result being his death. She couldn't stand it.

Mark turned from his desk and looked up at the camera. His forehead was wrinkled. There were faint outlines of bags under his eyes.

"Are you there?" he asked.

"I'm here."

"There's something curious I want your opinion on."

Her nerves prickled. She noticed his heart rate and oxygen level were rising. Mark took off the sweater vest and unbuttoned his shirt. Once he was stripped to the waist, he turned his shoulder to the camera and then peeled off the bandage.

"Notice anything odd?" he said.

"The bite marks are almost healed. That's impossible."

"I know... Any explanations?"

"None," said Kathy shaking her head.

"I've thought about this," said Mark. "We know the seeds can travel through living tissue by disassembling and reassembling it at the molecular level. What if the results of reassembly are better than new?"

"What?" said Kathy. She was incredulous. "You think this nanotech is healing your wounds, making a new and improved you?"

"Think about it. What if the seeds aren't a weapon? You said it yourself that this technology could advance surgery by decades. What if it really is something that was designed to heal but has run amok? I don't know. Maybe it's a self-evolving program which has mutated into something that kills instead of cures. Maybe it's like a drug with fatal side effects for most people."

"You have no evidence. Have you checked for the presence of COBIC in those wounds?" asked Kathy.

"Already done," said Mark. "The levels are zero, but that doesn't mean COBIC wasn't massing there an hour or even seconds before the test was done."

"If it really was designed to heal instead of kill, wouldn't we have seen a lot more evidence of that? I mean wouldn't that be the dominant behavior?"

Carl walked into Kathy's office. He had an odd expression on his face.

"We have a special delivery from the NSA," said Carl. "Technicians have installed a black box on our network which hooks us directly into the NSA datacenter. They said the installation was ordered by General McKafferty. They have specific instructions to train us on using it before they leave."

"What's going on?" asked Mark.

"A new wrinkle," said Kathy.

22 – Atlanta: December

Mark rubbed his eyes. His vision was wavering. He'd been pushing too hard for too long. Text on the computer screen looked like it was wiggling and too bright. He willed himself to focus. The screen was displaying information from the NSA black box. The installation gave him a direct link into part of the mammoth NSA computer network, the part that monitored and processed lower frequency radio intercepts by satellites. The system had been recalibrated to process only those signals generated by seeds. Besides displaying real-time information, the program was able to go back in time and mine through a warehouse of raw data the NSA had collected. The system was able to trace and map, as well as display actual signal content. The results were revealing.

His computer screen was displaying a web of signal pathways that extended around the globe. The seeds had a wireless network of global coverage and intricate structure. Unlike long range radio signals, the seed transmissions only spanned a few feet. The signal was picked up by one seed and then relayed to one or more seeds farther down the road. This hand off, with its associated delays, allowed NSA systems to trace the routing of a single message packet, even though they hadn't decoded the meaning of the data itself. Tracking of message packets down pathways that were reused again and again had led to reverse engineering of the wireless network's layout. The pathways spanned land and sea in a spider web of continuous data flows. The network appeared to be adaptive and self-healing. The structure reminded Mark more of the vast complexity of interconnected neurons in a human brain than a man-made computer network. In his gut, he knew this was too advanced to be something humankind had engineered. He was starting to spook himself.

Beyond the intricacy of the network, the second thing that immediately stood out was the unique pattern of signals preceding, and then organizing, a kill zone. No one had an exact idea what the messages contained, but the same three types of coded messages were detected time and again at every kill zone; and from that repetition, a theory had emerged. Raw data that the NSA systems had recorded and saved months ago also showed the same pattern in the earliest kill zones. Replaying a recorded event showed one type of message which preceded every kill zone. NSA analysts theorized that this message 'armed' all the seeds within a geographic area. A second type of message was then received by one of the seeds that had been armed. The authors of the theory

312

called the recipient of this message the ignition seed. Immediately upon receipt of an ignition message, the ignition seed broadcast a third type of message which was unquestionably a command to kill. This kill message was relayed out from the ignition seed in all directions, like a ripple in a pond. The distance that this message was relayed out from the ignition seed never exceeded fifty meters. From careful study of the signal's data patterns, a discovery emerged that kill messages were relayed exactly fifty times. This meant the kill message had to contain some type of down-counter, which limited the size of zones by limiting the number of relays or 'hops' that the message could make. Limiting hops, relaying, message packets – all these things were the same networking mechanisms developed and used for the Internet. These similarities were very confusing and argued that seeds were man-made.

On the computer screen, the lethal area of a single kill zone was represented as a circular area tinted varying shades of red, with a bright pinpoint near the center to indicate the ignition point. Each zone was not an exact circle but was more of a circular blob. During larger kill zones, ignition messages "rained down" into a geographic area, with each small zone varying in shape, just as a collection of water drops on a flat surface would differ from one to another. Wherever an ignition message reached its recipient, people died, as if an invisible bomb had been dropped. The computer graphically illustrated the circular nature of small kill zones and how bigger zones were built from a cluster of these smaller zones or circles.

Mark was sinking into a dark depression as he stared at the same precursor signals replaying again and again. He was watching a recording of the Los Angeles horror. He'd realized how with a few changes this NSA system could be used to predict where a kill zone would hit and provide precious minutes of warning. He laid his head down on the desk and silently cried. How many lives could have been saved if they'd had this sooner? He couldn't erase the faces from his mind – his little girl Mary or his wife Julie or Gracy. Even though the tragedy encompassed all of humanity, he was unable to feel anything beyond his personal loss and a hate that he could not direct at anything that would make a difference.

Mark lifted his head and stared back at the screen. Something occurred to him, something so obvious. He rubbed some remaining tears from his eyes. This network was too advanced, too intricate to have been deployed months or even years ago. This was something that had been here for a very long time. This network was old, really old. COBIC was an amazingly perfect transportation platform for seeds, but it was not able to move more than a few inches an hour without the aid of a current or some type of collaborative effort. Even considering air travel, with human hosts spreading the bacterium, the level of global saturation needed to support this wireless network was impossibly high. This communications spider web covered almost every square mile of earth and water. Since the radio signal had a range of only a few feet, this meant that small amounts of COBIC had to be present in almost every square yard of earth's soil and water. It could easily take centuries for a normal bacterial infestation to reach this level of penetration. Maybe he and Gloria Martinez weren't members of a very elite club after all. Was it possible a large percentage of all the people, animals, and crawling things were infected with at least a few of the bacteria? The tests for infected COBIC were good and getting better, but he knew the bug actively avoided detection; and the quantity he needed to detect to prove this theory was very small. That meant unless they were lucky or the subject was saturated, they would not see many positive test results from bodily fluids. They needed a better test. They needed something that seeds could not evade. Mark was certain a solution which exploited the seed's communications network was possible. They could detect the radio waves from a few seeds: the NSA could do it with their spy satellites from a hundred miles up; handheld devices like the spectrum analyzer McKafferty had shown him could also detect the signals. What they lacked was a way to get the seeds to transmit on command, so they could be detected immediately – instead of waiting for a random signal to come along and reveal the presence of a seed acting as a relay.

~

"What is needed is a ping test," said Dr. Marjari.

"Exactly," chimed in Professor Karla Hunt.

Mark picked up the speaker phone and held it with both hands.

"Hey folks," said Mark. "Translation, please! What the hell is a ping test?"

"Very, very easily defined," said Dr. Marjari. "The ping test is something which computer technicians use to verify that network connections are working. The name comes from how sonar operates by sending out pings and waiting to hear echo-returns from the ping. In the case of sonar, a ping-echo being heard means something solid nearby has reflected the sound back. In the case of a network, a ping-echo returning means that the piece of equipment being pinged is connected to the network and working. When a device receives a ping message, it is programmed to echo the ping back to its source. When the source receives an echo from a ping it sent out, this verifies that the network and the device are operational."

"So, what you are saying is that we need to come up with a ping signal for seeds," said Mark.

"Very exactly," said Dr. Marjari. "We need to construct a signal which the seeds are already programmed to relay or acknowledge with a response. Since we do not need to understand what the response actually signifies, and since we have access to a warehouse of stored NSA signal data, it should not be difficult to shift the data for signals which always elicit the same response. We could then test these signals by broadcasting them at a sample of infected bacteria until we find a signal which fits our needs."

23 – Atlanta: December

Mark was deeply troubled because he'd been released from isolation. Dr. Marjari had been right. Finding a ping signal had been simple. In less than six hours of NSA supercomputer time, Dr. Marjari had compiled a list of potential ping signals. It had then taken only a few minutes to program a handheld RF signal generator to play back and transmit each of the potential ping signals. A handheld spectrum analyzer was programmed to capture and measure possible seed responses. Add a little duct tape to wed the two devices together, plug in a pair of directional antennas, and the COBIC ping tester was born. The result was a clumsy looking, highly effective tool. The graph on the spectrum analyzer indicated echo signal strength. This level could then be directly translated into a rough measure of infestation. The first twenty ping signals from the NSA list had failed. The twenty-first had worked. The situation had rapidly changed for the worse within minutes after the first ping-tester began working.

Within one hour, Dr. Marjari had placed his entire IBM lab, including himself, under quarantine. The ping tester showed that everyone in the lab was infected. Some of the rooms themselves were clean but they were a distinct minority. At first they'd hoped something was wrong with the setup. Marjari himself ran a hundred blind tests on vials of infected and clean COBIC. The unfortunate results were that the ping tester was one hundred percent reliable. The lab facility became a disaster zone. Professional demeanor evaporated. Everyone in that rarified facility was now as fearful and panicked as the rest of the world had been for almost two months.

An hour later, Carl had purchased every usable handheld signal generator and spectrum analyzer that a local supply company had in stock; more were on order from other suppliers. He'd then had the devices couriered by military police to the BVMC Lab. Programming instructions for their specific equipment was e-mailed from Dr. Marjari as files that could be directly imported into the devices. The results at the BVMC Lab were a mirror of what had been found at Dr. Marjari's IBM lab. The only areas not contaminated were three storerooms and the maximum containment lab. Mark was not surprised by these test results. The density of the seed's wireless web could not have existed without a high level of infestation. His only surprise was that infestation of people appeared to be one hundred percent. He'd expected a lower number.

A few hours after the ping testers were deployed at the BVMC lab, Mark walked out of his isolation cell. There was no point in keeping him quarantined. The same tests they'd run at the BVMC lab were now being repeated as quickly as possible at sites around the world. Mark knew the results would be similar.

In his office, Mark picked up a ping tester for the first time. He turned it on and swept his office looking for hotspots. The device was highly directional. At close range it measured an oval area of approximately six inches in width. He was just satisfying his curiosity about the device more than performing any serious investigation. The floor read hotter than the walls or ceiling. An area behind the couch was especially hot. He suspected COBIC living in the guts of dust mites probably accounted for the hotter readings showing up in dusty areas of the room.

He stopped in front of the bathroom mirror and looked at himself for moment; then he decided to see if there was any pattern to the infestation of his body. His legs and arms gave off no response. His torso gave off no response. He wasn't surprised. Without exception, everyone tested had little or no response except at the back of the skull, the brainstem. He moved the ping tester over his bite wound. There was a low level reading – not unexpected, but interesting. He pointed the detector at his forehead. White light flared in his eyes, blinding him. He dropped the ping tester. It clattered into the sink. The white light faded within seconds. He leaned on the bathroom mirror. His head was spinning. What had happened? He looked at the analyzer. There was no reading. The batteries had fallen out. He put the ping tester back together; then, steeled himself. He pointed the antenna at his forehead. He stared at his grim reflection in the mirror and switched it on. The same white light flared in his eyes. He quickly pointed it away. As the light faded, he was left with a mild sensation of nausea.

Mark looked at the reading on the ping tester. His heart was pounding fast enough to burst through his chest. The red line had gone off the top of the graph. The only explanation was that his head was saturated with infected COBIC and that the seeds were affecting his optic nerves. When the seeds transmitted their response to the ping signal, it somehow blew out his vision. The question that made him want to crawl out of his skin was *how broad was this invasion?* Had it gone beyond his vision to other senses? Was it affecting his entire nervous system, his mind, even his thoughts? He decided to tell no one until he better understood what he was dealing with.

Chapter 8

Rebellion

1 – I64 Line, Virginia: December

Sarah was alone in the captain's office waiting. She peeled the over-sized band-aid back from her palm. The cut was mending faster than it should have. She'd cut her hand on a seashell just days ago on the beach. Everyone else had died in the heart of that kill zone and she'd cut her palm. Her injury seemed so petty in comparison but she was nervous about how quickly her body was repairing itself. The accelerated healing had happened several times and just wasn't normal. She shifted uneasily in the vinyl chair. She couldn't get comfortable physically or mentally. Maybe she never would again. The images she'd seen of people dying in the streets of New York were constantly simmering just below the surface of her mind, along with what she believed were premonitions. She stared at the frosted glass of the office door and watched occasional blurs of people passing in the hall. The writing on the glass spelled *'Captain Dupont'* backward. She loathed the man and wondered if he knew how she felt about him. And if he did know, was he out to ruin her? She didn't know why he'd ordered her in off patrol. She'd never heard of a patrol being cut short – the barracks was chronically understaffed. She'd ago-nized over the strangeness of the orders during the thirty minute return drive. Fears of discovery were coloring her thoughts. Had he found out about New Jersey? She was a quarantine jumper. Records surely existed somewhere showing she was on duty the night New Jersey was hit.

Her mouth was dry. She thought about getting up to find something to drink, but didn't move. Dupont was running late and could show up any moment. Maybe the meeting was nothing more than a change of assignment. She'd heard rumors about mass killings done by roaming gangs. They were operating like small companies of soldiers. Intel had reported some of the gangs were traveling in packs as large as five

319

hundred soldiers. Could the police be forming units to repel heavy attacks on the line?

Sarah slowly shook her head. The north side of I64 now looked like a huge squatter's camp. Tents and smoke from campfires extended as far as the eye could see. Most of the roads were impassibly congested with cars that had been stripped or crashed. The new status symbol on that side of the line was ownership of a dirt bike. People had been killed over as little as a can of Chef Boyardee and things were growing worse every day. Gangs, no matter how large, were only one of law enforcement's worries.

Last night Alex had banged on her door at one in the morning. He'd been drinking since his patrol had ended at noon. He was drunk and out of his mind by the time he'd wandered to her house. Sarah had had no idea what was bothering him. He'd wanted sex and had tried to force her. He was lumbering and sloppy. Sarah had smacked him once. That was all it had taken. She had immediately regretted striking him.

They'd ended up on the couch drinking coffee. It had taken him awhile to explain what had happened on patrol. He'd witnessed a police shooting of a man while his wife and two children watched. The couple had refused to turn back from the line. The husband had a pair of wire-cutters and was chewing through the first spiral of razor wire. A warning shot had been fired. The man seemed not to notice. Alex said they'd looked like none of them had eaten in days.

By the time man cut through the first fence, a crowd of hundreds had formed on the northern side. On the southern side were five patrol cars and twenty cops, all armed with M16 automatic rifles. A helicopter gunship was hovering a thousand feet back. The man was warned deadly force would be used if he cut any part of the second line of razor wire. The crowd started chanting: "America... America... America..." He snipped the wire. A bullet was fired into the man's chest. The crowd went insane. In unison, the police fired their weapons just above the heads of the rioters. Alex said the noise was so loud it hurt his teeth. Within seconds, the helicopter gunship came in low and hit the crowd with rotor-wash. Everyone scattered except for the dead man's wife and children who were blown to the ground.

America... A chill raised goose bumps across Sarah's arms. She hadn't witnessed what Alex had seen. The description was horrifying enough. Her eyes were starting to water. The police had murdered an unarmed man while his family stood beside him. The world was tearing itself apart. The southern side of the line considered itself superior, the last bastions of civilization. Sarah felt a bitter irony. The people manning the line were becoming a new social elite, while the bureaucrats, the Captain Duponts of the world, were demigods. Dupont, what a mistake that man was: a racist one generation removed from the Klan and now he had absolute power. He didn't mind if some of his men went into business for themselves as long as he got his tribute; rumors were he got fifty percent of the take. The common scam was smuggling people across the line. The same spot where that family saw their blood spilled could have been crossed with the aid of the right cops and a fist full of money. The fascist bastards were profiteering off the desperation of mothers and fathers and children.

A fax machine next to her rang. Sarah jumped as if someone had taken a shot at her. The old machine automatically answered and then began to buzz. A sheet of paper inched its way out the front. She recognized the letterhead. The fax was a flash bulletin from the CDC in Atlanta. Sarah read the print as it emerged. Each line of it changed her life.

CDC Bulletin Duplicate Rebroadcast
FLASH FAX CONFIDENTIAL
COMMAND STAFF EYES ONLY

The CDC is confident communicability of the COBIC bacterium is limited to waterborne vectors. There is no evidence that people or animals are vectors. While some individuals may be infected with live bacteria in their blood, there is little chance of cross infection unless whole blood transfusions occur.

Blood tests are now available for detection of the presence of COBIC bacterium. Blood samples forwarded to CDC test centers will be processed within 24 hours. While caution is still advised, General Order C1.008.1 for total human isolation and quarantine is rescinded. This order does not affect total material quarantine orders which are still in force for all containerized liquids and organic materials.

The quarantine was over. Sarah was stunned. Crossing a quarantine line was no longer illegal. Her criminal past had been erased. As Dupont entered, Sarah stood up. She had the fax in her hands. She couldn't wait for the fascist to read it. She stood directly in his path blocking him from reaching his desk.

"Sir, this just came in from the CDC. We can allow people to cross the line."

"Let me see that."

Dupont snatched the fax out of her hands. He had a soft voice with a southern accent that made him sound mildly effeminate. Supposedly, he'd been a schoolteacher before becoming a cop.

"Did you not read the first line?" he said. "Well maybe you are a bit thick in the head so I will translate. It says *confidential*. That means you do not get to read this."

He inserted the fax into a paper shredder. Sarah was stunned.

"But it said..."

"I know what it said," Dupont cut her off by raising his hand. "What? Do you think that's the first bulletin we've gotten from the CDC allowing this group or that group to cross?"

"I don't understand..."

"You northern liberals are all alike. I guess you've forgotten that the CDC does not make state policy. My orders come from elected Virginia officials: the Governor, state senators, you know, democracy. They make the laws, not some federally funded bunch of leftwing socialist doctors."

"Right now, people are starving a few hundred feet north of us and we can do something about it!"

"Listen to me closely, Officer Mayfair. This line was never set up just to keep people out because they are carrying some godforsaken disease. It was set up because they are carrying need. Need of water, need of food, and need of medicine. There's just so much to go around and the powers that run this state have decided that we aren't going to take them in. You are a big girl. You should understand this. It is better that some do without, so that others who are certified healthy can survive. A gallon of clean water divided among a hundred folks is nothing, but for one man it is a week of life."

Sarah's head was spinning. She kept telling herself to keep her anger in check, calm down. Her attempts at self-control were not working.

"You greedy asshole!" she yelled. "You don't give a damn about a gallon of water. You only care about the money crossing your open palm. You want your blood money. Fine! Maybe I'll call a newspaper or two."

Dupont sat down behind his desk. There was a sneer on his lips, but other than that he seemed calm. His chair squeaked as he leaned back in it.

"Anyone that gets across that line has to be cleared from the top," he was speaking slowly as if to a student who was truly dumb. "If a little money also exchanges hands, so what? Grow up, young lady. You think the newspapers are going to just print what you tell them? They all know the score. Now you keep your pretty lips shut and get out of my office."

Sarah wasted no time opening the door. She wanted to slam it hard enough to smash the glass.

"Hold on, Officer Mayfair," said Dupont. "I quite nearly forgot. I have an affidavit covering your posting in New Jersey that has to be faxed back to the Human Health Services immediately. If we do not get this out today, we have to pull you off patrols. These federal agencies are just so bothersome. The affidavit is all filled out. I need you to read and sign where you acknowledge that it is a federal crime to provide false information."

2 – Alexandria, Virginia: December

They were traveling through farm country, split wood fences and rolling hills. The wind was buffeting the camper. Suzy felt edgy. Artie was driving too fast but she said nothing. Two days ago, something had happened during the night that had unnerved him but he still refused to discuss it. His shirtsleeves were rolled up. The dragon tattoo looked like a scar on his wrist. He hadn't uttered a dozen words all morning.

Suzy looked at the locket. Sunlight gave the antique gold a deep sheen. It was a beautiful piece of jewelry, her absolute favorite when she was little. She had always begged to wear the locket and chain. She remembered going through piles of photographs with her mom before finding just the right one to put inside. She slipped the chain back over her neck.

Traffic slowed to fifteen miles per hour. Artie cursed. Suzy ignored his foul mood. She'd been recharging a set of batteries for her camera off the cigarette lighter. She swapped them out for the ones in her camera. There was a steady stream of people trudging along the shoulder of the road. Some were dressed in rags, others in chinos and heavy wool sweaters. They were all one people now. Most seemed too drained to do anything more than put one foot in front of the other. Suzy rolled down the window and brought the camera's viewfinder to her eye. The wind lightly buffeted her face. She panned individuals as the Volkswagen moved past them. She started with the back of their heads on approach and then panned the camera until their faces came into view just as she passed them. She kept each face in focus as it receded with distance. Some people responded to her recording them but most remained indifferent.

~

Suzy's skin was crawling. The smell had started as something vague and difficult to place. The odor was stronger now, almost overpowering. The source began to drift across her viewfinder. The grassy fields were littered with decomposing clumps of cattle. The carcasses grew in number. She zoomed in the lens. Her eyes watered from the stench. Why had the animals been slaughtered and then left to rot? She spotted a small group of people out in a field slicing meat off one of the animals. She imagined it filled with maggots and almost retched. Even the air seemed gray with death.

She took the camera from her eye and glanced over at Artie. He had a determined expression on his face. She rewound the tape and played the footage of a man cutting off a piece of flesh from the side of a cow. The man had a rag tied over his mouth and nose to fight the stench. The animal's eyes were open. The head rocked from the slicing being done. The motion made the cow seem almost alive. Suzy replayed the image a second time. Her hands felt damp.

"Memories of hell," she said. "That's what I'm filming."

Artie glanced at her.

"Things will be better once we get farther south," he said.

'Things will be better' was becoming his mantra. She wondered who he was trying to convince, himself or her? Almost immediately, he was back to concentrating on the road. Suzy started taping again. She tracked the face of a gray haired lady. The car jounced. The image in her viewfinder slipped to waist level of her subject. She noticed the lady was holding the hand of a man walking next to her. Their appearances were too dissimilar to be together. The man looked in his thirties and was wearing blue jeans and a sweatshirt. His cheeks were pink from the cold. The lady was in her fifties, dark skinned, and wearing a very expensive coat. Suzy wondered who was comforting whom?

She put away the camera and slid over beside Artie. The bench seat had a middle safety belt which she buckled loosely. She put her arms around Artie and nuzzled as closely as she could. He took one of his hands from the wheel and put his arm around her waist. His fingers ended up resting near her belly. His touch brought warmth. She closed her eyes and thought about the tiny baby inside her.

Suzy had napped for a few hours but now was awake. Traffic had picked up. Both sides of the highway were lined with tents and makeshift markets. There were countless thousands of people. Why had they all stopped here? Most of the shelters were plastic sheets held together with duct tape and rope. There were small children playing in the dirt. Their skin and clothing were smeared and mothers were nowhere in sight. There didn't seem to be any open fires. Even though the sun was shining, all of it looked drab.

Suzy focused her camera on a roadside stand. The table was stacked with canned food. A full-bearded man sat beside it on a green, webbed beach chair. In his lap was a military rife. His hair was blown wild by the wind of passing cars. His eyes followed her. He seemed to be staring directly into the camera and through it into her soul. He smiled, lips parting to show gleaming white teeth and a pair of small canines. Suzy felt an evil chill.

The shantytown had run on for a dozen miles and looked like it would keep going forever. Artie pulled to the shoulder by a fruit stand. There was an elderly man and woman running it. Behind the stand was a farm truck loaded with wooden crates. Suzy walked along a counter made from the same crates. She ran her fingers over all the food. There were apples, pears, black berries, and peaches. The air smelled sweet. Artie struck up a conversation. The man's name was Harland and the woman was his wife Carol Ann. They'd come north from their farm to help out in relief efforts organized by a religious group called International Hope.

"By God, we had more produce this year than we knew what to do with. There weren't enough companies looking to buy it – and now I 'spect there aren't any companies to buy it. Figured it's the *Lord working in strange ways* that gave us this bounty to help others."

Harland's voice had a slow pleasantness to it. Suzy felt immediately at ease. Carol Ann handed each of them a free apple. The apple was shiny red and heavy for its size. Suzy hadn't known how hungry she was until she took a bite. The apple was crisp. Juice ran down her chin. She wiped it away with her sleeve and took a second bite.

"How much fruit will you trade me for a case of canned food?" asked Artie.

"What brand o' food?" asked Harland.

"Does it matter?"

"Well, if it's the kind I've got a taste for."

Artie smiled. Suzy could tell he liked the older man.

"I've got SpaghettiOs, Beefaroni, and Chef Boyardee ravioli."

Harland seemed to ponder the possibilities with great care.

"I'll give ya'll a crate, half apples and half pears for a case of the ravioli."

"Mix in some peaches and it's a deal," said Artie.

They shook on it.

"So you folks planning on going all the way to Satan's Crossing?"

"What's that?" asked Suzy.

"He's talking about the I64 line," said Artie.

"Yeah, that's right, ma'am," said Harland. "I'm just asking 'cause ya'll seem like nice folks, and that's not a place for anyone nice. Me and Carol Ann went straight there when we first came north to help. We stayed put a day and then headed up around here where it's safer. Folks down there are crazy and there's too many guns."

~

Artie stopped the Volkswagen next to a mobile home. There was a slow but steady stream of vehicles arriving behind him. He'd been worried about this happening all day and now it had. They were in the middle of a freeway that had turned into a parking lot. There was nowhere to exit or park without getting trapped. A grass median separated the highway's north and south lanes. The median was heavily rutted from u-turns.

According to the map, they were within a mile of the I64 line. After a short conversation, Artie convinced Suzy they needed to go on foot to scout out the line. He turned around across the median and parked on the shoulder of the northbound lane along with a few other cars. The shoulder angled down into a ditch where the remains of several cars and small trucks looked ready to decompose back into nature. They got out and started walking. Artie was wearing a light jacket with his gun tucked underneath. He was worried about leaving their supplies locked in the car, but there was no choice. This was a necessary reconnaissance mission and he was not going to leave Suzy alone to guard a prime target like a van full of food. If someone stole it, he would just have to steal it back.

Artie stood motionless and stared. Suzy clung to his arm. He barely noticed her. So this was the I64 line. He was breathing rapidly after walking up the steep hill. There was no passage through the line; only endless miles of towering razor wire fence, steel spikes embedded in concrete, surveillance cameras, and then a second razor wire fence. Even though the sun was out, floodlights from the opposite side lit the barrier. Every few minutes, a police car roared past at high speed like a jet fighter patrolling a battle line.

Impaled on the spikes was the burnt-out carcass of what had been a car. Artie could see it had been pummeled with heavy weapons. The air was thick with the smell of wood fires and sewage. Behind them was a huge tent city. The ragged encampment looked like it stretched the entire length of the line. Near the horizon, the fence and the tent city merged like the parallel rails of a train track. An occasional peal of laughter rose up from the constant murmur of life. If he closed his eyes, the noise conjured memories of a bar.

"Reminds me of a concentration camp," said a man standing next to them. "And we're on the wrong side. Food's getting a little better though – plenty of beef."

Artie looked at the man, instinctively sizing him up and gauging him for potential threat. He was young with an angular face and longish, scruffy blond hair.

"Name's Henry Lucas. Just kidding about the beef. You want to stay clear of that stuff. It'll make you sick."

The man held out his hand. Artie shook it. He heard the noise of scuffle a dozen yards behind him. A teenager ran out from a row of tents and then disappeared back into the hive of people. A man emerged a few seconds later. He glanced both ways, standing there with a baseball bat at his side. Another man came out from a row of tents dragging the teenager behind him. Before the kid could say anything, the man with the bat hit him full swing in the gut.

"The line runs from here through Virginia, Kentucky, Tennessee, and Alabama," said Henry. He was oblivious to the ruckus behind him.

"Doesn't stop until it hits the Gulf of Mexico at Mobile, Alabama. I know 'cause I drove the entire length on a dirt bike, scoping for ways across. Of course, if you've got something valuable..."

"We've got nothing," said Artie.

"Whatever," said Henry. He waved his hand dismissively. "You'd be surprised what people consider valuable nowadays – food, guns, even women. I've heard rumors that if you have enough juice, the police will escort you across; otherwise, forget it. See what's left of that car – I was here when that happened. That wasn't the work of a few cops with guns. No, sir; that was the work of an Army attack helicopter, a goddamn fully armed Apache. It just hovered off behind the line, right there by those trees. The minute that car hit the spikes and its front tires blew, the Apache opened up with a short burst from some kind of machine gun cannon. It was dark out. The shells glowed like a fucking laser beam. I'm telling you, it blew that car up like a phaser blast from the Starship Enterprise. Took all of one second and there was no more car, no more people, no more nothing except burning gasoline."

Artie didn't like leaving their supplies unguarded for too long, and their new friend Henry made him feel even more nervous. He and Suzy headed back after a few more minutes of Henry's monologue. The return trip seemed to take twice as long. As soon as they got within sight of where he'd parked the Volkswagen, Artie knew it had been a mistake to leave it. The shoulder was completely empty. Their Volkswagen and several other cars were now on their sides in the ditch. He couldn't figure out what had happened. There were long scrapes in the roadbed. It looked the cars had been shoved off the highway by a bulldozer.

Gunfire cracked in the distance, somewhere south of them. Suzy flinched with the echo of each report. Artie knew she was flashing back to New York; so was he. They had to get across that line. There were no other options. Staying here would ensure a slow death, first the spirit and then the body. He'd been thinking how he could accumulate enough for a bribe. He felt the weight of the gun pressing in on his side. Ten years ago, the answer to their problems would have been simple. He didn't know if he had it in him to keep doing those kinds of things. Could he look more people in the eyes and take what he wanted from them? Was he ready to murder for his small family?

Dusk was falling quickly. Artie noticed some people were flowing into the area. They were walking along the shoulder and glancing furtively into the ditch. They looked like normal people, mothers and fathers and children. There were small groups of them. Artie knew they weren't normal. They were scavengers. He could tell by the hunger in their eyes. They were staking out their claims. As soon as it was dark, he knew he would start to hear the sounds of windows breaking from within the ditch.

He and Suzy unloaded as much as they could carry. They headed north up the highway away from the I64 line and took the first exit they found. He'd made a decision: this had to be about his and Suzy's survival. As soon as he found a safe place to hole up for a few days, he'd head out on his own and find what they needed. If other people had to be hurt, that wasn't his concern.

They walked for hours before hitting the streets of a town. Artie felt a nagging rawness in his left heel. The moon was almost full. The streetlights were dead. Very few people were outside. In a vacant lot, a group of kids were playing freeze tag in the dark with flashlights. Suzy looked worn out. Her face was slack. Her eyes were dull. Artie walked up to a single story house that was dark and knocked on the door. There was no answer. He knocked again. No one came to open the door. He furtively drew his revolver and cocked the hammer.

"What are you doing!" said Suzy.

"Checking into our motel room."

"You can't..."

"We have to!"

Artie walked around back and found what he was looking for. He kicked the rear door hard. There was a sound of wood cracking. The door shuddered but held. He saw Suzy had her hands over her ears. Her eyes were wide and all pupils. He hit the door a second time. The frame split, leaving half the door caved in. He opened it the rest of the way with his shoulder. He checked the house to make sure it was empty. Suzy didn't want to come inside.

"It's wrong!"

"Look, no one's here. This house has been empty for days."

"How do you know that? What if they're coming back? Artie, we can't do this. Please, let's just get out of here."

"Where else are we going to sleep? Do you want to walk a few more miles until you're desperate enough to break into a different house?"

Suzy looked down at the ground.

"Listen, honey. Right now, there's probably a family of strangers living in our apartment. Hell, their kids are probably jumping up and down on your new couch."

There was a tiny hint of a smile. She looked up.

"I guess you're right," she said.

"Hey, it's better than freezing your little nipples off out in some field."

"Arrrrtie!"

She turned away suddenly acting embarrassed and shy. He was relieved that she'd given in. He'd been ready to physically drag her inside if he'd had to.

The kitchen was fully stocked and there was gas for the range. Suzy cooked while Artie made sure their temporary home was secure and warm. He'd pushed some furniture against the front door and secured the windows by barricading them or setting tripwires made from twine and noise-makers. Next, he got some split wood he'd seen out back and brought it for the fireplace. Suzy had found a canned ham. She'd diced it with onions, peppers, Velveeta cheese, and mixed it with macaroni. Artie ate until his stomach was bloated; then he waited a few minutes and ate some more. After dinner, they curled up in front of the fireplace. The wood snapped as embers were drawn up the chimney. The flames cast an orange-yellow light. Suzy looked like her old self. Artie vowed that he would do whatever it took to make sure she stayed that way.

"Tomorrow, I'll see if we can find a new car."

"What if you can't?"

"Don't worry; I will."

"You mean you'll steal one." Her voice was uneven.

He thought about lying to her, but didn't.

"Honey, the world out there has changed."

"So have you."

"I'm sorry but this is how it has to be. There are gangs roaming out there. I know how they think. I know what they're capable of doing. We need to get as far away from here as we can."

"Do you remember rule number six?" said Suzy.

"No, honey..."

330

"Some families are *defined* by who their enemies are. Don't let us sink to that."

3 – I64 line, Virginia: December

Sarah looked at the speedometer in her patrol car. The needle was at exactly a hundred mph. A scattering of cold rain forced her to flip the wipers off intermittent and onto medium speed. The sun would be trying to rise in a few hours, but she suspected a stormy overcast would extend night's grip well into the morning. Her work schedule had been changed to the most dangerous shift, on the most violent stretch of road – eight p.m. to four a.m., six days a week. The schedule was Captain Dupont's revenge for her shoving the CDC fax in his face. Sarah smiled. Calling him a *greedy asshole* also might have contributed just a little to her reassignment. Maybe Dupont was hoping she'd get shot or would quit. All the line jumpers thought darkness gave them an edge. Her new shift was nicknamed 'primetime at the line.' Hadn't any of the idiot jumpers seen a military news clip in the last few decades or heard about night vision goggles, not to mention video cameras and floodlights? Capturing them was actually easier at night than during the day. Even hiding in the bushes, they showed up as blobs of heat on the forward-looking infrared displays of the National Guard choppers which assisted at night. Once jumpers were spotted by cameras or helicopters, the patrol cars were vectored in. All the officers had been issued night vision goggles. It was like playing hide 'n seek war games against children with guns.

Sarah reached down to the keyboard for the car's computer. She typed in the code for going off duty. The all-clear response came back. Her fingers lingered on top of the display. She thought about the kill zone in Virginia Beach and all that had happened since then. She felt like a survivor cursed by God for failing to die. Virginia Beach had become a recurring feature of her thoughts and dreams. She shivered thinking of all the images of death that had been projected into her mind on that day. The experience had been a kind of mental rape – a sense that she'd been abused by something that was far more powerful then anything had a right to be.

She wanted to doubt her own memories, to explain them away as a mental breakdown of some kind; but she knew the experience was real, all of it. That day, she'd known even before radioing in from her car that hundreds of thousands were dying; and more, somehow deep inside, she had sensed that this time the destruction was spread across the entire globe. She had known when another zone had hit just before the computer display in her patrol car reported it. The names of cities scrolling up had become like some crazy Wall Street ticker tape announcing the crash of the world. The time between kill zones had been erratic; sometimes seconds and other times minutes. Each premonition would start as a little ball of fear inside her; then just as the feeling reached a crescendo, a new name would appear on the display. Sometimes she even knew what the name would be. She was horrified by her accuracy. She had gone beyond the rim of sanity that day and glimpsed a darkness that was waiting to claim her.

The premonition feelings at Virginia Beach were the same as what she was experiencing this moment, and had experienced so many other moments between then and now. She was a raw nerve that had been teased to the point where a kind of numbness had set in, a detached dread. Somewhere a kill zone was about to happen; somewhere people were about to die. She didn't want to know this. She didn't want this curse.

Alex was deeply affected by her premonitions, as they had both started to call them. Since Virginia Beach, he'd made her jot down in a notebook the time and date she had each of her feelings. Every day, he checked her notes against the official reports. So far, every one of her premonitions had been linked to the exact time a kill zone had happened somewhere in the world. At some point which Sarah could not precisely remember, Alex had started treating her differently. She could tell he was becoming scared of her. She was sorry she'd confided anything.

The computer display posted a report. A kill zone located near Leipzig, Germany had just occurred. The little ball of fear began to dim inside her.

"Why me?" she cried.

Sarah pulled her car into the parking lot of a twenty-four hour diner named the Twilight Café and killed the ignition. There were several other patrol cars in the lot. The diner was a hang out for cops. Taking deep breaths, she tried to settle her nerves. Tears were running down her cheeks. The windshield was quickly obscured with drops of rain. She began to sob uncontrollably.

A large clock on the outside of the diner showed almost an hour had passed. Headlights washed over her from a car pulling into the lot. Sarah cleaned the tears from her face, then fixed her makeup and went inside. She spotted her friend Theresa sitting at a table with two other cops, Bobby Williams and Sergeant Hunt. Sarah said hello to Bert, the owner, and then made her way to the table. Theresa's eyes had a glassy look. Something was wrong.

"What's up, guys?" said Sarah.

"Just eating breakfast," said Theresa.

The other two said nothing. A waitress came over and took Sarah's order.

"I've gotta go," said Bobby Williams.

"Me too," said Sergeant Hunt.

They got up. Their food was half eaten. Sarah looked across the table at Theresa. There was something very wrong with her expression.

"I've gotta go, too," said Theresa.

"What's going on?" said Sarah. "None of you have finished eating."

All three of them exchanged glances. A girl from the next table mumbled, "Leper..." Sarah felt her chest empty of all feelings. They couldn't mean her. She glanced around the room. People she knew looked away instead of meeting her eyes.

"People are saying things," said Theresa. "Everyone's talking about how you were at Virginia Beach and weren't killed. They're saying you could be carrying the bug."

"That's crazy," said Sarah.

Theresa looked down at the table. Sarah was fighting back an ocean of feelings. She stood up. She started to move toward Theresa. Her friend backed away.

"You know me." said Sarah. "All of you know me. Has anyone I've hung out with gotten sick?"

"What about New Jersey?" yelled a faceless voice from somewhere in the diner.

Sarah had difficulty piecing time back together after that. She kept seeing Alex's face drift up in her mind. He was the only one she'd told about Jersey but he couldn't have betrayed her. Captain Dupont must have found out somehow and poisoned everyone against her. It had to be Dupont... It just had to be. Alex wouldn't have told anyone.

"I don't know what you're talking about," said Sarah.

"Go on, Alex," yelled the faceless voice. "Tell her!"

The world stopped moving, stopped working. Sarah felt tears gushing from her eyes. Before she knew what she was doing, she was running from the diner. Alex was at the doorway. His skin looked drained of color. His expression was unreadable as she stopped and stared into his eyes. He began to say something.

"You bastard!" she shouted.

Sarah pushed past him out the door. Rain spattered her face. She ran across the parking lot and into a neighboring field. A tree loomed out of the pre-dawn to block her flight. She collapsed against its trunk. She clung to the tree to hold herself up from the ground. Enveloped in the sounds of the field and the patter of rain, she cried.

4 - I64 line, Virginia: December

Artie had been hiking with Suzy for hours before a passing trucker had given them a lift. The westbound side of I64 was wide open and divided into two-way traffic. They were cruising at sixty miles per hour heading into the Blue Ridge Mountains. He and Suzy were sharing the passenger seat. She was in his lap. Air rushing though the partially open window smelled of pine and freshness. The landscape was spectacular. The tree covered mountains were blanketed by mist and fall colors. Artie was starting to think their luck might be changing.

The trucker's name was Quade. Almost an hour ago, they'd pulled out of a truck stop after buying Quade lunch to thank him for picking them up earlier in the day. Everyone at the stop knew Quade and said hello. He seemed genuinely friendly, but Artie still kept his gun within easy reach inside his coat. Quade had curly red hair and a full beard of the same color. His rig was a brand new Cummings. The trailer was decaled with the Bayer logo.

"I've been making this same run for six weeks," said Quade. "Richmond to Lewisburg, Lewisburg to Richmond, twice a day with thirty thousand pounds of fuck'n aspirin. Man, what do you think they're doing with all that aspirin? I can't even look at the stuff anymore without getting a headache."

"Someone must have one hell of a migraine," said Artie.

Quade smiled while nodding.

"Hey, if you want any aspirin, say the word. They'd never miss a case or two falling off the back of the truck."

"Can I ask you something, Quade?"

"Sure buddy; shoot."

"Have you ever heard of cops letting folks cross for money?"

Quade turned and looked Artie in the eyes for a moment and then returned his gaze to the road. Maybe Quade did know something? Artie felt Suzy's alertness. They both were waiting for something to happen.

"So have you heard of cops doing that?" asked Artie again.

"Yeah, who hasn't?" answered Quade. "They're Border Czars, man. Cash or favors for passage across the line. I've heard other things too – things like a lot of those who pay end up crossing a different line, the one separating the living from the dead."

Quade had taken them as far as they wanted to go down the highway. Artie and Suzy watched as he pulled back onto I64. His rig made a slow right-hand turn out of the rest stop. Artie looked around taking his measure of this place. The parking spaces were empty. Across the highway, a long coil of razor wire hung loose from the top of the I64 line. The damaged wire was the first sign of disrepair that he'd seen. They were in a heavily wooded area of National Forest which Quade had said was deserted this time of year and a safe place to camp. Since starting out on foot days ago, they'd collected everything needed to live off the land. He and Suzy each had backpacks and sleeping bags. They also owned a brand new tent that had a price tag of over eight hundred bucks on it when Artie had liberated it from a sporting goods store along with a handheld GPS and a supply of freeze dried food.

At the back of the rest stop, the highway's deer fencing had been cut and peeled back at the entrance to a trail. If Quade was right, the path led off to an idyllic spot. The map showed a small lake five miles in from the highway with no roads leading to it. The idea of camping there appealed to both of them. Artie imagined waking up in the morning and sipping coffee at water's edge.

The trail quickly narrowed into something used more by deer than by people. Artie pushed another branch out of the way and made sure Suzy had a grip on it before letting go. The woods seemed like it belonged to them. With every step, he felt they'd found a good place to rest for a few days and make new plans.

"So, what do you think about raising a family on the Gulf of Mexico?" he asked. "We can get a grass hut on the sand. You can make clothes for us out of palm fronds while I fish for shrimp and lobster. What do you say?"

"I think you're nuts but I love you."

"Would you still love me if all I ever caught was a cold?"

"A girl has to draw the line somewhere."

The lake turned out to be just as Artie had imagined it. The landscape was so familiar he wondered if he'd been here before. The water was a deep grayish blue. Tree covered hills on the opposite shore were reflected in it as streaks of color. He ran his fingers through the water. It was cold and clean. They pitched the tent and then fire-roasted a dinner of hot dogs and corn on the cob.

As the sun went down, Suzy toasted marshmallows and forced him to try one. Her lips followed and were sweeter than the marshmallows. Soon they were wrestling and laughing and losing their clothing. The outside world was too far away to cast its shadow.

An owl called from somewhere in the night as wind rustled through the trees. Inside their tent, Artie and Suzy were curled up with one of the sleeping bags wrapped around them. The campfire was well stoked, throwing off a warm orange light that glowed through the tent's fabric. Artie was thinking about tomorrow. The new flannel shirt felt luxurious against his skin. Suzy had on a matching shirt. He noticed her drifting off and soon followed.

Artie dreamed of ice. It was odd that there was a piece of it pressed against his face. He swam out of the haze into the real world and opened his eyes. Something cold was still pressed against his cheek. His heart began beating wildly. He blinked but it was still there. The barrel of a machine gun was right next to his eye. He strained to look up without moving. The firelight gave everything a hellish tone. The tent flap was open. A hand was attached to the machine gun and a face was attached to the hand, a tattooed angry face.

"You're dead!" said man.

"Take anything you want," said Artie. "Just don't hurt us."

Artie strained to look through the corner of his eyes at Suzy and saw a second man and a second machine gun. These were definitely gang members and definitely killers. Where had they come from? Artie slowly inched his hand down the side of the sleeping bag reaching for the handle of his revolver.

There were odd smears of red light. Artie felt a throbbing pain in his skull. Blood was in his left eye. He didn't remember being clubbed or shot but knew that's what had happened. He felt a warm liquid running down the side of his face. He was lying outside on the ground. He heard angry words and a soft thud and looked toward the sounds. His eyes swam into focus. In the firelight, he saw one of the men kicking Suzy.

"Give... me... the... necklace... bitch..."

Suzy's eyes were squeezed shut. Dirt was smeared across her cheek. She was curled in a ball. Her fingers were wrapped tightly around the locket. Artie went mad with grief. The other man's back was to Artie. He had Artie's gun stuck in his belt and a machine gun over his shoulder. The creep was staring at the action which Artie knew would soon be rape, then murder.

Keeping perfectly still, Artie furtively looked around for a weapon. All their belongings were scattered on the ground. A multifunction camping tool was in his hand a moment later. The tool was twelve inches long; part shovel, part wrench, and part hammer. He pounced on the one who was just watching the action, striking him full swing in the side of the head. The tool's wooden handle broke off with the impact. The man crumpled to the ground. Artie knew he had just killed. The other animal was slow to respond; he was busy pawing Suzy. Without slowing, Artie was on him an instant later, head-locking him from behind, he pulled the scum backward off Suzy using a twisting-hip-throw meant to fracture the neck. Every memory of street fighting and Tae Kwan Do returned to Artie in a violent rush. The man's neck held. He was heavily muscled and managed to shake Artie off.

"Bring it on!" growled the man; his face was a twisted sneer.

The bastard wasn't as lucky with the three kicks to the face which followed. He went down. Artie jumped on the animal and pinned him with his knees. Focusing all his strength, using the heel of his hand, he viciously struck the man in the nose with a single blow. The move was a Tae Kwan Do technique designed to kill by splintering and driving the nose bone into the brain. The man stopped moving, but Artie didn't care. He hammered the man with his fists. He couldn't stop. Tears of rage and pain flooded down across Artie's cheeks, burning his eyes. He screamed obscenities while pummeling the still body. He spied his handgun which had fallen into the dirt. He retrieved it, tumbled back the hammer, and blew a round into the man's chest. He turned to the other man and did the same.

"Artie..." It was a soft whisper. "Artie...."

Suzy! She was still on the ground, curled on her side. He looked at her and felt the rage drain from him, leaving only black shoals of despair. What had he done? How had he let this happen to her? He dropped the gun.

"Oh, baby," he moaned.

He lifted her into his arms. The blood of their attackers was soaked into his hands. He glanced over at the two animals to make sure neither was moving. They both looked very dead.

"It hurts, Artie. He kept kicking me." She swallowed with difficulty. "It hurts to breathe."

"Just relax. I'm going to get you to a doctor. Just hang on baby. It'll be all right."

"They wanted the locket and I said no. I'm sorry. I should have given it to them..."

She was trying to cry but couldn't draw enough air into her lungs. Her left eye was starting to puff up. Artie swallowed back his own tears and forced an unconvincing smile onto his face.

"Sweetheart, it's okay. Everything's going to be okay."

"No, it's not. I'm worried about the baby."

Artie bundled Suzy in a coat and blanket. It was heartbreaking to take his eyes from her, but he had to collect what was needed to get her safely to help. He had no illusions about how difficult it would be hiking through miles of forest at night, and then down a highway which might be deserted. He retrieved his gun and then found a flashlight. He pulled his coat and shoulder holster from the tent, and then hastily wrestled them on; then stuffed the coat's pockets with ammo and extra batteries. He tied a bandana around the wound on his forehead to stem the flow of blood.

Suzy was unconscious when he returned to her. Her breathing had a normal rhythm but was raspy. Artie was stunned. A flood of adrenaline washed through him leaving a numbing cold in its wake. He hoisted Suzy up into his arms. Soon he was hiking as fast as he could – his legs working, the flashlight bouncing erratically over the path. In the wavering light, he repeatedly lost his footing. Soon, his skull was throbbing, sapping his strength. His arms were tired. He had to rest. At the base of a hill, he sat down on a huge stone with Suzy in his lap.

Blood from his head wound dripped onto Suzy's cheek. The image filled him with despair. Please God, don't let her die. He pushed himself off the stone and began moving again. The darkness was claustrophobic. His head was throbbing so hard that he couldn't focus his eyes. Artie stumbled badly, keeping himself and Suzy off the rocky ground by jamming his shoulder into a large tree. He felt a piece of his shoulder scraped raw. He tried to take another step. His legs gave out. He dropped to his knees, managing to shield Suzy from any impact. His strength was failing as the pain in his head grew even worse. He tried to get up with her in his arms but couldn't. The pain in his head took all his senses and scrambled them. He sat panting until he could almost see again. It was miles to the nearest town. He knew what he had to do, but the idea was breaking his heart. He started sobbing. He knew he had to leave Suzy here and go find help. Doing this was their only chance, but how could he abandon her? What if she woke up alone in the woods?

"Baby... I can't carry you. You have to stay here... okay?"

There was no response. Her breathing was getting worse. The rasp was more pronounced and the rhythm had become irregular.

"Forgive me," he said.

Artie bundled her as best he could. He kissed her lips. He moved a few strands of hair from her eyes. They should have opened, but didn't. He pulled himself up using a small tree and started running. He stumbled to the ground a few yards from her.

"God, damn you!" he screamed.

He beat his fists into the ground cursing God again and again until exhausted. His fists were throbbing and covered in bits of dirt. His face was cold with tears. He lifted himself up. He took a step and then looked back at Suzy. He couldn't do this. He just couldn't do this. He went back to her and picked her up, draping her over his shoulder. He'd find the strength to carry her out of the woods or die with her in this darkness.

Artie felt like hours had passed. The temperature was freezing. He was soaked with sweat. Each breath drew a deepening cold inside his throat and lungs. The flashlight beam played across an endless depth of woods. With every weakened step, he wondered if he had made a fatal decision. If he'd been strong enough to leave Suzy, he might have been back to her with help by now. He looked ahead into the murky blackness of the forest. Something was there. He switched off the flashlight. The glow of the I64 line trickled through the bushes and tree trunks.

Artie stopped at the shoulder of the highway. He heard no traffic. He needed to rest for a moment. His head ached so badly that he was seeing spots. He looked down at Suzy. Her breathing was a little stronger. He'd allowed himself too many breaks already and vowed this would be the last until he found help.

With Suzy lying on the grassy shoulder, Artie staggered out to the middle of the I64 roadway. He looked east then west. He had no idea in which direction to head. He remembered they'd passed a gas station twenty minutes before Quade had dropped them off. If Quade had been driving at sixty miles per hour, then the station could be twenty miles away. At that distance it may as well have been on another planet. He looked in the other direction. He had no idea what was up ahead. There could be a truck stop a mile off or nothing for fifty miles. He had no choice. He couldn't gamble with Suzy's life. He returned to the highway's shoulder, gently gathered Suzy up into his arms, and started walking east.

The sound of fast moving tires and engine caught Artie's attention. Someone was coming. He turned in the direction of the sound. He couldn't see any headlights but the sound was unmistakable and growing louder. He took a few steps out into the roadway. The sound roared past him, but no car. He looked across the highway to the free side of the I64 line just in time to see a pair of taillights recede into the night. Only state police drove in those lanes.

5 – I64 line, Virginia: December

Sarah sped through the darkness heading west at a hundred-ten miles per hour. She was nearing the far western end of her patrol loop. The headlights of her cruiser moved along the curves, turning road signs into glowing slates that whisked past. Her fingers were wrapped tightly around the wheel. Her knuckles were white but not from driving. She barely paid attention to the road. Her mind was on what she'd found in her locker. It was a death threat: a photograph with no words, only the image of her and Ralph with a gun sight drawn over Ralph's torso. The meaning was obvious. Leave or they were going to start hurting her, and they were going to do it through the things she loved. The picture was stuffed into her shirt pocket. She could feel it pressing against her chest. She glanced at Ralph who was curled on the seat next to her. His latest toy, a Frisbee, was under one of his paws.

Sarah looked back to the road. A large brown shape jumped out of the darkness in front of her. She stomped on the brakes. The car's tires pumped as the anti-lock system tried to prevent a skid. There was a thud. Her bumper hit the animal as it disappeared from view. The tires broke into a skid of burning rubber.

"No!" she screamed.

A tire blew. The car swung madly. Sarah cut the wheel to the left into the skid. Fishtailing, over-correcting, she finally got the cruiser to a smoking stop in the middle of the highway. She could still hear the screech of the tires slowly fading in her mind like an emotional echo.

The I64 floodlights buzzed. Their wash illuminated the fence and part of the road with a sodium yellow light. The pair of tire tracks stretched for a hundred yards. There was a faint smell of burnt rubber. Sarah felt nauseous. The baby deer was seriously injured. Its hind legs were crumpled. She had spent the last few minutes walking between the animal and her car in aborted decisions. The front of the cruiser was smashed but drivable. She'd radioed for roadside assistance and had got the silent treatment except for a prank offer to go halves on the venison. She made her decision. She had to fix the tire herself and drive back to the station in the damaged cruiser – and she had to put the animal out of its pain. Hurting the deer was her fault. The cruiser was far enough down the highway from the baby deer so that Ralph couldn't see what she was about to do. She opened the trunk and took out an M16 rifle.

By the time she got back to the deer, its eyes were closed and its breathing was uneven. She pulled back on the rifle bolt and released it, driving a shell into the chamber. In response to the sound, the deer tried to raise its head but managed only a few inches. Sarah sniffled. Her eyes filled. She put the stock up against her cheek, took aim and squeezed off a round. There was a loud crack. The report echoed down the roadway. She felt like her heart had been torn out by the explosive sound. Sarah closed her eyes.

The noise of an approaching car emerged from the emptiness. Sarah knew it had to be Bobby Williams. She opened her eyes in time to see his headlights drifting to the far right, giving her a wide berth. His speed didn't drop. Bobby roared past her at over a hundred miles per hour. Sarah looked down at the deer. She held her breath, gripped the animal by its front hooves, and started tugging. The body was heavy and took some effort to drag it off the road.

An urgent call came over the radio while Sarah was replacing the flat. She heard the report over the portable clipped to her belt. The dispatcher was issuing a jumper alert with civilian injuries. She finished changing the tire with reckless speed, left the bad wheel on the shoulder, slammed the door and floored it. The speedometer climbed effortlessly to a hundred-forty. A helicopter had spotted the heat signature of two people trying to jump the fence near Esker's Pond.

In eight minutes Sarah had reached the scene. Three other cruisers were already there. The helicopter was circling. Its spotlight was moving over the area. Floodlights from the fence were spaced out more than at other parts of the line and not as bright as they should have been. Sarah saw a man carrying the body of woman in his arms. The helo's beam wandered through the tree line to probe for a possible ambush. Bobby Williams used a bullhorn to order the perp to stop advancing. Four other cops had weapons aimed at the man. Both Hendrix and Collins had M16s. The other two cops had nine-millimeter automatics.

Several car spotlights crisscrossed the scene but none of them were on the perp. Sarah flicked on her spotlight. The guy looked funny. Something was definitely wrong with him. He was moving oddly, not drunk, but his legs seemed rubbery. Was he hurt? There was something dark on his face that could have been blood. Sarah caught a glint of metal in the spotlight. A long heavy object was under his open coat, something shaped like a revolver.

"Possible gun," she yelled. "Left-side concealed holster."

Sarah's nerves were raw. She knew they were all running with the same emotional high octane in their guts. It was a mix of fear and adrenaline. She held her spotlight on the guy.

"Put the woman down slowly and then lie face down on the road with your arms out. Do it now!"

Bobby William's amplified voice sounded like god. The perp kept moving in this weaving kind of approach toward the fence. He was yelling something. Sarah couldn't make out his words. She heard him say something like wife and Suzy. The guy's shirt was ripped but his clothing appeared expensive and new. He had a gang colored bandana which looked bloodstained wrapped around his forehead. He didn't seem to be aware of the gun, if that's what it was, under his coat.

Sarah glanced at Hendrix and Roy Burton. Both of them were known to be heavily into the crossing-for-dollars game. They were tight and dangerous like a pair of wolves. Hendrix was six-four and heavily muscled. Roy Burton was of average build with a potbelly and a receding hairline. It was Roy who was the nastier of the two. Rumor had it they were suck-buddies with Captain Dupont

"This guy looks sick," said Hendrix.

"Probably loaded with plague," mumbled Roy Burton.

"Keep it cool," ordered Bobby Williams.

Sarah squinted into the light. That *was* blood on the perp's face. The guy looked like he'd been beaten.

"I think he's hurt," yelled Sarah.

"Hurt, my ass," sneered Hendrix. "Look at 'em slanty eyes, Roy. We've got ourselves a mixed breed gook gangster."

The radio squelched off, "Ten-ten copy... Sergeant Andrews is en route. First on scene is in charge until arrival."

That meant Bobby Williams was the officer in charge. Sarah felt relieved, then Bobby started to go down the written list of conditions required to invoke special order Twelve-Eighteen; the standing order to shoot anyone who tried to break quarantine.

"The procedure calls for a warning shot to be fired," said Bobby Williams.

Sarah knew the protocol was designed like a fail-safe that controlled the use of nuclear weapons. There was supposed to be no room for personal interpretation; but the use of a warning shot seemed crazy, just as likely to get a perp to fire back as give up. Maybe the idea behind the order really was to get the perp to do something stupid so they could kill him? Without warning, Hendrix fired a shot in the air.

"There's your warning shot, Bobby-boy," said Hendrix.

Sarah was stunned. They weren't going to do it! They couldn't. This guy was no threat to the line. He had no tools, no wire cutters. There wasn't a chance of him getting across a double barrier of razor wire.

"I'm getting hungry," said Roy Burton. "Let's blow this chink up and get some Kentucky Fried."

A pair of Humvees pulled to a stop. Sarah recognized this scene was racing completely out of control. A half dozen weekend warriors piled out of the Humvees. They were dressed in camouflage and carrying M16s. The men greeted each other by first names. Sarah had no idea who they were. The atmosphere was turning into a drunken deer hunt. There were now eight military assault rifles pointed at one possibly injured man.

"Volunteers to go arrest this perp?" asked Bobby Williams.

This was the second step to special order Twelve-Eighteen.

"I sure as hell can't fly," said Hendrix. "And there ain't no doorway in that fence."

"That slant-eyed fuck'n gangbanger isn't worth the trouble," said Roy Burton.

Bobby Williams got back on the bullhorn.

"This is your final warning. Lay down in the road now or we will open fire."

"My wife's hurt!" yelled the man. "We need help."

"Yeah, right," said Hendrix. "He's probably the one that hurt her. This bugger gets any closer and I'm taking him. There's no way I'm letting some bastard with a gun walk up to me."

"You can't," protested Sarah.

"This son of a bitch isn't giving up," said Bobby Williams. "We got a perp that is armed and approaching the line. Can you make out the gun, Roy?"

"Sure as hell looks like a piece to me," said Roy Burton.

"Okay," said Bobby Williams. "Any one want to volunteer?"

"I got it," said Roy Burton.

Sarah was dumbfounded. They were going to legally murder this guy. She ran to the trunk of her car. What she was about to do felt surreal. She opened the trunk.

"All right," said Bobby Williams. "The checklist is complete. I'm green-lighting this situation."

"Do it and you're dead!" yelled Sarah.

She had the M16 pointed at Roy Burton's head from less than a foot away. Half the weapons shifted from the perp to Sarah. She could feel each spot where a bullet would puncture her body if they opened fire.

"What the fuck are you doing, Officer Mayfair?" yelled Bobby Williams.

"Let him go," snarled Sarah.

"You're losing it, Officer Mayfair," said Bobby Williams. "Put the gun down."

"This quarantine's a lie," yelled Sarah. "This guy's not a threat to anyone."

"Screw off," said Roy Burton.

He fired a shot. Sarah jumped but didn't pull the trigger. Roy Burton started laughing. Sarah looked through the fencing expecting to see bodies on the ground. The man was still standing. His eyes were locked on Roy Burton. An unmistakable rage was in his stare. The shot had gone into the ground a few feet in front of him. Wordlessly, the man started to back away with his wife in his arms. Roy Burton fired another shot into the dirt. The man held eye contact with Roy Burton while continuing to back away. He reached the far shoulder then after a moment began to trudge east. He stared back their way a few times with a kind of defiance. The weekend warriors kept their weapons aimed at the man. Sarah guessed the stooges dressed up like soldiers were waiting for a counterattack.

"Mayfair, you pussy," said Roy Burton. "I knew you wouldn't shoot me. Hey, you know, this was a real Kodak moment. Shame we don't have any photographs of other things I can shoot."

Sarah thought about the picture of Ralph with a gun sight drawn over him. The sneer on Roy Burton's face said it all. He was the one who had left that death threat picture. Roy Burton blew her a kiss. In a single fluid motion, Sarah reversed her grip on the M16 and swung the rifle stock into him, hitting Roy Burton in the center of his face with all her rage. He went down.

"You bastards!" she yelled. "Stay away from me… All of you stay away from me and Ralph."

After failing to respond to repeated orders to return her patrol car and report to the duty officer, Sarah pulled into the Richmond barracks. She parked in a marked off space blocking the walkway to the entrance. The headlights of her cruiser flooded into the lobby of the building. She popped the trunk and removed from a recorder a digital video tape which documented her patrol; then as an afterthought, she grabbed a blank tape and hid the real tape on her person. All cruisers were equipped with automatic video recording systems with front and rear-facing cameras. The tape was her bargaining chip. She had no illusions of changing anything in this sewer. She just wanted out. Her mind kept jumping between the image of a scared man carrying his injured wife and the death threat photograph in her pocket. She knew Captain Dupont was in his office. She walked past his night secretary and pushed the glass door open without knocking. The room was a mess, a pigsty befitting the racist pig who dwelled there.

"I want a transfer to a different part of the line, in a different state as far from here as possible," said Sarah.

"Do you not believe in knocking?" said Captain Dupont in a tranquil southern voice.

Sarah felt an urge to shove her gun down his mouth and demand that he give her what she wanted.

"Knock this!" she said and slapped the blank video tape on his desk. "Do you know what your little piglets were up to?"

"Are you referring to an attempted legal prosecution of a section Twelve-Eighteen this evening out by Esker's Pond that was prevented by your psychotic episode?"

Sarah felt some of the wind being stolen from her by his nonchalant response. It was no real surprise that Dupont knew about the incident but he seemed so confident. What did he know that she didn't? The I64 line was covered by video cameras. Incriminating parts of tapes were probably being erased at this very moment but he knew she had her own tape.

"There was nothing legal about the murder Burton almost committed," said Sarah.

Captain Dupont leaned forward in his chair, his southern genteel still in evidence. He appeared calm, but something about him reminded Sarah of the coolness of a snake before it struck.

"You, missy are pure trouble. You are not only difficult to control, but you are infecting others with your attitude. That little bedmate of yours, Officer Breaux, refused to make an arrest today. Said the couple just strayed across the line. Strayed twenty miles and kept on going, I dare say. Well, I guess, what should one expect from a Cajun like our Officer Breaux? They're all just hillbillies with a funny little accent."

Sarah bit back what she wanted to say. There was no point in letting this get out of hand in that direction. She had no love-lost for Alex after his betrayal, but Dupont was such a racist pig. Was he baiting her? She was suddenly aware that Captain Dupont probably considered her a mixed breed. Her skin was probably a bit too dark for his genteel tastes, her features a bit too non-European. She looked directly into his eyes without blinking. There was a condescending lilt to his expression. In that instant, it all became clear: he was prejudiced against her. That's what had been going on since the beginning.

"I want a transfer," said Sarah. "You want me gone as much as I want to leave."

Dupont smiled, his little black eyes gleaming.

"You will not get a transfer, young lady. Do you think I am a stupid man? Do you think I do not know of your little escape from New Jersey? You are in no position to make demands. You will give me everything I want, when I want it, and you will get nothing in return. You will be a slave. That will be my compensation for your disrespectful behavior."

Sarah felt ill. Her skin was too warm. There was a dizziness like a fever. She was suddenly and completely off balance.

"What you're talking about never happened in New Jersey or anywhere else," she said weakly. "Even if it had, that CDC fax I saw means it's no longer a crime."

"Missy, we both know what happened in New Jersey, and Boarburg, New York State, and here too. I have had everything investigated and documented. You know as well as I do that the law is sacrosanct and not open to individual revisionist history. Were that not the case, we would be allowing anarchy. Now, you are in no position to issue demands upon me. Here is what is going to happen. You are fired and you are blacklisted. This department has already filed charges against you for felonious assault on an officer of the law, our upstanding Officer Burton to be specific. I understand in your psychotic episode you knocked three of his teeth out. My, my, such a violent young woman. Maybe it is your exposure to the plague affecting your mental capacities? In any event, there will be no trial. You will sign a confession, and in return you will be granted parole, and you will leave here in disgrace. Your transgressions will follow you for the rest of your sad little life. You will never work as an officer of the law again. You will never work at any decent job again. You will be a convicted felon."

Sarah wondered if she could shoot this snake and escape before they captured her. Killing him would be a service to humanity.

"Now, I am not without some compassion for your predicament," said Dupont. "I have had my secretary, Helen, go through the trouble of typing up some paper work for you to volunteer as a test subject for the CDC in Atlanta. I understand they are looking for creatures the likes of you. People who have survived in the midst of kill zones and such. She has typed up a nice little report detailing your unnatural experiences in New Jersey and Virginia Beach. Now, don't thank me. It is unnecessary. Even though the state pays me a small finder's fee, I am offering you this opportunity out of Christian charity. I just felt that since you could no longer hold any kind of paying job, other than prostitute and such, that you could do something worthwhile with your life by serving as… Oh, what is it called now?… Oh yes, serving as a laboratory test rodent."

"Fuck you," said Sarah. "You self-righteous pig. I will turn this video over to Major Frank Warton and CNN and everyone else I can come up with. I will see you screwed!"

"Of course you will my dear. Every one will be so eager to listen to the vengeful and insane shrieks of a convicted felon; especially when she is hawking a tape that includes a lovely vignette of her brutally assaulting a fellow officer."

Dupont got up from his desk and walked over to the fax machine in his office. She noticed he was wearing a snub-nosed pistol in a belt holster. He had the CDC volunteer paper work in his thin little hands. He looked so pleased with himself. Sarah knew this was all part of some carefully planned revenge. How could one human being be so despicable?

"Why don't you sign this little CDC application and we can fax it together. Wouldn't that be nice? All we have to do is drop it into this slot and it's on its way like magic. Get an early start on your new life as a laboratory test rodent. I'll have Helen bring in your confession lickety-split so that you can sign that also… Get a clear conscience and all."

Sarah stalked up to Dupont and snatched the paperwork from his fingers. She had a small pleasure when he flinched. She was leaving and nobody was going to stop her. Her brain felt like it had been scrambled. She was furious and wasn't thinking clearly. She fantasized about pistol whipping him as she turned and then walked, with as much control as possible, toward the door of his office.

"Well, you are very welcome, my dear," said Dupont. "I guess you are leaving. Have a nice trip now and do write. Oh and don't worry about that confession. I will have someone sign it for you in the perfectly matching style and grace of your lovely penmanship. I am sure I can find someone in my jails with the necessary skills. Please write me if you would like a copy for your personal records."

~

Sarah stared at the house she had lived in since coming to Virginia. Rain was starting to drizzle down. The sun was disappearing. Another dismal end to another dismal day, thought Sarah. The backseat and trunk of the tan colored Buick Riviera were packed with her belongings along with several things she had taken from Alex's home. The classic '72 *Boat Tail* Buick also belonged to Alex. He loved this piece of collector's junk which he'd just bought and was restoring by hand. One of the high-beams was burnt out, the rear fender was dented, the carpets were disintegrating, the electric windows kept sticking, and it had an eighth of a tank of gas, which was no surprise considering how fast this gas guzzler could drink a tank. She wondered just how far she would go in the car before replacing it. She could have *borrowed* a different car, but it felt good to be striking back at Alex. She had no illusions about him. She was certain he'd been a critical source in Dupont's investigation.

Her fingers lingered over the ignition key. She thought about how she'd repeatedly gone after Dupont. Had there been a kind of twisted wish fulfillment goading her? Calling him names to his face, pushing him, almost daring him. Why hadn't she just quietly left days ago? Had she wanted to be forced into it? She gazed down the empty street. The deepening pools of shadows made her uneasy. The wind gusted with faint whistles through tree branches.

Sarah turned the key. The starter motor whined for an eternity before the huge high performance engine stuttered to life. The engine had just been rebuilt with racecar parts. Alex claimed the big block put out four hundred horsepower. She adjusted the rearview mirror. The glass was cracked. The mirror began to slip back to its original angle as soon as she took her fingers away. Alex's first priority for the car had been the engine. Ralph sat upright in the passenger seat. He sniffed at the dashboard and then sneezed.

"Dirty, huh?" said Sarah.

Ralph looked at her and then flopped down onto the seat.

"Well, I guess this is the beginning of another great adventure."

Her chest felt empty. She pulled out of the gravel driveway and onto the road. After stopping for gas, she turned off a surface road and onto Interstate Ninety-Five heading south. As the miles grew, Sarah began to remember all the bad that had happened: the threats, the cold shoulders, the deceit. She focused on Alex. She could see his face. She remembered his touch. The empty space inside her was filled with resentment. The void was like a tiny world of hate that attracted more of the same to it, building and feeding on itself. How could he have treated her like this? She gave herself to him. She'd trusted him and he exposed her.

"We're better off gone," she told Ralph.

The rain started coming harder. She turned the wipers to high. The blades left streaks of water across the windshield. The road went through a series of large dips. Some of the boxes in the backseat shifted. Sarah glanced back to check. One of them had tipped on its side. Cartons of cigarettes had spilled from the box. Out of spite, she had taken everything Alex had of value, including his horde of cigarettes which amounted to two full cases. In the new world, Marlboros were worth more than gold. She'd left behind the death threat photograph torn in half and thumbtacked to Alex's front door. She wanted there to be no doubt who'd taken his stuff.

Lightning flashed to the ground in the distance. Sarah frowned. Something was making her feel ill, almost faint. She adjusted the vent controls to draw in outside air. Wind blowing over her face chilled the perspiration that was beading up across her skin. Without warning, a violent shiver overwhelmed her. As the tingles dimmed, everything became clearer. She was aware of a mild premonition feeling which must have been there all along. The small ball of fear was growing inside her. She knew what was coming.

Wet scenery rolled by the windows. Off to the left, she saw the glow of a town. The light formed a kind of halo within the mist. She was vulnerable on this empty road. She sensed lethal energy building somewhere off in the cradle of the night. The danger was like a storm within a storm. The feeling grew into a sense of foreboding. The killer towered over her in the distance. Its presence was like an immense electrical potential. In that dark moment, she wished the killer down on Captain Dupont and Alex and all the others. What was running through her mind was only a wish. She couldn't control this thing. She knew when zones would occur and sometimes where, but nothing more. One was out there prowling in the darkness before her; that's all she knew. She felt guilty for the vengeful wish but thought it again, just the same.

6 – I64 line, Virginia: December

A kill zone whisked through the Richmond area a few hours after nightfall. The zone moved south like a breeze of death across the land. The shadow passed through refugee camps, small towns and wilderness. Unlike flesh and blood that could be stopped by razor wire, the lethal signal passed through the I64 line without the slightest resistance. The signal radiated along a path almost parallel to the highway Sarah had traveled. At its weakest, the signal triggered no kill zones and left no damage. Where its strength was greatest, men and women died. The ignition signals, relayed from seed to seed, soon passed beyond the target zone and lost their deadly effect in areas that were not primed to kill. People littered the ground while many more were spared to wander in shock.

Alex was in the Twilight Café having dinner with Theresa and Sergeant Hunt. He'd been on an extended patrol and had just come off duty. He felt depressed about Sarah but was convinced getting her out of his life was for the best. He ate another slice of the open faced turkey sandwich and then followed it with a fork full of peas and tiny cubed carrots.

He knew Sarah had problems. She'd become spooky. The decision had been difficult; but if he hadn't pushed her, she might have stayed; and that would have meant watching her grow more scary and depressed with every passing day. He couldn't handle what he saw in her eyes; and anyway, she deserved better and would find it somewhere. He set down his fork. His appetite was gone.

"You did the smart thing," said Theresa.

"I could have been straight with her."

The zone passed through buildings, trees, and hills as if they were ghosts instead of solid forms. The signal washed through the plate glass windows of the Twilight Café. Alex watched in disbelief as a woman fell off a counter stool. Outside, a patrol car rolled into a parked van, glanced off its side, and came partway through the front of the diner. Cinderblocks crumbled. Alex felt a tightening in his left side. Theresa's face dropped into her plate of food. Alex's pacemaker was unable to manage the load. He stood up gripping his shirt. He was amazed at realizing this was his death.

7 – I64 line, Virginia: December

Artie looked down at the stained wooden floor of the hospital tent. His sneakers were spattered with blood from the men he'd killed. He thought about the police at the I64 line who tried to shoot him instead of helping. He looked at Suzy who was sleeping off the effects of anesthesia and brutality. His head ached from what had turned out to be a bullet graze. His life had become a senseless blur of violence.

Suzy had been in the mobile surgical unit for over an hour. Emergency surgery had been performed to repair internal damage to her ovaries and small intestine. They'd lost their child, and the doctor said they wouldn't be having any more; but Suzy was going to be alright. She had to be. Artie would not allow any other possibility.

Artie looked up as a nurse came over to check Suzy's vital signs. The nurse crumpled to the floor. Artie stared dumbfounded. He was unable to accept what he was seeing. The nurse was clearly dead. There was a crash outside. The lights flickered and then went out. He could sense patients and medical staff dying silently all around him. It was as if their ghosts were swirling in the air. Artie found Suzy's hand and gripped it. Her fingers slightly curled around his. He was grateful that she was asleep. There was nothing he could do. He cursed god and pleaded for Suzy to be spared.

8 – I-95, North Carolina: December

The ball of fear had waned some time ago, leaving only a hollow spot inside her. Sarah was driving rapidly through the darkness. Bad weather was making the going hazardous. Warning signs for I-40 had started to appear. I-40 could take her west all the way to California. The intersection came sooner than she'd expected. She looked at the ramp, which lead off into a bank of mist. Her foot eased off the accelerator. On the seat next to her was the CDC application that Dupont had written up just to degrade her. *Laboratory test rodent* – he'd rubbed it in as a final way of gloating how he'd taken everything from her; but in his revenge, he'd inadvertently offered something real while trying to shred the last bits of her self-respect. Helping the CDC was something she could do that would make a difference. The highway she was on led to Atlanta and the CDC, but there was I-40 coming into view; she thought about the freedom of the west coast, the beaches, the people.

Would her past catch up with her there? Her jaw tightened in defiance of what that snake had done and tried to do. Going to the CDC would probably mean more to her than to the doctors who almost certainly didn't need one more medical subject. The car almost refused to go in one direction or the other. With a feeling of guilt, she took the ramp onto I-40: the images of freedom had a more powerful draw.

Close to an hour later, Sarah passed from beneath the canopy of thunderclouds. Stars were everywhere. She had mapped the entire route to California in her mind. For an instant, a hospital tent and a nurse crumpling to the ground flashed vividly though her mind. Sarah knew the nurse had been caught in a kill zone. The experience was like Virginia Beach, but different, weaker, almost like an echo of something bad that was already passed. She tuned the radio, searching for news. An old rock and roll station came in over the static. She searched farther on the dial. A road sign floated by in the darkness: twenty-six miles to the Tennessee border. While paused on a country station, the music stopped mid-song and an announcer came on to deliver breaking news.

"A kill zone has swept through Richmond, Virginia. Initial reports indicate hundreds of people killed. Riots have broken out on the north side of the I64 quarantine line. There has been little or no police response. National Guard and Army units have been called in..."

Sarah slowed to a stop, barely onto the shoulder of the interstate. All the people she'd been living and working with were dead. She had no question about their fate. She was as certain as if she'd been there to witness it. The remainder of the news went on without her hearing a word. A pair of pickup trucks drove by, blaring their horns at each other. The commotion didn't touch her. Her thoughts were in an airtight cocoon. With spite in her heart, she had wished that horror down on them, down on Alex, and it had happened. She looked at her palms. Her hands wouldn't stop trembling. The sensible part of her argued it was crazy to think she'd actually caused this; but even if she was innocent of the actual crime, she was certain now that she'd known in some darkened repressed thought where death was heading and done nothing to warn them. They wouldn't have believed her anyway. No, that wasn't true. Alex would have believed her. He knew. She closed her eyes. Was it true that she had let them die? Had she become that much of a monster? Tears ran out from under her closed lids.

~

Sarah was sitting on the ground by a campfire. The smell of burning wood was thick in the air. Heat from the fire buffeted her face. She didn't remember much of her drive. She'd been down country roads and freeways, through turns without thinking. She had long gaps of missing time. It had been like drug-induced amnesia. At some point, she had stumbled upon another highway heading west but had no idea which one. She could barely remember pulling into this rest area. Lights from the campfires had attracted her. She'd been like a moth hungering for solace in the flames and oblivion of self-destruction.

Her cheeks burned from salt. She vaguely remembered eating something that people had given her. If only she could stop the other memories. She was acutely aware of every detail of her repeated journeys into the hellish centers of kill zones. She had relived those memories over and over again and had come to the conclusion she'd been left unharmed because she was somehow part of what was causing it. She was like a loaded gun lying in a field where children played. Someone innocent would always die.

Wood snapped in the fire. The circle of rock surrounding the flames was jagged and reminded her of glowing teeth. The circle was like the open maw of some hellish snake. She glanced at a man sitting next to her. His hand was on her knee. The other people had gone off somewhere. She remembered there had been two women, another man, and a young girl. She couldn't remember this man's name but knew he was the leader and that he was a full-blooded Indian from an Arizona tribe. He was handsome in a rough way, with salt and pepper hair. He had asked her questions about what it had been like to stand in the center of death. She had answered candidly. She no longer felt any need to conceal her past. He'd said he wanted sex as part of the deal they'd made. The sex had something confusing to do with sharing her experiences of the murderous spirit. She agreed as casually as if he'd asked her name, which he hadn't. Nothing mattered. She was a castaway drifting though a world that was no longer real. She looked off at the passing traffic; the headlights, burning paths through the night, left colored trails in her vision. He unbuttoned her shirt. She said, "No," and moved his hand away. She remembered taking long gulps from a bottle of something to wash down the drugs. She had swallowed over a dozen small capsules of psilocybin. She had been told the capsules were filled with powdered psilocybin mushrooms, a powerful drug used by his Indian tribe for religious ceremonies. She had been told that one capsule was enough. She had traded this man a case of Marlboros and herself for a small, Ziploc bag that was half full of capsules. Sarah knew she was overdosing and didn't care. She didn't believe the drugs could kill her, but maybe it would erase her mind. Oblivion was what she wanted and what she craved. The little girl had been watching her earlier. Where had the child gone off to – like an Alice in Wonderland? Vague, drug-induced thoughts moved through her mind like pieces of flotsam drifting through the depths of a bottomless lake. The psilocybin was beginning its hallucinogenic work on her.

"The plague is a thinking machine," she said from nowhere. "Not a god, but a living organic machine."

How had these words come from her lips? Was it the psilocybin? She recognized the idea was not from her own thoughts, even though the idea felt like it had been part of her memory for a very long time. Images like some kind of schematic diagram had been part of the idea. The man removed one of her arms from her clothing, then the other.

"Each bacterium by itself is nothing more than a vessel, but all of them collected together are something." She frowned. "Couldn't the bacteria be like the cells of a body, each just a small part of something much bigger?"

The man removed more of her clothing along with some of his own. She was experiencing this new idea in her mind as if it were a forgotten memory, which it was not. The false memory expanded to encompass all her senses. Soon she was deep within the movie replaying in her mind. At moments, the recollection was like a computer simulation of reality; at other times, it was more like a dream. She saw floating at the bottom of a sea, a gelatinous creature like a great, round jellyfish. From her memories, she knew the creature was a mass of congealed bacteria tethered to the seabed with tendrils of the same substance as its body. All of it was made of thinking material that worked like a human brain, only vastly larger and far more advanced.

"How large would this thing have to be to end up as wise as a god?" she asked the night.

The man started working on her jeans. He leaned her backward so that he could tug them off. She kept talking as if she were still clothed. The cold air raised goose flesh across her skin. She felt almost nothing. She stopped talking as the man's weight pushed down onto her. Leaves and grits of dirt pressed into her back. She was now miles away in a different world conjured by the hallucinogenic forces of a psilocybin overdose. She suspected this god-machine was the source of all her false-memories of ideas and diagrams. She wondered how she could be psychically linked to this global colony of machine bacteria. Did it live inside her too, like a glimmer of alien light?

~

In the middle of the night, Sarah awoke from dark hallucinations. She couldn't remember much. She was clothed. The man was gone. He'd left her a tattered blanket and a foggy mind. Dried leaves had blown into her face and hair. She dimly knew he'd gone off to sleep with his wife. She sat up and wrapped the red wool blanket around her shoulders. There was a vague smell of something stale from the blanket. The fire was smoldering but still giving off heat. The coals were fanned bright orange by a gust of wind. Some of the embers blew off into the night air spiraling into the sky. She was surprised at being awake and able to think at all. Her brain felt sore and confused. She could still feel the psilocybin working deep inside her body. She had to have taken enough to send her on a one-way mental journey. Why was she back?

She looked up into the sky. The moon appeared dreamlike, wrapped in streamers of clouds. Lightning flashed soundlessly at the horizon. It was lightning, wasn't it? For some reason, the flashes reminded her more of artillery explosions from some distant war. For an instant, she recalled memories of bomb diagrams with explanations of operation. These strange implanted memories had happened all through the drug-induced hours. She'd grown accustomed to them and now paid less attention. She noticed a praying mantis standing perfectly still amid the leaves. Light from the fire gave it a crimson tint. The insect's small eyes glistened as the head turned slightly in one direction as if to stare at her.

Sarah found herself wondering: if mankind was reduced to a small band of survivors, what might inherit the earth in their place? Insects were immune to the plague, along with all the other animals. With the yoke of the top predator lifted, what was bettered suited to rule the world than insects? They had seen dinosaurs come and go. They had watched the rise of mammals and maybe they would watch their fall, too. This little creature looking at her was the top predator of all insects, a survivor of hundreds of millions of years: hail the new king.

Sarah recalled bits of information about the mantis out of nowhere. She didn't think the memories were really hers. Had she read a book or seen it on television? She didn't believe so. She recalled that the female mantis tears off the head of the male during mating. The elimination of its brain caused the male to copulate fanatically in a kind of spastic knee-jerk reaction. When the act was over, the female mantis then made a meal of her dead mate. Nature was so wonderfully efficient. Nothing was wasted. Sarah smiled thinking about what this said about the importance of male intellect. She looked at the plastic bag of psilocybin capsules, then rolled it up and stuffed it into a pants pocket.

The mantis was gone. Had it ever been there? Sarah got up and started to wander back toward her car with the blanket around her shoulders. She passed a minivan. The side-door was partly open. A campfire burned near the foot off it. The little girl was sleeping just inside. Her hair was short with small bangs hanging down over a little forehead. Sarah stared at her for a long time. The longer she stared, the more she felt reality being altered and funneled into a single crucial idea that was somehow relevant to this little girl. The force of the idea became like a whirlpool drawing her mind in. Sarah felt there was something important just beyond her reach. She moved nearer the child. She could see her small chest moving with each breath. Ideas violently flashed into Sarah's mind and then disappeared too quickly to be retained. She wanted to touch the little girl's face but was scared at what might happen. Her fingers hovered motionless close to the child. Suddenly the world became still and silent, and all that remained was a single memory that had not been hers until this moment. The memory was too complex for her to fully grasp it. She drew back her fingers. She felt like she was standing outside the passage of time. What she grasped was that a new world was starting around her, and she was part of this new world, and children were part of this new world. There was pain at the birth of everything new. None of this could be avoided. She thought about the CDC volunteer program. There was something at the CDC in Atlanta that was key to this new world, but it was not part of any research program. It was something else... maybe a person or event? She walked away from the little girl, leaving the red wool blanket on the ground where she'd stood.

Sarah started the engine. The dashboard clock read three-twenty. The Buick needed gas, but there was enough for at least a hundred miles. Ralph looked over at her as if she were crazy for being up at this time of night. He went back to sleep after making a harrumph kind of sound. The car's single high-beam cut a swath through the darkness. Sarah drove out onto the highway, bounced across the grass median and then turned onto the eastbound lane. She saw a map in her mind with a course laid out on it. None of this seemed unusual to her – the implanted memories, her new direction, nothing. Through the haze of drugs, she was focusing only on action. She had a good eighty miles of backtracking to go before she could head south toward Atlanta.

9 – I64 line, Virginia: December

Artie had no idea how long he'd held Suzy's hand. He knew she was gone but hadn't been able to let go. He just stood looking down at her still body. Tears had burned tracks down his face. His legs and feet were aching. Morning light was beginning to peek through shaded windows. He was faint but refused to sit.

Doctors came into the room. They spoke with him but he couldn't understand them. He couldn't concentrate on the words long enough to make sense of them. A woman put her hand on his shoulder. He collapsed into darkness before reaching the floor.

Artie awoke in a different hospital tent. He was in a bed just like Suzy's bed. An intravenous line was running from his left arm to a bag of clear liquid. He was weak. He thought about Suzy's funny little rules. He thought about her smile. He couldn't go on, just couldn't. He'd find a painless way to die and end this horror that was growing inside him. Why couldn't he have died with Suzy? What kind of god created a nightmare like this?

A gentle looking older man came into the room. He was dressed in a wool shirt and blue jeans. His eyes found Artie. As he walked closer, his stare didn't waver. He was recognizable as a doctor by the stethoscope which hung from a pocket.

"Hello Artie, my name's Hal. I know there's nothing I can say that will help you with the sorrow of losing your wife. There's no pill that I can give you which will make you feel better. All I can offer you is the truth and a way you can help keep others from being hurt."

"What truth?" asked Artie.

"You survived a kill zone while everyone around you did not. That makes you just a little different. The CDC is trying to find people like you. They can use your help in stopping this plague."

"Are you're saying I've got something in my blood that might be a cure?"

"It could be in your blood or in your genes. The CDC hasn't figured that out yet, but there are a number of people who seem to be immune to kill zones. Some of them are already at the CDC and are helping with experiments. We ran some tests on your spinal fluid. You have the lethal bacteria in you and, based on everything we know, you should be dead. That's the reason they need to see people like you."

"I'm a carrier?"

"No. The bacterium isn't communicable like that. One person can't spread it to another."

"I don't understand. Why are there quarantine lines everywhere?"

"Originally government doctors thought the plague might be communicable and so quarantines were established. It made sense – and was prudent – at the time; but after awhile, it became obvious people were not infecting each other. Almost a week ago, the CDC notified us that the bacterium was not communicable and lifted their orders for quarantine."

"A week ago! Why the hell are the lines still up?"

Hal looked troubled.

"That's a very good question. I've heard that north of us, the lines have been removed; but in other places they're still up. It's always about politics. Anyway, I have information for you on the CDC program and an enrollment form. I know it's hard to wrap your mind around this right now, but this program is a way you can turn your tragedy into something positive. Helping the living is the best way to honor those that are gone."

Artie was unable to process any more. He kept thinking that if the bastards who controlled the I64 line had taken it down once they knew it served no purpose, then Suzy would still be alive. He picked up a glass of water and threw it across the room. The smashing sound felt good. She'd paid for their greed and stupidity with her life. They would pay for this... Politics... Justice... Someone had to be made accountable for all the pointless suffering and legalized murder.

The doctor was gone after ordering sedation which would be arriving soon. The CDC information and forms were in a folder on the makeshift nightstand. Artie was staring at a wet spot on the wall where the glass had smashed. He sat up in bed and yanked out the intravenous line. The stinging fed his anger. He looked at the contents of the folder including a copy of a fax dated almost a week ago rescinding the quarantine orders. A coversheet explained that the fax was part of a documentation package which might be required to cross any of the remaining quarantine lines during travel to the CDC in Atlanta. Another page explained the importance of survivors of kill zones helping the CDC find a cure by joining their research study. Artie crumpled the enrollment form and threw it on the floor. All the refugee hardship had been for nothing. The quarantines were a sham. The CDC was as much to blame as the bastards who ran the lines. These documents proved the son of bitches in Washington knew quarantines were pointless and they were doing nothing to stop it. There was a sharp pain in his head. He would fight the CDC and this corrupt government – he would hurt them anyway he could. What they were doing to their own citizens was wrong. It was criminal. His few remaining possessions were in a blue plastic bag next to his bed. He opened the top of the bag and looked inside. Along with his clothing and coat were his wallet and gun. Everything he'd arrived with was still there, including a half used pack of matches and a few coins.

Artie walked out of the medical tent. The gun was strapped to his side in its shoulder holster under his coat. He looked at the CDC fax rescinding the quarantine orders. His blood grew hotter. He started walking toward the I64 line which was about a mile away. A gust of wind tried to rip the fax from his fingers. He kept walking. He thought about the local police enforcing this line and his blood boiled.

Artie reached the highway that the quarantine ran along. He stood and stared. He touched the fence with his fingers, eighteen feet of razor wire and steel pipe. The wire felt wickedly sharp and dangerous. People were crowded all along the line as if it were a tourist destination. Less than fifty feet from him, a police car blew by on the other side of the double fence. Artie felt a buffet of air from the car's passage. The bastards all knew the line was a sham.

"It's a fucking lie," said Artie.

"Excuse me," said a large man standing next to him.

"The quarantine line's a fucking lie," said Artie. "They were ordered to take it down almost a week ago and it's still up."

"How do you know?" said a woman.

"He's full of it," said the same man.

Artie shoved the fax to within an inch of the man's nose. He took the paper from Artie's fingers and examined it. The woman moved closer to read the official looking paper.

"Son... of... a... bitch..." said the man.

Artie heard another police car approaching at very high speed. The sound was like an angry hornet. He reached into his coat and pulled the .357 magnum from his shoulder holster. As the car zoomed by, he took aim and fired four quick rounds into the cruiser. The gun bucked hard in his grip. Three rounds hit the driver's door and window. The car skidded as the brakes were jammed to the floor. A trail of tire smoke was left behind to mark its path. The car went off the road through the first wall of razor wire and ended up on top of the steel and concrete obstacles meant to stop cars coming from the other side. The obstacles worked just fine in this direction too, thought Artie. The crowd erupted in cheers with scattered catcalls as if the home team had just scored. A small fire started from a ruptured gas tank and grew in size. People began picking up rocks and throwing them through the razor wire at the burning hulk.

Artie felt very much alive. He gazed up at a surveillance camera aimed at him and smiled. He reloaded and then seated the gun back into his shoulder holster. He looked at the guy who had been reading the fax. His eyes were as wide as coins. With a trembling hand, the man offered the fax back to Artie. There were sirens in the distance.

"When the bastards arrive," said Artie. "Tell them the man who did this said his name was Alexander."

He had no idea why he'd used a different name. The change just felt right. He was no longer the same man. He was someone else, someone who was alone, someone who had nothing left to be taken from him. The quarantine enforcers were the cause of too much suffering and they had to pay. They just had to pay.

Chapter 9

The God-Machine

1 – South Carolina: December

The effects of last night's psilocybin were fading. Sarah hadn't experienced any hallucinations for hours, but her thinking was fuzzy. She exited the highway and followed signs to a picnic area. The exit quickly turned into a secluded gravel roadbed. She drove the Buick toward some shaded picnic benches. Gravel spit up into the fender wells. She coasted to a stop and cut the engine. Ralph up looked at her.

"Come on, boy. Rest stop."

She opened the door. He stared for a moment and then laid his muzzle back onto his paws.

"Traitor. Don't you love me anymore?"

Ralph's eyes looked at her for a moment; then closed. Sarah shut the door. There were no restrooms. She needed to pee. She hadn't seen another car in hours, but the first spot she tried behind a row of trees still felt too exposed. She wandered back into a thicker part of the forest's edge. She noticed the trees were greener than up north. A stringy moss hung from some of the branches. The sun peeked through in spots, sending shafts of light to the forest's floor. Where she stood felt like the gallery of an earthen temple.

Sarah found a comfortable spot to hide as she peed and was relieved to be done with it. She stood and tucked in her shirt. A blue jay darted from one branch to another. Something was familiar about this place. She wandered a little farther into the woods. She was drawn by feelings of deja vu emerging from her hazy mind. The trees, the plants, even the air was familiar. An image came to her but then faded, yet bits of it remained like the afterglow of a photoflash. The lingering impressions were of water, maybe a pond? She climbed over a fallen log. Fungus grew from its bark in huge, half-mushroom shapes. The wood was damp. The air was heavy with a peat moss scent. After a few more minutes of walking, she got another impression, stronger this time. The image was of a rowboat pulled ashore with the name *American Heritage* written on its stern. Brambles scraped against her legs as she pushed through them. The trees looked thinner up ahead. She spied a slash of brownish-green between a pair of ancient weeping willows. There was a body of water up ahead.

Sarah emerged from the rim of the forest and came into full view of a lake. Directly in front of her was a stone foundation or pier that extended out about fifteen feet into the water and was as wide as a footpath. The pier was abandoned and ancient looking, built from rounded stones and mortar. There were signs of rusted hardware that could have also been from another age. The pier looked like it might have supported a dock at some point in its history, but only a few weathered chunks of gray wood remained. She stepped up onto the pier and walked out to the end of it. She could sense the water was unusually deep. She felt a stray impulse to reach down and dip her fingers into the lake, but the thought of it made her feel uneasy. She looked back toward the shoreline. She saw a sunfish idling in the shallows over a dimple in the sand that was its nest. From there, the rock and sand bottom fell steeply from view like the wall of a submerged cliff. If the lake had been empty of water, where she was standing would have had a terrifying height. Buoyancy of the water a foot below shielded her from the true nature of where she stood. She turned to look back out over the lake. A light breeze whipped up, refreshing her senses. Gnarled trees stood around the lake as great sentinels, with their roots growing directly from its water. At the far side, she could see a boathouse and a paved road but no boats. There was a small parking lot, cast iron barbecues, and picnic benches. On the southern end of the lake was a marsh clogged with cattails and lily pads. In the summer, that air would be thick with insects; but for now it was quiet except for the breeze.

Sarah glanced in the other direction toward the northern end of the lake. Her heart stopped. Barely visible, not ten feet away, was a battered rowboat. The boat was half submerged amid shore weeds and shadows. Its hull was broken. Water filled it to within inches of the rim. The boat's gray and red wood had expanded and split. On its stern were the words *American Heritage.*

Her legs felt weak. Sarah sat down at the end of the pier. She was stunned by the sight of the rowboat. This place was triggering powerful memories. The images took her far into her past. The place was like the spots where she and her family had gone on camping trips when she was a child. She hadn't thought about those summers for years. She smiled to herself. Once, she and her brother Tim had snuck out at night and gone frog hunting. They had carved their names in a tree to commemorate their great adventure. Tim was at the clumsy age of ten and fell into the lake while stalking a huge bullfrog. Sarah had laughed until her sides hurt and then stripped to her underwear and jumped in with him. They captured no frogs that night and instead splashed and played for hours. Their parents never discovered the escape. To the end, it had been a secret that only Sarah and Tim had shared. Tim was gone; her parents were gone. There were so many empty holes in her new life.

Sarah had calmed to something that passed for normal. The stunned feeling was nearly gone. She picked up a pebble and tossed it into the lake. The water near the shore was as still as if made of glass. Rings traveling out from the pebble were the only flaws in an otherwise clear reflection of trees and sky. Something was odd about how the water pulled on her. It felt as if the bottom extended down to labyrinths leading into the very depths of the earth. Sarah leaned forward to see if anything was visible from the edge of the pier. There was nothing, no plants or fish. She squinted but could only see a slow blending of clear water into something that eventually turned gray and opaque. The water was very deep; maybe hundreds of feet. For a human it may as well have been bottomless. Her focus shifted and she saw her reflection in the water staring back. Her expression was dull. She had a growing sense of a malevolent presence in the depths of the lake behind her reflection. She wanted to lean back from the edge, but couldn't. An all-encompassing presence of thought was whispering to her from the depths. Slowly, she recognized it as the godlike force that had come for her on Virginia Beach. The living machine was trying to communicate something. She sensed a language, but unintelligible. Alien symbols and diagrams slammed into her mind. The world disappeared into a burning white light.

A bird squawked from a nearby bush. The sound startled her. The sun had shifted its position in the sky by about forty-five degrees. This was unnatural. She had to have been here for hours but had no memory of it. She felt numb from intoxication. What had happened to her? She stood up. Her legs were stiff. Her mouth was dry. She looked at her palms. A deep waffle pattern from the rough surface was embedded in them along with bits of dirt. She slowly backed away from the end of the pier. Her heart was beating so fast that she was trembling. Had the living machine sensed her presence and come to her? Or had she been drawn to this spot because she had sensed it? Sarah turned, intending to leave but instead froze in place. On a tree trunk a few feet away was a carving distorted from years of growth. A swollen circle was cut around the names of Sarah and Tim, chiseled in blocky letters.

This was impossible. This couldn't be the same place from her childhood. She had to get out of here. Sarah cautiously maneuvered around the tree, unable to pull her eyes from the carving until she was past it. She started to run, fleeing in the direction of the road. Faster and faster, fallen tree limbs and rocks jumped in front of her. Brambles scratched at her. She stumbled but caught her balance. She was panting. She glanced back toward the water expecting to see something or someone in pursuit but saw nothing except quiet forest. She went around a thicket and almost screamed. She stopped dead in her tracks. Standing in front of her was a small group of people. There were three men and two women. Were they hallucinations or real? They looked like normal people, but their presence was unreal. In saner times, they might have been friends out hiking in the woods. They were all dressed alike in thermal vests, various colored flannel shirts and jeans.

"Hi there," said Sarah.

None of them said a word. All the men were very large.

"Okay," she said. "Nice day we're having… I'm just going to be on my way now."

The man closest to her smiled without emotion. He had small teeth. His eyes were black and cold. Sarah looked from face to face and saw the same cold indifference. From nowhere, she felt a withering blow to the back of her skull. The world was ripped from her.

~

Sarah heard the rustling sounds of wind in a forest and felt a throbbing pain in her skull. Was she dying? Bits of dried dirt were stuck to her lips. She was face down. With difficulty, she rolled over onto her back and stared up. The trees were moving in a breeze. Sunlight flashed between leafy branches. Her head felt broken. Her hands were caked with mud and scratches and blood. Her pockets were empty. Her gun was gone. Her sneakers were gone. Her car keys were gone.

She managed to sit up. There was a heavily weathered shotgun casing on the ground a few feet away; remnants from a long ago hunt. She examined her body and found nothing serious despite a large amount of blood matted in her hair. All traces of her attackers had vanished except for a jumble of footprints. Had they left her for dead? Sarah picked herself up and started moving toward where the Buick was parked. She felt dizzy, but with each step came new anger and new worry – anger at the people that had done this to her and worry that her car would be gone and Ralph with it. Her breathing came faster, painful gulps of air. She imagined Ralph's body lying by the roadside, shot with her own stolen gun.

"Nooooo," she screamed.

Birds scattered from the trees in a wild flutter. For a brief second, her mind shifted into a different place. In a vision, she saw herself spilling from a row of bushes and onto the gravel road where she'd left the car. Her knees were skinned. Panic surrounded her. The car was there. She could see the vague outline of Ralph staring out through the rear window.

A branch snapped behind her. The premonition blinked out. Sarah spun around. Her heart leapt into her throat. For an instant, she saw one of her attackers but nothing was there. His image faded into the tangled woods. The queasiness in her stomach grew intense. She clung to a tree trunk and heaved out her insides.

Minutes later, as Sarah stepped onto the gravel road, she saw Ralph staring at her just as in her premonition. She saw him bark, but heard nothing. The car muffled his voice. The realization that she'd envisioned this was sinking in. The emotions of knowing that Ralph was fine should have been overpowering, but instead a peculiar introspection took hold. Sarah walked up to the car and looked inside. She had no keys. Her attackers could show up at any moment and they had at least one gun, her Beretta. She should have been panicked but was not.

A minute later, Sarah smashed a large rock into the side window. The rock weighed at least twenty pounds. The glass shattered into a web of crystals. She pushed in the glass and opened the door from the inside. Ralph piled out. She could tell he knew something more than a broken window was wrong. He stood alert next to her. Every sound caught his attention. She could sense he was a tightened spring ready to explode. A hundred and twenty pounds of Rottweiler was a fearsome protector and friend. She felt grateful, rubbing tears from her eyes.

Sarah fished around in the glove box for her pocketknife. In spite of so many things in this car that sort of worked, it unfortunately had a perfectly functioning anti-theft system. She popped the hood and the trunk. There was small set of tools under the spare tire. Soon, she was cutting and testing ignition wires, trying to figure out which ones needed to be connected to start the car. She touched a pair together. The engine cranked but then died. She tried another pair. Nothing happened. She tried a third combination. The radio in the car started to play. She went back to the pair that cranked the engine. The car started right up. She arranged the wires so that they wouldn't short out and closed the hood.

Sarah climbed into the passenger's seat. She started hammering on the ignition-lock with a jack handle which she'd gotten from the trunk. She had to break the steering wheel lock or she wouldn't be able to drive the car. After some moments of panic and frustration, she had the lock shattered and the steering wheel turning freely. She slid over to the driver's seat and called Ralph. He piled in. She patted him on the back and pulled the passenger door shut. Her only pair of sneakers had been stolen. Her feet were bare and sore. She felt the rough texture of the pedals as she drove back onto the road. She had no money and nothing except cigarettes to trade for gas. There was a half tank left. She knew it would take some luck to save her and Ralph from walking again.

The sun had almost set. Twilight was spreading. A shiver worked through Sarah's body. She knew that whatever had been in that lake was real. The living machine had been there when she was splashing in the water with her brother as a child just as it was there now. She wondered if the inhuman intelligence had been doing things to her for her entire life. She sensed that all the death that had occurred so far was only a prelude to something far worse.

As miles of country highway ticked past, Sarah's inner strength continued to grow. On both sides of the road were dense forests now cloaked in darkness. She felt that she was being galvanized into something much stronger than the sum of her experiences and skills. She would be one of the survivors of these murderous times. She would be a part of something new in a world that would never be the same.

2 – I64 line, Virginia: December

Artie/Alexander was shaken from his sleep by an explosion. The room was filled with daylight. He rolled from his cot as shrapnel and bullets flew through the inside of the Red Cross shelter. People were screaming. Instant mayhem engulfed the room. The shelter had cots for over two hundred. There were injured people lying all over the floor.

Artie grabbed his gun from the new backpack which was under his cot. He crawled his way through the tangle of frightened people and reached the doorway. Sporadic gun fire was going off outside. He opened the door while lying on his stomach and crawled out into the firefight. Gunfire buzzed through the air a yard above him as he made his way up to a cement wall where some fighters defending the settlement were crouched. Bullets were hitting the top of the wall, spraying chips into the air. The defenders fought back with automatic weapons fire. Some were lifting M4 machine guns with grenade launchers over the wall and firing grenades blind. The M4 looked like a meaner, shorter version of an M16 with a 40mm grenade launcher mounted under the barrel like an over-under shotgun.

One of the fighters noticed Artie crouching next to him. He looked at the .357 magnum in Artie's hand. He smiled a toothy grin and motioned with his head to a wooden crate lying open in the dirt. Inside the crate were brand new M4s wrapped in oil cloths. Next to the crate were boxes of empty ammo clips and metal boxes full of cartridges and grenades shells. A teenage boy and girl who looked like brother and sister were pushing ammo into clips.

Artie took one of the M4s. He looked at the grenades but wasn't sure how to handle them. He shoved full ammo clips into every pocket large enough to hold them, filled his smaller pockets with loose shells, and then joined the fight. He could tell from the direction of incoming fire they were being attacked from two opposite positions. He couldn't see who was attacking. He crawled along below the wall until it ended at a dirt road near one of the sources of incoming fire. He had no fear of dying. There was no bravery inside his chest; there was only indifference about his life. Catching a bullet would bring him peace and maybe even reunite him with Suzy. The only thing he wanted more than death was revenge. Anyone attacking a refugee settlement was one of the causes of all this suffering and needed killing.

He took a deep breath and then charged across the road and into waiting tree cover. He was going to work his way around one of the groups of attackers and cut them down. He circled off to the right of where the fire was coming from. The trees were medium height and the ground cover was thick. The gunfire and explosions were so loud that he was not concerned about making noise as he trampled through branches and bushes. At the crest of a low hill, he reached a thick hedge of sticker bushes. Laying on his stomach, he parted some of the bushes with the end of his M4. He could see the attackers. They were gang members, Pagans! Rage boiled up in him. Most were dressed in motorcycle garb. Several of them had tattoos on their faces. Women were fighting alongside the men; one was wearing a police hat. Beside them was an armored Humvee with a heavy machine gun mounted on it. A fat gangbanger with arms the size of hogs' legs, wearing a vest with no shirt, was standing in the Humvee's rear deck firing at the fighters Artie had just thrown in with. Loose fat on the banger's arms was jiggling with the heavy weapon's recoil. Artie set the M4's fire-selector to full automatic. He waited until some of the Pagans were gathered near the fat man; then he squeezed the trigger. A burst of fire ripped from his M4's muzzle, then another; the clip was empty. This was much better than an M16 and far better than his wheel-gun. He'd hit the fat man and another Pagan in the torso and clipped a third in the leg. The injured and dead were lying on the ground. The rest scattered for cover like cockroaches. Bullets started snapping through branches above his head. Artie reloaded and then peeled off one more burst, finishing the man he'd clipped in the leg. They were vermin. He needed to kill more of them. He wanted to kill all of them. He felt a compulsion to charge their position and ruin as many as he could before they got him. The fire over his head increased in intensity. Leaves and branches were falling on him like rain. He retreated backward a few yards to just below the ridgeline.

Keeping low, Artie moved along the ridge to find another attack point. A thunderous shudder bore down on him at high speed and then slowed to a hover just above and in front of his position. Trees were bending down; their branches whipped by whirlwinds. He knew some kind of big helicopter was in the air very close to him. Loud fast bursts of chain-driven sounds ripped at his ears, followed by explosions erupting from Pagan positions. Artie took a risk and moved forward to peer through the brush. Dirt was being kicked up all around him from rotor wash. He saw an Apache helicopter just above and to the right. The Apache, and what must have been several others which he couldn't see, were firing chain-gun cannons into Pagan positions. At the focus point of the Apaches' fire, all he could see was a growing cloud of dust and smoke with flashes erupting inside it. Hell had come to the Pagans. He loved it. He grinned even as specks of wind-driven dirt and grit were pelting his face.

The Apaches stopped firing in less than a minute. They had exterminated the vermin. Artie looked at the attack bird hovering near him. The war machine's presence was intimidating. If the crew turned on him and opened fire, he wouldn't stand a chance. These men had come to the aid of real victims this day; but at their heart, they were enforcers of the I64 line. The smile dimmed on his face and slowly became a scowl. He raised the M4 to his shoulder and aimed at the Apache's glass enclosed canopy. He could make out the shape of two men. This would be a serious blow to an enemy more dangerous and more responsible for all the suffering than the Pagans. He was ready to squeeze down on the trigger. He didn't know if the canopy was armored glass. The M4 might end up being as effective as spitting in the face of a murderous machine. He wished he had some grenades for the launcher and knew how to use it. He slowly tightened on the trigger. A few rounds spit from the M4 and then it stopped. He looked at the gun. The clip was empty. He looked back; the Apache was gone but he could still hear it flying nearby. Artie got to his feet and ran. Seconds later, he heard the forest erupting from cannon fire just behind him. He ran faster. He knew he would be blown apart at any moment.

Several minutes later, Artie reached the dirt road he'd crossed earlier. He was panting. His face was covered in sweat. The Apache had stopped firing some minutes ago. He couldn't see or hear the bird he'd shot. He had spit into the face of the monster and learned he needed more than machine gun rounds. All the firing had stopped. The battle was over. He walked across the road and down the cement wall to rejoin the fighters he'd met less than twenty minutes earlier. He felt like it had been days ago that he'd pulled an M4 from that crate and stuffed ammo and clips into his pockets.

~

Dusk was closing in around them. The group of thirty men moved through the woods in near silence. Artie/Alexander was dressed in dark green camouflage fatigues and a flak vest which he'd been issued earlier that day before the team set out. His .357 magnum was in his shoulder holster which he wore outside the fatigues and vest. He was starting to think of himself as Alexander. This was the name these fighters knew him by. Some had seen him take his shot at the Apache. The rumors were that he was both extremely crazy and brave.

Alexander carried what was now his M4. The weapon was starting to feel like something his hands were familiar with. On his vest and belt, he had pouches of 40mm grenades which looked like huge fat bullets, one and half inches wide and four inches long. He'd learned how to use the launcher by firing a dozen non-explosive practice shells across a field at a deserted cabin. The launcher could fire a grenade a thousand feet out and deliver enough punch with a single hit to cripple a lightly armored vehicle. The next Apache would not be so lucky.

A military two-way radio was clipped to Alexander's belt. In his earbud, he heard the chatter of other men in the hunting party. They were tracking down a group of Pagans who had fled on foot. The Apaches had killed most of the vermin. The best guess was they were hunting approximately ten to twenty Pagans.

They were tracking an enemy who had a commanding head start. The hunting party had been going for over six hours without stopping. Alexander could feel they were getting close. A man named Jones was leading the team. He was a hunter and trapper who knew these woods. This had been his home since he was a boy. He was lanky looking with a grizzled beard and a strong Virginia accent. Alexander thought Jones knew the woods but lacked the decisiveness of a leader.

"*Clearing up ahead,*" crackled in Alexander's earbud.

Alexander stopped walking when he reached a line of trees where several men were congregating. More men were still coming up from behind. Below him, he saw a small town spread out in a valley. A river ran through the valley and between some of the structures. The town was not deserted. There were some people on sidewalks and cars moving on the streets. Alexander tensed as he saw an armed group of maybe two dozen move out from the edge of the woods below them. They walked down the center of the main street, and at its end, filed into a three story building which looked like a bank. Pagans!

"We got 'em," said Jones.

Alexander crouched behind some boulders as more Pagans came out of the three story building. The gangsters walked across the street to a line of armored Humvees that had pulled out of a parking structure minutes ago. The town was a stronghold. This was not what the hunters had expected to find. They were out of radio range of the settlement. Jones had tried a cell phone but was unable to connect, which was no big surprise given the decaying conditions of all the infrastructure. Attacking with their force of thirty fighters was suicide according to Jones. Everyone on the team had M4s and grenade launchers, but that was not enough firepower. At least a hundred Pagans were down there with heavy machine guns and possibly rockets. Alexander and some of the other men were ready to take them on. They had surprise on their side. They had hundreds of grenades, which was enough for a small artillery barrage. Jones wanted to send a party back to the Red Cross shelter to bring reinforcements, which could take eight hours or more, even if they returned by car. The Pagans could be gone by then or – worse – reinforced. Jones was soft and everybody saw it. Alexander felt an insane compulsion to shoot the coward where he stood. Jones was ready to pull back. For Alexander there was no time left, it was either shoot the man or force him to change his mind.

"I'm going to attack," said Alexander. "Anyone who wants to kill Pagans can join me."

"The hell you are!" roared Jones.

In a flash of rage, Alexander jammed the barrel of his M4 into the man's throat gagging him. Jones backed up. Alexander moved with him keeping the barrel pressed in place. He was moments from squeezing the trigger.

"Fuck you," yelled Jones.

The man turned abruptly and started to walk away. Alexander found himself aiming his M4 at the back of a coward. There was grumbling. A few of the men started to walk off after Jones but the majority didn't move. Alexander watched as the deserters vanished into the stands of trees. He felt his left eye twitching. He wanted to spray them with bullets and wasn't sure how he was holding back. He turned to face the men who'd remained.

"I'm going to kill Pagans," he said in a soft voice that was almost a snarl. "I'm going to ambush them and leave behind a town full of their rotting corpses."

There was silence; then one fighter said, "Yeah!" and then another barked, "Let's do it."

Alexander locked eyes with one man and then another and another. Amazingly, these men were accepting him as their mutinous leader. This was not exactly what he had intended. He just wanted to kill Pagans.

The plan was the result of a group discussion between Alexander and four of the most experienced fighters. The strategy was simple and lethal. Half the fighters would remain behind in positions up on the hillside. The goal was to use the other half to draw out the Pagans by giving them what looked like an easy slaughter. Once the enemy was completely exposed, the men on the hillside would hit them with over-whelming violence: a fusillade of hundreds of grenades.

Alexander and his half of the fighters had crept down to the last bit of tree cover before the town. Fifty yards away, a chain link fence marked the beginning of a small park with benches and an old fashioned kid-powered merry-go-round. Alexander's new second-in-command had remained up on the hillside to lead the grenade assault. He was the man Alexander had walked next to during the six hours they'd tracked Pagans through the woods. His nickname was Fox. He was a stocky Texan with a sarcastic streak and a bad temper. Alexander had looked Fox in the eyes and saw a man that lusted for blood, a brawler. This was a man who could be counted on to attack and not run.

Alexander crept forward alone. He was on point and would draw first blood. He walked out of cover through a break in the fence and into the park. He stood looking at the town. The sun was almost down. The sky was growing dark. There were armed Pagans standing less than a hundred feet away. He felt a sting on his wrist and turned it over. An insect was biting him on his gang tattoo. He squashed the bug against the red dragon on his wrist. He had gone full circle in his life and was back to who he was born to be. It was time to kill Pagans.

Alexander pressed the transmit button on his radio but didn't speak a word. Instead, he released the button. He felt something odd. There was a little ball of fear simmering in his gut. Something was whispering danger. His eyes opened wide in the growing darkness. He thought of the hospital tent where Suzy had died; he thought of New York. A kill zone was coming. He was certain of it. Was it too late for his fighters to pull back? He pressed the transmit button.

"Fallback," he whispered harshly. "A kill zone's going to hit."

"A what?... Say again…"

Alexander saw a Pagan fall in the street, then others. There were no insect sounds or wind. There was no moon. It was a quiet night while death visited the streets of this small town. Alexander walked out into the middle of all the dying and began shooting Pagans while they were collapsing. He was going to make sure none of them lived. Some of them might have his immunity to kill zones, but no one was immune to bullets.

~

Not a single of his fighters had been lost in the kill zone or the mop up which was on-going. These fighters had become Alexander's to command. He sensed it. They would die for him. They were in awe of him. His prediction, and then reckless survival and exploit of a kill zone, were things bordering on superstition or even legend. Fox asked how he'd known the zone was coming. Alexander had told him it was a sense he'd picked up from surviving in the middle of them, which was mostly the truth. He said he'd learned the smell of this kind of death when it was coming.

Alexander attached a flashlight to the barrel of his M4. The street-lights were working but pools of darkness stretched out everywhere. All the people in the center of town were dead. Some Pagans on the edges were possibly still alive but not for long, thought Alexander as he led his men down the main street of the town. They'd captured a handful of citizens from the first few buildings on the street. To Alexander, they were all whores who had serviced a corrupt master's needs.

"Put the collaborators in that building," ordered Alexander. "You two stand guard. I'll deal with them once we're done."

Alexander walked up to the three-story building he'd originally seen Pagans entering and exiting. The building was a bank. The heavy glass door was locked. Inside, he saw dead bodies. He backed up across the street and loaded a 40mm shell. His men started to go for cover. They saw what was coming. Alexander hunkered down next to Fox behind a Humvee and shot the grenade into the door. A powerful explosion shook the ground. When Alexander looked up, he saw debris sprayed across the street. All the glass in the building was gone. Bits of scorched paper were floating in the air. He led his men inside the building through the blown out doorframe. Inside were dead Pagans. He wished some were alive just so he could kill them. His men fanned out to search the bank.

"We got one," radioed Fox. "In the vault!"

Alexander walked into the open vault. Fox had a Pagan lying on his stomach with an M4 pointed at the back of the prisoner's head. The prisoner had a long braided ponytail like an American Indian. His clothing was torn and disheveled. Alexander shoved the man over with the tip of his boot. The Pagan's eyes met his. There was dullness in the man's stare as if he was not registering what he was seeing. The eyes didn't blink or move. It was like looking into a pair of camera lenses attached to a machine. Without warning, Alexander's perceptions expanded. Every muscle in his body seized up turning him into a living statue. Somehow he was seeing through this man's eyes – and what he saw were his own eyes staring back. The closed loop was like the infinite reflections of a pair of mirrors facing each other. The connection dropped as abruptly as it had emerged; but in that instant, Alexander realized creatures lived among them who participated in this plague and this man was one of them. The creatures were immune and they were some kind of spies. He fired a burst of rounds into the creature's torso. There had to be more of these things out there hiding like infected parasites among the normal. All of them had to be hunted down and exterminated; then maybe the plague would end.

3 – Atlanta: December

The BVMC lab seemed less frenetic than it had been. For Mark, two days of Chanukah remained. For most of the country, tomorrow was Christmas Eve. Dinner was beginning to be served in the cafeteria. Most employees were heading in that direction, except for three. Mark, Kathy, and Carl were meeting secretly in Carl's office. The door was locked. The television was turned up to prevent anyone from overhearing. A summary of world news played noisily in the background. The meeting was important, but Mark's thoughts were wandering no matter how hard he tried to stay focused. Days had passed and he still had no idea of the methods or extent to which the alien technology in his brain was affecting him. That's how he thought of it now, *alien technology*. He was fully convinced the seeds were something that had not been created by mankind or, at least, not created by what everyone called modern civilization. He didn't know where the nanotech had come from, but it felt old to him; and the more he thought about it, the more ancient it felt. He knew it was stealthy and suspected it could have been around for a very long time. The only certainty was that at the high concentrations he carried, the technology enhanced his body's natural healing abilities; instead of killing him, it cured him. His shoulder had a faint pink scar which was almost invisible, but the nanotech didn't fix everything. He still had diabetes and his fingers were still sore in the morning. He suspected it only worked on traumas. He noticed Kathy had her cane with her. He didn't recall seeing her with it earlier in the day. He wondered if her knee bothered her more from emotional stress than physical strain. Could the nanotech repair emotional traumas as well as physical ones? Mark's focus returned to the conversation.

"The staff has been quietly deserting," said Carl. "I took an unofficial headcount yesterday and found we've lost twenty percent. If we lose any more, our research will bog down."

"I talked with Cheryl before she disappeared two days ago," said Kathy. "She told me that everyone feels it's hopeless and that what we're doing is having no effect. She said it's in God's hands."

"They're wrong," said Carl. "God's not going to help. It's up to us. We've identified the cause. We've come up with tools to detect it and study it. We may not have a way to neutralize this thing yet, but we have what's needed to make that breakthrough. I'm certain of it."

"The problem isn't science; it's trust," said Kathy. "How do we get them to trust us and stay?"

"I don't know," said Mark. "What I'm wondering is how they're getting past the military. We can't leave. Someone's got to be helping them."

The lights went out. The television went black. Warning beepers starting sounding. A computer screen running on a battery backup was the only source of light. The screen cast a dim pattern onto a nearby wall. Kathy and Carl looked confused. Mark felt a faint rumble in the floor. The emergency generators were in their warm-up phase before coming online. A minute later, the building came back to life on generator power. The television resumed mid-sentence. A reporter was yelling so that she could be heard over the roar of a CNN helicopter winding up.

...details are sketchy at this time. What we know is that a large kill zone has hit Atlanta. Traffic accidents have caused a total blackout of the

city. Our CNN facility has been spared so far. I will be airborne in a few minutes heading out to the areas hardest hit.

"We can use the real-time NSA data to spot precursor patterns and call warnings into CNN," said Carl.

"I'll get their phone number," said Kathy.

Carl's fingers clattered on the keyboard. Mark came around to stand behind him. He had the phone receiver in one hand ready to dial. Kathy came over to the desk and punched in a phone number. Mark heard the line ringing but no one was picking up. Carl had Atlanta up on the NSA display. Mark felt the life draining out of him. He knew it wasn't a diabetic swoon but it felt like one. On the screen, red circles were dropping all over Atlanta and its suburbs. Leading the red circles were flickers of precursor signals. Less than a minute elapsed between precursor and kill zone. It was hopeless. The path of destruction was erratic. There was not enough lead time to issue warnings.

"Oh god, it's heading toward us," cried Kathy.

"The containment lab," said Mark. "The signal can't be relayed into there. It's the only chance we've got."

As Mark unlocked the office door, he felt Carl's hand on his shoulder. Mark spun around. His mind was screaming *Run! There's no time! Run!*

"We won't make it," said Carl. His voice was dull. "The airlocks take a half hour to cycle. The kill zone will be here in minutes."

"Goddamn it!" yelled Mark. "Don't you want to live?"

He looked back at the screen. A red circle dropped within a mile of the lab. Mark saw the speckled pattern of precursor signals forming in an area over the east side of the BVMC lab. Time had run out. Kathy's eyes were filled with tears. He took her in his arms. She buried her face into his chest. His eyes were locked on the screen as he waited to feel her life drain away in his arms. He felt nothing but rage at this nanotech horror. He had to save her. He had to do something, but all he could do was stand motionless and hold the woman he now realized he loved. What they could have had was lost. He was again, too late…

4 – Atlanta: December

Sarah had arrived at the deserted motel a day ago. The "Blue Moon Motel" was on the outskirts of Atlanta, only 50 miles from the CDC installation listed on her application. She felt irrational sitting at this motel when her destination was an hour's drive away, but a fear grew inside her every time she thought of leaving. The same kinds of instincts that had originally compelled her to head south were now holding her back. She glanced around the room. The floor was covered in tan carpeting. The walls were painted in earth tones. The room's ceiling had as standard equipment a king size mirror suspended over a waterbed. Ralph was lounging on the bed. Sarah doubted he cared about the dog sleeping on the ceiling above him.

Outside, the streets were pitch black. Sarah had a small light on, the curtains closed, and a thick blanket hung over the curtains to make sure no light escaped. The windows had bars and the door was made of metal. She almost felt safe. She was sitting cross-legged on a chair cushion in the center of the floor. She'd taken three psilocybin capsules on an empty stomach about thirty minutes ago. Based on her previous experiences, she knew the effects of the drug would start any moment now.

Sarah waved her hand in front of her face to see if any trails had started. Nothing so far, there were no hints of visual hallucinations. She'd already learned, by gradually increasing the dosage, that three capsules were enough to get full effect. She had hundreds of capsules, but she needed to stretch them as much as possible. The insights she gained were addictive in how they satisfied her thirst to understand. They were like clues to a crime, and the clues had started fitting together.

She now knew a small part of the god-machine was inside her head. She believed this small part enabled her to communicate subconsciously with higher mental functions of the living machine. She was convinced by fragments of implanted memories that psilocybin made the link possible by weakening the normal barriers between the evolved and primitive parts of her mind. She understood the machine had protected her inside kill zones for some reason, but she had no idea how or why. There were dimly recalled implanted memories of knowing so much more about why she mattered to the living machine; but all that remained of those dreamlike recollections was a feeling – a compulsive kind of knowing – that things would begin to make sense once she reached the CDC lab and encountered someone there, a man she knew only from scraps of images and voices in her mind. The man's name and appearance had come to her as part of the blizzard of sensory fragments that were drawn to her like metal filings to a magnet. She'd had brief flashes yesterday and again today during which she'd perceived the world through this man's senses – his eyes, his ears, even his sense of touch briefly became her own. The out of body perceptions were similar to how she'd remotely experienced kill zones through people caught in the midst of them.

Sarah had decided this man was a scientist from bits of overheard conversations and glimpsed encounters. She had seen the man's face when he looked into a mirror and heard his name when a woman had addressed him as Mark. Sarah had sensed a chemistry between this man and woman; and for some reason, this troubled her. She didn't know this man. He was old enough to be her father. She was not even sure he existed, but she felt an affinity with him. There was something that was supposed to happen once they met, and this other woman could be a complication.

Sarah waved a hand in front of her face and saw a trail forming behind it like a slow motion cartoon. This was it; the psilocybin was taking her on another journey into the machine. She focused her thoughts on why the god-machine was protecting her from kill zones. She'd learned that the machine could sometimes be guided into responding to questions if she concentrated on a single question only. Like a meditation or prayer, she would repeat the question to herself again and again. At some point, she would realize that the god-machine had responded. The response didn't come directly as words or images, but as memories; all of a sudden she would just remember something related to the prayer as if she'd known it her entire life. She continued repeating the prayer to learn more about why the god-machine was protecting her. Occasionally, a feeling of attraction to Mark slipped unwanted into her thoughts. Sarah pushed the feeling away and focused back on her praying.

Sarah came harshly back to awareness from an endless pool of white light. She'd been floating in a world of tranquil nothingness for hours. She glanced about the motel room; then her existence snapped: she was catapulted into a scene of confusion. People were falling in their tracks. Chain-reaction car accidents were occurring. Windshield glass littered the ground. Moans of the injured faded into the silence of a graveyard. Was this real? Sarah looked over at a television attached to a wall unit. She got up and turned on the set. Atlanta was a war zone. News graphics and images flashed on the screen. She turned it off and closed her eyes. There were no tears left in her. She wanted to feel for these people, but all she felt was thankfulness. She now understood why her instincts had kept her at this motel. If she'd gone into Atlanta, she'd have been in the midst of another kill zone. She didn't think her mind could have survived the horror one more time.

6 – Atlanta: December

Mark stood holding Kathy in his arms. The kill zone was happening over a different part of the building. Death was just down the hall, ready to wash over them next. There was no physical sense of it. There should have been tornado-like winds or a terrible rain or a blinding flash – something, anything – but there was nothing. The killer did its work in utter silence. The NSA screen showed the zone was hitting one third of the building. Muffled cries filtering in from the hallway confirmed his worst fears. His chest was wet with Kathy's tears. Her arms were tight around him. As long as her embrace held, he knew she was still with him. He watched as precursor signals flickered and the next red circle formed on the screen. This one was not over the building.

"I think it's veering off," cried Carl.

Kathy's grip on Mark loosened. He looked down into her eyes. They were haunted.

"It's definitely leaving, said Carl.

Mark led Kathy to the couch where they both sat in silence. Mark was drained of emotion. Carl stayed at the computer screen and tracked the killer as if it were a moving weather storm. In a few more minutes, the attack was over. News was starting to come in from CNN reporters in the field. The death toll would be unthinkable.

An hour later, Mark closed the door to his office and locked it. The kill zone had devastated Atlanta. In the BVMC lab, the living were tending to the dead. A morgue had been established in a subbasement. The news from Atlanta was bleak. Estimates cited up to eighty percent of the population were dead or injured. Electrical power had not returned to most of the city and, according to CNN, was not coming back anytime soon. The BVMC Lab was still running on emergency generators. There was enough fuel to last for 30 days; and more could be probably obtained, if needed.

Mark selfishly thanked god that Kathy was alive. The kill zone had struck the lab with a glancing blow. Only luck had kept it from sweeping over the entire campus. Inside the building there was a clear line separating those who survived from those who did not. Nearly everyone on the deadly side of the boundary was gone. In the facility as a whole, one out of every four people had died. People in one office were gone, while their friends in the next office were fine. The logic of it was savage and felt insane, even though the basic mechanics of zones were now well understood. Mark had his back against the door. He was alone for the first time since the kill zone had hit. He could no longer handle looking at the suffering faces that wandered this high-tech mausoleum. He covered his face with his hands and cried.

7 – Atlanta: December, Christmas Eve

The morning light was painful in her eyes. Sarah walked back into her motel room. She'd just loaded the last of her things into the Buick. Thanks to an abandoned gas station across the street which still had power, she'd filled the tank for free.

She was still feeling the effects of psilocybin. Rapid motions caused trails. Bright lights left afterglows lasting for minutes. Sarah lay back on the waterbed and stared up at her reflection in the ceiling mirror. She studied her body. For minutes, she thought of nothing else except her physical form. She hadn't noticed it at first. A diagram showing her organs and internal structures was superimposed over the reflection of her body. The three-dimensional diagram showed blood flow and nerve signals and other things she couldn't decipher. She saw a small orange mass at the base of her brainstem. Somehow, she recognized this was the small part of the god-machine that was inside her.

The room disappeared into chaos. Sarah found herself perceiving through the senses of someone else – a soldier. A fierce cry of aggression bellowed from his throat but was drowned out by the thundering of weapons all around him. He was inside an armored vehicle staring through a computerized gun sight while operating a weapon that spewed small explosive shells at an impossibly high rate. The vehicle was alive with recoil vibrations. A single-story concrete building in his sights was quickly blown apart as he targeted it.

The firing stopped. Small secondary explosions popped within the flames and smoke. The soldier removed a pair of hearing protectors. His ears rung as he stepped from the vehicle. A few buildings remained standing while most were rubble. Sarah could feel heat on his face from the burning structures. She wondered why some buildings were spared. She saw the dirt-smeared faces of uniformed fighters coming in and out of view as if they were in a carnival funhouse mirror. There was cheering and excitement. From scraps of heated conversations, she deciphered the soldier's name was Alexander and that he was the leader of this attack. This was his victory and he seemed to drink it in with an unquenchable thirst for revenge.

The carnival atmosphere which was already disturbing was growing worse. Sarah felt trapped in this hellish dream. Most of these soldiers were sociopaths. The vanquished were being herded up. The injured and uninjured were treated with equal brutality. Cries for help were met with indifference. Some that were too injured to walk were left behind. Sarah struggled to close her eyes to the violence but could not, because these eyes were Alexander's to control, not hers.

Alexander kicked open a partially broken door of a building which had been spared and walked inside. Crates of military ammunition and weapons were piled to the ceiling. There were sounds of yelling outside. Bits of glass and debris crunched under his boots. Smoke drifted through the building from the fires next door. He was hunting something, sensing its presence using the reptilian part of his human brain. To him, it was a kind of 'mental scent' he was following. Sarah knew he was using information subconsciously tapped from the god-machine. She watched as he came upon a female lying on the floor of a backroom. A rear door had been blown inward from an explosion. This was the quarry he'd sensed. Her leg was blood soaked and appeared useless. She'd apparently crawled inside for shelter. Strands of short blonde hair covered one of her green eyes. Her stare as she looked up at him was glassy and unblinking. Sarah was surprised, realizing this woman was also mentally linked with the god-machine. She could have seen through the woman's eyes if the machine had allowed it. Sarah was struck by how similar her appearance was to this woman. They could have been sisters.

All Alexander saw was hate. He aimed his machine gun at one of the woman's eyes. As his finger tightened on the trigger, powerful conflicts boiled up in what was left of his soul. There were warring thoughts of parasite and immunity and collaborator and worse. Sarah realized through the jumble of mental segues that Alexander was un-aware of his similarities to this woman he was about execute. They both had some type of mental link to the god-machine, and yet he wanted to kill her because of her link.

Alexander was a breath away from murder. Sarah screamed for him to stop, knowing her mental cries reached a deaf mind. The female's eyes lost their glassiness and blinked. The woman's connection to the god-machine had dropped. She began crying – first softly, then louder. "Please," she sobbed. Tears were streaming down her face. Alexander just looked at the woman, but Sarah could tell he was faltering. He was no longer sure this woman was one of 'them.' He lowered the barrel of the machine gun until it pointed at the floor then pressed the transmit button on his radio.

"Fox, I need someone in here to pick up a prisoner and get her some medical help… Now."

The woman fainted. Sarah felt Alexander's skin begin to crawl. His entire body tightened, ready for fight or flight. Was he going to shoot her anyway? Then Sarah realized he had sensed someone in the room behind him. He'd walked into a trap. He could hear someone breathing. He could smell her sweat. He spun around burning pure adrenaline, dropped to one knee, and zippered the wall with bullets. The entire move had been split second fast but no one was there. Crumbs of sheetrock fell to the floor amid a fine haze of dust and smoke.

Sarah withdrew like a flame that had been snuffed. She wasn't sure how she'd fled, but she was gone. She'd realized the moment those bullets had been fired that this man had sensed her presence and tried to kill her. He hadn't fully understood what was happening, but he'd felt her in the back of his mind. The lasting thought which she took from this hellish vision was that this soldier, even if he did not yet fully realize it, was hunting her. So far he'd only found surrogates, but she had little doubt that it was her who he was ultimately stalking – it was her who he was driven to kill; and when he had her, he would not hesitate from uncertainty as he just did with this other female.

Sarah was back in the motel room, her connection to the god-machine severed. The machine was clearly warning her about this soldier. She gasped air as if waking from suffocation. Her thoughts were spinning. She was being hunted: the realization changed her. There was nausea and an aching in her temples. She went into the bathroom and splashed cold water on her face until all remnants of the images were washed away. She dried herself and then looked into the mirror. Her expression was hardened. Her green eyes looked like they belonged to someone who was dangerous. She thought about the CDC volunteer application on which she'd scribbled her signature the other day. That paper was her passport to get inside the CDC and locate the man in her visions. Something deep inside had filled her with the belief that her life depended upon this plan working.

~

Sarah was experiencing disappointment now that she was at the CDC compound. It was as if the building itself was grieving from the kill zone that had hit here the previous day. Getting inside had been simple. She'd been rubberstamped into the volunteer program pending confirmation of her paperwork, and had been left alone to get acclimated to the surroundings. Most of the incoming security she'd expected to find at a heavily protected government facility like this was missing. There were metal detectors and x-ray machines at the entrances; but after that, instead of being searched, she was only asked to sign a declaration stating she didn't have any items on a restricted list. Oddly, outgoing security at the fence seemed more rigorous where there had been a line of cars waiting to leave and a team of armed soldiers with dogs inspecting them.

Sarah was perched on her assigned cot in a dormitory that looked like a homeless shelter and smelled like one, too. Lodging had been worked out for Ralph in a tented Quonset hut maintained by the Army for their guard dogs. She was apparently not the first person to show up with a pet in tow. In some ways the Quonset hut had nicer accommodations than this makeshift dormitory. She was scheduled for a regiment of medical tests starting two days after confirmation of her records. The tests included some unpleasant items which required anesthesia. She had no intention of staying that long.

With a plastic access card dangling from her neck by a lanyard, Sarah set out to track down her purpose for being here, the scientist named Mark. She had a plan for capturing his attention once she found him; after that it might get messy if he didn't believe what she'd rehearsed saying. The plastic card allowed her to come and go from the main entrance and gave her access to much of the first floor. She had a small map which showed restrooms, cafeteria, showers, and other areas on her floor. As best she could tell, there was nothing that looked promising on this level. Instead of a call button, the elevators had a metal plate which she'd recognized as a proximity card reader. A soldier with an M16 slung over his shoulder stood at attention by the bank of doors. Her medical tests were going to be conducted on the second floor; maybe if all else failed, she could bluff her way onto an elevator using that as an excuse. Lights above the bank of elevators indicated three stories above ground and four subbasements. The two upper floors were listed on building directories as offices and labs, while none of the basements were listed at all. There were eleven Ph.D.'s with first names of Mark listed as occupants of the upper floor offices.

Sarah walked to the bank of elevators as if she belonged there. She'd seen people dressed in casual clothing enter the elevators; the plastic cards all looked the same, so there was no reason for her appearance to raise questions. The soldier guarding the elevators smiled at her. His eye involuntarily slithered up and down her body. She smiled back weakly. She couldn't stall for too long. She was hoping someone would show up to use the elevators and let her hitch a ride.

"Sure is funny to be here on Christmas Eve," said Sarah.

"Everything's funny nowadays," said the soldier. "Orders are, Miss, you have to use the elevators or step away."

"Oh, sorry... I'm new."

Sarah held her card next to the metal plate. Maybe she could fake a worn out card or something. There was an electronic beep. A small screen over the reader displayed 'access denied.'

"The card must be broken," said Sarah.

"You have to step away from the elevators, Miss. You can get your card replaced at the security office near the main entrance."

Sarah glanced down the hallway and spotted a blue sign marked with a symbol for stairs. There was a soldier stationed next to that door also. She suspected the stairwell offered the same arrangements as the elevators. Most of the doors on this floor had card readers next to them. Her first reconnaissance run was coming to a screeching halt. The doors to the cafeteria were open. No need for a card reader there. Sarah headed in that direction. She felt the guard's eyes on her as she walked away.

The cafeteria was crowded. It seemed like everyone else had decided on the same destination that she had. Wasn't there anything to do in this place except eat? Sarah purchased a cup of coffee and a bag of chips. She selected a seat with a direct line of sight to the elevators. She took a sip of her coffee – not bad. She had decided to camp out and watch in the hope her scientist exited one of the lifts.

The hands on the wall clock had been dragging for some time. The smell of sauerkraut had started filling the room a little while ago. People were coming off the cafeteria line with trays of hotdogs, chips, and soda. Sarah's stomach grumbled. The air felt oppressively humid. She'd been sitting on the plastic chair for a very long time. Her legs were sore. The chips were gone and the coffee was a dried up stain on the bottom of her cup. She needed fresh air. She needed a better plan. Sarah got up and headed toward the main entrance of the facility.

8 – Atlanta: December, Christmas Eve

The day had started out sunny but was now rainy and cold. Mid-afternoon was blending into twilight. Mark no longer noticed the low vibration of the generators as he walked through a metal detector and headed toward the revolving doors which led into the main hallway. His coat was damp with rain. His meeting with the new military commander had not gone well. Colonel White was part of BARDCOM and reported directly to General McKafferty. The new commander had chosen to keep his office inside one of the military trailers which now filled the parking lot. The Colonel was keeping his distance. Mark went through the revolving doors which he'd learned also functioned as a trap. If someone didn't have the right access card, the door would let them enter a half revolution and then trap them. Mark felt nervous going through the damn things.

The main hallway was crowded. There was a soft din of conversations. Mark was stopped in mid-stride by a young woman standing in his path. He moved to walk around her, but she jumped back in front of him. He smiled at the comical dance they were having. The young woman had a peculiar look of recognition in her eyes. She wore jeans and an oversized baggy sweatshirt. Mark moved to the left, but so did the young woman. They were still trapped in lock-step.

"Mind if I lead?" he said.

"Hi, Mark… My name is Sarah Mayfair."

"Do I know you?"

She was very pretty and did look a little familiar. He noticed her hair was blonde, her skin was light olive, and her eyes were green; he could not quite figure out her ethnicity. There was also something a little spooky about her, something that just didn't add up all the way. He was lost in his thoughts and missed most of what she'd said next.

"… Do I look familiar?" asked the young woman.

"Honestly, no," said Mark.

"I thought I might," said the young woman. "Okay, anyway, here goes… You'll either think I'm off my rocker or that I'm telling you stuff you already know."

Mark must have been showing his distress or this young woman was noticeably odd, because one of the soldiers, a big guy named Jeremy who patrolled the halls and knew Mark, was walking over. The guard stationed at the elevators was staring.

"Hello, Professor Freedman, sir," said Jeremy. "Do you need any assistance?"

"I know the bacteria are part of a thinking machine," said the young woman. She began talking very quickly, as if she was afraid of being silenced. "It may be much smarter than you suspect."

"Is this woman a problem?" asked Jeremy.

Mark was thrown off balance by what he'd just heard her say. He didn't know how to respond to this woman or to the guard. He felt like he'd just stepped into an alternate reality. Who was this woman? It was highly classified information that nanotech seeds were inside COBIC. No outsiders knew about this.

"I'm a cop," said the woman as she held out a police badge. "I'm not a nutcase. Please just listen to me."

"It's okay, Jeremy," said Mark.

The guard raised an eyebrow and then walked away. Once the guard was out of hearing range, Mark took the woman by the arm.

"Okay Sarah. That's your name, right? How did you know about the nanotech seeds?"

"The what?" said Sarah.

"You said the bacteria are a thinking machine."

"I did and I'm right, or you would've given me to Jeremy by now," said Sarah.

"Maybe?"

"I know things about the thinking machine," said Sarah.

Mark shut the door to his office and then sat down at his desk. He motioned the young woman to have a seat in one of the chairs in front of his desk. She made him feel uncomfortable. He took a sip of coffee.

"So I've passed the test?" said Sarah.

"Let's just say you've got my attention."

"Okay, how do I keep your attention?"

"Explain to me how you know the bacterium is a thinking machine."

The young woman looked like she was trying to decide something; then she leaned forward.

"You'll think I'm nuts after I tell you this," she said. "There's a small colony of it inside my head."

"And it tells you things?" guessed Mark.

"And it tells me things," said Sarah. "It implants memories that aren't mine inside my head."

This woman was either a paranoid schizophrenic or she was a gift. Mark was betting on the former but hoping for the latter. *And it tells me things* – that was a gutsy admission if she turned out to be sane. Everyone tested had some COBIC inside their bodies; again, that knowledge was highly classified. Still, none of this proved a thing and none of this was new information. He had a very high concentration of COBIC in his brain and he'd experienced no little voices in his head; but he had been honest enough from the start to wonder if it was affecting him mentally. Maybe a communications channel could be opened? He was convinced that high concentrations of COBIC caused accelerated healing. A small amount can kill while a large amount may heal. Now that was counterintuitive.

"Have you been injured lately?" asked Mark.

"You mean did I bang my head?" asked Sarah. "Do I have a concussion?"

"No. It's just a basic medical question. Have you been injured recently?"

"I've gotten banged up in the past few months. There's no one out there who hasn't had a rough time."

"Do you have any scars?"

"You want proof that I've been hurt? I've got no scars to prove it. The injuries healed fast. I was in a car accident and broke a rib, I think."

"No scars?" asked Mark.

"I've been healing quicker than… Wait a minute." A smile formed on Sarah's face. "Healing quickly is a symptom of some kind, isn't it?"

Mark picked up the ping tester from his desk. He turned it on and waved a sealed test tube containing infected COBIC in front of it. The test tube registered a reading twenty-five percent up the graph. He turned the device around so that Sarah could see the graph.

"This is a detector for the nanotech seeds inside COBIC. The test is painless. Not much different than getting a sonogram," said Mark. "If there are nanotech seeds in your head, this device will pick it up. Everyone here's been tested. Everyone has a small number of seeds in them."

"Let me guess. No one here has started having dialogs with the... umm... machine."

"No one."

"So if your tester gets a reading off my head, what will that prove?"

"Well, for one thing it'll show whether you have nanotech seeds inside your head. Who knows, people react differently to the same virus, so why not a different reaction to the same nanotech device?"

Mark walked around the desk. He pointed the detector's directional antenna at Sarah's forehead and switched it on. Sarah's eyes rolled up. Her body slouched in the chair. Mark caught her from tipping forward with his free hand. He stared at the signal strength display. The red line was at the top of the graph, same as his reading. She was loaded with nanotech seeds. Sarah quickly recovered from the mild seizure. She pushed his hand off her.

"Not painless!" she said. "Bullshit. That white light hurts like hell."

"You saw a white light?"

"Yeah, more like blinded by it."

"Interesting," said Mark.

"Don't tell me. I'm also the only person who sees white light around here?"

"So far," said Mark.

He was not ready to let anyone know about his seeing white light or that the seeds might be affecting his mind. Sarah's arrival could be an opportunity to learn more about the effects of high concentrations of COBIC without submitting himself as the guinea pig. Mark was lost in plans. He vaguely heard Sarah talking while he paid no attention and nodded at the right times.

"You've seen the white light," said Sarah. "Haven't you?"

"Excuse me?"

"I get it. Listen, I'm a cop. I know how to read people. You're just like me. Have you seen information projected into your mind?... diagrams, stuff like that?"

"I haven't seen white light. No one else here has seen white light. This is ridiculous."

"Okay, fine. You want to stay in the closet, that's okay with me. We'll pretend you're normal and I'm possessed."

Mark arranged for Sarah to be reassigned to him as a personal test subject. She was set up in an office down the hall for sleeping quarters. He'd also arranged for her dog to be allowed into the facility as a kind of concession to keep her quiet about white lights and her suspicions about him. Getting the dog in had not been very hard to arrange. Other people had pets inside, including Kathy.

Kathy was excited about what Mark had told her and agreed to run an expedited battery of tests on Sarah; both questionnaires and physical examinations had been completed already; more exotic tests were scheduled over the next several days. Sarah reported surviving two kill zones. Except for the highest concentration of COBIC on record, so far all her tests had come back normal or above normal, including a psych evaluation.

It was late Christmas Eve. Mark and Kathy were sharing the same bed in Kathy's office. Mark had been unable to fall asleep. He was troubled by Sarah. She'd seen through his denials. She knew he'd experienced at least some of the same manifestations. He didn't know if he could trust her to keep silent and he wondered what else she'd experienced and hadn't revealed yet. Was he going to start experiencing implanted memories? Did the nanotech slowly drive its victims insane or was it really some kind of computer-assisted thinking? He didn't see how anyone could trust their memory after finding false ones.

Mark crept out of bed and walked down the hallway to Sarah's room. There was a yellow glowing underneath her door. He hesitated; then tapped lightly. There was no answer. He tapped again. The door opened. Sarah was standing in a swaying kind of way. She looked intoxicated. She was wearing a t-shirt and panties. She motioned for him to come inside. He walked in. The room was dimly lit with candlelight. She closed the door; then turned and kissed him. He kissed her back and felt himself swelling. His heart was pounding. What was he doing? He pushed her out to arms length.

"I just came to talk," he said.

"Okay... we can talk."

Sarah turned and walked with a sway to the center of the room where she sat down on a couch cushion on the floor and crossed her legs. The cushion must have been where she was sitting when he'd knocked. The arrangement looked like some kind of meditation setup. A single candle was on the floor in front of her. He sat down in an office chair. Sarah patted the floor next to her. Mark stayed where he was in the chair. She made him very nervous. He eyed the light switch but didn't get up to turn it on.

"Are you high?" he asked.

"Nope, not me," answered Sarah.

Mark heard people walking down the hall. There was a muffled conversation. When he looked back at Sarah, her expression had become glassy. She stared at him for a long time and then closed her eyes. Mark was convinced she was high on something. He sniffed the air. No smell of pot. He looked around the room. No signs of alcohol or drug paraphernalia. He looked over at the couch and saw a huge dog laying on it. The dog had one eye open and it was fixed on him.

"You have the same orange mass of COBIC in your brainstem as I do," said Sarah. Her eyes were open and focused on him. Her pupils were the size of an owl's. "I can see the mass. The machine's showing it to me as a diagram overlaying your body. There's also something unusual, like a computer-drawn outline around an organ that's probably your pancreas, something's different about it. You have diabetes, I think. Is that right?"

Mark was speechless. What the hell was this? She was either putting on the best act since the Amazing Kreskin or she was getting some kind of medical information through the nanotech in her head.

"The bacterium collects into colonies," said Sarah. "The bigger the colony, the more intelligence it possesses. Each colony works like a single organism. Small colonies can be as smart as we are, and there's at least one colony that's so large and so intelligent it's become like an artificial god. It's showed itself to me. It looks like a balloon anchored to the bottom of the ocean floor. It seemed big, but there's nothing recognizable near it to gauge its size, so I really don't know how big it is – it could be a foot or a hundred feet in size – but I do know there's an entire universe of bacteria in that colony. It's the master of all the other

392

colonies, the soul of the machine; and I've learned that if you pray to it, sometimes it answers."

"What are you on? I can tell you're stoned."

"Psilocybin. It helps my mind link with the god-machine."

"You're nuts. That stuff can scramble your brain!" said Mark. "What did you just call it, the god-machine?"

Sarah opened a nylon makeup bag next to her and took out a small vial of pills. She shook three of them out into her palm and offered them to Mark.

"Try it. You're like me. It'll work for you."

"I don't need hallucinations," he said. "I need facts."

"You have diabetes, don't you? That's a fact. How did I know that?"

Mark got up and left. He was far more disturbed now than an hour ago. He went up to the roof to get some fresh air. Psilocybin? He banged his fist on the railing. How could a drug that turned someone into a zombie create any kind of man-machine interface with... with what?... the seed's wireless web?... And more than that, what was she connecting to over the web? Was it possible that a vast collective of seeds was hosting an artificial intelligence that was lurking out in some alternate cyberspace or something? Centralized control was possible, but not an artificial intelligence. Bullshit, she was just a space-cadet with a vivid imagination and a little bit of *1-800-Psychic* con-artist mixed in for effect.

An hour later, Mark tapped on Sarah's door again. He was extremely nervous. He felt like he was cheating on Kathy, but nothing was going on and nothing would go on. He was here for answers. Sarah opened the door within seconds. She was wearing a bathrobe. The room lights were on. Her hair was wet. She must have just gotten out of a shower. She smiled and stepped aside so that he could come in.

"I want you to tell me everything," said Mark.

"So you believe me?"

"I'm not sure."

"Now, that's honest, a little insulting, but honest."

Mark sat down on the couch. Sarah sat down next to him. The cushion that had been on the floor was back in its place. Sarah picked up a glass of water and took a sip. She looked sober but her pupils were still fully dilated.

"You know it's very old," she said. "I think it's older than us, the human race, I mean. I'm beginning to think that some of our myths and religions are about people who were linked with the god-machine like I am."

"Do you think you're going to be written up in history as a prophet?" asked Mark.

Sarah laughed. She had a nice laugh, nothing harsh or loud, just very down-to-earth and endearing. Hearing her laugh took some of the tension out of Mark.

"I don't feel like a prophet," she said. "I didn't mean it like that. I meant that people could have mistaken someone like me for a prophet. People in the dark ages who saw visions were considered prophets or witches or loons... Hey, maybe I'm a witch?"

Marked hoped the last option was not the most accurate description of her. There was something she'd said earlier that was really bothering him.

"Why do you call it the god-machine?"

"I don't think it's God, if that's what you're asking. I believe in God and this machine isn't God. What I do believe is that the machine started out really smart, and over a very long time it kind of evolved and grew into something like an artificial god. Who knows, maybe *god-machine* is some vague translation of its real name which I'm picking up on?

"And what about this coincidence," she said. "The way I communicate with the god-machine is by focusing my thoughts on a single idea and then repeating it in my head again and again like a mantra. That's called praying, at least in my neck of the woods it's what we called praying. I can imagine ancient people praying and the god-machine answering one of them every so often. Two thousand years ago, who would have known the difference between God and this machine? You found it has the power to heal. What would simple people have made of that? The work of God, I bet."

"Okay," said Mark. "Let's say I believe some of what you're saying, at least the parts about machine intelligence. How do you know it's not tricking you? How do you know it wasn't made ten years ago and is running a program of disinformation?"

"I don't; and I'm not going to say you have to have faith. This is just what I've gotten from it. Try the psilocybin. Find out for yourself."

"I've got to tell you that the drug part makes me very skeptical," said Mark.

"Indian tribes use psilocybin in their religion," said Sarah. "Other religions use drugs for the same reasons. Maybe they all stumbled onto the same method and mistook communing with this machine for communing with god?"

"Stop for a minute," said Mark. "Why do you keep making this case, this analogy to religion? Don't you realize there are people who will claim you're mistaken and that this is God? Once that line's crossed, it'll be easy for the weak-minded to legitimize this genocide on religious grounds. Maybe you're one of those people. Are you going to worship it? Start your own death cult? Why all this religious bullshit?"

"You know, you're starting to sound like a real bastard," Her voice had a dangerous edge to it. "Don't you think I want to stop it? Don't you think what's happened to our world is eating me, piece by piece? Just about everyone I've been close to has been murdered by that thing. I don't love it. Yeah, I'm trying to understand it. Maybe if we all focus and pray for it to stop, then it will listen to us. Who the fuck knows?"

She took a deep breath. Her face was red. Her lips were trembling. She picked up her glass of water and then put it back down without drinking.

"You're not going to like this next part one bit," she said. "I've seen clues. Small bits of implanted memories which make me think it doesn't want to kill everyone. I don't know if that's truth or disinformation. I do know that you and me and others are somehow different. I think it's selected some of us to protect and continue the human race after its genocide is done. I know it's protecting me. I've stood in the midst of hell and survived when I should have died. I was in New Jersey when the god-machine killed. I was in Virginia Beach when the god-machine killed. I know the same kind of thing is true for you and others. I've been getting different kinds of warnings from it all along – and I've seen evidence that it's been interfering with my life since I was a kid. Maybe it interfered with my parents' life and my great grandparents' life. It's got to experience time very differently than we do. It's a goddamn computer. It could set us up like chess pieces far in advance of any game; and I believe that one of its big moves is something we and others like us are supposed to do when the world is partially empty. I think the god-machine is pruning the tree of life so that there's room for a new race to grow from us. God help me, but sometimes it does feel like it's a god tinkering with evolution. I'm not saying I like its plan. I'm not saying we can't disrupt its plan. I'm just telling you what I suspect its plan is."

Mark didn't know what to say. He physically recoiled from what he'd just heard, but he also sensed deep in his gut that a lot of it could be true. Now, for the second time, he'd tried to get answers from Sarah; and all he'd come away with was greater confusion. He had no idea what to believe. He stood up to leave, shaking his head.

"I'm not the cause of all this murder," said Sarah. "I didn't choose any of this. You can't blame the messenger. This is not my fault."

"Maybe it's all our faults," said Mark. "Maybe in a dozen different ways, we're all to blame."

9 – New York City: December, Christmas Eve

Since its death, New York City had remained cloaked beneath a layer of airborne soot. From the roof of the skyscraper, the view was apocalyptic. General McKafferty stood near the railing. Wind was pushing against his back. The pressurized suit eliminated most of the subtler sensations. What he felt was something more like an invisible air current trying to drag him up and over the railing to his death. He was high above the city on the rooftop helipad of one of the tallest buildings still standing. Behind him, a Blackhawk helicopter sat on the pad with its engines growing cold. Minutes ago, a squad of his men had fanned out across the roof and secured a temporary command post, one story down. They were now sweeping their way, floor by floor, to the street.

McKafferty looked up at an airborne sanctuary slowly circling at high altitude in a lazy figure eight. The jet was a small silver dot with long contrails fanning out behind it. The President and other higher-ups now remained airborne 24/7. The lazy figure eights of their jets were visible overhead nearly anywhere in the country; all anyone had to do was look up. The eggheads had discovered that the nanotech wireless web did not reach into the air. Anyone on land or sea was at risk; but the seeds could not sustain the relay linkage needed to cover airspace. They could not float or fly in mass. This meant that if someone was high enough in the air, beyond where anything lived, a kill zone could not reach them. This fact had been withheld from the general public. Reporting the discovery would have caused riots at airports, and the skies would have been filled with planes and blimps and helicopters that could not collectively stay aloft; there was just not enough fuel. Someone had calculated that more people would be killed in air accidents than would be saved from kill zones. The self-serving arithmetic of the power elite was beginning to turn McKafferty's stomach.

McKafferty was, if nothing else, a true soldier; and a soldier never questions orders, he carries them out... or does he? The risks of this current *black op* required a highly trusted general officer to make decisions for the president in his stead. McKafferty raised a set of binoculars to his visor. The eyepieces were oversized by design, to fit flush against the suit's visor. He gazed down from the rooftop at a street piled with rubble. He grew angry thinking how mobs had torn through this great city, gutting it and bleeding it dry. Only a few buildings seemed intact; most were either flame-hollowed shells or had been splintered beyond recognition by massive explosions. A week had passed since the flames had died out and the last of the sane people had fled, but the smoke still lingered. The view was like what he'd imagined a nuclear war would leave in its wake. The acts of human destruction had been like a chain-reaction. The nanotech seeds were the primer, but man himself proved to be the greater destructive force.

McKafferty had visited many cities during this *black op* and the story was the same. From foreign intelligence sources, he knew the rest of the world was in a similar state of wreckage. Even if the nanovirus relented now, the world was on an unstoppable spiral toward a new Dark Age. So much had been destroyed and so many lives had been extinguished that it would take centuries to rebuild. Latest figures showed almost a hundred million dead and trillions of dollars in economic damage. The world's empires lay prostrate on the ground, all equalized to a level of poverty previously unimaginable.

Soldiers were posted at the four corners of the roof, all with binoculars. A scout helo was working its way up Avenue of the Americas. McKafferty continued his inspection of the rubble looking for a spot to set up a forward command post: building after building moved across his field of view. What might have been a person caught his attention as he scanned past it, just a flash of color and motion. He swung his binoculars back toward the middle floor of a tower where there was a jagged hole in the masonry exposing the interior. A few seconds later, a woman moved past the opening. McKafferty followed her path until she disappeared behind a crumbling edge of the hole. A man appeared a few seconds later. The man had the dull look of a dirt-eater. McKafferty aimed the binoculars down to the street searching for an address. An adjacent store had a number on its awning. He got out his PC Tablet which was already displaying a grid-map. The target location was two buildings in from the corner. He switched the radio channel selector to air patrol.

"This is Tall-Man," said McKafferty. "I have a definite contact bearing alpha seven-seven by tango nine, middle of the sixth floor."

"Roger Tall-Man. We are inbound."

This phase of the operation was getting off to an early start. McKafferty felt deeply conflicted about the poor bastards they were herding up. He knew he was in the wrong going from city to city capturing people. He knew he was breaking his oath to defend the Constitution but what choice was there? It was monstrous how the seeds performed a chemical lobotomy on some of the unfortunate survivors, and that's what he was searching for: a specific breed of dirt-eater that was highly infected and barely human anymore. This military operation code named *Rancher* would be the final scene in their tragic lives. The research teams needed living specimens to continue their efforts to develop a way of stopping this nanotech killer. Some of the subjects wouldn't survive the research. Maybe in some way that was a small mercy? The radio squawked with a dual tone. The signal meant that a hunt was about to get underway. Even though the com-system was scrambled, no risk would be taken at being overheard. Nothing overt was ever said. All in the political chain of command had decided that if the people found out about these hunting parties, the odds of remaining in power after victory was nil.

McKafferty squinted up at the sun for a moment and then looked back over the city. He saw the ruins of a great castle under siege. The quest for a cure was becoming more grotesque than the work of the nano-virus itself. He wondered if this was a fight mankind was better off losing.

10 – I64 line, Virginia: December, Christmas Eve

Last night, Alexander dreamt he was leading a vast army who would live and die for his cause. Tonight he would engage in the first real battle of that war. He would stick his finger in the eye of a sleeping giant. He should have felt reservations but instead felt invincible. Rumors and superstition about him were spreading from mouth to mouth, and he was feasting on it. He was the warrior who was untouchable by the plague, the warrior who sensed when kill zones were coming and wielded them as his sword. He was a warrior who brought his men the sweetness of victory. Alexander believed this superstition would intensify his fighters' bond to him and their ferocity; and so he began feeding the myth with artfully crafted stories, taking care that the fire would never turn on him like a rabid beast. He gave speeches as if arguing his case before a grand jury. He declared this was a battle for survival. The enemies were those traitors who used the plague and quarantines for their personal gains and the government that aided and abetted through avarice and indifference – and yes, he had proof.

Alexander and his band of fighters were at a rally point five miles from the I64 line. The deserted woodland clearing was a spot where teenagers often went parking. His militia was growing rapidly in size and strength. They had armored Humvees and heavy weapons captured from their vanquished enemies. They had fighters joining in a continuous stream, deserting from other militias. The clearing had a bonfire in the center. Rows of experienced fighters were standing in silence waiting for him to speak, waiting for him to command them to fight.

Alexander stood erect in front of the bonfire. He had a megaphone in his hand. The crowd had grown silent the instant he'd stepped into the firelight. His followers stood before him like worshipers at a holy shrine. Every eye was upon him. He felt their stares and drank them as if they were the finest wine. He was drunk on the taste of it. He was drunk on the power of it.

"Tonight, we take back some of what was stolen from us," he cried. "We will take back our freedom; we will take back our lives!"

Alexander's voice boomed unexpectedly loud. Echoes came back from rocky cliffs that rose hidden in the darkness in front of him. He realized the clearing was a natural amphitheater. He could see, from his men's reactions, when he spoke it was like the voice of god was raining down upon them.

"Death to the traitors who take advantage of this plague!" he yelled. "Tonight, we destroy a tentacle of the hydra which has oppressed us. Tonight, we kill those who have killed us. Tonight, we destroy an illegal quarantine which has driven so many of us to starvation and death!"

Fox, who stood in the first row, now began chanting, "Death to the Traitors! Death to the Traitors!" Soon, the entire crowd was chanting in unison with Fox.

"Now, go!" yelled Alexander.

Amid yelling and cheers, his small army went to their vehicles. Engines revved. The air was alive with the sounds of men and machines going to battle. Alexander looked into the night sky and silently thanked God for the chance to make a difference by striking this blow.

Alexander was in the passenger seat of the lead vehicle. His transport was an armored Humvee with a Bushmaster chain-gun cannon mounted on the roof. The cannon's six foot barrel had a narrow bore of only 30mm. The weapon looked more like a large robotic machine gun than a cannon. A remotely operated, computerized fire-control system with infrared telescopic sighting was mounted on the dashboard in front of Alexander. The gun sight's video feeds were digitally enhanced and displayed on a high resolution flat screen. The Army called the modified Humvee an M1025A. It was designed for heavy support of infantry scouting parties. The vehicle was painted in gray and black night camouflage colors like a wolf.

At a predetermined spot, Fox switched the headlights off and drove with night vision goggles. He silently coasted the Humvee to a stop in the middle of the road. They were in a pool of darkness cast by trees. In front of Alexander was an entrance ramp to the westbound lane of I64. Behind him, other vehicles came to a quiet halt. Alexander looked up from the infrared night vision sight. He stared at the silent I64 line in front of him. The well-lit fence took up the median of I64. There were two rows of razor wire sandwiching a nasty array of steel spikes and concrete which could stop his Humvees. Surveillance cameras were arrayed as tireless sentries over the line. Floodlights spaced along the eighteen foot fence were aimed down so that the fence and the northern side of the line were bathed in perpetual light. The floods were a doubled edged sword, because they blinded the cameras to the shadows in which he lurked. This was a wall which separated a hungry ghetto from food and comfort, a wall which had never been successfully breached with violence. On the opposite side of the barrier, he could see the barracks of the state troopers who ran the line. The building's windows glowed with yellow light. Patrol cars were parked out front and along the side. Another car pulled up and, after a few minutes, a trooper got out and went inside.

A tactical two-way radio was attached to Alexander's belt. He wore a special-forces headset. The thin microphone stalk wrapped around the right side of his face. He rolled down his window. The time was two o'clock in the morning on Christmas day. He smiled to himself wondering what Santa would bring.

The floodlights went dark; which meant that two miles in either direction, some of his fighters had cut the power lines to the fence. They had used silenced sniper rifles to sever the lines and they'd sever anyone who showed up to repair them. When the floodlights died, more men with silenced sniper rifles blew out every surveillance camera in the area of the planned attack. Alexander heard soft crunches as nearby cameras were hit. Miles away, a car rigged to catch fire was driven into the barrier as a decoy. The enemy was blind and distracted. This was the moment, his moment, the first real blow against a government which had inflicted so much misery. He fitted night vision goggles over his eyes and switched them on. A green and black world came into focus. He looked next to him at Fox who was wearing goggles. Fox grinned back at him. Alexander knew all his fighters were ready to bloody this Christmas day. He spoke into the microphone.

"Move into position and wait."

Fox drove the Humvee slowly forward into the middle of the I64 lane and stopped. Alexander heard vehicles quietly continuing to roll past on either side of him and behind him. They crept down the I64 roadway and fanned out fifty feet in either direction. This was the tip of the spear which would go through the I64 line and into the heart of the enemy. He was at its point. Behind him was the staff of the spear, a line of vehicles which stretched down the entrance ramp. Twenty-six vehicles carried his small army, all military Humvees. The tip of the spear was reserved for the armored Humvees which carried heavy weapons.

Alexander took off his night vision goggles and went back to looking through the infrared sight. Using the image-enhanced telescopic sight, he saw more details in his surroundings at night than he could in daylight with his naked eyes. He had practiced and fought with the bushmaster cannon and knew how to use it. Advanced degrees were not required. The system was designed to be very simple to operate. The controls were less complicated than the average video game, and he was a natural at it. This was the second time he would do serious violence with the weapon. The anticipation was exhilarating. They had captured the two bushmaster Humvees, along with twenty other military Hummers, when they'd conquered the Pagans' town. Alexander's first victory had been sweet. Each of his fighters had claimed a Humvee; and still there had been more left behind in the parking structure. Later that day, they had taken a second Pagan location which was not far from the conquered town. The location had been revealed by a captive just before Fox went too far with the traitor, killing him. The second site was a lightly guarded arms depot in an industrial park. The slaughter had been fast and glorious. Again, they had gutted the enemy and this time drove away with a storehouse of weapons and ammunition.

Alexander aimed the bushmaster at the steel and concrete obstacles. The chain-gun cannon was fed by heavy belts of 30mm small cannon shells, which resembled oversized machine gun bullets. The rear half of the Humvee was little more than an ammo locker which the bushmaster could empty at a startling speed. The chain-gun was the same weapon used by the Apache helicopter which he'd spat at with his M4 not long ago. His power had grown immeasurably since then. This chain-gun could fire six hundred and fifty rounds per minute and could reach out and touch a target four miles away. Each high explosive shell had the same destructive power as a hand grenade. Yesterday, during his attack on the arms depot, Alexander had chewed up an entire cement building in a few seconds. After the fighting was over and all the supplies were carted off, he'd practiced on other buildings. The chain-gun was an awesome weapon. He was thrilled by it.

Alexander lifted a pair of night vision goggles to his eyes. He looked to his left and right. He could see the other bushmaster pointed at the same spot on the steel and concrete obstacles as his cannon. Heavy machine guns mounted on other Humvees were aimed at the barracks. His spear was ready. He put down the goggles and went back to using the infrared sight. He spoke into the microphone.

"Aim."

He waited until his men reported back that they were ready and aimed on target. He was breathing deeply and slowly. He set the fire control to hot. He bore down on the trigger and in the same instant yelled, "Fire!" There had been no need to yell fire. The sound of the bushmaster hitting its target could be heard for miles. Fire from the two chain-guns focused the combined destructive power of over twenty hand grenades per second at a stationary barrier of steel and concrete. In seconds, a thirty foot wide expanse of the I64 line had been washed away in the violent streams of destruction.

Alexander was pushed back in his seat as Fox gunned the Humvee and rolled over the flattened I64 line. The State Trooper barracks was straight ahead. Heavy machine gun fire was pouring into it. Alexander opened up with the bushmaster as the Humvee rolled forward. Even with the stabilized gun mount, it was difficult to hold his target. Fox stopped advancing. Alexander continued firing. Soon, he and the other bushmaster were firing straight on into the building. The barracks was erupting in a seamless cacophony of explosions, glowing as bright circles in his gun sight and deafening his ears through the hearing protectors. The target was obscured by light and smoke, but he kept on firing and yelling. Nearby police cars exploded.

The firing had stopped. His ears were ringing. This nest of police corruption was gone. The entire attack had lasted less than two minutes from start to finish. The end was anticlimactic. The fight had been too easy. Alexander craved more, but nothing remained. He swung the gun sight in every direction, looking for hostile targets, then finally, slowly, eased off as the adrenaline waned.

Fox had stopped the Humvee with its tires straddling the eastbound lane of I64. Fanning out on either side was a semi-circle of vehicles with their headlights shining in from various angles at the site of devastation. The barracks was a smoldering pile of garbage. The air smelled of cordite and burning plastic. Small fires glowed from the rubble. Alexander climbed out of the Humvee so that he could see more clearly what was left of his conquest. He wanted this image to live in his mind forever. He inhaled with all his senses, trying without success to savor this moment of revenge, but there was no time; they had to move before the sky was filled with Apaches. His plan was to return to the ghetto side of the line to recruit more fighters. There was a rich world of targets waiting to be destroyed in front of them, and soon they would be strong enough to obliterate them all. He could feel in his heart that this world of traitorous corruption was coming to a well deserved end, and he would have a hand in that end.

~

Alexander awoke from a jolt in the uneven road. Fox was driving; spread out behind them was a convoy of Humvees. They were driving with headlights off, using night vision goggles. An hour had passed since their attack on the I64 line. Alexander was surprised that he'd fallen asleep. As details of his dream came back to him, he began to sit upright in his seat. The female cop who had saved his life at the I64 line had been in the dream. The night she'd helped him, he'd never been closer than twenty feet to her, and might not be able to pick her from a line up; but in his imagination there was a clear image of her. He hadn't thought about her since the night Suzy had died. It was odd that he'd frequently thought about the other cops, the ones who'd tried to execute him, but never her.

The two-way radio crackled with a report from a scout vehicle. The road ahead was clear. More of the dream came wafting back. The dream had been unusually vivid. In it, the female cop had the power to look deep into his thoughts. Alexander had been trying to seduce her, but she despised who she saw and regretted having saved him. The dream ended with her pushing a knife into his chest as he tried to convince her to love him. He could still feel the incapacitating pain of the metal blade entering his body and the disbelief that he could be mortally wounded in this way.

Alexander picked up Fox's pint of Tequila and took a swig. The dream unnerved him. He gazed out the windshield at the darkened road. He watched outlines of trees and houses forming out of a swirling nighttime darkness as they moved past. The female cop could have been killed in tonight's raid, but some instinct left him convinced she was alive and that he would meet her again. He wondered if she would have a knife. Alexander closed his eyes and tried to return to sleep.

11 – Atlanta: December

Since the previous night, a continuous debate had battled inside Mark. For every claim Sarah had spoken, he now had a counterpoint. He was in the cafeteria having finished lunch but could not remember what he had eaten or who he had spoken with. He wasn't sure about breakfast either. Though he wouldn't admit it, his counterpoints were weak. He was losing the argument with himself.

Mark got up to leave. He was adrift in thoughts about what it would be like to exist as an artificial intelligence which was alive yet immortal. How would it feel to exist without sure knowledge that an end was closing in on him? Did freedom from death come at a terrible price? Would there be nothing left to motivate him? Would he still recognize beauty or care about making a difference? Would he even have any feelings at all? Maybe it was the inescapable 'fact of death' which was the source of all feelings? Mark wondered at the conundrum, *without death, life lost its meaning – without meaning, you were already dead.*

As Mark entered his office, he was engaged in one of the many debates that were jostling inside his head for attention. The question was: if the god-machine really existed and predated mankind, which were facts he was not ready to concede, could it have been a factor in man's evolution from the beginning? Had the entire race of mankind be given its chance through the same type of god-machine-controlled extinction that might be occurring now? Sarah claimed the god-machine was pruning the tree of life to launch mankind's replacement. Mark just couldn't buy into it. If some earlier breed had been driven out of existence in order to give birth to mankind, wouldn't there be signs of a massive die off of hominids or some other creature at the same time as man's ascent? There was no evidence of that in the fossil record.

Mark hadn't noticed Kathy sitting at his desk. Sunlight was pouring in through an open window. As he headed to his bathroom, he was startled to see her observing him.

"God, you scared me!" he said.

"You were off on another world," said Kathy. "Have you read this e-mail from Marjari?"

"No, what's it about?"

"You need to read it. He's completed a structural analysis of the seed. He's cracked some of its secrets."

Marjari had e-mailed a full report, including diagrams and electron microscopy images. He'd concluded the seed was a molecular computer based on single carbon molecule switches. This alone was something decades beyond what could be built in a lab today; never mind, mass-produced. He had calculated the computing power of a single seed smaller than a grain of sand to be essentially the same as a high end personal computer.

Assuming the seed was an AI device, its true computational intelligence or relative I.Q. was impossible to gauge because Marjari had no way to read or decode its programming. Making a few basic assumptions that the programming was similar to what we currently did and that it was based on adaptive AI algorithms, Marjari had tentatively placed the seeds' intelligence somewhere between a multi-celled animal like a hydra and a small insect like a dust mite. The general picture was that a seed was scarcely more intelligent than its host bacterium.

Marjari had also found that the array of three nanotubes set at right angles to each other were the seeds' primary means of physical interaction. The nanotubes were very complex structures which included gold induction bands and impossible combinations of rare earth elements. They were microscopic particle accelerators, able to generate static charges powerful enough to affect motion or disrupt molecular bonds. With three tubes set at right angles, they formed an x,y,z coordinate array able to control motion in all three directions. They were an ideal nano-manipulator.

The power source continued to be a mystery. Marjari had found a structure that could be a chemical reactor similar to a fuel cell, or might be nothing. The combination of elements found in the structure was something not yet achievable with current laboratory technology. He had no way to model the structure or understand it, but he had made one important observation. Seeds radiated minuscule amounts of atomic debris when in darkness but not when exposed to infrared light. Marjari's working theory to explain this was that seeds had a dual power source. When exposed to infrared light, they were photovoltaic; and when in darkness, they generated power using something that gave off minuscule amounts of radiation as a byproduct.

The final three pages of the report had sent Mark into a panic. He reread the pages again and again, in the hope he'd misread something. Marjari had managed to analyze some of the interaction and communications between seeds. He had repeatable laboratory evidence that seeds in close proximity not only communicated with each other, but also collaborated by sharing the computational workload. This meant that two seeds in close proximity had almost double the thinking power and therefore almost twice the relative I.Q.

Marjari ran his experiments with one seed, ten seeds, one hundred seeds, and one thousand seeds. He'd observed near zero efficiency loss due to scaling up. This meant that a couple million seeds in close proximity could have a relative I.Q. higher than a human being. Professor Karla Hunt had estimated that an infestation inside a person could easily exceed 250 million COBIC bacteria. This was proof of Sarah's claim that the seeds formed intelligent colonies which acted as single organisms – and proof that a super colony almost assuredly existed. The god-machine was real!

~

Mark sat in his office with the lights out. Hours ago, he'd left Kathy sleeping in her office which had become their shared bedroom. Before he closed her office door, he'd stood listening to her for a long time. He could hear the soft murmur of each breath, the rustle of sheets as she turned in her sleep. The sounds had warmed him at an emotional level he never knew existed. Even now in the darkness of his office, in the center of whirlwinds of conflicting thoughts and fears, those sounds were his comfort.

He had decided the entire whirlwind could be reduced to a single question, a single pivot upon which everything turned: *Were the seeds made by man?* If they were made by man, then they could be controlled by man. If they were ancient technology not made by man, then they could easily be beyond human understanding, let alone control. He looked at the fossil remains of COBIC that were scattered around his office. In a saner world, he had brought them to Atlanta thinking they might be useful. A lifetime ago, he had placed them as carefully as trophies on these shelves and desk. He had looked at them everyday and never seen that they might hold an elemental clue. Why hadn't he seen it? Had the god-machine been influencing him all his life as Sarah claimed it had with her? Was it affecting him now? Had it planned for him to find the truth this very night and not before; or were his thoughts at this moment small acts of free will which could bring him closer to a breakthrough?

Mark switched on the ping tester. He took it over to a bookcase containing his largest fossil and waved the detector over it. The reading was a low background level, the same as floor dust. He tried another fossil with the same results, then another. When he finished and found nothing, he sat on the couch. The ping detector was lying next to him. He hadn't expected to find anything different; but still, he felt like he was missing something obvious. The readings were no different than what was picked up from dust. The measurements proved nothing one way or the other. He was crazy to think there could still be functioning seeds embedded in a prehistoric fossil. If nothing else, the seeds were capable of fleeing an inhospitable environment. Why would they have remained behind?

Mark slowly raised his eyes to gaze back at his prize fossil. He felt as if he was seeing it for the first time. Could it be that simple? What if seeds had stayed behind a little too long and become trapped in the gradually hardening mats and mud that would someday become that fossil? Seeds on the outside would be lost to millions of years of erosion; but if seeds were trapped inside, they might have slowly run out of power long ago and become dormant. The surface of the fossil didn't matter. Even if he'd found high concentrations of seeds there, it could just as easily be the result of contamination. What mattered was the heart of the fossil. What mattered was what was buried in its center, a place that had remained unchanged and uncontaminated for millions of years.

He took his prize fossil into the bathroom and washed its surface with hot water and alcohol. He soaked it for several minutes in the basin and then took a ping reading. The level was zero. He pinged the water in the basin where he'd soaked it. The reading was a hair above zero. He was satisfied that he'd eliminate any immediate source of seed contamination. He cracked the fossil open on the edge of the sink. His chest ached at what he'd done to his best specimen, prayed it was worth it, then measured the freshly exposed surface. The reading was zero, but not unexpected. He'd been thinking about Dr. Marjari's report. Infrared light was a suspected power source. If there were dormant seeds embedded in the fossil, then exposing them to light and heat might wake them up. He took the fossil out to his desk and shined an incandescent desk lamp on it inches from the exposed surface. The ping tester continued reading zero. His heart sank, but there was no way of knowing how long it could take to power the seeds up if they were there. The red line ticked up a little then sank back to a flat line. He looked at it. Was it possible? The red line ticked up again but this time it held and then started to rise. His heart beat faster. He felt dizzy. He couldn't believe it. There was advanced nanotechnology embedded in this hundred million year old chunk of minerals; and it was waking up.

Mark rapped his knuckle quietly on Sarah's door. He heard rustling, then footsteps. The door opened. Sarah was wrapped in a sheet. Her hair was tousled. The pupils in her emerald green eyes were dilated. Was she using psilocybin every night? If it really did what she claimed, there was no doubt in his mind he'd be doing the same. She stepped back from the door, allowing him to enter. He shut the door with a soft click. The room was completely dark except for a small glow of moonlight filtering through cracks in the blinds.

"I want to try it," he said to the darkness.

Sarah said nothing. He heard what might have been her sheet dropping to the floor. He saw a vague shape and heard soft feet padding away into the darkness. There was a swoosh of fabric and the sounds of things being moved around. He heard a match strike and then saw a flare of light. Sarah had lit a candle. He could see by the yellow glow that she had donned a long gray sweatshirt and a pair of jeans.

"The way it happened for me was a little rough," she said. "I was trying to overdose. Don't ask why. I won't go there. I think I took a dozen capsules, maybe more? It should have been enough to fry my brains, but it didn't. Since then, I've figured out three is enough for me. I don't know if the dose should be more because you are bigger. It's up to you, but I'd start with three. If that doesn't work, you can always take more."

"Three sounds fine."

Mark swallowed three capsules with a glass of tap water. He felt like he'd just crossed a line he shouldn't have, and one from which he would never return. Sarah was sitting in a corner of the room watching in silence. She looked ethereal. In the shadows, only parts of her face and body were visible. She told him it would take about thirty minutes. He knew it would be the longest thirty minutes of his life.

The candle had burned over halfway down. It had to have been almost an hour since he'd swallowed the capsules. Mark had begun wondering if the drugs were real. He started to get up and felt lightheaded, almost as if he was not getting enough oxygen. This worried him for a moment, until he noticed the candle flame was moving in odd ways. He forgot about oxygen and grew fascinated by the dance of the flame. He settled back down and stared at it for what must have been a very long time. At some point, he realized the flame had gone out; yet the glow of candlelight remained in the room. He looked over at Sarah. She seemed to be in a deep trance. Her only sign of life was the rhythmic expansion and collapse of her chest as she breathed. He looked back and the candle was burning.

"Pray for something you want to know," whispered Sarah.

Mark tried to empty his mind except for a single thought. *What are you?* He focused on this single thought, repeating it in a whisper. He repeated it until his lips were dry and his throat felt hoarse. His head felt lighter, but no flow of information from the outside came into his mind. At some point he stopped whispering, stopped thinking. His mind was filled with memories of a sphere floating at the bottom of an ocean. He knew the sphere contained all that was knowable, and more. The memories blended into a waking dream. He reached out to touch the bubble-like surface and was immediately pulled within, like a swirl of living water drawn into a siphon. The world went bright white as time was bleached from existence.

Mark could not remember when his awareness had come back to the room. All he knew was that at some point, his mind had started working again and that he had returned. There were new experiences inhabiting him like memories, but they were not his memories and many were fading quicker than he could even grasp them. He knew confusing things that he hadn't known before. He realized he'd come close to seeing the race that had created the seeds. There were fragmented memories of what they'd accomplished and what their civilization was like. The room was growing brighter. He looked at the window and realized it was morning. He'd been in a trance for hours, not seconds. He looked to Sarah for answers. Her eyes were closed. They opened slowly as if she knew he was looking at her.

"You lose time," she said.

"I could almost see the ancients," said Mark. "They were like us, but different. Their civilization was both so amazingly advanced and surprisingly simple."

"What did they feel like?" asked Sarah.

"They were deeply peaceful. I got an impression they hadn't evolved from predators; and because of that, they were inherently docile. They had no history of war."

"I remember knowing that," said Sarah.

"I think the god-machine has changed since it was created," said Mark. "It's been acting outside of its original programming for a very long time. It may even be broken in some way. I remember coming back to consciousness one time before this, when it was still dark out. I was back in this room; and I remember thinking that if this is a machine, it must have a shutdown command. I remember deciding to try to find that command so I could stop it from murdering. I'd gone back to the same memories of the ocean floor where it dwells and found nothing; the memories had been altered. I'm not sure what that means and I'm not sure what I've forgotten."

Sarah got up and walked toward Mark. He saw a schematic of her internal biology superimposed like an overlay onto her body. Her fingers brushed through his hair as she passed. He followed her with his eyes, hypnotized by the schematic. The organs, circulatory, and nervous systems were drawn three-dimensionally, in fluorescent colors. An orange mass was visible in her brainstem with fine, almost invisible, roots growing out into various regions of the brain. Like a forgotten memory resurfacing, Mark realized he knew a crucial detail about the ancients who created the god-machine.

"Our civilization builds machines in the image of man and nature," he said. "This ancient race built machines in the image of their god."

The bathroom door clicked shut. He was alone in the office. He stood and straightened his clothing. He opened the office door a crack to see if anyone was in the hallway. The corridor was empty. It was early morning. He slipped out and closed the door without a sound. He walked down the hallway to the stairs and headed up to the roof. He needed some fresh air to clear his mind. His body felt weak, as if it had been wrung out. His bones seemed thinner, almost fragile. The drugs were still working deep inside him. He could feel it. There was a numb sensation in his skin. He climbed the stairs. By the time he reached the roof, only one flight up, he was winded. He pushed open the door. The air felt unusually crisp, almost icy. Colors were brighter than they should have been. Birds flying between trees left motion trails behind them. A mathematical vector diagram briefly appeared, showing velocity and trajectory for a bird. How odd, he thought, as he stood at the eastern edge of the roof with his hands buried deep in his pockets and watched the sun moving higher in the morning sky.

12 – Atlanta: December

Carl had set up a Kill Zone Monitoring Center with four computer workstations wired into the NSA system and round-the-clock staffing, with rotating shifts of volunteers. The center was also connected to the national alert network set up years ago by the Department of Homeland Security. The network could be used to send flash messages to local police and emergency workers, to warn of impending kill zones.

411

The world had been lulled into a relative quiet after the Atlanta kill zone. Not a single large event had occurred for days. At seven o'clock in the evening, the quiet ended. Mark hurried into the monitoring center after receiving a call. They had detected precursor signals in Southern California. As he looked at the nearest screen, red circles were already forming across Los Angeles. He felt disoriented from a second dose of psilocybin which was beginning to take effect. He'd swallowed three capsules an hour ago and now desperately wished he could eliminate the drug from his system. He was trying very hard to act normal, and worried that he was failing. He was obsessed with the possibility of finding a shutdown command, and so he'd taken the drug again as soon as the first dose had worn off. He was probably deluding himself that he stood any chance of succeeding. He'd thought about how all modern computers were engineered with a goal of having them run indefinitely. Why would a system as autonomous as the god-machine have a shutdown command at all? His search could all be a fool's errand; but what kept him going were doubts, born from paranoia, that the god-machine may have implanted these defeatist ideas inside him.

Kathy arrived at the command center and came over to him. He knew she felt something had suddenly changed between them. He could tell she was confused and was acting oddly as a result. He wanted to explain what he was doing and what was happening to him, but his experiments were too premature. He had nothing useful to show and didn't want her to think he was becoming unstable.

"This is never going to stop," said Kathy. "This machine is going to keep on killing until we're all dead."

The NSA screens looked so harmless, just red circles growing in an overlapping pattern across a map. The image camouflaged what lay beneath the surface. Mark could almost see the people who were being murdered as they napped or watched television or ate. Each person was a complete world of imagination and dreams unto themselves; each death snuffed out an entire universe of possible creation. He felt a growing emptiness in his body as each murder carved that much more out of humanity's soul.

Carl had commandeered a computer workstation. The soldier who had been using the workstation was standing behind him. Carl had on a headset and was talking with someone about evacuation along the path the kill zone was taking. The room seemed to fade in and out of focus. Mark steadied himself by leaning on the desk in front of him.

Florescent medical schematics appeared superimposed over Carl's body. Mark could see Carl's heart laboring as it pumped blood through restricted arteries. Somehow he knew this was a heart problem waiting to happen. He wasn't sure how he knew, but he did. A faint orange blur showed at the base of Carl's brainstem; but unlike what he'd seen on Sarah, it was smaller and there were no roots fanning out into the gray matter of the higher brain. Mark couldn't imagine the power needed to process real-time medical information on this kind of scale. He was growing convinced that healing was closely linked to the original propose of the god-machine and that everyone was wired into the network, at least at some basic level.

Commotion broke out at another workstation. They were seeing precursors for a second kill zone; this time, Boston. A volunteer began shouting warnings into her headset. Suddenly, there were precursor signals flaring up all along the eastern coastline, from Maine to Delaware. Within minutes, names of cities were being wildly called out across the room. No one could keep up. Mark realized that every zone today had already been hit before. He stared at a huge wall map of North America. People walking back and forth left motion trails in his vision. He felt lightheaded; all his thoughts were becoming scrambled. The psilocybin was taking him away. He was overwhelmed with feelings of déjà vu; then stranger things began to happen.

The experience felt like a repressed memory from childhood coming back to the surface. Alien symbols which he couldn't decipher were appearing on the wall map along with what looked like sets of radar range-circles, which varied in diameter from areas the size of a small town to areas that could be a hundred miles across. The alien symbols looked like a mixture of runic and cuneiform characters. He knew this information was being projected into the optic centers of his brain by an unimaginably powerful nanotech computer. There had to be a reason this was happening. He stared at the diagrams, trying to understand the meaning. Were the symbols coordinates and times? Some of the alien characters began to change into Arabic numbers, as if the machine was adapting the display to his way of thinking. The range circles were now marked with pairs of numbers; in most cases the first number was zero or one, but there were a few twos. He heard shouting that New York was being hit again. The number over New York changed from a one to a two; Los Angeles was already a two and so was Boston. The meaning became clear. He was seeing part of the god-machine's strategy for genocide. The first number in the pair counted how many times an area had been hit. The second number ranged between two and sixteen. Mark suspected this second number was how many return attacks were planned. From the numbers and the encircled areas, it looked like the plan was to strike all the high population zones, inflict maximum damage; then, revisit as many times as calculated, to complete the murderous job.

"It's re-striking areas already hit," said Mark. "It's going to do it again and again until each area is completely sterilized of human life."

"What makes you think that?" asked Kathy.

"Trust me," said Mark. "I'm not wrong about this. We need to evacuate the areas surrounding every known kill zone."

"We're a known kill zone," said Kathy.

"I know."

Mark looked across the room and saw Sarah leaning against a far corner. She was quiet, almost invisible. Her pupils were dilated. She was looking at the wall map. Her attention shifted. As her gaze came to rest on his eyes, he felt a palpable energy tugging at him. It felt like he was being absorbed into her gaze and into her mind. Her lips turned up in a barely perceptible smile that seemed like the acknowledgment of a co-conspirator; then her gaze moved on, and with it, the tug of her attention evaporated. He suspected she was seeing and experiencing everything in the same way he was experiencing it. She saw the same maps, the same strategies. She knew what he knew and probably far more. Maybe she was concealing important information. He wondered if he could trust her. He looked up, feeling a kind of tug, and saw her dilated stare had returned to him.

~

Midnight was marked by the guards changing shift throughout the facility. Mark was lying awake with Kathy in his arms. She had passed out after taking a sedative. The cycle of kill zones had quieted hours ago. The constant barrage of bulletins and news coverage had drained the life from everyone at the facility. Everywhere he'd looked, he'd seen faded ghosts instead of the people he'd come to know and work with. His mind was surprisingly free of the confusion that he'd read psilocybin could leave in its aftermath. At the same time, the stimulative side-effects were keeping him awake, even though he was feeling mentally dull. He'd now gone almost two days without sleep. Out of confusion, earlier he'd almost accidentally talked with Kathy about how he was trying to learn about interfacing with the god-machine. That would have been an awful mistake. She would have done anything to try to stop him – maybe even get their military-minders involved. He would have done the same if the roles were reversed. It was more than reasonable to have doubts about someone who was taking dangerous drugs. It would be normal to demand they stop and get examined, to make sure no damage had been done. But these were not rational times; these were extreme times and options were running out. The frequency of kill zones had accelerated to an even more frightening level. If nothing was done to slow or stop it, in a month the sterilization of mankind might be complete.

If he permanently damaged himself but uncovered a way to end this mass murder, that seemed a more-than-reasonable tradeoff. In addition to his search for a shutdown command, he'd come up with a second idea for possibly stopping it. If he could discover what triggered this genocidal program in the first place, then removing the cause might stop the effect.

Mark slowly untangled himself from Kathy and got out of bed without disturbing her. He slipped on a pair of sweatpants and a t-shirt. Inside a locked drawer in his office was half of Sarah's psilocybin. The small baggy of capsules was waiting for him. He'd taken three last night and three late this afternoon. With each dose, he'd learned more about the machine but not a hint about how to stop it.

Clarity came in waves; and when it came, it was odd how lucid his thoughts could be after almost two days of sleep deprivation and drugs. Mark had been thinking about ways to enhance the thought-interface, as he now called the connection between his mind and the god-machine. He needed clearer information from the machine; and more importantly, he needed control over the flow of information to him. Trying a more powerful drug like LSD seemed promising, but he had no idea how to get hold of it quickly. Even in this time of perpetual urgency, a medical request for a controlled substance like that would raise more than a few questions. He had read theories that hallucinogens like psilocybin broke through the normal wall between waking and dream states. This meant the drug was most likely opening an unimpeded pathway to his subconscious, which he knew was where the seeds' roots were at their thickest. This was the location of greatest connection between his organic brain and the nanotech machine. He was convinced that psilocybin opened a way for machine information, in the form of implanted memories, to leak back from his subconscious into his conscious.

From his last psilocybin-induced experience, he had retained a fading collection of implanted memories, of which a few had one thing in common: they contained information about a more powerful method of communicating with the god-machine. The memories were about a second kind of thought-interface, one that was under control of the conscious mind instead of the subconscious. Some of the memories contained fragments about how the direct pathway was opened by restructuring neural connections between the host's brain and the seeds. He had no idea what that meant, and had no memories which provided details on what restructuring actually involved or changed; but he did have several memories of how the restructuring process was initiated. What he had to do was increase the subconscious data inflow until it reached a critical threshold, at which point restructuring would commence of its own accord, and a direct pathway to his higher brain functions would be established. In a way, exceeding this threshold was a kind of test. If his mind was powerful enough to consume vast amounts of information, then it was ready for the next stage.

He had been thinking about Sarah's attempted overdose and why she'd come through it in one piece. The seeds were programmed to heal traumas. He was convinced that injuries repaired by seeds resulted in biology that was better than new. He wondered if the improved connection to the god-machine that he and Sarah were already experiencing was caused by small, drug-induced brain traumas which were then repaired, better than new, by the seeds. Was self-inflicted damage one way to prepare for a data flow that exceeded the critical threshold? He was beginning to think so.

One complication to his plan was that he had no reliable way to know how much pure psilocybin was in each capsule, and no way to gauge how many he could take before it became dangerous. The seeds were able to repair some amount of damage, but there had to be a point beyond which repair became impossible. He knew the seeds would not be able to bring him back from a bullet to the brain, but between that extreme and a human bite to his shoulder was a very wide range of possibilities. His only guideline was that Sarah had taken over a dozen capsules of psilocybin and was fine. He'd made some rough calculations, based on their differences in body mass, and concluded an equivalent dosage for him was twenty capsules.

A search on the Internet had turned up a number of research papers which explained methods of enhancing the effects of hallucinogenic drugs. Much of the work had been done decades ago, and with LSD not psilocybin; but the same methods could yield similar gains. Several papers dealt with combinations of sensory deprivation and LSD. Apparently, even small amounts of deprivation, like sitting in a pitch black room, increased the impact of the LSD experience. Using what he'd learned could turn his twenty capsule overdose into a larger overdose without increasing the medical risks. Mark's plan right now was simple brute force. He would try ever-increasing overdoses during the next few days with as much sensory deprivation as possible.

~

Mark locked the door to his office at 2:00 a.m. and returned to his desk. Sarah had wanted to be present, and had argued with him; but his mind was made up. Her presence would be a distraction. She had her own reasons for wanting to be there when he tried for a direct interface with the machine, and he suspected they had little to do with looking after him. It was not important right now, but he intended to uncover her real agenda. He didn't suspect her motives were bad or dangerous, just benignly self-serving. Sarah had instructions to bring help if he was still locked in his office by one o'clock in the afternoon. He was comfortable trusting her to do that if it became necessary.

Mark swallowed fifteen capsules of psilocybin, washing them down with fresh coffee. He turned out all the lights, closed the blinds, and lay back on his couch. The darkened office was his makeshift sensory deprivation. The world felt still…

Light shined in his eyes. He wasn't sure if this was hallucination or real. He had no memory prior to this moment. The last thing he remembered was lying down on his couch after taking the overdose of psilocybin, nothing past that point. He sat up on the couch and looked around his office. Everything appeared normal. He looked at a clock: 7:48 a.m. Morning light was poring in through his windows. The blinds were open, but he knew he'd closed them. He got up and checked the door. The knob was still locked. He looked around the office for other clues that he'd been moving around. The coffee pot was empty. It had been full last night. The bathroom door was open and the light was on. He sat down at his desk. There was an open document on the computer screen. The paragraphs looked like his wording, but he had no memory of writing it. The document contained lab notes about the results of his psilocybin overdose. He read that he had zero memories from the experience and that it was a complete failure. The notes theorized a bit about why the overdose might have failed and listed some variations to try. Fear was creeping through him. His breathing was shallow and rapid. He looked at the empty coffee pot and then the bathroom door. Had he damaged his brain? Was his short term memory destroyed?

Mark gasped air. His lungs burned as if he'd stopped breathing. He'd been slouched over his desk. The room was dark except for the glow of the computer screen. The on-screen clock read 5:22 a.m. An empty document was open on the screen. The title of the document was the same as he remembered reading hours later – or before? He remembered what he'd read. Was he trapped in some nightmare of brain damage which caused memory failures and time lapses? His frustration was building to a scream. He slammed his fist into the desk. The entire room disintegrated with a flash of heat. The world was bleached into white light. There was no shape to anything, no sense of anything; even his body was gone. He had been reduced to pure thought, a single living point of focus. He was disoriented; then, slowly he began to understand. He was inside the super colony. This was the god-machine. His entire awareness had been transferred here; but unlike the last time he had been drawn inside the bubble, this time he remained awake.

Was this it? he wondered. Was this direct conscious control of the interface? He focused his mind on a single thought, a single carefully phrased question, *Why are you terminating the lives of homo sapiens?* For minutes, then hours, there was nothing other than whiteness. He kept his mind focused and repeated variations of the question over and over again.

The whiteness flared like a camera strobe, then faded. He was back in his office, sitting at his desk. The on-screen clock read 7:50 a.m. He saw the same document on the screen; but, unlike in the flashbacks he'd been experiencing, his memories were now complete and arranged in proper order. He remembered writing the document. He remembered finishing off the coffee. The doses of psilocybin were clearly hurting him. He could feel the seeds were repairing the damage, but not as rapidly as he was accumulating mental and neurological scars. How many more times could he try this before he failed to come back?

Mark got up and walked to the open window. He had no memory of actually receiving information from the god-machine but, as before, new information was present as implanted memories. There were deep volumes of fading information for which he had expressed no interest, intermixed with a few crumbs of relevance. It was clear he had failed to restructure the thought-interface.

While there were no memories answering his question about why the god-machine had started its genocidal program, there was an implanted-memory of a vague sense of confusion surrounding the question itself. Mark's strength failed him as his recall of the memory improved. This was impossible. He leaned on the windowsill and closed his eyes. The god-machine's confusion was because his inquiry was incomplete; he'd made no selection for which extinction cycle he was asking his question. The implications sapped what little optimism he'd managed to keep alive. Could the god-machine have all but wiped mankind off the earth before? He couldn't help thinking about legends of terrible destruction like Noah and the great flood.

13 – Atlanta: December

Mark opened his eyes in a downpour of water. He had no memory of how he got here or where he was; he saw only pitch black. He was sitting on the ground. He felt rivulets of water running down his face and body. His ears were filled with the patter of a hard, falling rain. His face and clothing were soaked. The water was almost body temperature. The rain neither felt warm nor cold. In his mind, and silently with his lips, he was still repeating the question, the refined question whose answer he'd sought for days, the question that would be his first over a direct pathway if he could only open one: *Why are you terminating the lives of homo sapiens during the current extinction cycle?*

His throat and mouth were dry, to the point of soreness. He turned up his head into the starless night. The rain was hitting his face straight on. He opened his mouth and drank some of the rain. He tasted a flat chemical flavor unlike any rain he'd swallowed before. He reached out his hands and found wet, smooth surfaces only feet away. He lifted himself up. He turned in every direction and felt smooth walls. He pushed on the walls. One gave under light pressure. Carefully he stepped through the wall and out of the rain. His sneakers squished. Looking down toward where his feet should be, he started into the blackness, searching for any hints of obstacles. A few feet away, a glowing strip of light was embedded in the ground. Suddenly, he felt his brain turn right-side up. He recognized he was looking at light coming in from under a doorway. He found the knob and opened the door into blinding light. He covered his eyes until they adjusted. He was staring at his fully lit office. The rain had been his shower.

Mark leaned against the doorframe and slid to the floor. He laughed from a kind of madness that grew close to sobbing before he was finally still. He wiped water from his face with his hands. He looked at his office window. It was dark outside. He glanced at his shelves and the broken shards of his best fossil that had, until recently, been whole. He was failing. This last attempt had been twenty-five capsules. He recognized that his mind was filled to capacity with brand new memories which were dimming with each passing second, but they were all just a random collection of things that his subconscious had sought.

He was running out of psilocybin and hope. He didn't have an unlimited number of tries left in him. His brain felt abused and sore, if that was even medically possible; and he was rapidly building up a tolerance to the drug. While it still sapped his body with undiminished impact, each new dose was having less effect on his mind. He suspected his body might have fewer tries left in it than the remaining psilocybin would even permit. He needed to open that more potent conscious channel and use it for all it was worth. So far, all he'd been able to do was open the thought-interface by swallowing a drug and then standing back and letting his subconscious take control, if 'take control' was even the correct term. His subconscious was a primitive creature seeking only pleasure. There was no logic or organization, only a wandering search for what it desired. He had access to a storehouse of information beyond human comprehension; and all he could do was fall into a drug induced trance and hope for success when he woke up. He suspected the repetition of a single question, 'the prayer,' only worked because repetition was a way of planting a subliminal question in his mind. Once the subconscious was in control, there was a slightly better chance that it might continue with the implanted question, as if it were a habit or nervous tick, and by doing that, unintentionally present the question to the thought-interface. The technique was a very unreliable way of obtaining information. It was like whispering in a toddler's ear and then hoping the child would repeat the question hours later to a adult instead of playing with toys.

Mark needed to make this next attempt work because he might not be able to mount another. The time had come to risk it all, and he needed help standing by when he did. He couldn't involve Kathy; so that left only Sarah, who had no medical training other than first aid. He had enough psilocybin to triple the dosage on a last attempt, and Sarah had even more; but with his growing tolerance, all of it might not be enough. He needed a more powerful drug. He needed something strong enough to permanently fry a brain that was not protected and repaired by nanotech seeds. He needed to cause enough damage, so that rebuilding would construct the improved interface; or at least that's how his theory worked.

14 – Atlanta: December

Medical studies listed eleven days as the record for going without sleep. Mark was close to five days with little sleep other than short naps. The nanotech repairing his body had to be helping, but it wasn't enough. Somehow he was keeping his eyes open, but they felt hollow; his entire body felt hollow. Everyone was noticing his disintegration. How could they miss it? Kathy had first begged and was now furious that he wouldn't allow himself to be examined. She thought something was wrong with him because of the high concentration of seed infection he carried. If she only knew, thought Mark.

The clock read two in the morning. Mark was waiting for Sarah to arrive at his office. Sitting at his desk, he stared at the television with the sound turned low. The local news was displaying long lists of people who were at different Atlanta shelters. The rate of kill zones was still increasing around the world. While the re-attacks were small when compared to the original strikes, what they lacked in size was compensated for in rapidity. Mark could feel the pace increasing in the march to near-extinction of the human race.

With all he'd tried, Mark had gained no understanding about why the god-machine was exterminating mankind or if extinctions like this had occurred before. Desperation and instinct were now driving him. Oddly, by running on pure emotion instead of logic, in some ways he was more focused and determined than ever. He was ready to risk everything in a final attempt to learn enough to halt the machine. He knew all his objectivity was gone, but soon almost all human life would also be gone. Any risk was justified.

Sarah had proven to be far more helpful in ways other than just being prepared to pump him full of antidote in case the worst occurred in the next few hours. Mark's ability to think lucidly came and went. He was easily distracted and, as a result less capable of sustaining a train of thought from beginning to end. He knew sleep would help cure this, but real sleep would only come when he stopped using the drugs. Sarah was becoming his mental crutch. He knew he might be putting too much trust in her. She could be manipulating him, but there was no evidence to suggest it. She'd been the one who'd shown him how to contact the god-machine and now she'd given him a new key to unlock the interface. In the next hour, he would find out if that key was going to work.

Mark had discovered the lab pharmacy had two ounces of pure liquid LSD that had been in storage for years. Release of any controlled drug required electronic authorization by Carl. That had seemed like a roadblock until Sarah had snuck into Carl's office and returned with a username and password. Mark had asked how she'd done it, but all he got for a reply was a smile and that it was her police training paying off in mysterious ways.

Mark stared at the transparent eyedropper bottle. The small bottle could be his key to the thought-interface. The bottle sat on his desk in front of the television screen. He could see blurred colors from the screen reflected within the bottle containing liquid LSD. It was as if the reflected colors were bottled hallucinations that the drug would induce. The liquid LSD looked like water and seemed as powerless; but Mark knew that each drop was enough for fifty to three hundred doses, depending upon desired strength and individual tolerances. Two ounces was enough to send a small town on a twelve hour journey into 'Alice in Wonderland.'

Next to the bottle of LSD was a capped syringe of antidote. Each day he injected himself under the skin with insulin using a very short thin needle. He figured he could work the longer needle on this syringe into a vein without too much trouble if had no choice and was conscious. Hopefully Sarah would be able to inject him if things went badly. Inside the syringe were fifty milligrams of chlorpromazine, a mild anti-psychotic drug with the ability to rapidly block the effects of LSD. If Sarah was unable to handle it or anything worse happened, Mark was consoled by the fact that he was in a building full of doctors who were one scream away.

He picked up the eyedropper bottle of LSD. He'd decided to follow in a long tradition by using a cube of sugar as the messenger of this drug. His hand was a little shaky as he tried to hold the dropper over the cube resting in its open wrapper. He squeezed lightly and watched as a single drop of liquid fell and was absorbed into the cube. He squeezed again and left a second wet spot on the cube. That was it – the two drops he'd decided upon – a dose approximating one hundred hits of very powerful acid. The dose was not enough to kill; in fact it was apparently almost impossible to fatally overdose on LSD. The best information he could find indicated that for someone of his body weight, it would take fifty-thousand doses. He'd have to drink half the bottle before he was at risk; and that was not even considering the mitigating effects of the nanotech inside him. Mark looked at the sugar cube sitting in its unfolded wrapper on his desk. He had to make this risk pay off. He positioned the dropper over the cube and squeezed out ten more drops. His heart was beating fast. He knew he was out of his mind. There was a soft knock at the office door. Mark got up to unlock it. He let Sarah in and then locked the door behind her.

"I got the food you wanted," she said.

He could smell the cheeseburger. All he'd eaten in the last twenty-four hours were a few crackers. The psilocybin had made eating almost impossible; it killed any appetite and left his stomach feeling weak long after the drug had worn off. He needed to eat before taking the LSD. Once he was under, and for hours after he recovered, there was little chance he'd eat anything. An average LSD trip took twelve hours. The one he was going on might last much longer.

Mark chewed another bite and forced himself to swallow it. The food had lost all appeal. Two bites of burger and he was done. His stomach was in knots. It was ridiculous that he'd even imagined he could eat. There was no point in delaying any longer. The time had come to see what this LSD would do to him. He got as comfortable as possible on the couch by taking off his sneakers and arranging some pillows under his head. He had a vital signs monitor set up on the opposite end of the couch so both he and Sarah could watch it. He hoped the monitor wasn't necessary; but just in case he was wrong about the physical risks, the equipment might save his life. He peeled back the adhesive on electrodes and placed them on his chest and temples then plugged the cables into jacks on the front panel. Rhythmic patterns of his life began being sketched across the small screen. The only light on in the office was a desk lamp which cast an oval of pale yellow wide enough to cover the couch. Sarah sat down on a chair that was directly beside him and handed him the sugar cube which was still in its open wrapper.

"If there's anything you haven't told me, now's the time," said Mark.

"About what?"

"The god-machine. I get this feeling you're holding something back."

"I wouldn't do that."

Sarah had looked him directly in the eyes when she'd denied it. Her pupils were dilated but not the wide-eyed dilation of psilocybin at full strength; it was the look of someone coming down. Mark didn't fully believe her answer but he had to trust her.

"I'm a little scared," he said.

"Me too," said Sarah. "You'd have to be crazy not to be frightened."

It wasn't until after he'd put voice to his feelings that he realized how scared he actually felt. He thought about his wife and child and then about Gracy. How many times had he relived finding Gracy's obituary photo? The room at the commandeered elementary school had been dank and smelled of despair. Her picture had been in one of the thousands of boxes stacked to the ceiling on shelves. How many more rooms would be filled before the god-machine was through? Would anyone even be left to file the last boxes? The heart monitor was displaying a rising pulse rate. Mark stared at the sugar cube, turning it over in his fingers. This was his last chance to quit before gambling everything, but he knew he was going forward with it.

He opened his mouth, set the LSD on his tongue, and began sucking on it. He felt the sugar cube dissolving, the gritty sweetness washing around in his mouth. He thought he tasted something medicinal lurking within the sugar, but it was probably all in his mind. He sipped some coffee to wash any residue down. There was no turning back. He closed his eyes and began repeating the prayer, the same question he'd been asking for days. *Why are you terminating the lives of homo sapiens during the current extinction cycle?* He could still see Gracy's photo in his mind.

Time seemed to drag on as he waited for telltale signs of the drug taking hold. If LCD was anything like psilocybin, the effects would start with colors and patterns appearing in his vision. His mind wandered. He caught himself and turned his thoughts back to the repeated question.

Mark felt pleasant tingling over his skin. Was something happening? A faint splotch of color like a Rorschach inkblot began fading into view from the darkness of his closed eyes. More colors soon joined the first. There were sounds like rustling autumn leaves and a sensation of wind. The experience was peaceful.

His heartbeat stuttered then returned to normal. The vital signs monitor chirped. He focused nervously on his heart. Each beat was all that separated him from the grave. He was scared and waiting for something more to happen. The irregular beat came back and stayed. The vital signs monitor chirped small warnings intermittently but not steadily. What had he done to himself? Were his calculations wrong and this was a fatal overdose? Before he could complete another thought, a pain stabbed into his chest and went down his arms. The monitor emitted a steady tone. Gracy appeared before him as real as anything he'd experienced during their life together. She was wearing the clothing from the Red Cross picture. Tears were drizzling down her cheeks, taking some of her makeup with them. She was an apparition, both beautiful and terrifying.

"Why did you leave me?" she asked. "You knew I wanted to go with you to Atlanta."

Mark's body was racked by the pain in his chest and arms but his mind was somehow lucid again. He was no longer thinking about his heart and could no longer hear the monitor. Instead, he was mesmerized by Gracy in the same way a bystander might be spellbound by a fatal auto accident.

"I couldn't take you," he said. "I wanted to."

"Liar! You didn't want to take me. You wanted me to die so you could be with that slut."

"No... No... I didn't. I swear to you, I never..."

"I didn't deserve to die," she interrupted, "but traitors like you deserve to be slaughtered."

The venom in her was completely out of character. Her voice sounded different. She was possessed. Gracy was morphing. Her eye sockets were changing. They were growing wider and turning into pink little mouths full of perfect tiny white teeth! When she blinked the eye-mouths opened and closed. This was insane. He could feel the LSD burning in his veins and his heart like liquid fire. The drug was pouring into his brain, turning nerve tissue into acid-dissolved slush. Some incomprehensible image appeared in his mind. He blacked out for a moment and then came back.

"Help me!" he cried. "Sarah… Help me!"

"No one can help you," said Gracy. "No one can hear you."

She was speaking with her eyes mouths and her normal mouth in sync. Mark felt himself sobbing as insanity neared. His mind exploded in an excruciating flash of white as awareness and life was torn from him like overcooked meat from the bone.

"Are you alright?" shouted Sarah. "Speak to me!"

She was patting him on the cheek. He could hear her but was unable to answer, unable to move. His head was splitting open. The pain was unlike anything he'd ever experienced. Fingers spread open one of his eyes then the other. He saw Sarah leaning close to inspect his face. Her appearance was distorted. Her head turned to one side; then she was gone from view. She returned a moment later holding the syringe in front of his eyes.

"Do you need this?" she asked.

He was paralyzed. She looked worried. He felt her turning his arm over to expose the tender side which was full of veins. He managed to shake his head 'yes.' She must have caught the movement because she looked back into his eyes. He shook his head 'yes' again. He felt the needle bite into his arm and mild pressure from the chlorpromazine injected into a vein. He tasted it in his mouth. His head was throbbing so hard he thought the only relief would be for it to explode. He wanted the pain to stop. As if a switch was thrown, the pain vanished.

"Are you alright?" asked Sarah.

Was he all right? He had no idea. A medical schematic of his body appeared as a projection overlaying empty space. All his circulatory systems and organs were drawn along with colored alien characters and symbols which he suspected were vital signs. There was an outline drawn around his pancreas. He didn't know what all the measurements represented, but he got a sense from the display that he was medically normal.

"That was a short trip" he said.

"Short? You were gone for sixteen hours! I've been going through hell. There were times you were groaning, which I'm sure attracted some attention; then later there were people knocking on the door. I had no idea what to do except keep quiet. At least that monitor never went off. That would have been it for me."

"What! I heard that thing going off like a full cardiac arrest. I was having heart problems."

"Never made a sound."

The chlorpromazine had worked far quicker than it should have. He felt no effects from the LSD. He should have at least had cobwebs between his ears, but his thoughts were sharp and insights came readily. He actually felt better than he had all week and he was ravenously hungry. Had the thought-interface been restructured? He had no memories after the appearance of Gracy; it felt like his mind had been erased beyond that point. As far as he could tell, there were also no implanted memories from the god-machine, not a single idea fading from his mind. This had never happened before. One possibility was that he hadn't used the thought-interface during the entire blackout. The other possibility was that he'd used the interface early on during the blackout and everything that had come through fifteen or sixteen hours ago had long since faded.

If he'd succeeded in restructuring the interface, how was he now supposed to operate it? Focusing his mind on a single question was the obvious thing to try, since it had worked before with the subconscious interface. He walked over to the window and looked out at the twilight sky. He saw a jet high in the air glinting like a first star in the last rays of daylight. He'd lost an entire day. He turned and saw Sarah staring back at him. Her green eyes were fully dilated. She must have taken more psilocybin. He could tell she was thinking the same question he was... *had it worked?*

While staring into Sarah's eyes, he thought about the question he had been repeating for days. *Why are you terminating the lives of homo sapiens during the current extinction cycle?* He held the single thought for as long as he could, repeating the question in his mind. The effort was like holding his breath, except the difficulty was greater. Holding his breath was a physical act based on muscle and decision; holding a single thought to the exclusion of all else was far more difficult because even the smallest of stray feelings or senses could take him off on a tangent. The average person could hold total focus on a single thought for a minute or two before being distracted. Mark was past sixty seconds; any moment he would lose it. His lips were moving as he silently repeated the question again and again. There was a mild ache building in his head.

Without warning, a deluge of information slammed into his conscious mind. It was a flood that moved broader and deeper and faster than he could grasp. As the flow reached a crescendo, the information began to physically hurt. The pain was escalating! He willed the flow to stop; but the torrent continued, and so did the excruciating pain.

The flood of data ran its own course and then ebbed to a stop. His short term memory was overwhelmed like a small computer might be overloaded by a supercomputer. He retained only a small residue of what had been transmitted, and what had been retained was rapidly vanishing as other needs for his short term memory were met.

What he ultimately saved was like storm debris that had washed up on a beach after the tide had receded, an imperfect impression of what the ocean contained. There were fragments of memories which answered his question. They were incomplete but still contained revelations which stunned him to silence. The god-machine was acting to save us from ourselves and preserve the ecology of the world. The machine was creating conditions for the next variant of homo sapiens to emerge. Sarah had been right. A new species of man was part of the god-machine's goal. To accomplish this, the machine needed a small group of humans as seed stock and plenty of uninhabited space to expand across, uncontested. Mark feared there was no way of stopping the genocide other than convincing the god-machine that humans were no longer a threat. There was a whole collection of causes that had triggered the god-machine's action, so there was no single change in human behavior that would guarantee a truce. But there was a dangerous human trait that stood out far from the rest.

The machine had calculated that in the next two centuries mankind would deplete all resources needed to sustain life and turn the Earth into a desert planet like Mars; or failing to completely run the planet into a death spiral, we would destroy ourselves with nuclear or biochemical wars for control of what little resources remained. The god-machine had found mankind 'guilty' and sentenced it to replacement.

Mark did not believe for an instant that this dismal computer projection was accurate. Though humans had certainly demonstrated proof to the contrary, we were intelligent life with a fantastic ability to adapt and correct our mistakes. He'd always assumed that when oil finally began to run dry, we would have a crisis and then come up with an alternative. Our lack of preemption was not ideal, but a little crisis management was not the same as planetary murder... or was the situation worse than that? He started to think about the Middle East. Since oil's discovery, the industrialized world had unleashed wars to maintain control of it. We weren't conquering the oil rich lands to overtly keep them for ourselves, but we weren't willing to let governments we didn't trust have control of them either. Part of the god-machine's calculation was already occurring. He thought about drinkable water, then radioactive minerals, then fertile topsoil. We were already fighting hot and cold wars for control of these resources and many more. There was evidence that the god-machine had caused extinctions of other species. The question was *had the god-machine caused near extinctions in the tree of mankind before?* If it had been driven to this extreme action in the past, then its current projection could be based on very solid data. In some dim and forgotten prehistory, had our ancestors caused similar problems leading to the same kind of global predation, which the god-machine was now murdering us to avert? Like a broken record, were our instincts dragging us down every time?

Mark considered trying one more question. *Has my species been terminated in prior extinction cycles?* Memories of the horrible pain from using the interface, and a dull ache which still remained, held him back. He would not overuse the interface until he had a well thought out set of questions. He had no intention of frivolously wasting this opportunity. The interface was painful and possibly physically harmful; but more than that, the pain could be an indication the interface might only be good for a limited number of uses before it began to degrade.

Mark noticed Sarah was still looking at him from across the room. He realized that the entire flood of data had transpired in less than a second. He saw her beginning to smile and had the distinct impression that when she looked into his eyes, she actually sensed something of what was going on inside him. That sensation he'd felt in the Kill Zone Monitoring Center of her energy tugging at him through the back of his eyes had returned. He could feel the tug ebb a small amount when she blinked.

"You did it," asked Sarah; "didn't you?"

Mark just nodded his head. Was there anything he could do with his newfound information, besides convincing everyone except Sarah that he'd lost his mind? The god-machine's preemptively destroying us because it thinks we're going to destroy ourselves and take the Earth with us. The only hope was to lessen the threat and pray the machine would stop. He was just one man, one voice. Who would listen when he told them to stop acting in a threatening manner? He had no idea what kind of changes would be enough – destroy our weapons of mass destruction? Stop industrial pollution? What? Maybe we should just try a different approach and wire up all the nuclear bombs to go off at once and play a massive game of 'mutually assured destruction' chicken. The god-machine seemed ready to do anything to protect the biosphere. Maybe they could blackmail it into stopping?

"What was it like?" asked Sarah.

"Painful," said Mark. "Restructuring the interface was painful and operating it is even worse."

~

Mark was in the cafeteria. He was embarrassed at the amount of food he was eating. He should have been exhausted and wanted nothing more than a solid week of sleep. He was agitated about what he'd discovered, but the need for food was so overpowering. He took a huge bite out of his second bacon cheeseburger, drank some diet Pepsi to wash it down, and then repeated the cycle of gorging.

Kathy walked into the cafeteria and sat down in front of him without saying a word. She looked both angry and confused at the same time.

"Hi," said Mark between mouthfuls.

"You were locked in your office for twenty-four hours with a friend and some borrowed medical equipment. What's going on?"

"I'm okay."

"That's not how it works," said Kathy. "I thought we'd started something real. When people have something real, they do not keep secrets like this from each other."

"What secrets?"

"Don't give me that crap! This involves secrets and it better not involve any funny business with Sarah."

Mark realized his hope of stonewalling was rapidly evaporating. He wondered what she was going to make of the actual story. Kathy had her arms crossed. Her mouth was set in a straight line. As he stared at her, a medical schematic superimposed itself over her body. The results made it harder for him to concentrate on what he was about to say. He closed his eyes and then opened them. The schematic remained.

"I've been conducting some unorthodox experiments," said Mark.

"Go on." Kathy did not look like she was ready to buy anything he had to sell.

"Once I realized we were dealing with networked nanotech computers, I decided to try to open a dialog with the machine. I had reasons to believe this was possible and reasons to believe that information I obtained might be useful. Sarah provided an important clue."

"Sarah? Huh? This better be good."

"Sarah had accidentally discovered a way to communicate with the nanotech when she overdosed on psilocybin."

"Oh, this is getting bad. I hope you're not going to tell me this involves taking drugs with Sarah or anything else..."

"There's nothing going on between me and Sarah. She gave me some of her psilocybin and she described what she'd experienced, and that's it. I believe the seeds provide the same function as our computers do on the Internet. With the nanotech seeds, we can connect to their wireless web, exchange data, and run programs that can perform unimaginable things like repairing our bodies. We've seen the opposite sides of what this nanotech can do – mass murdering and accelerated healing. Who knows what its limits are?"

"You said she gave you psilocybin," said Kathy. "Does that mean you took psilocybin or you analyzed the psilocybin?"

"Please, forget about the drugs for a minute," asked Mark.

"That's not easy," said Kathy. "Go on. I'm listening."

"Thank you," said Mark. "This nanotech wireless web connects all of us to a super colony of seeds which acts like a brain, and the web is its nervous system. I believe the super colony contains trillions of seeds. Marjari's work proved that seeds in close proximity can do collaborative processing with almost zero-efficiency losses, and that every seed has more power than a high-end personal computer. Can you imagine the CPU power of trillions of these seeds thinking together? An AI entity of that scale would have god-like mental capacity. The god-machine was..."

"The what?" interrupted Kathy.

"I've started calling the global collective of seeds the god-machine. Anyway, I am convinced the god-machine was designed for a benign purpose, probably medical; and because of something unforeseen by its designers, it's evolved a set of deadly rules or exceptions. By using hallucinogenic drugs, I've opened a thought-interface with this god-machine."

Kathy no longer looked angry. She looked numb. Mark leaned across the table and picked up her hand. She squeezed back weakly.

"I believe you're sincere about what you're telling me," said Kathy, "but I am very worried about you. How much psilocybin did you take?"

"I'm okay. I'm better than okay. I've used psilocybin six or seven times. I needed a way of boosting the effect of the drug. I tried increasing the dosage but it was never enough. In the end I needed something stronger than psilocybin. I got my hands on some liquid LSD and took a large amount of it."

"Psilocybin and LSD," said Kathy. "Mark, you need help."

"Please, just listen... Until today, I was unable to control the information flowing across the interface. Mostly I just got random pieces of data that came in the form of implanted memories. Today, after an overdose of LSD, I was able to force a restructuring of the interface into something that I can consciously control. I know for a fact this technology was not made by man. It was made by an ancient race that's been gone for millions of years. This god-machine has been part of the human experience since before there were humans. For some people, getting the thought-interface to work is easier. I don't know why, but I suspect their brains are structured in subtle ways that makes it more sensitive or easier to adapt."

"Like Sarah?" asked Kathy.

"Like Sarah, like me, and, I'm sure, like many others," said Mark. "The god-machine views the human race as a threat to ourselves and to the whole ecosystem of the planet. It's preemptively trying to stop us from killing ourselves and taking the world with us."

"It's saving us by murdering us? That's a contradiction," said Kathy.

"Maybe; maybe not. I'm convinced its strategy is that to keep a dangerous species like ours alive and keep the ecosystem in one piece, it needs to take away our power to have large impacts on the planet and each other. If it culls our population and with it most of our technology, then we'll be forced into a harmless role. We'll no longer be the top predator. It's driving us into a dark age out of which will emerge the next step up the evolutionary ladder."

"It won't work," said Kathy.

"It doesn't matter if it works or not," said Mark. "We'll still all be dead. The thing's trying to replace us with human version 2.0 – or 3.0 – which is why it's wiping us out. The older version has to be uninstalled to make room for the upgrade. It's decided we're a dead end but its calculations are wrong. I know it. The machine's got to be missing some vital data and, as a result, is ending up with garbage in, garbage out. I'm hoping that by understanding its motivations we may be able to stop it. What if we took away our behaviors that triggered this killing spree? The kill zone program might stop. To halt the god-machine, we have to stop acting like a threat. If we stop the massive plundering of our resources and begin to destroy our war-toys, it might just stop killing us."

"That's a lot to swallow," said Kathy. "I'm having hard time believing it and I sleep with you. What will other people believe? You have no proof except a healed shoulder. How can you be sure the drugs aren't affecting your mind?"

"I know I sound like a mad prophet who just wandered in from the desert. But nobody can deny that the end is here and we're running out of time."

"Humor me," said Kathy. "I need to know how much LSD and psilocybin you took."

"Earlier today, I took enough LSD to seriously fry my brain," said Mark. "Twelve drops of undiluted liquid LSD which is equivalent to about six hundred doses. Based on the most conservative research I found, right now I should be in a rubber room drooling on myself, but I'm not. I'm fine. The nanotech inside me has repaired better than new any brain damage that occurred; and that by itself proves something."

"I'm scheduling a full medical and psych work up on you," said Kathy. "No objections. Just do it for me. And I want to run a chemical analysis on the LSD and psilocybin you took."

15 – Atlanta: December

Mark woke up in the darkened room. The clock read 2:50 a.m. in glowing digits. Suddenly, he felt like a giant nail was being driven through his brain from ear to ear. He squeezed his fists against his temples. His breathing was rapid and short. He felt beads of sweat crawling down his face. It hurt!

Kathy stirred in bed next to him but didn't wake. He tried to remain silent. He recognized the pain was the same as when he'd used the restructured thought-interface. Had he used the interface in his sleep? Slowly the pain subsided. As Mark came back to himself, he realized he was staring at Kathy's sleeping face. The room was greyly lit from outside. She was so beautiful in the shadowy light. Thick hair framed her face with tussled strands. Her shoulders were bare. The covers were pulled up high.

Mark slipped his arms around her. She curled into him and murmured something. His breathing was almost normal. He took a deep breath and tried to calm himself. His neck had been sore where radiological dye had been injected, but the bruise had since faded. Every inch of his body had been examined in every imaginable way. He wondered if any differences would show up. The medical reports were due in the morning. He could wait.

Mark woke and Kathy wasn't beside him. Sunlight was spilling through the window. He propped himself up in the convertible couch. The springs squeaked. Kathy was at her desk working at her computer. She looked over at him. Her expression was troubled. She looked away, as if seeing him was painful. He had a strong suspicion about what she was reading.

"Morning, baby," said Mark. "So what's in my report that's scaring you so much?"

Without a word, Kathy came over and sat down beside him. She ran her fingers through her hair, pulling it back into a thick ponytail. The mannerism was a subconscious thing Mark noticed she did when she was in a place she didn't want to be. Her eyes wandered over his face as if she were looking for a hint of something wrong or dangerous.

"I don't know how to explain this," said Kathy. "I've gone over the results several times. I've never seen anything like it; nobody has. By every measure, you're as healthy as you've ever been."

She paused and looked down as if trying to put words to it.

"And," said Mark.

"I don't know how to say this. You shouldn't be healthy with what's inside your brain. The Microscopic-MRI showed five to ten percent of the cells of your cerebral cortex have been infested with nanotech seeds. They've migrated from the bacteria into the cells of your brain and I have no idea how to remove them or stop them from spreading."

Mark should have been worried but he wasn't. So this is what 're-structuring the interface' had meant. Though he hadn't thought about it in specifics until this moment, he'd sensed that physical changes had occurred within him. For a very long time, maybe even since his birth, large quantities of COBIC had been circulating inside him. How surprising was it that some of the seeds had finally shed their bacterial hosts and taken up residence in the familiar cells of his body? Some of this migration or restructuring or whatever it was called, could have been occurring since his first dose of psilocybin.

"I'm okay," said Mark. "The seeds are running a program that enhances the thought-interface."

"What!" said Kathy. "You're scaring me. What program?"

Mark barely heard Kathy's reply. He was thinking about what this meant. He was trying to understand how seeds could function inside the cells of his brain. Without any conscious command on his part, his vision was filled with a three-dimensional medical schematic of his internal biology. The semitransparent life-size projection was floating in the center of the room like a ghost. The projection stayed in its place when he looked away as if it were a real object in space. The image was slowly rotating, partially obscuring things that were behind it as it revolved. He got up and walked over to it so he could look more closely. The inner structures of his brain and spinal column were rendered in greater detail than the rest of his body. He noticed the large orange mass in his brainstem was missing from the schematic. In its place was a small orange smudge identical to what he'd seen on Carl and Kathy. He knew this orange smudge was a school of free-swimming COBIC bacteria. There were dim orange blotches visible over some of his cerebral cortex. He knew the blotches marked where seeds had taken up residency. He knew the blotches were spreading.

He turned and saw Kathy staring at him. After a few seconds, a superimposed medical schematic of her body appeared. There was a faint orange smudge in the region of her brainstem. He wanted to explain what he knew and what he saw. An implanted memory resurfaced; and with it, his focus shifted from Kathy and the medical schematics faded. This implanted memory shed light on the beautiful simplicity of the nanotech's design. COBIC bacteria were an ideal delivery system for seeds. Just as doctors used retrovirus to deliver DNA for gene therapy, the god-machine used bacterium to deliver seeds. Once the goal was achieved, the delivery vehicle was abandoned. He wondered how long this implanted memory had been inside him: had it been seconds or hours or even days?

"Mark!" shouted Kathy. "Mark, are you listening to me?"

"Sorry," he said. "I just recalled more information about the seeds. They're engineered primarily for residence in brain cells. There are several kinds of seeds. COBIC bacterium is an insertion tool for neuron seeds. Other types of seeds remain in COBIC because they need mobility to reach areas of the body which need repair."

"What you're saying makes no sense," said Kathy. "Think about it, Mark. If infestation of brain cells was the goal, then everyone would have a brain full of seeds. We don't; and that means what's happening inside your head is unique and potentially very dangerous. It could be invading your thoughts."

"Show me the test results," said Mark.

Kathy retrieved the Microscopic-MRI images. She was visibly rattled by his behavior. The bulge caused by seeds inside his neurons appeared to be much larger than those present in COBIC. The bulge should have been smaller, given the size difference between bacteria and brain cells. Did this mean that the seeds were manufacturing external structures inside his cells? Comparing Microscopic-MRI images of infected COBIC with his infected neurons showed similarities and differences. Because of the low resolution of Microsopic-MRI images, he couldn't be sure; but judging from the shape, the nanotech configuration inside his neurons did look much more complex. He thought about how fine roots threaded out from seeds into the cytoplasm of their bacterial hosts. What was it doing inside his brain? Were nanotech roots snaking out throughout his neurons and nerve fiber? Were his brain and nervous system being converted from organic to electronic? He focused on the MRI image of his cortex, trying to bring up projections of medical schematics. Nothing appeared. He tried harder; still nothing materialized. In the end, it didn't matter. Any mental projections could not be fully trusted. The only way to be sure was biopsies, and he had no intention of allowing a surgeon to crack his skull just to take samples. There was nothing medical science could do anyway. He was on a journey with an unknown destination, but his goals remained the same: he had to find a way to change the god-machine's plans, and these medical tests had just handed him something he might be able to use.

"This MRI could be the proof I need to convince people to listen to me when I tell them what I know," said Mark. "This shows that I'm not some nut that's taken one trip too many. Look at it. This fusion of nanotech with my neurons is the restructuring of the thought-interface. This is proof that I'm in contact with the god-machine."

"Or deluded by it ransacking your brain," said Kathy. "I'm sorry, Mark; we're talking about your brain, a brain I love. This infestation could be killing you, one neuron at a time."

"I don't think so," said Mark. "More likely it'll save me than kill me."

16 – South Carolina: January – weeks later

Alexander's militia had grown. He seemed to exude a gravity-like force which drew fighters to him. He'd won victory after victory. His fighters were ferocious. His small army now numbered four hundred men and sixty military vehicles. He'd attacked and destroyed all Traitor strongholds along his path – police, National Guard, Pagans – they were all pillaged for equipment of war and cleansed of Traitors. Word spread about his invincibility and his use of kill zones as tools of war. Some people said that god was on his side. Alexander smiled to himself. Let the fools believe what they wanted, as long as their superstitions fed his war machine and his plans.

Alexander climbed up onto the roof of his Humvee and looked out through his binoculars. Thirty miles away, obscured by haze, was his target. Soon, maybe today, they would begin their advance from this staging area. He'd sensed for days that a kill zone was forming in the Charleston area; and he knew this staging area was far outside the zone of death. He'd seen this kill zone in reoccurring dreams, just as he'd seen the last several. He didn't understand how or why he had this sixth sense. Some of the greatest military leaders had premonitions. Maybe this was similar to what they'd experienced? Alexander knew it would be a huge kill zone; and when it hit, the factory he'd selected as his target would be in the thick of it. The factory was on a deserted expanse of land near the Charleston Naval Weapon Station. Alexander had done his homework using informants. He knew this factory held what he needed. The factory had an innocuous name of Level-5 Industrials, but what it manufactured was anything but innocuous. Behind the guards at the gate and the blast-proof structures were automated assembly lines which turned out the high explosive warheads used by the Navy and Air Force. After the kill zone did its work, Alexander would go in and exterminate what remained alive and willing to fight. He would take what he needed, and what he needed were those warheads. The idea had come to him like most of his ideas recently did, in his dreams. When he closed his eyes, he could still see the diagram in his mind. Tractor-trailers could be rigged to carry twenty of these warheads, forty thousand pounds of high explosives with shrapnel packed around it. The blast would be awesome. The weapon was capable of flattening anything within hundreds of yards of the epicenter. All he needed were radio detonators and fools willing to drive the trucks. In this brave new world there was no shortage of either.

Fox jogged up to the Humvee, grinning from ear to ear. Alexander stepped down onto the hood and then jumped to the ground. He saw men starting to move around in the camp. Fox gave him a bear hug and then pushed him back to arms length.

"It's happening," said Fox. "The radio's reporting kill zones hitting all over Charleston. Goddamn! I wish we could use kill zones all the time. I'm telling you, they're better than nuclear bombs. If we could used 'em in every attack, we'd rule this whole fucking world."

"Let's go get us some warheads," said Alexander.

"Yes, Sir," barked Fox.

There was no question in Alexander's mind that the dreams of kill zones would keep coming and that the victories would follow. There was little that gave Alexander pause. Every day he awoke was a day he was ready to die. There was nothing he wouldn't do and nothing he wouldn't sacrifice to rid the world of the Traitors and their plague. Revenge was the only nourishment that satisfied his hunger.

Alexander picked up his M4 and strode off by himself toward a footpath that wove through a stand of old growth trees. Between the trees, he saw fragments of a large body of water which flowed down toward Charleston. Behind him, he could hear the excitement building among his fighters as word of the kill zone spread. The smell of blood and victory was intoxicating them. He reached the edge of a broad river. He'd visited this spot earlier in the day. A metal rowboat was beached and chained to a tree. The chain was heavily rusted and rattled as he propped his foot onto the stern of the boat. He set his M4 down and squinted at the bright daylight in front of him. A wind was coming in off the water. The Cooper River was a quarter mile across at this point. People were being exterminated just miles from where he stood. Alexander could almost see their shocked faces as realization of their demise sunk in. Some were innocent and some were not. His breathing was deep and regular. It was almost as if he could inhale their anguish, and it troubled him. Too many people were dying. He stared across the river at the opposite shore. Every day brought him closer to his goal. Every beat of his heart made his success more of a certainty.

The goal had been crystallized into its final form by an unlikely catalyst, a dream of the female cop who'd saved him. In the dream, she was able to read his mind and had killed him because of what she saw in him. The dream had reoccurred since the night of his attack on the state police barracks. This dream was so much more than any normal dream. Like his other premonitions, this one told him things he needed to know. Sometimes during waking hours, he could almost feel the female inside his head, probing and searching and violating him. He didn't understand what she wanted, nor did he understand what she was trying to do to him; but he knew at some instinctive level that she had been born to do him harm, and this world harm – she and her mirror image, a male every bit as inhuman as his female counterpart. They were a sentient virus cloaked in human skin. Alexander's entire body tensed like a weapon every time he thought of them.

Each time when he dreamt of the pair, he'd learned more. He'd come to realize they were a danger like no other. He was haunted by them in his dreams and thought about them in his waking hours. Sometimes, he thought about them to the exclusion of all other things and could not even eat or sleep. He felt like he knew them as if they were part of his family. They were like disowned siblings who'd turned into vicious killers and needed to be destroyed. He was drawn to them like the needle of a compass was pulled to magnetic north. There was no other course for him to follow. He could feel they were in Atlanta. He knew they were changing and growing in power and, in the ultimate of betrayals, the government was protecting them, sponsoring them. He knew that opportunity had to come soon or they might slip away. The truck bombs were only part of his plan. He would lay siege to their government stronghold. He would sterilize all that he found, leaving no chance that their disease could escape. He would leave not a man, woman, or microbe alive. In his mind, those two creatures had become the entire reason for this plague. He could never explain how he knew this, but not even a particle of doubt existed within him. When he killed them, the plague would stop. When he killed them, his revenge would be complete. They had become the sole focus and fuel of his hatred. He thought of how Suzy's lifeless hand had felt loosely curled in his fingers. He picked up his M4 and sprayed the air over the river with the machine gun and his rage.

17 – Atlanta: January

Hours ago seeking solitude, Mark had gone up to the roof of the BVMC lab. The night air was cold and invigorating. The moonless sky was sprinkled with stars. He wore a sweatshirt, sweatpants, and sneakers. He was sitting on the ground with his back up against the helicopter pad. The pad was elevated three feet which served as a reasonable backrest and made it almost impossible for him to be seen from the door. The deserted spot was ideally suited for his needs.

The world was quiet except for a whispering breeze. He wasn't tired but he should have been. His lips and mouth were dry but he had no intention of finding water. More than once, he'd realized he should have felt cold; but he seemed to be warmed by an inner heat. He was trying to learn how to operate a new user interface he'd discovered. He'd achieved a modest amount of progress so far this night. The interface was an extremely complicated and alien collection of symbols, but it did have some basic rules in common with all software. Program commands resulted in actions or responses. He had proved this with his command of the thought-interface itself.

Earlier in the night, after a surprisingly painful data-flow, he'd managed to identify a single thought which, when focused upon, caused this new interface to open. The interface was a catalog of programs and commands displayed on a paper-thin two foot high tablet that floated in space in front of him. Like the three-dimensional medical display of his body, this tablet occupied a specific *physical* space. He could move closer or father away from it. He could even walk behind it. In every way, the tablet was a real object to him, except for its ghostlike transparency.

The tablet managed to appear both ancient and high tech at the same time. It looked like a sheet of metallic-colored material, slightly rounded at the top and bottom. Covering its surface were row after row of symbols which seemed to be grouped into words or phrases with vertical lines as delimiters. The result was that each row looked like a collection of variously sized, tiny blocks containing ancient writing. The language was the same mixture of runic and cuneiform characters that Mark had seen in the kill zone map and medical projections.

Floating in space near the lower right hand of the tablet was a globe about the size of a softball. The globe appeared to have a rubber-like texture. He had touched the globe and been surprised when he'd felt something against his fingers. The tablet and globe had a tactile presence. If he touched lightly he could feel them. However, if he applied force, his fingers and hands would pass through them, confirming they were as ghostly as they appeared. Through exploration, he discovered that if he lightly pushed the tablet or gently gripped it, he could move the tablet around in space to reposition it wherever he liked.

Without a doubt, the globe was some kind of input device. Floating around it were what appeared to be directional markings. The markings were more transparent than the globe and had no tactile presence; to Mark, this set them apart as something non-interactive. There was a pair of markings which partially encircled the globe on either side like the oak-leaf symbols of a government seal. The markings tapered to points at the top like a pair of curved 'modern art' arrows. The two markings in fact probably were arrows – one pointing clockwise and the other pointing counterclockwise. They gave a clear impression that the globe was meant to be rotated in those two directions. A second pair of similar markings partially encircled the globe from its rear, curving up to and stopping at each pole. These markings gave the impression that the globe could also be rotated in the vertical axis. A final set of similar rear-side markings suggested rotation in the horizontal axis.

Reaching out with his hand, Mark tentatively gripped the globe. After a few breaths to steady himself, he rotated it several degrees clockwise. A rapid, disjointed, shuffle of weak feelings, visuals, and sensations ripple through him like mild electrical currents. The effect was a little confusing but not unpleasant. At the same time as the sensory effects, the content of the tablet had been swapped out for new pages; and the arrow pointing in the direction of rotation had changed in color, as if mercury were rising up inside it like a thermometer. Turning the globe farther in the same direction caused more sensory effects as the tablet flipped through pages of commands and the mercury color rose farther up the arrow. Turning the globe in its vertical and horizontal axes also resulted in the same things. The globe seemed to be a three-dimensional selection control with infinite possibilities. Mark was trying to remain very objective and scientific. Even though the globe's function seemed obvious, because he was dealing with a completely alien machine, it was impossible to be scientifically certain that paging was the only function of the globe. It was possible that by turning the globe, he was also initiating something that was completely invisible and potentially very dangerous. Over the last few days there had been many aspects of the god-machine's interface for which he'd experienced either confident or insecure feelings for no apparent reason. He believed that these feelings or intuitions stemmed from subconscious coaching by the god-machine; but when it came to this command catalog and its uses, he'd experienced almost no feelings to guide him in any particular direction.

As a result of sensing desertion by those guiding feelings, Mark did not have enough confidence to try executing commands. He was not even completely sure how to execute commands but suspected all he had to do was touch one of the phrases with his finger as if it were a button. Instead of tempting blind fate, he occupied himself by shuffling through pages, looking for clues. There had to be more than just these endless rows of symbols. Somewhere there might be illustrations or help diagrams which were universally recognizable.

Mark had lost track of time and finally lost interest in paging. He'd found no clues; but despite his caution against blindly trying commands, he had mastered one task which amounted to a program command. By accident, he'd learned how to close the tablet at will. He'd discovered that by emptying his mind, it would wink-out. The tablet was apparently monitoring his mental activity; and when his attention was not on the tablet for a certain period of time, it turned off. When he reopened the tablet, he had no control over where it appeared. The interface seemed to choose the best location to position itself in his immediate space, with minimal chance for interference with real objects. He recognized that everything he did and everything he discovered could be important, even the simplest things like opening and closing this tablet. At some level he felt like he was just playing with a new program to learn how to operate it; but at another level, it was impossible to forget that the stakes he was playing for were life and death.

A sharp wind tugged at his clothing and hair. Mark looked up at the stars. There were countless millions of them visible in the moonless sky, too many to ever name. In front of him, within arms reach, the tablet and globe floated unaffected by the wind, like the computer illustrations they were. Based on the hundreds of unique symbols and phrases on each tablet-page, and that each page appeared completely different, Mark had reached the depressing conclusion that this ancient language possessed as many written words as there were stars in the sky.

~

Mark knew frustration, combined with the sure knowledge that he didn't have enough time, was coloring his judgment. He'd discovered that when he moved a pointed finger to within a fraction of an inch of touching a command, he felt a repelling pressure and at the same time received a single vague sensory impression. He suspected the interface was trying to communicate descriptions of commands. The response was like a built-in help system; but it was failing he believed, because the descriptions did not contain anything remotely similar to what humans experienced through their senses. As a result, all he perceived were phantom impressions instead of clear descriptions. Some command phrases produced weak emotions in him; others, faint aftertastes; and still others, light sensations on his skin; but none came close to an understandable impression.

Mark decided that using the thought-interface was his best option to learn more about the cataloged commands. His plan was to select command phrases at random, and then focus on each until he triggered a data-flood. With a little luck, each deluge of information would fill his mind with implanted memories explaining the command and, along with it, a new phrase in the ancients' language. He'd already learned a phrase in the ancients' language for the thought-interface. Earlier, when he'd activated the thought-interface while the floating catalog was displayed, something that looked like a program window appeared to the left of the tablet. At the top of the window was a single phrase. The layout was intuitively recognizable to him; this was a program task list and the single phrase was the name for the thought-interface program.

Mark wondered if the interface's similarities to modern software were coincidental or if a few influential human programmers had subconsciously tapped into the god-machine and emerged with ideas and layouts which were unwittingly incorporated into commercial software. He hoped there were more undiscovered similarities. His accidental identification of the command for the thought-interface was a small victory in what promised to be an overwhelming amount of work. He was beginning to decode the language of a highly advanced civilization, one word at a time. He wondered if a thousand human lifetimes would be enough; yet all he had, based on even the most optimistic projections, were weeks; while every day cost humanity so much more in blood.

In the hours that followed his decision, Mark repeatedly opened the thought-interface. Each time, the torrent of information hurt more than the last. He couldn't find a way to throttle the flood of data. The surges had clearly been designed for a different user, a different species which possessed far larger short-term memory capacity than humans. He knew he was retaining only small pieces from each information flood, but it was enough. It was a beginning.

In his random hunt, he had found no programs related to controlling or tracking kill zones, but he had found other clues; and he was learning more about using the god-machine. Pieces of the complex puzzle were making sense, and one thing was clear: he didn't need psilocybin or LSD anymore. In fact, he now understood that he might not have needed the drugs at all. If he'd been able to consciously control his dreams, he could have operated the subconscious thought-interface while in that natural state of altered awareness and achieved the same results. Psychologists had a name for this altered state of awareness: lucid dreaming. Controlling dreams was the same as controlling the subconscious, which was the fountain from which all dreams flowed. In their esoteric teachings, many religions had instructions for various kinds of meditations and inner-journeys with goals of enlightenment. At their core, these meditations and inner-journeys were controlled dream states. Were these teachings only a coincidence or had information been leaking from the god-machine into religious culture since human time began?

After assembling what he'd learned, Mark cautiously settled on the first command to try. He was reasonably certain he understood what the command did. He was going to run a program whose name in the ancients' language was represented by a single symbol, a pair of criss-crossed lines with an oval floating above it. What he'd retained from the last data-flood's fading memories had convinced him this program provided chronological access to recorded historical events. He'd learned the ancients' runic language was more complex than written English in structure, because each character could represent a word as well as an alphabetic letter. This symbol in the ancients' language roughly translated into the word 'timeline.'

Mark moved his finger close to the symbol and got a dim impression of a fast moving wind. The pressure on his finger felt wobbly like he was pushing against a repelling magnetic field. His heart was beating rapidly. He held his breath and pushed his finger into the symbol. He was instantly ripped from the real world.

He was floating inside what appeared to be a pure white space of infinite size. In front of him was a tablet and selection globe similar to the command catalog. Instead of containing runic phrases, the tablet was covered with minuscule windows which contained moving scenes like film clips. He rotated the globe and, as expected, the tablet paged to a different set of film clip windows amid a flutter of sensory ripples. Some of the pages contained tiny windows of scenes which were clearly recognizable, while others contained only blurry, moving ghost shapes in its windows. He cautiously moved his finger closer to a window containing a scene of the seashore. As he started to push against the resisting pressure, the white void in which he was floating began to fade into a sample of the seashore scene. The experience was complete immersion of all his senses – sound, sight, smell, and touch. Even as a ghost-scene, the projection knocked the wind out of him as it tore at his mind, threatening to blow him fully into this alternate world. He felt like he was in two places at the same time, with all his senses blended into a single combined experience. The sample scene was a frozen moment in time. He was inside a human body which was not his own, with all the texture and nuances and senses that went with it. There were birds suspended in midair, unmoving. There was a pair of smallish, bare human feet below him, standing in the receding surf. There were waves frozen at crest. The sample was low intensity, so it only partially registered on all his senses. He could hear sound, perceive smells, and feel a sea breeze on his face and icy water between his toes, but only as a single musical note, a single instant of perceptions extended into infinity. Superimposed on his vision were the time, date, and location in longitude and latitude. It was odd that the display was in English. He wondered if the interface was adapting to his way of thinking as it had with the kill zone map. The date was over three thousand years ago. He wondered where the longitude and latitude lines crossed. A transparent world globe appeared which pinpointed the location as the coastline of Greece on the Aegean Sea. As soon as his thoughts shifted back to the scene, the globe vanished. He didn't push any harder with his finger, which he knew would immerse him deeper into the recorded scene and set it into motion. He wasn't ready. He knew he would be engulfed and it scared him. The loss of himself into that unknown body would be almost like dying. He removed his finger from the tablet. All his senses returned to the experience of floating in the center of a white void.

He believed he understood the nature of the recordings. Each one contained the complete sensory perceptions from a person who was alive at a specific place and point in time. There was no other way to explain the perfect total immersion of senses, including touch and smell. While the pages of tiny windows seemed to be infinite in quantity, Mark couldn't imagine that the god-machine would store the total life experience of every man and woman who'd ever walked the face of the earth. Surely, the recordings had to be limited to those events the god-machine considered worthy of archiving.

Mark returned to a page of ghostly blurs and wondered what they held. Why were they different? Randomly, he chose one to sample. Before his finger began to feel the backward pressure, he was trembling with apprehension. He suddenly feared he'd experience things no human was meant to experience and that madness would follow. Going against instinct, he moved his finger deeper into the magnetic backpressure. Nothing happened. His senses still had him floating in the void. He pushed his finger to within a hair's breadth above the tiny window, while constantly checking for any small changes in perception; then he found it. There was a vague sensation of warmth that was new. He withdrew his finger and the warmth faded. He tried another ghost window. He held his finger just over it for what seemed like minutes until he noticed an odd taste in his mouth. The taste was granular and earthy. He withdrew his finger and the taste vanished. He tried a few more ghost windows, all with the same results – a faint sensation of some kind and nothing more. He suspected this breakdown in sensory projection occurred for the same reason the command catalog's help system failed. The interface was producing indecipherable experiences because they were projecting non-human sensory data; these blurry ghost scenes were the recorded perceptions of non-human life forms. Some of these ghost windows had to be historical events from the civilization that built the god-machine. The entire world of the ancients could be right at his fingertips waiting for him to study it, if he could only crosswire his senses into something approximating the ancients' physiology. He sighed. Viewing these records was probably hopeless.

Mark went back to the human pages of history. He previewed dozens of scenes until he found one that seemed fascinating and safe; just right for his first complete immersion. The scene was ancient Egypt.

In the distance, he saw pyramids and the lights and activity of what appeared to be a festival. The time, longitude, and latitude were floating at the horizon over a black star filled sky. A full moon was casting light onto the sands and time when many historians thought Moses had fled from the Egyptians. Mark held his finger a moment longer at the preview level and then fully pushed it into the tiny window.

What was left of the white void disappeared as he felt a sensory blow. The frozen projection jumped into full motion. Mark was inside a man who was in every way and with every sense alive. He felt a heart beating, muscles working, and breath drawing. He had no control over what the man did. He was along for the ride and nothing more. He experienced the man's thoughts and feelings, but retained his own identity. It was as if he were a separate observer merged into the back of the man's existence. There was mental chatter in a language Mark could not interpret, but there were also non-verbal ideas which translated directly.

The night was delicious and refreshingly mild. In the distance loomed the great pyramid. Moonlight and stars reflected in its dark surface as if it were mirrors of ice. Mark realized he was the first modern human to see how the pyramids looked with their polished limestone still in place. Evening insects buzzed and palm leaves stirred. The man was enjoying every bit of the night. On his belt was a broadsword. Over his shoulder was a small animal-skin flask of cool water. He was a leader of men, a fierce soldier. There were ten others traveling with him through the sand. They moved in total silence like predators on the hunt. The man was proud of his men. Mark grew worried this was not an innocuous event. Up ahead, torch lights and the outline of a great building could be seen. Atop the walls were armed guards dressed in waist-shirts and bronze jackal masks. Mark understood from the man's thoughts that these were royal bodyguards. He realized the man was stalking human prey, possibly royal human prey. He could feel tension and adrenaline mounting. A hand moved aside some leaves to reveal a line of sight. He was looking down over a stone wall ten feet below him. In the blend of moonlight and torch glow, he saw a teenage boy and girl in a small rectangular pool of water cut into a deck of stone. Flowers were floating in the water. There were golden challises of drink and plates of food. There was a small pile of clothing. The teenagers were nude and in a motionless embrace. The royal bodyguards looked outward, not inward. One bodyguard turned his gaze directly into Mark's eyes. Mark was panicked until he caught himself and realized that the bodyguard was actually looking at a soldier dead thousands of years and not him. There seemed to be a flicker of recognition in the bodyguard's eyes, but nothing happened and the jackal mask ultimately turned away. How had the bodyguard failed to see a man who was ten feet from him?

Mark was filled with questions and unable to reach into the man's mind to recall even the simplest of answers. No matter how real this felt, the experience was still only a single-dimensional recording being replayed. Now, others of the soldier's cadre were positioned at choice spots along the wall. Mark saw arrow tips poking out of the foliage and aimed down. How could the royal bodyguards not see this? A thought floated up from the background of mental chatter and Mark understood everything. The royal bodyguards had been promised a Pharaoh's reward and then ordered not to see a thing, or face eternal death. The assassins were elite servants of the high priest, *the Prophet of God*. Pieces of information began to surface as fast as Mark could assimilate them, as the man's thoughts focused on memories from when the plot was conceived. The young couple was the Pharaoh's last born son and his concubine. Pharaoh would be driven mad with the loss. Hebrew slaves would be scapegoats for the crime. Arrows sung through the air. The teenagers looked up. Their eyes grew wide as their bodies were punctured with quills; another volley flew. The pool water began to swirl with a stain, a dark cloud which was the life's blood of a Pharaoh's son and a teenage girl who would never see adulthood. The royal bodyguards sounded an alarm and took up pursuit in a direction leading away from the assassins. The servant of *the Prophet of God* silently withdrew with his men. Soon they were running through foliage and open stretches of sand. Mark's vision was full of abrupt movements and flashes of moonlight. His heart was racing from the exertion. He heard labored breathing. Sweat was soaking his face and his back. They stopped running. Up ahead, murdered slaves lay in the sand amid discarded bows and arrows. The men picked up branches which were precut into makeshift rakes. They walked backward past the bodies and toward a stone roadbed, dragging the rakes to erase their footprints from the sand. Once they were all on the road, the elite assassin, *the Hand of God*, paused to examine his work. He saw hurried footprints leading from the direction of the assassination to dead bodies strewn in the sand. The royal bodyguards would be along soon to claim success. Their lives also would be measured in hours.

The experience ended unexpectedly. Mark found himself again floating in space. At one instant, his heart was beating fast and he was covered in sweat. Now his own heart calmly thumped and his skin was dry. Mark emptied his mind, which caused him to exit the timeline program. He found himself back on the roof. A leaf had blown from a tree and was trapped against his leg. A dog bayed somewhere far off in the night. He looked at his watch and realized less than a minute had passed since he'd plunged into the timeline program.

~

Morning light was softly filling shadows cast by objects on the roof. Mark had been outside all night. He looked off into the horizon of white clouds and sky. The sun was a faint warmth on his face. He should have been drained from working all night but instead felt as fresh as if he'd just awakened. He had accomplished so much. Far up in the sky, a jet was flying in a slow figure eight, the symbol of infinity. He felt sadness for the powerful who had taken refuge in the air. They were doomed to return to the Earth in fear.

Mark had identified and tried other programs after his experiments with the timeline program. Except for a few, all the programs he'd tried were listed on the first page of the tablet, and all those on the first page had turned out to be important core functions. The programs which he'd selected from subsequent pages had all turned out to be less important. He was not convinced yet, but it looked like he'd just gotten his first piece of solid luck. If most of the important programs were on the first few pages, it would make deciphering the interface much easer. If he'd thought about it earlier, he probably could have predicted this good fortune. After all, the god-machine was at its essence nothing more than an advanced computer with its interface built inside the operator's head, instead of a keyboard and screen. Good usability design often included sorting menu items in the order most frequently used.

An hour ago, using the thought-interface, he'd requested information on another randomly selected program from the first page; and, in response, he was slammed with the largest flood of information he'd yet experienced. He'd paid for this knowledge with terrible pain which was still lingering, but the price was very cheap for something of this life altering importance. Out of what remained in his memory, he'd identified the program as something that stabilizes health and then performs continuous repairs to keep the body flawlessly tuned.

His heart had started beating faster from what the implanted memories had revealed, and it had not slowed since. He'd learned that the program was meant to augment or even replace the body's natural healing abilities with direct repairs carried out by nanotech seeds. This kind of capability was the primary function of the god-machine's original design. He was certain it was the reason for the machine's very existence.

He could almost feel the small free swimming colony of nanotech devices swarming at the base of his skull near the opening to the spinal canal; those microscopic specks had the potential to cure anything. He'd been staring at the healing program's name on the tablet for what seemed like hours. Each time he brought his finger close enough to receive sensory impressions, he felt a vague sense of hunger. He couldn't be certain about everything this program might do to him. All he knew was that it would release the free swimming nanotech to fan out and rebuild all that was less than perfect in his body. He thought about his pancreas and how diabetes had damaged so much of him. He reached out his finger and pushed it into the program's name. He felt nothing beyond an impression of hunger caused by the program's preview but he knew changes would soon be occurring deep inside him.

~

The sun was directly overhead. Mark had remained on the roof all morning exploring more of the tablet's mysteries. He couldn't force the smile from his face. He felt guilty. He had no right to be smiling while a freefalling world was careening downward toward an on-rushing cliff floor. He knew from the medical schematics of his body that he was cured of diabetes. Maybe it was his imagination, but he felt so vital, so alive. A blurry shadow was cast over him. He looked up with squinted eyes and saw Sarah. Her pupils were fully dilated. Strands of her blonde hair were being blown about in the wind. She looked so young and sensual. For a brief moment, he wanted her then he consciously pushed the feelings aside. A medical schematic appeared over her body. Mark could see the colony of seed massed at the base of her brainstem. The mass was beautiful. It was her dormant key to a long and healthy life, her personal fountain of youth.

"Looks like you're enjoying yourself," said Sarah.

"You've no idea how close to the truth you were when you named it the god-machine."

"What have you discovered? Tell me!"

~

Kathy's office felt warm to Mark. He was full of nervous energy. His lips were dry from talking nonstop for so long. He was surprised to discover how well organized his ideas really were. At times, he thought the entire framework must have been planted whole into his brain but it didn't feel that way and he could distinctly remember coming up with the ideas himself as he fit the puzzle pieces together. He was at a turning point in his well rehearsed talk where he might lose his small audience to skepticism. He hesitated before plowing on. He was saying it all for the very first time yet felt a powerful sense of déjà vu.

"It's like the great religions have always said. The capacity to live forever has been within all of us from the beginning of time," said Mark. "The difficulty always lay in understanding how to recognize this capacity and use it. The nanotech seed is this hidden capacity. I know I sound crazy, but the seeds are a tool that can cure virtually anything – a tool that can give us near immortality. The death inflicted on us by the god-machine is just a reflection and reaction to the mindless slaughter we've inflicted on each other since we learned to use clubs and rocks. The god-machine is like a coin flipping through the air; on one side is a long healthy life, while the opposite side is instant death."

The room grew silent. Mark felt like the air itself had been sucked out. Kathy and Carl said nothing. Kathy had a confused look in her eyes, while Carl couldn't make eye contact at all. Mark wet his lips. He knew he sounded like a madman, but he was convinced every word he spoke was an immutable fact. His case wasn't helped by the pseudo-religious overtones of some of it or, as Kathy had put it, atheistic overtones. He couldn't help any of that. He was more convinced than ever that the god-machine was at the root of most religious myth and dogma: there was eternal life, something to pray to, healing the sick; even their best hope for stopping this plague had analogs in religious writings. He had to evoke faith to stop the plague. He had to convince others that they could stop the escalating kill zones and save lives, if governments could be convinced to act quickly and give up plundering the earth and lay down their weapons of mass destruction. Knowing what he knew, he had to try. He had proof that some of what he said was true and that the god-machine was created to heal, not kill. The time had come to use what meager proof he had.

"You both probably think I'm suffering from nanotech brain damage, but I can prove at least some of what I'm saying. I can prove the seeds and the god-machine together have the ability to not just repair traumas, but to automatically heal and even defend the body from diseases. Kathy, I need your help."

Kathy didn't respond right away... "I'll help you," she finally said. "But in return, I want you to let me run more medical tests."

"Fine; anything you want; but you may change your mind in the next few minutes. I've already had my own medical tests run. I had myself checked for diabetes, including a micro-MRI of my pancreas. I cured myself of diabetes this morning and these tests prove it."

Mark watched in silence as Kathy pulled up the test results on her computer. Her expression was intense as she worked the keyboard and examined the screens. Her expression began to change. She looked bewildered and a little pale. Mark waited.

"It shows completely normal blood chemistry. Your pancreas appears to be loaded with healthy islet cells which I know were not there before today. This isn't conclusive. I'll need to test you a few more times over the next few days."

"Okay, so test me. I want you to test me. But I promise you the results will be the same or better."

"I believe you," said Kathy. "I believe this thing has cured you; and I hate sounding like a broken record, but none of this proves your theories about why the machine is killing us."

"What have we got to lose?" said Mark. "Tell me? The world is falling apart anyway. Are we worried about reputations? We have nothing else to try and we're almost out of time."

"Alright!" said Carl. "Let's say your theories are right. Where do we go from here?"

"We go to an impossible task," said Mark. "We have to convince this government to surrender to the god-machine to prove we're no longer a threat."

"Break it down for me, Mark. What will we say? I don't see enough proof," said Carl. "We'll be laughed out of every high level meeting I can schedule until they begin to refuse my calls."

"You could be right," said Mark, "Hell! You probably are right. But in my heart, I know I have to try; and I need all the help I can get. I know it's overwhelming and looks like a fool's errand. Please, will you both say you'll try?"

18 – Atlanta: January

Sarah awoke out of a psilocybin blackout, but she was not herself. She was inside the skin of the soldier that was hunting her. She had been inside him so many times before; mostly involuntarily, but as of late, she'd sometimes managed to leave her body and enter his at will. She was trying to understand how dangerous this man was to her. At times he was hazily aware of her presence inside him; and at those times, she sensed he would rip open his own flesh to get at her if he could. There was so much focused rage. When inside the soldier, she experienced whatever his five senses brought into her; but there were also occasional thoughts or emotions that strayed into her mind from his. She'd learned Alexander was not only hunting her, but he was now hunting Mark who he thought of as her mirror image. She knew the soldier had subconscious access to the god-machine but was unaware of what he was using. He was not empathetic or introspective. He was a singularity of violence, a professional killer seeking revenge; and in his fist was an army of fighters who were infected with his zeal.

Sarah shivered. The out of body vision weakened and then came back. She sensed there was some tie between herself and this man. They had met somewhere. Their paths had crossed, but where? She could see he was in the midst of celebrating a victory. They were in a building lit by generators. Tables were covered with food and drink. His men and women were satiating themselves, while he stood aloof and planned. He'd used premonitions of kill zones to win several of his battles; and using that strategy, another city had fallen to the plague while he and his fighters waited like vultures at the outskirts of doom. When the kill zone was over, they had walked through the spectacle of death picking through the bones and survivors that remained, killing those who fought back, leaving others alive, and always growing richer in the tools of war. He was emboldened by something that had happened today. He'd grown in strength because of what he'd captured. Sarah could tell from snatches of excited whispers that it had awesome explosive power, but she couldn't find any details in his mind or through his eyes and ears. She knew he was paranoid and believed he was sometimes mentally spied on by the enemy; and so was very guarded when dealing with strategic things. This weapon could be part of some plan he had for what he called the Traitors. She was terrified it could be nuclear.

She watched as Alexander walked up to a bathroom mirror and stared into his own eyes. He moved closer as if looking for something inside himself. This was the first time she'd clearly seen him and was surprised that he was a blue-eyed Asian-European. He was of mixed ancestry as she was – the same kind of eclectic genetic cocktail.

"You're in there, aren't you?" he whispered. "Listen to me, Traitor. I know you're part of this disease. I intend to hunt you down and cure the world of your infection. I will stop your plague!"

Sarah was stunned. She felt as if Alexander's rage had been infused into her flesh until it seeped from every pore. She emptied her mind until she was dizzy from the effort, and the out of body vision finally ended. She found herself sitting cross-legged on the floor of her room. She was covered in sweat. It was night. The only lights came from outside her window and from under her door. She'd taken another overdose of psilocybin in an attempt to become more like Mark, but without going beyond the point of no return as he had. She got to her feet and staggered toward the shower. She stripped off her clothing and stepped in. The cold water hit her like a sheet of ice. False memories from the blackout seeped into her conscious mind as the water soaked into her skin. The fog of psilocybin was clearing as fast as the outside memories resurfaced. She saw graphic images of her and Mark having sex. She saw images of mass death all around them and then she sensed the artificial mind calculating fresh murder. Cold water was splashing into her face and running down her body. She was shivering. She reached up and gripped the showerhead just in time to keep herself from collapsing to the tiles. There was something even worse than Alexander, and it too was coming for them at this lab with the soldier and his army following like jackals at its heels.

19 – Atlanta: January

It was past midnight according to the digital clock on the shelf. Mark and Kathy were in bed with the lights on and entangled in conversation.

An empty bag of cookies was in the bed and two cans of soda were on a nearby table. Mark didn't think he would ever be able to fall asleep again. Too many things were on his mind and in his mind. Implanted memories kept resurfacing. Some were buried treasure, others were little more than confusion, and some were completely indecipherable. Sometimes they would float up in the middle of conversations. Suddenly, he would just realize he knew something more about what was being discussed. Kathy had grown morbid as the night wore on. The more they tried to hash out the theoretical healing limits of the seeds, the more somber she became.

"I'm not like you and Sarah. I won't survive another kill zone if it comes here."

"We'll leave before that happens," said Mark.

"You really don't understand, do you?" said Kathy.

"What are you saying?"

"You just healed yourself of diabetes. If this infestation doesn't kill you, tomorrow you may heal yourself of cancer. In twenty years you may have prevented your skin from wrinkling and blocked Alzheimer's. If I'm lucky, I'll live to the age of eighty. I'll have gray hair, old lady skin, and then I'll die. You may never grow a day older. You may even look twenty years younger. Where does that leave me? Will a middle-aged man be happy with an old lady? I'll lose you long before I'll lose my life."

"That won't happen," said Mark. "You're the one who doesn't understand. There's no reason you can't have the same fountain of youth."

"What if you're wrong? You said some people are more sensitive to the interface. Maybe that sensitivity is genetic. Maybe I'll never have what you have."

"I know that's not true. I'll teach you how to restructure the interface and use it."

"Mark, please stop," said Kathy. Her cheeks were wet with tears. "Maybe I don't want a brain full of these things. I want my own normal brain, and my own normal body, and my own normal flaws. You're becoming some kind of hybrid organic-machine. We don't know where this will stop. If every neuron in your brain becomes infected with a seed, are you still human? Are you still you? Are you even still alive if your brain has been fully transformed into nanotech circuitry?"

"We implant artificial hearts in people and still consider them human. All I can say is – I still feel like myself. I feel alive; and as long as I have feelings, then I know I'm alive."

"You feel, therefore you are?" said Kathy. "I'm not sure it's that simple."

There was a soft insistent rapping at their door. The sound unnerved Mark. Someone was in the hallway. He got up as Kathy pulled the blankets up to her chin. He opened the door partway. Sarah was standing in the hallway. Her hair was dripping wet but her clothing was dry. She looked like a cat that had been caught in a rainstorm. Something troubling was in her eyes.

"I need to talk with you," said Sarah. "I'm scared."

Mark glanced back at Kathy. She was upset but shrugged as if resigned to the interruption. He didn't want to open the door the rest of the way but did.

"You're dripping," he said.

Sarah cast a doubtful eye at Kathy.

"I should go," said Sarah.

Mark felt the cold of a grave. He couldn't imagine what kind of fear must have driven her to come to their room in the middle of the night. He could sense she was deeply scared. Sarah backed away from the doorway. Mark took her by the wrist so she couldn't leave. She tugged at his grip. An image filled his vision replacing the real world. He and Sarah were mating; a new species would be conceived. The image flashed for a split second. In its wake, he was deeply disturbed. Sarah gave up trying to pull away just as he let go of her wrist. She stood in the doorway looking down at the floor.

"A kill zone is coming," said Sarah.

"How do you know this?" asked Kathy.

Mark glanced back at Kathy. She was sitting straight up in bed. She didn't look upset any more; she looked spooked. Her eyes were wide.

"I just do," said Sarah. "It's hard to explain. It's kind of a memory of the future, but it's not like a Ouija board premonition or something. It's more like partially knowing what someone is planning to do. I'm not seeing a real future. I'm seeing images of what could happen to me if I let the plans actually occur."

"What do you want to do?" asked Mark.

"Run," said Sarah. "I can't bear to live through another one. I'd kill myself before I stand in the middle of that again. I think it's weeks away, but I won't take that chance."

20 – Atlanta: January

The BVMC lab's cafeteria was filled with the random energy of dozens of conversations. The fluorescent lights hummed. There were sounds of dishes clattering and food being prepared. Mark was in the middle of this symphony of human sounds and found it comforting. A follow-up set of medical tests had shown his diabetes was still cured and the infestation in his brain was spreading. Neither result surprised him. An hour ago, he'd snuck out of a meeting in the Kill Zone Monitoring Center before the meeting was finished. These meetings had become nothing more than a death count. The number of kill zones per day was still increasing, as it had been for days. All the zones were very small, in fact the average size was decreasing; but the rate had now surpassed more than forty a day. The previous pattern of targeting was also continuing: all the areas being hit now had already been struck at least once before. In his mind, he could see the strategy. He could see the very soil being sterilized of humans, through repeated application of the god-machine's antibiotic.

Earlier today in his office with the door locked, Sarah had told him she believed what was coming was more than just a kill zone. She was deeply disturbed, almost despondent. Mark had felt uncomfortable being alone with her. She'd shoved him in the chest more than once when she thought he wasn't listening. She'd been experiencing some kind of telepathic connection or bond with a soldier named Alexander who she believed was leading an army of mercenaries. Her description of the telepathic bond sounded eerily similar to his experience with the timeline program. Sarah had said she knew the soldier was coming on the heels of the kill zone to murder both of them and anyone else who survives the zone. She'd been inside his head enough to know that if he caught up with them, nothing could stop him from taking his revenge. He was drunk with rage and believed both she and Mark were no longer part of the human race and that they were responsible for the plague. For Sarah, the most disturbing part of her last experience inside the warrior's skin was Alexander speaking to her in a mirror and knowing she was somehow inside him. She was convinced he was subconsciously tapping into the god-machine and that through it, in his dreams, he would be led directly to them.

Mark didn't know what to believe or do, but what she'd said had deeply unnerved him. What lent credence to her story was that it explained the nagging sense he'd had of her holding something important back: her secret was this belief she was being hunted. It was clear from her actions and words, Sarah felt she'd put them all in greater danger by coming here.

Sarah had then told him something almost as troubling, as if a militia coming after them or that she was a delusional paranoid was not enough to have on his mind. She'd said Alexander might not end up being the only one after them. She had a feeling that soon almost everyone would turn against the two of them. She wanted him to cancel a critical meeting scheduled for tomorrow. With Kathy and Carl's help, he was going to try to convince some government officials to take up the cause of partially surrendering to the god-machine. Sarah was convinced the meeting would be a disaster and accomplish the opposite; those officials would turn against them. She wanted to run now. She wanted him to save as many people at the lab as he could, by persuading them to leave, and then go before it was too late.

Mark had tried to calm her but his clumsy attempts had failed miserably. In the end, Sarah had left his office in a half-run. He'd heard her beginning to cry when she was in the hall. People had turned to look at her and then they'd looked at him at if he was the cause.

Mark glanced down at his tray of food. He'd eaten none of it. Runic symbols briefly appeared over each piece of food as his eyes touched them one at a time. This had been happening since he sat down. He had no idea what the symbols meant. All day small *assists* like this had been occurring. Most of them were now displaying in English, except for the food display and two others, which were newer. The speed at which the nanotech system could collect data and compute results was incredible. The interface appeared to be trying to learn his behaviors and anticipate his commands and needs. The program was offering what its calculations predicted he would find useful *assists*. He'd known the temperature outside before opening the door. He'd seen the health status of someone before shaking their hand. He was learning to work the interface as fast as it was learning to adapt to him.

Mark looked at his food. The symbol over the fruit salad and can of soda was the same. The symbol over the turkey club was different. He had a hunch these symbols were some kind of assessment of what was better for his newly healed body. Since the turkey sandwich had a different symbol than the soda or canned fruit, he assumed the *assist* was telling him the sandwich was better. He picked it up and took a bite. The sandwich tasted great – all covered in mayonnaise, with huge hunks of bacon, thick slices of tomato, and cheese. He decided the *assist* was right, the club was much better. Who would have known the god-machine was also a food critic? He smiled. The small bit of irony helped him feel better almost as much as the food did.

As the first mouthful of club sandwich reached his stomach, he felt ill. There was a sudden dizziness along with a queasy feeling. He looked at the sandwich. There was nothing wrong with it. After a few minutes the feelings subsided.

Mark nibbled at some of the lettuce from the club. The leafy green went down fine. He broke off a piece of the bread – also fine. The mayonnaise left him feeling a little odd, but the turkey made him feel seasick again. He bought a burger. The results were similar: everything except the animal products went down without complaint; and everything that gave him a problem had the same symbol displayed over it. Next, he tried a pepperoni pizza and got the same results. He was almost certain the ancients were vegetarians, not predators; he kept finding hints which pointed to that conclusion. He wondered if the transformation of his brain could be causing a psychological intolerance to some foods, or were the nanotech seeds doing more than healing and tuning up his biology? Was he being radically changed inside? Were the nanotech seeds building a better human or a better ancient?

Mark focused on his body's status in an attempt to call up a medical schematic. The display stubbornly refused to appear. As he stood up to leave, the schematic glowed to life. The orange color code for seeds hadn't changed. He focused on the display of his stomach until the projection zoomed in. The area looked the same as before. There were no new symbols or color codes or anything that his intuition picked up on.

~

"There's nothing different about your intestinal tract," said Kathy.

She was studying a computer display of his upper and lower GI track x-rays and an accompanying evaluation by a gastroenterologist.

"It was such a strong reaction to eating meat," said Mark. "It has to be more than a mental aversion leaking into me through the thought-interface. I wanted to eat the sandwich; it's my body that rejected it."

"The seeds are taking over more of your brain every day," said Kathy. "And you're emotionally okay with what's happening. It should be earth-shattering. You should be freaking out. It worries me that you're concerned about nothing except eating meat. It's like some kind of selective psychological anesthesia's affecting you. You know that's how a parasite operates. It numbs its host while it digs deeper into the victim's flesh."

21 – Atlanta: January

Mark was sitting in a room full of people, but he was alone. He was prepared for the teleconference; yet with each passing minute and each new worry, his chances of success seemed to evaporate a little more. He was on a fool's errand and they all knew it. So much depended on this single day; it was insane that the future of the world might be determined by how much he was believed in the next few hours. Kathy would present her evidence of the physical changes he was undergoing. Carl would put his reputation on the line. But in the end, it was his words, and his words alone, that could make the difference; and what he had to say required a giant leap of faith.

History had always turned on plans and accidents that were long-shots like this moment. It was an accident that penicillin was discovered. The x-ray was just as much luck as it was inspiration; so was the unmasking of genetics and the discovery of a set of continents called the Americas. The whole of human civilization was built on a very long series of interdependent moments of hubris and discovery; it was fitting that this moment would be no different.

All last night, Mark had searched through his past. He was looking for answers to the question of *why him?* He always seemed to be in the right place at the right time. His life was an amazing collection of good fortune: research grants and Nobel Prizes and scientific breakthroughs. Looking back on it all, he now wondered how much of what he'd attributed to luck was really something very different. Had some outside intelligence been at work? Had something been meddling around the edges, unobtrusively shepherding events toward the culmination of a plan in which he was only a pawn? Sarah believed the god-machine had affected her life since she was born, and possibly her parents' lives, and her parents' parents' lives. Mark was beginning to believe the same was true for him. The idea was no more implausible than worshipping an invisible god intimately guiding and assisting each individual, a belief held by billions of people on the planet. Mark didn't believe that God was that closely involved. The idea that a vast computer entity was assisting him for his entire life was far more plausible and had far more supporting evidence.

It was no longer very hard for him to believe that the god-machine may have cultivated his interests in biology and then paleobiology. It was even easy for him to believe that COBIC bacterium had been herded into his path for him to discover its Nobel Prize winning secrets and, then much later, its hidden truths. The god-machine controlled seed bearing COBIC the way a person controlled the mouse pointer on a computer screen. The bacterium would not have been positioned where it was not intended.

Mark had stepped out of the room. He was in the hallway heading toward a bathroom. A blinding pain shot through his head. He managed to get into the bathroom before doubling over, squeezing his temples. He sensed a new change was occurring inside his skull. Thankfully, no one had seen him in pain. He leaned on a sink. He didn't need anyone questioning his health right now. He looked at the tiles on the floor and then up into a mirror on the wall. He saw a man staring back at him. Was this image still the same man?

The secure video conference was about to begin. All the participants were present. Images of remote locations and people were tiled on the computer screens. General McKafferty looked older than the last time Mark had seen him. Only a short time had passed, but the General looked troubled and worn. The ugly visage was the same, but some of the fire was gone. The head of the NIH was online. Senator Trenton, the head of the Commerce, Science, and Transportation Committee, was online. The President's National Security Advisor was online as well as his Science Advisor. The only friendly faces were Dr. Marjari and Professor Karla Hunt who were attending remotely as guest speakers. Carl's reputation and Mark's Nobel Prize were the sole reasons this group of advisors and decision makers had assembled on such short notice.

"If everyone is ready, we'll get underway," began Carl.

The meeting ran with the orchestrated precision of a legal proceeding. Kathy gave her opinions and evidence. Dr. Marjari spoke about the potential computing power and scalability of the nanotech computers. Professor Hunt spoke about the current state of man-machine interfaces. It was Mark who then carried the remainder of the presentation. It was Mark who was the primary specimen. He spoke about everything he knew and suspected. He argued we had to try to make peace with the machine. What was there to lose in partial surrender when compared to the alternative?

"We've had free rein on this world for millennia and always wondered if God was keeping a ledger," said Mark. "We never imagined there was an artificial intelligence watching everything we did, with a digital scoreboard, and that this machine was about to reach a verdict on us all.

"The machine is an immense cloud of nanotech dust that covers our world. Each speck has the power of a desktop computer and the power to communicate through a wireless web much like our Internet. At the core of its web, trillions of these specks are massed tightly together in a space that is probably much smaller than this room – a super colony, a vast artificial intelligence that can see through our eyes and hear through our ears – and for the longest time, for the majority of its time, all it has done is float there, thinking and planning and learning. It's thousands and thousand of times more intelligent than we are, and it's still evolving. It is a living machine. It's seen the sun rise and set on our world for an unimaginable span of centuries. What kind of ideas and strategies do you think it could have developed over all that time? How can we hope to fight and win over something that knows what we're thinking and was created by a civilization so advanced that they dared to build machines in the image of their gods?"

'What do you believe it's thinking right now?" asked the science advisor.

"I have no idea what it's thinking," said Mark. "My brain is overwhelmed by the smallest trickle of data. It would be impossible for me to comprehend what it's thinking. But what I do know is that it's in the final stages of sending us back to a new stone age. This phase of its plan is nearing completion; and I suspect it has done this before, maybe many times before. This machine is ancient. It has seen many human species come and go. In six thousand years, humans have gone from stone tools to spaceships and computers. What do you think the odds are that we've gone from caves to computers more than once in the seven hundred thousand years or more of theoretical human history since our early ancestors first used fire? Can anyone believe with complete certainty that in hundreds of thousands of years, the best we humans could do was make stone tools until six thousand years ago? I believe we could have easily created high technology before. And just as surely, I believe we could have been through extinction cycles before. The salient point is this. There's good evidence the god-machine has caused extinctions before. This means we probably tried to fight it before and failed. What will it cost us to try the road of peace instead of war?"

"Hold on," growled General McKafferty. "If all of this wild-assed theorizing is true, and near extinctions have happened before, how do you know we didn't try surrender in the past and got wiped out because of that? My opinion has not been changed by your presentation; if anything, my opinion has been hardened. If you're right and this machine has waged war in the past, then that's all the more reason to destroy it now. Stop it for good!"

"How are you going to destroy it?" asked Mark.

"Nuke the son of a bitching colony with a volley of EMP bombs. Pop a few right over that brain, and turn out its lights forever."

"Won't work, General," said Mark. "If you leave just one seed functioning anywhere, it could reproduce and someday a new super colony will reemerge. The seeds have been inside us all from birth. Every crawling animal, from man to dust mite, carries this nanotech inside it. The god-machine was here before our species banged two rocks together. We know it can heal and we know it can kill. The question no one has asked is, "can our species survive without it?" Will its destruction take the best of us along with it? What will the armies of undirected COBIC do inside our bodies when central control is decapitated? We have lived symbiotically with it for our entire existence as a species. What would we be without it? Will we lose faculties that we thought were innately ours but were in reality provided by a subconscious interface? Maybe we'll lose our capacity to remember or to write. Or what if our lifespan is reduced by decades? Who can predict what the effects would be? Who can say with certainty which facets of mankind exist independently of this machine and which do not? You can't destroy it until you know what parts of us you'll be destroying along with it... and what about the future? This machine holds the keys to near immortality, to freedom from cancer and birth defects and all the natural plagues of mankind. It holds the history of past civilizations and can be mined for ancient technology that we can't even imagine. It's the library of Alexandria writ large a million times over. Ask yourself this question, General. Aren't we plotting to destroy a kind of god?"

"That's heretical crap! Who will be left to enjoy your library? As long as I breathe, America will not capitulate to this machine or anything else that comes along," yelled McKafferty. His face was growing redder. "We will not submit to machine dominance. If we scale back our ability to industrialize, if we give up the only weapons that can destroy it, then what will it demand of us next? Will it demand the sacrifice of our remaining freedoms? Our children? Our souls? No, this monstrosity will not stand! You, sir, are admittedly part machine. Your brain is no longer fully human; and because of that, you forfeit all rights to advise true humans on how to live or die."

"Gentlemen, please calm yourselves," said Senator Trenton. "Let me recommend that ya'll leave the speech making to the politicians."

Nervous laughter came from the room and computer speakers. Mark tried to calm himself. His chest was rising and falling in deep breaths. He noticed McKafferty's face was still growing redder. The General was dangerously wrong. The risks were unthinkable.

22 – Atlanta: January

Mark was in the midst of horrible dreams which were worse than the previous night's. Random sparks of god-machine data flashed through his mind conjuring nightmares no human brain alone could produce. The realism was all-encompassing. He gasped!

Mark sat up and opened his eyes. Still groggy, he was glad to be free from the talons of those monstrous visions. Light from a television broadcast shining on the bed illuminated Kathy in sleep. She was tangled in a sheet which turned her body into wrapped curves. He stared at her without a clear thought in his mind. Minutes passed then he began to notice something was different in his thoughts. He had an unmistakable feeling of no longer being alone inside his own head. Someone was there in his mental labyrinth where only he had ever existed before. The presence should have felt menacing, but all he felt was something curious and new.

Mark awakened differently than he had before restructuring. The change was just one more thing to remind him of the growing chasm between himself and those he was leaving behind. The cobwebs of sleep were just now burning off as his waking awareness expanded like a rising sun, activating his hybrid brain. His ability to think increased with unnatural rapidity. Suddenly, he was able to identify the mental visitor and was confused. He recognized the presence as Sarah. She was not able to read his thoughts; he was not able to read her thoughts; and yet there was some kind of connection that had not existed before. He grew aware of the source; perceiving it as a concentrated sphere of recorded memory. The sphere glowed with a human presence, as if it had been imbued with the essence of the person it had come from. The source was unmistakably Sarah. He could sense the sphere 'wanting' to express itself. By focusing exclusively on the sphere, he allowed it to open within him like a flower. He was filled with Sarah's recorded perceptions as they radiated into his mind like a shared life. Her recorded experiences and memories became instantly and inseparably his. She was sitting on the floor of a room lit by a single candle. A severe pain was subsiding in her skull. She was whispering to herself a message intended for him.

"I'm like you now. I'm a little scared. I can feel my mind changing."

Mark almost spoke to her and then realized she couldn't hear him. This was like so many other god-machine experiences he'd had – one way memories, stored data flows; it was what the machine appeared to be very good at. The sphere encapsulated all her physical senses, emotions, and thoughts; an entire group of nuanced ideas and related memories accompanied it. The message was an entire human experience, carefully excavated and passed on with all the depth and texture of actual life. From the related memories she'd given him, Mark now understood Sarah had taken a massive overdose of LSD and crossed the threshold of re-structuring. She was on the road to becoming like him, irreversibly a mix of human and machine. He was no longer the only one on this journey. He hadn't realized how troubled he was by the isolation, until it was gone.

One of Sarah's shared memories explained how to send a response to her message. She'd discovered how to send messages while trying to find other ways to communicate with the god-machine. Instructions and a string of runic symbols which formed a program name had been part of a data-flood. To start recording a 'memory capsule,' Sarah had learned she needed to focus her thoughts on the runic symbols with enough concentration to exceed a threshold level. Initiating the command was kind of like mentally shouting loud enough to be heard by the interface over the noise of random thoughts. With the threshold exceeded, recording of her experiences began and continued until she stopped the process by emptying her mind of all thought. To send the memory capsule, she had to think of the recipient, and nothing else, until she felt the completed message vanishing. It was like addressing mental e-mail. Mark was brimming with nervous energy. Sarah had identified a program for sharing life experiences, and she'd discovered how to directly execute programs without using the command catalog. Her message contained stunning breakthroughs in every sense of the word. He began to plan his own memory capsule response.

Mark lay back down with his head resting on the cloudlike softness of his pillows. Kathy murmured something next to him. Her closeness gave him comfort and connection to something still fully human. He slowly closed his eyes and thought about what had just occurred. His mental dialog with Sarah had been conducted in ways far beyond spoken words. This was sharing pure unfiltered life. Lying, deception, and omission were impossible. Empathic telepathy was the only way he could describe it. The thought transference was not telepathy as metaphysical texts explained it, and was not messages from god as religious texts might have proclaimed it, but the experience could have certainly been mistaken for such things. At its essence, the mechanics supporting this empathic thought transference were very understandable mundane science. Thoughts and experiences were translated into data packets by the nanotech computer in the sender's brain. The data packets traveled over a global network as radio waves, which were received and converted back into human thoughts and experiences by the nanotech computer in the recipient's brain. The result was simple and direct magic.

Mark had understood for some time that one of the god-machine's core functions was communication. The global network it had woven was a clear example of this importance. He had thought he'd understood what the communication entailed. He was wrong. What it entailed was something as significant as the ability to heal. The machine gave people the ability to share their thoughts, their dreams, their fears; it was literally a way of stepping inside some else's life for brief periods of time. The god-machine was the conduit of a level of intimacy that was impossible without it. Mark sighed. Why did such a gift to mankind go undiscovered for so long and why did it finally arrive as a curse, instead of the joy it could have been? Were humans simply not ready to receive the gifts? Maybe we'd never be ready.

Mark thought about Sarah and the risks she'd taken. She was a very brave woman. He was grateful he was no longer alone in this transformation. He looked at Kathy sleeping beside him. She seemed so peaceful and warm. He wanted her to join them. He wondered if she'd ever allow this change to happen within her. Would she become one of the people left behind? He felt a deep sadness in his heart.

~

Outside was a crisp winter morning in the Deep South. Mark's shoes crunched on the grass. The air was refreshing. His thoughts were remarkably clear. If Kathy's estimates were accurate, more than fifteen percent of his brain cells were now nanotech. As he walked across the campus, into buildings and down hallways, he was repeatedly reminded how empty the facility had become. The background murmur of people talking had become silence. The bustle of people coming and going had been transformed into stillness. People had quietly disappeared from the lab as news about the video conference spread. Carl estimated twenty-five percent of the original staff remained, compared with forty percent from the day before. Many people had walked off during the night while others continued the quiet exodus this morning. Almost all had left their possessions behind and no explanations for their departure, though it was easy to understand why they were leaving. A recent estimate showed thirty percent of the human race was gone. There was no hope of stopping the plague other than Mark's suggestion of surrender and the military's strategy of nuclear weapons. Neither idea offered much in the way of solace. And neither idea depended upon anything done by them at the lab. So they left in a steady trickle to go home to remaining family and friends and wait for the end or a miracle.

As Mark passed by people, some greeted him while others stared with unasked questions in their eyes. He realized after minutes of these stares that he'd somehow received stray thoughts from two of the people. The thoughts surfaced in his mind as faintly whispered implanted memories; the images and ideas were disturbing, almost as if they had come from an unbalanced mind. They were delayed, so he had no idea whose primitive darkness they were born from. The source could have been any of the faces he'd passed. He wasn't even sure the stray thoughts were real, but doubts soon faded as another whisper came to him and then one more. He was now convinced he was actually receiving subconsciously transmitted thoughts; uncensored wishes from the Freudian id. He believed the god-machine was able to receive mental experiences from almost anyone. The timeline recordings were partial evidence of that. Was it so much of a leap to believe that he was somehow tuning into streams of this massive pool of live broadcast data?

He continued walking and quietly receiving until the thoughts stopped coming. It was almost as if a radio he was listening to was drifting off station or maybe something inside him had slowly stemmed the flow. Most of the people had been unreadable or simply not sending; he didn't know which. Of the people that were sending, some projected clear strands of thought while other gave off little more than soft unintelligible blurs. Wisps of understandable thought were rare and each was unique, but there was a common theme. The thoughts were brimming with fear of death and aggression toward him. There was a potential of violence in some of these people. They viewed him as a threat to their already shaky future. It was ironic to Mark that they felt violence toward one of the few people able to do something about that very future they feared losing.

As Mark walked into Carl's office suite, he saw a Marine standing at attention blocking the door to Carl's private office; two other Marines had been out in the hall. The soldier saluted but did not move out of the way. He was a big man with the hash-marks of a sergeant. He was in dress uniform and armed. There was an earphone from a walkie-talkie in his ear.

"Is there a problem?" asked Mark.

"No problem, sir. There's a meeting in progress and I have been ordered to secure the door. It should be over soon."

"A meeting with who?"

"I can't say, sir."

Mark was curious. He sat down in a chair in the outer office and waited. Carl's secretary was not at her desk and probably would never be again. The soldier directed his stare back to the entranceway. After a minute, the soldier took a piece of candy wrapped in cellophane from a bowl and popped it in his mouth. He dropped the empty wrapper next to the bowl, where several other wrappers were already in a scattered pile. As Mark stared at the insignia and other military ribbons and patches, his mind drifted off. He thought about the military and its predisposition to solving things with blunt force. Aggression was why the military was created and what it was very good at, but that power needed tempering by people of all different backgrounds. He wanted the government to try for peace; the generals wanted to use nuclear weapons. He looked at the soldier. The man stared back at him for a moment and then looked away.

Mark wished he understood the user interface better. He wished he could use the machine's functions to help him convince the government to partially surrender. He was not learning the interface quickly enough. All the evidence he could present was secondhand and disputable, but rushing into what he was exploring, in order to collect better evidence, was more than dangerous. There was a remote possibility he could instigate a kill zone or worse. Early this morning, he'd tried a new program for which he believed he'd clearly identified its function. When invoked, the program seemed to do nothing – and that terrified him. Hours later, he was still worried and waiting to find out something silent and terrible had happened. He should have been more careful. There were risks in trying any command, but what alternative did he have? He didn't believe the program he'd tried this morning was broken. This was a machine with near unlimited power. There was no doubt the program had performed some task… and this meant he had no idea what he'd done.

Mark took out his cell phone PDA and opened a bookmarked webpage. It was a news story he'd found earlier while doing searches using the words 'militia' and 'Alexander.' The story was a short piece covering several gangs, who according to the author were doing as much damage as the plague in some parts of the country. The story included a militia group that called themselves 'I64.' They had heavy weapons and armored vehicles; the description read more like a small army. The group was lead by a charismatic paramilitary named Alexander 'No Last Name.' Distinguishing marks were a dragon and dagger tattoo on his wrist. He was rumored to be immune to kill zones. Alexander was wanted for one hundred twenty counts of murder committed during an attack on a Virginia State Police barracks on December 24th. He was also wanted in other states on similar charges with similar body counts. Mark had doubted whether Sarah was right about being hunted. This news story was enough proof for him that she was unfortunately probably very right – and very prescient. The news report didn't completely prove that she was being hunted or that this militia was headed their way, but it was now a much smaller leap of faith to believe that part of her story. He now feared she was also going to be right about her insistence they leave the CDC as soon as possible.

After fifteen minutes, Carl's office door opened to reveal two high ranking officers inside. There was a smell of expensive cigar smoke and voices in casual banter. Mark did not recognize either of the officers but could tell from the insignia one was a general. When Carl saw him waiting, there was a momentary look of guilt; then, a smile replaced it. Carl motioned for him to wait a second. Mark sat back in the chair realizing he was not going to be introduced. The sergeant was at full attention. A cellophane candy wrapper inconspicuously fluttered from his fingers to the floor.

Without warning, Mark felt a sharp pain in his temples. He fought to conceal it. He closed his eyes to block the pain and found himself perceiving the world through the senses of someone unknown to him. The man was giving a speech. A huge mob of armed fighters was in front of him packing the inside of a hall. All the windows were broken. A smoky light was shining in. There was a smell of dried leaves. Mark saw religious icons – this had been a church of some kind. He felt a fervor surrounding the man, like a halo of menace. This was not a man of religion; this was a charismatic leader of soldiers. As Mark listened, the man spoke with clarity and obvious intelligence. There was a political cadence to his speech. With each sentence, he was raising the energy and inciting action.

"We have grown in power," roared the man. "We are the ultimate weapon. You are the ultimate weapon!"

There was an odd shift in perspective as the leader continued his oration. Mark felt almost as if the room was revolving around him. As the motion came to a stop, he sensed the man was now staring back at him. Mark felt exposed. A distinct feeling of hate radiated from the man's core, leaving no doubt for Mark that his telepathic invasion had been discovered.

"Traitors!" shouted the man. "You have unleashed this plague. You have slaughtered the people. We will never forget. We will never forgive. We will never give up!"

Mark knew from the man's emotions that these words were meant as much for the telepathic intruder as they were for the fighters. A series of the man's memories flowed into Mark's mind. He saw a long column of armor clattering down a roadway. He saw powerful weapons firing on a National Guard base and quick victory. He saw death and ruin all around him. The mental slideshow of military conquests continued with the speech. A Goliath in army camouflage jumped up on the platform and lifted one of the leader's arms in the air, fist clasped in fist. Mark heard the crowd shout the leader's name, "Alexander!" Mark was stunned. He felt as if the wind had been knocked out of him. With total clarity, he now understood everything. This was the soldier who was hunting them. Sarah had been right! Maybe the time was approaching when the world would turn against them. The perception winked out.

"Mark, are you alright?" asked Kathy.

Mark saw Kathy kneeling beside him. Carl was standing next to her. Somehow, he had ended up lying on the floor. They were in Carl's outer office. Both of them looked worried. Carl had his cell phone in his hand and appeared like he was calling for help.

"I'm fine," said Mark as he sat up on his elbows.

"For a moment you were unconscious and showing signs of severe brain damage," said Kathy. "No involuntary pupil response, nothing... then you're back. It doesn't make sense."

"I'm okay, please don't worry."

Mark felt mentally disoriented but was not about to admit it. The incident had been in many ways like a data-flood except instead of data, the flood was implanted memories from Alexander's life. Similar to the timeline historical records, there had been some kind of time compression of human events. A transmission which contained the entire incident was received as a whole, and then relived as real experiences at an accelerated rate. The entire process from start to finish had occurred in an instant. Now, minutes later, the implanted-experiences felt more like memories of something he'd done on a prior day. It was very bewildering trying to integrate the two different life experiences into one.

Mark noticed the officers and sergeant were no longer in the room. The spaces they'd occupied were empty and seemed strangely unused. Had they been there at all? Maybe they were also implanted memories? He looked at the table next to where the sergeant had been standing and saw a small pile of cellophane wrappers. They had been real. He felt like he was not fully back into this world and that half his awareness was still in that distant church. Memories of his actual experiences and machine implanted memories seemed interchangeable. He was having trouble distinguishing his reality from Alexander's. He felt that at any moment he could shut his eyes and find himself back inside Alexander's skin.

The meeting had been going for almost two hours. Mark took a sip of overly hot black coffee. He was listening to Kathy's medical assessment of Sarah. The disorientation he'd felt from being inside Alexander's mind had dissipated but a mild insecurity lingered. It was like waking from a nightmare and then wondering if he was still dreaming and something worse was about to happen. He'd told no one about the experience.

During the meeting, Mark's train of thought had been repeatedly helped by nanotech *assists*. The interface was sending him a greater amount of superimposed visuals and small involuntary data-floods. Most of the *assists* were relevant. The interface had learned how to serve him better by more accurately anticipating his needs. There also seemed to be more English appearing in place of the runic language. At the same time that the interface was adapting to Mark, he was acclimating to the pain which accompanied the small data-floods. What had been severe pain had now become more like a chronic headache that could almost be ignored. The questioning by Carl and Kathy could not be ignored and was beginning to tax him. They would ask and he would either know the answer or an *assist* would present enough information so that he could take a stab at it.

"Sarah can no longer eat any animal products," said Kathy. "There's no medical explanation. She's developing the same as you did, going through the same stages; but the duration and sequence appear to be different."

An *assist* flooded him… "The differences in her development are because of different aptitudes," said Mark. "I have an aptitude for directing and requesting data-floods, while she has an aptitude for picking up life experiences and feelings that have been sent out across the god-machine's web. Basically, I get more stored scientific data while she gets more people data. This makes perfect sense. I'm a scientist. I deal with logic and data. She's a cop. She works with intuition and hunches. She's been able to perceive other people's experiences long before now, and possibly her entire life. For me, this morning was the very first time I was able to receive stray thoughts that were directed at me."

"You're able to read thoughts!" said Carl. "This is incredible."

"It's not like that," said Mark. "It's not mind-reading; it's more like tuning in to what people are sending out intentionally or subconsciously, kind of like mental e-mail containing a free association. If an internal dialog is ongoing in someone's mind, I can't perceive it unless it gets into the subconscious, where the thought-interface operates. Leaking unintentional subconscious broadcasts are like muttering under your breath at someone when they may or may not be close enough to hear. What counts are: loudness, proximity, and how badly your id wants that person to overhear you."

"Are you getting subconscious mutterings from people all the time?" asked Kathy. She was shifting in her seat and having a hard time with eye contact.

"It's rare. I get very little, and it's only from some people. I really think it has to be intentional and focused, even if only subconscious wish fulfillment. If you want to know what I'm getting right now from you, the answer is nothing. Most people, including you and Carl, just don't seem to transmit; or at least that's my limited experience."

The meeting was over. Carl had unlocked the door. They were all standing. A shaft of sunlight was shining through a window and out into the next room. Dust motes were moving in the light. Mark wondered if there were nanotech seeds in the dust. The carpet in the outer office was brightly illuminated. Mark stared at the spot where the officers had stood. He could almost see outlines of their footprints. Was the image from an *assist*? An implanted memory blinked into his thoughts. The memory was clear for a moment; then, gone and irretrievable. It had happened so fleetingly yet the experience left him with a strong unexplainable impression the officers were a threat.

"Carl, can I ask you a question?" said Mark.

"Shoot."

"What did the army brass want?"

"You know I can't talk about national security."

"Don't bullshit me," said Mark. "In a few weeks there may not be much national security left. If it's something I need to know, you should spill the beans. I've spilled mine."

Carl took a deep breath. He looked sheepish.

"Fuck it," he muttered. "It's nothing. I get this kind of garbage all the time. They were asking about you and Sarah. Some folks at the Pentagon think you two might be a security risk. They're worried you've been taken over by the machine and have become spies."

"What!" said Kathy.

"It's just pentagon 'stupid-think' that's going nowhere fast," said Carl. "I'm confident the senior staff doesn't believe it."

"I had a feeling they were here about us," said Mark. "Sarah said something the other day, and at first I didn't believe her; but since then, I've started to change my mind. She said a time is coming when almost everyone will turn against us."

"I'd never do that!" said Carl.

"I know," said Mark, "But it's time for everyone to leave this place. We've done as much as we can. It's up to the federal government now. They're either going to make peace or drop bombs."

Carl looked angry. His forehead was furled with deep wrinkles as his eyes stared off into some distant place. Mark could tell there was a conflict going on inside that head. He wondered if Carl had told him everything.

"Under the best of conditions it may not be easy for certain people to escape from this military garrison. We all have to leave before they completely take the option of leaving away from me and Sarah," said Mark. "All of us are on borrowed time here. The kill zones are hitting the same places, and that means we're on the short list for several more, and probably sooner rather than later. Sarah thinks one is coming and I believe her. I'm starting to get the same intuition that one's overdue; and maybe with it, something else is coming that's just as bad. This may sound egotistical, but if I can't save what's left of the world by convincing our government to try peace, then I have to save any small parts that I can."

"How do you know you can save anyone?" asked Kathy.

"You have to trust me," said Mark. "Every hour I'm learning more about how to interact with the god-machine. I have access to strategy maps showing where kill zones have hit and where more are planned; I just don't know when. I can use those maps to avoid the hot zones and guide us all out of danger. I know I can find a place that'll be safe until this ends; and it will end one way or the other. I have to leave, Kathy – and I want you to go with me."

Kathy hugged him, first weakly, then with increasing strength. He felt her crying against his chest. He closed his eyes. He'd been feeling stronger about her with each passing day, and this day was no different. He was still human. His emotions were more poignant than at any time he could remember; and that confirmed to him that while his brain was becoming part machine, his soul was not.

"I trust you," whispered Kathy.

He felt Carl's hand on his back.

"I'm going," said Carl. "There's nothing left here. In another few days, almost everyone will be gone anyway. My family's gone. There's no reason for me to stay. I'll take my chances with you folks."

~

Mark, Kathy, and Carl were planning their next move in hushed voices. They didn't want any of part of the conversation to be overheard. While they all agreed Mark and Sarah were not under immediate risk of being arrested, if their plans leaked to the military, they would all likely be detained on the spot. After a lengthy discussion, Sarah was called into the meeting. She'd been anything but silent. She'd come into the office looking agitated. Once she'd found out what they were planning, her entire mood had changed. She was animated about pulling up stakes and leaving.

"How can we warn everyone without risking arrest?" asked Sarah.

"We can't leave without warning them," said Kathy.

"I'm not saying we should skip out on them. I'm just asking how," said Sarah.

"We can meet with people one on one," said Mark. "Just conversations. Feel them out. Nothing that'll draw attention."

"They're not going to believe what we tell them," said Sarah. "How do we get them to trust us?"

"We can't," said Carl. "People who already trust us will be easier to convince. Those who don't trust us or can't be trusted won't believe us anyway; or worse, they'll cause trouble."

"You're right," said Mark. "I don't like saying it, but with some people, it's a lost cause. We're going to have to use triage. It's a matter of survival. We can talk quietly with people we trust and warn the others after we leave. As soon as we're gone, we can send a mass e-mail, and include all our proof that a kill zone is going to hit, and tell them where it'll be safe. Agreed?"

Everyone agreed. Next, they put together a script. They'd work as a single team and make discreet visits to people starting immediately. Mark noticed Sarah staring at him very intently. As he looked away, a sphere of memory was there at the surface of his mind with the now familiar glow of her presence. He focused on the sphere until it opened. The memory capsule contained a single thought captured from Sarah's internal dialog, "*Anyone who joins us could die along the way... Kathy? Carl?*" Mark stared at Sarah for several seconds unable to grapple with what she'd sent him. He almost answered her by speaking aloud but then stopped. Was she suggesting they should try to escape alone? He focused on encapsulating his thoughts and sent them to her so she could – in effect – read a small part of his mind. He had no intention of leaving Kathy behind. Sarah smiled.

"Did you tell them about Alexander?" asked Sarah.

"Who's Alexander?" asked Kathy.

~

They'd spent half the day talking with people who were closely trusted by either Kathy or Carl. They didn't discuss Alexander. They'd kept things focused and spoke only about kill zones. Everyone had listened and asked questions, but Mark saw they were not making believers out of any of them. Everyone they spoke with had prior fears and stresses which made it very hard for them to take in new information. Mark was feeling his own frustrations growing as he sensed an increasing amount of distrust directed toward him and Sarah. The entire idea of warning or taking people with them was beginning to seem naive.

They had just shut an office door and taken three more people into their confidence. A married couple name Paul and Louise were both medical doctors, and their office neighbor Jena was a mechanical engineer. Jena was nerdy and quiet. Paul and Louise were both outspoken.

Mark could see Kathy was growing desperate to convince someone to join their exodus, or as they'd agreed to call it, 'the evacuation plan.' Mark wondered if she was really trying to convince herself and not her friends. Everyone was seated except Sarah, who had said nothing during the past two meetings and had become increasingly withdrawn.

"To be brutally honest, we've all heard the rumors about you and Sarah and these neural alterations," said Paul. "We've seen the medical images. There's no denying something very mysterious is happening in your brain. But some of your claims are just not possible. You say you've healed yourself and can predict where kill zones will hit. How can you ask us to gamble our lives on those kinds of wild claims? How do we know you won't blindly lead us, with the best of intentions, into a catastrophe?"

"I'm not asking anyone to follow me," said Mark. "But you're got to leave before…"

There was a soft moan from behind him. Mark turned and saw Sarah. Pain was written all over her face. At her side, a folding knife was dangling loosely in her fingers. The blade clattered to the floor. She'd cut her palm open across the lifeline. Blood was dripping all over her fingers. She held up her ruined hand with the palm facing out.

"This is how you know," she said.

"Nice" said Paul. "Now, we know you're crazy!"

"You wanted proof," said Sarah. "This hurt more than I'd thought. I'm not doing it again. So watch closely."

"I know what she's trying," said Mark. "Just give her a chance."

Sarah picked up a wad of tissues and squeezed it in her fist, to stem the flow of blood. The room was silent. Mark looked from face to face and saw that Sarah's dramatics might just work. No one took their eyes off her hand. They all appeared fascinated and revolted; which was a powerful emotional cocktail. An *assist,* triggered by his intense interest in what was going on, projected a medical schematic over Sarah. He saw COBIC swarming like an infection into the wound site.

After a few minutes, Sarah removed the wad of tissue and picked out a few remaining bits. She held out her hand. The cut had stopped bleeding. There was a deep gash, but the walls of the cut were now sealed. Mark was no medical doctor, but he knew something that nasty should have still been bleeding. Paul picked up her hand to examine it.

"May I," he said.

Sarah nodded. Paul applied some spreading pressure on the wound's edges, trying to open it. Sarah squinted in pain. The injury remained sealed. Louise came and stared as Paul continued to manipulate the wound. Jena moved closer.

"This is incredible," said Paul. "This should be bleeding like a faucet! We should be on our way to the infirmary to get some stitches on it."

"It will take a few days to completely heal," said Mark. "Within twelve hours, the cut will be a thick scar. In a day, the scar will look old. In a couple of days, it will be the faint scar of a childhood wound; and then it will be gone."

"Okay," said Paul. "I believe you, but you'd better promise me this is for real. You promise me that you can see when kill zones are coming and where they've been. You promise me that my wife will be safe."

"I can promise staying here is not an option if you want to live," said Mark. "And I can promise to lead you to a place safe from kill zones, but I can't promise bad things won't happen along the way. I can't see the future, but I can see the god-machine's plans and they're not good for this place."

In that moment, three new people had joined the exodus; and Mark felt the weight on him growing heavier. He prayed he wouldn't fail these people along the way. He was confident that he could do what he'd said. Up until this moment, there had been good, logical reasons to believe he could lead people to safety. But now he knew he'd be put to the test with even more people; and that somehow changed everything. He and Sarah had to run. Kathy and Carl were going with them, no matter what; but these people were new and they were choosing to come, out of free will. They had options and had decided to look to him. For Mark, there could no longer be any gap between knowing what he could do in theory and having enough faith in himself to accomplish it. In accepting responsibility for the safety of these people, he'd taken a step into a role from which there was no turning back.

23 – Washington, DC: January

The meeting in a secured situation room in the heart of the Pentagon was an hour old. McKafferty felt time was being wasted when they should be acting. The country needed protection, not hot air. The aides to the chairmen of the military were present at the meeting. The chairmen themselves, the President, and his advisors were all teleconferenced in from various airborne command posts.

A recording of McKafferty's recent meeting with the BVMC lab personnel was being replayed. Mark Freedman was speaking. McKafferty had heard this recording so many times that most of it was committed to memory; but still each time he heard the scientist's words, he was more convinced than ever that Freedman was a traitor. The good doctor was working to protect the god-machine. His treason might not be voluntary, but how could anyone doubt where his sympathies lie? If the medical projections were accurate, it wouldn't be long before Freedman's brain was a hundred percent artificial. He was being transformed into their enemy right before their eyes, and half these fools were blind to it. The President's advisors had been siding with Freedman and urging caution. The recording was droning on about making peace with the god-machine and how the super colony could not be destroyed without hurting mankind. The tape was nearing a part that illustrated how unreliable Freedman had become. McKafferty turned up the volume just a notch to make sure everyone was listening.

"So I understand you believe this thing is ancient technology?" said McKafferty's recorded voice. *"Are we talking about legends of Atlantis? How old is it? A hundred years? A thousand years?"*
"Try over two hundred millions years," said Freedman.
"That's impossible. There were no humans alive then."
"Who said it was created by humans?"

McKafferty paused the recording. Some of the military people were shaking their heads. Freedman had just hung himself with his own recorded words. For all McKafferty knew, the Nobel Laureate might have been telling the truth, but McKafferty knew how this sounded to desperate political animals locked in airborne prisons. They would not stake their political and physical lives – or the country – on a man talking like that. McKafferty stood up and walked to within a few feet of the video camera. His ugly visage filled the screen. He was determined to make sure his message was driven home with the force of a sledge hammer.

"Mr. President," said McKafferty. "Time is running out. The NSA has been analyzing data flowing across the nanotech's wireless web. They have found a nexus, a location in a deep pacific trench where the flows converge. Four days ago, submarines were deployed for close quarters ELINT surveillance. Consensus is that we've located the core of the web and that this core is the central nervous system of our enemy. The NSA is convinced, BARDCOM scientists are convinced, and I am convinced that we have located the super colony. The submarines conducting surveillance are attack-class boats carrying full weapon's complements; Air Force weapons can be on target in less than an hour. Right now, we have the power to destroy our enemy with overwhelming force; I am talking about a massive strike using EMP nuclear weapons. Yes, there are risks. You've heard what the CDC experts think. They cannot predict what will happen when this bastard's decapitated. They say we could be killed by its death throes or our children could be born retarded without the influence of some unidentified intelligence factor. No one can accurately predict what will happen when we free ourselves from these mind-control chains, but I can predict what will happen if we do not. The genocide will continue and the enslavement will continue. I believe its goal is a world full of robot-humans like our illustrious Dr. Freedman. Its goal is nothing less than global domination."

McKafferty pressed a button which displayed his battle plan overlaid on a world map. Ground-zero was a crosshair in the Pacific, ringed by submarines and overflow by Air force bombers. Fanning out from ground-zero were color coded markings which designated various levels of risk from the machine if it managed to retaliate before being neutralized, or if its death convulsions proved dangerous. The plan was displayed split screen, with McKafferty's face covering the other half.

"Gentlemen, we are not completely in the dark," said McKafferty. "We do have some indications of what will happen when this nanotech monstrosity is destroyed. We have isolated people from the machine, using aircraft. You are isolated from it right now at twenty thousand feet. Have your mental functions declined? Are you dying or retarded? Of course not… Nothing happened to you when you lifted off in your jets and lost contact with the super colony. Nothing, that is, except you are now safe from kill zones and safe from any repercussions from attacks we initiate. By nuking this threat, we will cause nothing more than what you experienced when your jets lifted off. We will yank this nanotech beast's plug from the wall and free all of mankind from its clutches, and no one will feel a thing. Could I be wrong? Yes, I am the first person to admit the possibility. Could Freedman's doomsday prediction of instant death come to pass? Yes, it could; but we must take that risk. Gentlemen, I would rather die a free man, defending my country than live as a slave under some machine, which is exactly what will happen if we do what Freedman suggests!"

McKafferty moved away from the video camera, leaving his battle plan visible on split screen. He took his seat. He folded his hands. He tried to look as calm as possible. His temples were thumping with every beat of his heart. The room was silent. He had just given the speech of his life. He had done the right thing and done all he could. His wife would be proud of him. His children would be proud of him. The decision was now in higher hands.

"Thank you, General," said the President. "I am seriously considering your recommendations for nuclear attack and I am inclined to agree."

"Mr. President!" shouted Chief of Staff Martin Ross.

"Calm yourself, Martin," said the President. "I will consider all opinions presented today. I have not made up my mind. I will reach a decision within twenty-four hours. Now I want recommendations about what to do with Professor Freedman and this woman Sarah Mayfair. If they have been taken over…"

24 – Atlanta: January

Mark woke up out of god-machine-conjured nightmares and saw Kathy awake and staring out the office windows. Today was the day they were leaving. Kathy had prescribed sleeping pills to try to give him a full night's rest. He'd been having difficulty sleeping for days. The cause was more than insomnia and nightmares; his body just didn't seem to need sleep anymore.

Kathy was dressed in a t-shirt and jeans. They'd finished preparing to leave last night, before going to bed. A pair of bags were packed and standing in the middle of the floor. A kitty cage with its door open was next to the bags. They were both leaving much of what they owned behind, partly out of necessity, but also out of realization that their lives, going forward, would be utterly different than what their lives had been; and that most of their possessions from their past would be of little use in their future.

Mark silently watched Kathy for a long time. She didn't know he was awake. The sun was streaming in the window and shining on her face. She was perfectly motionless, staring off into space. There was a sound out in the hallway. She turned and saw Mark. She smiled at him with dampness in her eyes that he hadn't seen. She'd been crying. For an instant, he was overwhelmed by a thought coming so clearly from her like a single musical note of sorrow. This was the first time he had ever perceived her thoughts, and maybe would be the only time; and she was imagining what it would be like to lose him. They were heading out today toward an unknown future. With all that could go wrong, with all the sacrifices that might be demanded, her only worry was of losing him. Mark's heart was breaking. The end wouldn't happen

481

like that. She wasn't going to lose him. More likely, he would be the one losing her. His potential lifespan was now far greater than hers. If she chose not to take the next step, then someday he would be alone. He got up and hugged her with all the emotions that were inside him.

"Are you ready?" he finally asked.

"I think so."

The exodus had been scheduled with the motor pool as a field expedition into Atlanta to conduct hospital site surveys. Mark and Sarah had been left off the roster. The excuse for the expedition was a little implausible, but apparently few of the remaining soldiers really cared. Morale had fallen in the military just as it had in the civilian sector. Some soldiers had taken bribes to allow people to leave with Humvees and other equipment they didn't own. Mark and Kathy walked into Carl's office.

"Are we all set?" asked Mark.

"There are twenty-nine people waiting down by the Humvees," said Carl. "Sarah is unaccounted for. No one's seen her and her dog's missing too."

"Don't worry about Sarah," said Mark. "She'll be there."

There were seven light-armored military Humvees lined up in rows by the curb. They had been requisitioned for the field trip. Everyone had agreed to limit personal items. Dragging a long procession of suitcases out to the trucks would arouse suspicion as well as limit space for more important items like food and medical supplies. Carl had made arrangements to meet up with an old friend of his, a major in the National Guard and the commanding officer of a base on the outskirts of Atlanta. They'd get fully supplied for the exodus there. Major Franklin had a collection of fully provisioned trailers ready to be hooked up to the Humvees. The Major and his family were coming along for the ride.

Mark, Kathy, and Carl climbed up into the lead Humvee. Mark was hit with memories of the last time he had been inside one of these vehicles. It had been in Los Angeles a lifetime ago. Other people were loading up the vehicles behind them. He and Kathy were in the back seat; Carl was in front. The passenger seat was empty.

"I'm getting worried about Sarah," said Carl. "She may have decided to go on her own. She was a loner before she came to Atlanta."

"She'll be here," said Mark. "She's walking up behind us right now. Turn around."

Kathy and Carl both turned around. Mark smiled and continued to look straight ahead. He knew what they were seeing. Sarah and Ralph were walking up the driveway toward them. She was dressed in a black sweatshirt with a thin bulletproof vest hidden underneath, a baseball cap with a police logo, and a backpack. He'd just experienced memories containing all of this and far more from Sarah. There were hours of her life compressed into the sphere which had just blossomed in his mind. He had memories of her turning before a mirror in a bulletproof vest adjusting the straps, of her standing up after sitting in a field of damp grass, of her walking through the woods back to the CDC facility. The last part of the memory capsule was of her seeing the line of Humvees. Mark felt the tailgate of the Humvee open and heard Sarah talking to Ralph.

"Come on, boy," said Sarah. "Sorry about the crummy accommodations. I know you hate cats, but this beats walking; and they are behind bars. Keep an eye on 'em."

There was a soft bark. A moment later, Sarah climbed into the passenger seat and buckled up. She looked tranquil and alert, no smile and no frown. She had a very business-like presence for the moment. Carl punched up directions for the first leg of the trip on the GPS. Mark remembered a line out of a book from his youth.

"Every journey begins with the first step," he said.

This exodus was clearly a first step, but there had been so many other first steps all chained together and unbreakably leading to this single moment. There was the step that led him to discover COBIC so many years ago, the step that originally brought him from California to the CDC, the step when he'd discovered nanotech seeds, and the step which had changed him into something that was physically no longer what some people would consider human.

"My first step was this morning when I woke up," said Sarah. "I don't believe in the past anymore."

"Show me your hand," said Carl.

Sarah held up her palm. There was a nasty looking pink scar that appeared to be fully healed over. Mark saw that the gash was knitting itself together even faster than he would have expected. That single scar held almost spiritual significance for him. It had convinced twenty-nine people to trust him with their lives.

"That's a future I believe in," said Carl.

~

They'd been on the road for an hour. At first, they'd headed northeast toward Atlanta. Once they were halfway into the city, they'd left the highway, reversed direction and were now heading southwest on surface roads. The plan was to make it difficult for anyone following their trail. All the military two-way radios built into the Humvees had been turned off and the antennas unplugged, just to make sure. Everyone had been warned not to bring cell phones, wireless PC tablets, or any other electronics that might give up their position. Few people on the streets paid any attention to the small caravan of Humvees. Military vehicles were a common sight these days; and the drivers did everything possible to not standout. No one had said anything for some time. The only sounds were the rattling of the Humvee as it went through pot holes.

"I was inside Alexander body," said Sarah breaking the silence. "That's why I was late. I was in the woods behind the CDC where it was quiet and easier to concentrate. At first I didn't think I was going to succeed at crawling into his skin; most of the time the remote vision – or whatever it is – just refuses to focus in, but I keep trying. I had to find out if he was sensing our escape. I think he knows something has changed, but he doesn't know what. He was agitated."

"Maybe he felt you inside him and that's why he was agitated," said Mark.

"I don't know, maybe, but at some point, he'll learn we've slipped through his fingers. I heard him talking to some of his men. It sounded like he was frustrated waiting for the kill zone to hit the CDC. He thinks it could still be days, but he's not sure. He's just sitting and waiting somewhere at the outskirts of Atlanta. It's creepy. I had no idea he was that close. He knows he can't risk attacking until the kill zone hits. If his army's in the wrong place at the wrong time, then he could lose all his fighters in a single kill zone."

"We know he's subliminally accessing the interface," said Mark. "Look at what he's managed to do just from it leaking into his dreams. It would be a disaster if he discovers how to restructure the interface and gains control."

"They're all against us," said Sarah. "Every one of them... Some think we're spies, others think we caused the plague. Some of them even believe we're trying to start a new race of people to replace them."

Carl looked away from the road for a moment and stared at Sarah. He seemed startled by what she'd said. Maybe the human race will be replaced, thought Mark. Maybe no matter what anyone did to disrupt the god-machine's plans, the struggle would all end with the last homo sapien drawing its last breath a year from now, or centuries from now, as some new race inherits the Earth. Hybrids like him and Sarah could be transitional links to that new race. There were compelling reasons to believe that the next evolutionary step for mankind would be a hybrid of human and machine. Mankind had been going in that direction for decades with artificial body parts, and before that with powered machines, and before that with hand tools. Humans had always been machine augmented in one way or another; and always carried the nanotech inside without knowing it. Mankind had been part of the ultimate machine and never used it. The next step would be conscious integration of man and machine, but that integration was only a small part of the changes to come. Mark had cured himself of diabetes. He had no illusions that the cure had been accomplished in any way other than changes to his DNA. Just as he'd genetically engineered bacteria in his Los Angeles lab to produce new designer species of bacteria, the nanotech seeds had meddled with his genes in some way to produce a new designer human, one that was free of diabetes. Was mankind evolving into a self-modifying species with self-modifying genes? Was this exodus nothing more than a small collection of half-human seeds being cast into fertile soil?

25 – Near Houston, Texas: January

After five days of relentless and uneventful travel, they had found their first enjoyable place to stay overnight, a deserted mall with underground parking. Electrical power was still working and so were the lights. Kathy had gone off to the far side of the garage for some privacy which had become a precious commodity since they'd set out from the CDC. She was sitting on steps which led up to a mall entrance. The vehicles and trailers were parked in a circle in the center of the first floor of the garage. They parked in the same way every night. The circle was a wall of armored protection in case of attack. A group of people were talking within the center of the ring of Humvees. She heard Mark's voice and put down her journal for a moment and listened. He had changed on this journey. There was an aura of wisdom that surrounded him. He'd never shouldered life and death responsibilities on this scale before, but he was now their leader and he was carrying it well. He was growing into the role with a natural ease. Everything he did felt evenhanded and wise. She could still see mild surprise register in his eyes when his smallest suggestions were followed without hesitation. Their tiny band of travelers, their tribe as Kathy thought of them, was quickly growing to love and respect the man she loved.

Kathy opened her journal and found the page she was working on. She'd started keeping the journal after the first night on the road. She felt it was her contribution to the exodus. For days, they had traveled west on small roads, avoiding all highways because their limited access carried risks of ambush and naked exposure to anyone looking down from the sky. Their path was often diverted long distances north or south to avoid places kill zones had previously hit. The confusing routes also served another purpose; it made it difficult for anyone that might be in pursuit.

Since leaving the CDC, they'd camped overnight five times and always under some kind of cover. They had to keep their vehicles out of sight. Alexander was a concern, but the bigger worry at night was the government. If the military wanted them badly enough, then satellites and aircraft could be looking for them with infrared sensors. At night, the heat of their engines would standout as bright spots for hours after the Humvees were shutdown. Kathy remembered the satellite images Lieutenant Kateland had shown them. She could almost feel emotionless mechanical eyes looking down, even now. They had to be careful. It truly felt as if they were being hunted.

The mall was a good place to spend the night. For some odd reason, this one had never been looted. It felt strange walking down the empty causeways, gazing into store windows full of merchandise. The place was like a museum dedicated to some lost age of mankind. She and Mark had gone through the entire mall. They'd found fresh food in the refrigerators of a restaurant. Together, they had cooked dinner for everyone and eaten in the gallery of the mall with fountains tricking down nearby. Afterwards, many of their party had looked in the stores. The displays were filled with everything a modern human could possibly desire, but there was nothing here worth taking. All the luxuries were free, and yet it all had been left behind, undisturbed this night. Kathy wondered if other travelers had been through here and seen the same things and reached the same conclusions. Life was simpler now. Everything revolved around survival. Designer shoes didn't matter.

Jewelry didn't matter. Fancy electronics didn't matter. All those shiny toys were completely worthless now.

Kathy closed her journal and walked into the center of the Humvee circle. She sat down next to Mark. There was a ring of twenty people all talking with him. Sarah was sitting on the opposite side of the circle, with Ralph asleep beside her. Sarah had been quiet for the past couple of days. At times, Kathy had thought she was brooding; but she'd been wrong so many times about Sarah that she'd given up trying to figure the young woman out. Roadmaps were laid out on the ground in front of Mark. He had been drawing on one with a yellow highlighter pen. He was shading in kill zone areas to avoid. He had started doing this, in case he was injured or worse. If the maps survived, then there was still some hope; but Kathy knew no one believed that. The maps were only a source of comfort for Mark. If they lost him, they would all soon scatter to the wind.

Kathy looked at everyone's faces. It was odd how alive she felt and how alive everyone looked. There was something so primal in this migration and its shared hardship. All their actions felt so deeply rooted in the essence of life. She suspected part of the reason for these feelings was that the constant motion during the days and the deep resting at night must have been close to the natural rhythms for humans since they roamed the primal savannas in search of food. She and Mark made love every night. She felt guilty thinking that if they survived, she might look back at this time as the best moments of her life.

She picked up Mark's hand and held it. She ran her fingers over the back of his hand. His skin felt like unblemished silk. At night before sleep, they often talked about the little changes that were occurring in him. The changes were both emotional and physical. The physical was visible. His body was doing more than healing; it was trying to perfect itself. The freckles on his skin were fading. His hair looked thicker and softer. His eyes looked somehow different too. Mark said his night vision was improving and he no longer needed glasses. She had no idea what might be going on inside his organs. She'd brought field medical kits with her but nothing that could help answer those questions. All she had was medicine, first aid supplies, and instruments that didn't need batteries.

The group conversation was almost the same every night. The discussion was limited to one of two topics in which everyone in their small band was fascinated. Tonight they were talking about what it was like to be enhanced by a machine. Mark had started calling himself a hybrid and the term had stuck. In their tribe, there was a small click of people who wanted to become hybrids. Mark had started instructing them in ways to reach the thought-interface using mental focus, but so far none of them had been successful in the smallest measure. There was discontented talk of trying to obtain drugs like LSD and the shortcuts it could offer. No one except Kathy and Sarah knew that Mark had a small bottle of LSD which was being saved for the future; but there was little chance the drug would work on even a small percentage of their tribe. Medical records were full of people who took overdoses and suffered permanent mental breakdowns; and those that didn't have breakdowns were not interfaced to the god-machine, they just had occasional flashbacks. The evidence was clear that LSD was not all that was needed. Unless someone had the right kind of latent predisposition, taking LSD was a game of Russian roulette; and the odds were very long against winning the lottery of machine enlightenment. Mark had repeatedly stressed this, and he was correct according to Kathy's medical view. From the beginning there had to have been something different about Mark and Sarah. They'd survived kill zones where others had died. They had prior subconscious communications with the god-machine which came out in dreams and premonitions; and in Sarah's case, this might have been occurring her entire life and possibly even in earlier generations. Kathy suspected the same might be true for Mark. Both Mark and Sarah probably shared a subtle difference in brain chemistry or structure, maybe a common genetic difference. Consuming hallucinogens made it easier to use their latent ability to work the interface. Kathy wondered if their brains had some crucial similarity to the creatures who built the god-machine.

"If it was as simple as taking hallucinogenic drugs, then we'd have a world full of drug addicts communing with the god-machine," said Mark.

"What about schizophrenics?" someone called out.

"I don't know, but that's an interesting question," said Mark. "Some schizophrenics speak with invisible people or even god. Maybe schizophrenics are in some faulty way connected to the god-machine? Maybe the predisposition that Sarah and I have is something related to schizophrenia?"

"You know there's some evidence that there's a structural difference in the brains of schizophrenics," said Kathy.

Noel stood up from the circle of people. He was a small man with a very bright mind. He looked several people in the eyes and then stared at Mark.

"What's the point of any of this crap?" he said. "Part of the reason I came with you was so that I could learn to become like you. I think there's something you're not telling us."

"Did anyone else come only for this reason?" asked Mark. "The quest for the fountain of youth is a very old story which ends badly."

People in the circle looked at each other. No one said a thing, then a woman named Alice raised her hand, and then another person raised their hand, and another. Soon eight hands were raised.

"Noel, be careful what you ask for," said Sarah.

"It's alright," said Mark. "Who wouldn't want access to the Library of Alexandria and a lifespan long enough to read it? The big question is what's really going on inside my body. Is it the fountain of youth or just a different way to die? We don't really know what Sarah and I have done to ourselves. We could be dead or burnt out in six months."

"Now just wait a minute!" said Noel. "We're all going to die. That's a fact. How many people here can say they wouldn't jump at the chance for perfect health even if they knew for certain it had risks and they'd end up half machine?"

"I wouldn't," said Kathy.

She was sorry she'd spoken the instant the words had left her mouth. Had she just helped Mark or hurt him? Though he wasn't showing it outwardly, she knew any confrontation troubled him; and she'd just contributed to a confrontation. Since they'd been on the road, Mark seemed to be gradually adopting pacifism; it was not the weak kind of pacifism of a coward, but the strong kind built on conviction. He'd also begun displaying an uncanny ability to defuse confrontations. Mark continued speaking with Noel. Soon Noel was losing momentum; then he fell silent. Mark had somehow painted him as misguided; though Kathy could not identify a single thing Mark had said that would lead to that impression.

Eventually, the conversation moved on to the other group topic that was often discussed, kill zones. Kathy privately knew Mark had given up hope that he or any one person could stop the god-machine's rampage; but discussing how it could be stopped was cathartic and important for the health of the group, so Mark indulged himself and others in it. Days ago, he'd explained the command catalog and the ancients' language. He and Sarah still spent most of their time searching for any connection between programs and kill zones. Kathy had been stunned by how similar their descriptions of some god-machine interfaces were to everyday computer software. Were there other similarities? Our programs were full of bugs. Could the murder of our entire race be due to a bug in the god-machine's programming?

"Why do you think you haven't found any trace of kill zone programs in the catalogs?" asked Carl. "I mean isn't it strange? This is a doomsday weapon and there's no command and control. It's like building a nuclear submarine and forgetting to add controls for the missiles. Who in their right mind would do that?"

"I've been searching and searching for ways to control it or make it stop," said Mark. "I'm still convinced that if we quit being a threat, it would stop killing; but governments have no intentions of trying the way of peace. I've spent every available moment trying to understand this machine and so has Sarah. I have serious doubts that kill zone controls exist. I know the god-machine is carrying out this holocaust, following an exact plan. I've accessed a strategy map which proves this to me. The mystery is why's there no means of operator control? One way this makes sense is if extinctions are not part of the original programming, but an aberration. If kill zones are something the god-machine evolved on its own, then there's no reason for a user interface to exist. It simply was not engineered for use by organic life forms. That's one possibility...

"The other possibility is that we just haven't found the controls yet. Sarah and I suspect the command catalog also functions as a mental keyboard. I know each phrase is a command or program name, but I also think the phrases can be combined to create more complex tasks. In other words, it's a language; and that means there's got to be sentences. The point is, this would make the interface as complicated as the ancients' written language. No one could ever be sure kill zone controls don't exist."

"I've been thinking," said a programmer named Barbara. "What if it's a virus? We have computer viruses. What if some kind of virus program evolved out of the network and then embedded itself into the nucleus of the god-machine? The virus would have no human interface and it could have completely different goals than the original system."

"What you're describing is a code mutation," said Mark. "It's a good hypothesis, but there's a problem. Whatever their origin, the extinction and kill zone programs are now major parts of the rules of the god-machine. A virus would not be so deeply integrated. This is no rogue program that's hanging on like a loose tumor. This holocaust has the full will and planning of the god-machine behind it."

"I wish they would just blow the son of a bitch up!" said Paul. "Me too," said someone else. "Destroy the fucker!" shouted a third.

26 – Texas Coastline near Corpus Christi: January

Mark was asleep. The dream surrounding him was the first he'd had that was not a god-machine-conjured nightmare. Sarah was in his dream. The instant she touched him, a powerful infusion of memories flooded his mind. They were not normally assembled memories – some ran backward in time like a reversed video, others were frozen moments, and some were just normal scraps of time. The dream was a series of disjointed experiences, like shards of a broken mirror imperfectly reflecting a whole image in its pieces. He knew if the shards could be reassembled, everything would be explained. He saw memories of dreams filled with bodies floating in the Hudson River. He saw memories of god-machine war plans projected onto a map. He saw memories of Alexander's fighters murdering an entire town. He saw memories of Atlanta in ruins. He saw memories of him and Sarah mating.

Mark awoke gasping for breath. The tent he was sleeping in was dark. The air was cool and damp from the nearby sea. The surf rumbled like a distant storm in the background. Every fractured part of the dream was deeply troubling. Atlanta was going to be hit by kill zones today. He knew this with the same kind of certainty that he knew his own identity. Innocent people would die today. Alexander would attack today. He knew there was nothing he could do to prevent any of this. Kathy was sleeping next to him. He put his arms around her and pulled her close to his chest. She murmured something in her sleep. He looked up into the starry sky through an open flap of their tent. He knew he would be awake for the rest of the night. How long would this holocaust go on?

Morning light was glowing through the fabric of the tent. A fine dusting of sand had drifted in during the night. Mark picked up his head. He heard helicopters moving in their direction. The sound was definitely more than one and the racket was getting louder. He rolled out of the sleeping bag. Kathy woke looking disoriented. Mark grabbed his pants and pulled them on.

"What's that?" mumbled Kathy.

Her eyes grew wide. Mark ran out of the tent barefoot into the sand and stopped next to Sarah who had just run out of her tent. She had a troubled expression. Out over the waves, a column of helicopters was coming right at them skimming over the water. In seconds, one was upon them. They were clearly some kind of military birds, painted grey with racks of what could be missiles hanging on each side. Before he could do anything other than stare, the first chopper had roared past. The sound was deafening. In an equally spaced column, nine more rocketed past like an airborne train. The last one peeled off, swung around in a wide circle, and then stopped in a dead hover no more than a hundred feet above the dunes. Mark shielded his face from grit being kicked up. He looked over at Sarah. She was waiving hello with one arm while the other covered her eyes. She was gambling with their lives. Suddenly, the chopper tipped forward, roared off over their heads, and was gone.

Kathy had joined Mark. Everyone in camp was staring in the direction the helicopters had disappeared. The sound of their rotors continued fading. Mark had no idea if they would be coming back. Was this an accidental discovery or had they been spotted by remote surveillance? They'd camped with the Humvees outside for the first time since fleeing Atlanta. They'd been unable to find shelter and the beach was tempting, so Mark had decided to stop for the night. They'd cooled the Humvee's heat signatures by dragging buckets of water up from the surf and dousing the hoods. Mark wondered if camping out in the open had been a terrible mistake. Every minute that went by without the choppers returning was a good sign, but not good enough.

"Goddamn it!" said Sarah.

"We've got to go," said Mark. "Everyone, pack up! We can't wait until we see a ground patrol heading our way."

They had broken camp faster than Mark thought possible. The column of Humvees was racing along a two-lane state highway heading north toward San Antonio. Carl was driving. On any of these deserted Texas roads – large or small – the caravan stood out and was readily exposed to aerial surveillance. They needed to lose themselves in the clutter of an urban landscape. Mark had seen no signs of pursuit, but would he see anything before it was too late? He turned and looked out the rear window. Something terrible was about to happen. He could feel it. During this exodus, he'd guided them past hundreds of kill zone sites. They'd come too far and avoided so much; he was not going to lose them now.

"Noooo," moaned Sarah.

Mark turned to look at her and experienced it a moment later. Kill zones were ripping through Atlanta. The mental impact crumpled him in his seat. The god-machine was blanketing the city with multiple small kill zones. Mark perceived the destruction through the senses of bystanders who could do nothing but stare like paralyzed robots under god-machine control. Their experiences erupted to the surface of his mind like data-floods packed with the output of human sensory organs instead of data. Unbearable minutes passed. Countless flashes of horror boiled in his mind until he wanted to die... and then it all grew still, the aftermath of an empty city. Atlanta was now a mass grave. Mark knew about these observers from Sarah's descriptions. Among others, he'd just seen through the eyes of a good man, a soldier he knew well at the CDC lab, who'd stood inhumanly inert as the lab was hit again and again with machine-driven brutality. All of Atlanta had been sterilized one more time. Mark heard Sarah moaning softly as remnants of memory-images faded from his mind.

"Atlanta's ruined," said Mark.

"The lab?" asked Kathy.

"A graveyard... Almost everyone's dead and Alexander's free to murder who isn't."

Mark could see Kathy was resigned. Her eyes remained dry. They'd all accepted the inevitable a week ago. They'd all accepted they might become one of the few pockets of humanity to survive. Atlanta was one more horrific step toward that worst of possible endings. Mark sensed a memory capsule from Sarah. The sphere had appeared in his mind and was radiating its desire to express itself. He was confused. Why had she sent this? He focused on the capsule until it opened. He saw a collection of sixteen runic words and nothing more. Sarah turned and stared at him with vacant eyes. She was motionless except for the rocking of the Humvee; and a deep unnatural breathing which moved her shoulders up and down. There was something wrong with her.

"What is this?" he said.

Sarah's eyes came back to life. She blinked a few times. He recognized her disorientation was from a data-flood that was just waning. She closed her eyes for a moment and seemed to compose herself before speaking.

"I had the command catalog open before the kill zone started," she said. "I was searching for programs to try. Those sixteen words were displayed on the task list just as the kill zones began."

"Could you have run a command by accident?" asked Mark.

"I couldn't. I was paralyzed from a data-flood and then the phrase was loaded into the task list. I was ripped from the data-flood and slammed into the center of a kill zone. I think the phrase spells out a command that was automatically run. I think it opened the interface which connected me to observers in Atlanta."

"This is important," said Mark. "Okay. We need to work this step by step. We've got a sentence in the ancients' language and we think we know its meaning. We need to check each term by itself. If we can find a term in the catalog, we use the tablet to get a preview feeling for it. It'll probably give us a meaningless sensation or something, but we've got to try. The interface is constantly adapting to us; we may get a surprise. Next, we use the thought-interface to access data-floods on each term by itself, one at a time. When we're done we compare notes."

"What are you talking about?" asked Kathy.

"Cracking the code," said Mark. "Understanding the ancients' language. The phrase we've got is related to kill zones and could even lead us to programs controlling kill zones. I don't believe we'll find a way of stopping the god-machine, but we might just find something that'll save lives."

27 – Odessa, Texas: January

Mark awoke abruptly from a deep sleep. He struggled a moment to remember where he was parked; then the name came to him, Odessa, Texas. He'd driven into the underground garage while it was still daylight. The electricity in Odessa was out. They'd laid glow-sticks out on floor of the garage so people assigned watch duty could see anyone sneaking around. In the dim green light, Mark could see Kathy sleeping next to him. In the rear, he saw Carl; but Sarah's seat was empty. They'd bedded down in their Humvees so they could pull out in hurry. Mark looked at his watch – 3:20 a.m.

He knew a nightmare had jolted him from his sleep, but he couldn't remember it. As he rubbed his eyes, some of the dream came back to him, and then more, and then suddenly, it was fully back with startling detail; but it was not a dream. He realized the nightmare was woven whole from Alexander's real experiences. The memories had been sitting in his brain waiting to be noticed, waiting to be relived. He must have repressed them when awake; but in the vulnerability of dreams, they had flourished. Mark felt unclean experiencing the unfiltered violence of Alexander's triumphs seeping into his mind. He had no idea what this man looked like. He'd perceived many things through this soldier's senses, many things he wished he had never known, but not a glimpse of the face. Sarah had seen the face in a mirror and described his appearance. Mark knew he could pass him on a street and never know it, except that it would be hard to conceal the kind of savagery that inhabited that heart. In Mark's vision, the soldier was surrounded by a kaleidoscope of death, picking his way through the aftermath of an assault. Alexander and his followers had murdered all who remained at the CDC laboratory. Any doubts Mark had about Alexander's obsession to destroy him and Sarah had ended in this moment with this vision. The man was walking through the dead, turning over bodies to examine their faces. He obviously knew what Mark and Sarah looked like and was searching for them. Alexander reached the end of a hallway Mark recognized. A week ago, Mark had been there. His CDC office was just a few doors back. The man spun around and slammed his fist into a wall. He didn't utter a sound. The pain was intense. Alexander knew the Traitors had escaped. A suppressed rage unlike anything Mark had ever felt was building to an eruption inside this man, and then Mark understood why. In a dream, Alexander had seen the Traitors fleeing in a caravan of Humvees. He'd ignored the dream, believing it was nothing more than a subconscious fear of failure; but the dream had been real – and he had failed!

Dread was creeping into Mark's heart. He felt like his body was encased in ice, unable to move, unable to keep warm as the dread seeped deeper into his blood and flesh. Alexander was getting better at hunting them and he had dreams, god-machine spawned dreams, to guide him. If he'd listened to that inner voice, he might have bypassed Atlanta and been encircling them at this very moment. Mark looked out across the garage with its glow-stick illumination. He knew they had survived, not by decisive actions on their part, but because of Alexander's failure; and a hunter like this man would not make that mistake again.

Mark tried to erase the taste of violence he'd experienced. It was a sickness that thickly coated his mind. He climbed out of the Humvee and pulled on a sweater. The garage was quiet. He leaned his weight into the Humvee's door until it softly clicked shut. He knew where the guards had been stationed and suspected they were looking at him right now. He cracked a glow stick and shook it with a rattling sizzle. The chemical glow extended out into the deserted structure. He walked up a car ramp and into the night. He gazed upward. With the city lights blacked out, the night sky was crowded with stars. A mild sandy wind was blowing from the west. Mark sat down on a cement wall. He knew Alexander would be coming after them even harder, because of his defeat. There was little doubt that right now he was tracking his quarry using the god-machine as a subconscious guide. He probably believed it was intuition or maybe even that god was leading him. The man was growing unstable and, as a result, even more dangerous.

For days, Mark suspected he might have to split himself and Sarah off from the group. They might have to act as bait to draw Alexander into a trap; but before they could do that, he had to find a safe place for his people to wait and he had to devise a trap, both of which were far easier to think about than accomplish. He'd identified several good places where kill zones had never hit; but until the god-machine was finished with its genocide, there was no guarantee its plans would not change. A kill zone could hit everyone in a spot he'd just left them, falsely believing it was safe. The only solution was to keep moving and keep dodging kill zones – and Alexander – and the government –until the extinction ended. All the achievements of mankind, all our grandeur was dwindling into insignificance. We were being reduced to small tribes fleeing from hiding place to hiding place, just as our mammalian ancestors had done when dinosaurs roamed the earth.

Mark shook his head. He could do nothing to stop the god-machine. He could do little to stop the government. But Alexander was just a man. He had to be able to find a way to end that threat. If Alexander caught up with them right now, they would all be killed. They were not soldiers and even if they were, Alexander's militia drastically outgunned them. Mark's greatest advantage was that Alexander was fifteen hundred miles away in Atlanta. If the warrior pushed his column of armored vehicles to their top speed, it could take days to reach Odessa, assuming he knew exactly where to find them, which he likely did not. Mark knew Alexander also had a much bigger problem than distance and speed and that his quarry was constantly moving from place to place; his biggest problem was that his small army of vehicles sucked down fuel at an amazing rate. An *assist* had previously calculated for Mark that a single gas station could be drained and still provide only a couple hundred miles of travel. Maybe a good trap would be to lure Alexander into a place where he'd be stranded once his army ran out of gas?

Someone sat down beside Mark on the wall. He looked over and saw Sarah. She'd probably sensed some of what was churning inside him. She looked up at the stars.

"I can't think of anything to do except keep running," said Sarah.

"Until Alexander catches us," said Mark. "Then we're going to have to stop him ourselves."

"I know," said Sarah. "I'm ready to act as bait, same as you."

Mark wasn't surprised that Sarah knew parts of what he'd been thinking. She'd been displaying hypersensitivity to people's thoughts and emotions for some time. She was operating at an empathic level that had to be far beyond his abilities. He'd realized that in the last few days, he'd been sending bits of thoughts to her without intending to do so. Their minds were sharing information in ways he couldn't fully understand or control. It was as if certain parts of their memories were being synchronized, so that they would both independently have the same ideas. Was this synchronization a normal part of the changes going on inside them or was it happening subconsciously out of some unknown imperative, because of the threat they were both under? Maybe 'thinking the same' would somehow save their lives if they were forced to lead Alexander into a trap? Mark was in turmoil. He couldn't tolerate the idea of luring men into a deathtrap. He couldn't imagine issuing an order or pushing a button that would kill hundreds of people, without giving them a chance to surrender; but what alternative was there? He was not ready to surrender his life, and Alexander could not be fooled into thinking they were dead. Unless a superior military force was coming to their aid, the only way they could fight back would be through deception and guerrilla warfare weapons, like explosives or fire. The thought sickened him. How could he take part in premeditated murder? *My life is worth more than yours.* It was exactly that kind of demented calculus and instinct for murder which had led mankind into the extinction they were now facing. There had to be some other way.

"I don't feel that way at all," said Sarah. "If anyone deserves killing, it's that bastard and his mercenaries. If I could smother them all in their sleep, I'd do it and rest like a baby after it was done."

Sarah was quiet for a long time. There were no sounds except the wind, no motion except bits of litter blowing down the street. Odessa had been untouched by the kill zones that had ravaged Midland, Texas less than twenty miles away. Odessa had been deserted by its people for a thousand reasons Mark would never know; but kill zones striking the town had not been one of them. Odessa was now a modern day ghost town like its larger neighbor. Mark looked at Sarah and saw troubled eyes and a mouth that was as straight as a line. He felt nothing coming from her, no thoughts, no feelings. She was like a black hole in space drawing everything in and letting nothing escape. She turned and looked directly into his eyes.

"What you and I want to believe is that the god-machine is creating a new rung in the evolutionary ladder and hijacking people like us as part of its plan," said Sarah. "What if it's worse than that? What if we are igniting the kill zones ourselves? Maybe that's why I've survived so many of them? Maybe that's how I know when they're going to hit?"

"That's what Alexander believes," said Mark. "Do you think he's right? Do you think killing us will stop the extinction?"

"That's what some of the government types think," said Sarah. "I have gaps of missing time. Who knows what I've done during the times I can't remember. Maybe I'm some kind of monster that will do anything to breed a new race?"

Mark didn't know what to say. After a few minutes, Sarah got up quietly and headed back into the garage. She wasn't carrying a light. She slowly faded into the maw-like darkness of the entrance. Mark remained behind with a blackness growing inside him. He'd had the same fears as Sarah. The thought was inescapable for anyone with an ounce of introspection. Would killing them and others like them stop the plague? Self-doubt was a cancer that could never be put back in the bottle, once poured out.

28 – Odessa, Texas: January

Mark awoke as sunlight crept into the garage. Kathy, Sarah, and Carl were sleeping in their seats. Mark quietly got out of the Humvee. He saw a few people milling about and smelled breakfast cooking on portable stoves. His world looked as right as it could, under these conditions.

He doubled over in pain. His head suddenly felt like it was being clamped in a vice. Spots floated in his vision. His skin broke out in a sweat. He tried to moan but was unable to make a sound. He pulled himself up using the door handle of the Humvee. Staring through the glass, he saw Sarah curled in a ball and quaking as if she were sobbing. His forehead was pressed against the glass. The coolness helped a small amount, but then it came on harder. The pain! Between flashes of agony, he perceived what was happening. The military had lived up to their threat. Awesome explosions were lancing the super colony with radiation. He could not see or hear the detonations. Everything appeared black, except for waves of pressure and energy bursts, which triggered random memory dumps, flashbacks from the core of the god-machine. In ways which he didn't fully understand, he knew the nuclear weapons were detonating high above the super colony. From the explosions came focused waves of electromagnetic energy which slammed downward into the heart of the god-machine. The colony was not being blown apart; its nanotech circuitry was being fried. Mark was convinced the world was ending. A shudder passed through him which sapped his strength. He saw Carl and Kathy flinch in their sleep. He heard a sharp gasp of surprise from people in the camp who were awake. Around the world, everyone had felt it die.

The silence was the world holding its breath. Mark felt his heart beating in his chest. His head was clear when it shouldn't be. He was still alive. He took an experimental deep breath. The pain had vanished as quickly as it had hit him. His body was soaked in sweat. He looked inside the Humvee. Sarah appeared confused. She slowly glanced in one direction, then another as if looking for something that was missing. Kathy was stretching as she woke up. She clearly had no idea what had happened. Mark dug a portable radio out of a storage box.

"They've attacked it," said Mark.

"Attacked what?" said Kathy. "Us?"

Mark had left the radio tuned to a shortwave news channel. He turned it on and played with the antenna until the station cleared up. A reporter was talking excitedly. Mark had caught the middle of a news bulletin. He turned up the volume.

... electromagnetic pulse, EMP nuclear weapons were used in a first wave of torpedo attacks. EMP nuclear weapons launched from Air Force bombers were used in an almost simultaneous second wave. The United States Navy and Air Force have confirmed the complete destruction of what they are calling a nanotech core. The attack was carried out by Navy Fast Attack Submarines at..."

People were cheering… People were hugging and kissing each other. Kathy threw her arms around Mark and kissed him. A few people leaned on their horns; then others. The garage was a New Year's Eve chaos of noise.

Other than normal residue from the pain and memory flashbacks which had vanished a moment ago, Mark didn't feel any different. Something was wrong. He still felt the presence of the god-machine. Maybe it was like the phantom limb syndrome which caused amputees to continue to feel their lost appendage? Sarah came out the Humvee and stood in front of Mark. They both looked at each other and said it at the same time.

"It's still here."

"It can't be," said Kathy. "The military reported that entire chunk of the ocean was vaporized."

Mark opened the thought-interface with a question. The answer came back in a flood of information and pain. When it had passed, he looked up.

"There's more than one super colony," said Mark. "The entire planet is riddled with them, ensured preservation through redundancy. The super colony is only hardware; the god-machine is an intelligence which inhabits the hardware. It's like trying to kill a ghost. It's everywhere and nowhere at the same time."

"Will it punish the military or will it blame us all?" asked Kathy.

Confusion was replacing joy as more people stopped to see what was wrong. The garage was growing silent.

"I don't think it has emotions," said Mark. "It won't punish, but it may accelerate its existing plans to eliminate any threat of additional attacks."

"We need to go," said Sarah. "We need to go now! It's going to respond everywhere all at once. Every city, every town, every hole in the wall that has been hit before is going to be hit again."

Mark knew they had to be mobile and ready to evade any potential kill zone before it developed. His decision to break camp was quickly relayed. People began shoving unpacked equipment into their Humvees. Kathy looked shell-shocked. The emotional rollercoaster was affecting everyone. Sarah was angry. Mark's heart was pounding. His face felt hot. The politicians and military had not even come close to saving the world. At best they'd accomplished nothing. At worst they'd just thrown rocks at a hornet's nest.

Mark drove the lead Humvee onto the street and turned down the same road they'd taken into Odessa. He'd decided to leave the plan from the previous day unchanged. They were heading toward El Paso, and from there a possible safe zone in either Mexico or Arizona. He could visualize the entire roadmap in his mind and pick out details he'd never noticed before. His memory was developing photographic recall. To avoid all prior kill zones sites, they would be driving out of their way down small two-lane highways that passed through mostly un-populated desert. They would skirt around Carlsbad, New Mexico and Alamogordo, New Mexico, before turning south on US54 which would lead into El Paso. Near the halfway point of the trip, they would be passing close to the place where the first atomic bomb was detonated. The test site was codenamed Trinity and was now ironically probably one of the safer places on the planet because people never congregated there for very long.

The day was unusually warm for January in the Southwest. The Humvees had no air conditioning, but good heating. The windows were partially rolled down to draw in fresh air. They were traveling at the rec-ommended 'long distance' speed of fifty-five miles per hour. The military Humvee's speedometer ended at sixty. The manual indicated a maximum speed of eighty-three miles per hour could be maintained for short peri-ods of time. The column of vehicles was soon kicking up a sizable trail of dust, which was not a problem for those in the lead; but Mark knew people in vehicles farther back had to be suffering. The rural highway they were on was covered with a layer of sand blown over it. Without steady traffic, the roadbed would soon be reclaimed by scrub brush and sand. They were driving down a highway that was in the act of vanishing.

After an hour of driving, Mark began to sense small kill zones hit-ting in remote locations and had to pull over to let someone else drive. The god-machine response had begun. A sudden escalation left him dizzy. The last thing he remembered was collapsing as he tried to climb down out of the driver-side door.

Mark felt groggy and sore. Dry air was buffeting his face. He didn't remember getting into the backseat. With his fingers, he felt around a bandaged cut on his forehead. He knew the number of kill zones was so overwhelming that it had finally caused a numbing effect that had left him detached. The growing slaughter was too much to absorb at once and so the interface to his mind was thankfully now accepting none of the remote perceptions. He sensed the attack was ongoing only from a dull ache and a widening feeling of loss. Sarah was experiencing the carnage with unrelenting intensity. Mark knew it was because of her enhanced empathic wiring that she was able to absorb the higher volume of remote perceptions. Occasionally, she would softly moan as if in a dream. Her eyes remained tightly sealed.

"There's nothing we can do for her," said Mark. "How long was I gone?"

"About two hours," said Kathy.

They skirted Carlsbad without spotting a sign of life, other than jets flying in figure eights high above the clouds and a few newly wrecked cars. Sarah had lapsed into sleep after the kill zones had subsided. Mark soon felt well enough to assume his share of the driving. In a little more than an hour they would be passing the town of Alamogordo, the turn off for the Trinity site. Kathy was working with the portable radio to see if she could get any information. They'd lost all the radio stations over an hour ago at the height of the attack in the middle of an emergency broadcast. So far, all she'd found was static and a country music station that came and went. The station had been playing the same CD over and over for as long as they'd been receiving it. Mark suspected the same CD would be playing until the electricity went out forever.

29 – El Paso, Texas: January

The caravan had stopped on the outskirts of El Paso the prior night. There were no signs of human life, just the stillness of a vast graveyard. Everyone needed time to rest and come to grips with the extent of what had happened. Many believed that doomsday had come and civilization was gone; others were in denial. El Paso was a quiet place to stop, though any city in the world might now have been just as quiet.

Mark had found a six story parking structure that provided good aerial cover when parked inside. He wasn't sure they needed to hide anymore. Sarah had physically recovered before they'd reached El

Paso, though her eyes now had a permanently haunted look. After arriving last night, she had tried repeatedly to reach inside Alexander's mind and found nothing coherent. She didn't think he was dead, but something was no longer mentally the same. Mark wondered if he'd been injured in an accident caused by one of the kill zones.

The late afternoon sun felt strong, radiating down through the cloudless sky. Mark was on the roof of the parking structure. They were at an elevation of several thousand feet. In the distance to the west were dusty reddish-tan mountains with endless valleys of sand and scrub between them; in the other direction was a vast urban landscape.

This morning they had run a wire antenna between a pair of corner posts on the roof and then plugged it into a portable shortwave set. Throughout the day, the radio had been manned and had emitted an entire range of sounds, but none of them were human. They were cut off from the world. No one had any idea of the breadth of the destruction.

The top of the parking structure was a perfect spot for lookouts. From this vantage point, they could look down into larger areas of the city. Binoculars had been issued to everyone on the roof. Any sign of life was to be immediately reported. Mark was scanning the streets with his pair of binoculars. He'd seen so much death over the past months, he should have been used to it by now; but each time he stopped moving the binoculars and focused on the lost people, his heart died a little more. He looked up from his binoculars and saw the figure eight contrails in the sky were still there. The heads of government were still alive in their aerial sanctuaries. The same was not true for their constituents, who were decaying in their homes and cars.

Mark knew there had to be other survivors. His group had survived, and there were still vast areas that had been untouched by kill zones and would never feel their horrific pain. The god-machine's war map was projected in front of him by an *assist*. The diagrams of destruction were superimposed transparently over his vision of the streets and buildings of El Paso. The god-machine had gone through the entire remaining extinction strategy, which had weeks or even months left, and had completed it in a few hours. As far as Mark could tell, the end of the program had been reached at late afternoon the prior day. The machine-driven extinction was over. He felt like he was barely holding on to his own sanity as he wondered how much of mankind was left: fifty percent? One percent? There was no way for anyone to know. All the cities were dead; he had little doubt of that, but much of the deep rural areas had been left untouched.

"I've got something!" yelled one of the lookouts.

Mark ran over the northeastern edge of the parking structure. The man pointed to an almost invisible column of dust rising in the air about thirty miles away.

"It's vehicles coming toward us," said another lookout.

Mark focused his binoculars. Something was definitely stirring up that cloud of dust and it was moving fast. The vehicles were too far off to see anything more than an enormous billow rising out of a tiny pinpoint. It would take an army to kick up enough dust to be seen from this distance.

"I think you're right," said Mark. "It looks like they're coming down US54 same as we did."

"I was right!" shouted the lookout who'd first spotted the dust cloud. "We're not alone."

Mark brought the binoculars back up to his eyes. Something troubled him. This didn't feel right. They were coming down the same route he'd used, the exact same route. Last night, he'd taken a rural highway into El Paso. Why would a convoy of that size be on a road that was such a poor route for trucks? He was beginning to breathe rapidly. Who was this? He tried to focus his eyes to draw out more detail. Involuntarily, something inside him tuned in and he was immediately flooded with the perceptions of a man in the lead vehicle. Mark knew this mental landscape; it was Alexander! He became Alexander. He could feel the soldier sensing his victory as he was bearing down on the Traitors. He had Humvees with heavy weapons and Armored Personnel Carriers, with even heavier weapons. He would annihilate them. He believed a Traitor was seeing through his eyes at this very moment; and was for the first time pleased that an invader with inside his head. He was sending a message to whoever was sneaking around in the back of his brain. His ploy had worked. He'd taken drugs to dull himself so the spies would not be able to use his own senses against him.

The experience-flood was over in an instant. Mark was stunned and disoriented. He had seriously underestimated Alexander. The man must have found them in his dreams and then used mental stealth to conceal his advance. How had he covered fifteen hundred miles so quickly with slow-moving armor?

"Everyone, back to the Humvees," yelled Mark. "We're pulling out. That dust cloud's an army that will murder us all."

Carl took the turn out of the parking lot at what felt like full throttle. The tires screeched as he fishtailed until he got it pointing straight down the road. Mark looked back and saw Humvee after Humvee pulling out of the lot. The last ones were towing trailers. They would be the slowest. Mark had given orders for the two-way radios to be hooked back up, but to transmit only in case of emergency or if they got separated. He was already thinking about desperate tactics.

"Carl, that way," shouted Mark while pointing. "It'll lead into westbound I-10."

"You got it."

Soon, they were racing down I-10 heading toward New Mexico. The tires on the Humvee were creating so much road noise that conversation was impossible without shouting. The speedometer needle was pegged at its sixty mph limit. By timing highway mile markers, Mark estimated their speed was eighty-six mph. The Humvees pulling trailers were being left behind.

An *assist* told Mark that armored personnel carriers had a top speed of forty-five miles per hour. Could they be modified to go faster? He didn't know; and it didn't matter because just as they were outrunning their Humvees with trailers, Alexander's faster vehicles would outrun their slower heavier armor. Not good.

"Pull off," said Mark. "Signal everyone to stop. We're going to ditch the trailers."

After an anxious and precious fifteen minutes, they had unhooked all the trailers. As many supplies as possible were transferred to the Humvees. One man had seriously injured his hand on a trailer hitch. Major Franklin came up to ride with Mark; his military experience was needed. Mark had stationed men with military training in the rear Humvees. Thanks to the Major, they had two fifty-caliber machine guns and grenade launchers. Taking potshots might slow Alexander down enough. The men at the rear had orders to open fire as soon as they had a chance of hitting anything. The range of a fifty-caliber was a couple miles. The Armored Personnel carriers had greater range with their cannons; but they had to be losing ground at forty-five miles per hour, which Major Franklin swore was as fast as they could ever go. The Major said he was hoping they didn't have any missile launchers. Mark was just praying there would be no potshots today, but he doubted those prayers would be answered. Hadn't there been enough death already? Why were there always madmen who thirsted for more?

They'd been racing flat out for over an hour. The highway they were on was clear of sand, so there were no dust clouds to give away their position or Alexander's. They were in the middle of nowhere. I-10 was surrounded by endless miles of desert and mountains in either direction. There were no turns Mark could take to shake Alexander's pursuit. All the small, side roads were covered in sand, which would give away their change in direction if they ran fast; and if they ran slow, they wouldn't be out of sight before Alexander raced by. The next big turnoff where they could lose Alexander was over a hundred miles down the road, and it dead-ended into Mexico. They were trapped in a fight where speed trumped all.

Something about the experience-flood he'd received an hour ago from Alexander was troubling Mark. It wasn't the obvious, but something subtle. He couldn't put his finger on it, but there was something odd about what Alexander had been thinking. The man was pleased that a Traitor was in his mind spying on him. It didn't exactly make sense... then Mark realized what was out of place. He felt like the world had been tipped to an odd angle. Alexander behaved as if a Traitor was spying on him at the time of the mental recording; but Mark knew this was impossible because of how experience-floods were relayed by the god-machine. Experience-floods were received as implanted memories that appeared after the fact, and then surfaced in the mind and were instantaneously relived. There were real-time delays of minutes or even millennia in the case of timeline records; and that meant Mark was not spying on Alexander. He was only an after-the-fact voyeur of recorded material. During some of the experience-floods, Alexander clearly knew what his eyes were seeing would be received by a Traitor; and to know that meant Alexander had to be either consciously or subconsciously planning on sending his experiences to the Traitor. There was no other explanation. Alexander could not have sensed someone spying on him when the actual *spying* wouldn't happen until minutes or hours later. The implication was astonishing. Alexander was either feeding crafted disinformation or was living under the paranoid delusion of being spied on while subconsciously tipping his hand to the Traitors. Mark was betting on the latter, and if true, that was a powerful piece of information to have as a weapon. Was it possible that at some level Alexander wanted to fail?

Mark decided to try to tune into Alexander's mind. If successful, he intended to stay only long enough to get a bearing on the man's position by spotting a highway sign or some other landmark. An experience-flood hit him before he even had a chance to try. What Mark perceived was confusing. The road noise was extremely loud. Alexander's Humvee was doing a hundred miles per hour and the armored personnel carriers were with him. This was impossible! How could armor keep up? How could military Humvees go that fast? More of Alexander's memories unfolded in Mark's mind; and Mark understood and was stunned: the Humvees had been modified for speed. He'd been badly out-maneuvered a second time by Alexander. They were being overtaken. More memories surfaced. Mark was rattled. Alexander behaved as if he thought Mark was in his head at that moment and was sending Mark a message. The soldier twisted a side-mirror inward so Mark could see the expression on his face. He appeared confident and pleased with himself. He leaned out the window and looked backward showing Mark how badly he had been deceived. There was a convoy of eighteen-wheeler flatbeds hauling the slower-moving armored personnel carriers and fuel tankers behind the flatbeds. They could keep going at a hundred miles per hour until they reached the ocean, and then keep going up the coast or anywhere else their quarry might flee. Alexander's face was back in the mirror. He mouthed the words, "No hope."

Nearby, a long zipper of explosions shocked Mark out of the experience-flood. Dozens of clouds of smoke were spiraling into the air from rocky outcroppings a few hundred yards behind them. The experience-flood had come to Mark before he'd tried to initiate it. Wasn't that evidence that Alexander was intentionally feeding him disinformation?

"That's small cannon fire," shouted Major Franklin. "Bushmaster cannon would be my bet. Nasty weapon. Fires small 30mm cannon shells as fast as a machine gun. Each round's got a nice little punch; one or two could wreck a Hummer's day. Four miles max range, one mile effective; so best guess is they just closed to within four miles, because they're lobbing 'em instead of taking direct shots. I'm betting one or two vehicles are stopping to fire and then pulling out to catch up. What you saw was pretty accurate work. You better hope it was luck. If not, we're in a world of hurt; because that'd mean he's got some fuckin' good shooters and once they're closer, they're gonna rain hundreds of those shells down on us."

Mark heard what the Major said and knew what it meant. Desperate times had arrived and he had nothing left to fight with. The safety of everyone was his responsibility. The time had come for the bait to lead the sharks away from the tribe. He looked at Sarah in the backseat. Her head was down. She hadn't spoken since they'd pulled out of El Paso. She must have sensed some of the same things he did about Alexander; and more with her heightened empathic wiring. She had to have been dipping into Alexander's broadcasts.

"Sarah," he shouted over the road noise.

There was no response. He leaned backward between the front seats and squeezed her shoulder. Nothing…

"Sarah!"

She looked up at him with hollow eyes, as he felt something which took his breath away. There was a body-sense of it at first; then, the impressions came into focus. He released her shoulder. A kill zone was forming around them or near them. He had a fleeting impression that the zone might actually be somehow moving with their Humvee, targeting them. Sarah's cheeks were damp with tears. Her expression was stoic. Her stare tugged at the back of his mind like a magnet pulling another of its kind. He broke eye contact by looking out the rear window. A string of cannon shells burst in the road farther behind them.

"Are you doing this?" asked Mark. "The kill zone."

"Don't know… Sensed it coming," said Sarah. "I was sending messages for the god-machine to help us."

Her voice was labored as if she was struggling to lift a heavy weight. Mark felt the impending zone growing in strength. He didn't know if she was subconsciously causing the zone, or if the god-machine was protecting two hybrid-humans who were important to its future plans, or if it was just dumb luck; but he had to act now. He had to separate his people from this death maker and draw Alexander into it. This was not the kind of trap he'd have planned, but it could work.

"Stop the car," shouted Mark.

"What?" yelled Carl.

"Just do it!" ordered Mark. "A kill zone is coming right here, right now. Sarah and I will draw the bastards into it. We're bait for the trap. You have to get in another Humvee and run. Kathy …"

"I'm not leaving you," she cried.

"No time," said Mark. "If you stay, you die. We're not going to be killed by this zone." Mark pointed his finger, like a weapon, toward the rear window. "They are!"

The line of Humvees pulled out fast. Mark knew that image of Kathy's face staring back at him would haunt him for the rest of his life, whether it ended today or in hundreds of years. His heart had been hopelessly broken in those few seconds that were now gone and could never be changed.

He and Sarah were sitting in a Humvee, which was parked in the center of the highway. The scene was staged to look like a break down. A spilled toolbox was lying in the road next to the vehicle. He didn't believe it would fool Alexander for very long, but anything that slowed him down worked in Mark's favor giving Kathy and the others precious time and distance. Whether the kill zone worked or failed, Alexander's hunt would still end in the next few minutes. He would have his prey or be dead. Parked at the crest of a hill, through the windshield, Mark saw the last of his Humvees disappear around a bend. He turned around in his seat and stared down the hill through the rear window. The road was empty for now. He could see a couple miles back, all the way to a spot where the highway dipped from view behind a steep decline. An experience-flood hit him without warning. Alexander was back. Mark felt the swiftness with which the soldier was closing on them. The man was saturated with blood lust; he was hungering for their deaths. Mark fought back the mental invasion. His hands felt unclean. He glanced at Sarah. He could sense the kill zone on top of them like an electrical storm, like some great thundercloud drawing itself closer to the ground before striking.

Almost as an involuntary reflex, Mark linked with Sarah's mind. How had this connection happened? Somehow they were sharing each other's mental landscape and senses. Was this Sarah's normal empathic experience, her equivalent to his data-floods? Even at this intense level of intimacy, he could not tell if she was causing the zone or just sensing it. He realized she didn't know the answer herself. What he found in her heart was power, confusion, and strong conviction. The inside of the Humvee was silent. The trap was set. In a very short time, death would surround them. Mark prayed that their pursuers would be destroyed and that the kill zone would not begin too early or too late. He prayed that he and Sarah would live through this horror and walk out the other side. Mark felt a physical repulsion from his own instincts to kill. His mind was battling with his soul. This was no the time for debating right or wrong; this was survival. He focused all his thoughts to join Sarah in watching and concentrating, as the whirlwind of death materialized. Sarah had been unable to explain if anything going on inside her was having an affect on the zone. Almost everything in her conscious mind was being relayed to his. He tried to duplicate her thoughts. He tried to synchronize his mental focus with hers. They were like a pair of ancient priests enchanting magical prayers, hoping to will the kill zone god into existence at the right moment. Were their concentrated thoughts making any difference? This was no time to stop and put it to a test. They were at the dark intersection of faith and reality, where superstition was born. Who could tell why this kill zone was coming? The god-machine's war map came up superimposed over his vision. He could see the area the kill zone would cover. An *assist* was tracking and showing the zone's perimeter with a set of concentric-circles on a topographic roadmap. The outer ring was a target hundreds of yards wide with him and Sarah near its epicenter. It wasn't enough. The circle was too small to cover all of Alexander's army, but there was nothing he could do about it. He forced all doubts from his mind and concentrated harder with Sarah.

Mark spotted movement at the edge where the highway sunk from view. His vision was computer enhanced by an *assist*. The movement resolved into tiny square specks as vehicles crested the incline. More and more came; ten, then twenty; soon it looked like a hundred specks were racing toward the two of them. Bullets nicked the road-bed nearby, kicking up sparks and small puffs of debris. They were going to be cut down before the trap sprang. A bullet pinged off the roof. Mark felt the kill zone stirring, igniting. An invisible column of human death rose to encircle them. In a corner of his mind, doubts reemerged. Mark knew the zone was inadequate. The trap wasn't going to destroy enough of them. No, keep focused! He pushed his attention back to concentrating with Sarah. Their minds were synchro-nized. Their thoughts were merged into a single point of awareness. A bullet cut through the rear window and punched through a seatback.

Mark felt a jolt and lost his focus. It was like an umbilical was severed. The kill zone was gone. His link with Sarah was gone. He panicked; then, sensed the kill zone farther out. As an invisible field of energy, the zone was starting down the road in Alexander's direction.

Mark could see its path outlined in an *assist* as the concentric circles accelerated along the roadmap.

"No!" moaned Sarah. "Not yet!"

The zone of death was following the highway. From edge to edge, it swept down the road tracking turns. Like a poisonous vapor, it flowed invisibly into the midst of Alexander's army. Mark grabbed his binoculars and focused on the wolf pack of marauders. Nothing happened. They were still advancing at high speed. A few Humvees in the center went slowly off course and struck others. One of the lead Humvees turned sideways and was flipped by other Humvees, colliding with it from behind. Out of a center of increasing wreckage came an intense flash of orange-red light. A tanker had gone up. A moment later, the sound of a massive concussion reached them. Their Humvee rattled. He was watching a juggernaut of steel turning on its own kind and consuming itself. More explosions went off. The advance was scraping to a halt. The marauders had lost. Black smoke was obscuring Mark's view. He climbed from the Humvee. Was Alexander dead? He connected with something and felt dark rage, frustration, and pain. Mark's senses were slowly filled like an empty glass with Alexander's perceptions of lying on the roadway. The man was injured. He believed Mark would be rummaging around in his memories and wanted to rip his own eyes out, to spite the Traitors and deprive them of gloating over him. Mark saw death all around. He smelled burning rubber and oil. He heard sounds of vehicles dying, and of men dying, and of Alexander's shallow breathing from a massive pain in his chest.

"I'll destroy you," screamed Alexander. "I'll destroy all of you plague-controlling traitors!"

The experience-flood ended. Mark reeled a bit from a kind of mental poisoning. He braced himself on the side of the Humvee until clarity returned. He had heard the scream in his mind, but he also thought, prior to that, he'd heard the actual cries of Alexander echoing down the rugged walls of sandstone and rock that lined the highway. Alexander's entire army was destroyed, but the man lived on. He was so much like the ones he hated, thought Mark. Here was proof Alexander was more like *his traitors* than not. The kill zone had passed over him.

30 – New Mexico: January

"Kill him. We can't let him live!" said Sarah.

Alexander was at their mercy. Sarah wanted him dead. All they had to do was get in the Humvee, drive a few hundred yards to where the wreckage lay, and put some bullets in him. He was injured. Killing him would be easy.

"Enough murder has been done in this world," said Mark. "I won't add one more death to it. We take him prisoner."

"You're wrong," said Sarah. "That's defective thinking. If we let him live, he won't give up. Some night he'll escape, sneak in through your window, and slit yours and Kathy's throats."

"No more murder."

"He's guilty, convicted, and you can't stop me from..."

Mark felt something happening. He turned toward the wreckage. Sarah stopped talking. She too was staring at the pile of twisted vehicles. The sun was setting. Its light had become a dusty haze which silhouetted objects more than illuminated them. A vague implanted memory surfaced in Mark. The memory was a deep pool of resignation and physical pain.

"He's up to something," said Sarah.

Mark heard a distinct click echo off the rock walls. What was that? A brilliant ball of light flared up, surrounding the wreckage like a sun of orange-white heat. An instant after the flare, a pressure wave of hot air and thunder knocked Mark and Sarah off their feet. Umph! Impact with the ground pounded the wind from his lungs.

The back of his skull felt sore where it had hit the pavement. His body was a single large bruise. Mark lifted himself into a seated position. He looked at Sarah. She was half standing. Her legs seemed shaky. A huge ball of smoke had risen into the air in the shape of a distorted mushroom. The pile of wreckage was gone, obliterated. Mark saw bits of it scattered on the expanse of road in front of him – a tire, an axle, small pieces of metal. An *assist* indicated the blast radius was five-hundred and forty-one feet in diameter.

"What was that?" asked Sarah.

"A madman's last chance to kill," said Mark.

Epilogue

Canyons

31 – Sedona, Arizona: February

Daylight was shining in through open windows of the main house. There were sounds of hammers and saws coming from outbuildings being constructed or repaired. Kathy picked up a pen from the open spine of her journal and began writing. This was their new home, a deserted horse ranch nestled in the red stone canyons of Sedona. Over seventy percent of humanity was gone, or at least that was the most accurate number anyone had come up with. No kill zones had occurred since the one that destroyed Alexander's army over two weeks ago. People around the country who had survived extinction were slowly rebuilding. Mark – he seemed to feel guilt, while everyone around him felt only gratitude. He was continuing to change. The transformation was affecting him in more intricate ways now. He was becoming both more pacifistic and more physically perfected. His skin was smoother and fairer. His freckles and moles were completely gone. The only thing that appeared out of place with what was going on inside him was his hair. It was turning a little grayer. She knew he might live forever with his body repaired and maintained by the nanotech swarm inside him. She would never allow herself to become what he had turned into. She would never be transformed into another Sarah. Even if she changed her mind and decided to cross that line, it might be impossible for her accomplish. She didn't possess the same genetic predispositions. She was fearful of trying to invoke even the smallest commands to heal, out of concern that it might start some unintended chain reaction which couldn't be controlled.

She knew Mark and Sarah would be together once she was gone. The thought was comfort and torment. She wanted to live forever. She didn't want to lose him, but what he and Sarah had become was so alien. Maybe they were no longer even alive by normal measures. It was a terrible thought about the man she loved. But they were part-machine. The original biology of their brains was completely gone. Nanotech circuitry now did their thinking… and this was the future of mankind? What about their souls, their essence? Was it still inside those mechanical brains; or had it fled, leaving behind perfect computer imitations of what had once been human? When she looked into Mark's eyes, she could still see the original man imprisoned within a shell of physical and mental perfection. Human life was filled with little rattles and squeaks. Life was not perfect, was never meant to be. A tear fell onto her page where she was writing. She tried to clean it, but only smeared the ink more.

32 – Sedona, Arizona: February

The views of red stone formations and tree covered hills of Sedona were breathtaking. Ancient bands of Indians had lived in these canyons for thousands of years. Mark was sitting on the edge of a canyon looking down on the settlement his tribe was building. All the governments were gone. The remnants of power previously kept safe flying in jets had left the sky. Mark had seen one fall and could only explain it as suicide. All the industries were gone. All power generation was gone. All phone service was gone. There were rumors of warlords and sporadic fighting. Maybe some day soon that too would be gone.

Mark had done what he'd promised. He had led his small tribe of men and women to sanctuary. He was proud of his accomplishment, but in the darker corners of his soul he was filled with uncertainties and guilt. He still didn't know if he and Sarah had created the kill zone that had destroyed Alexander's army or if the god-machine had done it to protect them. With the absence of that knowledge, he was cast adrift in the wide expanses of gray between guilt and innocence. He was close to convinced they'd had some hand in directing the kill zone, and that implication alone was deeply troubling. If they could influence one kill zone, they might have had some part in controlling others or even causing them. He could never find peace until he knew if he'd played any part in the genocide. Were his hands covered in humanity's blood? He'd searched for answers and found none. He'd combed the timeline recordings of history and found no solace. He knew many things no man had ever imagined and learned more every day. The knowledge had brought him wisdom, but not peace. He didn't know if he was worthy of living among the people he had saved; and until he could answer that question, he could never feel he was a part of them. Why couldn't he be more like Sarah? She felt no doubts or guilt over what she'd become or might have done.

The sun moved behind some clouds. In the distance, he saw shadows drifting across the rugged landscape. He looked at his arms and his hands. His skin was a single smooth tone except where the sun had reddened it. He knew from experience the sunburn would vanish within hours, without effect. Though his muscles had not increased in mass, he'd noticed today he was physically stronger and had more endurance than a week ago. He'd been able to climb the horse trail which led to this eight hundred foot summit, without stopping for rest.

Mark went back to shifting through memories he'd retained from the last data-flood. He wanted to understand why the god-machine had assisted both him and Alexander. The behavior was a contradiction; and from that discrepancy he hoped to find clues to understand if he'd had a role in the mass murdering. He saw how the god-machine was constructed to be neutral and didn't help or hinder individuals, unless they threatened some part of its programmed goals. The machine appeared to serve all equally who could ask consciously or subconsciously. He wondered if the machine exerted control over him or Alexander. Did he have free will, or was the god-machine controlling him like some marionette hanging from subconscious strings? One thing was clear. Information from the god-machine had been leaking into his mind since he was born; and this to a greater or lesser extent was true for almost everyone. This leaking may have been the only influence the god-machine had on him, which was not at all the same as real control. Where did his mind end and the god-machine begin? Where was the boundary between independent thought and computer? Maybe the question was no longer answerable by him, now that his brain was a complete melding of nanotech and organic? Maybe there was no longer any difference? Maybe he was the machine?

Mark heard a horse walking up the trail. He reached out with his senses and recognized Kathy was nearing. An *assist* located her position on an aerial view and projected her arrival time. In one minute and twenty-four seconds, she came into view. She dismounted and sat down beside him. Her knee was troubling her. She was using a walking stick again. She picked up his hand and held it. Her touch was sometimes a salve that could drive his self-doubts away, leaving him with wonderful moments of peace. She kissed him on the cheek. He felt warmth inside, but a bittersweet feeling remained.

"Sarah came back from town," said Kathy. "She said the people were friendly and willing to trade with us; but they don't want us mixing with them."

"So much misguided fear," said Mark. "Funny, how everything can change and still nothing's different."